Barnaby the Wanderer

Being the astonishing adventures of a widow's son journeying the Land of Saints, with a magic cat, a dark ghost and the map of a cursed tower; and all that became thereof.

By Raymond St. Elmo

2023

"You are all turning your brains into getting into this country. I say we should be scheming how to get out of it."

"I am surprised, sir," boomed Challenger, stroking his majestic beard, *"that any man of science should commit himself to so ignoble a sentiment... I absolutely refuse to leave until we are able to take back with us something in the nature of a chart."*

Arthur Conan Doyle, **The Lost World**

Part I

A Gathering of Wanderers

Chapter 1
On the Road

Barnaby walked in no least hurry, amazed with all the different greens of a slow rich summer. Grass blades bordering the country lane showed a simple innocent green. While cabbage rows in farm plots offered a darker green touched with the purple of old bruises. Fields of wheat waved stalks of yellow-green, half-ready for the scythe. The shy creek courting the path shimmered the color of a baby cricket. As he passed beneath a tree, the leaves turned sunbeams to emerald dapples touched with a king's gold.

Barnaby halted, looking back. He could no longer see Mother Miller waving from the steps of the chapel. Even the vanes of the mill had vanished, as if sunken beneath the earth. Barnaby pictured the ground opening, swallowing down mill, chapel, smithy and all the little cottages. Like a pike gulping mayflies. Maybe he should go back, make sure all remained un-swallowed?

But it'd look foolish to return so soon after brave goodbyes. His stepmother, stepbrother and the squire all waving him on to adventure; giving him a treasure map, a copper piece and a fine lunch. He'd just have to trust that his home still shared this sunlit earth.

Barnaby turned again, considering the road ahead. The countryside made a quilt of farm fields; the tree-shaded lane wandering in and out, taking no more hurry than Barnaby.

Once a year the folk of Mill Town walked the South Road together to the Jahrmarkt, where people wore strange clothes and faces. But this road went west. Entirely a mystery that Barnaby walked alone.

Far, far in the distance a house crowned a hill. Large and brick. His eyes widened to realize he did not know the faces, names and family history of whoever lived there. Didn't know their dogs' names. Their dogs wouldn't know his smell. They'd all have to stare and sniff astounded, unable to comprehend one another.

On consideration, the folk ahead mightn't even *have* a dog. He was beyond the bounds of his world. Well, so be it. He took a deep breath, smelling fresh cut hay, leaf rot and summer dust. And the bread, ham and cheese in the bag given by Mother Miller. He weighed sitting under a tree, having lunch. But she'd ordered him not to so much as sample a crumb till evening light. And Da always said '*work done, then the fun.*'

Barnaby walked on, kicking at dust. Da had been a cheerful sort, always whistling. Barnaby wished he knew how to whistle. Behold a blue sky and an open road. Absolutely made for walking while whistling. The birds flitted about, showing off. *They* knew the trick. But Barnaby's stepbrother Alf had solemnly assured him that boys with names beginning with 'B' could never whistle. Shouldn't even try. It had something to do with how you shaped your lips for the letter 'B'.

"I might have been Frank," he told a robin. "Or Fortinbras or Philodendron. Then I'd puff music out same as you."

The robin cocked an eye, considering, doubting. It gave a quick rolling trill in open challenge.

"That's not whistling," Barnaby argued. "Whistles are when you puck out your lips like you're going to kiss the Goat Girl. Then you puff." He showed the robin how this would work for those not christened 'Barnaby', 'Beelzebub' or 'Brendon'. To his shock, out came a string of sound. Not near so pretty as the robin's trill. But definitely, clearly, undeniably: a whistle note. He stopped, meeting the robin's gaze. It gave a wing shrug to say 'hmm', returning to stalking worms.

How strange, thought Barnaby. Had it something to do with the air beyond the village bounds? He walked on, puffing out, pulling in. By the time he came even with the farmhouse on the hill, he'd turned bits of air into a song.

A girl leaned on the fence separating the lane from the house, watching him approach.

"What are you at, boy?" she asked.

"I've made a song," he declared proudly. "Do you want to hear?"

"No."

"Very well then."

"But if you fill this bucket with water from the creek, I'll give you a kiss."

Barnaby weighed this offer. The girl was his same young years. Prettyish but with a sour look. As though in her eyes all this bright earth summed to a sea of vinegar.

"Can I have the kiss first?"

"No."

"Very well, then." She handed him a heavy wooden bucket. "Best leave your pack," she advised. "'Tis a slippery climb down the bank, and twice that up."

Barnaby nodded, dropping his pack by the fence. He crossed the lane, descending a grassy slope. There waited the brook, muttering to itself its watery thoughts. Barnaby found a dry bit of bank and knelt over the water. Splashing the dust and sweat from his face. The water felt wonderfully cool. For a while he watched a dragonfly dart about, wings sunlight-shimmering. It looked so happy to be a dragonfly that Barnaby felt happy for it too. He laughed, then scooped water in cupped hands, drinking his fill.

At last he dipped the bucket into the brook. Pouring a minnow out that wanted to leave home, go adventuring in a bucket. "Best stay home," he advised in tone wise as the Friar's.

He turned and carried the bucket back up to the lane. Trying not to slip, not to splash.

He found the girl still waiting, leaning on the fence, kicking a foot back and forth impatient with Barnaby and the turning world. He passed the bucket over the fence. She received it in strong arms, setting it down.

"Now hold out your hand," she ordered. He did so. She reached, carefully placing a pebble into his palm.

"There you go. Bye now." She took up the bucket, headed towards the house.

Barnaby studied the object. It was shiny and smooth and not a kiss.

"What about my wages?" he asked.

The girl did not stop nor turn as she answered.

"That's what we call a kiss. What do you call them?"

"Pebbles?"

The girl laughed. "You're from foreign parts." She hurried up the hill and away.

Barnaby sighed, then laughed. He'd best learn the greater world's words or there'd come conflagrations. He'd be asking for bread and be given a beating. Offer a hand and they'd take his shoe. Shout 'fire' and folk would grab forks for a feast. He put the kiss in his pocket, retrieved his pack, set off down the lane again, whistling.

Farther down the road a butterfly began stalking him in fluttering circles, fascinated by Barnaby's straw-colored hair. He walked all a mile joying in its random dance. So different than the dragonfly he'd seen by the creek. Dragonflies darted about on *serious* concerns. But not the butterflies of the world.

"You and me, friend," he informed the butterfly. "We're no dragonflies." It felt a strange thing to declare; strange as whistling. He began pondering all the things he was not. Not a tree nor rock, not cloud nor king or any special thing. Not the heir of his father's mill nor the sun in the sky. The afternoon sun that he was not, now shone in the eyes of what he was, making him squint. Was it close enough to sunset to suit Mother Miller's instruction of when to eat his lunch? He looked about for a shady spot, just in case he decided it was.

On the path ahead he spied a donkey. With a long dangling burden across its back. Barnaby saw neither rider nor drover. Probably the beast had scampered from some farm. The donkeys that brought grain to the mill were sly things, always sneaking off. Then Barnaby had to chase after them while folk laughed, making timeless jests about one donkey chasing another.

Barnaby quickened his pace. The beast flicked long rabbity ears at his boot step. It hurried down the road, defying him to catch it. But soon stumbling, slowing again. Shaking its head as though debating grand themes of life and donkey-hood. At last it stopped, come to final decision.

Barnaby approached, panting, puzzled at what he found. The beast stood splay-legged, trembling, head down in defeat. Across its rump flies drank from the wounds of whippings. The donkey turned its head towards Barnaby, eyes rolling in despair.

"Peace," whispered Barnaby. He made the *'ssh, ssh'* sound that Smith gave to horses when removing a rock from a hoof, or salved some cut. A calming whisper that assured 'all is well, all is well'.

Not that all seemed so well as that. Thick twine wrapped the donkey's muzzle. The beast had been set upon the road unable to eat nor drink. While across its back was bound the corpse of a man. Naked, with wounds of a whipping worse than the donkey's. Face livid; eyelids half closed in dark consideration of the earth and its paths. Atop his head was tied a conical cap.

Barnaby puzzled. He knew that shape of cap. The Friar made him wear it in his lessons when he confused 'pax' with 'pox', 'venerable' and 'venial', 'potentate' with 'potash'.

"Ssh, ssh," he repeated, absently. To the dead man as much as the donkey, and to himself. Not that there was aught to do for the first or the last. He put palm to the donkey's head, patting. It shivered, eyes pleading. Barnaby nodded, drew his knife, cut at the cords binding the muzzle. Freed, the beast opened wide its jaws, gave a soft bray. Then it tried to bite him.

"None of that, now," whispered Barnaby, not bit nor wit surprised. The donkey gave over violence, staggering to the roadside. It bent head to weeds and grass, devouring what it found.

"Best leave that alone," shouted someone. Barnaby looked about. A man stood leaning on a spade, eyeing Barnaby, the donkey and its corpse-burden.

"Why?"

The farmer straightened his back, his straw hat; then idled over. A low wall of loose rock separated field from lane; the man hopped across, considered beast and burden. Nodding to himself to say, *'just as I thought'*.

"That's a thrice-condemned criminal. Bound, broken and shamed. The creature isn't allowed to stop for bite nor sip, but must wander the roads forever as warning to them that does evil."

"What evil did he do?"

The farmer frowned. "How would I know? And why might I care?"

Barnaby pulled the cap from the corpse. It had writing upon it.

"Says he was a traitor," declared Barnaby.

"You're reading it upside down, you tomnoddy."

Barnaby shook his head. The Friar himself had taught him letters, the great book of saints upon his knees, pointing to words for Barnaby to read; striking Barnaby's knuckles with each error.

The farmer grabbed the hat, turned it point upwards. "Aye, but it does declare that very crime. Traitor he was, then. When you see such beasts upon the road, 'tis an honest man's duty to curse it, toss stones to drive it on, wandering forever."

"There'd be no wandering forever. Why, the poor donkey is near falling down dead now."

"'Tisn't for the likes of you to say."

"Well, I shall bury the man," declared Barnaby, feeling defiant.

The farmer looked up and down the road, spying no tattletale eyes.

"No harm in that," he decided. "You bury him. And I shall take the donkey."

"That seems fair." Barnaby took knife, cut the cords binding the corpse. It was loose and liquid, far past the stage of rigor. Barnaby pulled his kerchief about his mouth to shelter from the smell; then worked to bring the dead man to the ground. Arms, legs and head flopping as though the bones had separated.

"Will you lend your spade?" he asked.

"No," said the farmer. Then reconsidered. "Unless you have coin for the favor?"

Barnaby searched pockets, knowing what he'd find. Just the lonely penny given by the Squire at their parting. He looked to the corpse upon the roadside, and readied to say *apologies, stranger*. The dead man gazed upwards, eyes empty as a blind man staring into a sky equally blind and empty. Not beseeching pity nor demanding justice. Just puzzling, staring up at Barnaby and the sky, wondering what the world was about, what would the world do next.

"I have a penny," said Barnaby.

"Fair enough," decided the farmer. He began gathering up the bits of cut cord, making a halter for the donkey. While Barnaby pushed and pulled the body over the low wall. He considered apologizing to the corpse for the bumps and scrapes. But that was him being silly, as his brother would say. And Mother Miller would say. And the Squire would say. And the Friar would say.

The farmer pointed out a quiet corner of field. "Will help the potatoes grow, if you can believe it." He tossed Barnaby the spade, then led the donkey towards a distant barn.

"Make sure it gets water," said Barnaby. "Poor beast can't have supped or sipped in days."

"Hmm," agreed the farmer. "Finish up your burying. I need my spade back."

Barnaby set to digging. The ground was soft enough. He turned over clods of earth, sighing to consider the dead man's size. Large and tall in life. Someone important, perhaps. Not now, save to the potatoes.

When at last he rested, he stared into the hole. Watching grubs squiggle, worms wiggle. Ready to gobble the corpse quick as thin friars at a fat bishop's feast. He looked about the field. Beheld quiet crops in evening sunlight. Clouds passing, sun passing, wind passing. Simple and peaceful a scene as some Eden embroidered on a child's blanket.

Barnaby recalled a mouse scurrying among the gears of his father's mill, happily nibbling the loose grains. Till the world's winds blew. And so the mill vanes turned the shaft, the shaft turned the cogs... there'd come a mousy death-squeak. When the wheel turned about again Barnaby beheld no mouse. Only a red stain, a furry blot.

This world's a thing of turning parts, thought Barnaby. Soon or late it catches all us poor mice in the wheels. A sad thought. For Barnaby, a very strange thought. He'd never thought such things before. No doubt it was more work of the air beyond his village bounds.

Barnaby considered the shallow grave. He felt weary and hungered, knew the day fast ended. This scrape of earth would have to do. He took deep breath, then dragged the corpse into the grave, wishing for proper winding sheet. He folded the hands across the chest. Brushed the flies from the face. Then stood, considering, wondering what and who and why.

The farmer returned, without the donkey.

"You going to say words?"

Barnaby considered. The Friar's speech at Da's burying had been astonishing orations and incantations; authoritative and incomprehensible as writing carved upside down in stone. What words Barnaby found now were of simpler sort.

"Luck to you, friend," he told the beaten face of the dead man.

"Friend?" puzzled the farmer. "He was a stranger given shameful death." He stared down at the dead man, verifying that indeed no one better lay within. "You're clearly a fool."

Barnaby nodded. It was the common opinion of his village. The farmer looked disappointed for lack of argument. Held out a hand.

"Let's have my penny now."

Barnaby dug out the penny, placing it into the farmer's palm with the reverence of priest giving communion wafer. Exact as when the Squire put the coin in Barnaby's hand. Barnaby had smiled to receive; but the farmer only scowled.

"This is tin, colored copper," he growled. "In a town they'd have your head for pretending it honest coin."

Barnaby shook his un-had head. "Was given me by Squire Semple himself," he assured. "Said it was true coin of the realm."

"Bah," spat the man, tossing the coin to the dirt. "Your squire knew you for the fool you are." He picked up the spade. "Be off before I set the dogs on you." He turned and stalked away.

Barnaby stared after the man; then bent, retrieved the penny. Examined with cynical eye, it felt light as a wooden button, and of less worth. Perhaps it had fooled the Squire, though the man was said to know his coins same as God knew his separate angels. Barnaby turned to the man in the grave. The stranger lay contemplating the sky with half-open eyes. Hands upon chest, legs crossed. Looking more at peace than slumped across a donkey damned to wandering. This change cheered Barnaby. He reached down, closing the man's eyes. For final touch he placed the dubious coin on the man's chest. Formalities done, he began pushing the clods of dirt with hand and foot, covering the man best he could.

At last finished, he gave a nod to fresh grave and buried man. Then turned and climbed over the wall, back to the work of his own wandering.

Chapter 2
In the Witches' Wood

Evening light faded to night; the first stars bright. A cool wind set Barnaby shivering. He looked about for a millhouse where he'd hurry in, curl up by the hearth with a wool blanket woven by his gran. But his home had not followed him down the road. Was foolish to fancy it had, any more than to fear it'd been swallowed by the earth.

He weighed knocking on some farmhouse door, asking to sleep in their barn. At harvest time the villagers let the loaders, hay cutters and threshers do just that. But Barnaby spied no farms, no barns. Only a dark wood ahead, the trees arching over the lane, turning it black as mountain cavern.

Barnaby waivered. Perhaps it were time to turn about, head home? But he knew himself too weary to retrace the day's miles, even if he could bear the shame of returning without treasure. No, best rest in the shelter of the woods, enjoying his long-delayed lunch. This plan cheered him. Decided, he entered the tree-gloom.

The air within was full of owl hoots and fireflies, bat flitter and the choir of crickets, the scurry and hurry of small creatures seeking shelter for the night, exact as Barnaby. The sun's light faded with each step onwards. He felt weary; more than when the Squire brought five full carts of barley to be ground all in a day.

Barnaby looked for a spot dry yet soft, with moonlit clover for a pillow. Alas, all he found were hard tree roots, with brambles in between. No comfortable beds here. He chose a likely trunk in view of the path. The roots made sitting uncomfortable. The bark made leaning uncomfortable. But he gathered dead leaves, making what uncomforting bed he could. At last satisfied, he pulled his pack open, took out the lunch sack his stepmother had gifted him. He no longer smelled the bread, the cheese, the ham. Feeling about within the sack, he found within no lunch; just a lump of rock, a clod of earth.

What in the world? he asked the world. Had Mother Miller fooled him? With Barnaby she kept short of words, shorter of temper. Wasting no time with jests. Though his brother Alf oft found the time. Handing Barnaby a cup of horse piss vowing it was ale. Putting burrs in his socks, a dead cat in his blanket... Serving Barnaby a lunch of rock and clod would set Alf braying laughter like a tickled mule.

Yet Barnaby remembered the earlier, glorious smell of fresh bread, ripe cheese. The sack hadn't held clods and a rock when the day began.

"It was that sour girl at the fence," he told the night. "She had me leave my pack when I fetched her water." *Ah; that explains it nicely*, replied the night.

Barnaby debated laughing or cursing. Neither seemed worth the trouble. His stomach thought it worth a growl. He tightened his belt, told the growling thing to quiet before it drew bears. He wondered if there *were* bears about. Or lions? He lay back and decided he'd rather like to see a lion. For sure there'd be wolves. What wood in a tale ever lacked for wolf? Perhaps he'd best find a tree to climb. No; tree climbing could wait till wolf howls sounded. He shifted about in the gathered leaves, thinking it so prickly he'd never sleep.

He awoke deep into the night. The moon now hung above the treetops, casting strange shadows. Moths flittered in the shine, dancing exact as butterflies in sun's beams. Barnaby shivered, wishing for a fire. Not just for the warmth. A hearth-fire would keep him company. He pictured the flames dancing like courtiers at a fine ball, twisting and turning, leaping and bowing...

Barnaby found himself holding out his hands to the imagined warmth. Sitting and staring into the hearth had been much of his life. For all that his brother and mother, the Friar and the Squire cuffed him, called him dreamy fool. Chided him to get busy, cease staring into ashes.

They had the right of it, he decided. Better to be out and about to some purpose. Whether carrying sacks of flour or going down the road with a treasure map in one's pocket. Da would have agreed, for sure.

Barnaby reviewed all the things he'd seen on the road today. A girl and a butterfly, several strange houses, and a cloud that'd resembled a castle. His mind kept coming back to the dead stranger. That dunce cap on the dead man had said 'traitor', clear as dog said 'bark'. The farmer read the same; but holding it with the pointed side up. Had the Friar taught Barnaby to read upside down? That, or beyond his village the world was upside down. Who knew but that it was?

He heard voices, looked about. Perhaps it'd be hunters who'd share fire and venison. Else bandits who'd take his shoes and shirt. Of a sudden, a high mad laugh sounded, sending shivers. Barnaby turned to whence came the laugh: upwards. Spied a silhouette passing between the moonlit clouds and the trees. Laughing wild as all a flock of drunken geese.

Someone just flew overhead, thought Barnaby. On a broom. At night. Well.

Barnaby gaped at the treetops, eyes wide as the night sky. Hoping for a whole host of witches to pass overhead. And a dragon, perhaps a wizard riding a comet? Alas, nothing further passed but cloud whisps. At last he sighed, looked down to the dark earth again. To spy a creature coming along the path. A rooster, strutting proudly into the woods. Its cock's comb straight, eyes so fiery aglow they served for a lantern to light its way. For tail it had a serpent, writhing like flag in storm wind.

Barnaby kept still as millstone on a windless day, watching it pass. The creature's light faded into the trees. Soon as gone, another entered. Here now came a goat, with wool blacker than the night. It pranced forwards, backwards, sidling ahead, leaping to the side, bobbing horns as though batting and butting the shadows. Eyes bright, yellow as amber held to the sun. When it opened its mouth flames glimmered within. For a moment it paused, glancing Barnaby's way. He held still, letting no least leaf rustle. The goat could not long hold still; it pranced onwards.

Just as Barnaby dared take breath, here came a third creature. A great boar, tusked and hairy. It moved absurdly, ungainly hopping on back legs while reaching upwards with its front trotters. *It wants to walk upright,* thought Barnaby. The creature's eyes were hot red embers threatening to set the woods alight.

The boar halted in the path. Turning this way and that. Sniffing into the night shadows of the trees. Barnaby's heart beat fast as soldier's drum signaling *retreat, retreat.*

More voices sounded. The pig looked back, then grunted, hurrying onwards as if afraid to be caught dawdling. Soon as it vanished, Barnaby jumped up, darted behind a tree trunk. Peeking out wide-eyed as two-legged folk moved in and out of the moonlight along the path. Dancing as they came, which should have set them tumbling in the moon shadows. But no, they came sure-footed as the Squire into his counting house.

Suddenly one stopped, sniffed.

"Smell that?" she asked. "Someone hides in the trees."

"Belshazzar!" cried another. "Come fetch a sweet for us."

The great boar trotted back into view, casting red light from its eyes, bloody flames from out its opened mouth. For a moment it sniffed; then pushed into shadows and bracken towards Barnaby's tree. No further use in hiding. He turned, running into the dark, catching clothes on brambles, bumping into branches. The human folk laughed to hear him scurry.

"Leave be," said the leader. "Art too young to know that bouquet? 'Tis fresh grave dirt."

"Ah, just a revenant, then," declared another. "Poor thing, poor dead thing. Leave him for a darker night."

"Want to see it," complained a third. "Want to play with it."

Barnaby fled through the trees, away from their voices. Till he crashed into a wall of thorns and bracken. Impassible to all but rabbits. Barnaby decided he'd best *be* a rabbit. He lowered himself to the dirt, where brambles grew less thick. Then wiggled and crawled through dead leaves. Leaf mold and wet decay filled his nose and lungs till he near drowned in a sea of forest rot.

At length he popped out into fresh air, the half-light of moon shine. Scrambling out and up from the brambles; finding himself in a quiet clearing. Centered by a great oak, branches out to hold up the night sky. Barnaby hurried to the tree, grabbing the lowest branch, pulling himself up. Reached for another and another, till he felt hidden high within the dark canopy. There he rested, holding tight to a thick oak branch. Gathering breath as his heart ceased its drumbeat panic. At length he even dared look downwards.

He spied nothing but quiet glade, the silent moonlight. Heard nothing but cricket choir, nightingale concert, owl parliamentarians debating. The night wind blew, sounding a bit like voices, a bit like laughter. The thought came to Barnaby that he'd dreamed the whole chase, witches and Infernum-beasts and all. He'd popped up and run from phantoms, same as when his brother chased him with a candlelit turnip-ghost.

Something moved about beneath the tree. The rooster with snake's tail and eyes shining brighter than any turnip ghost. *Wasn't a dream, then*, thought Barnaby. With a certain sense of satisfaction, a definite sense of awe. He pictured telling his brother and mother of the creature. They'd listen astounded.

The rooster carried sticks and treefall branches in its serpent tail. Barnaby watched as it set them in a proper pile for a fire. Then up came the dancing goat. Bearing a dark iron pot, handle in its mouth as bone in the jaws of a dog. The pot sloshing with something dark and thick. The goat set the pot atop the pile of wood.

Now the great boar trotted from out the trees, still making its absurd half-steps. Given over chasing Barnaby, else turned to other duty. The beast pushed aside rooster and goat; snuffled at the kindling. At once red flames leaped up, like fresh-wakened servants anxious to appear busy before their master. The pot began to simmer as though it'd stood in the fire all the night.

Now came the human folk; three cloaked figures chatting, laughing. Entering the moth-and-moon haunted glade proud as courtiers into a king's hall. A fourth followed behind, not quite so confident. She pushed back her cloak hood, and Barnaby knew her. Behold the sour-faced girl for whom he'd fetched water, receiving a kiss. Or a pebble, depending on one's village vernacular.

"And here is our precious Jewel," declared one, turning to the newcomer. "Our new sister. Shall we summon a familiar to serve her?"

"Such was the bargain," said their precious Jewel, crossing arms.

"And bargains we keep," affirmed another. "As you keep yours, poppet."

"What's it to be?" asked another. "Shall you have a mare to ride through dreams, casting palsy upon sleepers? Else a snake to keep within your bosom, whispering dark wisdom? Perhaps a solemn raven who will circle the world each night, tell you who's been murdered, whose house is alight?"

"I want a cat," declared Jewel. "A great black cat to serve for shadow, teaching me magic."

"That's rather dull, moppet," chided a witch.

"A cat," repeated Jewel. Stamping foot.

"Very well," sighed the witch. She produced a long stick unpleasantly like a leg bone; began stirring the pot. "Have we the ingredients?"

Barnaby watched while one after another brought forth some item, dropping it into the bubbling brew, making a 'plop' sound like rock dropped into mud. The stirring witch began to sing.

Tithe from a miser, pinching each cent.
Tooth from a womanizer, dirty old gent!
A bride's hair, a hunter's snare.
A splinter from the bishop's chair.
A bauble from a lover with bad intent.
Last a trifle, stole from an innocent.

The oldest witch bent down, dropping something within. Whispering as she did.

"What are you saying, Eldest?" demanded Jewel. "Do you add to the casting?"

The old witch straightened slowly, as if her back ached. "I but say farewell to my darling Trent. That was the last tooth I had of the dear old lecher."

The other witches chuckled; then looked to Jewel. Her turn to place something within the pot.

"What do you bring for innocence, little sister? Naught of your own will serve, for all your sweet child's face."

Jewel scowled. "I'm perfectly innocent, you old thing."

This declaration was met with laughter. Even the rooster, pig and goat shook with amusement.

Jewel growled, emptying a sack into the boiling pot. Barnaby spied a quarter-wheel of cheese, a portion of ham big as his fist, a half loaf of bread. He sighed, stomach growling.

"That last was strangely spiced," observed the one stirring. "Did I not know better, I'd declare it Lifebane, ground fine."

"'Twas the lunch of a gormless boy on the road," scoffed Jewel. "Not the archbishop's poisoned cup handed the king."

"Hmm," said the witch. "Hmm, yes, I smell the innocence right enough. Well, so long as you sip, so shall we all. Drink, girl; then choose a patch of moonlight where your new friend shall appear. The summoning shall serve the one who first gives it kiss."

"Did you kiss Belshazzar?" asked Jewel, looking at the boar.

"I did," affirmed the witch. "He's a finer kisser than the queen's confessor."

The boar grunted proudly, flames shooting from its jaws.

Something went 'plop' into the boiling pot.

"What was that?" demanded Jewel, staring about.

"An acorn," judged the witch stirring. "Fret not, dear. Shan't spoil the broth a wit." She found a ladle, scooped into the brew, handing this to Jewel. The girl made a face. Still she sipped, sipped till the ladle held not a drop. Then scooped up more, handing it to the next witch.

"Hot," declared one. "But proper. That bitter taste must be acorn."

"Womanizer always makes a stomach burn," complained another.

"Too strong a taste of innocence," declared the third, smacking lips. "Must have been a true fool you found, Jewel my dear."

Jewel gave no answer. She moved out into the clearing. Stopping before a bright patch of moonshine. Pulling back cloak sleeves, raising two pale arms high. She began singing soft words that melted into wind, melded into shadow.

The witches watched. Their familiar beasts watched. Barnaby watched. While wood and world went quiet. The wind stilled, crickets ceasing all song. At length, at last, and then... into Jewel's chosen moonbeam strode a cat. Large and lithe, slanted eyes shining white. White as the feathers of a stained-glass angel in the king's cathedral, with summer sun shining behind. The cat stretched itself in luxury, in no least hurry. Then it sat on hind legs. Tail curling about its forefeet, elegant as a banker's fox-fur stole.

The creature blinked its angel-white eyes up at Jewel. She blinked down. Finally, she bent low, putting her face to the cat's. Lips puckered. At which act of familiarity the cat gave a terrible hiss, an ear-spiking howl. It slashed with claws fast as light from moon to earth.

Jewel screamed, fell back, covering her face with hands. The cat whirled, disappearing into the trees. But from the shadows of the woods it continued its outraged yowl.

"Something is amiss," said a witch. "I feel most dreadful ill." She sat upon the grass, holding hands to stomach.

"Weary," said another, and sank against the tree trunk.

Jewel rose to her knees. She began to retch and cough, spewing pot-brew across the glade.

"Oh, sisters, we are poisoned," cried a witch. "The innocent's food was spiced with Lifebane."

"Jewel, you have betrayed," began another. Struggling to say more, but falling into silence.

One witch worked to climb onto the back of the goat. Soon as astride, it raced away. A second clambered atop the boar; it trotted off into the night. But the third witch lay exact where she fell. The rooster circled about the still form, writhing its snake tail in worry. At last it threw back its head, gave a horrible cock's crow lament. Out the beak burst flames enveloping it. This fire soon died, leaving naught but drifting smoke tainting the night air. The witch did not stir.

Nor did Barnaby. He hugged the tree branch tight, watching Jewel. She crawled slowly, slowly into the woods and away. This last witch gone, the fire beneath the pot went dark quick as snuffed candle. Barnaby considered climbing down, making his own exit. But he felt too tired; and here seemed safe as anywhere within the mad woods. So he held tight to the oak branch, watching clouds scudder across the night sky, bats swoop upon moths, owls swoop upon bats. He watched the dead witch sink slowly into the earth. He watched the cat sitting deep in the moon shadows, while its great moon eyes watched him.

Chapter 3
Could a Road Speak

Lord Michael:

My death was a weary business. I recall only the interesting moments, as one recollects the more striking steps of any journey. The months within a lightless cell have vanished. What would there be to recall? Just a dull dark, dank with despair. But I remember the whipping post, down to the fine details of wood grain. Fresh pine from the mountains. It had swirls of yellow grain etched with rougher red lines that leaked sap. I tried to picture myself in the mountains from where this wooden thing began. Seeing the cool green shadows, feeling the cold clean wind. Each crack of the whip brought me back screaming to the execution dock.

I forget my trial. A tedious stage-play of sly faces, stomach-turning betrayal. And I only dimly remember days in the stocks, while folk who once tugged forelock in respect to my noble person now tossed horse apples and cobblestones, jeering at my fall. Dull business; angels and devils alike agreed to strike it from the records of the human story. Exact as did I.

And yet, I remember the smallest details of the hangman's absurd leather hood. Soft calfskin, dyed black as a courtier's funeral best. Eyeholes cut big and round, giving the burly man the air of an astonished child. With a slit to show lips; wide red lips, for all the hairy naked chest. I remember a brief comic urge to give him a kiss. I did not; I was too broken in body and spirit for japes. There came a last gaze at the sky, the tightening grasp of the noose while I kicked legs, gave last farts and gasps... But what came after? I've no least recollection.

Death passes same as birth. One cannot recall the moment. It is forever hidden. One only realizes later that it must have happened. Think back to your earliest memory. It cannot be of your birth, struggling in the womb, pushed out into light and air as your mother howls. No, it will be some childhood recollection of a burned hand, a lost toy, a soft song sung beside the bed. Memories from years after the start of life. So also, beyond death.

My first recollection after dying is walking beside the donkey that bore my remains. Turning random ways as villagers drove us ever on. And yet I knew I'd been walking so for hours; perhaps for years. I almost remember that I argued as we walked. I do not recall with whom. But I feel we debated the goal of my journey, the purpose of the road itself and the injustice shown the donkey. With whom did I argue? Perhaps with the donkey; or my corpse upon it. Perhaps I argued with the road itself. Could a road speak, surely it would ask what purpose did I have upon it?

I remember the passing countryside as mere bits of tattered light, a crude sketch of a world upon a tapestry torn by wind and storm. The long miles of trudging, the dead man slowly, slowly turning to something sad and liquid. The donkey plodding ever on, at times putting muzzle to grass it could not eat, into water it could not drink. A creature suffering without purpose. A symbol of pain borne patiently for lack of choice. A weary damnation lacking the comforting drama of Infernum's fire.

And then, ah, and then upon the infinite endless road, I recall the boy. Absurd creature; not yet grown into his large hands and feet. Freckled, with hair wild and yellow as straw. Face bright and innocent as summer sky. I never saw a face that had less to do with me or mine. A pleasant, peasant face. Features declaring at once to all:

behold a dreamer, an optimist, a gormless fool no wiser than the donkeys of the world.

I watched fascinated as the farmer hefted the spade, weighing whether it were best to add the boy's corpse to the hole, lest he reveal they'd taken the donkey from its civic duty. The boy did not notice the clenched hands, the narrowed eyes. Instead he whistled while digging my grave, dragging the pathetic clay within. At last for final word: naming me 'friend'.

Friend! As though I were neither a noble far above his peasant station, nor worm food at his feet. No; I was *friend;* something common as him. And holy for being common, as all truly holy things are. I sighed; and then before my grave, beside the road, beneath the declining sun, I laughed. For I knew now the purpose of the journey given me. Not in life, but on the long road after.

Chapter 4
Meeting with a Green Lady

Two more days of walking left Barnaby ragged and hungry, but in high spirits. He'd slept one night in a hedge, to be awakened at dawn by farm dogs howling at the scent of trespass. The second night he'd been granted the corner of a barn by a kindly farmer, who in return only asked that he chop wood, carry water, card wool and weed the garden. Barnaby did these things; leaving with a pocket of rough carrots and cheerful blessings.

The country lane had matured to a wider cart-rutted road. Not bricked as were the great roads of the world (according to the Friar, who knew such things). Still, this new path was traveled by horse and wagon, tillers and tinkers, monks and millers, fiddlers and farmers. Worn as he was, Barnaby drank in every face met, each voice heard. Calling out 'hallo!' to all he passed. Most oft getting greeting in return. At times mere jeers, else indifferent silence. No matter. Weary, hungry, he walked delighting in all sights seen, all sounds caught, all folk met. The open world was an orchard of wonders, he the happy wanderer sampling the windfall fruit.

Occasionally he consulted his map. It gave him no least idea of where he was or where he needed to go. But doing so reminded him that *he* was no lost donkey, but a bold seeker of treasure. Somewhere on this journey, the map and world would agree. Then he'd get down to the work that pulled him from staring at the hearth fire.

At times upon the road he'd look back, feeling followed. Spying a small creature far behind; lurking in evening light or morning shadow. It was the cat from the moonlit wood, he felt sure. Whenever he slowed to let it catch up, it merely halted.

Other whiles he would spy a figure walking far ahead. A tall man in black coat, black hat. When Barnaby hurried to catch up, the figure moved effortlessly onwards, just beyond clear sight. No telling who *that* might be.

On the third morning he walked chewing on thoughts and carrots. He wondered what everyone did back home. Without Barnaby, his brother Alf would have to tend the wheels, patch the vanes, oil the cogs, mill the grain, sack the flour. His mother would be fetching kindling, weeding the garden, churning the butter. Try as he might, he couldn't picture them doing these things without grumbles to rival thunder.

They might get the Goat Girl to help. Though they'd best keep eye on her or she'd feed the butter to the cats, and mill cow-shit while riding on the turning vanes, singing her mad songs.

Maybe the friar would help tend the wheels. He was knowledgeable about machinery, for all it had naught to do with saints and scripture. At least, not that Barnaby could see. But who knew, perhaps a mill wheel turned with the angels, or the stars spinning overhead?

Whether turning by winds angelic or earthly, for sure all at the mill cursed Barnaby's absence, wondering when by Infernum's warm blessing he'd return with bags of gold. They'd have to be patient. As Da said: *let the stones turn slow, so long as they go.*

Barnaby pictured marching into Mill Town, treasure chest upon his shoulders, same as a hunter returning with a fine deer. He'd drop the treasure before brother and mother, friar and squire. The chest would be so heavy it'd burst, spilling coins and crowns to roll in the dirt. What would everyone say?

"Hey!" shouted someone. Someone complaining of scattered gold and rolling crowns?

Barnaby shook himself from daydreams, looking about. There in the road ahead stood a child. A girl, seven or so. Wild hair and wide eyes.

"What is it?"

"Mamma's about to calf and she can't get over the stile."

Barnaby blinked, prepared to ask questions. But the girl whirled about, running down the road. Barnaby hurried after.

Around the next turn, he spied her climbing rough planks making rough ladder over a low wall. He called for her to halt; but she only waved, leaping into the world beyond.

Barnaby climbed after, peering into a cabbage field. Right beneath him against the stone wall, sat a woman holding hands to a swollen belly.

Birthing, thought Barnaby, and winced. It wasn't a subject he knew well. He'd sat the night by a few cows in the Squire's barn, talking to them of whatever he could. *Keeps them calm*, said the Squire. Twice or thrice he'd held a nanny goat fast while the Goat Girl reached in, pulled out the wet and kicking kid.

But a people-lady birthing... that was new territory. Not for men to be stepping into. The little girl stood beside him, chattering fast.

"We were just gathering but she screamed and poured out and now she can't get over the wall to get home."

"Is there someone hereabouts who knows birthing?" asked Barnaby.

"Missus Green," said the girl. "But she's long ways off."

"I could run," he offered. "Where does she live?"

The woman gave a howl of pain. Barnaby jumped, anxious to begin running. The girl ran in a circle, close to panic herself.

"You go down the road to the forked oak and then follow the creek till you pass the rock that looks like Uncle. Then go through the wheat field. Not the radish field 'cause that takes you to the farm where the dogs are mean. Go into the woods towards where it smells all moss and lavender. Missus Green's got a cottage. But stay this side of the tree stump or you'll wind up in mud and flies. Uncle has a beard if that helps with the rock."

Barnaby tried to order that in his head, but the woman ceased moaning. Doing her best to speak.

"Steph, you'd best be the one to fetch Missus Green. He'll get lost."

"It's long ways," said the girl, bending down to the woman. "He's a big man. Can't he carry you home?"

Barnaby considered the woman, measuring her equal weight in flour.

"I could pick you up, get you over the wall," he decided.

"I'd do no better that side of it than this," said the woman. Smiling weakly. "Nor on the kitchen floor. No, here is where I'd best stay. Steph, fetch Missus Green. Stranger, thank you kindly, but you can be on your –"

She interrupted herself with a fresh howl. Barnaby watched pinkish water trickle from the woman's outstretched legs. Realized he was trembling.

"Right," said Barnaby, turning to the girl. "Go fetch your wise-woman. I'll stay and keep your momma company."

The girl jumped, whirling between her mother and the road. Then she nodded, clambering over the wall and disappeared.

Barnaby sat. The air tasted of cabbage field and summer-warmed earth. A pleasant place, at least.

"You staying?" asked the woman. She panted as if she'd run for the last nine months.

"If you let me," said Barnaby. "Wouldn't feel right to just walk on."

The woman nodded. "You were raised right, young sir."

Barnaby did his best not to smile. Past pale face stretched by pain, the would-be-mother didn't look to be any older than Barnaby.

"This'un is my first," said the woman, closing her eyes. "All say that's the hard one."

"Ah?"

"Steph calls me 'momma' but she was my sister Maria's first."

"Oh."

"Maria, she died same day Steph was born."

"Ah."

The woman opened her eyes, peering at Barnaby, making a weak smile. "Not to talk so gloomy as to catch the ear of Friar February, you understand."

"Yes'm," said Barnaby. "Can I fetch you anything? Water from a creek or well? I've got some carrots, though they're pretty hard."

He watched in horror as the woman's stomach rippled beneath the cloth of her dress. She bent her back, stared up, groaning, panting. He fought an urge to jump up, wish her well and run.

Finally, she shook her head at offered carrots.

"Just sit by, so's I'm not here alone." She reached out, grabbed his hand, held it tight.

"Easy enough work," he declared. Thinking privately how it wasn't.

They sat together so. Barnaby watched birds and clouds pass overhead, feeling the woman shake, hearing her pant and moan.

You'd think clouds and birds and the sun would stop and ask us if all were right, he thought. *But that's foolish. They fly right over births and deaths every day.*

"Oh, I wish Rog were here," the woman gasped. "I'd curse him out hotter than the pokers St. Lucif shoves up the behinds of the specially wicked."

"Rog your husband?"

"More or less. Mostly less. Ow! Gone for a soldier. Drink beer, fight the Festians, the Tarchs."

"Sounds adventurous."

"More adventurous, ow! – than raising babies and cabbages. Why are you on the road? What's your name? Where's your home?"

Barnaby grasped she wanted him to talk, to take her mind from pain, from fear. So he described the things he knew. The mill, and his Da, and the stories of the saints the Friar read aloud by the fire on winter evenings. Going to the southern *Jahrmarkt* with the Mill Town folk, seeing more strangers than crows in autumn, all gathered in a riot of tents and booths.

He described a pantomime puppet show he and Alf paid half-pence to watch. Cheering the gold-caped hero, booing the wicked lord of the manor, laughing at the comic robber.

The woman said 'Oh?' and 'I see', to encourage him to keep talking.

She interrupted with a howl. "Dang child isn't going to wait polite for Missus Green," she gasped. "Oh!"

She pulled her skirt hem, parting legs; Held hands to her crotch, turning a face of pain up to the evening sky.

Barnaby put his hand on her shoulder, patting it, feeling a useless fool.

Blood and water poured out from between the woman's legs. Barnaby watched in horror and awe as the red wet head of the baby pushed forth. The woman screamed. Barnaby felt close to screaming himself. Then, of all things, the baby opened a mouth red and round as rose bloom, giving a howl to join with theirs.

"Help me," gasped the woman. "Pull 'er forth."

Together they tugged the tiny being free of the womb, bloody and squirming, cord still dangling.

"A girl, then," gasped the woman. "Poor thing. Knew it so." She cradled the child in folded arms, crying, laughing, babbling. The babe gave gasps and howls, entirely upset by the business.

"Have you knife?" asked the woman.

"Yes'm."

"Good. Cut the cord, leaving a hand length. Then knot it close."

Barnaby did this, surprised how his hands trembled.

The woman pulled open her blouse, pressing the baby to a breast. It did not feed, merely squirmed, gasped, howled, smearing her bloody.

The mother closed her eyes. Barnaby stared at the wet red ground beneath them both. Astonishing as if the babe had rising from the earth.

"Are you, are you well, miss? I mean ma'am?"

For a long while she didn't answer. He thought her dead. Then she nodded, even smiled. "I'm fine. Just damned weary."

Barnaby nodded. He felt drained himself. Though he'd done naught but sit, but talk. He studied the blood on his still-shaking hands. He wiped them on the ground, which didn't help much. He got up, walked back and forth, realizing his head was swimming. He'd fall in a faint. He sat down again.

"Well, now, and who and what are you?" asked a voice. He looked up into evening sky while a woman peered over the wall, staring down from the very same sky.

"I am Barnaby and my father was a miller and this is a woman I don't know her name, and I don't know the babe's name either." He considered, then added, "Because the baby's new." Which was true, if rather absurd to point out.

But the stranger nodded to declare she thought his words summed to excellent sense. She clambered over the wall, then reached, lifting the tangle-haired girl Steph, placing her upon the wall.

Steph jumped down, knelt, poking mother and child with a finger.

"Momma's breathing," she declared. "But the baby's ugly."

The woman laughed, setting a large bag down upon the ground.

"This is Missus Green," said Steph. "Missus Green, this man is someone I don't know but says he's a miller. Doesn't look much like our miller so I don't know."

Missus Green pulled forth a blanket, draped it about the new mother. Then drew out a second one, handing it to Barnaby.

"You look more worn than this new matron," she declared. "Get some rest."

Barnaby wrapped himself in the blanket. It was scratchy wool, poorly carded, just something to cover calves in winter.

Still, it served Barnaby fine. He prepared to thank the woman, ask if there was aught he could fetch. But the words never came. He tumbled into a hole filled with rich warm sleep. The night grew cold, but he just curled the tighter.

He woke only once, deep in the night, the stars so bright they seemed to have crept closer to spy upon the doings in the cabbage field. Missus Green sat beside a small fire, holding the new baby, singing to it soft and low as evening breeze. Wasn't a word in the song that Barnaby knew. Still, he felt he knew the tune. It seemed part of some grand hymn to breath and flame, field and star. Some piece of music he'd heard before. At his own birthing, perhaps.

It made no challenge to curl warm and content, to return to sleep.

Chapter 5
The Crater that is my Crater

Shadow Night-Creep:

Witches I have served, seven times seven; and six mages, and thrice the High Priest in the temple of St. Bast, wherein I lay upon pillows of hummingbird feathers. Servants brought me fish upon platters, silver scales agleam. And when I rose, and stretched, and chose to prowl? They rushed to open the sacred doors for me, close the sacred doors for me, open the sacred doors for me, close the sacred doors for me.

And once did I serve a fat wealthy merchant in a cobbled city to the South. At his demand I told dark tales of war and hunger, sorrow and loss. I spoke of mothers feeding hungry babes upon their own heart's blood, and villages plagued by drought till the house dogs turned wolves and devoured all. Stories I purred of city streets where children and rats played chase, winners devouring losers. Grim things I told, and dark; till the man's mind grew disturbed with visions of hard lives and winter winds. He ordered me from his golden house. Ah, but as he lay in his soft warm bed I perched upon the window ledge, staring in, staring in, staring in. At length he went mad; hanging himself in the golden gleam of his treasure vault.

And oft have I attended convocations of devils beneath the earth, prowling beneath tables of dragon bone and onyx, rubbing against the feet of princes of Infernum seated on their thrones of fire. At times they gravely consult me, inquiring my opinion concerning the troop strength of the Upper House and the weakness of human souls. In answer, I only blink my eyes, my beautiful eyes, to say that what I know, I will never share.

In gay revels of forest Fae and woodland spirits I have sat, watching silent, entranced by their mad faery japes and near cat-like grace. But never dancing, never taking part. Kings, priests, faeries, devils, and all manner of witch and wizard have I served. But they knew me not, for I give myself not.

But never and never and never have I served a farmland fool wandering the world's roads innocent as some duckling out from a mill pond. A tasty succulent tempting duckling, hopping and peeping up to wolves who stare astonished. While I watch, equally astonished.

I creep and spy at the boy's heels. He knows I follow; but he knows me not. I watch him greet crooked tinkers and bloody soldiers, a band of thieves he takes for acrobats, and once a mad dog. He wishes to all that the sun shine bright upon them, the wind blow cool. And they smile, and wish him the same. Even the mad dog, the stinking piddling drooling fool of a cur. They return his smile and pass on, hoping to find for themselves the joy that he holds in his idiot empty head, his sad empty pockets, his rumbling empty stomach.

Oft I return to the moon, where I curl in the crater that is *my* crater and no other cat's crater for it is *my* crater. And there I gaze at the unmoving earth, the evermoving stars. And I consider my time upon it, and my new binding to the idiot boy. To teach; but not to aid. Surely this is the strangest service that ever a witch's cat was summoned to.

Chapter 6
Introduction to a Stone

Dawn found Barnaby alone in a cabbage field. He stirred, yawned, looking about. Were it not for the blood-muddy ground, the scratchy blanket and a bundle of barley bread left for his breakfast, he might have thought he dreamed the previous day.

He rose, sitting on the wall, enjoying the sun, eating the bread, staring at cabbages and crows. Wondering what they would name the baby. Maybe they'd name it after the noble stranger who nobly sat by the woman in travail? Not to any least noble use, granted. And anyway 'Barnaby' would make a silly name for a girl. Not even considering the issue of whistling.

Thoughts and breakfast completed, he took up his pack, heading down the road, glad to be moving again. Whistling whatever song that wind, heart and breath requested he so blow.

A farmer throned upon an oxcart rumbled up the road. Barnaby moved aside, but the man invited him to ride with the hay. Barnaby accepted gladly, rested in scratchy straw while the farmer declaimed upon kings and wives, angels and chickens. He didn't want Barnaby's opinion of these things any more than he wanted the ox's. Just an ear to receive the *Truth Declared*. Barnaby lent ear gladly, fascinated by all he heard.

The farmer left him at a crossroads, his cart rumbling on, his talk upon kings and chickens rumbling on. Barnaby stretched, brushing itching stalks of hay out his jerkin. He approached a stone fountain centering the crossroad. Water dribbled out the mouth of a carved face, too worn to discern whether man or beast. No matter; it offered cool drink to weary folk. Barnaby drank his fill, then sat on the rim, consulting his map. Glancing from the parchment to the world, then back again. Searching in different directions for a great mountain with a tower atop it. A tower higher than the clouds, the glow of treasure shining out the windows.

He spied clouds and fields, a thatch-roofed cottage, a pasture of goats. A flock of crows in a just-threshed field huddled together, muttering of murder. An approaching horseman riding a fine beast, with silver jangles that rang pleasant as light summer rain. Barnaby observed how the rider threw head back, declaiming to the sky. Singing, for sure.

What a fine thing, he told himself. To ride the road singing. Even better than whistling. I shall get a horse and do the same. When I know how to ride a horse. And to sing. Do folk learn to ride? Do folk learn to sing?

As he pondered these important questions, the rider halted before font and boy. Dismounting with a flourish that set all the bells jingling. The crescendo made Barnaby laugh, which made the rider laugh. The horse rolled its eyes at their easy amusement, pushing towards the stone basin. Barnaby moved politely aside. The horse slurped, eyeing him in suspicion.

The newcomer stretched, clearly glad to be on foot. Put hands to backside, facing Barnaby. "Do you know that old stone?" he asked, nodding to the fountain.

Barnaby considered. Did people know stones? Certainly he knew the greater and lesser grinding stones of the mill. They were old friends. He turned to the fountain, wondering whether he should introduce himself.

A tall stone construction, with water dribbling out the mouth of the time-dimmed face. Words and symbols carved into it; weather-worn as worm-rot on old wood. Barnaby decided he'd never met this rock before; shook his head.

The newcomer crossed arms, clearly pleased to instruct. "Well as it happens, we stand at St. Herman's font. That worn face is Herm himself. Has little shrines up and down all the older highways. Patron saint of travelers. Looks out after them, they say, they say."

Barnaby widened eyes, impressed. He studied the ancient stone face. If one stared sideways, the features grew clearer. Surely that was a smile? A rough rogue's grin, welcoming all in their coming and going. A trick of sun-shadow upon the carving granted Barnaby a sly wink.

In return, Barnaby stood, gave the stone a deep bow. "I am honored to meet you, Saintly Herman. My thanks for the drink, and all your kind service to the thirsty."

Herm said naught; but the trickling water laughed; the rider laughed. He had a high voice, almost girlish. Barnaby pondered this person as he had the stone. Noting the thin wrists and delicate face. Was he a girl? He thought about asking. But, *'take folk for who they say they are'*, Da always advised. *'There's holy truth in what folk pretend of themselves'*.

Barnaby had never found use for that advice within Mill Town. All the folk he knew were just who they were. What else could they be? Meanwhile, the stranger stood giving the same measured consideration to Barnaby; who was after all, only Barnaby.

"You wouldn't by chance be the third son of a poor woodcutter's widow sent off to win a princess, are you?"

Barnaby shook his head. "Ah, no; I'm the second son. There's no third. True enough, mother's a widow. But the mill wheels turn oft enough she can winter in fox fur. While I'm on my way to find treasure, not a princess." He pondered. "Still, I'd like to find a princess. Oh, she'd be all in silks eating chocolates, declaring her pillow too hard and the porridge too cold.

She'd wave a hand, send me to fetch strawberries in winter, ices in summer."

The rider grinned. "That's the creatures, exactly." He hobbled the horse in a shady spot beneath trees that must have been saplings when Saint Herman was green and spry. The horse fed upon the green summer grass, while its master pulled a book from its pack. Circling to the back of St. Herman's stone, where yet more writing waited. He produced quill and ink horn, began a studious sketching of the stone.

Barnaby looked down the road. He should be *getting on with the sun*, as his Da would say. But the stranger fascinated. He considered the harp across the back, gold-painted. The green velvet jerkin, the fine cloth hat over hair bound with silver band.

"Are you a bard?"

"Of a sort," declared this personage. "Just a journeyman." He paused, deciding to share a secret. "And so I journey a man, in search of a famous cup. I've been told to ask St. Herman for hints. So far he's not been forthcoming."

Barnaby shivered in appreciation of such quest.

"A golden cup, all aglow with holy light and music? In a haunted church or castle, surrounded by angels singing, knights praying, maidens swooning?"

The journeyman laughed. "You know your tales, right enough. Ah, I've dreamed twice of it now. Didn't spy the angels or knights. But there was music. As if it were a bowl filled with golden song, waiting for the thirsty to drink."

For a moment the bard's face took on a look that Barnaby could not interpret. A mad gaze into impossible distance, like the Goat Girl sitting on a rock by her herd, staring into the sun. It gave Barnaby a strange feeling.

Then the bard shook head, returned gaze to the visible world.

"When I find the cup, I shall call myself a master bard."

"Sounds a wondrous thing," said Barnaby. "A miller is a miller is a miller and no more, not if he finds a thousand magical cups."

He turned to study the stone fountain. Finding the words upon this side less worn.

Ware winter ice and summer heat.
Ware the wolf upon two feet.
An open hand for those in strife.
A wary eye for the brigand's knife.

"Sound proper wisdom," declared Barnaby.

"So you can read?" observed the bard. "But why tilt your head so? One eye not set right?"

Barnaby confessed. "Seems I've learned my letters upside down. We'd naught to read in Mill Town but the Friar's books, and he must have held them proper to his eye, wrong to mine."

"Ah." The bard considered. "Hmm." He blew awhile upon his own book page, letting the ink dry. Then set paper, quill and inkhorn aside.

"You made old Herman's acquaintance, but not mine. I am Val the Bard. Not decided yet if 'Val' shall be for Valentine, Valerian, or Valiant."

"Can a bard choose what they are called?" asked Barnaby. The idea had never occurred to him.

Val grinned. "As can a miller. If he wishes. How are you calling yourself today?"

Barnaby pondered. Absurd names came to mind. 'Felicitation'. 'Falcon'. 'Fish'. What would it be like to be called 'Fish'? Or 'Jellyjamtoast' or 'Abracacadamian'? He shook his head, undecided.

"I'm just 'Barnaby' for today. Perhaps I'll choose something grander, later."

Val offered hand; Barnaby took it, shook it.

"Pleased to meet you, Journeyman Bard Val."

"You as well, Barnaby the Miller's Son. And you are truly off to seek treasure?"

Barnaby scratched his head, looking towards the paths of the crossroads.

"Yes. It's in a tower on a mountain the saints avoid. The tower goes up taller than five pine trees one atop the other, if you can believe." He stood on tiptoe, hand in the air to indicate how high this must be. "It has a thousand black marble steps just to reach the door."

Barnaby sighed, gestured to indicate the fields and missing mountain. "I've followed my map but haven't so much as bumped into anything higher than a hill."

Val weighed this, frowning.

"There is such a place," he/she admitted. "But it's far to the north, past Hefestia. And it isn't a place to journey towards. Holy Bridget's private bits, that's the sort of place you run from. Screaming, most oft. Who sent you on such path?"

"My younger brother Alf," declared Barnaby proudly. "With a map from my Da himself."

The bard sat on the rim of the fountain next to Barnaby, eyeing him.

"You said you were the second of two. How is your brother the younger?"

"Well, he's Mother Miller's eldest. I was my Da's eldest. I had a different mother, long ago."

"Then with your Da dead, the mill should be yours."

Barnaby looked up at a cloud. He wished it was a hearth fire. Perhaps it *was* a hearth fire, and he'd imagined it into a cloud? A butterfly fluttered by, and Barnaby considered whether it might not really be a flame, to go with the cloud. Certainly it danced like flame. Then again, perhaps the butterfly was a cloud.

Val waited, not hearing this inner examination of fact and flame. At length growing impatient.

"Besides lessons in reading upside down and a map to a death trap, what else did your loving family give you for the road?"

Barnaby spent a long time before answering. Finding he didn't really want to answer. He watched the butterfly circling Herm's fount. The butterfly and Herm were clearly old friends.

But it felt impolite to keep silent. At length Barnaby told the butterfly. "The Squire gave me a penny. Though it seems to have been painted tin."

"Ouch," said the bard. "Dangerous thing to have."

"And mother gave me lunch. It was strangely spiced."

The bard followed his gaze to the butterfly. Then stood, returning to the horse. Adjusted his pack, then mounted, setting tin bells jingling. From that height he looked down at Barnaby, expression a mix of puzzlement and pity.

"Well, your family wants you dead, Barnaby. Sure as your friar wanted you ignorant, your squire hopes some township hangs you. And if by 'strangely spiced' you mean 'poisoned', well, I'm thinking the folk at home do not expect your return. With treasure or without."

To these words Barnaby made no answer. Keeping to a silence stony as St. Herman's. The bard waited; at last gave sigh and shrug.

"Well, anyways. I'm off in search of my cup. Good luck on your own quest, young miller." Val clicked heals, set the horse trotting. The bard tossed some last advice over his shoulder: "And were I you, I'd mind the wolves on two feet."

Chapter 7
The Knight of Cups

Val the Bard:

I am a practical person set upon impractical quest. Exactly as it should be. Realists are the souls best suited for impractical challenges. To seek the grail is a thing of dream. And it is only those awake who understand dreams.

And so, blessed St. Bridget's bust but that Barnaby made my hair stand on end. You'd think I'd laugh to meet someone so gormless wandering the road. I didn't. I shivered same as coming upon some ghost from childhood. Knew him for what he was, soon as spying him.

The Holy Fool: striding blind through perils whilst luck and a good heart guides through the fire, past the lion pit and around the storm. Hero of a thousand fireside stories. All those third sons, dreamy ash-lads and cinder-girls taken for idiots… my storybook friends when I was young and stupid, whining how cruel was life.

Fired by such tales, at thirteen I fled to St. Demetia, enrolling in the absurd St. Euterpe's School for Female Bards. And there I learned, not fairy tales, but the world's truth.

The instructors of St. Euterpe's know that those who sing of heroic deeds had best learn the facts of real heroes and real deeds. On the shelves of St. Bridget waited books that told me what the world was, not what I imagined it to be. Stories where life did not favor cheerful fools. It devoured them. Spitting the bones out with a laugh.

True histories, fascinating as fiction and much more bloody. Instead of widow's sons rewarded with a princess's kiss for acts of kindness, I read the history of King Thrastus the Glorious, a sailor turned brigand who converted a band of hill-robbers into an army of conquest. Still robbing and raping; but beneath a golden flag. I devoured tales of the brilliant artificer Artaphrax, inventor of ways to fly in the clouds, swim in the sea, and endless devices to kill, maim, poison and enchain.

In bard school I read the truth of my ancestor Kurgus, celebrated for establishing the St. Martia Yearly Fair. Fascinating to read in footnotes how he exterminated the entire previous nobility. Selling the dead lords and ladies to the necromancers of Plutarch; their children to the Fae folk of Nod.

Point being: with enough facts in my head and hairs twixt my legs I understood that the truth of the world lies in history books, not the pages of children's tales. Walk a real road, and every dead dog in a ditch, any quiet cemetery where flowers bloom, and every last flag waving in the wind are all reminders: *this world is a devouring thing.* And nothing is more quickly devoured than the innocent fool.

Yet, meeting Barnaby on the road, returning his cheerful cloud-free smile... Bridget's tits and Taliesin's shits, I confess. For one idiot moment I found myself looking about for dragons who'd play at riddles, for princesses calling for rescue from a tower. Maybe a kindly forest robber who'd invite me to feast with his merry band.

Perhaps I should have dived into the dream, joined the boy's quest, become the companion encouraging him to keep chin up, heart clean and smile bright.

Screw that. I told the idiot son of a miller the sad bad truth. Clearly his 'family' sent him to his death. His friar taught him to be a fool. No doubt his stepmother and brother coveted the mill.

I watched the boy's eyes as he gazed into the sky. And I saw something that threw me. *He already knew.* Knew the folk of his home meant him ill, his path led towards dark ending.

Knew; and yet kept silent, watching a butterfly battle the breeze. Perhaps even within his own head he did not put it to words. Why? Maybe he could not bear to think ill of his home. Or maybe he could not comprehend such malice, was reduced to staring blankly at innocent things: clouds, hearths, butterflies.

The children's tales never say what keeps the Ash Lads and Cinder Lasses gazing into the hearth, poking at dreams and embers. Surely it is the shadows of a dark home that fixes their gaze on the firelight? Until at last they rise up, go down the road to find what they cannot face at home.

Logical; but... bah. I don't believe it. Barnaby the miller's son hid no tangled drama behind his eyes. He was a happy idiot delighting in the summer day, smiling at the pleasant road before him.

And yet, and yet...*he knew*. So why go on an adventure meant for his death? Why laugh with the breeze, greet birds and mankind with a smile? I can't comprehend it. Holy foolishness, I suppose.

One thing else. I swear by the patroness of bards, Blessed Saint Euterpe herself. When Barnaby bowed in greeting to the font, the damned stone face *winke*d. It did. Returning greeting with greeting. Old Herm knew a proper fool on the road.

While I stood blinking, turning from old saint to young fool. And I shivered to know I was no longer comparing reality with the pages of old tales. No; I'd wandered into the child's tale itself. Sure as if I'd stepped into the woodcut illustration.

A terrifying thought to a bard. And so I declared my warnings, made my farewells, spurring tits and tail from sly saint and gormless boy alike. Quick as I did from my home in St. Martia. Quick as I did from St. Euterpe's School for Female Bards, upon the back of a stolen horse.

Chapter 8
On Orders of General Stomach

Barnaby took the north road from the fountain. Expecting with each mile for the sky to blacken. Snow would fall thick as winter quilts, the wind carrying the howl of wolves on his trail. Their eyes would glow red as embers, their fur white as lace on ice...

Yet in open defiance of tales, all that day the sun stayed hot, the wind remained warm, the fields remained green, the sky kept the usual dusty blue.

At sunset he spied a camp beside the road. A dozen folk gathered about a fire. Singing, laughing, roasting meats that traveled the distance to Barnaby's nose, setting it twitching rabbity. He pondered walking past, unsure of such loud folk. But they spotted him quick as robin does the worm; calling for him to join their circle.

They looked rough; scarred veterans of life, knife and strife. Swearing oaths that astonished Barnaby for the originality of obscenity. Still, they shared their fire, their songs and sizzling bits of venison. He sat listening wide-eyed to tales of towns and lands that sounded like fairy palaces or devil haunts, according to the shading of the tale. At last he fell asleep by the fire, dreaming of far places, mad battles, courtly dances.

In the morning he awoke to find the troop up and packing. They informed Barnaby they were heading south to the coast. For a second, he felt tempted to ask if their mad troop had use for a miller? But his path lay to the North. So he thanked them for their charity, wishing them well on their path. In reply they laughed, leaving Barnaby with a bit of venison, a dying fire and their own well wishes. The words came with grins, as if they knew to what end he went, and what end they went.

Barnaby felt sad to see them go. And yet, glad to be on his own again. He'd never met such loud confident folk. They made him feel like a spring lamb wandering beyond the summer shepherd's eye. He continued up the north road, staring up at a fleecy cloud.

"Am I just a sheep?" he asked it. "I'm strong. I can lift the middle grindstone, and Da could never do that. I can read real letters, if upside down." He considered what else he could do. Whistling had grown old. "I can look at the mill cogs, tell just which turns what and why the vanes have slowed."

Of course he could also dig and chop and carry, sew cloth, snare rabbits, tend a garden. But so could anyone excepting his stepbrother Alf, whose back was always poorly for such chores. What did folk learn that made them proud to be themselves?

Bards, shoemakers and stonemasons, blacksmiths, tin smiths and gold smiths, merchants and miners. Tailors and sailors too.

On consideration, the finest learning came marked with a glorious sign: *a hat*. Wizards, captains, doctors and bishops wore hats that declared the head beneath it of special worth.

"Just 'Barnaby' doesn't impress much," he admitted to the cloud. Staring into the sky exact as he did the flames of the hearth at home. *Sailors*, he considered, and the cloud shifted sheep shape to become a ship. *I'd like to sail a ship*, he informed it. I'd be captain at the wheel, shouting orders during a terrible storm. And I'd be forever fighting pirates with my cutlas.

I shall learn to sail and fight, he decided, recalling the acrobatic folk's tales of dueling in dungeons, tumbling in taverns, fencing upon fences. What else to learn? He considered Val, the bard he'd met at the fountain.

I'll learn to ride a horse. And to sing and tell of ancient stones and kingdoms from before grandam's time. Also I'll learn to smith shoes for my horse when I have a horse. Oh, and do magic like a wizard.

That last made him laugh right up to the cloud. He pictured himself chanting orations, drawing lightning down from the sky, summoning ghosts up from the earth. The idea turned his mind to the witches in the woods. Had that been real? Perhaps he'd dreamed it. Perhaps dreaming was his true calling. Just wandering daydreaming down the road, talking to clouds... he frowned, searching the sky. The cloud had hurried away on business more serious than talking to daydreaming millers.

Barnaby shook himself from consideration of clouds, looked about. Finding himself practically at the gate of a building bigger than the mill. A sign on a post declared its happy purpose: a tavern.

* * *

Within, the warmth was a wonder. As was each separate smell; sizzling sausage, wine and ale and fresh bread. A woman in leather smock gave him a measuring glance and a shake of her head. She seemed about to speak. But shouting from a table by the hearth prevented her words. Barnaby turned, spying three soldiers ruling a table as they would a battlefield. All a host of bottles, mugs and plates lay defeated before them.

They called Barnaby over with smiles and waves of hand.

"Who are you and where do you go?" asked one. A young fellow, long nose projecting from a face that grinned at world and comic noses alike. His more elegant uniform, more polished armor declaring him the leader. Barnaby stared open-mouthed while the man smiled.

"Well, I'm Barnaby."

"Excellent name. I'm Capitano."

Barnaby was not sure if that was name or title. He studied their matching blue tunics, the steel helmets, the bright buttons. Swords to the side. "Are you real soldiers?"

Capitano laughed. "We are that. And so we recognize a man on a long march when we see one. Hungry? Tired? Chilled? Feet complaining of too much road?"

Barnaby laughed. "I am all these things."

"Then sit and give your feet some rest. Ah, a man's feet are soldiers, you know. Infantry. They keep you safe, either charging bravely forwards or running fast away. And when faithfully following the orders of Captain Nose, they get you safe to your next meal."

"General Stomach agrees," declared Barnaby. He sat, staring wide eyed at swords, uniforms and scarred faces. While Capitano himself called the tavern maid to bring the newcomer a plate of bread and sausage. She did, her eyes down, avoiding Barnaby's. He wondered if she felt his ragged presence defiled this martial gathering. But General Stomach bugled a growl; he fell upon the food before him quick as cavalry charge. The soldiers laughed in delight to see his enthusiasm for battle.

When the plate was empty their leader pushed forwards a mug of ale, inviting him to make a toast to St. Demetia.

"How?" Barnaby asked. He'd never made a toast before.

"Stand," explained Capitano. He did. "Raise the mug high." He did. "Hmm, higher. You're speaking to the Upper House of Saints, not the tavern ceiling." Barnaby raised the mug higher. "Now say these words: 'I pledge my life and honor to the flag and sword of the lands of blessed Saint Demetia'."

Barnaby solemnly repeated these words, while the soldiers grinned, the barmaid shook her head.

"Now drink up!" ordered Capitano. The two other soldiers pounded fists of approval upon the table.

Barnaby did his best. Stronger brew than anything served in Mill Town. It made him cough, and set his head whirling like the mill vanes in high wind. But he finished it off, trying to sit again. But the two regular soldiers stood. One taking Barnaby firmly by the shoulder.

Capitano remained seated, waving his own mug of ale in toast to Barnaby. "Welcome to the army, soldier," he declared.

Barnaby shook his head, attempting to clear it of muddling words and ale. He decided he disliked the grasp on his shoulder. So he shoved the man away, with more strength than the soldier expected. It sent him tumbling to the floor, cursing. The second soldier only laughed. Then put a fist to the side of Barnaby's head, knocking him flat.

Chapter 9
First Lessons

Barnaby lay bound hand and foot upon a rough wooden floor. The room held scarce light, but shadow and echo declared it someplace large. He spied boxes and barrels. Beyond the ceiling sounded conversation, laughter, boot steps going and coming.

I'm in the cellar of the tavern, he decided. This explained the memory of being dragged down steps, as well as the aches and scrapes from that dragging. Granted, the ache in his head came from the blow struck before the dragging.

'*Ware wolves on two feet*'; that had been wiser advice than he'd understood. At the time he'd pictured real wolves walking upright, as the witch's magic pig Baltazar attempted. But now the meaning shown bright, for all the basement dark. Some folk were wolves on the inside, no matter the human face they wore. Barnaby sighed to admit it.

But: *don't gaze overlong on dark things,* his Da always said. Barnaby nodded, and did his best. Bound in the dark, he pictured the wonders of the last three days. He'd watched witches at work; met a bard with a golden harp. Said *hallo* to a stone saint. He'd helped a poor donkey, buried a stranger and rode in an ox cart. Not that riding an ox cart was extraordinary. But he'd sat by the fire of loud acrobats, listening to tales that would make his stepmother scowl and his father laugh.

No, he'd met no one more unpleasant than a cow that chased him when he'd sought to drink from its trough. Well, and that farmwife who'd struck him with a broom before he had chance to bargain work in exchange for meal. All said, the world was full of good folk, everywhere; until he'd sat with the three smiling soldiers anxious to share cheese, ale and army service.

"Might have been my fault," he considered. "Perhaps I did the toast wrong. Who knows what words mean so far from home?" But no; Capitano had said he was a soldier for reciting the oath. He didn't feel like a soldier. He felt like a bruised miller, tied up same as a sack of flour.

He considered his bound hands and feet. Leather straps; the kind Da used to bind the flour barrels. Wrap the leather wet, let it dry and it became tight as chains. These felt dry and tight.

He struggled to free himself, not expecting any success and not finding any. A rat darted across the floor. He considered whether he could get it to chew through his bindings. More likely it'd prefer to chew him. Barnaby gave struggle a rest. He drowsed for a while; dreaming that he discussed life and bindings with the rat.

"You fellows are always chewing on what you shouldn't," pointed out Barnaby. "Candles and shoes, toes and the Sunday pie. You might make yourselves useful for once."

"Ha," said the rat, showing yellow incisors. "You sound like your stepmother."

"Oh, I'm sorry then," said Barnaby, not wishing to hurt the rat's feelings.

Mollified, the rat bowed. "For all the ancient war twixt Miller and Rat, I'd gladly aid one so polite caught in trap. But I dare not." The rat looked left and right, twitching nose, then confided in the low whisper of night creatures. "The cat's coming." With that he scurried off.

Before Barnaby could call him back, he awoke, shaken by a distant boom that echoed like cannon fire. Perhaps it *was* cannon fire, from the army hurrying to claim its new recruit. He listened for the call of bugles and marching feet. Then the boom came again; a clap of thunder from the world beyond. He smiled, catching the faint rush of rain-heavy wind. He felt parched, longing to be drinking honest water. And yet, the patter and roar of storm comforted. Bound in the dark, it lightened Barnaby's heart to know that in the wide world beyond waited clean drink, free air.

A trickle of rain began splashing down the wall beside Barnaby. He moved away, wiggling like a caterpillar. Then thirst made him wiggle back, putting mouth to all he could catch. It tasted of stone and dirt, but he drank all he could. When that sufficed, he held his bound hands beneath the trickle. Wetting the leather straps, seeking to soak them. It was a long slow business that left him wet and weary. He fell asleep again.

He awoke more slowly this time. Not to a thunderclap, but a calm and measured voice. Barnaby felt the speaker had talked some while, gradually drawing him awake. He opened eyes to the shadow-filled cellar. A beam of moonlight now shone from a high window. Someone paced in and out of the faint glow, hands clasped behind in pose of concentration.

Behold a short little man with fat belly covered by a fur vest. He wore a cap turned up in points on either side, like the ears of a cat or fox. The man's eyes were bright white, flashing like lightning as he made some declaration that moved his heart.

"And so we see that magic may occur in the intersection of any two realities. This land of St. Demetia is a place of life and growth. While its neighboring terrain of Plutarch is dark with decay and rot. The magic of one intersects with Life; the other with Death."

The little man reached the wall. He turned, pacing in the opposite direction. Behind him something waved in time to his words. *A tail*, realized Barnaby. Fascinated, he watched the tail as it twitched this way and that, same as a hand guiding music.

"Consider the Republic of St. Hefestia, land of mechanical wonders. With what strange world does it collide to derive its magic? Why, from the world of the mind itself. From the laws of math and logic, the power of observation and experimentation."

At mention of Hefestia, Barnaby grew excited.

"Do the Festians truly have ships that fly in the clouds?"

The little man frowned at this interruption, stopping his pacing. He spent a while giving his fur vest a brushing, in case any moonlight stained it. At length he answered.

"They do. Giant whale-like things, brittle as eggshells, swimming like great slow fish through seas of cloud and star."

"I'd like to see that," declared Barnaby, delighted to hear a wonder of the world confirmed.

"Indeed the sight is something," admitted the man. "But, let us continue. Now, many and various are the mysteries called 'magic'. But the magic of the House of Saints is simple. Call it *theurgy*, if you wish an academic label. It comes from using the power of the saints as your mill uses the power of the winds."

Barnaby pictured glowing robed figures puffing from their icon mouths, spinning the mill vanes, setting the wheels to clatter, the stones to grind. A fascinating thing.

A question had long bothered Barnaby; now he had chance to ask without getting a knuckle-rap.

"The saints are there for all, same as the wind. Why doesn't everyone do magic?"

"Excellent question. Consider it, hmm, like music. Some lack the talent. Many that do, never try. As well, consider that the saints themselves have a choice in the matter. They give of their power to those who show affinity to their area of patronage. Saint Martia hears the war cries of soldiers, not the curses of tinkers. Sainted Plutarch reveals his dark secrets to those with the courage to face their own mortality. Hefestia sends his bolts of inspiration to those seeking truth, not those wishing to light their pipes. And Sainted Mother Demetia smiles most warmly on those who reverence life. And so each saint hears their proper oration."

"But why even have spells? Why not say '*Sainted Demetia, undo these ropes?*'"

"'Spell' is vulgar. Never say 'spell'. Nor 'cantrip'. 'enchantment' nor 'glamour'. Those are words for witches, sorcerers and riffraff magic mongers. A proper petition to the saints shall be called an 'oration'. Which is to say, a prayer. And the phrasing of a proper oration must be learned and practiced."

"Why?"

"Hmm. Have you ever submitted a petition to the potentate of a foreign kingdom requesting a commission be formed to delineate a treaty defining wheat tariffs between your borders?"

Barnaby considered, then shook his head. He never had once.

"Just as I thought. Well, if you had, you would know that such requests require formality. Those that dwell in the Upper House of Saints live by rules far more complex than the government of empires. And so the words to address them are ritualized, lest you forget you beseech powers that dwell farther from you than the stars. Do try not to anger them."

"What is this foolishness?" whispered a new voice. A low, deep voice; rough and impatient.

The little man showed no surprise at the interruption. Though the tail twitched, annoyed.

"I am beginning the long process of educating this blank slate of a being, this empty bucket of a boy, you sad shadow of an ignorant."

"Why not to teach him some *cantrip* to free himself?"

"Oh, far too advanced. He knows no more of magic that a fish knows of fire."

"Then untie him."

"Hmm, entirely outside the curriculum," declared the little man. "The rule of my summoning was: '*to teach, not to aid.*' He put hands behind his back, began his pacing again. "In any case a bound student is far more attentive than a free one."

Barnaby stared into shadows, seeking the second speaker. There, by the wall. Behold a man in long dark coat, a wide-brimmed hat. A face darker than the basement shadows. This personage leaned nonchalant, letting Barnaby judge him. Barnaby judged him *eerie*. He turned back to the little man.

"You are the cat the witch summoned," declared Barnaby.

Again the man stopped his pacing. Giving Barnaby a measuring glance. "Indeed," he admitted. "Hmm. Quicker than I took you. Perhaps more than luck let you steal a summoning from a coven." He gave a bow. "I am... Professor Shadow Night-Creep."

Barnaby laughed in delight. He'd always wanted to talk to a cat. Well, he'd talked to plenty of cats. But now he'd found one who could talk back. Unless the others had been able to reply but chose not. In any case,

Barnaby did his best to return the bow while sitting bound on the floor.

"I am Barnaby the miller's son," he declared. "Very pleased to make your acquaintance, Professor Night-Creep. Am I really going to learn magic?"

Night-Creep examined the fingertips of a gloved hand, inspecting. "Hmm. It remains in doubt whether you shall *learn*. But certainly, I shall strive to instruct. In magic's various forms and logics, flavors and systems."

"Bah," declared the man slouching in the shadows. "Useless. He needs far different instruction." He took a step into the moonlight. Its dim silver glow revealing a tall, wide-shouldered figure in heavy coat. Hands deep in pockets as though he walked in December wind. The cat-professor backed away, making the hiss of an angered teakettle. The dark man ignored this.

He leaned towards Barnaby, staring down. Barnaby gaped up. The man's face was familiar. But he'd never seen eyes so dark; two caves with firelight a mile within.

"First lesson," whispered the dark man. "Never, ever trust strangers in taverns who are over-free with welcome and ale."

"I think I did their oath wrong," admitted Barnaby.

"Ah, no, you did it right," corrected the dark man. "But if you toast St. Demetia, vowing to serve her before an officer and two witnesses, why then by law you have enlisted into the army."

"Ha," said Barnaby. "That explains it nicely." His eyes widened in realization. "So, am I a soldier now?"

"By law," affirmed the Dark Man. "For what the law is worth. That worth summing to one well-measured bushel of dog shit. No, it is a mere trick to pull fools into a net of rules and flags, orders and songs, medals and mindless obedience."

"I suspect we hear the voice of former soldier in this observation upon military service," said Professor Night-Creep.

"Be silent, witch-spawn," growled the Dark Man. In reply the cat-man also growled. His eyes glowing bright, tail thrashing like a wheat stalk in storm wind.

"I was instructing," declared Professor Night-Creep. "Begone, ghost."

"Bah. You give theory when he needs a knife."

"Have you knife?" demanded the cat.

"Experience is a knife. I know what he needs to learn. To fight, to defend, to walk wary."

"You," said Barnaby. "Sir. Ah. Are you a ghost?"

"Of a sort," shrugged the man. "Not the usual shrouded thing moaning through eternity in some idiot ruin." He considered. "Call me... Dark Michael."

"Dramatic name," scoffed Professor Shadow Night-Creep.

"Since my death, I am feeling dramatic," declared Dark Michael. And for the first time Barnaby saw him smile, following with a laugh sad as autumn rain. The man pulled a hand from pocket, grasping something. Crouching near Barnaby, he opened the fist to reveal what it held.

A copper penny, looking light and thin as tin.

"Ah," said Barnaby. "Ha. Well. You are the very fellow I buried then?"

"I am."

"I am pleased to see you again," declared Barnaby. "You look far better than when I saw you last, Master Dark Michael. And have you seen the donkey?"

At which question Professor Night-Creep laughed. A high laugh that hurt the ears, like icicles worming towards the brain. While the ghost shook his head.

Rising again, he returned hands to coat pockets. Then stood awhile studying Barnaby with those cavernous eyes.

"The donkey?"

"Yes," affirmed Barnaby. "You recall him, surely? I worry that farmer might treat him ill."

"You are bound in the dark, prisoner of those who beat you. Trapped with a mad ghost and a witch's familiar. And you ask about a donkey?"

Barnaby considered. Was he being foolish? These two did not seem to mean him ill. And what an amazing thing, to talk to a ghost and a cat. On the very same night in the very same basement. Who knew but the donkey could talk as well? Barnaby had not thought to ask it. But what would one ask a donkey? For that matter, what would a donkey ask a miller?

While Barnaby pondered, the ghost-man sighed. Then began pacing in and out of the moonbeam, exact as the cat-man had done, lecturing the attentive-bound student.

"When you realized the soldiers meant you ill, you should have smiled, sat again." His long legs quickly brought him to the wall; he turned, began pacing the other way. "You should have pretended to be delighted to join them. Waiting for them to be distracted by time and wine. Then... hmm, I'd grab the pepper pot, toss it into the captain's eyes. Then taken up a bottle, striking the man to your left. That leaves but one. If he remains sober he'll move beyond reach of the bottle. But if you stand, take your chair and strike him, it leaves the field to your flag."

Barnaby pictured himself performing these dance-steps. It seemed an unlikely dance. "I don't think I could hit a man with a bottle or a chair. I suppose I could manage the pepper."

Dark Michael exchanged looks with Professor Night Creep. One shrugged, one twitched tail.

"Can you free him?" asked the cat-man.

"I may walk beside him, advise as is fit," declared Dark Michael. "But three times only may I reach hand out to aid this boy. Then is my service ended." He turned to Barnaby. "Do you wish me to untie you? If you do not get free you will soon be marching on the road while some sub-captain beats time with a baton upon your backside."

"Three times only," considered Barnaby. "It's like wishes. I get three, and must not waste them."

"Exact so," said Cat and Ghost together.

Barnaby shook his head. "Da always said '*never waste a grain of flour or a bright day's hour*'." The two stared blankly. "He meant that I should keep what I can for when I need it."

"You need it now, boy," growled Dark Michael.

"Indeed, the graveyard brute is correct," agreed Professor Night-Creep. "Dawn comes. You have little time to be free of your bindings."

"Oh, I'm free of them already," said Barnaby. He rose, slowly; sore and stiff. Stretched, then held out the leather straps to show his teachers. They dripped damp. "Once they had time to soak, it was easy to pull them off."

Chapter 10
Council of War, with Cheese

"I shall speak as necessary," whispered Dark Michael. "None but you will hear my voice. But you must not reply, or you awaken the foe."

Barnaby started to say *understood*, but caught himself. Nodded wisely.

"The door creaks," observed Michael. "Open it slowly and steadily, neither stopping nor hurrying."

Barnaby took breath, then did so, trembling with fear and excitement. There came a gentle metal creak from the hinges. Barnaby stared past into the tavern scullery.

"Now scan about," declared Michael. "And use your ears. There will be folk asleep by the hearth fire; perhaps some already awake and about."

Barnaby peered into the dim light, squeezing his eyes into slits.

"Not that way," chided the ghost. "Open eyes wide to get the most light. Turning head left and right. In dark, one sees best out the corners of the eyes."

Barnaby opened his eyes wide as an owl's, twisting head solemnly left, right as did an owl. He desperately wanted to give out an owlish 'whooo' but did not.

"Excellent," declared the ghost. "Now go on. But don't tiptoe. Place each foot flat. Slowly and evenly upon the seam between the floorboards. Keep close to the walls as possible. Floors squeak loudest where folk most often walk."

Barnaby nodded, making slow steps through the scullery towards the front of the tavern.

"Stop and spy the battlefield again," whispered Michael. Barnaby halted, peering through a doorway into the common room. There by the fireside lay a soldier wrapped in blanket. Upon a bench, pack for a pillow, lay another. The barred door awaited on the far side of this lion's den. Barnaby made his slow way around a chair into a corner. There he stopped, contemplating the field. Biting his lip, deep in decision.

"Let me guess," said the voice of Dark Michael. "You feel you must keep your oath to become a soldier."

No, I don't, Barnaby wished to say. *That'd be a mutton-head thing to think.* But he'd been commanded to silence. So he pointed at a great wedge of cheese upon a table. The ghost considered this object.

"Ah," he said. "Rations. Sensible. Seize it. With care."

Barnaby stepped slow as the greater millstone turning on a mild summer wind. But floorboards nearer the table creaked and squeaked for a choir of mice. He froze, waiting, listening. The soldier by the fire stirred, muttering of ale and victory. Barnaby worked not to breathe, until he had to breathe. Then it came out a loud whoosh that made the instructing ghost curse.

A creature glided through the dark room, silent as hawk-shadow passing. A great black cat, eyes white as snow in full moon's light. It leaped upon the table, strode to the plate, sat with tail curled. There it batted a paw at the cheese. Clearly telling Barnaby: *See? Here it is. Come get it.*

Not daring to step farther upon the treacherous floor, Barnaby bent forwards, reaching out, stretching his arm, wiggling fingers, grasping the cheese... and then near tumbling over. He recovered, all but dropping the cheese, all but falling backwards against the wall.

The cat closed its eyes. Dark Michael hissed. Barnaby stood straight, steadied himself, placing the cheese inside his pack.

"Now for the door," said Michael. Voice rough and low as gravel from a burial pit. "Step light. Be most cautious of careless moves when you are almost to safety."

Barnaby opened his mouth to say 'Of course'. The cat hissed, eyes wide. Barnaby snapped mouth shut again. Continued his slow progress to the door. It was barred and latched; but had no lock. He lifted the heavy bar; began the slow process of pulling it open without least squeak of hinges. And then at last, he faced the open night.

"Who's at the door?" called a sleepy voice. The soldier by the fireside.

"Run," whispered Dark Michael.

"Agreed," concurred Professor Night-creep.

Barnaby lay on a large flat rock in the clearing of a wood. Warmed by morning sunshine, comforted by the bird song and free wind. The tavern lay miles behind, as did the shouts of soldiers calling him to halt, to return to duty, to take his beating like a man.

"Boy shows a good set of heels," admitted Dark Michael. Leaning against a tree, arms crossed. "A soldier's best friend."

"You surprise me," yawned the cat. "I expected you to order him to turn and deliver battle. Suggesting this kick, advise that blow." The cat began a thorough inspection of its tail fur.

"Fighting is wise when sensible retreat against greater numbers doesn't offer itself. Granted, I expected a witch's familiar to turn itself to a lion, devouring soldiers like mice cornered in the kitchen."

Professor Shadow Creep continued his patient wash and groom.

"I might have," brooded the cat. "I have done things far more bloody. And entertaining. Alas, the witches who summoned me put binding upon my actions. They did not trust their new sister Jewel, and decided it were best to limit my powers in serving her."

"What limits?" asked Dark Michael.

Barnaby rolled over upon the rock, letting the sun warm his back. Putting chin upon his folded arms, watching his two counselors. And he shivered, not with morning chill but sheer delight. What glorious fun, to lie free on a warm rock in the morning light with two companions so exotic and wise, so different from a miller's son.

Professor Night-Creep gave a lick to tail-tip, then recited.

Not to aid or abet.
Mere purring, talking pet.
Never hunt nor harry.
Not to fetch nor carry.
No fighting, no fending.
Only instruction lending

Barnaby sought to recall; yes, the oldest witch had muttered an addition into the pot. Not trusting Jewel. And really, the girl had stolen his lunch. It was only sense they should not trust her. Not that they seemed any more trustworthy. Barnaby wondered how such folk even got along? They'd be stealing each other's lunches and casting spells on one another like crows feuding over a dead rabbit.

"So, you are useless," growled Dark Michael.

At that the tail twitched from out the cat's grasp. Writhing back and forth, a furry, furious snake.

"Few things walk the earth as dangerous, as terrifying, as lethal in power as the instructional knowledge held in my little kitty head, you wispy pointless remainder of a thuggish noble."

Dark Michael pushed back his long coat, hand reaching to his side, the pommel of a sword.

"Oh, please," yawned the cat. It seized the angered tail, returned to ordering fur.

There came uncomfortable silence, except for bird song. Barnaby ended it.

"Are you both coming with me to find the tower and the treasure?"

His two advisors exchanged looks. The cat released its tail, walking daintily to sit beside Barnaby. "Perhaps. First let's see this fabulous treasure map."

Barnaby sat up, stretching sore muscles. The pains of yesterday's blows had faded, but the long run from the tavern after lying bound, left his legs complaining of misuse. He searched pockets, finding the cheese. Of a sudden his stomach howled, declaring that cheese preceded treasure in importance. Barnaby agreed with General Stomach. He broke off a piece, placing it before the cat. Broke off another piece, placed it towards Michael. Began to munch upon the remainder.

The cat promptly took his portion in his mouth. Leaping down from the rock, devouring the cheese upon the ground.

"Why do cats do that?" asked Barnaby. "You have some tidbit on a table or counter, and you always take it to the floor."

"It's mere manners," declared the cat. "How crude, to simply eat where one is served. Really, that's the sort of thing a dog would do." He glanced at Michael. "Or a nobleman."

Finished, he wiped tongue to maw, then leaped up to the rock again. Eyeing Michael's portion of cheese, still unclaimed.

"The boy may have my share from the brave tavern raid," declared Dark Michael, emphasizing *'the boy'*. "I neither hunger nor thirst."

"A sad damnation, that," said the cat, with no faintest sympathy to his high voice. "More for us, alas."

"The map, now," growled Dark Michael.

Barnaby nodded, reached to pockets, pulling out the leather scroll. Thick calfskin oiled to avoid water's harm. Still, in morning light it looked a weary unimportant scrap. He laid it flat; the ghost and the cat peered close, studying.

"Interesting," said the cat.

"I expected something absurd," mused the ghost. "But that is certainly the Saintless Tower. And the sketch of the separate floors is expert done. No fakery there."

"Whence comes this map?" demanded the cat, sniffing at it. "It's suspiciously old."

"My brother gave it me," declared Barnaby. "Out from the locked trunk that held Da's things." It felt good to know that if his tutoring by the Friar was upside-down, and the coin given by the Squire was false, and even the lunch given by mother was, well, false... still, this map was real. He'd scarce have reason to go on otherwise.

"How does a miller come to have a map of such a place?" wondered the cat.

Barnaby stared fondly into the past.

"Oh, Da oft took oddities from farmers needing their harvest grinding done, when they could not pay tithe to mill and squire and shire. Once he ground all a wagon of wheat in exchange for a bronze bird from Hefestia." Barnaby grew excited. "You turned a key in the back and it waved its wings." He flapped his arms to demonstrate this wonder.

"Well, it's a map of a famous ruin," said Michael. "What does it have to do with treasure?"

"Da always said it led to treasure at the bottom of the tower. The farmer must have told him so. I'm thinking the treasure must lie in that red circle in the lowest part here." Barnaby pointed a finger to the side sketch of the tower. "My brother Alf said it was nonsense."

"But he told you to follow it," puzzled the cat. "As you seek to do. Why?"

Barnaby said nothing for awhile. Taking Michael's portion of cheese, he split it in half, putting one part before the cat, keeping the other half for himself. Not eating it yet; just considering. He pictured jumping down from the rock, eating the cheese on the ground like a polite cat. Did manners of a cat count for a man?

"You aren't going to explain why you follow a path openly declared nonsense," said Michael.

Barnaby searched for words. "Alf had no good opinion of Da. Called him foolish. He calls most things foolish. He dropped the Hefestian bird down the well. But just a week ago he handed me the map. Told me it'd lead to treasure, I'd bring it back, and we'd live like kings. Howsoever kings live, exactly."

He considered awhile, then ended. "I wanted to go. Past time I went and saw the world for myself."

For a moment, for just a quick-passing shadow of a second, the face of Barnaby the miller's son grew clouded; grew sad and lost as any man that ever stared at a dark hearth in a heartless home. There followed silence, his two counselors exchanging glances.

"Well, it makes as good a reason as any for a walk about the world" declared the cat at last, giving his chest fur a quick washing.

"I find myself agreeing," said Dark Michael.

Chapter 11
Warrior Princess of St. Martia

Val the Bard:

Twice have I seen the cup in dream, and once in waking life. If any true border separates the lands of Dream and Waking. *The Gospel of St. Taliesin* says true visions come as they wish, and care naught for eyes open, eyes closed.

The first dream came when I was seven. I awoke to find my chamber full of light. I supposed I'd overslept, would be whipped for missing practice upon the field.

But this was not dawn's glow. A shining thing waited at my window, like a friendly sun peering in. I rose, approached. Not frightened, but awed.

It was a cup. Brighter than the sun; and yet not burning the eye to gaze upon. One felt that here was the true purpose of sight; to see this cup, this light.

Ah, and it sang. Perhaps it held music the way lesser cups held wine, and it poured out song as a kindly fountain might give to this dry world. Then again, perhaps it was the light itself that sang, for the joy of shining upon the cup.

I sat on the floor before it, listening, gazing. The song never repeated, never faltered. I felt it was a living thing. It knew me, and was happy that I was happy just to sit and hear its song. At times I dared hum in my child's voice, trying to sing along. When I did so, it flashed golden as though laughing in delight.

I feel I sat there for lifetimes, for ages of the world. After infinite bliss, I awoke on the cold stone floor, curled before my window. It was difficult to recall where I was, who I was. My room, the house, even my parents seemed things of long years passed.

My father declared me ill, a statement St. Martia frowns to hear. As her testament says: *if one be not strong enough to fight, be strong enough to die.* I lay in bed a week, tossing and turning, looking for the cup at my window, in my dreams.

Four years passed before I saw the cup again. The day of my father's pyre after glorious deeds upon the border with Hefestia.

I woke hearing the cup's golden song. I leapt from bed, whirling about, not finding its gold glow. I went running barefoot through our great house, full of sleepers who did not hear the song.

The light of the cup shone out the library doorway, so bright one might think the books afire. I rushed in. The old servant-librarian sat at a desk, copying pages from dusty scrolls. He looked up at my entrance but did not speak.

I ignored him. The cup awaited me in a far corner. Perched like a bird upon a shelf of dusty tomes from other lands less practical than Martia.

The cup looked different than I recalled. Larger now, more like to a bowl. And brighter, yet less clear. I gazed into it as if it were the sun rising through golden clouds. But the song was the same. I sat happily beneath the cup, shivering, crying with joy.

I sang with it whenever I felt I understood some fragment of the song. The old servant rose, came and stood behind me. I wondered if he intended to sing as well. Servants of St. Martia are to keep quiet, heads down, eyes down. But in this light, before this cup, such rules seemed dust.

"What do you see, child?" he asked.

"The cup," I said, frowning at '*child*'. I did not worry he might take the cup away. One might as well worry that a sly thief should pocket the sun.

"What sort of cup?" he asked.

"A golden one," I sighed, wishing he would leave me be. "It sings."

"Ah," he said, and no more.

As before, I awoke alone, curled upon cold stone. I rose, hurrying through the library looking for the cup, calling like a lost child for its mother. Gone; but upon a table waited a book, large and old. Surely left by the old man.

Resigned that the glory had flown again, I peered at the book, unwilling to return to bed and all the life of a St. Martia warrior-child. But my heart beat faster with each page turned.

For it was full of pictures that teased with bits of the cup's song. Behold knights in vigil, and minstrels singing before kings. Lover staring into one another's eyes with the intensity of the moon peering into a mirror. Magicians waving wands, and the sun dripping golden light. Ships in storm, and glimpses of towers, stars, angels, devils, lions, swords, hearts.

I turned a page, coming to a rider pursuing a golden cup. The picture gave me chills. It was the cup of my vision. The rider rode a prancing horse through a green summer day. The cup flew high before him, bright with golden rays casting no least shadow. Perhaps it guided, perhaps he pursued. Farther down the road waited a crossroad; a fountain of old stone.

I returned to bed, returned to life of duty and instruction. But from then on came dreams. Not of the cup, but of ordinary things that hinted and teased of the cup. A tree in summer's shine, a candle flickering in the dark, else a wind carrying bits of music from across far hills... always some dream-trifle seemed a thing of infinite significance. And I would gasp *'it's the cup.'* Then awaken bereft.

Before, music had played little part of my life. But after each dream of the cup, I awoke singing. And weeping, like a pathetic fool, like a lost child.

I haunted the library, convinced it held clues to the cup. The old librarian never spoke; he'd have been whipped for so doing. But sly man, he left books and scrolls that served for marks of a trail.

One in particular led me far. It was *'The Gospel of St. Taliesin'*, patron of the *troubadours* who wander the roads of the world singing of the mysteries of the House of Saints. All the mysteries above, below, or within this middle house, that moved hearts to joy or sorrow, whether neat or mixed together.

Inevitable, that I would decide to become a bard.

Chapter 12
Tin bells and a Dead Horse

Barnaby waved his war saber before a host of foes. They howled, snarling fangs sharp as pitchfork tines, spitting venom green as pond scum. Noble Sir Barnaby prepared to cut them down, wheat stalks before his autumn scythe.

"No, don't pose like a farmwife beating a dog with the laundry stick," admonished Dark Michael. He took a stand beside the boy, one leg before the other, back straight. "Your foe is before you. He extends sword thus. He intends to move his blade beneath yours and stir your guts. You must be ready to move back. Or forwards. Else left or right. Infernum, be ready to jump into the air. Swordcraft is a matter of feet as much as hand."

"Perhaps I could have a shield?" asked Barnaby.

"That's a whole separate art," said Michael. "Let's grasp the basics of blades first."

Professor Night Creep sat on a tree stump watching the practice. Following each wave of sword and stick. Now he turned, tasting the wind with nose and whisker.

"I smell death," he observed.

"I am cutting down the foe," declared Barnaby, slashing the air again.

"No, I mean something organic, non-imaginary, and in point of fact actually dead," said the cat. He looked at Michael. "Of more recent demise than your instructor in sharp things." That said, the cat leaped down, stalking through grass, tail raised.

Barnaby looked to Dark Michael, who sheathed his sword, nodding permission. Barnaby dropped his stick, hurrying after the cat along a path shadowed by tall trees. The high branches sang in summer wind, the sunlight beaming through green leaves to cast dapples of gold.

"Ware brigands," whispered Michael.

Ahead on the road lay a dead horse, a dead man. Two living men stood staring down, shaking heads. One led a goat on a rope; the other held a pitchfork towards the woods to ward off trees, or those within the trees. The goat, pitchfork and rough clothes implied they were farmers, not brigands. Barnaby turned to Michael to declare them so; spinning completely about in astonishment. Dark Michael was gone.

But he was a ghost. Maybe he still stood beside Barnaby. A strange thing to imagine. Barnaby listened for steps behind him, perhaps ghostly whispers. Even reached out a tentative hand to left and right, testing if the air felt chill. Perhaps he passed hands through the man. That seemed rude; he stopped himself from further testing. "Sorry," he whispered.

In this way he came up to the dead horse, the dead man, the two living men and the goat. The goat eyed Barnaby with distrust; clearly suspecting him of the crime before them all. The man holding the goat stood with arms crossed, defying accusation. The other fellow bent down with a knife, cutting at the horse tack and bridle, pulling it free. It tinkled pleasant as pennies on plates. Dismayed, Barnaby recognized that happy jingle.

He turned to the figure lying dead. But it was not Val the Bard. No, it was a fellow in brown jerkin, with a hard rough face death worked to soften. The stomach was a puddle of red, cloth and skin showing ragged knife slices. Flies swarmed in delight.

"We didn't do this foul act," declared the man with crossed arms. "If that was what you were thinking. Just came upon it ourselves." He jerked on the goat's rope to call it for witness. The goat rolled its slotted eyes, grinning to say it was no witness worthy of trust.

Barnaby nodded, ready to take them at their word, even the goat.

"That's Val the Bard's horse," he said sadly. "Where is he?"

The farmer looked about. "Not seen anyone else. Crows would be cawing over other dead folk nearby. Either the rider ran off, or robbers took him to their evil lair."

"Would they want a bard?" asked Barnaby, puzzled.

The two men exchanged glances. "Aye, they might. Dead, he could be sold to the evil Plutarch wizards. Alive, he'd be worth coin to the bloody fools of Santa Martia."

Barnaby stood in sunshine upon a pleasant road in a warm summer day, and yet shivered. Feeling as though a ghost beside him whispered of the darker side to this pleasant summer world. As perhaps the ghost beside him did so whisper.

"It's that band of Saint-Lucif-take-them chicken thieves who scurry in these woods," said the man freeing the horse gear. "Think they're wolves for leaping out on folk from behind. But they're just local dogs who've gotten a taste for sheep."

He lifted the bridle and tack to his shoulder. Gestured into the shadows of the trees. "For sure they waited here till some poor soul passed with something that looked worth taking. Then put an arrow into the horse's head."

"Ah, but the rider wasn't caught all unaware," pointed out the other. He gave a kick to the dead man. "This is one of the band. Seen him in the tavern, drinking ale bought with honest folks' coin."

"What good was killing one, if the others beat you down?" asked his fellow, beginning to walk away. "No doubt just earned him crueler blows." The two turned and walked away, arguing the point of defiance against superior numbers. The goat following behind, giving Barnaby a last mad grin.

Barnaby stood alone with the dead horse, the dead man.

"I don't think I want to bury you," Barnaby told the corpse. "Not if you behaved so. Shame on you." The man did not stir; the flies buzzled amused. Barnaby prepared to say more, then stopped himself. Seemed mean to berate a dead man. He settled for grasping the corpse's feet, dragging him off the road. Closed the eyes, folded hands on chest.

He returned to the horse. Far too big to move. A shame. How fun it had been to hear the horse's tinkling bells as it came up to St. Herman's font. But no doubt in a week there'd be nothing but a few bones, gnawed by honest wolves, pecked by honest crows.

Barnaby stared into the trees, past the corpse of the robber. A path wound through the bracken. He took a breath, then placed a slow careful foot upon it.

"What are you doing?" came the growling gravel-voice of Dark Michael.

"Val the Bard has been taken by a band of robbers," explained Barnaby. "We have to go help her."

"Her?" asked the cat, perched on a branch above his head.

"I think he was a girl dressed in man-clothes," said Barnaby. "But that's no matter. He or she, they were nice. Introduced me to St. Herman. And the horse was nice. It trotted making all a song of jingling bells."

"That is the world, miller's son," said the cat. "Travelers take their chances. Careless travelers take arrows. If you turn aside for every lost lamb, you'll never reach your treasure tower."

"You won't reach the end of the day," declared Dark Michael. He now stood leaning against the trunk of the tree in which perched Professor Night-Creep. "From the tracks hereabouts, I'd say you face four men. Probably they have no skill. Farm boys who ran off to steal crowns from kings, settled for stealing their neighbor's pigs. Still too much for you to front."

"Your bard must face her fate, miller's son," agreed the cat. "You can do nothing."

Barnaby turned, considering the flies circling the dead horse. They buzzed excited, talkative as thirsty workers entering a tavern at day's end. He looked down the road where his destination waited, if not his destiny. He should keep on, shaking a wiser head at the good and bad of the world. Forgetting those left on the wayside. What choice did he have?

Barnaby laughed. It was rather fun to think in this way. As if he were wise and old, with scars on face and heart. Instead of the miller's fool son, whose only wisdom was staring into dreams and the hearth flame.

"Ah, I can't do much," he told the flies. "But I have a friend who can."

"Who?" demanded the ghost.

"You, master Michael," declared Barnaby. "Did you not say, three times you might come to my aid?"

"This is not to your aid," growled the ghost. "It's for some careless stranger on the road. Who may well be dead, else sitting safe miles away lamenting their horse."

Barnaby nodded, began to walk the shadowed path deeper into the woods. "I'd best find out, then. And if that brings me in need of help, good master, then comes your turn to rescue *me*."

Chapter 13
Wisdom is This

Jewel of Stonecroft, Novice of Sister Hecatatia:

I want to walk on their faces. Yes, just that. Give me a path of all the faces I ever saw in city street or country road. Set them like cobbles beneath my feet. You will have to bury the bodies in ordered rows. Leaving each head a bit above ground. Angle them so I don't walk on top of their heads. That wouldn't do. No, I want to grind my feet into their noses and eyes and mouths, without really paying attention to their stupid idiot expressions.

Damn all the faces of all the people in all lands. What has any face ever given ME? Just leers and sneers. All my life I have been servant to eyes and mouths you could exchange with chewing cattle, barking dogs, grinning monkeys. Oh, Sainted Sister Hecatatia, I treasure every honest glare of hate or anger given me. At least THAT says 'you exist'. I am at war with the world, and the idiot world is too mutton-headed to take note. Shit! I am beating my fists against a giant's leg while it stares stupidly away, too dim and dull to feel how I hate, hate, hate it.

So let me speak to every face of the world with my foot. Let my step declare that I am someone of worth. Not a gray faceless meaningless penniless servant in a boring tyrant's farmhouse. Nor a failed farmer's daughter. Not even a lesser witch of a lesser coven in the meager backwoods of a land ruled by squires and cows. Ha, my foot shall tell each face: *here passes someone of worth*.

When I spied the idiot boy chatting to clouds and butterflies, I could have eaten him alive. It's what the world does, you know. You're a liar or fool if you claim aught else. But I only had the boy fetch water. Then I stole his lunch. Nothing worse. Easy as taking milk from a nanny goat. Why feel guilt? Seriously, he was a kind of human cake walking down the road, calling out happy greetings to knives and forks.

And yet... I liked his face. Taking his pathetic meal was coven work. But I could have given him the kiss. He did fetch the water. He had that dreamer's look in his eyes, like pappa's when he'd look at mamma. Long, long ago. No reason I had to cheat the boy out of a kiss. But I've learned. Wisdom is this: take all you can, and give little as you can. Little? No; give nothing! Make it habit. Make it holy ritual! Even when need is little and the boy is comely. He had hair yellow as wheat straw; curling and tangling about a freckled face. Yes, I could have kissed. But better to cheat him.

And then to find that he cheated me! Tricked me out of my summoning! And set the coven to blame me for a broth of poison. I dare not return to the farmhouse; dare not face my coven sisters. And now my face, MY face is damnably scratched by that cursed and traitorous cat!

Best I walk the road myself now, seeking boy and beast. I will set things right. I will NOT be a thing walked upon by others, using me yet ignoring me. I will not. Not by farmers nor covens nor anything. For sure not by an idiot dreamy-eyed barnyard fool of a boy.

Chapter 14
The Merry Band of Robbers

"You need not step so careful," sighed Dark Michael. "The forest has no wooden planks to creak."

"There are sticks that snap," pointed out Barnaby. "Dry leaves that crunch."

"Then step around them," advised his teacher. "Your goal here is to move without being seen. Choose shadows over light. Seek to remain behind trees and brambles. Select a tree and move quickly to it; then stop to look about, to listen. Ask yourself where you would hide, waiting to put an arrow in a fool walking past."

"The path would be quicker," pointed out Night-Creep.

"The path will be watched," pointed out Dark Michael.

"And what exactly does our brave knight do when he comes unseen into the forest glen where reveling robbers roister?"

"He dies with a crossbow bolt to the head."

"What is that like?" asked Barnaby. He pressed close to a pine trunk, peering past.

"Can't say," yawned Michael. "Hurts, probably."

Barnaby stared into green shadow, brown forest floor. Was there a man by that bramble bush? No, it was a stump. He hurried to the next tree, looked about.

"No, but I meant dying. What is that like?"

"Wait and find out."

"That's no answer."

"True."

Barnaby prepared to protest this, when the cat interrupted.

"Stop," ordered the creature.

"Trouble ahead?" whispered Barnaby.

"No doubt," said the cat. "But that's no concern of mine. See the willow to the left? The branch pointing east. With a purple creeper wrapping about it."

"Yes?"

"Break it off."

"Why?" asked Barnaby and Michael, echoing one another.

The cat walked up to the tree, began to sharpen claws upon the trunk.

"*Willow green with life, kissed by lavender wife,*" explained the cat. This remark brought blank stares. "Makes excellent wand," he growled.

Barnaby stepped to the tree, tugged at the branch. Expecting a struggle to free it. But for all its green look, it snapped quick and clean, anxious to join his service.

"Keep it for later," advised his cat-tutor in magic. "Assuming a later."

Barnaby placed the stick in his pack.

"I hear screams," said Michael.

"I smell blood," said the cat.

There came crashing through the brambles, cracking sticks, stomping leaves. Someone ran in no fear of being heard. Barnaby felt suddenly sick, stomach and legs going loose.

He looked back towards the road, tempted to turn and flee. He'd done what he could for the bard. But all said, he was a miller, not a bold adventurer.

But I can't just turn around. Well, no, I *can* just turn around. I'll still be a miller. Just not a very brave miller.

"I don't much want a crossbow bolt in my head," he admitted to himself.

Dark Michael and Night Creep observed Barnaby argue with Barnaby.

"Might be just an arrow in the chest," said Shadow Creep. "Faster."

"Ah, no, that would be a slower passing," said Michael.

"Even to the heart?" asked the cat, seemingly fascinated.

"Oh, indeed," affirmed the ghost. "Takes a minute or three for a body to realize it's finished with life."

They don't want me to go on, thought Barnaby. They mean well. They know this is no adventure for my sort. But what do they know about me?

Well, what do I know about me? fairness forced him to ask. I can lift the middle mill stone. I can whistle though my name begins with 'B'. I have a magic cat and a ghostly tutor. And now I have a magic willow stick.

Whoever rushed through the woods now came into view. Barnaby crouched, wishing he could wrap himself in shadows like a blanket on a cold winter night.

He peered out at no angry brigand wielding bow or axe. Here rushed a boy younger than himself. Skin dark as the folk of the southern isles, eyes wide and white with fear of what he fled.

This newcomer spied him, slowing, near tumbling. For a moment he and Barnaby met eyes. Then the boy shook himself, rushed on, fleeing all a host of dragons.

Barnaby considered following behind. But then came an encouraging thought. Clearly, something happened among the robbers. Perhaps they fought one another for the bard's golden harp? How easy for a clever miller to slip in and save a bard.

Decided, Barnaby took a breath, using the path, giving up the slow creep through brambles. Best go straight on, see what frightened all a band of bold woodland robbers.

 The path led to a clearing bordered by high pines swaying slowly in summer's breeze. A lean-to stood at the far end; a haphazard construction of branches and sail canvas. Before it smoldered a campfire sending up blue smoke that drifted weary with the endless turning of wood to ash. Beside the fire lay a man with arms outstretched, hands pulling at the grass. No longer able to crawl yet still seeking to flee. The shirt on his back bubbled red with each desperate breath.
 A second man sat leaning against a tree, hands to a stomach that had become an open door to the world. He moaned, rocking, seeking to keep what spilled from between his fingers.
 A third fellow lay quiet and still upon his back, arms outspread, staring calm as a stone into the sky. Sky and man equally indifferent to his fresh-cut throat.
 In the center of this slaughter sat a figure, shirtless, blood-splattered as the slaughterhouse floor in autumn. Holding a scarlet knife to breasts just as scarlet, just as dripping.
 This person sat upright, swaying lightly, singing to the dripping blade and the bright summer day. Her voice sweet and soft, clearly trained to carry.
Green wife, give me the green life.
Forest ramble and bramble
In sweet summer tangle.
Glad wife, giving me no strife,
In green fern we'll roll and we'll gambol.

"Val?" asked Barnaby. Finding he trembled, backing into tree shadows. Then stopped. Hiding wouldn't do. He stepped forwards into the glade.

The shreds of the bard's fine velvet jerkin lay beside her, as did the splinters of her harp. Blood oozed out a wound in her side, leaking steady as a mouth drooling blood.

Spying Barnaby, she rose to her feet. Head cocked sideways, she began sidling, sideways steps towards him. Still singing.

Green eyes, too much of your sad sighs,
In green shadow your body now lies.
Gay wife, gave you the sharp knife,
No more ramble and bramble
In the sweet forest tangle.

The bard tilted her mad gaze straight at him, moving the knife in a slow wave that fascinated, distracted.

"Val?" asked Barnaby. Opening his hands to show them empty of threat.

"You look a bit familiar," she said, stepping yet closer. "Are you the fellow I first gutted on the road?"

"No, no, I'm just me," he insisted. "Barnaby. You remember. The miller. Second son, not the third. Introduced me to St. Herman?"

"Ah," said Val the Bard. "My mistake." Then she leaped towards him, knife raised.

Barnaby leaped back, every bit as quick. But promptly crashing into a tree. Bouncing off, falling to the green grass. The bard stood above him, staring down, the bloody knife weaving this way, that way, like a snake. Barnaby considered it. A kitchen knife, no fighter's blade. The bard considered it as well. Began to sing to it.

In forest glade there came a maid,

Sing ramble and bramble and tangle.
With her love she laughed and laid,
Sing tangle and ramble and bramble.

"That's very nice," said Barnaby.
She looked down at Barnaby, eyes doubting.
"Really?"
"Yes. Very pretty."
She bent low, confided to him in whisper.
"Personally, I loathe those old ditties. But, my thanks." She put a foot upon his chest, raised the knife. "Die now," she suggested.
"Help now," whispered Barnaby.

Chapter 15

Inform the Submister that the Chief Flayer is Out of Snake Venom. Again.

"Entirely a waste of my aid," brooded Michael. He stood in the dark just beyond the fire; somber eyes reflecting dancing flames.

"But entertaining," observed the cat. Sitting far closer to the flames. His angel-white eyes catching no least gleam of firelight.

"Will she live?" asked Barnaby. "Can't I use a second wish so you may cure her?"

"I am no healer," said the ghost. "Quite the opposite. But if she doesn't start spitting blood, and the wound does not turn green and she does not take a fever, she will live. Till she dies of something else."

"Granted, she might yet kill *you*," observed the cat.

"She wasn't herself," said Barnaby. Feeling a rare anger. "She's a bard, not a soldier ready to shrug at killing. She'd gone out of her head."

The cat smiled to fire and anger alike. "Heads are not really houses one goes in, goes out, goes in."

"She certainly knows her knife work," mused Michael. "One supposes it a requirement for pretty bards on the road."

Barnaby got up, saying naught. He ladled soup from the kettle into a bowl. Then carried this to the lean-to where Val lay upon a mat of straw and heather.

Her eyes were open, staring at the sky, the sparks rising. As he approached, she studied him.

"The miller's son, right?"

Barnaby smiled in relief. "Then you do know me. Hungry? I made soup from things I found."

The woman considered. "No."

"And I found you a new shirt. It's beside you."

"Where is my knife?"

"The kitchen knife?"

"No, my long knife. They took it when they first caught me."

"It's just under your mat. Michael said you'd rest better having it close by."

She reached about, found it. Raising the blade. Barnaby felt a moment's worry. Would she jump up, chase him about? Else wait till he came close, then lunge.

She spied the thought. Gave a sour smile.

"Worried I'll gut you?"

Barnaby considered. Honesty seemed best.

"Some."

She nodded. "Smart." She put the knife back under the mat. "Safe enough?"

She lay covered with the blanket. But still looked entirely a girl now. Or woman? Somewhere between.

"They were easygoing at first," she said. Staring upwards, recalling. "Didn't hold grudge for me slicing their leader. He wasn't popular, it seems."

"That'd be the fellow by your horse?"

She nodded. "Poor Destrier. Fell dead with an arrow to the head. Stupid of them. That horse was worth more than I am. But they didn't know rat-shit about proper robbery. They dragged me away, insisting it was nothing personal. Were going to sell me to St. Martia, but promised to leave a knife in my boot so's I could get free of the slavers."

"Would they have?"

She smiled. "No. They were lying. To themselves as much as me. Still, we got on fine. At first. They tied my feet but not my hands, so I could play my harp for them. Brigit's tits, I sang ten thousand songs about sly robbers, clever brigands, stupid sheriffs. They sang right along. The redhead, Marcus, had a decent voice. Then I got careless."

"How so?"

"Over-many high notes. They caught on I wasn't soprano boy, but tenor girl. After that it was all talk of rape in the shadows, no more noble brigands under the green wood."

Barnaby stayed silent, wishing he was at home, sitting by the hearth, staring into the kindly flames.

"The world's a fearful place," he sighed.

"It is that," Val agreed. "Are they all dead?"

Barnaby nodded. "They are now. Two I tried to bandage but it wasn't any good. A boy ran off through the trees."

"Dark skin, copper hair, white teeth?"

"Yes."

"That was Bodkin. Glad he got away. He's the one who slipped me the cooking knife."

"That was good of him."

"Quite good, for a thief," Val mused. "But Bodkin didn't really fit in with woodland bandits. More the kind to pick the bishop's pocket on the High Street, and then ask for his blessing. Who were you talking to by the fire?"

"A magic cat and a ghost."

Val closed her eyes. "Doesn't surprise me a bit."

This observation surprised Barnaby. "No?"

"No. Was it the ghost who grabbed me as I was about to gut you?"

"Yes. That's Dark Michael."

"Thought there was something funny about him. Was right behind me all on a sudden. His arm about my throat gave chills. I mean, worse than one usually gets from an unexpected arm about one's throat. Didn't see the magic cat."

Barnaby began describing Master Shadow Night-Creep, which required explaining the witches and the pebble-kiss. His words grew as tangled as the witches' wood, so he switched to Dark Michael, giving a long description of the poor donkey. At the burial he realized Val did not hear him. She slept, breathing soft but rapid, as though in dreams she ran for her life.

* * *

"If the boy goes to the Saintless Tower, he dies on the steps," observed Professor Night-Creep.

"If he goes as is," agreed Dark Michael.

"What, will you first teach him to waggle a sword? Give him soldierly advice on keeping feet dry, eyes and blade sharp? And in a week, he'll walk into the lion's den, returning with the lion's gold tooth?"

"Certainly, I can teach him to fight," said Michael. "As you might instruct in magics. Till then, we must steer him to other pursuits."

"I am his humble, most humble servant, oh ghost," meowed the cat. "Not his master. Whether the boy sets himself to wrestle dragons or climb cursed towers to dance jigs upon the pinnacle, I but follow meekly behind."

Dark Michael laughed; a sound sharp and cold as the crack of ice in far northern places lacking sun's light, sun's hope.

"Do not talk to me of servants. Whether magic-summoned spirit or farmgirl in the scullery. Servants are forever leading their masters by the nose. Exact as cats."

The cat yawned. "This is but a fool's summoning, to aid a fool in a fool's quest. I must return to work fitting a being of my fur and station."

"What? Fetching gold coins for wizards, baby breath for witches? Instructing a wrinkled sorcerer how to concoct potions to make him feel seventy again? Perhaps informing some sub-minister of Infernum that the Chief Flayer is out of snake venom?"

The cat growled. "The high and noble path such as I walk, is nothing a deceased butcher-lord can comprehend."

Now Dark Michael yawned, to say what he thought of *high and noble paths*.

Master Shadow Night-Creep licked a tail-tip. "But speaking entirely hypothetically, when one wishes to turn human feet down a side path, the heart makes excellent distraction. Or the groin, at least."

Ghost and cat met eyes, then turned them towards the lean-to, where Barnaby sat, head down, watching over the sleeping bard.

Chapter 16
First Instructions

Far into the night, Barnaby sat by Val. Wondering whether to wake her, offer her broth. Else bring her closer to the fire? In the end he let her sleep. Deciding he'd best sleep himself.

Of course, he could not. His gaze kept turning towards the dead men lying in the night gloom. Would they become ghosts? Might be angry spirits, complaining how Barnaby made free with their blankets, rations and firewood.

Perhaps they'd start following him, giving lessons in being a bandit. He didn't want their company or their lessons.

Closing his eyes, he found the view *there* just as dark. Grim images wandered his head, as though it'd become a wood full of robbers and sly soldiers, witches and ghosts.

He wished he were closer to the campfire, trading his dark thoughts for pleasant fancies with the flames, As he'd done at the hearth at home.

He gave sleep up; opening eyes to search about for Master Night-Creep and Michael. Perhaps one was ready with some lesson in magic or fighting.

Finding to his surprise that he was no longer in the robber's camp. He lay on the floor of his father's mill. But it was changed, grown vast to store a winter's supply of cathedrals. The wheels and cogs were become great mountainous circles turning slow and inexorable as the stars. Watching them made Barnaby dizzy, the sight more than a miller's head should be asked to hold.

Far, far above in the rafters, he spied the cat-shape of Master Night-Creep, watching Barnaby; white pupilless eyes small and bright as winter stars.

Barnaby turned away, spying his mother and brother rushing to feed grain to the grindstones. He'd never seen them work so hard. Pouring great baskets of oats, barley, millet and wheat into the funnels; but out the sliders came only the faintest puffs of flour.

"We've not nearly enough," howled Alf. "They grow hungrier with every turn."

And indeed the mill began to shake, as though the turning wheels began to rebel against their service of ceaseless grinding.

"Let's feed them Barnaby," shouted his mother. She and Alf rushed to seize his arms. He did not resist as they dragged him, threw him beneath the ever-turning stones.

He awoke to find himself shivering in the lean-to beside the bard. He blinked upwards, eyes searching for the great turning millwheels. Seeing only a night sky at the borderland of dawn. Cold and chill. And the face of Dark Michael staring down; also cold and chill.

"Up," said the ghost. "Blade practice."

Barnaby yawned, stretched, shaking dreams from his head. Checked on Val. She seemed no better, no worse. He went behind a tree, peed sleepily then wandered towards the campfire. The ghost stood before the fire, casting no shadow.

"Your bard has moved me to alter our instruction," said the ghost. "It's too early to learn the sword. Particularly when you have no sword. Find a knife. Something more fierce than your pocket blade."

Barnaby sighed. The dead robbers wore knives they no longer needed. He went to the corpse lying beside the fire. Flies buzzed about. He'd have to do something about the bodies soon, or the glade would be unbearable. He struggled at the belt, the swelling stomach holding it tight; till he'd pulled free a long knife of hammered iron.

Heavier than a kitchen knife, with a broad leather grip. In the firelight it looked practical yet sinister. Barnaby wondered if anyone had ever been killed with it.

"We begin with stance," said the ghost.

As time passed, as daylight filled the clearing, Dark Michael became increasingly difficult to see and hear. At some point Barnaby found himself alone, listening to birds chirp, squirrels chatter, waving a knife at the smoke of the dying fire.

"Like this?" he asked, making a downward slash that slaughtered the gray whisps.

Michael made no answer that Barnaby could hear. So he sighed; stretched; went to check on Val again. Finding her awake. He rushed to get her a bowl of broth from the pot by the fire, fearing she'd fall asleep before returning. But she remained awake, blinking at the ceiling of the lean-to.

"I was having the most absurd dream," she said.

"Were there mill wheels big as giants?"

"No. Just a fat little man in a fur vest. He gave me a long lecture on, on *romance*. Touching on all the major themes, with reference to the higher works. Quite impressive."

"Ah. That was probably Master Night-Creep. He's wonderfully learned, for cat or man. Can you drink this?"

"Yes. Let me sit up."

Doing so caused her pain. But once sitting, she held the bowl steady, taking small sips.

"Watched you. Been practicing knife-fighting?"

"Dark Michael decided that was more practical, as I lack sword. I suppose you inspired him."

Val went silent at that. Barnaby worked to hold a cheering smile; inwardly cursing himself for reminding her of the dead robbers. Her face looked drawn, pink-flushed. Beads of sweat glistening on the forehead.

Fever, he decided.

"Your tutor must have trained in St. Martia," said the bard.

"Could you see him?"

"Hmm. No. I watched you talking to smoke and tree shadow. Though sometimes it did seem like there was a tall man beside you, wearing a Demetian officer's coat. But that stand you made with one foot before the other, both hands to the side, is pure Martia. Except you should keep your knees looser."

"Ha, that's just what Michael said."

She set aside the bowl, lay back.

"What brought you into the wood?" she asked.

"Oh, we saw your dead horse," said Barnaby. "Farmers said the robbers captured you. We came to get you back." He decided not to mention that ghost and cat had argued against this decision.

Val studied him awhile, eyes slowly lowering, closing like flowers at sunset. When she spoke, it was the voice of someone drifting from the world.

"You know, when we met by the fountain, I thought old Herm winked at you."

"Oh?"

"Yes. He has an affection for fools who take to the road."

"Ah?"

"But now I think... I am almost ready to think, that maybe he winked at me."

That declared, she slept again.

Barnaby considered returning to sleep as well. But Da would box his ears for napping when there was work to be done. He began with the bodies of the robbers.

He had no spade for digging graves, nor was the ground here the soft earth of a farm field. In the end, he dragged each of the three corpses into the pines. Covering the bodies with scrapings of dirt, branches, pine needles, what rocks he could find. The trees' sharp scent masked all but the faintest trace of decaying bandit. Still, probably it would draw animals by night. Dogs, wolves, bears, foxes; who knew.

Unpleasant work that lasted till afternoon shadows filled the woods. At last Barnaby rested, considering the three mounds as he would sacks of flour, milled and ready.

He searched within himself, not finding any kindly words to say over *these* dead. He wondered why. Had he grown more callous than when he'd buried Michael?

One might call a stranger 'friend' and hope it true. But what did one say when all you knew of folk was that they'd hid by the road to murder a horse, stab a bard?

In the end, Barnaby said nothing; leaving the graves to the wind-whisper eulogy of the pines.

Walking back, he decided he would prefer to be buried under oaks. Oaks had a wisdom you didn't find in other trees. Granted, pine needles made a far better bed than oak leaves. Not that a dead Barnaby would probably care.

"Four burials now," he sighed to the woods. He recalled the cabbage field and smiled. "And one birth."

"Such is Life's mathematics," said a voice. "Addition, subtraction."

Barnaby looked up to see the cat, feline form shaped of night. There the creature perched upon a branch same as any squirrel. The eyes staring wide and without pupil; white and bright as sunlight on new snow.

"Instruction time," declared Professor Shadow Night-Creep.

By habit, Barnaby looked for his stool and dunce's cap. But this glade was not Friar Cedric's cottage. So he stood straight, readying knuckles to be rapped.

The cat leapt down beside him; circled once, nodding in approval of posture and attitude. Then turned, walking away. Barnaby followed, finding the cat sitting pert before the campfire.

"Now, as with any true craft, we begin by preparing our tools. Take your knife and place the blade within the fire. You'll have to build up the embers, so we get a proper touch of flame."

Barnaby knelt, adding kindling. While he did, the cat mused, to himself as much as his student.

"To my mind, a proper working requires a blade of purest silver held above a fire of spring rowan. Still, there are those who swear by tools touched with ordinary use. And truly, the things of daily life hold great power in St. Demetia. All things considered, which is more magic; a wizard's silver knife for cutting moonbeams, or a farmwife's kitchen blade for slicing bread?"

Barnaby pondered the question. He pictured slices of moonbeam. Certainly they'd be unusual. While fresh bread was entirely usual, excepting on the road. He decided that in his present life he'd prefer bread to moonbeams.

"Now fetch the willow wand," commanded the cat.

Barnaby prepared to ask *what wand?* Then recalled the stick put aside as he'd crept upon the robbers. Hurrying to his pack, he reached in, drew forth the magic branch. It looked astonishingly like an ordinary stick.

"Excellent. Take the knife from the fire and peel the bark away. Don't carve the raw wood. Good. Now cut the ends so they are not ragged."

Barnaby did these things. Stripped of bark, the stick looked naked and new. Seeming to shine faintly. The cat sniffed, whiskers declaring themselves satisfied.

"Now hold out your paw. Your palm, I mean. I am going to make four scratches. Along your life-line, your heart line, your spirit line and the line of your mind."

"Are these things truly there?" asked Barnaby, staring at his own hand in wonder.

"No," said the cat. "And yes. The concepts are there. And concepts are the flesh and bone of magic."

Barnaby held out his concept-laden hand. The cat sniffed; then, near too fast to be seen, raked claws across Barnaby's palm.

"Ouch," said Barnaby.

"Do you never swear, boy?" asked the dark voice of Dark Michael. Barnaby turned to this instructor, shrugging.

"No sir, not much, sir. Da never held with such words even when the mill wheels stuck or rats became ground with the grist. He said that my, my first Ma disliked profanities. I grew thinking she'd be pleased I avoided them."

Barnaby considered, then gave what for him passed as *wicked grin*.

"I heard some wonderful oaths from the acrobat troop. I've tried saying them, specially the one about the mother of the dog of St. Lucif. But it sounded silly from a miller's mouth."

"Wise decision," said the cat. "Leave foul oaths to soldiers and other fools. While we return to wise instruction. Smear your blood across all the wand, rubbing it into the wood."

Barnaby did this. Lamenting how the stick lost its bright white glow. Now it appeared brown-red, old as bronze. Heavier as well, though no doubt that was fancy.

"Draw a circle in the air around you," commanded the cat. "Start from the East, where Life begins. Turn to South, where Life is warm. Now West, where life journeys. Next to North, where Life is struggle. Last, back to East. Excellent."

Barnaby held the wand, examining it. Perhaps it would shoot lightning. Or he'd tap his head, turn himself to a hawk? No, better, a lion.

"We have now consecrated the stick to fire, to blood, to air. As willow it begins sacred to earth and water. Remember these five keys of life, boy. It is in these that the power of St. Demetia rests. In other lands it would be different."

"What shall we do first?" asked Barnaby. Then answered himself. "Val needs a horse. Can we change something into a horse?" He studied a squirrel, which studied him right back. Defying him to transmogrify.

The cat sighed. "A horse. Yes. Why not. Then we shall turn the moon into a great wheel of cheese."

"Truly?"

"No. Take the wand and come with me."

Barnaby followed the cat. Dark Michael remained behind, leaning against a tree, arms folded, chin on chest, deep in thought.

While they walked, Barnaby shook the wand at sticks, rocks, a passing sparrow. Nothing changed. He found himself unsurprised. In his hands, a magic wand became a dirty stick, nothing more.

The cat led to a small clearing, uncomfortably near where Barnaby had left the three robber corpses. The scent of death weighed heavy on the evening breeze. For sure it would bring wolves and bears.

The cat stopped, sat in a patch of evening sunshine, centered in a dance of butterfly and bee.

"Push the wand upright into the ground," said the cat. "Just here." He tapped a spot of green.

Barnaby did so, finding the stick went easily into the earth. The cat sniffed, turned, walking away, tail raised.

"What now?"

"Now you let it be till I say otherwise," said the cat. "Touch it not, or we must begin again."

"For how long?"

"A sunrise, a moonrise? Perhaps a year's full turn of the stars of the sky. Perhaps till seven kingdoms fall that have yet to rise. A proper wand must come into its own, upon its own time."

"Suppose a squirrel or deer chews upon it?" asked Barnaby, disappointed. "After only six kingdoms fall?"

The cat twitched tail in what was clearly a feline shrug.

"Then we begin again."

Chapter 17
The Seventh Wisdom is for Fools

Friar Cedric of Mill Town:

The saints know I never sought the boy's death. *"Teach him to be a fool,"* I was told. An easy task, but an evil request.

Request? No. Best I speak honest. It was command. Given by two scheming peasants as beneath me in breeding as in learning. By the Lord of Saints, I am no mere *friar!* I am an ordained priest of the Order of Saint Demetia herself.

But, alas, I am also a brother of the excommunicate Society of Lucretius; those who gather in secret places to whisper truth to shadows. Vanity and cowardice! It was not to shadows we should have preached. We should have shouted to crowds. Proclaiming aloud the truth of saints and stars, earth and stone, the order of beasts and men, the spinning world beneath us.

True, it would have earned us martyrdom. Branding, and a breaking on the wheel. But a man must speak the truths he holds, else the truth shall rot within his soul. Like forgotten grain moldering in a barn.

But we of the Society only shared our truths to one another, whispering secrets to shadows. Till shadows no longer protected; and the Society of St. Lucretius, the One True Saint, was pronounced anathema across the kingdoms. The Questioners hunted down my scholarly brethren, captured them, broke them.

The miller's sly wife and her evil consort Squire Semple gave me sanctuary in their little peasant fiefdom. So long as I obeyed, like a proper serf. Serf? No, like a *whipped dog*.

When the miller died, I made no question concerning the blackened tongue of the corpse. When stepmother and stepbrother declared the mill rightfully theirs, I nodded as if they recited catechism, not proud declaration of theft from the miller's son.

"Teach him to be a fool." A degrading task. And unnecessary as instructing a duck in the art of paddling a pond. Barnaby was born with head empty as the sky on a cloudless day.

And yet... and yet. At times I wondered if we all misunderstood the creature. Not that he deceived, pretending idiocy as Claudius did to deceive Caligula. But what the sly and clever of this world take for foolishness, can be a different wisdom. Neither the practiced innocence of those in holy vestments, nor the academic mind of the universities, nor the cool objectivity of we Lucretians.

If Barnaby read upside down, still he read. When the cruelties of his stepmother and brother drove him from his hearth corner, he would come to my cottage, sit by my shelves, perusing books. Yes, upside down. But who else but me held them at all?

For there be six wisdoms, says the Testament of Sister Sophia.

The wisdom of the Holy, who know the will of Divinity. The wisdom of the Serpent, who knows the wiles of humanity. The wisdom of the Scholar, who knows the world in words. The wisdom of the Beasts, who follow the rhythm of nature. The wisdom of the Young, who know the joy of Life. And last, the wisdom of the Old, who know the cost of Life.

Six. I always felt there should be a seventh that completes the six. Suppose... suppose it is the Wisdom of the Fool?

What does the fool know? How to read upside-down, how to trade a cow for magic beans, how to walk whistling into the dragon's den. The seventh wisdom is beyond scripture and logic alike. A mad path leading to the precipice, and beyond.

Once winter evening Barnaby sat by my hearth. Staring into the fire as he did whenever not set to some task of use.

"What do you see in the fire?" I asked.

"Faces."

"Whose?"

"My Da's, most oft. But also yours and the Squire's. Alf's and Mother's. Other folk too. Folk I've not yet met except in the hearth. All the faces of the world, sometimes."

"The world's full of faces. Why seek them in the fire?"

"The faces in the fire are the real ones."

I could make nothing of that. And yet, I wondered.

When his family sent the boy to die, I did not join the cheerful farewell. I remained in my simple cottage, seeking comfort in the texts of St. Lucretius. Looking for distraction in explanations of stars and sand grains, the absolute laws that turn the greatest and least wheels of earth and heaven.

Priest though I am, I said no prayers. How should I dare and why would I bother? There come times when seeking communion with the Absolute is pointless; for one already sits in the presence of Truth. As I did then.

And the truth was clear. I'd let an innocent be sent to his death. No doubt he left waving cheerful goodbye to his murderers.

Truth is light; and the light revealed all I'd done, and where I now dwelled. I looked about, seeing no friar's cell for prayer and study, but a prisoner's cell. And then, gazing into the hearth fire, I saw my own face. Not the noble scholar my mirror presented. The face in the flames was a thing of subservience, a visage worthy of some creature best suited to crawl the earth upon its belly.

Years past, I had a love. The novice, Beatrice Lucia. We parted when she vowed to devote her life to holy penance. *Penance*... for what? For warm nights a'bed with me. Sipping the saints' communion wine upon the bell tower. Wearing over-soft vestments. Trivial, laughable sins that could only trouble conscientious students of divinity.

But what penance suffices to absolve a soul truly tarred by an act of evil? Marked with betrayal of the innocent?

Bah. St. Lucretius has no use for penance. Only this does the *One True Saint* revere: acceptance of what is true.

This, then, is truth: I have done evil. There is no mending it. The boy is surely dead, his murder done. Yet I will hide in this hole no longer. I will seek his bones upon the byways of this world. Not in exile but in pilgrimage.

And should I ever find Barnaby's bones, I shall give them proper words, if the hungry wolves of the world have left aught.

Alas for the poor wolves of this world! And I a dog among them.

Chapter 18
Words Writ Rough

At noon of the third day of their conquest of the robber's glade, Barnaby sat beside Val. Her face drawn and grey, at times opening eyes that did not see Barnaby or the summer day. Her hand twitching at the blanket edge, perhaps seeking the security of her knife. But the motion reminded Barnaby of Grandda's final days, clutching blindly at the things of a fading world.

Finally, Barnaby rose, walking towards the campfire. He called for his magic cat instructor, his dark ghost tutor. Finding neither by mid-day's light.

"Master Night-Creep? Dark Michael?"

The wind made indifferent rustle; no shadow hinted ghostly form.

"Val still won't eat and won't wake and she's not breathing right," shouted Barnaby. Then, voice lower: "I fear she's dying."

No reply but a crackle from the embers of the fire. The dying fire... Barnaby knelt, placing the last of the gathered kindling upon the embers. Blew, wondering why one could not do the same for the sick.

Here I am staring into fire and ashes again, thought Barnaby.

Here you are, agreed the fire. Embers and ashes glimmering orange-red welcome.

This is no time for daydreams, Barnaby scolded. I must do something. He looked about, hoping to find his clever teachers had mysteriously appeared behind him. But no; here was just Barnaby and the fire, no different than the millhouse.

I'll have to do something on my own, he told the fire.

But what? asked the flames, dancing excitedly.

Barnaby answered aloud, tasting the words for hope or sense.

"I could make a broth of healing herbs to revive Val. Excepting I don't know which herbs. I don't even have any herbs. I might carry her into a town, so some surgeon gives her a healing poultice. Except it's over-far for her to go, even if I knew where a village lay or a surgeon lived or I had coin for the doctoring. Maybe I could fetch a wise-wife to cast healing spells. Though I don't know where such a person might be."

The campfire crackled encouragingly.

"You and wind, water, earth and blood," mused Barnaby. "Master Shadow Creep said you five held magic in St. Demetia."

Magic. Of a sudden he recalled his willow wand. He jumped up, setting off into the wood, crashing through brambles, seeking the small glade. Following the scent of the half-buried robbers.

He found himself on the edge of a sun-lit circle of trees; butterfly-haunted, bejeweled by buzzing bees. There in the center stood his wand. And beside it, a woman knelt. And Barnaby knew the woman.

He near laughed, happy to see this familiar face. Behold: Missus Green herself.

She was humming, some tune to which the light flickered, the butterflies danced, the bees buzzed. The melody filled Barnaby's head till he found himself breathing in time to it.

He watched as Missus Green reached a finger to touch a fresh leaf now sprouting from the wand, a leaf green as the sun seen through an emerald.

Missus Green did not wear the straw hat she'd favored when she'd come to help the birthing in the cabbage field. Today she wore a crown. No silly thing of gold or jewels. Just a circlet of wheat stalks set upon braids thick and rich as rope, more golden than gold itself.

Barnaby puzzled. How had she come to be here? And why did the sight of her make him feel so shy? She was just some farm wife keeping a field probably no bigger than the mill-house floor.

Neither young girl nor old crone. Lines on her face declaring she'd tasted from life's cups of sorrow and joy. Her waist spoke of children born and raised. The hand reaching now to Barnaby's willow wand was knuckled and strong. *Harvest hands,* Da used to call such. Claiming he could tell who spent their days planting, who spent their days milling or weaving or cobbling shoes.

The woman turned from studying the wand to studying Barnaby; showing no annoyance to find he should be studying *her*. No, she gave a smile warm as summer breeze. In return he gaped; wanting to run, wanting to stammer.

She seemed taller. Surely this was no peasant widow, but a lord's lady. A High Sister of Sainted Demetia. Else someone more fearful yet.

Whoever she might be, it went impolite to stare like a cow over a fence. And so Barnaby gathered courage and bowed, as he imagined lords did in city streets whenever a king passed by.

Missus Green laughed, clearly pleased. Then she rose, gathering her skirt about her. She bent a knee, curtsied in return to his bow. That done, she turned and walked away through the trees.

Barnaby stared after her, feeling abandoned. Wanting to call '*stay with me.*' He knew that for absurdity. Foolish as calling for the sun to linger in the sky to keep him company. He stared into the trees, silent, hoping for any last glimpse. Gone.

At last he took a breath, looking about as though come fresh awake. Why had he run here? Ah, the wand, of course. He went to the stick, still standing just where he'd set it yesterday.

He reached, hesitated. Master Night Creep had commanded: *leave it be*. But the cat was not here, and Val was dying. If this might heal her, then it were worth a knuckle-rapping.

Barnaby tugged at the stick. Puzzled, for though he'd set it lightly into the earth, now it seemed rooted as a young oak.

It took both hands to pull free. That done, he held it a moment, studying. Was it even the same willow stick?

It weighed heavier, smooth and cold, green with a patina of ancient bronze. Yet a new leaf sprouted from the tip; green and living.

Barnaby turned and ran back to the robbers' clearing, holding the wand before him to show the brambles he had no time for their foolish game of tangles. He did not rest till he stood panting again beside the sleeping bard.

Val did not stir. Her face looked gray as old milk. The blanket rose and fell with each breath, as though she sought to seize all the air before it was taken from her.

"I'm going to carry you near the fire," said Barnaby. She made no answer. He bent, scooping her up. The arms and legs dangled limp as the limbs of a hanged man. He recalled the dead robbers, their loose legs and faces...Barnaby had a sudden vision of burying Val.

Well, if it came to that, he'd do it. Then turn about, return to Mill Town. The road passed too many graves.

Determined not to drop her nor fail her, he carried the bard to the campfire. Laying her down soft as babe into crib. At that her eyes opened, rolling upwards, white and unseeing.

"Fire, wind and earth," said Barnaby to himself. "We have these things. What else?" For a moment he could not recall. "Oh, blood. And water." He raced to the lean-to, fetching the bucket. Recalling the minnow he'd met who'd wanted to go adventuring in a bucket.

Glad he stayed in the creek. This world's no pleasant pond.

Barnaby set the bucket beside Val. Considered, then cupped hands into the water, dripping it across her forehead. She shivered as though it were melted ice.

Of a sudden Barnaby doubted his plan to do magic was anything but a fool's dream. He was the idiot son of a miller, playing at high things. But no choice now but continue.

He drew his knife, took breath and sliced across his palm, across the lines scratched by the teacher-cat.

"Ouch," he said. Then, seeing none nearby but the fire and the unconscious bard, he whispered: *"Damn it to the dogs twixt St. Lucif's mother's legs."* An interesting thing to say, if not relevant.

He stared at the blood pooling in his palm. What now? He tried tapping it with the wand. Then walked in a slow circle about Val, waving the wand as Dark Michael had told him to flourish a branch imagined to be saber.

He found himself humming the melody he'd heard from Missus Green in the clearing. Deciding the tune needed words. What words? They'd be things of life and light, home and healing.

"Light," he said. "Life. Fire. Bright. Home. Hearth." Then,

Star light, dark night,
Fire is blood, flame is light.
Hearth is heart, Life is bright.

He walked about the bard and fire, chanting this rhyme like a child skipping a rope. Only ceasing when he'd circled the bard thrice.

"Now what?" he wondered. He bent down. Did Val seem less pale? Breathe easier? Not noticeably. He touched the wand-tip to her forehead, leaving a single red dot of his blood.

She did not stir. The green leaf sprouting from the wand waved in the wind's breath, not the bard's.

Barnaby reached, plucked the leaf. Bending lower, he placed it in the bard's mouth, just on the tongue. And of a sudden he felt weary past standing. Nearly toppling into the campfire.

Telling himself he'd done all he could, he sat beside Val and waited.

Barnaby awoke to find himself upon his back, staring up at clouds tinted in the softer tones of dawn. While two angel-white eyes stared down. Night-Creep perched upon his chest, weighing heavy.

He wondered if he should worry. The creature was a witch's familiar. Perhaps it had decided to eat him up?

"Sir?" he asked.

In reply the cat said... nothing. Merely continued staring, silent, unblinking.

I wonder if I could pet him, thought Barnaby. I'd rub his tummy. I miss the cats at the mill. Good folk to sit with through cold nights, lonely days.

Of a sudden he recalled the wand, Missus Green, the dying bard, his absurd attempt to do magic.

Barnaby sat up, sending the cat leaping. He looked to where Val had lain, gray and fading. There lay the blanket, empty of bard as cocoon with butterfly flown.

"Where is she?"

The cat collected itself, tail tip a'twitch.

"You used your wand," said the cat.

"Yessir."

"You attempted magic," stated the cat.

"I did that." Barnaby sighed, prepared to have his knuckles rapped.

The cat then did something no cat at any mill ever did. It *laughed*. Then leaped clean over Barnaby, graceful as deer over farm field fence. The creature tumbled, rolled, came upright and ran a circle about the boy, all while he stared astounded.

"Tomnoddy," said the cat. "Puddinghead. Nit-for-wit. It worked. You did magic."

"Truly?" said Barnaby, eyes round as cynic owls hearing good news. He stood, looked about. Studying the glade by dawn's light; the fire a mere pit of orange embers. "Me?"

Now came his turn to laugh. Which, granted, was a thing Barnaby oft did. Laugh done, he turned to his instructor.

"I'm going to rub your tummy, cat."

Professor Shadow Night-Creep, familiar of the lower Courts of Infernum, closet advisor to High Witches, privy counselor to kings and wizards, gave outraged hiss. Then leaped across the grass. Barnaby chasing after, waving his wand.

They circled the campfire thrice, then Night Creep rolled upon his back. Showing the night-fur of his underbelly, a small patch of white and four sets of claws extending like sickle moons foretelling destruction.

"Of course, boy. Rub my stomach, boy. You've naught to fear, boy."

"Excepting mutilation," said a voice dark and somber as the stones of forgotten tombs of forgotten kings of kingdoms long forgot. Barnaby turned, excited.

"Master Michael, I did magic!"

Dark Michael kept to his usual pose, leaning against a tree, arms folded, hat low. Low enough to hide the eyes. But not the smile.

"Well done, boy. Tell us about it."

Barnaby felt suddenly weary again. He sat upon the tree stump, recalling.

"Val was dying and so I went for my wand and Missus Green was there."

"Who?"

"Just some farm wife I met on the road. She was helping with a birthing in a potato field. Ah, no, wait, it was cabbage."

"Oh?"

"Truly," affirmed Barnaby. "Cabbage, not potato. The leaves are far different. But there Missus Green was yesterday in these very woods, singing with the bees. She made a leaf sprout from the wand."

Barnaby went silent, recalling the gold of her braids, the strength of her hands. The cat came upright, staring at Barnaby. Then turned to Dark Michael. The two exchanged a long look.

Barnaby shook himself, continued. "Anyhow, when she left I took the wand. Brought Val close by the fire and did what came to mind." He surveyed the empty blanket with satisfaction. "And it was magic, if you can believe it."

"I can," affirmed the cat. "But exactly how did you do it?"

Barnaby rubbed his head. "It's a bit muddled. I remembered your lesson. Blood and water, air and fire and earth. And there was a song that came into my head." He looked about.

"So, where is Val?"

The cat turned to the ordering of its tail fur, with careful licks of its pink tongue. Michael answered.

"She left. I watched her wend her way back towards the road."

"Oh," said Barnaby. "Well, that must mean she's truly better."

But he felt disappointed. It wasn't every day a miller cast magic healing upon a dying bard. She might have remained, just to allow him to tell a bit about it.

"I doubt this is a place she wished to stay," said Dark Michael.

Barnaby considered, then nodded. From Val's point of view this pleasant woodland glade was a place of fear and death. One could understand fleeing, given least chance.

"Wish she'd said goodbye," said Barnaby. "I wanted her to meet you."

"She left you a goodbye," said the cat. "Of a sort."

"Oh?"

"You sit upon it."

Barnaby stood, turned to examine the tree trunk. There in the light of dawn lay a plentiful pile of copper and silver coins. Barnaby stirred them with a finger, awed.

"Where did she get such riches? The robbers would have taken any she had."

Dark Michael laughed. "Clever girl. Must have spied where the sheep-bandits hid their coin."

"She counted out half, left that for you," observed the cat. "Quite idealistic of her. Do not doubt her gratitude, boy."

"Ah," said Barnaby. "Well, I hope she gets a new harp with her share. And a horse. With silver bells that jingle like pennies on a plate."

He poked at the coins, spying something beneath. Scratched in the rough wood, two rough words, possibly upside down depending on where you stood stump-wise. From where Barnaby stood, they read:

noʎ ʞuɐɥʇ

Chapter 19
Of Acorn Bread and Pockets of Emeralds

The next day, after blade practice with Michael followed by magical lecture from Night-Creep, Barnaby was given leave to do whatever deeds the merely living and breathing required.

He gathered wood, then took the water bucket to the spring, filled it, returning to the fire. He scrubbed the cooking pot; set about making a fresh mix of deer meat and gruel. Hanging this above the fire. That done, he went to a tree with a knotted rope.

Climbed, the rope led to a rough platform where waited a tin box of salted deer meat, a basket of nuts, a sack of flour. Provisions placed here by the bandits, out of reach of bandit animals.

He sat on the platform edge, legs dangling, nibbling on acorn bread, gazing out over the sunlit woodland. It looked wide as a world. He wondered what creatures it held. Bears? Wolves? More robbers? More millers? No, for sure he was the only miller present. No bards, probably.

He looked northwards, hoping to spy the Saintless Tower glittering with treasure. Seeing only trees, clouds, a blue line that might be mountains or clouds or an ocean or the world's fabled edge.

He felt anxious to get on with his journey. But each day his tutors cajoled and badgered him to learn some trick of wrist, some twist of wand. Clearly they thought he'd perish before ever reaching the tower, unless he received a proper education first.

Probably they were right. And yet, why linger in a nameless wood? They could instruct as he walked. Then he'd arrive at his tower wise and ready for war.

A thousand steps of black stone, guarded by wolves, snakes and spiders, leading to a doorway wherein waited ten thousand more dangers. So Friar Cedric described it.

Barnaby watched a storm move slowly from the east; the wind already fretting tree branches, tasting wet with rain. It'd reach here by evening. The lean-to would be poor comfort.

The robbers should have had a cave. Granted, a farmhouse would serve as well. But a cave seemed more proper. With candles and rugs, bags of coins and chests of weapons. And a waterfall and secret tunnels through hollow trees and a door that only opened with a magic password…

"You should be practicing," advised Michael. "Not daydreaming."

Barnaby nodded. It was the sort of thing said to him oft as a donkey heard 'whoa' and 'git'.

"Did you climb up the rope?" he asked the ghost.

Michael's reply came slow and sour as the honey gathered from the wasp nests of Plutarch.

"Why would I climb the rope?"

"Well, you might just feel like climbing a rope, I suppose."

"Climbing a rope makes no sense for a ghost. I have no need to climb a rope. No, I did not climb the rope."

"Very well, then."

"When we leave, take the road west."

"Isn't the tower north?"

"Yes, but west is the city of Persephone."

"Why go there?"

"Have you food for long journeying?"

Barnaby considered the remains of the robber's rations. "Some venison, carrots and acorn bread.

Truthfully, the venison is gone green and my teeth are tired of acorn bread and my stomach is tired of carrots."

"Exactly. And have you winter clothes for northern wind? Have you shovel for digging, pickaxe for breaking? Candles and lantern for dark tunnels?"

"No. But I have the robber's blankets. They aren't very clean."

"And when at last you find treasure, have you sacks to carry it away?"

This was a new and interesting idea to Barnaby. He pictured standing in a spill of glittering stones and shiny gold. He'd need a broom to sweep it up. Or a shovel. And a donkey or three for carrying. Would sacks serve best for gold, or would barrels serve better?

"I'll fill my pockets with jewels," he declared. "Then I'll go to a town, buy a donkey and return for the gold."

"Assume you have pockets of emeralds now," proposed Dark Michael. "What would you do?"

Barnaby considered, mouth watering. "Ah, first I'd buy a great feast of a breakfast, with sausage and goose and chicken and fresh bread and pudding and ale. And pies. Meat pies, mince pies, strawberry pies and peach pies."

"One emerald for one pie?"

Barnaby laughed. "No, Lord Michael, I'm not so wooden headed. First, I'll sell the jewels for proper coin."

"Who will you sell them to? A tinker? A tavern keeper? A baker?"

Barnaby scratched his unwooden head. Picturing himself knocking on village doors, offering to trade a shiny emerald for a mere fistful of gold. A bargain, surely. And yet farmers and shepherds did not commonly have fistfuls of gold. And anyways, what use did regular folk have for emeralds? In the world he knew, one might starve with pockets of rubies.

"Well, where does one go with a pack full of treasure?"

"To the grave, if you be not careful."

That from a branch above them both, where Shadow Night-Creep now perched. Barnaby doubted the cat climbed the rope. Granted, a cat did not need to climb a rope, any more than a ghost.

"Da always said *'don't get your feet too far in front of your head'*," Barnaby informed his teachers.

"Meaning?" That, from Michael.

"Meaning I have no packs of jewels to be worrying about."

"The boy has a point," said the cat.

"Someone approaches," said Michael.

Barnaby searched the woods below, hoping to see Val the Bard returning on a new horse, silver bells jangling. But no, there by the campfire stood someone else. This person was dark of face, light of hair.

"That's the boy who ran past the day we arrived," declared Barnaby. "His name is Bodkin."

"He'll be wondering about his friends," said Michael.

"Not if he has a nose," sniffed the cat.

"Val said he was a good sort," considered Barnaby. "Gave her the knife she used."

"The knife that killed his companions," observed Michael. "Be wary of such friendship."

Barnaby considered what he could see of Bodkin. He looked younger than Barnaby. Just a kid lost in the woods, staring dismayed about the empty clearing.

Decided, he climbed down the rope, walking slow through the trees, stopping on the edge of the clearing.

"Hallo, Bodkin."

This greeting made the boy jump.

"Who are you?"

"Barnaby. A friend of Val."

"Is she alive?"

"Alive and gone."

"Where are the others?"

"They aren't. Alive, I mean."

Bodkin gaped, then nodded. "Oh. That them making the stink in the trees?"

"I tried to bury them. Didn't have a shovel."

"Shit. All of 'em dead? Even Marcus?"

Barnaby nodded.

Bodkin shook his head. "I came to warn. The farmers have gotten up a band with a couple of real soldiers. On their way now. They catch you here, they'll hang you for a lawbreaker."

"Me? I'm a miller."

"They won't believe it. Best clear out. I'm going to fetch a few things and skedaddle myself." That said, he darted into the trees.

"He'll be back," said Night-Creep. Perching on the tree stump.

"Why?"

"He's gone for the squirrel's nest where the robbers hid their coin. When he finds it empty, he'll follow you."

"Oh."

"Fetch your pack," ordered Michael.

Barnaby reached the country road just as the storm reached the wood; darkening the sky, shaking the branches. Thunder rolled overhead like great barrels of flour across the mill house floor. A flash of lightning revealed the wood, the road, the ribs and skull of Val's horse.

Barnaby considered the bones, then the road's two choices. Why not go north, straight to the tower?

"The city is the other direction," declared Dark Michael.

"How far?"

"Hmm, some two day's march. As I recall. Long years since I journeyed this quiet nowhere."

"And I have not passed this way since that hoary oak was an acorn," declared Night-Shadow.

"Well, but I have food and a blanket and a map and a magic cat and a wise ghost counselor," declared Barnaby. "Why not go north to the tower? Da always said *'no point in circling the hill to enter the mill.'*"

"You aren't ready for the tower."

"My da always –'"

"-And if you babble one more of your ancestor's inane aphorisms I will grow wroth."

Barnaby crossed his arms, preparing to argue Da's wisdom.

"The bard will certainly have headed to Persephone," mused the cat, idly licking a paw. "She'll be looking for a new harp, perhaps a horse."

Barnaby uncrossed his arms.

Chapter 20
Notes from Underground

Marcus, Dead Brigand:

Scurry. We scurry. And scrabble. Best to keep moving. Here are worms that bite. Spiders that sting. Bats that scream with the wind. The light is bright, casting shadows sharp as knives. Ugly shadows of scurrying, scrabbling things. Shades of us.

The fire is bright, so bright, bright, bright. It shows our teeth, our tiny claws. It shows our soul, this cave that is us. This place of shadow and flame, rot and wind, worm and heat and hunger. Yes, the cave is us. We scrabble, we scurry. No getting out. We are in it. It's in us.

When we meet another rat-soul we fight! Tangle and screech and bite! Why? Ah, because we fear. And we hate. Hate! We loath. Loath! Disgusting creatures, the dead soul-rats that are us.

When I was a man outside myself, instead of a rat within this hot rotting Infernum that is myself, I walked and talked in grand ways. Such grand ways! But deep in the caves of my chest was always the rat thing, scrabbling, biting, whispering.

I did not wish to hurt the farmer I stabbed or the baker I hid in the well. Nor harm the maid or my brother. It was the scurrying rat inside me. I feared it, and it hated me. It hungered, it whispered. All my life it nibbled, gnawing at me. Eventually it ate me up.

When the miller boy dragged my body into the pines, I thought, *now at last I shall rest. I shall become a tree in the woods, drinking the sweet rain, the happy beams of light.*

But the rat scrabbled in my breast. The light within grew bright, bright. Revealing this cave of rot and heat and shadow and worm that is me. Fight, bite, scrabble, scurry! This is what I am. I am inside all that was me, and I cannot get out of me.

Chapter 21
Crossing Boundaries

Barnaby followed the road by storm glow, lightning flash. Wind-maddened branches waved as though the trees cast spells upon Barnaby's head. He wondered what orations a tree would cast, were they inclined to do such.

Friar Cedric claimed that in the forest of St. Sylvanus, the trees talked. When they wanted. Cedric never said what a tree would want to say. Tonight, it seemed the trees of St. Demetia wished to shout and wave at Barnaby. No telling the what nor the why. Probably they shouted 'idiot, get out of the rain.'

Meanwhile, Master Night-Creep perched upon Barnaby's backpack, lecturing upon things historical, mythical and mystical, laws natural, unnatural and supernatural.

"In earlier days this was an important byway twixt the city of Persephone, the southern city of Pomona and the eastern farmlands of St. Demetia," cat informed boy, shouting above storm. "Note the bricks still visible in patches beneath the dirt. The stonework wrapped in tree roots."

Barnaby dutifully paused to consider what seemed mere rock. Lightning flashed, redrawing it as jumbled steps leading down to dark places, inviting him to follow. He shivered, declining invitation, hurrying on down the road.

Rain conspired with wind to rush into his collar and fill his boots by way of chest and pants. The cat upon his back seemed indifferent to wet and wind. *Magical protection*, Barnaby supposed.

"I'm drenched, master. Might you not teach me a spell that sends away the rain?"

"Doubtful. Weather-working is a far-advanced subject. What spells have we practiced so far?"

"Lesser Healing. Lesser flame. Lesser Open. Lesser Light. What's the one where I tap the wand to my eyes?"

"Lesser True Seeing."

"That one, then."

Not that I've seen anything yet that isn't what it looked to be, grumbled Barnaby to Barnaby. Silently, unsure if the words aloud would sum to sense. He reached into his jacket, drew forth the wand to tap his eyes.

Quick as the lightning, a cat-paw batted the wand away.

"As I previously instructed, you do not use the spell more than once per day," growled the cat. "Else you'll ruin your sight. Or your mind."

Barnaby sighed, returned the wand to keeping. They continued down the road, while wind blew, storm shouted. Barnaby looked up at the sky, wondering what he'd behold with spell-touched eyes. Storm giants and spirits, perhaps. Or the Wild Hunt that was said to ride the night storm, led by the Archangel Michael himself.

Lacking magic sight and insight, he saw a sky dark as cavern roof, lightning crackles revealing it a vast sea of purplish glass etched with white fire.

He wondered if this same storm passed over the mill? If so, Alf had best see to the vanes, removing the cloth panels, placing the blocks in the cogs. Or else the wheels would spin till they burst afire. Probably his brother and mother argued who'd go into the rain and wind, get the work done. No doubt cursing Barnaby for being tardy with the treasure. When he returned, they'd sit back, counting coins whilst telling Barnaby to get to all the chores he'd missed.

He pondered that. Did he still wish to bring home treasure just to please his stepmother and stepbrother, impress the Squire and Friar? Why not keep it for himself? He was the one on the road in the rain.

It was an astonishing thought, like lightning flashing through his head, revealing things long pushed to dark corners.

They haven't been family. They haven't been kind. They meant me ill. I owe them nothing.

"Consider that statue," commanded the cat.

Barnaby looked about. A stone figure stood to the side of the road. Vine-wrapped, time worn, yet menacing in its indifference to vine and time.

"Behold, Saintly Sister Hecatatia. Her image is oft placed at boundaries of significance."

"What boundary?" he asked, peering ahead. Seeing only more rain, further dark. But perhaps they stood on the edge of St. Demetia itself. Or the world, though Friar Cedric said it had no edge. *Round as an apple*, he'd proclaimed, proud as if he himself had constructed the world so. Alf had laughed at the idea of folk living on a whirling ball, like ants upon an apple. Probably it was just Friar Cedric teaching him nonsense again.

"Centuries past, when that statue had a nose, she marked a grand estate," mused his cat-teacher. "Called, hmm, *Pentafax Abbey*. Owned by a sorcerer of unusual power and exotic tastes. Let us see what remains of his bright house."

Barnaby hurried past the statue. The saintly Sister held a snake in one hand; the other rested upon the head of a lion. By storm's light, her face shone proud and angry. Reminding Barnaby of the witch-girl Jewel, whose cat-familiar he'd stolen. But then, the girl had cheated him of a kiss and stolen his lunch, so the score went tit-for-tat. Granted, stealing his lunch had saved his life. Ah, but Jewel had not *meant* to save his life, just steal his lunch.

Barnaby weighed it all, deciding he didn't owe Jewel anything excepting a kick to her skinny rear.

At that he heard his Da's chiding wisdom: *Ware dark thoughts on dark nights.*

For a moment Barnaby considered arguing with Da. But that went too far. *This storm is making me think like a storm,* he decided. All the wind and thunder is getting inside my head. Best get out from it before I'm washed into someone else entirely.

He trudged on. The trees thinned, no longer a proper wood. But not becoming farmland. To left and right now lay empty fields, dotted with scrub and weed in a tableau more dreary than Barnaby had ever beheld. Broken stonework glistened wet and dark as gravestones for drowned sailors. Clearly, here St. Demetia withheld her smile of warmth and growth.

Past this dismal scene waited a hill; upon the hill perched a great beast of a ruin. Lightning revealing Pentafax Abbey as crumbled stone, fallen tower, vine-twisted wall.

"And so time passes," declared the cat. "*Sic Gloria Mundi,* as they say across the sea." Sounding not a bit non-plussed to see bright hall come to dark ruin. He leaped from Barnaby's pack, perching upon a rain-dripping stone. "Yet centuries past, it was a grand house. The windows aglow, the air music-filled as a spring morning bird-choired. Feasts in the great hall for folk of every sort. And fish! Many and various were the fish served the worthy guest. Trout and herring, tuna and eel, oyster and salmon. Ah, salmon pink and soft as the ears of baby mice."

The cat licked its muzzle, remembering.

"Might we take shelter there?" asked Barnaby. "I'm weary of this storm and the lightning is getting closer and my boots are falling to pieces."

"Do you not enjoy the adventure in walking dark roads by night in storm?" asked the cat.

Barnaby merely stared in reply. The cat considered.

"Hmm. I suppose it *would* be dry within, out of the wind. And no doubt with plenteous material to build a pleasant fire."

"Unwise," said another voice. Dark Michael, suddenly beside them, a black pillar of a figure holding up the night. "Such a ruin is not empty without reason."

"Afraid of ghosts?" asked Night Creep.

"I am not," said Michael. "But the boy had best be. You as well, witch-spawn."

The cat widened its angel-white eyes, tail twitching.

"Many and various are the methods for expelling haunting spirits," he hissed. "Particularly the lesser sort."

Lightning flashed, thunder crashed, making Barnaby jump. His instructors ignored it entirely, glowering upon one another. He felt suddenly annoyed.

Why am I standing in a storm listening to a cat and a ghost argue which is more dangerous, a ghost or a cat?

"I am going to get out of the rain before I drown, catch ague or Saint Typhon of the Lightning blasts me flat."

Defiance declared, Barnaby hurried along the path towards the ruin.

His counselors watched his journey, waiting till he stumbled beyond hearing. Then Dark Michael spoke.

"What mischief are you about, witch-spawn?"

"No mischief, oh dull shade of dull man. I am about my calling. To educate the lad in magic."

"Then why sly him into danger?"

"A tried soldier questions the worth of sending recruits before moderate challenge?"

"Moderate? That ruin stinks of death and dark magic."

"Indeed it does. It is Pentafax Abbey. But the boy wafts an even stronger perfume of life and luck."

"You would risk his life to try his luck?"

"Let us speak plain, ghost. We both have eyes, in our own way. We both know the world, again in our own way. This business reeks of secret purpose."

"Of what?"

"Consider that a barnyard simpleton has, against all probability, avoided various attempts at murder by his family. Instead, he skips whistling down the road with the map of a legendary tower in his pocket. Rather than properly ending dead in a ditch he stumbles upon a powerful tutor in magic, myself. And a skilled teacher in weaponry, the Cold Major himself and yes of course I know of you, spirit. Meanwhile during a quiet stay in a nameless wood the boy gains a major relic, clearly a wand touched by St. Demetia herself."

"Sister Fortuna oft smiles while the sun rises," said the ghost. "She says nothing of how the day shall end. I've seen a thousand good fellows pass unscathed through a storm of arrows and bolts, spear and spell. And then drop dead of pox the next week, be knifed by their tent mates arguing cards. Else fall to the sword of Fortuna's new favorite in the next battle."

"I spoke of purpose, for which fickle *Madam Luck* is mere servant, not mistress."

"Then speak plainer."

"Powers wish the boy to dare the tower."

"Why?"

"I've no least idea."

Barnaby slowed as he neared the ruin, awed. Dark and broken, still it stood a grander building than any that Barnaby'd ever imagined. Far larger than the Squire's pleasant manse.

Before the ruin lay the remains of a garden gone to weed and mud. Here and there stood statues looking ominously like guards. Rain turned the great steps to waterfalls trickling and glistening by storm-light, leading to a portico of blackest stone. In the shadows beyond waited a great archway inviting travelers into a darkness thick as cloth. Barnaby hesitated, no longer sure.

Then beside him stood a stout little man; vest of fur, cap with pointed ears. His magical cat-tutor taking man-shape, white eyes glowing, studying the dark.

"This just might be interesting," decided Night-Creep, and stepped within. Barnaby followed, glad to be second.

Within waited possibly interesting dark and the smell of potentially interesting mold, the theoretically interesting drip of rain through shattered windows, broken roof tiles. A rustle of wind through cobwebs and rotting curtains did what it could to interest. Barnaby stumbled, appreciating the cease of rain down his back, lamenting the lack of light.

"We don't need to go far within," he told the cat. "Here out of the rain is enough."

And then someone spoke. Not the cat; nor any voice he knew. A sepulchral voice, low and slow, fit for dark places, damp ruins.

"Welcome back, Master Night-Creep," said the voice.

"Sexton," said the cat-man. "How nice to be remembered."

"His lordship has been expecting you."

"Has he now?"

"Indeed, sir," intoned the voice. "Oft has he struck the bell, inscribed the pentacle, pronounced the seven shadow-words. But you appeared not."

"If he wishes those that come when called, let him summon a dog."

"Just so, I informed the master."

Of a sudden there came light. Barnaby jumped, seeing candles flickering all about. Set upon ancient tables, held in sconces, standing like ancient servants in cobwebbed candelabrum. The bright yellow glow illuminated a grand hall of dust and debris.

Before Night-Creep stood a man tall, thin and as reminiscent of graves as his name. Sexton, holding a candlestick high in sign of guide.

"This way. And your guest." He paused, corrected. "Your guests, I should say."

Barnaby looked behind, expecting Dark Michael. Instead he spied someone else, crouching by the doorway. A boy younger than himself, and far smaller. Eleven years or thereabouts. His long, tattered coat dripping same as Barnaby's. Olive skinned, white teeth chattering with cold, eyes staring about like a rabbit preparing to dart for cover.

"Bodkin?" said Barnaby. "What are you doing here?"

"Oh, he's tiptoed behind us since the brigand camp," said Night-Shadow. "Watching for the chance to retrieve what he considers his share of coins. We won't speculate whether he intended cutting your throat."

Bodkin shook his head, sending water splashing. Wrapped arms about himself to declare how very cold and wet and harmless he was.

"Just trying to get out of the storm." His high boyish voice peeping defiance.

"Is this footpad indeed with you, Master Night-Creep?" inquired Sexton. "I have quite specific instructions for mere intruders."

The cat-man turned his angel-wing eyes upon Bodkin, who writhed in the gaze.

"Yes, he's with us," Barnaby declared. Bodkin looked surprised to hear it. Night-Creep merely continued to study Bodkin, as he might a mouse beneath his paw.

At length the sepulchral Sexton nodded.

"So be it. This way, all."

They followed the glow of his candle down halls more dry, less surrendered to mold and time. Coming to an archway high and wide, the doors thrown back.

Sexton bowed, motioning them to enter. But Night-Creep raised a hand to Barnaby in sign to halt.

"A moment of privy counsel with my master, if you please, good Sexton."

Sexton nodded to say, '*I leave you to it*,' continuing through the arch.

Then did Night-Creep turn to Barnaby, whispering.

"Will you take my instruction in tonight's lesson, miller's son?"

Barnaby nodded.

"Excellent. Then do not speak tonight, excepting bare 'aye' or 'nay'. Nod pleased at all you hear or see, showing no least fear. Pentateuch was a powerful sorcerer, upon a time. What remains of him shall be mad and dangerous."

"Then why in the name of Lucif's barbed cockerel did you lead us here?" demanded Bodkin.

"No one led *you*, boy, but your own nose," hissed the cat-man. "As for my master, he decided this path. I but work to turn his choice to his advantage."

Before Barnaby could ask what *that* might mean, the cat-man hurried on. Barnaby hesitated, then followed his tutor. Bodkin hesitated, then followed Barnaby.

Within waited a grand feast hall crossed by a table of sufficient length to serve all a regiment. At one end bright candles glowed, flickered, danced. An ornate chair declared it the table's head. Within that throne, looking absurdly small, sat a skeletal creature in bright clothes, a feathered hat, a glittering shirt. Rings upon every finger; which summed to five, as one arm ended at the elbow.

This strange personage gazed into a tarnished silver goblet, silent in thought. The very image of lonely contemplation of wine long drunk, time long passed.

As the newcomers approached, he stirred, sitting upright. The man's eyes shone like black glass; reflecting the candle glow yet keeping the night's dark. Now they focused upon the newcomers. Then,

"Night-Creep!" shouted the man, standing. "At last."

"Pentateuch," acknowledged the cat. For cat again he was, night-furred and four-legged. He leaped upon the table, making a leisurely saunter down its length.

"We shall have a welcoming feast," declared the man, lifting goblet. "With salmon and eel, oyster and herring. And, hmm, what was your favorite? Ah, I recall. Baby mermaid. Sexton, see to it. And build up the fire, our guests appear drenched. Fetch towels and cloths. Oh, and awaken the orchestra. I have not heard a tune in long weary days."

Pentateuch waved hand in sign for all to sit. Barnaby took a seat far from the man as seemed polite. Bodkin sat one chair yet farther.

"Baby mermaid?" whispered Bodkin.

Barnaby prepared to agree; but kept silent, recalling his cat-tutor's warning. He turned to find Pentateuch's gaze upon him.

"Who is this young sir, Night-Creep?"

Barnaby opened mouth to speak, but the cat interposed.

"Dread sorcerer Pentateuch Draconicus, it is my pleasure to introduce you to my master Barnabys, Marquise of the Fief of Millstones, Lord of the Thousand Winds."

Barnaby blinked; smothering an urge to laugh. Instead he picked up the goblet that sat before him. Time-blackened silver with a draught of dust, not wine. A spider scurried out. Barnaby ignored it. Nodding gravely to Pentateuch, he lifted the cup in toast to the Fief of Millstones.

Pentateuch returned the gesture with his own chalice of vintage dust. Barnaby's eyes kept drifting to the missing lower arm. A shard of bone projected beyond the torn sleeve; bloodless, yet somehow the more horrible.

"The Fief of Millstones," mused Pentateuch. "I confess I know it not. But it is long since I fled Plutarch. No doubt entire kingdoms have changed since. Fallen, risen, riven, united."

"And yet, the world remains the same wicked garden of delights," said Night-Creep. At which declaration they both laughed.

Their laughter merged with twanging strings, puffing pipes. Barnaby looked upwards. In a balcony sat several figures. Wielding viola and flute, tambor and harp.

Slowly, as if awakening from long sleep, their melody filled the hall. The candles grew brighter in welcome to the music.

"And this child?" Pentateuch asked, gazing at Bodkin. "His face seems familiar. Has he not a rogue's face, Night-Creep? But by age we scarce can have met. What fiefdoms do you rule, boy?"

Bodkin returned rogue's grin, not a bit abashed.

"The kingdoms of my head, my stomach, my cock and my feet."

Pentateuch laughed loud. "Ha! Now here is a proper lord sitting to table."

Barnaby felt an urge to confess that Bodkin was a town pickpocket lost in country lanes; and he just a miller without a mill. Neither holding any importance to the world or their mirrors.

But defiance rose within him. As if some of the storm remained in his head. Why should he not call himself a person of import? He stared into a bright fire that now burned in the hearth, though he'd seen none set it alight. He considered moving his chair before it, drying himself while consulting with its cheerful flames. He'd ask them if every soul held the right to declare themselves a lord. Or he might ask one of the newcomers to the hall...

Barnaby blinked. He had not seen them enter, and yet far more folk now filled the chamber. Ladies in grand silk gowns, men in fine ermine, velvet caped. All wore masks; whether of animal kind or man kind, devil or angel, fish or fowl or creature too bizarre to be named by mortal tongue.

Some sat to the long table, sipping from crystal goblets that sparkled as if holding vintages of liquid diamond, of ruby, of amber. Others found partners and danced in whirls of step and bow, turn and leap. Danced to the music that now filled the hall, wild and strong as the storm wind left outside to the dark.

Barnaby gaped delighted; feeling all these lords and ladies danced for his joy alone. He strove to catch every swirl of silk and twirl of cape, absently reaching to his plate, nibbling on a savory bit of lamb...

At which he near jumped from his chair. When had this feast platter appeared before him?

"To business," said Pentateuch to Night-Creep, speaking over the orchestra, the dancing folk, the table conversation. "For some while I have been desiring your aid."

The cat was occupied with a plate of delicate silvery scales that Barnaby did not wish to consider overmuch. But at 'business', the cat raised its head, wiping mouth with pink napkin tongue.

"My aid, concerning?" he asked.

"You recall Belinda?"

"Hmm, the dancer. Yes."

"Years past my passing, exiled to this dead ruin, become myself a dead ruin, I longed to see my beloved Belinda dance again. Her little bare feet pattering upon the floor like a deer's heart beating. Twisting, leaping, swaying... Ah, such beauty."

"Allow me to guess. You attempted to raise her, the oration went amiss."

Pentateuch's remaining hand tossed the goblet to the floor, where it clanged and rang in outrage. For a moment the orchestra faltered, the gala crowd hushed. Then all continued, louder and gayer than before.

"It's this damned green country, Night-Creep. Demetia twists a proper Plutarchian spell, sends it in the wrong direction. I summoned my beloved, and she, she rebelled. Vowed she'd have nothing to do with me."

"And?"

"Ah, we argued. Inevitable. I'd forgot how oft she argued. Eventually I ordered her back to dust and dark. And she defied me again! A willful girl, in life or out."

"And?"

"She refused expulsion! Merely stood mocking me, bringing up old events time's mercy had erased from memory. At last, I summoned spiders. She always had a dreadful fear of spiders."

"And?"

"Oh, they wound her about, ate her up. But then came the *spiders* turn to rebel! They would not leave at my dismissal. Perhaps they were infected by eating Belinda. So I thought it clever to summon rats."

"And?"

"The rats ate the spiders, properly. Then refused my dismissal, predictably. The business became a bore. I locked the vermin in my study, assuming they'd take care of one another when they hungered. That proved, hmm, unwise."

Night-Creep sniffed the air of the hall, whiskers twitching at the mention of *rats*.

"They broke free?"

"Certainly not. My study is wound nine times about with spells of binding. But... I'd left a scroll lying. A scroll of Progression. One rat must have eaten it, then eaten the others. That final rat then broke into my cabinets, devouring all varieties of magical enhancements. Now it's quite, hmm, formidable."

He nodded chin to his missing lower arm. "When I attempted to expel it, I was forced to flee, leaving behind half an arm and all my dignity."

Night-Creep tasted the tip of his tail, wide white eyes wide in amusement.

"So you summoned a cat to kill the rat that ate the spiders that ate your true love," mused Night-Creep. "And when I devour the rat, what dog will you call to expel me? And then a cow to toss the dog? This can only end in dragons."

"Oh, mock me not," growled Pentateuch. "You at least have too much vanity to stay past your welcome."

"True. But if the creature is already safely imprisoned, then wherein lies the problem?"

"Problem? Damn it all to Lucif's summer house, I want my study back! There lie all my greater relics. I can't fix this arm properly till I have my work tools again."

"Well now," said Night-Creep, licking tail tip. "A rat king. Difficult. Hmm. But look, my plate seems to have gone empty as my stomach."

"Sexton." A second plate was brought.

"Gladly would I aid you," said Night-Creep, after careful consideration, diligent devouring. "Alas, my service is bound to the Marquise by powerful oaths rendering me his merest advisor."

Pentateuch turned dark eyes upon Barnaby. Who felt a sudden chill, as if the bright hall still contained the cold of the ruin upon the hill.

"And yet," continued Night-Creep, licking chops in consideration. "And yet."

"Yet?"

"Why, my master himself may serve you. For he is no usual warrior, my lord lich. But a week past he left seasoned soldiers supine upon a tavern floor. This very day he bid 'adieu' to three brigand corpses in the eastern wood. Why, I have seen the man wave sword as though it were the lightest of sticks, slashing foes easily as if they were the merest smoke."

Pentateuch focused upon this dangerous figure of war. Barnaby struggled to keep his face to the solemn ferocity of a seasoned warrior.

"Hmm," said Pentateuch. "He looks strong. But rather young, Night-Creep."

"Oh, I've no doubt but my master could vanquish your unwelcome rat."

"Will you indeed do this thing for me, Marquis? I vow rich reward."

Barnaby hesitated. Certainly, he'd slain his share of rats in the mill. But a magic rat might be more trouble. Perhaps it would breathe fire, or fly. Maybe its eyes would turn him to stone. Which would be interesting to see, granted, if one could see one being turned to stone...

Barnaby met the angel-wing eyes of his cat-tutor.

Night-Creep wouldn't have suggested this if he did not think it wise, decided Barnaby. And so he nodded.

"But, alas," said Night-Creep.

"Yet another 'alas'? growled Pentateuch.

"Adventures upon the road have deprived my master of his bright sword, his fine armor. 'Tis pity. Like you, he is a craftsman without his tools."

"Oh, that's no obstacle. Sexton!"

"Sir."

"See the Marquise to the better armory. Let him have his choice of what he may find."

"Of course."

Orders given, Pentateuch brought down his one hand upon the table. At once, the music ceased. The whirling dancers vanished. The plates of savory foods disappeared. The fire in the hearth roared up the chimney, leaving only cold ash and shadow.

Pentateuch rose from his great throne of a chair.

"When you have done for me this little favor, oh Marquise of the Fief of Millstones, then we shall have a *real* feast."

Chapter 22
One Tumbler Knows Another

Odd Bodkin:

I began as an acrobat. I mean in my real life, not this second, idiot return to boyhood. Before aught else, the acrobats taught me how to tumble and fall.

It was the most important lesson in my life: *how to fall*. For falls will come. When they do, wisdom is this: to save oneself by surrendering to the fall. Not by grabbing, not by screaming, not by flailing.

When I first saw the miller he was a stranger hiding poorly behind trees, sneaking towards Marcus and the band. He looked sensibly frightened. And yet he smiled as I ran past, clearly wishing I'd stop and chat, pass the time. I had no time for such. I had to get away before the band found I'd given the bard a knife. If Marcus didn't get the blade in his eager crotch, he'd be on my heels in a minute.

So I ran past the friendly stranger. wondering what the idiot was doing in the wood. He'd get his liver sliced for sure, the corpse sold to the darkrobes of Plutarch. Or else be beaten, tied tight, sold off to Martia.

Yet days later when I returned, there the fellow stood, clearly the master of the glade. While the death-stink of the former owners wafted through the trees. I wondered then: *was the man secretly dangerous?* He looked big; but peaceful as a plow horse giving a child a ride on its back.

True, I trailed Barnaby in the storm to regain the miserable pile of pennies gathered by Marcus's chicken-thieves. But I also followed in fascination. Watching as the miller walked through a lightning storm arguing with a talking cat, a somber ghost.

I have the insight of the old man that once I was, for all I have no least beard. And studying Barnaby by lightning flash and ancient's wisdom, I beheld a master of the art of falling. A creature designed by the House of Saints itself, to wander down roads or over cliffs, into haunted castles, tumbling and rolling, laughing for the adventure.

I, Mercutio of the Moon, greatest thief in all the Land of Saints, who at eighty years of age stole the elixir of youth from the altar of St. Cronos Himself, only to drink it and became fresh boy again... recognized in Barnaby the miller's son a master tumbler on life's roads.

What could I do but follow humbly behind?

Chapter 23
Deathbite Would Also Have Made a Good Name

Sexton led down long halls draped with tattered cobweb, torn tapestry. Barnaby shivered in storm winds that trespassed the shattered windows. His cat-tutor kept hurrying before them all, then trailing behind, then rushing ahead again, near tripping every foot.

Barnaby held to the silence ordered by the cat. For all he wished to ask of Dark Michael. Did the ghost walk unseen beside him? Tripping on the cat, perhaps. Did ghosts trip? And this was surely a haunted house. No doubt ghosts crowded the hallway now, drawing cold wet fingers across face and back. Granted, so did the wind.

Sexton halted before an imposing door of stout oak, banded with bronze. Producing a heavy key he fed to the mouth of a lock. With twist and click, the door opened.

Within waited a long chamber lined with stands of rusting armor, shelves of worm-riddled pikes, blades and axes gone to rust, bows with strings woven into dust.

The solemn servant set about lighting candles, an oil lantern.

"Thank you, Sexton," said Night-Creep. "That will do. Allow me to attend the Marquise."

"Certainly, sir."

When the man departed, the cat hopped upon a table littered with daggers blood-red with rust and murder. For a while he stared about the chamber, sniffing, whiskers twitching. At last nodding satisfied.

"We may talk freely here. Bodkin, shut the door."

While Bodkin obliged, Barnaby released all the words he'd been holding with his breath.

"I'm to fight a rat? The Marquise of Millstones? The soldiers in the tavern were asleep not dead. Baby mermaid? Anyway Val killed the bandits. And how big is the rat? Your friend is missing an arm. A real baby mermaid? Where is Michael? A giant magic rat?"

"Calm," said the cat. "A rat's a rat, no matter the size. It will menace with incisors, then leap for your throat. You jump high and sideways, bite through the spine just behind its head, and adventure ended."

"Bite?" asked Barnaby and Bodkin together.

"Strike, I mean," growled the cat, tail giving dismissive twitch.

"But why should I do this?"

"You entered Pentateuch's house of your own will. He accepted you as guest, you accepted his request. If you refuse now, he will take grave offense. And 'grave' in terms of a necromancer's displeasure, is a dark business indeed."

Barnaby felt the room grow colder.

"Yet, if you meet this modest challenge, the reward shall aid against the far greater dangers of your real quest.'"

"What quest?" asked Bodkin.

"What dangers?" asked Barnaby.

"What reward?" asked Bodkin.

The cat growled at the young thief.

"For you? None. For Barnaby, he gains weapon and armor, and what items of use we shall request from a rich and grateful host."

He turned to Barnaby. "To work, miller's son. Find a weapon that suits your grasp. I smell items here touched with spell-craft. Might even be a lesser relic or two."

At the thought of magical swords, Barnaby held off further complaint. He looked about. "Truly?"

The cat leapt from the table, pacing along hangings and displays, whiskers twitching.

"Ah," said the cat, halting. "This will serve nicely."

Barnaby and Bodkin approached, considered. Upon the wall from a rope of velvet hung a sheathed sword. Dusty but untarnished. The hilt caught the candlelight, returning it in sparkles.

Barnaby reached, took it down. Tugged upon the hilt. Out came the sword easy and light as poured quicksilver. Barnaby twisted it about, letting candle shine run up and down the blade.

The cat stood on hind legs, sniffing.

"Spell-wound to aid the aim, increase the speed," declared the cat. "Exactly what is needed."

But, "No," countered a rough voice.

Barnaby turned, beheld Dark Michael. The ghost walked slowly along shelves and displays, hands clasped behind, perusing weaponry as he might the book titles of a library.

"The master of this house is a powerful necromancer," observed Night-Creep. "I didn't think you'd dare cross his doorway."

Michael sniffed to imply just how little he valued the cat's thoughts. "I have served in Plutarch, witch's spawn. I know my way past the wards of necromancers, liches and all such dreary dead."

"Says a dreary dead," yawned the cat.

"Who are you?" asked Bodkin.

"Oh, this is Dark Michael," said Barnaby. "He is wonderfully wise about swords and fighting."

"Exact so," said Michael. "And my wisdom says do not choose a magic blade."

He continued walking the room, studying weaponry. Tracing fingers along spear shafts, tapping upon a wooden shield to beat a far and distant drum. He stopped before a bronze helmet, spoke to it, else to his own shadowed reflection.

"Why risk life and limb for a dark wizard's favor?"

Before Barnaby could answer, Shadow Creep leaped upon the table, thence to a stand of armor. Perching there, he faced the ghost, eye to eye.

"Would you have him go to the Saintless Tower untried? This is a mere rat. The boy risks little, to gain much."

"Risk," said Michael, tasting the word, finding it unwelcome in his mouth. "Only the living know what it means to put life at *risk*. Not your kind."

"Nor yours then, spirit."

"True," said the ghost. He walked on, repeated the word. "True." Then he halted before a dark corner.

"Here is your tool, miller."

Barnaby and Bodkin edged slowly closer, peering at something that neither glittered nor glowed. Night-Creep dropped to the floor, followed with tail thrashing.

"That's an axe," said the cat. "You have been training him for sword and knife."

"And finding him poorly suited for either," replied Michael. "But he is strong of arm and shoulder, with firm stance. He is an axe-man."

"Is that better than a sword that helps me fight?" asked Barnaby. Waving the sword same as he'd waved branches, making Bodkin duck.

"A magic sword will make you stupid," said Michael. "Which is to say, make you dead."

The cat moved closer. "Not even a proper battle axe." He sniffed, and then his eyes widened, the fur of his tail puffing out in alarm. "It stinks of blood and death."

"As proper weapon shall," said Dark Michael, giving dark grin.

"It's a butcher's axe," sighed Barnaby. "The long square blade has weight for chopping bones. This one looks made for chopping oxen. Or elephants."

"Have you used one?" asked Michael.

Barnaby nodded. "Not on oxen nor elephants, no sir. Just pigs and cows and such. Every autumn after the harvest milling. I don't like the work. But Da always says, said, *'if honest work pleased a body, princes would serve themselves.'*"

He turned gaze back to the glittering sword, giving it a finger caress. Tracing strange writing on the sheath; as incomprehensible upside down as right-side up.

"Little point in having a teacher if you do not follow his advice," said Bodkin.

"Wisely put," said Dark Michael.

"Entirely your decision, Master Barnaby," said Night-Creep. Turning, stalking away, tail lashing.

Barnaby nodded. Laid the magic sword on the table. Went to the axe, stood before it considering. While it leaned against the cold stones, considering *him*. Looking the very symbol of bloody thought, grim deeds. Barnaby picked it up.

Far heavier than the magic sword. There was no waving *this* about like a stick. For sure it did not shimmer. By candle's light it looked time-blackened, dented, the edge showing jagged places sharp as teeth.

But it felt firm in his grasp. No toy, but a tool. A leather sheath lay beside it. Barnaby recalled seeing the woodsmen of Sylvanus at the Jahrmarkt; they wore their axes across their backs, just so.

Barnaby sheathed the axe, strapped it to his back. The handle projected over his shoulder. He reached pulled it forth. Put it back. Pulled it forth again.

Night-Creep sighed.

I'll give it a name, Barnaby decided. *Deathblade? Warwife. Bloodhawk.* He shivered at the wonder of the wealth of excellent names

While he so shivered, Michael turned, proceeding to stands of armor. Perusing various types in various stages of shine and decay.

The ghost poked at a vest of silvery rings. "This will protect neck, chest and stomach. You'll have to guard arms and legs best you can."

But, "no," said someone.

All turned to Bodkin, who stood now before a stand of dull brown material. "Here is what he should wear."

"That's just leather," scoffed Michael. "It won't stop crossbow bolts or sword points."

"Is a rat going to shoot crossbows? Fence with sword?"

"We'll assume not."

"You already having him carrying a heavy axe. You'll crush him with your chain mail. This is light. Reinforced leather, boiled in oil. Protects against tooth and claw."

Michael and Night-Creep exchanged frowns, united in resenting this third voice. Finally Michael turned to Barnaby.

"The little thief may be right. Steel armor will protect; but it will also hinder. Leather will give more leeway to fight or flee. But less safety. It is your call."

"I shall call it Dragontooth," Barnaby informed the room.

"What?"

"What?

"Who?"

"My axe," he explained. He swung it, making Bodkin jump back yet again.

"Have you even been listening, you rural nitwit?" demanded Night-Creep.

Barnaby blinked, looking about. "Yessir. Armor. Leather or chain or heavy or light."

"And which is it?"

Barnaby considered carefully, knowing the importance of the decision.

"I *think*... the dark red leather armor would look best with Dragontooth. That thing of silvery rings is over shiny."

Bodkin laughed. Michael snarled. Night-Creep attended his tail. There came a knock upon the door. Michael vanished.

The door opened. There stood Pentateuch, Sexton behind him serving for a solemn shadow.

"Is our brave champion ready for battle?"

"Almost," said the Marquise of the Fief of Millstones. "Just let him get his armor on."

Chapter 24
Mind the Rug and Broken Heart

Beneath Pentafax Abbey lurked a basement maze worthy of such a grand ruin. Sexton led, holding a lantern before him. Barnaby followed, stretching shoulders, waving arms, seeking to become used to this covering of stiff leather. It felt the same as when he'd awoken to find Alf had wrapped him tight in layers of twine. A jest, of sorts.

They halted before a blank stone wall.

"I shall open the outer ward first," said Pentateuch. "You must hurry through. I cannot keep it open past the count of, hmm, three. Then it seals again. Beyond is a door, here is its key. Past the door awaits your foe." He considered further instructions. "See you do not damage my furniture. Nor my books." He considered yet further. "And mind my vases. Seek to slay the beast away from my rug. I suggest by the hearth."

"Seriously, Pentateuch?" asked Night-Creep.

"Well, never mind the rug then," sighed the necromancer. "If, or rather *when* you achieve victory, I will know, and open the wards. Ready, oh Marquise of Millstones, Lord of the Thousand Winds?"

"Yes," said Barnaby, hoping it was true.

"Yes," said Bodkin.

"You?" asked the cat.

"You?" asked Barnaby.

"You?" asked the necromancer.

Bodkin bowed, nodded. "Is there some reason the Marquise must fight alone?"

"Have you even a weapon, child?" asked Pentateuch.

"I've a sword," said Bodkin, pulling back his long coat. From his belt hung the magic blade Barnaby left behind. On his short frame the tip near touched the floor.

"Sly work," observed Night-Creep, admiring.

"That is a valuable object of my collection," declared Pentateuch. "If this heroic youth joins the battle, he must return it forthwith. And empty his pockets afterwards."

Night-Creep considered Bodkin, angel-wing eyes unblinking; then turned to Barnaby.

"Your decision, Marquise. Do you wish his company?"

Barnaby shook his head. "No. He's too young." Gave the discussed boy a rueful smile. "Sorry, Bodkin."

At which Bodkin stamped a foot, glaring upwards.

"I'm not near as young as I look."

Of a sudden, Barnaby felt old and wise. He'd never felt so before. Was this what Professor Shadow Night-Creep and Dark Michael felt? It was a sad, rueful sort of sensation.

"I understand. And I think much of your courage. But best you wait till you look older to the world."

With that, Barnaby turned to the door. *Dragontooth* before him.

"Let us to it, Master Pentateuch."

"Well, what about light?" said Bodkin. "Can't wave a torch while fighting two handed, can you? Let me take some candles."

"Ah, yes," sighed Pentateuch. "How quickly one forgets the frailty of mortal eyes." He waved his one hand. To Barnaby's surprise and delight, he found himself glowing.

"Well, now, look at that. I'm a lantern." He considered a glowing arm. "No, it's more like the glow on clouds before dawn."

The necromancer stared, but not in wonder of a glowing Barnaby.

"What is that you carry, Marquise? I sense something of power upon you."

Barnaby considered. "This axe?"

"No, no. I know *that* and all its dark story. But you bear something of power. Green and strong."

Barnaby reached to the side of his leather armor, drew from the belt his willow wand. It glowed just as he did; but brighter. Not with twilight, but day's light.

Pentateuch stepped back. Then turned dark gaze upon Night-Creep, who became of a sudden deeply concerned with the ordering of his fur.

"Clearly," said the necromancer. "There is some design here beyond an adventuring marquise. We must hear it."

"After dealing with the rat," said Night-Creep.

The necromancer looked ready to argue; then decided not.

"Ready, Marquise?"

Barnaby nodded, facing the stone wall.

"One," said the necromancer. Soon as said, the wall vanished. Barnaby found himself staring into a further hallway. A great dark door waiting at the end.

"Go," said Night-Creep.

Barnaby leaped forwards.

"Two."

Bodkin jumped after Barnaby.

"Three," whispered the necromancer. And the wall returned to its place.

Pentateuch and Night-Creep stared at cold and solid stones.

"Thought the little rogue would do that," said the necromancer.

"It was rather obvious," agreed the cat.

Barnaby rushed forwards, wondering what would happen if the magic wall should return as he crossed. Would he be trapped in stone? His face might peer out forever, like the ones carved on old rocks in the hills east of Mill Town; staring pop-eyed upon green fields of grass and goat.

He hurried to the door at the hall's end, stood before it. Finding that another stood beside him.

"Bodkin, go back!"

"How?" asked the boy, turning to stare at blank stone wall.

"Saint Lucif's mother take you for her tea kettle," growled Barnaby.

"What?"

"It's some words I heard."

"Ah. You mean, *Lucif's dam take you for her piss pot.*"

"Yes, that." Barnaby stamped to the stone wall, rapped upon it with Dragontooth. The axe blade chimed a heroic clang, but the stones cared not.

Bodkin drew the magic sword Barnaby had declined. "No help for it now," he said, cheerfully.

"You'd best stay here," said Barnaby, uncheerful.

"I said I was older than I looked."

"Yes, but you look ten."

"I'm well past eighty years, youngster."

'Youngster' came absurd from a high-voiced boy with head below Barnaby's chin. Barnaby shook his higher, hoarier head.

"You lack all the wrinkles and gray hair and yellow teeth."

"You are a miller's son with a talking cat and a brooding ghost," argued Bodkin. "You stand in a haunted house to fight a magic rat. Why should you not believe I am more than I seem?"

Barnaby considered. Da always said, *'take folk for who they say they are.'* But he'd meant take them for honest if they pretended honesty; take them for kind if they worked to seem kind. That way you helped them become what they promised to their mirror.

How did one take a youngster claiming to be eighty? Probably Da had never met such. A thought occurred.

"Are you one of those Fae folk from Aurelia that grow slow as trees?"

"No," snorted Bodkin. He stood straight, to match the pride now in his voice. "I was a famous thief. Mercutio of the Moon. Haven't you ever heard of me?"

"No. Sorry."

"Ah, no matter. But every thief's guild sung my praises. Every thief catcher knew my face and sought my head. Glorious days." His eyes gleamed by the light of the glowing Barnaby. "My last heroic deed was to steal the elixir of youth from the church of St. Chronos. Didn't mean to drink it *all* down. Thought I'd stop at thirty. But, ah, well, one sip led to another, till there I was a boy in man's clothes, holding empty cup."

Barnaby found this easy to picture. There'd be the sly old criminal, crooked of back and grin, standing in a candle-lit Chapel of Time. The holy clocks of St. Chronos ticking, tocking, while the wrinkled thief chuckled, grasping the forbidden chalice... then drank his fill, shrinking down to child...

"Then you have all that old-man wisdom in your head now?" Would be amazing to have the knowledge of some ancient thief, with the quickness of a boy.

"No," admitted Bodkin. "I just know what I knew when I was twelve."

At which Barnaby laughed, letting the sound echo off the stones.

"Then what the Lucif's flaming piss-pot difference does it make?" He pronounced these words with a certain pleasure. They sounded fierce and direct, if not strikingly obscene.

"Plenty," declared the boy, sketching the air with his sword. "I still have an old man's spirit. It remembers things. Like when I knew you'd best wear leather armor. Because my old self fought animals. Guard dogs for sure. But rarer beasts too, I'd wager. Old Mercutio saw it all, and did it all. He's in the back of my head, watching outwards."

Barnaby wished Michael or Night-Creep were present. They'd untangle things quick as blink. But would they care for this ancient child's welfare? Barnaby decided it was up to Barnaby.

"Let me deal with the rat," he said. "You keep your dusty young self to the back. If you see me losing, then do as your old man self thinks best."

"Fair enough, oh Marquise of Millponds."

"Millstones."

"Yessir."

Barnaby turned to the door, put key to lock, doing his best to turn it silently. But he knew rats. There'd be no catching the creature by surprise. Still, it's first thought would be to dart for safety. Probably it'd rush to a dark corner or under a table.

Barnaby readied himself, Dragontooth's hilt clasped tight. Whispered to Bodkin. "Push it open. Then move aside."

Bodkin nodded, dark face solemn. He stepped to the door, pushed. Of course, the hinges creaked. The heavy door swung inwards. Beyond awaited... a well-lit room, requiring no glowing Barnaby.

He and Bodkin stared into a large chamber. Once it would have been ornate, richly furnished. Now it was a battlefield of torn books, overturned furniture. Centering the shambles waited the rat.

Large as a grown man, it perched easily in a cushioned chair before a crackling fireplace. An open book resting in its lap. One delicate pink hand grasped a long feather quill, which went *scritch, scritch* across the pages. Spattering drops of blue upon its muzzle.

At their entrance it looked up, great ruby eyes agleam.

"Well, hello," said the rat.

Barnaby weighed rushing forwards, waving axe, shouting war cries. The act seemed absurd. The rat sat peaceful as Friar Cedric reading tales to the village young on a winter evening.

"Hello to you," replied Barnaby, unwilling to be rude. There followed a long silence. The rat eyeing the boys and their weaponry; the boys eyeing her, her book and quill pen.

"I'm Barnaby. This is Bodkin."

"Hello, young Barnaby. And younger Bodkin."

It talks, thought Barnaby. Pentateuch didn't mention that. Maybe he didn't know. What in the world should they do now? He couldn't leap upon this polite creature.

"What are you writing?" he asked, finally.

"Oh," said the rat. Turning head down shyly. "Uhm, a, a poem." The creature returned to scribbling, dipping the quill in an ink jar resting in a curve of her tail.

"Oh," said Barnaby. "What sort of poem?"

The rat giggled, then changed the sound to a cough and an unconcerned shrug.

"Romantic, if you can believe." Then asked. "Are you familiar with the verses of Sapho?"

Barnaby shook his head. The poems he knew were of the saints; excepting the bawdy verses that Alf sang, and the mad things the Goat Girl chanted.

The rat whispered in tone of confession, waving the book.

"This was Pentateuch's favorite volume of poems. I'm writing in the margins. I know, I know, I shouldn't. But it inspires me, you understand? Let me read you some of Sapho's words. Then you'll see."

The rat's voice was sharp and high. *It's a she,* decided Barnaby. He considered putting away the axe, giving Bodkin a sideways look.

The boy stared at the rat, mouth agape. But keeping sword at ready. Maybe that was his old-man's spirit saying '*keep your guard up*'. But old folk were dour creatures, Barnaby knew. He lowered his axe.

The rat took the lowered weapon as consent. "Now. This is my favorite of Sapho's." She began to recite.

"When I look at you
Even the quickest view,
Suddenly I cannot speak
As if my clever tongue is broken
And subtle fire has woken upon my skin,
I cannot see with these eyes,
My ears are deafened by sighs.
Chill sweat overtakes me,

*Trembling shakes me,
I turn paler than the roots of fresh grass.
Is this death? Oh, then never let it pass."*

The rat turned a scarlet eye upon the boys, waiting their judgement.

"I didn't understand it," confessed Barnaby. "It is it about a person taken sick?"

The rat laughed. To his annoyance, so did Bodkin.

"He'll learn," said Bodkin to the rat.

"So he will," agreed the rat. "Poor boy."

"Learn what?" demanded Barnaby. At which sensible question they both just laughed the louder.

Barnaby sighed; but being laughed at was nothing new to his soul or ears. Granted, he'd never been mocked by an ancient child, a giant rat. A rat big as a man; with wet yellow daggers for teeth.

"I see I'm confusing you," said the rat. "Let me explain. But first, please stop lurking in the doorway." She winked. "I won't bite."

The boys exchanged glances, then Barnaby stepped into the room. Bodkin following behind, sword still raised. The rat nodded at their good manners, crossing her legs.

"To begin. I wasn't always a rat. I am Belinda. Pentateuch summoned me from death to dance for him again. I spat in his bony face. So, he sent spiders. The spiders ate me up, and I became the spiders. When the rats devoured us spiders, we became the rats. Then we rats ate one another up, and I became the last rat."

She returned to scribbling. Speaking aloud while doing so.

"Pentateuch used to write me poems. So now I'm writing one for him."

"Was he any good?" asked Bodkin.

"Hmm," said the rat. "Hard to say. When someone writes you a love poem, it's judged by the heart, not the head."

It occurred to Barnaby that if Belinda recalled Pentateuch's affection, she might make peace with him. Then there'd be no need for axes.

"Would you share one?" he asked.

"Oh, no," said the rat, hurriedly. "I couldn't." Then, 'Well, I mean, unless you really wanted to hear."

Barnaby nodded. Bodkin nodded.

She put the quill behind an ear again. Fidgeted with her whiskers. Coughed, several times. Barnaby and Bodkin waited. She waved a pink hand.

"Have a seat, while I recall it in my head," said the rat.

Barnaby moved obediently towards a stool. But Bodkin held him back. "If you please, ma'am, we'll stand."

The rat lady chuckled. "I understand. Came to slay the monster, hmm?"

Barnaby felt shamed. But it'd be absurd to deny after entering the room waving axes and swords. The rat shrugged, unconcerned.

"Very well. 'Pentateuch's Lament', from memory."

She closed eyes, began to recite, voice solemn as church catechism, soft as silk cushion.

"My chest is hollow.
I pant but the air is gone.
My heart is a drum gone mad,
Beating out of time, racing, stopping, racing.
My head swirls with visions of you,
Yet my mind is empty of thought
Because these arms are empty.
This bed is empty.

I am empty."

The rat lady opened red eyes again.

"What do you think?"

Barnaby sighed. "That one didn't even rhyme. And just sounded like someone fell sick again."

"Sainted Venus's favorite penis, Barnaby," said Bodkin. "It's about heartbreak."

Barnaby and the rat-lady stared at the boy, who returned defiant gaze, waving sword blade to emphasize point. "You can't breathe, can't rest, can't think. You drink, sleep, drink, wander the night muttering nonsense to yourself. It's awful. Shit, you'll shove a hand in the fire just to feel something besides all the emptiness the world has shoved inside you."

"Oh, here's a wise heart," said the rat. "Bit disturbing, such knowledge out beardless boy."

Barnaby felt left out. "Well, what about the poem you're writing for Pentateuch?" he asked. "Does it sound like having plague, palsy and pox too?"

The rat showed teeth at that. A smile, possibly.

"Nothing so dull," she declared. Laying the book carefully upon a table. Then she stood. Her body was round-bellied, with proper rat's feet. The hairless tail twitching like a scaleless snake. She looked entirely a rat, if big as Barnaby.

And yet she moved gracefully, with no crouching rat-motions, no rodent scuttling. Now she stretched, arching; exactly as a young woman luxuriating in youth and beauty.

"Quite attractive, once." She raised furred arms, pirouetted on a rat toe. "Finest dancer in the Eastern kingdoms." She tapped rat feet upon the floor. "Pentateuch fell in love with my dancing. I fell for his love of me. Ah, he would watch for hours. Then we'd both fall. To the floor, hmm, when no bed lay handy."

"Then why fight?" asked Barnaby. "If you loved each other, I mean."

"Why?" asked the rat, ceasing dance in mid-twirl. She opened jaws wide, revealing wet yellow incisors. Snapped them shut. "Because he chose magic over love. Chose death over life. That's the price to become a lich. End your life, your love, to become a chattering thing of spell and dust."

She began swaying slowly to some sad tune from long years past.

"You will hear a lich is a cold and evil thing. Quite right. But the cold and evil was in the living man. There's no difference between a lich, and the man who would be a lich."

Barnaby considered. Pentateuch had seemed friendly enough; but certainly unearthly. Not human. Hard to picture him as ever a young man in love.

"But if you were, were lovers, why does he want to kill you?"

The rat turned head upwards, showing white throat. Her ruby eyes glistened wet. Barnaby felt an urge to go to her, pat her upon the back, promising it would all be well.

The rat spoke softly, still swaying.

"Whatever comes after death, Barnaby, it does not continue what passed in life. Death is ending. Remember that, when you deal with such as Pentateuch. Or Belinda."

"Well," asked Bodkin, "Now you're quite over one another, why fight? Why'd he send us to kill you?"

"Mere greed, my boy. This is his workroom and treasure chamber. Without the things scattered at your feet, he's scarce more than a wraith. Wretched old fool."

"You could let him back in," suggested Barnaby.

"Why should I?" demanded the rat. Stamping a long foot. "I delight to defy him. Sitting in his best chair, eating his precious scrolls, writing bad poetry."

She gave another dancer's twirl, tail tip between fingers to serve for fringe of a lacy dress.

"Since then, that dratted corpse has been sending his summonings and servants. Quite amusing. I doubt the old bone has a single lackey left besides that bore Sexton."

She gave another twirl, then bent entirely down, giving the floor a graceful brush with whiskers.

"What happened to them?" asked Bodkin.

"Whom?" asked Belinda, head still down, lifting one leg straight behind her. Barnaby judged that quite a difficult pose, for rat or woman.

"The servants and summonings. That came here. To kill you."

"Oh, them," said the rat-lady. Dismissively. "I ate them up." She stood upright again, pointing towards a corner less lit by fire and glow. Barnaby turned, studying what seemed just another pile of clutter. Well, but it was a clutter of bones, skulls, gnawed limbs.

Belinda leaped upon him then.

The attack knocked Barnaby backwards, raising the axe to keep the yellow fangs from his throat. He stared into her blood-red eyes, breathing the creature's hot meaty breath. The pink hands that had seemed so ladylike, now clawed at his leather armor.

But Bodkin had not been distracted. He swung the magic sword. Belinda leaped away with all the grace of a dancer, the quickness of a rat.

She moved back, crouching, hissing at Bodkin. Barnaby rolled, stood again, readying, recalling the cows and pigs of autumn harvest seasons passed. Belinda lashed her worm-tail, then leaped...

And Barnaby swung.

Striking just behind the head, as Night-Creep advised. The creature gave no shriek before the head flew from the body. Dark liquid fountained out; not animal blood, but something like smoke, like mud. Yet the body continued scrabbling onwards, claws seeking Bodkin. He backed away, crashing into the far wall. His brown face grimacing, mouth whispering oaths or prayers.

A foul stench filled the room; the body slowing its blind march. Bodkin edged around it, waving his sword as though to warn it off. While Barnaby stared at the rat's head. For a second, he met the bright red eye of Belinda.

I feel sick, he thought. Exact as he'd told Da that first autumn, watching the blood pour from a young cow upon the floor of the slaughterhouse.

Then the rat's eyes closed, weary of the world's light.

Trembling, Barnaby stepped around the body, went to the chair. Picking up the book of poetry. Studying words in the margin. Belinda's poem to Pentateuch.

"You're holding it upside down," said a cold and dusty voice.

There in the doorway stood Pentateuch himself. He looked about the chamber, tilting his jaunty hat back upon his hairless head.

"What a horrible mess. It shall take Sexton a week to straighten this."

Night-Creep rushed between his legs, leaping upon Barnaby's shoulder. There he perched, angel-wing eyes observing. Barnaby felt a comfort in his presence. His panicked heart and breath slowed.

The necromancer ignored them, stepping into the room. Bent down, lifted up the rat's head with his one hand. Considered it.

"You'll find it hard to believe, but I used to write her poetry," he said. "Sad stuff about being empty, feeling lost. Bad verses explaining how I was in agony, that every second was torment of love and confusion. And do you know what she thought?"

He did not turn to indicate to whom he spoke. The room kept just as silent as the rat's head. Pentateuch grinned, shaking his own head.

"She actually believed that the agony of love was something *wonderful*, to be enjoyed forever."

He dropped the rat's head, gave it a kick to send it rolling.

"Love is something to survive, to get past. Like life. Exactly like life."

He looked about, defying any to argue it. None did. He settled for kicking at a leaf-drift of torn scrolls, shattered bottles.

"I don't even *see* my good rug," he grumbled.

"She wrote you a poem," said Barnaby.

"Did she now?" asked the necromancer. He bent, gathering up shreds of paper. Sighed, and let the tatters fall again, drifting down like autumn leaves.

"It's titled 'To My Dear Pente'."

"I assume, oh Marquise, that you will not be content till you have read it to me. So let's hear, and have done."

Barnaby read aloud.

"Die." He paused, continued. *"Die. Die. Die. Die. Die. Die. Die. Die. Die."* He stopped, turned several pages. "Die. Goes on and on. Just that."

"Well, it rhymes well," observed Night-Creep.

Pentateuch laughed; a dusty exhalation from out hollow chest. Barnaby closed the book. Pentateuch grabbed it. Kicking through magical debris, he stomped to the fireplace. There he began ripping pages away with his teeth, feeding them to the flames.

"Well done, master," whispered the cat into his ear. "But now be ready with your second of three."

Second of three? Barnaby puzzled; then understood. Surely the cat referred to the times he might call for Dark Michael's help.

But the rat was dead. What danger did they face now?

Barnaby watched the necromancer feeding verses to the fire, muttering to himself of times passed, love lost. Then nodded.

Chapter 25
This Fish is Overcooked

They sat again in the necromancer's feast hall. Not a fever-dream masquerade of ghostly dancers, nor yet the cold dark chamber they'd left.

Now a modest fire crackled in the hearth, doing its best not to smoke. A few candles flickered close by the guests, surrendering the rest of the hall to shadow. No mad dancers twirled, no bright lights glowed, no eerie orchestra piped and strummed.

The plates before Barnaby and Bodkin held bread and venison, not the delights of princes. Within the tarnished silver cups: mere wine mixed with rainwater.

"Where's the salt?" asked Bodkin.

"I don't have it," said Barnaby.

"Well, there was a silver salt pot here. Where's it wandered?"

"Into your pocket, like enough," said Night-Creep.

"Not mine," insisted Bodkin.

"I promised a real feast," sighed Pentateuch, leaning back in his great chair. "But that dratted rat made hay of my scrolls and rings, wands and summoning ingredients. Poor Sexton is still setting things aright."

Barnaby felt famished. Yet despite the food before him, he could not turn his mind from the dancing rat, her shy recitation, her dying glance. He watched Bodkin devouring his meal untroubled. Was that a boy's quick adaptability, or an old man's wisdom?

Night-Creep sat upon the table, nibbling at a river trout. Nothing of baby mermaid, thankfully. The necromancer himself sat before a plate of black bread, holding a crystal cup of dark liquid. Wine, perhaps. If so, it failed to yield any least sparkle. Pentateuch stared into its depths, shaking his head.

Barnaby wondered if the creature recalled the dancer; or merely regretted the meager meal before them.

"Enough is as good as a feast," offered Barnaby. One of Da's favorite sayings. The cat looked up, giving a warning eye in reminder of silence.

"Not so," argued Bodkin. "Any lucky beggar can fill his belly with bread. But there are delights served the rich that would astonish the Prophet Epicurus himself."

"Wisely said," declared Pentateuch. "Entirely too wise. You are very a strange child."

"It makes a long story," admitted Bodkin.

"We'll hear it later," said the necromancer. "Or not." He stood, lifting crystal cup, readying grand words. Then considered the shadowed hall, the meagre food, and growled. "Not only the salt. We lack music." He turned towards the dark, gave order.

"Play, little harp."

The guests waited, puzzling. But from out the shadows came the faint thrum and hum of strings plucked in soft melody. On the balcony railing perched a harp, as bird upon branch. This instrument now shone with a gentle firefly light, flickering in time to its own crystal song.

That's what magic is for, Barnaby told himself. *To make music and light and wonders.* He pictured such a harp at the mill. Ah, he'd say 'play, little harp', and hear its sweet music as he worked. And as he ate, and even slept.

"The tune pleases our Marquise," observed Pentateuch. He tilted his pirate hat at a jaunty angle, yellow teeth displaying grin. Posing so, at last it came possible to picture Pentateuch as living man in noisy tavern, entranced with the motions of a dancer.

Barnaby opened mouth to share this thought; caught another warning from his cat-tutor's angel-wing eyes. Settled for nodding.

Pentateuch looked from one to the other, nodding to himself as though reaching conclusions. Then he raised his cup high.

"First, oh Marquise of Millstones, Lord of the Thousand Winds, we extend unto you our fullest thanks. Your heroic actions have freed my house of a most troubling threat."

The room went silent; even the harp. Barnaby found all eyes upon him, awaiting his reply. But life in Mill Town did not teach the ways of lordly toasts. Beneath the table, Bodkin kicked his foot. Barnaby jumped, stood, considering tales of princes and kings, knights and formal riffraff.

Inspired, he scooped up his own goblet, returning the gesture of a toast. Bowing his head in noble but humble acknowledgement of well-earned praise. Pentateuch nodded satisfied. The harp continued its gentle music.

"In recompense, Marquise, please accept as my gift the armor you wear. As well as the dark blade of slaughter you chose to carry." The necromancer shuddered. "Truthfully, that thing is well out of my house."

Barnaby reached to the side of his chair, where Dragontooth leaned. Gave it a pat to say: *take no offense.*

Pentateuch continued. "Your *advisor* Night-Creep tells me that you are now embarked upon a noble quest, but the usual misadventures upon the road have left you without resources, excepting his knowledge and your courage."

Something in the emphasis of 'advisor' worried Barnaby. He turned to Night-Creep. The cat now sat observing with wide white eyes. Calm as stone figurine;

excepting the tail, which gave regular twitch this way, that way.

"To aid in your quest, please accept what few coins this fallen house can spare." Pentateuch placed upon the table a small bag, which gave a pleasing clink.

"As well, there are one or two items of magical nature I have recovered from my study, which might be of use to the traditional bold adventurer in the field." He followed this with a larger bag, placing it beside the first.

"I helped," reminded Bodkin.

"Did you?" replied Pentateuch. "Excellent. Always remember, virtuous action is its own reward."

Bodkin sighed. No one else spoke. Barnaby prepared to sit again; stopping, seeing his host had not yet finished.

"And now that I have fulfilled my duty," said the necromancer, "in merest recompense I desire to hear how the son of a miller comes to my door with Shadow Night-Creep himself for a summoning, and a greater relic tucked casually in his belt."

"A what?"

"Cease pretending," said Pentateuch, tilting back his pirate hat, slapping his ringed hand upon the table. "I am not to be mocked in my own house. You carry a wand touched by the Green Lady herself, the patroness of this life-infested land."

Green Lady? "Oh," said Barnaby. "You mean Missus Green." Just recalling her warm smile made him smile. "She's nice. Do you know her?"

The question made the necromancer go silent. But Night-Creep chuckled, returned attention to his fish. Speaking between bites.

"Really, Pentateuch, you jump at shadows."

Pentateuch recovered his voice.

"Show the wand. Lay it upon the table."

Barnaby could think of no reason to refuse. He drew it from his belt. As always, it felt heavier than mere wood. More solid; and yet warm and alive as if still a branch of a tree feasting on summer sunshine.

He laid it before him, noting that a new leaf now sprouted from the wand.

Pentateuch stood so rapidly that his chair moved back, throne of stone that it was.

"Yield it to me," he commanded. "Now. Or I shall destroy you."

"Oh, please," yawned Night-Creep. "You have already complained how far you stand in arrears concerning magical power." He gave the river trout a dismissive tap of paw. 'Quite obvious."

"And you have foolishly confessed you are constrained to the role of mere advisor," snarled Pentateuch.

"Perhaps I lied," replied the cat. Eyes aglow, tail a'twitch. "In your enfeebled state, would you put it to test?"

"I need not *test*," snarled Pentateuch. "You are bound, Shadow Night-Creep. You can speak, lecture, advise. Naught else. You are useless." The necromancer grinned teeth yellow as old parchment, and as dry. "I know you are so bound. I inquired of one of your fellow spirits."

"Belshazzar?" asked the cat, licking a paw idly. Though his ears tilted back in anger. "He's no peer nor fellow of mine. I shall require satisfaction for his little betrayal."

"I care not," said the necromancer. Turned to Barnaby. "Enough. The wand, boy."

Barnaby considered the wand upon the table.

"I don't think so," he decided. "It was my work, and I think Missus Green meant me to have it. But thank you for Dragontooth. Though I wouldn't have agreed to killing the rat if I'd known it was a dancer named Belinda who liked poems."

"Such a simpleton," sighed the necromancer. And reached within his bright shirt, pulled forth a wand of his own. It looked to be bone, blackened in fire. He raised it.

Bodkin dove beneath the table.

Barnaby closed eyes, holding hands out against the impending magical blast.

None came. He opened eyes again. Bodkin peeked out from under the table. While Night-Creep chuckled.

"What is this?" demanded Pentateuch. Waved the wand again in greater emphasis. Nothing happened. He attempted to walk around the table, stopped same if he'd hit stone wall.

"It would seem you have a circle of salt drawn about you," said Night-Creep. And returned attention to his fish.

"How? Who and when?"

"While you were blustering," said Night-Creep, "not to mention threatening, making a fool of yourself and attempting murder of guests in defiance of the most sacred duty of a host." The cat nibbled thoughtfully, then adding "And I will add that the fish you served is over-cooked."

"Sexton!" shouted the necromancer. "Sexton!"

All waited. The servant did not appear. Within the shadows, the harp upon the balcony continued its soft strum of beauty.

But: "He's not coming," drawled a slow, gravelly voice. All turned to study a dark figure leaning against a stone pillar, arms crossed, hat low over eyes.

"And who in Lucif's seven fires are you?" snarled Pentateuch. Again pointing the blackened bone; again to no effect.

Dark Michael gave what for his grim visage made bright smile.

"Sexton was busy ordering your study. I borrowed the key you gave Barnaby, and locked him in. Those are excellent wards. I doubt Sexton will be able to free himself anytime soon."

"Yes, but now we can't get in," complained Night-Creep. "There were wondrous items of power and worth lying about that chamber."

Dark Michael shrugged. "Deadly things, that would only work to evil."

"True," said the cat. He gave the trout a last nibble. Then leaped to the floor. "Well, let us depart. This feast is over, and well over."

Pentateuch growled, eyes the glittering black match of Night-Creep's angelic white.

"And you think my wrath will not follow upon your heels?"

"Hmm," replied the cat. "It occurs to me that it might."

"Why?" demanded Barnaby. "We have done you no harm, Mister Pentateuch. I killed your rat who told us poems. And you didn't tell us she could even *speak*. Now you threaten us for something of mine you want? That's just evil."

At which judgement Pentateuch laughed loud, echoing against the stones, making the candle flames flicker, the harp notes falter. Laughter done, echoes faded, he sat in his throne again,

"Yes, yes," he chuckled. "I am evil and cold and greedy and vengeful. Quite nasty." He tilted the jaunty feather hat back to let his dark eyes shine, amused.

"I am entirely unfair, unjust, unkind, unpleasant and in fact, *undead*." He held out his one good hand, a beggar beseeching alms. "Pity me, Marquise. I intend ten thousand evils. This is what I am, what I must be. Hmm. How did the poem go?"

He considered, then recited.

"Yet my mind is empty of thought
Because these arms are empty.
This bed is empty.
I am empty."

Bodkin came out from under the table, looking from one to the other. Dark Michael continued to lean against the wall, hat low, waiting.

"Alas, poor Pentateuch," said Night-Creep, attending his tail-tip. "If only this cruel world held some way of healing your hollow heart, your empty arms, your loveless life in death."

Pentateuch sniffed at the idea. But Barnaby considered the cat's words, and then the necromancer. Indeed the creature looked dead, broken, bitten and bitter; for all the jaunty hat, glittering rings. Lord of a cold ruin of a once-bright house.

Did Pentateuch deserve pity? Probably not *now*. But surely once he had. When alive, in agony for the love of a dancer. If he were less dead, could he find peace?

Decided, Barnaby raised his wand, and whispered what words came into his head.

"Life. Light. Fire. Night and Day, moon and sun, shadow and ray. Be warm, be light, be alive."

Pentateuch sat upright in sudden alarm, eyes wide as the sockets of any skull lying quiet in its grave. Raising his one hand to fend away words of *light* and *life*.

From Barnaby's wand sprang green fire so bright that all eyes drowned in the blinding flash. Pentateuch shrieked. Bodkin returned to hiding beneath the table.

Barnaby stumbled back, dropping his wand. Through the haze he watched the necromancer writhing in emerald flames. Twisting, flailing his one arm, eyes and mouth agape in agony. At last the necromancer fell to the floor in a clatter and patter of ash and bone.

At that, Barnaby tumbled as well, lying upon his back, staring up into a blur of green spots. Feeling he'd just run to Mill Town and back.

He lay for a while just so, listening to the soft strum and hum of the harp. Blinking to clear his vision, he spied folk gathering about him, staring down. Not his companions. These were the mad dancers and masked revelers of earlier in the night. Now circling solemn and silent about Barnaby.

"Hello," he said. Feeling he should stand, unsure he had the strength.

A grand gentleman in velvet nodded to him, then a lady in red satin. While others bowed, else curtsied, or bent low doffing hats. He lay surrounded by a silent crowd, making whatever signs of respect they chose.

That done, they turned, walked into the shadows and were gone. While Barnaby settled for sitting upright. Bodkin brought him a wine cup.

"What just happened?" asked Barnaby. Looking to Pentateuch's chair. Nothing of the necromancer remained but ash and bits of bone. A few glittering rings. And a pirate hat, the feather looking wilted.

His cat tutor walked lazily up before him.

"You cast a spell of healing. Quite impressive, and verification that indeed you bear a greater relic, impossible as that sounds."

"But it didn't heal him," pointed out Barnaby.

"Ah," said Night-Creep. "Hmm. In review, I see I neglected to share a fascinating fact concerning the undead and spells of life."

Now came Dark Michael turn to speak, still leaning insouciant against a pillar.

"If you cast healing upon dead creatures such as liches, it hurts them. Or destroys them outright."

"I see," sighed Barnaby, contemplating the scattered dust. "I destroyed him." He picked up the wand. The green leaf trembled, or the wand did or his hand did or the world did.

"A good thing," said Night-Creep. "He would have pursued us, seeking our murder with sendings."

"I suppose. But... I liked his hat. I bet he was nice when he was, was different."

The cat yawned. "I grant he was a connoisseur of the finest. Alas, he was also dead, not to mention a rude host. Now to work."

"What work?" asked Bodkin.

Barnaby stood, still trembling, staring at the trembling leaf of the wand.

"Hmm," said the cat. "First, gather up the two bags upon the table and so help me Bodkin if you sly-pocket a single penny I will use your guts for a cat collar."

"Ha," said Bodkin.

"Second, take a napkin and gather up those rings the late Pentateuch dropped. But do not put any on, else you risk hand, mind and soul."

"We can sell them, at least," agreed Bodkin.

"Exactly," said the cat. "Excepting the 'we'."

"There must be more treasure hereabouts," said Bodkin. "Plenty for all."

"There is," said Dark Michael. "But there are also various guardians who may take offense. Sexton shall free himself at any moment. You will find him a powerful foe."

"Could you defeat him?" asked Bodkin.

"Doubtful," said the ghost. "I will not catch him unawares, as I did his master. In any case Barnaby has but one more time to request my aid. While he has yet to even reach the lowest step of his tower."

"What tower?" asked Bodkin.

"We'd best leave," said Barnaby, not feeling up to explaining just yet. He grasped a candle, stepping into shadows towards a stairway.

"Our exit is the other way," said Night-Creep.

Barnaby continued into the dark.

"Where are you going?" demanded Dark Michael.

"I want to get something first," said Barnaby, looking up at the harp on the balcony, still flickering with gentle light, still singing soft string song. "For, for a friend."

Chapter 26
The Box that Holds the Magic

Val the Bard:

My father's house in the Free State of St. Martia stood far larger than most. We (or *they*, as I've abandoned family, saint, and kingdom alike) pride ourselves on despising wealth and decadence. Sneering at the ponderous castles of St. Demetia, the dark palaces of Plutarch, the insane mechanical mansions of the Hefestians.

We, I mean *they*, of Martia live starkly as the tedious *Little Brothers of Poverty*. A regimented life we devote not to lives of prayer, but to the arts of war. Our children grasp a sword pommel soon as releasing their mother's teat.

Martia houses are plain brick boxes, simply furnished. Decorated only with swords, spears and flowers. The Free State does not tolerate symbols of wealth. No gold rings, pearl diadems, silk dresses. No fur robes, liveried servants, ornamented carriages. Houses of important people have no marble steps, no grand lawns, sculpted ponds. Such things are for the decadent Plutarchians, the absurd Demetians.

But wealth come in many currencies. In other lands riches may be vaults of silver or deeds to castles, flocks of sheep or a bishop's miter upon the head. Anything can symbolize wealth, so long as it serves as currency for power.

We of the House of War, chief family of the Free State of St. Martia, descendants of bloody Martia herself, patroness of *Worthy Battle*, owned the wealth of our family name: *Kurgus*. And so my father's home had plentiful rooms, silent servants, hidden gardens. And even a library.

When Barnaby healed me in the robber's glade, I came to myself staring up at stars, thinking I'd fallen asleep in my father's garden. No doubt a book lay beside me, pages growing damp with dew.

Only gradually did I recall long ago leaving garden and library, family and land. What followed? Ah yes; bard school; then that glorious day when I'd spied the cup itself outside the window of the instruction room. Floating down the road like a soap bubble on the wind.

I'd tossed instruction aside, stealing the horse of the headmistress herself. Then came days of riding the green country roads of St. Demetia. Seeking the cup. No longer daughter, no longer student. I was my own thing, finding my own path. Singing my own songs, if mostly to my stolen horse.

Thought of Destrier led to recollection of the horse shying at the arrow suddenly projecting from his head. Then came tumbling to the road, the shouting bandits, the idiot embarrassment of being the prisoner of idiots. The mad joy I'd felt slicing the sons of bitches dead. A joy soured by my own slow dying.

That last memory seemed long years of fevered burning, watched over by a worried miller.

At thought of Barnaby I sat up, astounded to find myself able to sit up, even to breathe. But was this true breathing? Perhaps I'd died, come to the Fields. Definitely the air tasted of smoke and death-rot, mixing with pleasanter woodland smells.

But no, I was still in the damned woods. And there lay the miller himself, beside the fire. Did he live? Perhaps I'd knifed him in mad fever.

No, he breathed. I sat awhile watching him breathe, as he'd watched over me. The boy has a pleasant face. Young and round. The Demetians are paler folk than we of Martia. They have freckles, which I find fascinating. But Barnaby looked older than at our first meeting by Herm's Font. Thinner of face. Dirtier, in truth; and more worn. I wondered what adventures he'd been having besides sitting beside a dying bard.

He twitched. What dream did he have now? At which question, I recalled my own last dream.

In fever, I watched him pull me from a pool of hot blood and cold shadow. Placing me down someplace warm and bright. Whispering '*ssh, ssh*' as though I were a horse to be shod and comforted.

Then... he'd waved a torch of green flames above me. It dripped emerald sparks that sank into my cold self, warming places death had claimed. And then so help me Lucif's mother in bed with the goat, the son of a miller *commanded* the earth to return the life dribbling from my side.

A strange dream. But stranger still was when the earth trembled *and obeyed*.

In St. Martia we, *they*, forbid spell-craft, except in weapon making. Of course, as a bard I learned basic cantrips of healing and restoration. Simple orations. If I hadn't smashed my harp into Marcus's face, I might have healed myself. Or not. Such magics extract high price. Stabbed in the gut, trying to heal myself would probably have ended me.

But what I witnessed in fever was more mystical than magical. Well, we all know there is magic; and the forever mystery behind the magic. Our first day of cantrips, the headmistress gravely informed us:

There is a box that holds all the magic of the world. This box rests on a chair that holds all the magic of the world. The chair is in a room that holds all the magic of the world. The room is in a house; the house is in a town; the town in a kingdom that is in the world that contains the town that holds the house that has the room where the chair sits quiet, holding the box that holds all the magic of the world.

She was quoting the *Testament of Sister Hecatatia*, of course. I was so new I supposed she meant a real box, real chair, etcetera. Though it sounded like a child's skipping rhyme, not an explanation of thaumaturgical theory. I asked why we sat in a classroom, instead of seeking this magic box.

When I grasped the business as parable, I sniffed, annoyed; the way one does when catching elders being tedious again.

And yet, when I awoke in the robbers' glade, watching the dawn, hearing the morning bird-choir, sitting beside the sleeping Barnaby, recalling my dream... I understood. Or felt I understood.

No matter how deeply buried, how far off and hidden, if there is magic in the world then it is within something that is within something bigger. And so on, till we see that the magic and we are in a box together. We live with magic we don't see. Whatever lies hidden, in the end it is with us, within whatever or whoever holds all things.

Teaching recalled and lesson learned. Healed, I staggered to my feet in a hurry to get *out* of those damned woods.

I know, I should have stayed till Barnaby awoke. But truly, looking down at the sleeping boy, I felt as I had at Herm's Font. There is something uncanny about the miller's son. Sets a bard's hair standing on end.

As well, the sweet woodland wind blew perfumed with death. Each shadow of dawn looked like a corpse lying quiet. I *had* to get the Infernum *away*.

But I did not run from him or the watching trees. No, I calmly fetched what I needed. My knife, the strings of my broken harp. A pack, the trivial hoard of copper and silver Marcus hid in a tree hollow.

I fled the robbers' glade, dawn kindly lighting my path, birds twittering a farewell choir. I felt new; reborn, even. Just as the penitents claim after fasting in vigil alone through a night and a day. Ah, I felt drunk, in truth.

Just a day before I'd lain gasping in darkness that pressed ever closer, smothering me as though I were already in the grave, choking on wet clods of earth. Now I staggered weak, yet shaking with life.

Demetia is a perilous land. For all it seems a kingdom of bumpkin farms, thatched villages, clumsy towns of wattle and wood. There is a power in its air, hidden in its fields, carried with each breeze. The power of Sainted Demetia herself, I suppose. She's just beneath the dirt, lurking behind the trees, whispering with the wind, ordering life to rise and bloom and fruit.

Yet neither land nor saint is only all about green life. Hurrying through the trees, I felt alive, but I shivered with each touch of boot to the earth. Knowing I walked over the thinnest crust of dirt, beneath which waited an infinite abyss of dark and rot, root and worm. The green rising life of Demetia is matched by a pull down into the waiting earth. Demetia is a land of Death and Life together.

Wherefore not? The Patroness is said to have been charged by the Lord of the House of Saints with explaining to mortals the mystery of life and death. Not 'mysteries'; for they are one mystery.

In that damned glade, I'd had stern lessons in ancient and solemn secrets. For which I hurried to get the Lucif's fifty fornicatoriums out and away.

And yet... I wished Barnaby had woken. Or I might have lain myself down beside him. Counting those freckles, till the boy woke to find me close and warm and thankful. Bardic training insisted there was purpose to our meeting. And if not, why, we could have found our own purpose.

But I was in a fever to leave. The freedom of the road called. The search for the cup called. So I quite nobly left half the robbers' squirrel-trove in sign of thanks, and headed for Persephone.

It made a sensible destination. I needed a new harp. Clean clothes as well. With mere pennies, a horse was out of the question. And clearly riding made me a careless traveler. I resolved to walk more wary.

Two days of wary walking brought me in sight of the cathedral spire, the roofs of the greater houses, the smoke of Persephone.

An ancient city straddling the river Lethe. Long ago it belonged entirely to St. Demetia. Till the Plutarchians captured it. Then the Demetians took it back... so it went, year by year, battle by battle, till Demetia's green warmth turned sear and dark as the robes of Plutarch's somber priests.

Now the two saints shared. The Plutarchian half ruled by the Deaconry of St. Plutarch. Dead folk, mostly, and their living partners.

St. Demetia's side of the city was ruled by a peaceable, breathing duke. I knew his daughter Alexandra. She'd visit my family in Martia during the summers. For the usual political alliance-building between important families.

Alexandra had been fun, if absurdly determined to become a warrior like the women of St. Martia. Supportive of my dream to become a bard. Euterpe's tuned tits, Alex had been the one to tell me of Demetia's school for bards.

I decided to seek her out. She'd aid me for the fun of it, if not for friendship. If I could contact her without anyone alerting those of St. Martia that I was here.

At the city gate I nodded polite to the guards, who asked my name and business in the city.

I informed them I was Val no-one-in-particular; just a bard in need of fresh harp, clean clothes. They doubted. I offered to sing them a song. Grinning, they agreed. So I sang.

The gate-guards were impressed, as they should have been. So also the onlookers. Though the Captain insisted I took liberties with the lyrics of Greensleeves. I didn't, by the way. I improved the dreary lyrics.

My claim to bardship established, the gate captain himself produced a fresh white parchment showing an excellent drawing of my face. Complete with name, and promising reward from St. Bridget's School for Female Bards.

And so here I now sit in a Persephone gaol, facing whipping and branding for horse theft.

Chapter 27
Spit, spite and burn

Jewel of Stonecroft:

Demetia is a fat farmwife of a hayseed saint. Her magic is for bumpkins in huts reeking of goat-shit. She's the patroness of barnyard oafs who chant of seeds and sunshine while holding piss-wet babes off the floor so they aren't gobbled by the pigs.

Demetia has no law against witches. Oh, no; not unless they *call* themselves witches. And so 'holy sisters', 'forest-mothers' and 'good-wives' set their little magic huts all about the land, taking strings of onions and half-pennies in return for poultices to cure warts, sniffles and drooping penises.

Hard to believe that St. Demetia is sister to Hecatatia, patroness of *serious* magics. Magic that changes lives. Or ends them, ends them, la, la, la.

I tracked the boy on the road to Persephone; and that by questioning spirits I could scarce keep from devouring my soul or removing my skirt. The wrath of my former coven following me like a storm cloud. I *feel* Sister Agat and Mother Hemp's shadows on the road behind even now. They hate me, hate me now. So much for *sisterhood!*

Not that any of it was MY fault. How was I to know of poison in the broth? Damnation, ruin and death seven times seven upon them it was THEIR fault my promised servant was stolen. Stolen! Mine!

I've come to a crossroad with no least idea of where to go next. I sit on the edge of some dreary stone fountain, staring at weary green farmlands. I hate these idiot fields. They mock me, reminding of times passed.

My fool of a father could not keep his land. My lunatic of a mother could not stop singing to the moon. One day he hung himself, she ran into the hills. Screaming, laughing, being a useless idiot. Leaving me with his corpse hanging from the rafter, swinging back and forth. Forth and back, back and forth, like a fat ham. Leaving me. Leaving me alone. Leaving me to be a sniffling brat. A brat *oh-so-kindly* taken on as scullery girl for the big fat farm that swallowed our little croft like a sow eating its piglets.

I sit on the rim of the fountain and stare at farm fields and I want them to darken. Why won't they darken? They should feel what I feel, and wither away, turn to dust and dead weed. Oh, and the fruit on the trees should turn to sacks of worms. Or wasps? Yes, yes, wasps would be better. And let the milk cows give snake venom. Green poison that bubbles in the milk pail. And let the pigs devour the babies. Oh, and let's have the goats turn to wolves, leaping from the sties hungry and grinning.

I'd do it, if Hecatatia gave me the power. Why doesn't she give me the power? Infernum, maybe she will. Maybe she has. Give it a try.

I grasp my broach of Sainted Hecatatia. No true relic, but it's old and bears her sigil and was thrice dipped in the baptismal font of her chapel in Pomona. I stand, raise left arm to say my prayers.

"Death." That's a good beginning. *"Blight. Bones and night. Ash and dust and rust and pox and worm, wasp and spit and spite and burn. Ache and spurn and spite and blight and drought and rot-"*

A bee all but flies into my mouth. I brush at it; it dodges and buzzes. Behind comes loud clamor, I whirl, find a family of crows now splashing in the font, cawing for the joy of bathing. I snarl, raise arm again and a butterfly slaps my face, floats away satisfied. I snarl curses, not in magical casting but pathetic frustration.

Three rabbits now poke their heads up from the grass, whispering to one another, discussing why the lunatic girl is shouting at empty fields and insects. I wonder too.

I lower my arm, release my broach, my determination. So pointless, this useless rage. Useless, useless. The ultimate curse word, fouler than fuck or Infernum or a thousand citations to Lucif's mother's crotch. Nothing is worse, is more obscene, than the word *useless*.

I give it up, all up, sit again on the rim of the font, listening to crows splash, wind blow, bees buzz.

There was a song mama used to sing. Comes to me whenever I surrender to uselessness. It's like sinking into fever or rising water. I wrap arms about myself and sing. The fountain behind splashes along.

"La, the moon is our boat.
Through the sky we float.
Through the sleeping night,
Through the happy light.
Clouds and stars are ours.
Through the sleepy hours. La."

Look at me. Now I'm rocking back, forth, back, forth, like a mother cradling her child. Or a hanged man swinging, back, forth. Singing, hugging myself. Pathetic. Absolutely useless. But what the Infernum does it matter? I sink to the dirt, curl up, singing to myself.

I come awake in the dirt beside the font. I'm hungry, I'm thirsty, I'm stiff, I'm cold. My face hurts, the scratches of MY stolen cat-summoning only half-healed.

I stand, looking about. Where am I? Oh yes, the crossroads fountain. Moths flitter in the moonlight, dodging bats. Bats flitter about, dodging owls. Meanwhile the font water trickles out a stone face I can't see. Too worn by time. I put my hands to my own face, wondering if it is worn. Stupid thought. I bend down, splash and drink like a crow. The water is cool on the cat-scratches. Well, that's a start.

Voices far off make me turn, spying lights on the east road. A red glow, a yellow glow. Two riders. One upon a giant boar who lights the way with the bloody flames out his eyes and mouth. The other is a prancing goat, yellow sickly light shining out eyes like two mad lanterns.

Behold Mother Hemp, and Sister Agat. On Belshazzar and Ptolemy. Their very useful servants. Pity I don't have a servant. I have n*othing*.

Except my head, and if I want to keep it I'd best use it. The moping fit is over, I am myself again, coldly weighing paths.

I can run down the road or into the trees. Useless. They'd be on me like hounds after a sick fox. I can fight, picking up a rock, casting a curse. Neither Agat nor Hemp are so great in magic as they pretend. And their servants are dim creatures, good for fetching and riding. But I'm tired and hungry and have no servant. If *no* to running, *no* to fighting, then best I hide. Where?

I look to the font basin. Taking breath, I climb over the rim, slip into the water. It's cold as St. Plutarch's marriage bed but I curl my body beneath, till all but my face lies beneath the water.

I put hand to my broach of Hecatatia, willing myself to become invisible, unseen, unimportant. I'm hiding in the font of some old saint, probably Herm. The water shall shield somewhat from the spell they use to hunt me. Being in St. Herm's shadow may help more. He's a trickster with a wink for a soul on the run.

My ears under water, I can't hear exact words. By the sound, Agat and Hemp argue. Over whether to flay me or turn my guts to snakes? Agat would favor flaying. But maybe they argue over where to go now. Perhaps I'll fox them. With luck.

Not that Fortuna ever smiles on me. Nor the Upper House It's only been the saints' frowns I've seen when I bother looking up. No, any moment Belshazzar's muzzle shall poke over the rim, grinning like a great turnip-ghost filled with blood set afire.

So I wait in cold wet, face to the night sky, expecting the worst. I must look like a maiden drowned for love or lunacy. The picture makes me want to laugh at the stars. Those cold distant stars where no moon-boat floats, no happy sleepers fly.

I'd *never* drown for love. I'd drown my beloved, if I had one. Teach 'em respect for a sweet girl's heart.

I spent a long while lying so, staring up at the passing clouds, the shining moon. Scripture say the waxing moon is sanctified by St. Demetia to bless the sleep of the faithful. But the moon's waning chastises those same faithful to consider the martyrdom of Demetia's beloved novice, Sister Persephone.

This moon waned; just a pale sliver of bone and silver. Didn't set my mind upon martyrdom nor damnation. But it set me thinking upon a new direction.

When I could take the chill of the font water no longer, I peeked out. The hunters were gone. I took scripture's advice, considered the road to Persephone. It made as good a choice as any.

Three days of walking brought sore feet, an empty belly, the curses of a farmer whose dog thought he owned the road and found he owned a broken leg. *Keep your dog on a rope, bumpkin.* I stole cabbages from a field while rabbits sneered, crows jeered. Gathered windfall pears hard as wood from an orchard. Wrapped a rock in my scarf, swung it about my head to fend away an amorous tinker.

After these amazing adventures, I trudge into sight of the rooftops, steeples and weathervanes of Persephone. Walled, for all that fighting with Plutarch ended a century past. A long line of folk on foot, on horse and cart wait upon the road before the gate, grumbling at the slow passage.

Damned if I'll wait in the hot sun. I slip in, out of the carts and folk afoot, come to the front.

"Heya, girl, get back," growls a fat woman pushing a barrow filled with weavings.

"I was here," I lie, studying what makes our passage so slow.

"Now, that's not true," admonishes a man holding baskets of onions.

"Sure an' it's true," I insist. "Was right behind you and your nasty onions, sure as shadow."

He lectures but I ignore him to study three figures in green robes. They stand beside the gate pillars, studying each before allowing entry. Holding leashes to two great mastiffs. While the gate guards hold pikes ready, ensuring the crowd passes slowly before the dogs.

"Woe to those who defile the orations of Sainted Mother Demetia with darkest spellcraft," says the onion-monger.

Shit! *Witchfinders*. I try backing away but the crowd is too thick.

"Who you pushin'?" growls the fat woman. "Aren't scared to near the Saint's servants, now are you?"

"'Course not," I snap. "You're the likely witch here."

"Not me," says the stout woman, stoutly. The onion-man now stands before the three in green. Eyeing the dogs, their great white teeth while they sniff suspiciously at his onions. Should I run? No, the crowd would grab me. Best keep calm.

But something is not right here. The shadows of the dogs waver like candle flame, though we stand in unwavering sun. And the witchfinders *smell* wrong.

I take my broach, touch it to left eye, casting *Soul Sight*. Blink, then study the world again. The onion-man now stands straighter. His ugly face turned noble as the statue of a rare and honest statesman.

The fat barrow-woman now seems a babyish thing, face wandering through expressions of anger and frustration, desire and boredom.

But the witchfinders... St. Erebus eat me.

The first witchfinder looks little different. A bony old man in green robes of St. Demetia, a face of devout and mindless duty. But the two behind him... their faces and form are entirely changed. The truth revealed, beyond mere enchanting.

Behold Sister Agat and Mother Hemp. Not in green robes. In truth they wear their usual black habits of Sainted Hecatatia. And what seemed their witch-sniffing dogs on leashes, are a red-eyed boar, a yellow-eyed goat.

I step backwards, but the fat barrow-woman shoves me forwards into the onion man, who pushed me yet farther on, to stumble in the dirt at the feet of my two coven sisters. They grin down, while boar and goat tug upon the leashes.

"Oh, here's a witch for sure," gloats Agat.

"Ripe for the burning," agrees Hemp.

Chapter 28
On the Nature of Lightning

Friar Cedric:

I am free.

True, I sit in a cell of the gaol of Persephone. But free to speak the truth. To the stones of my cell, the rats in the oubliette, the yawning guards, my fellow prisoners in their separate cells. To speak openly, as I never dared as secret Lucretian, nor hiding as mere friar in farmland oblivion.

Let us pray. But do not bow your heads. Raise them! Do not close eyes. Open them! For Truth is not catechism mumbled blindly to the floor. If prayer be truth, it is light to be seen, and to see by. Let us begin.

The world is round. Literate folk know it so; and were all folk literate all would know it so. And the sun is a great burning stone around which the earth circles. We dwell upon a point on the gear of a crystalline clock.

But what of the stars? Is it not logical to believe they also are fiery stones equal to our sun? Great burning fires so distant they appear only as bright points of light. As a bonfire on a hill might seem to distant eyes as a mere point of light, small and bright.

And if the stars are suns, shall they not also have their earths? And who can say what strange folk walk those lands? What saints rule? Only the Lord of the House of Saints himself knows what hides within the stars. Dark worlds of eternal night. And worlds of light, and realms of fire and ice. In the sky above us await unfathomable wonders and horrors, all the places of our dreams. The night sky is bedecked with the light of dreams.

A pleasant vision. I will be burned alive for saying it. And yet I declare it worth the fire. *There are worlds in the stars*. A beautiful truth. Twice so, thrice so, from this dark cell.

A pilgrim in search of absolution, I went down the roads of *this* world seeking Barnaby's bones. Thinking to spy his corpse on the roadside, where crows fed, dogs growled.

I wondered what sad method his mother and brother chose to ensure his death. A mere map to a cursed tower did not suffice. They could hardly suppose the innocent boy would find his way there. No, the map had been Alf's spiteful jest, to give Barnaby a fool's destination.

They wished the boy's death; but beyond village bounds, beyond village eyes and gossip. Elsewise, years past Alf would have shoved Barnaby into the millwheels.

The Squire might have arranged with some assassin to meet the boy on the road; murder him, hide the body. But the greedy man would be obligate to forsake his beloved coins. Then trust in a murderer's silence. Unlikely.

Perhaps they gave Barnaby a sealed letter to deliver to some official, confessing terrible crime? The boy would faithfully perform such duty. Proud to keep word not to open the letter. Bah; that was absurd theatre.

Simpler for brother Alf to follow on the road, knifing Barnaby from behind. But... sly Alf is not so direct. His style would be to convince Barnaby to fill his pockets with stones, leap into a river to visit the amorous merwomen.

His stepmother... she'd not hesitate at murder. But she walked warry. I recalled the blackened tongue of Barnaby's father. Knife-thrusts were superfluous.

Simply send the boy from the village with poison in his pack, and murder done.

So I journeyed from Mill Town, asking all I met whether they'd seen a large youth with straw hair, cheerful smile. Or his remains. They eyed my humble robe and staff bedecked with cockle shells in sign of pilgrimage, and gave respectful answer. Always *no*. None saw such a boy, nor such a corpse. It did not surprise. He might well have wandered into woods, over a cliff, down a well. Else wolves and crows had not left a bone to keep as relic of holy innocence.

So I journeyed, with purpose far grimmer than when I trotted a happy student from Pomona to Persephone, Pleasance to St. Daedalus, even the forests of St. Silenus. And yet I now walked in high spirits. Wherefore not? For overlong I lived as prisoner of my own cowardice. Though I now sought a dead innocent, walking in threat of arrest as heretic, I knew myself freed. There is no life lived in shadows. Any more than truth whispered only to shadows.

Warnings of bandits waylaying travelers on the road pushed me to join a band of tinker-traders heading to Persephone. Cheerful folk, they welcomed me for the blessing of St. Demetia.

Their leader was a cinnamon trader from Sister Parvati, skin as brown as his spice wares. An educated creature. We walked through a storm debating upon the nature of lightning as the bolts flew about us, while the others crouched in alarm, muttering prayers to Typhon.

The cinnamon-trader maintained the crackle and blast was the Upper House of Saints quarreling again with St. Lucif. As thunder rumbled, bolts flashed, I explained how what seemed war in heaven was merely a by-product of natural process.

"Consider a rain barrel," I told the shivering tinker, as we walked drenched down the road. "The rain fills it, makes it too heavy to even lift. And yet the same water floated happily above the earth. What kept the water in the air? Why, the same power that sends steam from a kettle. Fire, my friend. The fire of the sun's light sends water to the sky. This storm above us is the war of fire and water; sending rain and lightning upon us."

I raised arms to the thundering storm, and so help me St. Tinia if a bolt did not pass so close above that my hair stood on end, drenched though it was.

I laughed. The tinkers and traders laughed as well, but uneasily. Their look declared I was a holy man, touched by lightning. And so I am; and so is any man.

As we arrived at the gate of Persephone the road grew crowded with those anxious to enter. But gate guards made it a slow journey. We watched as they arrested first a horse thief, then a witch. When our band of wanderers came to the gate, the cinnamon-trader whispered to the guard captain, who looked to me, nodding wise as all a congregation of owls.

And there at the gate of Persephone I was arrested for being a Lucretian.

Chapter 29
Three Discussions

Friar Cedric:

"You were arrested for what?" asks the prisoner from the cell across my own. Their voice expressing equal disdain and disbelief.

"For declaring the truth," I repeat. "That the saints are but the shadows of natural laws cast on the cavern walls of our minds. We dress those shadows in clothes, give them holy names, assigning absurd human motives."

There comes argument up and down the hallway.

"Oh, go burn, Lucretian," shouts someone of faith.

"How do you put clothes on a shadow?" demands another, who fails to grasp the idea of metaphor. Which, ironically, is my point. The world fails to see that the saints are mere metaphor.

"Hardly seem worth death by fire," comments the prisoner two cells down. A female, from the voice. Clearly educated, though charged with theft of horse.

She has the right of it. *'The saints are shadows'*. Not a stirring truth. Might justify a burned thumb. Certainly not a fiery funeral pyre while one yet breathes.

"All truths are one," I declare. "As many stones to one cathedral. If a mind values the Edifice of Truth, it matters naught for which stone one gives oneself."

What brave words come from me since I left Mill Town! Seeking the boy's bones, finding only tavern argument, arrest as Lucretian.

"Caves and shadows," mused the prisoner down the hall. "That's old stuff."

"You seem educated for a horse thief," I observe. Then repent the words; they sound dismissive. Perhaps

I am jealous that she will only be whipped, sold to St. Martia.

The prisoner takes no offense. "I'm a bard. From St. Martia, actually. If they sell me I may wind up in my mother's kitchen. I'll spit in the soup for sure."

"I thought those of the land of the *Saint of Worthy Battle* only studied the arts of war. Not philosophy."

The prisoner was silent a bit.

"That's about right. But we, my old family, were important. We have the blood of St. Martia herself, before she took vows, determined to spread the word of the Saints' Just Cause."

"So?"

"So, we had a library."

"Ah," I say. For some reason I feel deeply sad, and yet amused. "Books led you astray."

At that we laugh together. The other prisoners make no rejoinder; entirely thrown by how a book might lead a soul to crime and flame, glory and truth.

* * *

Val the Bard:

I sit in a closet of rough stone, stare at iron bars blackened by dark thoughts from the ten thousand sad prisoners who sat here previously, their labored breath and sweat blackening the very same bars. Now I add my own dark thoughts, blackening the view yet more.

Beyond the bars I glimpse other cells, a table with a lamp, a bored guard reading a book. I desperately want out; and desperately wish to know the title of the book.

We prisoners make idle conversation from cell to cell; seeking escape from the dread that smolders in our stomachs, confuses our minds. Each awaits the moment when gaolers will come to our particular door, rattling keys and clinking manacles. To march us staggering and blinking out... then to be surrendered to a whipping post, a bonfire, a glowing iron, a noose, the headsman's axe.

So we chat upon what missteps and sad dice-throws led to our present sorrows. The fellow across and to the right is a heretic of the interdicted Society of St. Lucretius. He proudly admits his idiot crime of arguing reality with authority. I admit it makes a more glorious story than horse-theft. But more pointless. A horse at least has *use*.

At length he and I determine the real villains of our stories, the authors of our crimes: *books*. Yes, books led us on our separate paths of destruction. The cleric-heretic devoured tomes of natural law, forsaking the sacred texts. This diet poisoned his mind; or freed it, depending upon whether you stand within the bonfire, or comfortably outside it.

In a similar way, my father's library led me here. Glorious tales of wandering adventurers and heroic lovers, magical lands where people lived and breathed for reasons other than war. The stories sparked within my heart the desire for a different life than the endless practice of successful slaughter.

Up Lucif's flaming ass with the martial life. I vowed to be... *a wandering troubadour*. Singing songs of love, of beauty, of life lived free. And I'd follow the life I sang; living free, loving free.

Talking to the heretic, I do not mention the cup. That is my vision alone. For all that it led me to the library. And the books led me to become a bard. Which brought me to steal a horse. get captured by thieves who killed the horse. Then I slew the thieves, only to be arrested for the theft of the horse.

Priest though he is, the Lucretian declines to pronounce my theft a mortal sin. He sees extenuating circumstance in my being a bard.

"You wandering troubadours are trained to see the romantic side of actions. Not the practical results," the priest informs me from his cell. "You sing of rogues, pirates and highway robbers as glorious rascals, never taking into account the reality of such profession. How should any court of Earth or Heaven fault you for leaping dramatically on a convenient horse, riding off to adventure?"

His error makes me laugh. Strange sound in a dungeon of cold stone and old shit, iron bar and damp straw.

I don't tell him of gutting Marcus's band. Too many listen, guards and prisoners alike. But I explain the priest's error concerning the education of a bard.

"We have all that fairy-tale nonsense knocked out our heads first day we pass the school gate. Barding isn't just about learning to strum a harp. We learn history, politics, all the darker facts of life. A proper bard can trace historical blood stains from Cain's fratricide to the latest despot's patricide. Sure, we sing of glorious heroes and noble fates. While humming under our breath the truth, which is mostly death, war and theft.

"If you want to please tavern patriots or a court of princes, you sing lies. And to sing a lie correctly, you'd best know the truth."

The cleric goes silent at that. Some of the other prisoners argue how the lives of bandits, burglars and wall-breakers is more than cutting throats and purses. It's *rebellion against the chains of the rich*. An art form, a profession ancient and honorable as any priestcraft or bardic chanting.

"It's the damned priests that have the tomnoddy child's view," growls the coiner three cells down. "Always sayin' there's a story to things. But what's the story? It's anybody's guess. So far I've seen naught but '*be born, then live till you die.*'"

A prisoner down the hall has kept silent till now. A witch, according to the guard in the chair. Now she contributes her view.

"After death, all the devils and angels come from hiding, shouting over each wrong step we took in life. What for, when the journey is over? Why the Infernum didn't they whisper aught when we breathed?"

A funeral finality tinges her words, even in theologic anger. Clearly, she's resigned herself to the fire. Or seeks to, as does the heretic cleric.

I work to resign myself to a whipping and a branding. We of Martia are taught from infancy to wear scars as folk of other lands wear jewelry. As things of pride.

But in the back of my mind is the thought that if I can get word to Alexandra the Duke's daughter, I might, in an excess of humble self-abnegation, skip the glory of new scars.

* * *

Jewel of Stonecroft:

I lie bored on dirty straw, stare upwards where a great spider walks back, forth, back across the ceiling. Like a nervous prisoner. Though a spider seems more the gaoler sort, tying the poor bugs up.

Someone hisses, then hisses some more, till at last I look about for what idiot thinks he's Lucif's teakettle.

A louder hiss makes me look across the hallway into the cell of the heretic. He's seeking my attention. Dirty old men, all alike. Probably going to wave his flaccid member through the bars.

But no, he's drawing a finger slowly through the air. Is he casting a spell? Granting a heretic's blessing? A 'C'. An 'A'... well, he's spelling something out.

"CAN YOU READ?"

Insulting question. Of course I can. I consider spelling a sarcastic 'NO'. But this is *slightly* more interesting than the spider's pacing. I nod, watch as he scribes upon the air. He's writing backwards so it is easier for me to follow. Polite of him, I admit.

"WANT TO ESCAPE?"

Now *there's* an idiot question; as the flair of hope in my heart is an idiot answer. But I nod again, why not.

He gestures at himself. "PRIEST OF DEMETIA". Then points above my cell bars. I'm slow of brain today, it takes a minute to comprehend.

The gaol knows witches. Don't want prisoners casting in their cells, maybe summon a demon to bite the bars through. They took my broach away, first thing. Lucky they didn't take skirt and teeth.

And so above my cell door, out of reach, they've hung a Greater Charm of Sainted Demetia. Forged in silver light, dipped in sacred water. It'd take a Matron of St. Hecatatia to cast aught beneath it. Not me. I feel the thing like a lead blanket holding me still.

Ah, but an ordained priest of St. Demetia... he might snuff the charm. Like a lantern flame, tell it '*sleep, little charm, sleep*'. Still, this fellow's a Lucretian. Can he also be a real Demetian priest? Obviously the gaolers don't think so.

And even if the charm were to be snuffed, it's still a question of what the Infernum I might cast without candle, book or broach. But... it makes an *interesting* question. I sit a while, staring upwards at the pacing spider again.

Chapter 30
The City of Bones and Blooms

"Welcome to Persephone," said Night-Creep, perched upon Barnaby's shoulder pack.

Barnaby made no reply; merely stared; mouth open, eyes wide. Astonished by all he saw, all he heard, all he smelled.

Senses overcome, he lowered eyes to the street. Behold: orderly lines of stones round and regular as prayer beads on a string. Whose labor was this wonder of cobbles? Where could they find so many river-smoothed stones to fit so neatly? How could they bear to let a horse shit upon such work?

He turned gaze upwards. Gables of houses, flowered terraces and ornate balconies made stage backdrop fit for a grand play. Higher still, tiled roofs wore weathervanes like crowns upon princes commanding wind and storm. And higher yet stood a forest of tower tops and church spires. From these pinnacles flew banners bright in the afternoon sun, alive in the river-wind. Who dared the dreadful fall, just to climb into the sky, placing these symbols? Did they know what a wonder they performed, fixing a colored cloth to declare this city a place of beauty and victory rivaling heaven's draperies of cloud and star? Surely they knew, and so walked proud among the ground-dwelling commons.

Barnaby turned gaze upon those in the streets and walkways sharing this fantastical stage. Men, women and children streamed past, skipped past, limped past, rode past, sauntered past… each knowing their steps in the amazing dance.

The faces passed as a parade of dream folk. Some olive-skinned like to Bodkin. Else light and freckled same as any Barnaby. A tall man passed pale as milk, hair black as ink, cheekbones sharp as church spires. What land did he call home? Nix? Aurelia? A shirtless boy skipped by on hooves that clattered the cobbles. Bearing the same tight-curled hair and mad eyes of the Goat Girl. A *Silenian*, Barnaby thought, astonished. He'd never considered she must have relatives. Brothers and fathers and all the usual tribe of relations.

A fellow strode beneath a chimney of a hat, round lenses covering eyes. Meeting Barnaby's gaze, he grinned. Barnaby grinned right back. They grinned together, mutually pleased to meet one another upon a busy street in a summer day. A *Hefestian*, decided Barnaby. Alf said the folk of that land were addicted to strange hats, absurd spectacles.

Passing through the gate of Persephone, each soul whistled, chatted, called out to one another. Hummed and hurried, sauntered and strode. They also grumbled and cursed when finding a Barnaby hindering their grand entrance.

"It's like the *Jahrmarkt*," declared Barnaby. "The spring fair east of Mill Town. But instead of tents and booths, here are houses and churches and castles and taverns and towers and fountains and paving and statues and trees and so many people."

"Yes, right, now get from out the way," admonished Bodkin, tugging his arm. "Close gob and stop staring. You look like a farm dog stopping to piss in front of the duke's parade."

"Damn right he does," growled a gate guard. "Move the bumpkin from the path 'for I pull you both."

"Yessir," said Bodkin.

"Pull us where?" asked Barnaby, allowing himself to be pulled to a side-path.

"Means toss us into gaol," said Bodkin. "Truly, is this your first sight of anywhere bigger than two houses and a barn?"

"Mill Town has plenteous folk and houses. Just, well, not so many as here."

Persephone was not all stone and brick, plaster and wood. Trees stood in basins at every corner. Boxes of flowers hung beneath each window. Birds choired from tree branches and rooftops. For all the city-smell of wood smoke and horseshit, there remained a background perfume of summer flowers.

"Hasn't changed a bit," declared Bodkin. "That tower is new. Those used to be cherry trees, not elms."

"When were you here?" asked Barnaby.

"Oh, born and raised in 'Seph. Seventy-something years ago. I mean, that's the last I remember being here. For sure I came back oft enough. Probably old Mercutio had a grand house or two. Ancient mates to meet for a beer, cry about the old days the way wrinkled fools do."

Barnaby tried to picture *Ancient Bodkin*.

"Is being here now strange?"

"You'd think." The boy leaped into the air, clicked heels, landed dancing. "But it feels right. Young body, old soul, no plague of memories and regrets. Best of all worlds."

They walked on, staring about.

"Now, when *I* was last here," mused Night-Creep.

"When?" interrupted Barnaby.

"Hmm. Some centuries ago."

"Ah."

"Then," continued the cat, "war and death ruled these streets. See that pleasant trickling fountain? I watched monks of the Order of Plutarch fill it with the blood of sacrifices, till every stone shone wet and red as the tongue of a wolf devouring a lamb."

"What sort of sacrifices?" asked Barnaby.

"Hmm. Human females, mostly. Novices of Demetia and Vesta, who refused to follow Sister Persephone into Sainted Plutarch's somber order."

Barnaby stared at the fountain. A construction of marble in form of cupped flowers, with silvery drops of water wending from high blossoms down to a final basin. Birds splashed within, trilling, chirping, tossing diamond drops in delight. How could this have once been a thing of horror?

"I don't understand how saints can war with one another. Aren't they all servants together in the House of Saints?"

"Ah, servants oft quarrel how best to serve the house," said Bodkin. "With ever an eye to serving themselves."

"Exact so," agreed Night-Creep. "Doubly so in matters of doctrine. The theologics across the river declare Death to be the most holy sacrament of Life. While monks and nuns of the Green Saint affirm that the Middle House is for the living, not the dead. Both claim to serve a revelation given by the Lord of Saints. As perhaps they do, perhaps they do."

They walked past the fountain, Barnaby silent, pondering. He reached to touch the water, hesitated, deciding not. Though he smelled no blood in this place of peace and sunshine. The magic cat's recollection had been from ages past. Just something to give stories a taint of dark, touching songs with a sad tone.

Thought of songs turned to thoughts of Val. Was she in this city? Perhaps on this very street, strumming a new harp. So many streets with so many turns, it'd be easier to find her in the woods.

"Where do we go now?" he wondered aloud.

"First we find a base of operations," declared Bodkin. "A basement or abandoned house where we store our tools, keep out of sight, meet and plan our next move."

"Next move for what?" asked the cat. "Out of sight of whom? Are you hunted by authorities? Do you intend to burgle the Duke's citadel or storm the city garrison?"

"Well, no," said Bodkin. "It's just good practice. And you aren't going to *pay* for a room, are you?" He sounded scandalized.

"I hear singing," said Barnaby. Increasing his pace, turning down a side street, beside a great stone block of a building. Windows barred, with no flower boxes to brighten the view.

A young girl sat tailor-fashion on a rough blanket, singing. A wooden bowl set before her bare feet. The girl looked thin faced, wrapped in old clothes as though she sat in winter's ice, not summer's shine. She sang upwards, not to the passersby but higher, towards birds and clouds and sky.

"Hello," said Barnaby.

"Hello," said the girl, ceasing song. "My name is Whisper."

"Hello, Whisper. My name is Barnaby."

Names established, the two pondered one another.

"You sing wonderfully well, Whisper."

"Thank you, Barnaby." She looked down at the bowl, as if waiting for it to offer its name and opinion. Barnaby considered the contents: a half-penny, a wooden button, a brass buckle.... It took a moment to understand. Then he reached to pockets, seeking something gold and heavy. Bodkin reached to stop him.

"Let me," he said, producing a copper. Barnaby frowned at this. Bodkin sighed, produced a second, dropping them separately into the bowl. The girl shivered at each *clink, clank.*

"Thank you," she said. "What song would you like?"

Barnaby considered. "A song about all this."

"All what?" asked Whisper, puzzled.

Barnaby waved hands at something that felt too large to put into words. "The city. The streets. The sun. The flowers. The day. The people."

Whisper nodded. "Oh. I understand." She threw back her head, child voice high, sweet but strong.

"Out from cloud the sun comes free.
Return to me, Persephone.
Between the stones,
Beneath each bone
Lie flower seeds of Persephone.
Bring your smile to us again,
Let your touch warm our land.
Persephone, come home to me."

Whisper closed mouth, crossed arms to declare the song done.

Barnaby clapped, as did Bodkin, as did passerby. A passing cleric nodded approving, tossed a copper piece into the bowl to add its *clink.*

"You paid two pennies so's you can have another song," said Whisper. "What else would you hear?"

"Something about a cat," said Night-Creep, staring down from Barnaby's shoulder.

Whisper's eyes grew round. "Your cat talks. Are you magic folk?"

"It is," said Barnaby. "We're just Bodkin and Barnaby. I'm a miller. Bodkin is a, a kind of adventurer who's older than he looks."

She nodded. "That's fine then. But I don't know any songs about cats."

"Then I shall teach you one," said Night-Creep, leaping from his miller-perch. He landed beside the girl. Adjusted his tail, whiskers, chest fur, and last his voice. Then began to sing. In tones high as a church spire, and just as sharp, and just as unpleasant to find poking into one's ears.

> *"I am a cat, I slept on a queen's bed.*
> *I heard what an archbishop said.*
> *I leapt from a gargoyle's head*
> *To where the castle shadows led*
> *Down onto a poor man's shed."*

Whisper put hands over her ears. "Your voice is all nails poking into my head."

At which critique the cat's tail twitched. But it did not cease singing. It rose up on hind legs, put paws to chest and continued all the louder.

> *"I am a cat. I prowl the slimy city sewer.*
> *Ssshh, my footstep silent, sure.*
> *Whiskers taste the air's allure,*
> *Egyptian gaze a blazing skewer*
> *For every rodent evil doer."*

Passersby stopped to consider the singing cat. In amusement, not astonishment. Barnaby wondered at their easy acceptance. Perhaps such sights were more common in Persephone than in Mill Town? He recalled a choir of trained dogs barking in chorus at the *Jahrmarkt*. But a singing cat seemed far greater wonder.

Granted, the dogs had not made folk wince for the pain in their ears..

> *"I am a cat. I wash upon cathedral slates.*
> *While Lord and Lucif hold debate.*
> *A pigeon nods and hesitates.*
> *Angels stare in wry reproof*
> *While feathers flutter from…"*

Night-Creep drew the last notes out. *"the roooooof."*

The cat lowered arms, bowing deep, song ended. A small clatter of clapping followed, entirely from Barnaby and Bodkin. Onlookers shook their abused heads, moving on. Whisper took hands from ears, eyeing the cat warily lest he begin encore.

"Good trick, that," said a lady pushing a barrow of flowers. "Pity the little blind kitty can't sing. But what cat can?"

"Oh, no, don't be blaming the feline. It's the fellow with the horrible axe on his back doing the real singing," said someone else. "His beast is just trained by blows and cuffs to mimic."

"Idiots," hissed the discussed cat, ears flat in anger. "The last soul to cuff *me* is still untangling his guts in the midden flames of Infernum."

"Rude thing," scoffed the man. "No penny for your master." Which comment brought laughter. Argument won, man and woman walked away.

But an onlooker holding baskets of onions nodded, brought forth an onion and dropped it next to the bowl. Then continued down the street, humming of cats and kings.

"This's been good," said Whisper, taking two of the pennies, hiding them in her rags. "Got more coin?"

Bodkin jumped to answer before Barnaby.

"No. pity, sorry, empty pockets."

Whisper nodded unsurprised. "That's fine. Go away now please."

"Why?" Barnaby felt surprised, a bit hurt.

"You're big and have an axe and a beard and a singing cat. Scares the coins away."

Barnaby brushed at his chin, considered what he found. Indeed, it'd been days since he'd shaved. Or bathed. In Mill Town folk took such things as weekly duties, or monthly.

"Very well, then," said Barnaby. "Good luck, Miss Whisper."

"Good luck to you too, Mister Barnaby."

* * *

Val paced her narrow cell, listening to the conversations of other prisoners. The guard argued with his captain about reading books on duty. The false coiner shared bawdy tales with the fellow who sold fake titles of nobility. Their tales rang false as the wares of either. The cleric and the witch had gone silent. Perhaps sleeping. Else sunken into despair, awaiting when they'd be led to the fire.

From the narrow window that provided a bit of light and air to her cell, came the sound of singing in the street. Not the waif who sang of green fields and loving hearts. This was a voice like to a knife cutting into glass, with the broken shards digging into the ears.

Val covered her own ears, till she was sure it finished.

Chapter 31
Three Interviews

Friar Cedric:

The Questioner has come. He stands outside my cell, not approaching overclose. Velvet green robes, shoulders draped with stole of black to declare *ecclesiastic authority*. Thumping the floor with a staff wound with vine in sign of service to the Green Saint. We stare at one another. I don't know the fellow, though no doubt we've crossed paths in chapel and temple, in studies and sacred gatherings. He clears throat in sign that he now begins formal speech.

"Are you Cedric Weiland, born thirty years past in the village of Portunus, ordained Priest of the Order of St. Demetia under the authority of the Bishopric of Pomona?"

I debate whether to stand or remain seated upon the stone floor. This is ceremony, and I have come to loathe ceremony. But sitting is rude. And I do not resent this person. Nor do I long for the power to defy his pompous authority. I desire the power to open his mind to the truth. There is no greater power, nor more rare.

I stand, arms at side.

"Yes, I am Cedric Weiland."

"Excellent. Are you that Cedric Weiland who accompanied the excommunicate Bishop Amandine to the Republic of St. Hephaestus, to learn systems of thought contrary to the teaching of Sainted Demetia and the Lord of the House of Saints?"

"Indeed I did go to Daedalus. With full permission of the Counsel of Studies."

He declines to debate *permissions*.

"And did you not return from that land of mechanical abominations tainted with the Lucretian heresy?"

I smile. "I returned with a tinderbox that told me the hours of the day. And a book of formulae explaining the motion of objects, whether falling ball or whirling planet. But neither time nor motion are abominations to the saints. Say rather, they are laws of the creation of the Lord of Saints."

He stamps his staff, making an unimpressive 'bump'. "I am not here to debate. Such would be painful to my mind and to your soul. Let us in mutual mercy be brief. I ask now once. Cedric Weiland, who is Lucretius Carus?"

And there it is. The question that cannot be danced around, nor turned upon its head. If only the officious fool would argue the nature of the saints, the source of magic or the mystery of existence. Then I could draw forth a thousand clever words. And if he crossed into discussion of the worlds hidden within those points of light we call *stars*... Ha. In an hour I would have him questioning the very earth he thumps with staff.

He repeats the question, the thump. "Twice now I ask. Cedric Weiland, who is Lucretius Carus?"

'*Painful to my soul,*' he'd said. What is 'soul'? A word for the shadow that calls itself 'me'. The saints themselves are shadows; and the Lord of Saints too. All, all, mere shadow. But for shadow to be cast there must be light. Light is Truth, Truth is light. The light of the stars is the fire of infinite suns. The night sky is the only true host of heaven. Their light touches us; and yet knows us not. Light, truth, fire... for a moment I am overcome, shivering before the vision that contains all things, and yet only knows itself through my clay eyes, my trivial mind.

Words. Truth is no tangle of *words*. It is revelation. It may come in a book of perfected formulas describing time and motion. It may come in a quiet hour watching the dawn. Or in a cold night peering at the stars through crafted lenses, perceiving one tiny bit of their nature. No matter the medium, Truth is the only true fire from Heaven. Alas that we cannot pass it on to others, except in words. We must speak of light in words of shadow.

And so I think, and so I shiver, and so the Questioner waits. No doubt knowing full well my thoughts, if not the meaning of my thoughts.

To live dishonest, or die honest?

Such an easy question. Live, of course. Breathe. Give my life to studying shadows, the words of the world. Not end screaming in flames.

And yet... ah, no. No going back to hiding, to obsequious service to a system of idiot ritual. That is just a slower, more degrading fire.

"Thrice I now ask and done," intones the Questioner. Thump of staff. "Cedric Weiland, who is Lucretius Carus?"

I take breath. No doubt one of the few remaining to my life. Unless I escape, granted. That small hope remains, like slight breath upon an ember, keeping it alight. And so strengthened, I give answer.

"Lucretius Carus is the One True Saint."

From the other cells comes cheering, laughing, hissing. Well, I'd forgot we had an audience. Not one that agrees with me, or even follows the argument. Still, these are folk who can appreciate a dramatic stand.

The Questioner shows surprise. Obviously he expected me to equivocate. It occurs to me that my brave answer was meaningless, excepting unto me. They'd have condemned me though I howled my faith in their dogma. No doubt the writs of condemnation are already signed and sealed, the tinder gathered to the stake.

But the man keeps to ceremony. Nods, thumps his staff to say *'we are done now.'* Then walks down the hall, seeking his next subject for review.

I sigh, fold myself upon the floor again. I am trembling with exhaustion. Strange that merely being in a cell, reciting a few words should so tire one.

The guards turn from the Questioner to me, unimpressed. They'd hoped for a fiery debate, prayers, curses and spells shaking the stones. I'd have preferred it myself.

* * *

Jewel of Stonecroft:

"I am absolutely not a witch," I tell the fool of a Questioner. "That's a horrible lie put on me from two evil slimy nasty things named Agat and Hemp."

"And why, hmm, should they do that?"

"Because I found out *they* were witches." I want to add '*dimwit*,' but do not.

"And how did you discover their secret?".

I open eyes wide to show my girlish horror. "Oh, you can smell the dark on their souls like, like sweat off a plow horse. Geese hiss as they pass. Dogs growl and babies shit."

"Hmm," says the man. "And did these two fiends give you the broach with sign of Hecatatia?"

Well, no. I stole that from the farmhouse where I sculleried.

"Sure an' they did. Was ought wrong with it? My blessed mother always said St. Hecatatia was dearest sister to Demetia."

The Questioner nods. "Indeed, they are sacred sisters together. Ordained to the service of the House of the Saints, surely as night and day, as the green fields beneath the sky, and the dark earth below the fields. Demetia has been given sweet revelation of Light. But her sister Hecatatia guards a most dangerous revelation of Darkness."

I consider grabbing his staff, bashing his holy head. He's close enough, and looks stupid enough. But I'm not idiot enough.

"I'm just a kitchen girl, m'lord," I whimper. "How'm I supposed to know these learned matters?"

"No need for you to know, child," he says, and smiles. "What counts is that your betters know. As you said, the stench of dark magic follows a practitioner about. And so we know that you, Jewel Stonecroft, servant girl of the parish of Greencroft, are a witch."

Shit.

"No, no, I'm not." Putting hands to face as if to cover tears. Really, I'm covering teeth that want to snap into his throat.

"But do not despair," continues the pathetic worm of a priest. "You are young, and far brighter than you feign, and less evil than you believe. Poor girl, you fell into bad company. No doubt this Agat and Hemp were indeed witches who appealed to your dark desire to be more than an orphan farmgirl."

Infernum, that hits close. The officious worm has dealt with kitchen maids and widows who slip into the woods by night, seeking power to make the world pay respect.

I say nothing; he blithers on.

"And then came the day your coven sisters turned on you?" Sounding genuinely sympathetic. "Such is the nature of those who corrupt the gifts of our Green Lady Demetia."

I resist an urge to burst into tears, admit his point, my guilt. Neither Agat nor Hemp were *nice*. But I am not nice either. Don't want to be. Nice is for fools and frauds.

I consider his words. They seem suspiciously nice.

"Am I not to be burned?"

"Child, no," chuckles the man. "The parish of Persephone hasn't burned a witch in long years."

Well, *that's* good to hear. I peek between my fingers. He's put on a fatherly look. Now I really want to hit him.

"No, a witch's head is cut away. It's only the remains that are burned. Ashes given to the river, else the crossroads."

"Oh."

"Not that such sad matters apply here. You shall keep your pretty head, young Jewel."

"I shall?"

"Indeed. What point in praising kindly revelation, if we be not kind?"

I remove hands from face, give him hopeful smile. It's not entirely false.

"Then am I to be released?"

He nods. "After branding and a nominal whipping. We shall send you to the Cloister in Pomona. There you will devote your life as penitent servant, learning the kind ways of the Green Saint. And all will be well, and all will be well, and all will yet be well."

Well, shit.

* * *

Val the Bard

Two of my fellow prisoners had the honor of a visit by a fully ordained Questioner of St. Demetia. Parading in holy vestments into this dank place, standing before cell doors to discuss justice and mercy, heresy and truth.

I, mere horse thief, got a justiciar's assistant. He didn't offer conversation. He informed me I'd receive twenty lashes, a 'T' for 'thief' burned upon my right hand. Then I'd be shipped in chains as indentured servant to St. Martia.

He offered to reduce the whipping to fifteen lashes if I took off my shirt. I declined. We both knew he didn't have the authority to remove a single whip-stroke. I offered to kiss whatever parts of himself he put through the bars. Surprisingly, he knew better. Declined, went away.

Pity, that. I'd have made him scream. And not in pleasure.

We prisoners listen as the witch receives a sentence similar to mine; whipping, branding, life-long servitude. Better than having one's head removed. She makes grateful sounds; they ring false as the coiner's wares.

Some of us cheered when the heretic cleric defied the Questioner. I did not. Absurd to die for a philosophical argument. We bards know that folk should die for flags, for gold and glory, for loves and hates. Not arguing whether the wind blows because St. Demetia puffs her lips, or because the sun warms the sky.

Still, one admires courage when one sees it.

Courage is a thing of song, and song is all I have left. I consider that sad fact, and then consider again. An idea occurs.

I need to get a message to Alexandra, the Duke's daughter. The street-waif singing in the street outside the window earns coin from the families of prisoners, fetching items the guards won't mind, raising them to the window on a stick. And she carries messages. She has a strict rule to be paid first. Alas, my coins are all in the pockets of the city gate-guards.

I grasp the window bars, listen to the child. She has no training, and no special talent. But her voice is sweet and the stone wall of the city garrison gives a proper echo.

I wait till her song is finished, then I call down.

"Whisper!"

She doesn't answer. Maybe she can't hear, or chooses not to hear. I tug on the bars. They are thick but rusted. So many folk must have grabbed them just as I do, staring out. Maybe I can tug them away. I give it a try. No; I can't.

"Aye, miss Bard?"

I project my voice loud and confident, as if I sang before a tavern of rowdy drunks.

"If you deliver a message for me, I'll teach you two new songs guaranteed to bring in the glitter."

She is silent. Then,

"Four songs. And they must be good songs."

I know better than not to bargain. She'll have no faith in what I offer too easily.

"Three. But the third will be the best."

"Agreed."

A hard bargain, but I smile.

"Done for a song."

"*Three* songs."

"That's what I meant."

Chapter 32
Your Professor of the Street

Barnaby walked about the room, eyeing, smelling, touching. High ceiling, plaster walls, wooden floor, one wide window. The stench of tallow candles sweetened by fresh rushes, a summery breeze carrying flower smells and sounds of the busy town.

Three narrow beds with straw-filled matting. A table with water pitcher and washing bowl. Barnaby stood before the cracked glass-and-tin mirror, traced a finger along the crack, across his reflected face. Whisper said he scared folk with his axe and leather armor, beard and talking cat. Try as he could, he didn't see aught in the cloudy glass but a Barnaby. Nothing fearful *there*.

Was it the armor? Dark red as dried blood, scarred as some veteran of battle charges and bugle calls. Probably it frightened children. But the sleeves buckled to the shoulders. He unfastened these, pulled them away, enjoying the breeze cooling his arms. Leather was *uncomfortable*. He studied the mirror again. Still seeing just a Barnaby.

He gave reflection up; wandered to the curtain in the corner. Pulled it back to reveal a heavy wooden chair. Why this secret throne? Then spied the chamber pot inserted into the seat. Understanding, he laughed aloud.

"This room is a wonder."

Bodkin sniffed, less impressed.

"The Pomegranate's a decent inn, if you insist on wasting coin. Granted, this room is four bloody flights up."

"Well, I've only ever been to one inn before. Spent the night tied up in the basement. All dark and damp."

"Then this is better. Though a wet basement would be cheaper."

Bodkin took his pack and Barnaby's, began emptying items on the rickety table. The coin bag, the sack of useful items from the necromancer in reward for besting the rat. And the magic harp, shining soft and golden.

That done, the boy leapt on the table, nimble as thimble to thumb. Then jumped higher, grabbing a rafter, pulling himself up. There to meet the eyes of Night-Creep, white and wide.

"Didn't know you were up here."

The cat replied not; but the eyes blinked to say *without doubt, many, many things you do not know.*

Bodkin looked down at Barnaby.

"Right, now toss me the bags."

"Why?"

"Not smart to carry valuables about the town. Folk have a nose for it. We'll hide things up here, lock the door. It's middling safe. Best odds you get in life."

Barnaby nodded, threw the coin bag to the boy, keeping a few for his pockets. Then the bag of magical items. But holding the harp, he hesitated.

"Sure you can catch it now?"

"'Course."

Barnaby readied, then threw the magical wonder upwards; Bodkin snatched it, setting the strings to thrum and chime.

"Now you catch," said Bodkin. Tossing down a silver coin. "Put it under your bed mat."

"Why? For luck?"

Bodkin rolled from the rafter, landing neat upon his feet.

"No, because it's worth a silver to know if anyone has been sneaking about while we aren't here."

"Wise," declared the cat from above.

"Couldn't Professor Night-Creep or Dark Michael keep watch?"

Bodkin shrugged, looking upwards. The answer came down cat-paw quick.

"Beware such error, miller's son. Recall always, I am bound not to guard nor fetch, neither fight nor fend. And your soldier-brute of a dead teacher can but once more aide you with more than words. We *instruct*. If your coins be stole or your throat be cut, that shall be your day's instruction."

"Exact as I thought," declared Bodkin. Sitting himself in a rickety chair, a match to the table's rickets. He brought forth a cloth napkin; untying it to set five rings clattering across the table.

"First off, we sell these. Give me chills, they do."

"They are rings of Nix," declared the cat above. "Each binding seven very angry spirits."

Bodkin reached towards a ring, then pulled his hand back.

"Nix, where folk live in holes underground and scatter treasure to lure wanderers, and the women are beautiful cannibals, naked as newborns?"

Night-Creep yawned. "A reasonable description, if incomplete. You should add that they adore cats."

Barnaby went to the window, peering out at the street below. His eyes chose different figures, following them in their journey. He wondered who they were, what they thought of the day. From this grand height one didn't see faces. Only how arms swung in cheer or grim purpose, and who walked with whom, and at what pace.

He watched a child chase a dog, a woman in flowery skirt argue with a knife-grinder. An old man leaning against a wall, holding out hand to passersby.

A beggar, Barnaby thought. He'd never seen a proper one before. Sometimes folk wandered through Mill Town asking for what scraps of bread or cloth any could spare.

But a proper beggar seemed one of the folk in scriptures and tales. Like knights and kings, highway men, wizards and shepherds who were secretly princes. Barnaby considered tossing down a coin. Deciding it'd likely roll into the gutter, else knock the man dead.

He gazed across the sunlit rooftops where pigeons gathered, flags waved, chimneys puffed smoke, to glimpse a dark ribbon that must be the river Lethe. The city continued beyond that division; but strangely changed.

"Why does it look so different over there? Across the river, as if it were all in cloud shadow."

"That side of the city belongs to St. Plutarch and his clericals," replied Bodkin. "We call it Dark Persephone. We can visit, but you want to step careful when you do."

"Why?"

"The Tarchs put their dead in charge. Their great, great-grandfathers order 'em about, if you can credit it. As they see things, we living folk are just children. To be told what to do till we grow up and die."

"You *are* a child," said Night-Creep. "To be told what to do. Dead or not."

Bodkin made a gesture no doubt meaningful in the world of city alleys. The cat hissed.

Barnaby peered at *Dark Persephone*. Spying streets and houses similar to this side of the river. Fluttering banners, bird-filled trees lining pleasant boulevards. But the banners waved black with somber thought. The trees raised branches solemn as funeral ribbons. The birds circled in slow flight, autumn crows seeking carrion.

"Are the folk there cruel and evil?"

"Not particularly," said Bodkin. "Might even be a bit more civilized. Make us breathing sort look rough and tumble, you understand. But them in charge on that side spent more years being dead than alive. They think different than we do. It's not a wise way to run a life or a kingdom. Not that anyone asked me."

"The Dimarchy of St. Plutarch is ruled jointly by councils of the living and the dead," observed the cat. "Those last are ghosts, revenants and creatures similar to the recently late Pentateuch. Though they exiled him for his unnatural pursuit of natural pleasures."

"Plutarch," considered Barnaby. "Nix, Demetia, Silenus, where the Goat Girl came from. St. Martia, where Val came from though she didn't want to say so. Hefestia, where they made the bronze windup bird. Psamathe, where the ground is just hills of sand and sharp stones... How many kingdoms are in the world?"

"Excellent question," said the cat in the rafters. "We shall cover geography in today's instruction. For each land has its separate genius, and the flow of magic shall work in each by a different nature."

Barnaby sighed. He gazed down at the street, wanting to join the river-like flow of life.

"Meanwhile I'll take these, see what I can get," declared Bodkin, scooping the rings back into the cloth napkin. "There are places docksides that deals with such."

"I think not," said the cat, tone dry and sharp as the desert stones of St. Psamathe.

"You don't trust me?" asked Bodkin.

"Seriously?"

"Well, it's needing to get done. And if you send Barnaby to sell valuables, he'll return with a magic rock that makes soup whensoever you drop it in a pot, say the magic phrase 'soup, please', and then add water, carrots, onions and mutton."

"That would be a fine thing to have," argued Barnaby, suddenly famished. "Are there really such magic stones?"

Bodkin gave the rafters a smile bright as the eyes staring down. Which eyes closed now in pained agreement.

"We take your point. Very well. Return to your ancient thief haunts, oh ancient thief. But take Barnaby with you. We shall call that today's lesson."

* * *

First thing on the street, Bodkin hurried to a cart selling sausage and roasted apples.

"Lunch," the boy declared.

"Exactly my thought," agreed Barnaby. Had he been with Michael or Night-Creep, they'd have dismissed his belly-growls as the whining of weak and living flesh. Was that how things went in Plutarch? The breathing folk having to remind their older, wiser masters that eating and sleeping were necessities?

The two living boys purchased whatever smelled freshest, sizzled loudest. Then walked on, munching, enjoying being not dead. Barnaby looked at the apple, the sausage, the pretty town about him and laughed loud in total satisfaction.

A large dog ran in front of them, halting to block their path. Barnaby eyed it. White, almost hairless, with red eyes that studied the boys.

"Bide still a sec," advised Bodkin.

The dog extended muzzle, sniffed Barnaby, sniffed Bodkin. Gave a longing glance to the sausages, then darted away.

"That's done," declared Bodkin, walking on.

"What was that?"

"Hmm. Death Hound from across the river. The Tarchs send 'em to sniff for dead folk who've snuck across, pretending to be on live. Demetia puts up with it, since folk this side don't want Tarch misbegots wandering about either. Still, you hear those dogs serve as spies for the Black Robes."

"I can't picture a land run by ghosts and dead folk,' said Barnaby. "Are they like to Michael?"

"Is he about now?" asked Bodkin, looking left, right, up, behind.

"Dunno. He's not fond of daylight, nor being seen by others."

"Well, your friend seems different. More in the here and now. But nothing dead properly recalls what a living body needs." He finished the apple, tossed the core to the gutter. A flock of pigeons rushed upon it. "Not that most folk breathing are any wiser."

He hitched up his overlarge coat, revealing he still bore the sword stolen from Pentateuch.

Barnaby finished his own apple with a happy crunch; tossing the core to the pigeons.

Bodkin led on, skipping at times. Down an alley, up a tree-lined street of shops, past a pond where a swan sailed proud as royal schooner, followed by paddling cygnets.

"Up here's the Bright Market," declared Bodkin. "To be distinguished from the Dark Market across the river."

They entered a great airy plaza of flowering trees and sparkling founts. Booths and barrows, tents and blankets set upon the ground, all to display wares of use practical and impractical; edible, wearable, readable, thaumaturgical and inexplicable.

"Lucif's teapot kiss me to Nix," whispered an awed Barnaby.

"What do what?"

Barnaby shook his head, staring at the crowd. How many souls did he now see? He'd have to stand on a rooftop, tell everyone to stand still while he counted.

"Stop gaping like a miller who wandered into civilization," warned Bodkin. "Look bored and angry."

Barnaby did his best, wondering the purpose of such a face. They went to a flower-vined stand where a woman cooked something more aromatic than any delicacy upon the feast-table of the House of Saints. Behold tiny cakes dusted with sugar and cinnamon. Bodkin took five in exchange for a penny.

Barnaby tasted. It astounded his tongue as the crowd did his eyes. He tried looking angry and bored, the woman only laughed, gave him a wink and an extra sugar cake.

They wandered on, sampling other delights. Barnaby bought a leather-sheathed shaving razor, no common knife. Bodkin purchased a set of strange wires like keys come apart. Barnaby bought an awl and sinew for patching boots and armor. Bodkin purchased a hat of stiff felt, rather like Pentateuch's. He fixed the wire keys into the brim, set to a jaunty angle.

Another white dog of red eyes and hungry gaze stopped before Barnaby.

"Again?" said Bodkin. "Bother the suspicious critters. Hold still."

Barnaby did not; he met the dog's red gaze, held hand slowly out.

The beast sniffed, making a sound neither growl nor bark; some comment to itself concerning scents and millers. Commentary complete, it trotted away.

"They take an interest in you, Master Miller. Might be your association with ghosts and magic cats."

"Michael hasn't been a ghost for long. And sometimes Night-Creep looks like a man. I've a question."

"Excellent," declared Bodkin. "I am your professor of the street." He bowed. Barnaby laughed.

"So, Professor Bodkin, why do you keep stopping me from paying?"

Bodkin grinned. "As a rule I prefer folk who are quicker'n me to open their purse. Turn this way, it's a shortcut to the jeweler's borough.

Barnaby followed the boy down a side alley. The upper stories leaned over the walkway, making a pleasantly shadowed path.

"Me paying first is just till you learn the steps of the dance. How much a coin should fetch. When to trust, when not. When to keep mum, when to stamp feet and shout."

Bodkin leaped upon a doorstep so as put eyes near on level with Barnaby's.

"First rule, Master Miller. Never ever show a single extra penny on the street. Nor in tavern nor market. You'll be spied for a mark quick as lit candlewick."

"By who?"

"Hmm, cutpurses. Else the sort that cut throats."

Bodkin jumped down. "Here comes your first lesson."

Barnaby looked about. Spying no lessons. Only friendly town folk busy on a summer day.

"Where?" he asked. "Who?"

"New to the city, sirs?" asked a man in long coat, long beard.

Barnaby nodded. Bodkin nodded. The bearded man nodded.

"Knew it so. You'll be wise to hire a guide."

"Would we?" asked Bodkin, eyes wide in surprise. "Are there things to see?

"Oh, aye. See that spire?" The man pointed up into the strip of visible sky.

Barnaby stared up. "The one with the blue banners?"

"No, next to it. With the silver trim. That's the Duke's very own favorite balcony. His noble eyes stare down upon us all from there, they do."

Barnaby searched the sky for sight of a Duke, till someone crashed into him. Far smaller, they bounced away, scarce rocking Barnaby. Bodkin shouted in surprise, jumped, knocking into the bearded man. They flailed and pushed away from one another.

Barnaby looked down to find a child in tangles and tatters of red dress, sitting on the cobbles, staring up at him.

"Oh, sorry, sorry, sorry, sorry.. Ouch. Sorry."

"You hurt?" he asked.

"Sorry," whimpered the girl. She sat staring up wide-eyed with fear. "Aren't gonna hit me, no? Sorry, sorry."

Barnaby shook his head, reached down, offered his hand. She took it, jumped up again.

"Kind," she said. "Kind, kind, kind," and reached round, gave him a hug. Then ran off.

Bodkin laughed.

"Street riffraff," growled the stranger. "Pay them no mind, and give them no coin."

With that, he walked on. Barnaby watched him go, puzzled.

"I thought he wanted to be our guide?"

Bodkin continued to shake with laughter, till he had to prop himself against a wall. Barnaby grew annoyed.

"Is it so amusing to talk to folk?"

"Nah," said the boy, wiping his eyes. "It's amusing that I'm tasked to teach you city ways, and the lessons come upon us like ducks to fresh bread. We were talking about coin. How much did you have in the pocket of your pack?"

Barnaby considered. "One gold, four silver, eight copper." He reached, searched about. Puzzlement on his face to find... a scattering of smooth stone disks.

"What are these?"

"Fishnet weights," said Bodkin. He took the stones, walking down the street, tossing them to bounce against the wall.

"First the bearded fellow sized you up, figured where you kept your coin. Then signaled the girl, drew our attention. She bangs into you, swaps coin for stones. Easy as eating pie."

"She was a, a pickpocket?"

"Aye. A good one. They work in teams."

"You saw all that?"

"Ah, no, too fast. You don't see the good ones. You just know from the empty feel in your pockets, 'Less they've gone the extra dance step of adding stones."

Bodkin reached within his coat, pulling out three gold coins, "He didn't see it either, when I bumped into him, emptied his privy bank." He proffered one to Barnaby.

Barnaby stopped, shook his head. Took the coin. Staring at it. *Stolen gold*. Weighing heavy in his hand with sin and adventure.

"Now, the best place for coin is in a front pants pocket," declared Bodkin. "A fellow pays attention to what goes on thereabouts."

"Where are you keeping the rings?"

"Oh, those lovelies go in my inner coat. Don't want the nasty magic things too close to..."

Bodkin felt about, surprise taking his coffee-dark face "Oh, shove my idiot head up all seven of Lucif's asses."

"What?"

"They're gone! When I took his coin, he took the rings. Shit-shit-shit!"

Oath uttered thrice, Bodkin ran off down the street.

Barnaby hesitated, then hurried after. But the boy dodged in and out of passersby with far greater dexterity. Barnaby came to a corner, looking about, uncertain where Bodkin had gone.

Should he return to the Pomegranate? Seemed more sensible than wandering, getting lost. But Bodkin might be counting on him to follow.

A child in tatters of red darted past, fox before the hound. The very girl who'd stole *his* coin.

"Hey, you," he commanded. "Come back here."

She looked wide-eyed, hurried on the faster. Barnaby pursuing.

"Someone got their pockets emptied," laughed an onlooker.

"Get the brat!" shouted another. But most on the street simply stepped out of the way.

The girl darted into an alley where the upper stories to left and right overhung, all but making a tunnel. Barnaby could see little in the gloom; but followed flashes of red. Coming to a crossway, he turned left. There the girl stood some twenty feet ahead, at an open door.

"Go away, go away, go away," she shouted, making an awful face. Then vanished within the doorway.

Barnaby wondered what to shout back. *'Stop, thief?'* The girl had his money. But Barnaby had one of the bearded fellow's coins taken by Bodkin. Granted, the bearded fellow had Pentateuch's rings. Which Barnaby and Bodkin had *sort* of stolen but not exactly. And where was Bodkin, Professor of the Streets?

Barnaby settled for a firm *'come back'* and hurried after. Came to the doorway, wood framed, still open. Stepping inside, struggling to see.

He found himself in a dark cave of a building that smelled of wet brick, old mold. Direct before his feet waited a wide circular pit some twelve feet deep, twenty feet across. Barnaby all but tumbled over the edge. He leaned backwards, windmilling arms.

Balance recovered, he looked about. The pit was some sort of cistern, like the one where Mill Town stored water for dry summers. Where was the girl?

Her red rags glimmered on the far side of the pit. Had she fallen in? She might be hurt. But a rope waited at his feet. She must have climbed down, now she hid, knowing she'd reached flight's end. Excellent. He had her sure as rabbit in snare. He'd order her to lead him to the bearded man. That would lead to Bodkin and the rings. Lesson in city streets concluded.

Barnaby climbed down the rope, settling in the gloom of the pit. The girl did not move. Was she hurt? He approached, bent down, poked. Well, it wasn't any girl. Just a bundle of bright red rags.

A child's happy laugh from behind confirmed his suspicion. He'd been tricked. *The rope*, he thought, and rushed back. But it was already snaking up the cistern wall. He leaped for it, fell back with empty hands.

"Caught a fish!" shouted the girl. "Fish, fish, fish."

"Excellent," said a man's voice. "Your catch is bigger. But mine was slipperier."

Upon the cistern edge appeared the bearded man. Carrying a struggling Bodkin.

"I'm going to drop him down to you." He said to Barnaby. "All ready?"

"Fuck you to Infernum's fifth circle of catamites, you sod of a –" began Bodkin. The man released the boy. Barnaby held out arms, caught the falling boy. Set him down.

Bodkin pushed away, moving to the center of the pit, turning around warily to examine the trap. He stopped of a sudden, staring.

Barnaby followed his gaze. Upon the pit edge opposite their captors, perched a cat. Black against the shadows, with eyes white as summer clouds in bright sun.

The cat licked a paw in thought. Then stretched over the edge of the pit, letting itself fall. Halfway down it kicked hind feet against the wall, flew forwards to land in acrobatic elegance. Thence it strode casually to Barnaby. Leaping up, it settled itself upon a shoulder.

Bodkin growled.

"Don't start your lecturing, you mad feline."

Night-Creep yawned. "Today's lecture was *your* work, boy." The cat looked about at the dim pit imprisoning them.

"Proceeding, hmm, about as expected."

Chapter 33
Has he not a Rogue's Face?

"Look brooding and scary," whispered Bodkin.
"Me?"
"You. I'm the talker. You're the loomer."
"The which?"
"The nasty bruiser that looms behind, hoping for trouble."

Barnaby nodded. "Very well, then." He stood tall, stretching shoulders till leather armor creaked, working mouth and eyes into a scowl that said *dangerous*.

Bodkin turned attention to the bearded man, the girl in red. These creatures observed the boys from the comfort of standing above and beyond the pit.

"Let's start with proper introduction," declared Bodkin. Crossing arms, voice confident as king in the kitchen. "I'm Jack Knife. This here is my associate Mr. Axe. You?"

The man and girl gave no answer. They began casually circling the pit, towards a platform with a table and lantern. Arrived, the man sat in a chair, dropping Bodkin's magic sword to the table as though it were a thing of no importance. Bodkin growled low. Night-Creep chuckled.

Next the man began working to light the lamp upon the table. While the girl sat herself on the edge of the pit, staring at its prisoners. Legs dangling, kicking bare feet out, in, out. Clearly restless to be running or dancing.

Lantern finally, finally alight, the bearded man now began work on a pipe. Bodkin sighed, waited. At length the man puffed smoke in satisfaction, and spoke.

"I see you know the protocol, young sir. As it happens, I am Master Crow. This is my associate Magpie."

"Hi," said Magpie. She gave a cheerful wave. Barnaby waved back. Bodkin gave him a sideways kick while addressing Crow.

"We want out and our loot back. What's it going to cost?"

"He's a businesslike sort," observed Crow to Magpie. The girl nodded agreement. The man took a long pipe-puff of consideration.

"I recollect I offered myself as your guide. Allow me to continue sharing the wonders of Persephone. Now, where you stand this very moment is a retaining well for when the waters of dark Lethe rise. Generally in the rains of spring. You will have already noted the pipe opening, I assume? That leads by winding ways to the river."

Barnaby looked about, spying a dark hole in the floor. Too narrow for a miller's shoulders. Bodkin might navigate it.

"Now if you are thinking of exiting through those pipes, sir, makes sure to stop and appreciate the many and various rats, snakes and less canny nasties."

"Nasty," agreed the girl. "Nasty, nasty, nasty."

The man stopped to puff a smoke ring that drifted over her head. She giggled, attempting to catch it, near tumbling into the pit. The man smiled, continuing his lecture.

"Nasty indeed. The sewers of Persephone make an exciting maze of pipes, pits, tunnels and bends. Each with their separate and special fauna. Perhaps more exciting than a visitor wishes. I recall a particular area we locals call *The Bone Room*. The reasons for the name are dark but fascinating."

Night-Creep yawned, whispered to Bodkin. "Is he boring us with his travelogue for some hidden purpose?"

Bodkin did not look to the cat, but whispered reply.

"Yeah. Means to keep us here till sundown."

"Why?"

"Night gives him leverage. We're in the center of town, not the docks. Daylight, a wandering watch might take it into their heads to sniff about. If so, Crow can claim he's naught to do with our trespass. But come sundown he'll do as he pleases. Say, practice his crossbow, hauling any accident victims over the river, selling 'em to the Tarchs."

"That's awful," whispered Barnaby. Scowling at the bearded man. Who puffed smoke rings, passively observing their discussion.

Bodkin shrugged to declare his indifference to moral judgements.

"Well, he'd rather not have matters come to blood. Knows he's already made profit with the rings and sword. But... he's greedy. And curious. Needs to be sure there isn't more swag to be had. So we've time to think. Let's sit."

With that command, Bodkin moved to the center of the pit, sitting tailor-fashion upon the bricks. Barnaby did the same.

"Keep back to back," whispered Bodkin. "Don't know who might be hiding about with a crossbow."

"Right," said Barnaby. Turned, putting his back to Bodkin's. Finding the view less interesting. Just a circular brick wall. He focused on a patch of cheerful sunlight from a hole in the distant roof.

He wondered how Crow and Magpie lived. Were they father and daughter, or just master and apprentice? Did they eat supper at a table of family and friends? On winter evenings did they sit by a hearth, listening to tales? As they walked down the streets looking for folk to wrong, did they sing songs, make old jokes? Could Magpie whistle?

"I see you are settling in for a rest," declared Crow. "For a reasonable fee our tour service will provide food and drink."

"What about a rope?" asked Bodkin.

"It just so happens I have that very item. What length would you require?"

"Enough to get out of this hole."

"Ah. I should have guessed. Magpie, do we have on hand a rope of, hmm, pit-length?"

The girl nodded, pointing to the rope that Barnaby had descended, and she'd raised again. Crow stamped a foot, satisfied.

"Well, you're in luck today, Mr. Knife. Seems we have just such a rope for those in the market. I am now prepared to hear a bid on this object of amazing utility. Starting bid is two hundred gold, else an item of worth equal to said sum."

"I'll consult my colleague," replied Bodkin. To Barnaby he whispered, "Keep any spells in your pocket that can do aught here?"

Barnaby considered. "I can cast a light. Do a healing, though it will knock me flat for the day. I can make my eyes see things according to Professor Night-Creep though I haven't seen anything yet that wasn't already there to be seen. I can open things, and tell if there is something magic about. I can start a fire if there is anything to burn."

"Don't see use in any of that," sighed Bodkin. "Sorry."

"Don't be," said the boy. "This is my cock-up."

"Exact so," agreed the cat.

Barnaby looked about for a brooding ghost-soldier. "I could ask Dark Michael for his third favor."

"Lucif's hot shit pot," spat Bodkin. "Waste your last wish to deal with a trash-picking alley-sneak amateur like Crow? Never. It's the job of your Professor of the Streets to untangle this lesson. Let me consider. There's a hole in every net."

They sat silent while the boy ruminated for a hole. Barnaby watched the patch of sunlight travel slowly up the cistern wall. If he only knew an oration that turned folk to light, they could do the same. Granted, you didn't need orations to move things.

"I could toss you high enough to grab the edge," offered Barnaby. "You don't look heavier than a sack of flour."

Bodkin laughed. "Don't need anyone tossing me. Give me a run at that wall and I'd go more'n half up it before slowing. Grab the top easy. But Crow's keeping a crossbow undersides the table. Odds are good he'd do me in before I got out the door."

"And should odds favor you, still it leaves the miller in this pit," pointed out the cat, tone sarcastic as only a cat's can be.

"Still," pondered Bodkin, "if I *did* get out and away, I could run to the inn. Fetch gold, hire a couple of rowdies to come bounce Crow.... but that's still no good. Soon as I feel safe, Crow won't feel safe. At best he'd leave Barnaby here alive. For spite and quietude he might leave him dead."

Barnaby pointed to the floor beside them. "What about the hole into the sewers?"

"Same catch in the plan. I know those pipes like a popular whore knows the bishop's thumb. But you're too big. It'd still mean leaving you to Crow."

They sat silent again. Barnaby watched the patch of sunlight travel slow as minute hand up the wall. Evening settled upon the world outside; turning the pit into a well of shadows. Crow seemed content to let them sit. Was he watching? Barnaby turned, peering over Bodkin's shoulder.

Magpie lay curled sleeping on the pit edge, While Crow now held a great glass lens to something glittering. One of the five stolen rings. The bearded thief stared into the glass, seemingly fascinated.

"He'd best be careful of that Nix ring," muttered Barnaby.

"Now there's an idea," replied Bodkin. He yawned, stretched, then stood.

"Instruction time," declared the cat. Leaping from Barnaby's shoulder.

"Now?"

"My clever kitty head says you have need to learn a new spell now right now."

"What spell?"

"*Circle of Protection from Evil*. I'm going to teach you the basic oration now. Very much exactly *now*."

While they began class in the shadows, Bodkin addressed Crow. Young voice echoing across the bricks.

"We have reached a consensus."

At this announcement, Magpie awoke, sitting up, yawning, rubbing eyes, near tumbling into the pit. Crow laid down his jeweler's lens, leaned back in his chair, pipe-puffing away. Eyes bright by lantern light, shining with amusement.

"Have you now? Is your consensus to purchase our rope? I'm afraid the price has risen during your long consultation."

"Doesn't surprise me a bit. But a favor first."

"Favor? Alas, we do strict barter in this city."

"No cost to you, my word and spit."

Crow shrug. "Fair enough. What's your request?"

"Show me your face. Minus the silly beard."

Crow and Magpie exchanged looks; two matching scowls.

"That's not wisely asked, young sir."

At which warning Bodkin chuckled.

"If I were wise, would I be in a hole buying rope from an alley pick-me-pocket? Humor the customer."

Crow shrugged, finding no argument. He reached, unfastened strings about his ears. Tossed away the hairy thing to become of a sudden clean chinned as a fish.

"Ah, thought so," declared Bodkin. And of all things, he laughed. "You're a Swyke, am I right?"

Crow gave up his easy slouch, sitting straight. Magpie opened eyes and mouth in surprise.

"A who? Never heard the name in me life."

"Ah, now, now," chided Bodkin. "But the girl's no Swyke. Them's the red tangles of a Swynth. Could she be baptized for the talented Margaret Swynth? Ah, Maggie could steal the back teeth of a constable, just with her tongue."

"Oy!" shouted Magpie, stamping foot. "Oy, oy, oy!"

Crow waved her to silence.

"Maggie Swynth was my young associate's grandmother, as it happens. Who are you? I confess, you look kick-me-to-Infernum familiar."

"I'm exactly nobody. But out of curiosity, who'd Maggie marry?"

Crow laughed. "Was no *marrying*. Just the usual fornicate and fare-thee-well. With Mercutio Moon himself, tale says."

"Ah," said Bodkin. And kept silent, staring at Magpie awhile. The girl defied his attention by sticking out tongue, gesturing with fingers.

Crow shook his head.

"I deduce your rascal features declare you a Moon. Do they not, youngster?"

Bodkin sighed, nodded.

Crow laughed.

"No surprise there, nor overmuch shame. Not a family man, old Mercutio Moon, for all he kept the maiden population in a family way. Damn his busy member to Lucif's dogs, but between his glorious thefts he fathered all a nation of pickpockets, cut-throats, whores and wall-breakers."

Bodkin said nothing. Crow waited in seeming pity. At last Bodkin spoke.

"Well, that's all dust and no matter. Let's get to business. Do you know aught of the ring you hold?"

Crow sniffed at the object in his hand.

"Probably as much as you, Mister Moon. I mean to say, Mister Knife."

"Excellent. Then send the child out. Let's not see her hurt."

"I take that as a threat, youngster."

"You should, oldster. It *is* a threat. That's a ring of Nix. Imprisons the very nastiest sort of undead, it does. Drop one and you're in the soup pot."

"Dangerous, hmm? But that makes it valuable."

"Valuable to me. Deadly to you. If'n I pronounce the charm, they'll be out and about their business. Under my control. I'm hoping. Damned things haven't been fed lately.

"Uhm," said Magpie. Looking at Crow, the ring, then towards the door. "Uhm, uhm."

"You hush," growled Crow.

Bodkin yawned, smiled.

"I'll kindly give you half a minute to consult, then scarper. But not a full minute."

Crow bent down to Magpie; they whispered. Arguing, waving hands in emphasis of pro and con. Bodkin waited, studying the face of the girl in the lamplight.

Meanwhile, Barnaby and Night-Creep continued their quick magical lesson.

"You have the words in your head now?"

"Think so, sir, yes sir."

"Shame we can't test."

"I could try now."

"No point. Opportunity rushes upon you."

Barnaby waved the wand in the air, muttering to himself till Crow called loudly across the chamber.

"We have reached our own consensus, Mister Knife."

"And that is?" asked Bodkin.

"We believe… you bluff."

There came silence. Barnaby felt puzzled, as he'd not followed the discussion. But Bodkin nodded.

"You sure?" asked Bodkin. Shook one hand, then the other, holding them before him as though readying some master work. "There's no calling these devils back once I say the charm. My advice is you make a run for the door now, else peace with your preferred saint."

Magpie looked from Crow to Bodkin, fear on her face. But Crow shook his head.

"Bluff," he repeated.

There came a long silence; then Bodkin laughed.

"Got me good," he said. Lightly as laying down a bad hand of cards in a game of no stakes. "Was worth a try."

"I admire your spirit," declared the thief. "And so it pains me what comes next."

But what came next was Bodkin running straight at the wall of the pit. Directly beneath where Crow and Magpie presided. He leaped, running up the bricks, reaching high to grab the edge.

Magpie shrieked, kicking him in the face. Bodkin did not stop to complain. He pulled himself up and over, rolling past the girl, around a kick from Crow, and vanished in the shadows under the table.

Crow cursed, jumping from his chair. Reaching for the crossbow. Bodkin struggled to gain it first. Together they overturned the table. Five rings of Nix fell to the floor making cheerful metallic *clink, clank*, rolling purposefully towards the pit.

Magpie rushed to catch them, but they dodged her hands as though alive. She scrambled for one then another, at last tumbling with a screech over the edge into the shadows below.

One, two, three, four, five rings followed.

As each struck the pit floor there came no *clink*. No, each ring shattered with the crystal thunder of a solemn mirror struck by a laughing hammer.

"Well," observed Night-Creep. "That went about as expected."

The chamber filled with an awful smell of sulfur and rot; an unpleasant mist that glowed soft and red as sunset reflected from a pool of blood. Within the fog appeared eyes of various colors and shapes. Crimson eyes sharp as knives, and violet eyes round as sockets of a skull. Fiery eyes slotted like a goat's, and eyes like candle-flames of black.

A muttering came from the mist; growling, snarling, growing. More eyes appeared.

"Magpie!" called Crow and Bodkin together. Crow held the crossbow; Bodkin held the magic sword. Both peered over the pit edge into the red mist below.

"Here!" came her shout. "Help, help, help, help. Help."

"I'll get the rope," shouted Crow, and darted away.

Bodkin hesitated, then leaped into the pit.

Barnaby moved to join him, but the cat hissed, claws digging into shoulder.

"Idiot. Cast the spell. And do it above the grating to the sewer."

Barnaby resisted the urge to argue. Instead he took a firm stand, a firm breath, and held out the wand. Finding that the tip now gave a soft shine of green. A calming sight, just the shade of sun on a new leaf. The color reminded of green summer days. Sitting with the Goat Girl while she chattered in her incomprehensible tongue. And the cabbage field where he'd watched a baby be born. He smelled again the scent of pine and death as he'd sat with the fevered Val. All the bright growing places seen in his short life seemed suddenly before him, within him, part of him.

He began turning in a slow circle, chanting.

"We thank you for the life we have.
We thank you for the life we had.
Green days, bright fire.
Never let the light expire."

Strange, he thought. The words never come out the way Night-Creep teaches. Just something like them.

Still, he felt the now-familiar pull of strength from his body, as though he lifted a full barrel of flour upon a cart. His hand trembled with the weight of the wand. Green-gold light played out, dancing, weaving like strands of fire in the air as he struggled to complete the spell.

Bodkin appeared from out the red fog, holding Magpie, who struggled and cursed. Behind them, still in the mist, danced the shadows of strange beings. Ever more eyes, more figures; and their growling and howling grew loud as storm wind.

"Into the circle, idiots," shouted the cat.

Bodkin rushed to place himself near as could be to Barnaby, who continued to turn, chanting till at last the circle of light was complete. At which the strings of green and gold shivered, winding together. Now holding fast as words carved in stone.

Barnaby shuddered, feeling spent as if he'd done all a day's work in a moment.

Beyond the circle, the red fog filled the pit. Silhouettes of skeletal beings now gave the eyes shape and form. The creatures howled, snarled, edging closer to the green-gold circle of protection. At last, surrounding it.

Bodkin put down Magpie. She gave an outraged kick, then fell to the ground, wrapping arms tight about knees and head.

"That didn't go well," said Bodkin. Shouting above the howls.

"On the contrary," observed Night-Creep upon Barnaby's shoulder. Somehow not shouting, yet perfectly hearable. "With no slight to my pupil, I expected to be witnessing the dismal scene of you all being torn to bits."

"What happens now?"

"You stand here until the barrier fails, then you are torn to bits."

Bodkin stamped foot.

"How long till then?"

"At best, sunrise. At worst, any moment."

They stood silent, watching the red fog dissipate. But the creatures did not vanish. Ten, twenty, thirty and more forms of bone and rotted flesh, horn and teeth now crowded the pit, circling the gold-green barrier.

There came a shout from Crow, safely out of the pit.

"Can you get to the rope?" He stood by the door, waving the crossbow.

"No," shouted Bodkin.

"Infernum, that's a pity," replied the man.

"That one is climbing out," observed Barnaby. "And that one." They watched a skeleton slither up the wall easy as a cockroach. Followed by another and another.

Crow observed the same. "I'm out of here," he shouted. "Luck to all." With that, he disappeared through the doorway.

"Never cared much for the Swykes," observed Bodkin.

"Who?"

"Crow's clan. Thieves. Lacked the style the Moon's always kept."

"Oh?"

A thing like a man turned inside out rushed straight at the magic circle. When it hit there came a flash of green; the creature was thrown back, howling in rage and agony.

At that, more of the creatures climbed the pit wall, slouching and loping to the exit and out. But some continued to circle them, testing the barrier. Waiting.

"If it fails, can you cast the oration again?" asked Bodkin. To his eye, the gold-green glow already faded.

"Don't think so," admitted Barnaby. "It's like holding a barrel of flour over my head. I can do it once. Then I need a rest."

"Thought so. Here's the plan, then." Bodkin bent down, pulled at the rusted iron grating at their feet. With Barnaby's help, they pulled it away.

"I can get myself and the girl out through the pipe," declared Bodkin. "Then I fetch the watch, bring 'em here. Persephone's forever on the lookout for undead. They'll be on this lot like mastiffs on rabbits."

Barnaby considered the flaw in the plan. *Time*. But it'd have occurred to Bodkin too. So he nodded.

"Then do it. If the circle fails first I'll just cut my way to the rope with Dragontooth."

"Right. Magpie, let's be off. We're taking a tour of Seph's piping."

The girl uncurled, sat up, looking from Bodkin to the hole.

"Don't like it down there."

"You like it better here?"

She looked about at the milling crowd of angry dead. Shivered, shook head. "You first."

Bodkin nodded. "Mr. Miller, if I don't find you here, I'll meet you back at the inn.

"Can you manage crawling through such dark places?"

"Who, me? Done it plenty of times."

Bodkin grinned, bright smile on dark face. But his eyes held darker opinion of the venture.

Barnaby gave him a rap on the shoulder, like Da used to do when sending him on some chore for the day.

"Right, then, boyo. Good luck."

Bodkin nodded, and slipped into the hole easy as head to hat. His voice echoed up. "I'm down. Your turn, Magpie. Not a hard jump."

The girl swore softly if unladylike, slipping legs over the hole, then waist, then head, then disappeared within.

The cat on Barnaby's shoulder now jumped down, staring with angel-wing eyes into the hole. Whisker-tasted the damp and dank rising up.

"Miller's son, as my instruction is done today, I believe I will tour these fabled tunnels myself."

"Oh," said Barnaby. "Well then. Farewell."

The cat snorted. "Idiot. I don't abandon you. But I consider the rogue to be in your service. As such, I serve you by granting him my advice. He's going to need it down there. And I can do no more here. The next lesson is for your other, lesser instructor."

These words said, the cat slipped into the pipe.

But up from the dark rose his voice. Singing brightly, for all the pain it gave the ear.

"I am a cat. I prowl the slimy city sewer.
Ssshh, my footstep silent, sure.
Whiskers taste the air's allure,
Stygian gaze a blazing skewer
For every rodent evil doer."

And now Barnaby stood alone, circled by the capering, snarling, dancing dead. He counted ten. The rest had grown impatient, left to haunt the city.

He returned wand to belt, drew Dragontooth from its sheath on his back. The blade felt comforting to grasp.

Five shadow-fiends turned, climbing from the pit. Perhaps bored, perhaps not liking the sight of Dragontooth. The remaining creatures paced before the fading barrier, edging ever closer. Barnaby stared into their fiery eyes. Like the embers of burning rainbows. Beautiful and bright; mad and hungry.

Beyond the pit, Crow's lamp had fallen to the floor but kept alight, providing a bit of normal light. Now Barnaby noted someone standing at the edge of its glow. A somber form in soldier's coat, hat low over eyes, arms crossed in patient pose.

"Master Michael," said Barnaby. Heart jumping in relief to not be alone.

The ghost replied with the very slightest of nods.

"You'd best replace the grating, or risk stepping a foot into that hole."

Barnaby looked down. The soldier was right. Barnaby pushed the grating back with a boot. The barrier's glow dimmed further. Michael continued his laconic advice.

"Do not charge for the rope. They would tear you to pieces as you climbed. Seek to put your back to the wall."

Barnaby gave a longing glance to the rope, the doorway beyond. But nodded; his teacher surely had the right of it.

"These creatures are shadow-fiends of Infernum," observed Dark Michael. "Damned souls steeped in mindless anger. You have two advantages. One, the creatures do not work together. Two, you need no magic but your axe to send them back."

Barnaby nodded. Waved the axe at the watching eyes. They tilted their skeletal heads, studying Barnaby, the dented blade.

The last light of the magic barrier flickered, faded; vanished.

"And now to your work, pupil," said the ghost. The angry spirits charged.

Barnaby swung his axe.

Chapter 34
Three Escapes

Friar Cedric:

By nights there is but one guard for our corridor. Fifteen cells; ten occupied. Clearly Persephone is no hotbed of criminality. A door separates the corridor from the rest of the gaol; that door can only be opened from outside. Our cell keys are locked in a cabinet beside the lone night guard. He does not keep the key to the cabinet. That's kept in the outer guard room.

Our night watcher waits in his chair beside a bell rope to sound alarum should we somehow walk through stone and iron. Meanwhile he sits reading in the pleasant glow of the oil lamp. What a peaceful, excellent job.

The book is leather bound and heavy. The *'Baptismus Deorum'* by Brendon himself. Describing the conversion of the ancient deities, demiurges and archons of old, baptizing them into the blessed House of Saints. A problematic work only allowed the most advanced students of history and theology.

Its subject is forever on my mind. Vital to the truth of the Lucretians. I feel an urge to call out from my cell, ask his opinions, share my own. I resist. There is other work tonight, and should I argue eloquently, what would I achieve? Naught but the good man thrown to the fire as my fellow heretic.

So I ignore his book, and fix upon the flower in the pot beside his lamp. The sweet city of Persephone is full of flowers, even in this sad place of damp stone, dark iron.

The particular flower is a periwinkle. A pretty name, worth recalling in full. *Per omne vinculum:* 'through every bond'. Astonishing at times, these accidental meetings of word and reality.

I contemplate the flower while my fellow prisoners rest quiet. Even the bard, who has been singing all day to some urchin in the street. Pretty songs, I admit.

I close my eyes, thinking upon Sainted Demetia. Talking to her as I oft did in the cell of my quiet cottage in Mill Town.

Blessed saint, I believe in you not. You are a creation of men's minds. A face in the clouds, a voice in the summer wind blowing across the fields. Your heartbeat is the life of the earth, the warmth of spring, the light in the clouds. We hear your song in the hum of the bees, the choir of birds with each sunrise. Your voice, your heart, your face... these remain mere wind, light, cloud, animal motion and sound. As I myself am but shadow of self, composed of earth and water, dream and bone. And so to you I call, oh saint, and ask your blessing from one shadow to another.

Certainly not the authorized catechism; but I feel the peace of the saint calm me, strengthen me, as lines of prayer-book praise long ago ceased to do.

I open my eyes, staring across the corridor to the charm above the witch's door. The *Greater Charm of Inhibition*, preventing the witch from casting.

It is a thing well-made; a plate of silver and bronze melded to form a stern face, eyes open in determined guard. To my opened senses it gives a faint buzzing, like a bee nestled into blossom.

"Peace", I whisper to it. "Peace. Sleep now, and let others take the watch of the night."

The soft glow does not diminish; the inaudible hum does not lessen.

The usual voices of doubt chatter in the chapel of my mind. I have offended the saint, I have fallen into mad doctrine. Perhaps. But I have stood for the Truth, daring the fire. It shall suffice! It *must* suffice.

I raise right hand; not in plea, but in authority.

"I am Father Cedric of the order of the Most Blessed Saint Demetia. Sleep, servant of the saint. Your watch is done. Mine now the duty. Sleep, watcher."

The witch stands, hands grasping bars, staring at me. My body is beginning to tremble, as it does in true prayer.

"Sleep, now, servant of the saint," I command.

And the glow flickers, the humming dims. The eyes of the charm close, slowly as poppy petals at sun's setting.

Done. I feel exhausted. Because of course it was I doing the work, not any imaginary saintly lady in the clouds or under the floor. The floor to which I now sink.

The witch's face shows surprise. Well, she hadn't thought I could do it. I consider the creature. Not as ally in escape, but fellow traveler upon this world's rough roads. She is young, her face pinched with hunger and bitterness. No doubt she's spent her life in hard places, cold homes. Well, the House of Saints has other messengers than warm, green Demetia. Their lessons are harsh, their blessings leave scar.

Now the witch lifts her hands, stares at them, weighing the feel of invisible forces. Attempts to peer up at the charm, though it is beyond her view. Finally she nods to admit: *it worked*.

Her turn to reciter orations. Let us hope her standing with Demetia's dark sister shall suffice.

* * *

Jewel:

As if being locked in a cage awaiting whipping and branding, followed by lifetime servitude to simpering nuns were not enough... I must endure theologic lectures. Given by my fellow prisoner, the cleric heretic.

This idiocy makes me laugh. Almost.

'CAN'T', I sign to the cleric. 'TOO HARD'.

He sits his ass on the cold cell floor. Spelling his rebuttal with letters shouted upon the air.

'CAN'.

I cross my arms, a rebellious child refusing chores. So what? I am a novice witch in a cell built to hold matrons of power. Even if he *has* put the inhibiting charm to sleep.

'THINK ON WHAT HECATATIA MEANS TO YOU'. He ends this pointing at me, as though chiding me for insulting a dear aunt. And he doesn't even believe in the saints! Is he mocking? More like he is mad. Why else confess to the Questioner, give himself to the fire?

I turn about, facing the wall so as to ignore him. He doesn't understand. Not that I understand. And why should I? What the Infernum good does understanding do?

I'll be whipped. Understand that? It'll hurt. Demetia knows I've been beaten before. Branding is going to hurt *worse*. It'll be on my hand. Won't it? Not my face. Please, please not on my face.

I stare at the stones of the wall where I spent this day scratching a picture of Hecatatia; holding her scepter snake. I even gouged a cut into my arm, dripped blood before the rough icon. It hurt. It still hurts. Maybe it will always hurt.

Then I recited the twelve stanzas of her Testament. Putting what hope I have into the whisperings... Scratches in dirty stone, smeared with farmgirl blood... It doesn't count for any relic. But it makes for the idea of a shrine.

I stare towards this work, not seeing aught but shadows. Memory and weariness take these shadows, twist them into the wattling of our cottage. My mother singing by the window, shutters thrown back. Looking out every so often. She's waiting for the moon to rise, to shine into our dreary dark. Same as a maiden watching for sight of her true love.

Da snores in his cot, drunken as sailor in the hold of a wine ship. He groans and shouts in his sleep. Dreaming of failure and famine, no doubt. Dry cows, dead sheep, dust for harvest. Poor sot. Meanwhile my mother waits for her lover the moon.

And when it comes, when at last the light shines through the window, she lets her nightdress fall and stands naked in the silvery shine. She shivers and laughs, running hands along breasts and belly. She bathes in the moonlight. I'm seven; I watch amazed.

The memory hurts, if not so much as a branding iron. I close eyes to the shadows, not wanting to see more. Pointless. They are in my head, not on the wall. I must see, no help for it.

I watch the day that Da hung himself and Ma ran singing into the hills, While I sat beneath the swinging body, unable to cut him down. I felt that if I could get him to the floor, put him to bed, he'd be fine in the morning. For all the purple face staring down. But I couldn't get him down.

When it grew dark I could no longer see his face. But I felt the goggling eyes still staring, wondering when I'd get to the work. How? I couldn't reach high enough with the knife, even standing on the chair.

So I curled whimpering by the hearth, feeding it bits of trash, straw, old rushes from the floor. Creeping into the dark to find what might burn, give light, give warmth. Deep in cold night I found Da's Book of Saints. Leafed pages for a suitable candidate for the fire.

Apollonius, Demetia, Herman, Georgos, Plutarch, Silenus, Chronos, Hefestia, Martia, June, Dion, Claire, Walpurgis, Hecatatia...

The picture of that last showed a motherly figure at a crossroad. Bright moon casting dark shadow towards me, while a dog at her side grinned at me. She held a snake high for a scepter.

Moonshine and mothers. Mine had danced over the hills, leaving me alone with Da's pendulum corpse. I growled, ripping the page from the book, tossing it to the fire.

The flames rose, eager to devour... but did not. The page neither curled nor crisped. No, it lay unharmed upon the fire as though on cushions of flame.

I looked about me, wanting another to see this wonder. Perhaps I dreamt? I beheld the moonlight pouring through the window. Casting the shadow of a hanged man upon the wall. And a snake now pouring itself over the windowsill.

I shrieked, leapt up onto the table. Not high enough from the slithery thing. I reached down, grabbed the chair, pulling it atop the table. Clambered atop that.

Finding myself now high enough to face my father's dead face. And still the flames in the hearth blazed, and still the page of the saint lay unburned. While the snake coiled by the hearth, warming itself. I understood then.

I climbed down, fetched the knife, mounted table and chair again. Reaching careful, I cut the rope. Down came Da, thump and bump to the floor.

I think I fell too. Awoke in the morning curled beside him. Still holding the knife. No snake, no picture of the saint in the fire. But I understood. Hecatatia had taught me a practical lesson. *Think*, she'd told me. Think past the sadness, the moonlight and the madness.

My mother lost herself in trivial lunacy. I admit, I once hoped to feel that same mad release pursuing the teachings of Sister Hecatatia in the woods of Greencroft.

Instead, I found the opposite. I found a *practical* saint. A personage of power and no nonsense. She'd been my comfort in the hard days that followed. Such as now. Infernum, the heretic was right. I needed to recall what Hecatatia meant to me.

I stand in my cell, taking breaths to begin. No easy casting this, without my broach. But the cleric did his part; I'm no longer bound by the Demetian charm above the door. Excellent. To my work, then.

I stare up to the ceiling, where the spider paces back, forth, back. It, too, is eager to begin.

* * *

Val the Bard:

Something's changed. I can't make out what. As if a bell softly chiming since I came to this gaol, has now fallen silent.

And I hear movement and whispers. We aren't all asleep. I certainly am not. I keep checking if the little street-singer Whisper has returned. Unlikely that she will get any message to Alexandra. But the hope keeps me listening for her call.

I stand, look up and down the corridor. Interesting. The Demetian *Greater Charm of Inhibition* has gone dark. An innocent failure, possibly.

I peer towards the night guard's station. He's wrapped himself in a strange white blanket. No, not a blanket. *Thread.* He looks like a giant caterpillar bound to a chair.

His face remains uncovered, eyes wide with terror. Eyes twitching towards the bell-rope that sounds alarm, but arms are entirely bound.

Meanwhile the source of his terror sits in his lap; a large spider. Large? Lucif's left testicle in a pentacle, it's bigger than a cat. The eyes are clumps of facetted jewels, glowing blue. It clacks wet fangs in satisfaction to see its fly well-bound.

I back from the bars, though it pays me no mind. Such a creature is surely a summoning. Well now, someone uses magic to escape. *Good for them,* is my first thought.

I hear more whispering. It is the cleric-heretic, muttering with steady breath. Prayers? To whom? For what?

Now something new is happening. A snake weaves up the wall. No, not a snake. A vine, growing out the flowerpot. I peer close. Periwinkle. Rather pretty, actually. They grow all up and down Persephone. They don't grow so fast, usually.

Obviously, another magical working. I watch as the vine splits, multiplies, becomes a periwinkle swarm of vines that snake up the wall to the cabinet. The vines slither, testing here, trying there... I watch one enter a knothole of the oaken cabinet. For a long minute nothing happens. Then the cabinet bursts open, the lock snapped by the pressure of a thousand summer growths in a minute.

The spider leaps to the cabinet, reaches with one arm and another and another, grabbing keys. Then drops to the floor, scurrying down the corridor.

Passing by my cell, for a moment our eyes meet. Some of its eyes, to both of mine. I step away, shuddering. I consider shouting alarm. No doubt the guards beyond the night door would hear. If I cannot escape, why let another? Perhaps I will even be rewarded for my civic duty.

Bah. That's not civic virtue, that's petty spite. I watch, keeping silent.

There come more whispers, the sweet clink and click of copulating keys and locks. Other prisoners have awoken, sensing change. They stand at their cell doors peering.

A tall man of middle years exits his cell. The heretic cleric. Beside him is the witch. The cleric stops before the coiner's cell.

"What are you doing?" whispers the witch. She's my age, thin and mean-looking as steel dirk.

"One moment," says the cleric. Then, to the maker of false coins, "Do you wish out?"

The man considers the keys held by the heretic. Then shakes his head.

"I'd rather lose the hand," he says, waving one. "Failed escape means they'll take the head."

The cleric looks ready to debate that wisdom.

"Let's go," says the witch. "Leave the fool."

"Anyone wish to depart with us?" asks the cleric to the faces peering from the bars.

"How you getting past the door?" replies the seller of fake titles.

Witch and heretic consider the door. Thick oak, barred on the other side. And beyond that door is the main guard room. They won't be deep into books there.

"This fellow knocks three times, then once," said the witch, pointing to the spider-webbed guard. The man's eyes are still fixed on the spider. The monster is now draping itself in periwinkle blooms, like a village maid with spring garlands. Beautiful, and yet so very nasty.

"Oh, they'll open to the knock," agrees the falsifier. "But it'll open to armed soldiery with backup to call if they want. All of us together charging through the door couldn't do more than make 'em laugh while we bleed."

"Can you do any more spells?" whispers the witch. "I'm worn out."

The cleric nods. "I am little use in the front of battle. But this I can do." He reaches a hand to the witch, places it upon her head. The girl flinches, clearly disliking to be touched. But endures.

The cleric whispers. I hear 'Demetia', and other words. It does not sound a standard oration. But then, he is a mad heretic praying to the House of Saints he denies. His orations shall of necessity be original.

"That... helped," whispers the witch. Shrugging off the hand. "I felt it." Then, as if forced, "Thank you."

"You are welcome. Shall we face what is beyond the door? I do not think there is any going back for you nor me."

The girl bites lip, then nods. Looks to the flower-draped spider, who leaps to the floor, stands beside her.

"Wait," I say.

They turn, faces annoyed. I'm interrupting their dramatic dénouement.

"Let me out," I tell them. "I'm useful in a fight."

"You're a horse thief," scoffs the witch.

"And a bard," adds the heretic. "Though lacking instrument. Perhaps you were wiser to stay where you are."

Well, that's an afront. I point to the guard's short-sword hanging on the vine-bedecked wall.

"There's my instrument," I growl.

At my suggestion we carry the night-guard into a cell, still bound to his chair. Putting him out of sight. He doesn't complain, clearly relieved we aren't cutting his throat. But the heretic apologizes.

"I would dearly have loved to discuss '*Baptismus Deorum*' with you," he says. "It is a work that should be read from the rooftops, not hidden in locked libraries."

The guard mumbles a reply through the webs binding his mouth. Before I think to stop him, the cleric pulls these aside. A foolish act if the guard chooses to shout.

But, "nonsense," he spits, once mouth is freed. "*Baptisumus* is heretical fable reducing the House of Saints to a collection of ancient magical riffraff."

The heretic cleric smiles, raised finger in sign he instructs.

"Ah, it goes yet farther, young sir. In truth, Brendon realizes those ancient riffraff he baptizes *saints* are themselves but wind, sun, earth and fire. Those old gods are the brute forces of existence our child-minds give faces. As the House of Saints is but the world about us. Consider chapter-"

"Shut the Infernum's fuck up now," growls the witch. Beating me to it by a quarter second. She gives repeated shoves to the cleric, forcing him from the cell. I follow, after replacing the webbing that gags the guard.

I don the cape and helm hanging by his post, belting his short sword about my waist.

"Stand to the side," I order my two fellow escapees. Or three, if you count the spider. *I* don't count the spider. Though I admire the crown of periwinkles it's given itself. "I'll do the knock on the door. When the outer guard opens, I pull him in quick. We finish him, hide the body."

"Tying him up alive," corrects the cleric.

"If he lives," I shrug. "Then... we send the spider out. Seeking more conveniently unwary guards to bind. At some point they'll see it, start shouting. When it looks convenient we tiptoe out the main doorway."

The fake coiner laughs scornfully from the safety of his cell. "What a tomfool of a plan."

"Might work," I say, knowing it won't. "Anyone have a better one?"

Witch and cleric shake heads. But I see in their eyes they hold no more hope than I. They merely trade the certainty of torture and slavery for a quick death in noble battle. Exactly as I do. Exactly as I was taught in St. Martia.

Strange, strange, that the lessons of the saint I rebelled against should be my guide in rebellion now.

I test the grip and balance of the short sword. I miss my long knife, but this will do. The cleric stamps a wooden staff that previously served as the gaol's broom, till he unbound the straw.

I stand before the door, lift hand to knock, - and stop. There's shouting from beyond. And now bells begin ringing.

"Shit," says the witch. "They know already?"

But the cleric does not panic. Good man.

"No. Those bells ring from the city garrison. Three, two, three. What could that signal? Fire?"

The answer comes quick from down the hallway.

"Means you'd best get back in your cells where it is safe," shouts the maker of false Ducal letters. "And lock the doors tight."

Bah. The coward delights in the thought we will fail our brave escape. I consider cutting him; but we need answers more than his thin blood.

"Lock from what? Safe from what?"

The man chuckles.

"Ah, from ghosts. Skeletons. Revenants, liches. Three, two, three? That's the signal that the dead of Plutarch are attacking the city."

Chapter 35
Wind, Light, Shadow and Fire

Val the Bard:

Bells clanging, guards shouting, the door opening... mother of Infernum we are given no time to *think*.

"Out of the light," I tell cleric and witch. I place myself half in shadow, sword drawn, wearing the guard cape and helm. With Sister Fortuna's smile I'll pass for who he expects. Should I be holding the book, posing deep in theologic study?

The heavy door pushes open, a guard hurries in.

"Leave the lock up. All hands to posts, we've got rotters in the middle of town and who are you?"

I knee him to the side of the gut. As he folds I strike the back of his head with the sword butt. He collapses nicely. The cleric adds a ceremonial *thump* with his broom-stick staff. The witch gives a hard kick, unnecessary and rather mean. The man is *down*.

"Take his helmet and cloak," I order the witch.

"Who the Lucif's thorny cock put Missus Horse Thief in charge?" she demands.

I fight the desire to run her through. I'm trembling, not with fear but that same red thirst that shook me when Marcus ripped my shirt and I ripped his guts.

"Blessed Martia just promoted me on the field," I growl. "If you want to live, follow her holy light."

She returns growl for growl, but the cleric lays one calming hand to her shoulder, the other to mine. At which I struggle not to run *him* through. While she bares the teeth of a dog finished with being beaten. But the cleric whispers soothing words.

"The bard is clearly wise to this work. Let us make use of her wisdom."

I shake off the hand, peer beyond the door. Within is a disgraceful chaos. Folk shouting, bells ringing, horns blowing. Guards searching for weapons, straightening uniforms, stumbling towards the front gate.

"If we look like guards, with a cleric chanting protective orations, we might be taken as part of the incompetent garrison."

The witch's face says she wants to argue; but resists. Not a total fool then. She dons the helmet and cloak. The helmet falls over her eyes, while she waggles the sword like a feather duster.

"What about my spider, then?"

It scuttles across the floor to sit before her, a pet dog. Still garlanded in periwinkles. It waves clusters of eyes to say '*yes, what about me*'? I shrug. "Don't know, don't care, let's go."

And so we go.

Sister Fortuna is a comic denizen of the House of Saints. She has no holy testament, much less a full gospel. No churches bear her name, no chapel walls echo her orations. Most oft you spy her statue in niches bordering quarters where prostitutes lounge, and taverns with fountains of wine invite the unwary passerby.

Still, even a scullery maid is servant to the master of the house. The least in the House of Saints bears holy message to all creation.

But what exactly is Sister Fortuna's message? She sets you a feast, then slaps you with worries that end all joy in feasting. Drops a purse of gold onto your path, follows with a pack of wolves. And that is when she *smiles*. When Fortuna frowns, she settles for giving the worries and the wolves, skips the feast and purse of gold.

No sacred figure is easier to view in terms of the mad Lucretians' doctrine: *the saints are mere faces we put upon wind, wave and shadow.*

And yet, when the impossible happens, as it must in any life... when past all odds and obstacles one stands free and breathing, it seems to our eyes that the doors of the Upper House of Saints have been thrust wide. And beyond those doors we glimpse the mysterious purpose to all our trials. While the Novice Fortuna stands demurely to the side, smiling warm and wise as the summer sun.

We stood in the street between the garrison and the gaol, while guards rushed thither and hither, shouting orders one to another, taking turns playing commander. Bells clangled and jangled, dogs barked, a thousand awakened babies cried. Lights shone at windows, men raced down streets with torches in sign they bore important messages, same as the saints. A troop of soldiers on horse rode past, near trampling all. The riders wore proper armor, looking far more competent than the bumbling city guards.

"Head towards the river," shouted an officer on horse. "You lot on foot get to the bridges."

"Our chance to slip away," I whispered to the witch beside me.

"Don't even think it," came the growled reply. A man's voice. Shit, I'd taken him for the witch. "Daft to scamper here. Wait till we're close to the docks."

I looked about for my fellow escapees. Spying the heretic cleric on the steps of the gaol. Surrounded by guards; but they knelt as he raised staff and right hand, giving blessing of St. Demetia.

A warm light shone about the men, like a moment of summer sun. They cheered and stood, warmed with strength and comfort. I considered laughing; I also considered joining them. How did he recite such orations when he denied the saints? Bah. Theology is madness; and the night already went mad enough.

Soon the gaol would count its prisoners. I faced a choice; flee the city, or seek Lady Alexandra. Both were risks.

"Move, double-time!" shouted a guard in silver mail. An officer for sure. Disobeying invited suspicion. I began a dogtrot with ten other soldiers. Our swords drawn, capes flaring.

Quite dramatic, and yet familiar as a nursery song. St. Erebus bite Lucif's mum's bum, all my childhood I'd run in step with others, waving weaponry. Practicing battle. Just as I'd sung of glorious warfare in bard school. Well, no more practice, no more song. This night came the thing itself. *Battle*.

I wondered if we faced undead troops or living soldiers? Which would I rather? My father served in the hills twixt Plutarch and Martia. I recalled him telling of the horror of piercing a man through the heart, only to watch the foe grin for the gesture. What good was blade-skill against creatures already dead?

"Let's find out," I whispered, and spurred heels, meaning to get to the front of things. But someone grabbed my cloak, slowing me. I brushed their arm away, near slashing.

"Slow down, idiot," came their whisper. "Let them get ahead. You want to lead the charge?"

I did, actually. But here was my fellow escapee the witch. And she was right, I was being an idiot.

I slowed pace. Our marching band hurried down a dark boulevard lined with tall buildings, graced with trees. A place of beauty and birdsong by day, no doubt. At night it became shadowed and ominous. Above the larger doorways hung oil lamps casting a funereal memorial to sunlight. To left and right, alleyways waited like cave openings, inviting us to lose ourselves in the dark.

"Now," whispered the witch. She darted into a shadowed side street. I followed behind, feeling I betrayed the soldiers hurrying to the fight. For all that they were the same shilling-a-week brutes that would have marched me to the whipping post, holding me fast while a glowing brand burned 'T' upon my forehead.

We stood in night shadows, waiting till the echo of their boots diminished. Of course, soon as gone, here came the clip clop of approaching horses.

"Shit, that's going to be officers," I whispered. "Let's not hang around." We hurried on down the alley, round a corner into an intersection. And there we found the enemy.

Skeletal creatures. Some glowing red as heated iron. Others exuding a green foxfire glow of rot, else bearing black shadows like velvet cloaks darker than the night. No matter form or light, their eyes shone harsh and bright, with beauty to make one shiver. Fiery as stained glass before the flames of Infernum. Lovely eyes set in faces of bone, their teeth fangs, their hands claws.

Not at all like the staggering corpses my father described. These beings moved with grace, shadow forms flowing across the cobbles, waving arms, shifting legs in what came near a dance.

Fascinating, in a nightmarish style like to the fevered melodies of the choir-monks of St. Orpheus. These beings stared at us; and we stared at them.

Then the witch screamed. I screamed. The creatures screamed. They rushed upon us. We turned and ran.

Behind us came the bone-clicks of the shadow-fiends. Ahead of us came the horse hoof echoes of the Demetian soldiers.

"This way," I gasped, darting left at an intersection. With Fortuna's blessing, fiends and soldiery would make themselves busy with one another.

Farther into the dark, we stopped to rest, catch our breaths. Something scuttled along the wall beside us. I prepared to slash, but the witch grabbed my arm.

"It's Perry," she whispered.

Who? I almost asked. But of course it was the spider. Which she named for periwinkles, why not. It wiggled its eye-clusters at us, then scuttled off around the corner.

"We should follow it," declared the witch.

I wanted to argue. Why follow it? But I had no plan except to run about in the night dodging soldiers and fiends, waving a sword.

"Fine," I sighed, and we went on around a corner, down a street. There we found lamplight and all a festival of fiends.

"Back, back," I growled. But of course there came shouting of soldiers behind us, the sound of horses.

A man lay on the stones before us, throat a liquid mess. Some of the fiends tore into him, biting, drinking. Others milled before the doorway of a great brick edifice. Not a house but some municipal building. The shadow-fiends paid us no mind; they watched, awaiting someone to enter the stage.

Who came was a man, appearing in the doorway bearing a monstrous axe that cut two of the creatures down in one sweep. He did not wait for greeting, but darted into the street, taking position beneath a doorway lantern. Back to the wall, wise fellow. The creatures howled, gathering about him.

Large-shouldered, bearded, the fellow swung again, cutting a shadow-fiend clear in half. The creature gave a shriek, pieces tumbling to the cobbles, The others backed away, flower-petal eyes flickering rage.

A few turned, considering flight or easier victims. Finally noting the witch and me. Easier prey for sure. They capered in their graceful dance-steps towards us. Only to trip, fly faces first into the cobbles.

"Well done, Perry," whispered the witch. Upon a close wall I spied the spider, waving various legs. Well, the creature had set a trip-line across the street. Fast work, and clever.

I could no longer take merely observing. I rushed upon one of the downed skeletons. Meeting its eyes of autumn blue sky, I slashed. The thing raised an arm in defense. My strike removed the arm. The blade continued into its head. The creature screamed, I screamed. The blade became fixed in its bony head. I tugged, it struggled. The second shadow-fiend rose to its feet before I could free my weapon.

But the witch stepped beside me, holding a fist of purple fire. She tossed it upon the creature. It burst into lovely flames of lavender. Screaming. The witch screaming too; same as I.

I freed the sword, glanced to the man beneath the light. He still kept back to the wall. Several fiends now lay in pieces before him. But his bearded face ran with blood, and the axe no longer swung its deadly arc. Tiring, no doubt.

More of the creatures surrounded him, others turned to rush upon the witch and me. I took what stance I could, thinking it pointless.

"Good work," shouted a voice behind me. "But next time you show to muster without proper uniform, I'll see you whipped." A woman's voice, officious and annoying. I turned to see a Demetian officer with sword drawn. No ordinary blade; this one burned green as a pyre of emeralds. She tossed me the reigns of her horse.

"Get Valentine to safety," she ordered. "We'll handle the Infernum-spawn."

With that, she and her guards pushed us aside, rushing upon the shadow-fiends. I stared in outrage and relief.

"Well done, young bard, and you, novice of Hecatatia," said a newcomer. The heretic cleric, wielding his broom-stick staff. He lowered his voice. "Best you make your exit now."

"What about you?"

"Too late. They have noted my person and utility. They would mark my departure." He raised his staff. Green light glimmered along the length. "And I have orations yet to pronounce. Clearly, the saints require me in this battle."

"You don't believe in the saints."

The man leaned on his broomstick staff. Trembling some. Weary, as were we all.

"The saints are autumn wind in the chimney, the light on clouds, the shadows of the night, the fire of the hearth. But I believe in wind, light, shadow and fire." Doctrine declared, he hurried on to the fight.

I looked at the witch; she at me. Then at the horse. Well, the officious officer had ordered me to get it to safety. I put foot to stirrup, mounted. Reached down, holding out hand to the witch. She looked at the soldiers, the heretic, the fiends, then clasped my hand. I pulled her up behind me.

"You're going to steal this horse," she said.

I considered denying it. Decided not.

"Seems it has my name."

I gave a last glance to the fight, wishing I could join. The soldiers seemed to have the situation in hand. The officer darted about, slashing with what had to be a saint's major relic. Clearly she was someone of importance. With a fine horse, I noted.

The brave fellow with the axe was down, lying beneath the lamp light. For a moment I considered riding into the fight, defending his corpse. A foolish impulse, worthy of a bad ballad.

I kicked heels, hurrying the horse through side-streets, avoiding shouts of friend, foe or fiend alike, working our way towards the city gate.

Chapter 36
Sing Ramble and Bramble and Tangle

"What can you see?

"Nothing."

"Then how do you know where to go?"

"Who said I did?

"Heard you tell the big man with the axe you knew these pipes like the bishop knew his thumb."

"No, it was 'like the popular whore knew the bishop's thumb'."

"Why should she know his thumb, particularly?"

"That there's a fascinating question you should ask the very next bishop you meet. Coincidentally, hark to the chanting? We're right under the Church of St. Apollonius. Could get up and out through their ossuary but they keep it barred tight."

"Are you really a Moon? 'Cause ol' Mercutio was the only soul crazy enough to dance down here for fun and profit."

"That he was, bless 'im."

"I know Artemis Moon. Works at the docks. Calls himself a pirate but just nicks from the warehouses."

"Ha, anyone can do that. Just make friends with the dogs. Did you know your granddam Margaret?"

"Course not. Drowned herself years ago. In a big marble tub full of the finest white wine, they say."

"Was she happy?"

"Why would she drown herself if'n she was happy?"

"Yeah. Did you ever hear if she talked about old Mercutio?"

"Only to curse his soul and pecker to Infernum's forty hottest fornicatoriums."

"Ah. We can walk this next part. But have to step slow. There'll be holes deep enough to drop a body into St. Lucif's deepest chamber pot."

"Oy, what's that creature behind us?"

"A cat."

"Why's his eyes so bright?"

"Hmm, 'cause he's an angel cat."

"Liar. He's a witch-thing."

"You've a sound head for the truth, youngster."

"Yep. I can spot a mark or a thief-catcher faster'n a dog'll swallow your shit or your lunch. It's why Crow took me for prentice."

"That Crow is a bad 'un. All those Swykes are over-easy 'bout crossing knives and throats."

"Oh, sure. But the bad sort are the best to learn from."

"Well, but you'll be learning the wrong things."

"What are you, the bishop now?"

"Damn if I know what I am."

"I'm scared. Can I hold your hand?"

"Sure. Let me just put my coin and favorite teeth in the farther pocket first."

"Ha, I'd still get 'em. Got the Moon touch, I do. That's a bad smell ahead."

"We're getting near the river. And that means we walk sly and slow. Things from the water make these pipes their tavern. And we wandering strangers are their drink."

"I hear singing."

"And I see light. That's a street grate above us."

"Oh, that's a mate of mine, singing. Name's Whisper."

"Met her soon as come to town. She the one that tipped you and Crow to our coin?"

"Maybe, maybe."

Green wife, give me the green life.
Forest ramble and bramble
In sweet summer tangle.
Glad wife, giving me no strife,
In green fern we'll roll and we'll gambol.

"Oy, up there. Whisper!"

"Who's that down there?"

"Me. Magpie. An' a client."

"Well, you'd best be getting somewhere safer than the river pipes. Bells say the dead are pouring across Lethe."

"Yeah, but they're wrong. Hey, can you get the grate up for us?"

"No. Too heavy."

"Whisper!"

"Who're you?"

"Dearest friend of Magpie. Are you in the courtyard backside of St. Demetia's?"

"Yep. Here in the shadow of her holy house I'll be safe, safe, safe from dead things. Safe."

"Knew it so. Look towards the west corner. There still the statue of St. Sidon of the Waves?"

"Still? It's rock and iron. Not going nowhere, he isn't."

"Yeah, but that spear he's holding comes out his hand. Fits into the grate like key to lock. You just slip the tines under the side with the holes, and done."

"How would you be knowing that?"

"I'm just that clever and good looking. Do this for us and you get a silver. Do it quick and you get two."

"Ha. Two gold. And you toss them up first."

"You've a hard heart for a sweet voice. Well, Magpie, it's the river door for us."

"Fine then. One gold. But you toss it up 'fore I get to work."

"Maggie, can we trust your very good mate Whisper?"

"It's Magpie. I'm not my grandma. And *I* can trust her. Give her the glitter."

* * *

"You going to make the horse leap the city wall?" demanded Jewel.

"No, I'm going to ride it through the city gate, you sarcastic bitch," replied Val. "The city's under attack. Folk will be fleeing. We'll join them."

"Yeah, won't work."

"Why not?"

"Guard robes, guard helmets, war horse? We'll look like deserters."

Shit, she's right. "So, we ditch the gear."

"Then we look like who we are. Escaped prisoners, remember?"

"You got a better plan?"

"If we can rest up for a day I could recite an oration of disguise." *Maybe, anyway.*

Behind came shouts, whistles, the clop of hooves and jangle of bridles. Val guided the horse into an alleyway so narrow it offered no room for turning. If it proved dead end they'd have to dismount, leave the animal staring at a wall.

But it soon exited into a courtyard, moonlit. The Cathedral of St. Demetia of the Sheaves walling away one side of the sky. A glowering statue of St. Sidon of the Waves lurked in a corner. The courtyard offered no other exit; just the doorway to the cathedral.

"Trapped, dammit," declared Jewel.

"Then we'll turn around."

"I think they saw us go into the alley."

"Then we lose the horse and go through the church. What is that child doing?

In the center of the court a small figure maneuvered a spear thrice her length. She pushed it into flagstones, pulling, cursing.

Val kicked heels, rode closer.

"What are you up to, child?" she demanded.

"Who cares what she does?" demanded Jewel.

"Not doing anything, sirs or madams," insisted the child. "Wait, wait, wait, that you, Miss Bard? I got your message far as the Duke's third cook. Can't promise it'll get to her ladyship."

"Whisper?"

"Uh huh. You snaked out the lockup anyways, so no matter."

"I was pardoned by the saints."

"Ah, nuh uh. I'm hearing the whistles. Seems sly folk walked through gaol bars during the excitement."

"These are exciting times."

"Been practicing your song about Miss Fortune. Where you say 'give it up' but turn it to tupping. Ha, I know what that's about."

To Jewel's consternation, Val began to sing.

Miss Fortune pursued a cup.
Vowed to drink the vessel up.
Met a monk, just half drunk
Said, 'twere best you give a tup.

Whisper joined in, her voice a soft descant.

Miss Fortune cried 'alack'
On the hunt she'd gone off track.
Met St. Herm, who in voice firm,
Said, 'let us get her honor back'.

"Hey up there!" shouted a voice from the ground. "You going to let us out? Or practice choir?"

"Ah," said Val. "I see." She dismounted. Stretched, then took the iron spear from Whisper. Fit it under the grate, pushed.

Jewel clambered less skillfully down from the horse.

"What in the name of the sainted cocks of all the Lower House are you at?" she demanded. "We have to get away."

"*She's* a peppery sort," observed Whisper.

"She is that," agreed Val, levering the heavy grate up. It flipped over with a crash and clang, revealing a dark hole.

Immediately hands appeared on the edge; then a girl's face peeked out and about.

"Two guards up here," she warned someone below. Then corrected. "No, just folk wearing guard things. Bet they nicked 'em. And oh for the love of Holy Mother Demetia they've stole the Lady's horse, Valentine. Yow, she'll be pissing fire."

Whisper pulled Magpie up and out. She emerged painted with all the liquid colors of the under-city, which summed to browns, greens and grays.

"Oy, you stink like the shit-lake where St. Lucif boils the tax collectors," declared Whisper.

"Shit isn't the nastiest stuff down there," declared Magpie.

Two more hands grabbed the edges of the hole. A second slime-draped head peeked out, cautiously studying the scene before emerging. At the same time a less cautious creature leaped entirely out, settling upon the stones graceful as butterfly upon lily cup. A cat entirely lacking any paint-brush touch of excrement.

The white angel-wing eyes stared about, considering the night, the two children, the bard still holding St. Sidon's spear, and lastly the witch; who returned the stare. Putting hand to her half-healed face. Then she shrieked.

"You!"

Shadow Night-Creep hissed, ears laid flat. Jewel reached to grab him. He leapt back into the sewer hole. The boy immediately dropped from sight as well. Jewel rushed to the hole, screaming after them.

"Come back here! That cat's mine!"

Other shouts than hers now echoed from the courtyard walls. Val looked towards the alley entrance. A guard stepped warily into view; followed by another.

"Shit, they're on our trail." She remounted the horse, still holding St. Sidon's spear. Magpie and Whisper stared up at her. Something about the way Val sat in saddle, spear before her, gave a soul shivers.

"You going to fight 'em?" asked Magpie.

"Course not," Val replied. "Probably not. Maybe yes. Witch, we need to leave."

But Jewel only muttered curses; then lowered herself into the sewer hole. Disappearing with a last shout of *'mine'*.

"Well, crap," declared Val. Counted; there were now five guards in the courtyard. Two stayed back to block the exit; three approached, swords drawn. Coming slow; not liking the sight of rider and spear

"Go through the church," suggested Whisper. "Door's not barred."

Val wheeled the horse about. Spurred towards the church doorway. She prepared to dismount and open the great door. Unnecessary. It swung wide as if the saint had long expected her. In the doorway waited yet another guard.

Anonymous guard and heroic bard contemplated one another's existence and purpose. Then,

"For Saint Martia of Just Causes!" Val screamed, spurring the horse forwards. The guard leapt aside. Val ducked her head to pass beneath the frame, rode clip-clopping into the cathedral.

Jewel hurried down a tunnel, walls echoing *splash* and *squish* at each step. The air a fog of excrement and slime.so thick she pushed against it like a swimmer. Only once, far ahead did she spy the white eyes of her stolen familiar, looking back. They blinked in mockery, then disappeared, leaving her to smother in stink, in dark, in frustration.

I'm being stupid, she thought. What am I going to do, grab it by the scruff? She looked for the hole she'd foolishly jumped down. Gone. She stood lost in dark and dank.

She leaned against the dripping wall, trembling with hunger, with weariness, with despair. *Weak. Useless. Might as well chase the moon over the hills. Like Mama.*

Stop, Jewel ordered Jewel. Focus. You need out. To get out you need light. You're a novice of the Sainted Sister of Dark Places herself. She'll lend some light.

She held out a hand, gathering breath, gathering courage, and began to whisper.

"This night is your dark. Grant me your spark."

She repeated this thrice. And for one moment a faint glow appeared above her palm. Then the hand trembled, the glow faded… was gone.

"Shit," she whispered. Closing fingers, seeking to keep some tiny bit of light. Opened her hand, finding she held only darkness. Of course. What else had life ever given her?

But a faint starshine appeared on the wall. Weak and watery, too dim to illuminate. Just clusters of pale blue stars, blinking.

"Periwinkle?" she whispered.

The eyes waggled; possibly in greeting. Then moved along the dark tunnel. Jewel collected herself, following. When the eyes began rising upwards, she puzzled, nearly tripping on the first step of a stairway.

The stairs spiraled; bringing her at last into faint light. At the end step waited a small door. Jewel had to bend low to peer within.

Beyond shone candlelight, with distant sounds of shouting. She hesitated, then crept through, smelling old wax, incense, stone and wood polish. The fragrance of an old church, for sure.

Jewel stood upright again in a small chapel aglow with rows of candles, crowded with statuary figures of matrons holding moons, mothers holding snakes, queens guarded by dogs and lions.

Something glittered on the floor. She tiptoed forwards. Feeling watched by eyes of stone and glass. She bent down to find a silver pendant in shape of a spider. Tiny clusters of eyes blinking blue as summer periwinkles.

She lifted it by a silver chain, spider-silk thin, dangling it before her. Touched, the pendant felt warm, fresh-forged. The certainty came that this was Periwinkle, the spider she'd enchanted. Bound now in silver and crystal.

She stared up at the statue directly before her. Tall, stern, entirely and only stone. Motherly without least hint of maternal weakness nor mad fancy. Smiling, not in affection nor humor; but in confidence that what she ruled, she ruled well and rightly.

Jewel shivered. Feeling a desire to drop the pendant, leave it for another to find.

Who? she demanded of her doubts. For someone more worthy? Bah; that wasn't humility. It was weakness. The pendant came as gift to Jewel of Stonecroft farm and no soul else. She could refuse it and run, keeping head down, spirit down, for all the days yet left her. Snarling like a beaten dog at the world, whether it gave kicks or smiles.

Or she could put the necklace on. Accept the gift; and so admit that such things as *gifts* existed in life. Cruel and stupid as she knew life to be.

For a moment she wavered... then looped the chain over her head, pulling tangled hair out the way. Settling the spider between her breasts, where it rested warm and comforting.

"Thank you," she said to the statue. Then to all the gathered statues of Sainted Sister Hecatatia. Making what farmgirl curtsey she could with weary legs and slime-drenched skirt. No reply came from the stones; and that was best.

But the shouts and clamor she'd heard before, now drew her attention. She tiptoed to an archway, finding herself on a high balcony overlooking the main hall of the cathedral.

Behold a great marble statue of Demetia, full Matron of the House of Saints, commanding one end of the chamber. Tall as five men, the base wide as a cottage. Round and about this statue raced a horsewoman and four guards. Jewel could not tell who chased whom. The horsewoman waved spear before her, the guards waved swords behind her.

At the fifth circuit, when the guards obviously tired, Val turned horse, galloping down the aisle for the entrance of the church.

Only to halt halfway, as the doorway before her filled with fresh guards.

Jewel observed their entry. These were not comic city guards tripping over cloaks, waving blades like schoolboys waggling sticks. The newcomers looked proper soldiers, in smart green mail, black helmets that showed wary eyes, set mouths. These efficient beings spread through the church, swords drawn, moving to circle Val.

Should I help? wondered Jewel. How? The girl is caught. Good as in the noose. A vision of her dad hanging from the rafters made her shudder.

But I'm not caught. I can escape. I have the favor of St. Hecatatia.

She watched the horse thief consider the field, no doubt reaching the same conclusion concerning fate and noose. The woman tossed aside the overlarge helm, sending it clattering across the stone floor. Then dropped the overheavy spear. That done, she drew the short sword, raising it in defiance to the encircling soldiers.

Idiot, thought Jewel. To herself as much as to the girl on the horse. She put hand to the spider-broach. Perhaps she could cast some spell to diminish the light, snuff the candles, give the bard a chance to flee.

But before she could focus upon the least oration, one of the soldiers stepped towards Val. Speaking as she walked down the long aisle, in no hurry.

"That's a saint's spear you just desecrated." The voice of a young woman; hoarse from shouting all night.

"True. And my horse just shat behind Demetia's altar."

"No, that's my horse," the woman corrected. "Her name's Valentine." She pulled a crossbow from a sling across her back. Began checking wire and bolt. "You lack title. Also, you lack future. Hmm, unless..."

The incomplete observation hung in the cathedral air like to the wafts of the most sacred incense.

"Unless?"

"Unless in plea of forgiveness to the saint you sing of St. Sidon's spear."

"What?"

"Right," sighed the lady-officer. Waving official hand. "Pull her down. Mind no harm comes to my horse."

"Wait, wait," insisted the bard. And then... *laughed*. "Lexia?"

For reply the officer removed her helmet. Revealing young face, freckled, blond hair cut short. This personage cleared throat, and then recited.

Miss Fortune chased the grail.
Night and day to no avail.
Met a centaur, hot to kiss her.
Said, 'What a pretty pony tail'.

The soldiers traded puzzled glances with the stony gaze of St. Demetia, the weary city guards. One looked up to the balcony, met Jewel's eye. They shrugged in shared confusion.

But Val threw back head, began to sing. Her strong voice echoing off stones laid ages past for the most holy orations unto the House of Saints.

Miss Fortune met St. Sidon
Sea bathing, no clothes on.
Waved his spear, glad to see 'er.

Said, 'well now here's a hard one.'

What the Infernum? wondered Jewel.
Both Val and the officer sang the next verse. The bard had far the better voice, but struggled more not to giggle.

Miss Fortune lost her way,
Crying out 'alack a day'.
Met St. Hefestus, who with a 'bless us',
Said, 'She looks to make a proper lay.'

The officer-lady nodded. Then put away the crossbow.

"Off my horse, Valentine Kurgus."

"You named your horse after me?"

"Yeah, it has a way of farting that reminds of your soprano."

Lady Alexandra, Duke's daughter, looked up at the balcony where Jewel stared down, puzzled and transfixed.

"You, lurking up there. Our escaped witch? Get down here. And quit whatever idiot oration you're about to recite."

Jewel scowled, tempted to continue just to show she didn't follow orders from lunatics. Which was absurd. The lunatic was in charge. Best go along. For now. Jewel searched for the stairs.

While Val dismounted the stolen horse 'Valentine'. Held the reigns out to Alexandra. For a moment they studied one another, then stepped close, exchanged awkward hugs, laughing some.

Then they turned, leading the horse towards the door. Ignoring the soldiers following behind. Singing as they passed through the cathedral door.

Miss Fortune journeyed long,
Singing every lyric wrong.
Met St. Lucif, who gave a sniff,
Said, 'Now here's a proper effing song.'

Chapter 37
When the Goat Girl Dressed the Milk Cow

In the pit. Bodkin and Magpie vanished into the sewers. Barnaby watched his circle of protection fade awau, the fiends make their dance-steps forwards.

"They shall strike faster than you swing," observed Dark Michael. "You must begin before they move."

Barnaby did not answer. He was too busy waving the axe, backing towards the wall of the pit.

"Granted, if you swing uselessly, you will tire and die," considered the ghost. Voice calm and dry. He leaned against a wall, not bothering to raise hat above eyes.

"Sainted Lucif's piss pot take you for its kettle," whispered Barnaby.

"What take me for *who*?"

"Ah, sorry. Sir."

A shadow-fiend with eyes of rose petal flame leaped past the next swing. Clasped Barnaby in its arms, black teeth seeking his neck. Too close for Barnaby to strike. So he turned, rushing at the wall of the pit. Crashed into it, stunning the creature. It fell to the floor. Barnaby kicked it away, then swung. The head rolled, rose-petal eyes dimming to dark.

He wheeled about, putting back to wall. A second creature launched itself. Barnaby brought the axe down upon the creature's head. It shrieked, clawing at the blade. Barnaby put a foot upon the writhing creature, tugging free his axe.

"Well done, boy." That, from Michael.

Barnaby took a moment to gather breath. There remained three shadow-fiends. Their fiery eyes considering Barnaby, the two fallen denizens of Infernum, and the dark red glimmer of Dragontooth.

Consideration done, they backed away, crawling up the sides of the pit, scurrying towards the door and the freedom of the night.

Barnaby watched them depart. Panting as if he'd run five circuits round Mill Town. Arms trembled till he could scarce hold the axe; while legs shook so he needed the wall to stand.

"Close your eyes, take a deep breath," ordered Michael. "Count to ten."

Barnaby closed eyes, took breath, counted. Opened eyes at *ten*, exhaling. Then shook himself, feeling better. At length he began walking towards the rope, working not to stagger.

"Where are you going?"

"After the creatures, sir."

At which answer Dark Michael at last raised hat brim to gaze upon his pupil.

"Why?"

Barnaby considered. "Well, sir, they'll be eating folk in the streets and maybe in their beds. Sir."

"That's Persephone's problem. Hark to the bells? The alarm already sounds, they know the danger. You've done your part."

Barnaby shook his head. Sheathing Dragontooth so he could climb the rope.

"We brought those creatures into the city, Master Michael. Da always told me *'Face your mistakes as you face your mirror'*. Not that we had a proper mirror. Just a polished pan to shave with." He tugged at his beard in recollection of clean-shaven days.

Dark Michael made no reply. Not with sarcastic word nor glowering eye. He merely slouched in shadows, observing Barnaby climb the rope, draw his axe again. That done, the miller's son exited the chamber in search of fiends from Infernum.

It made no long search. The street outside swarmed with the creatures. Howling and hissing as though conducting discussion of deepest importance. But the infernal things had not expected Barnaby to follow. He had time to cut two down with one great scything swing; then put his back to the wall beside the door, beneath a bright lantern.

Not far from the doorway lay the body of Crow. The mangled throat still leaking into the street cobbles. More than one fiend knelt to drink from the cooling pools. While Crow stared up with eyes still wide and white with whatever last vision he'd pick-pocketed from this living world.

The sight angered Barnaby. Crow had clearly enjoyed being alive, acting all sly and dishonest, by turns now wicked, now polite. Exactly like a proper story villain. Barnaby shouted at the shadow-creatures, swinging his axe to drive them from their feast.

Some of the fiends leaped beyond the dreadful sweep. Others circled about, seeking to time their attack to his axe swing.

But the night air rang with alarm bells and horns, shouts and whistles. The city knew itself under attack. Two figures appeared at the edge of the lamplight. City guards, by their cloaks and helms. One waving sword, the other wielding a purple fire that turned a shadow-fiend to a glowing violet torch.

I'm not fighting alone, Barnaby thought. *Just have to stay alive a bit longer.*

A shadow-thing danced beneath his axe-swing, wrapping claws about his waist. He struggled to free himself, but another stepped in, struck him aside the head, claws gouging down his face.

Barnaby screamed, staggered, found himself beneath a rising sea of teeth and claws. *I'll call for Michael,* he decided. But the creatures put their faces to his, pressing upon his chest, clawing into the armor. He could not breathe, much less cry out.

This is death, he thought. Bound to happen, sure as the autumn wheat harvest. With that came a vision of millstones turning, rolling, grinding all things to dust. Grinding every last Barnaby to dust.

The vision faded. He lay on cold cobbles staring up at moths circling the lamp. And a glowing staff held by a man in Demetian robes, warding away the attacking shadows.

More shouting close about. Guards ran here and there, waving swords, stamping feet. The remaining shadow-fiends fled into the alleyways of Persephone. The priest knelt beside Barnaby. Staring down with a look of surprise worthy of a beggar finding the king's crown on the cobbles.

"Barnaby?"

"Friar Cedric," replied Barnaby, happy to see this familiar face. "I was having the most amazing dream." He lifted a bloody hand to his bloody face. "Ah. Still dreaming. Which means you aren't here. Excepting as you are in the dream."

"No, no, I am here," said the man. He knelt, laying down his staff. "Where I never dared hope to be. You're badly hurt, boy."

"Yessir. Sorry, sir." Barnaby realized he was only seeing from one eye. With each breath he felt claws digging deeper into his chest. Perhaps the creatures left some behind.

"Don't apologize without cause," reproved Cedric. "Or, or I'll rap your knuckles with my staff."

Barnaby smiled. "Don't suppose you brought the dunce's cap?"

Friar Cedric threw back his head and laughed up to the lantern, and the night beyond the lantern, and the stars beyond the night. Bright tears said he wept as well. Laughing done, weeping done, he took his staff, whispering. Breathing into it as though stirring dim embers to flame again.

The simple staff became a bar of green fire held above Barnaby. Burning life into his wounds till he cried out in pain, in fright, in wonder.

While Cedric, of the Society of Lucretius, continued whispering quiet orations to St. Demetia, patron mother to life and growth. Face shining; eyes shining with the exact same wonder that Barnaby felt, returning to life.

"Where you fellows off?" demanded the officious lady in black armor who'd led the guards.

Cedric leaned on his staff, while Barnaby leaned on Cedric. Both looking ready to fall to the cobbles.

Cedric answered. "I'm taking this worthy civilian to the Chapel of St. Demetia, where he can rest and heal. There I shall pray for renewal of the forces I have spent tonight, returning to the battle refreshed."

The officer considered their weary faces, the bloody stains. Kicked a thoughtful boot at the surrounding debris of axed shadow-fiends.

"Right," she decided. "But don't take overlong. These creatures must have come up through the sewers. Makes no sense 'less more are coming. We need healers and augmentation orations. Fetch all of your fellow holy mumblers who aren't hiding under their beds."

"And so I shall," affirmed Cedric.

"Tell them we regroup at the High Bridge."

"Wise decision," agreed Cedric. He continued leading Barnaby and himself away. Leaving the officer to declaim, stamp and shout, in command of the theatre stage.

"And where in Lucif's seven assholes is my horse?"

* * *

Few folk dared the streets. Only the messengers running past with torches, and the guards hurrying this way, scurrying that way, seeking the enemy. But from every upper window faces peered out, watching the night.

Barnaby felt an urge to wave. Every now and then he did wave. Oft as not, when he did the onlookers waved back. Some even cheered, taking him for a brave defender of civic safety.

"I don't understand how you can be here," said Friar Cedric.

"Well, I don't understand how you can be here either," replied Barnaby. "Could we rest? I am dreadful weary."

"I as well."

They chose a shadowed doorway, settling on cold stone steps. The night air continued its symphony of shouts and bells, screams and horn-calls.

They watched a horse trot out from the dark, slowing at an intersection. Bearing two riders. Guards, by their helmets and robes. Cedric studied them, wondering. He considered calling out.

But the sound of more horses followed close behind. The lead rider spurred her horse down a side street, disappearing. A moment later a dozen more riders galloped past, continuing down the street.

Barnaby sat content, appreciating how the horse hooves clattered and clopped in echoes off the city buildings. Not that horses did not trot through Mill

Town. But iron-shod hooves did not ring so musically on the dirt lanes of home.

Now came howling and barking. From a side street rushed a skeletal being with eyes of burning violet, raging to itself as it fled a pack of dogs.

"Those are Death Hounds," observed Barnaby. Proud to know this local fact. "They chase down dead things."

They watched as the dogs circled the shadow-fiend ripping, tearing, growling. When at last they rushed away, nothing remained upon the cobbles but tatters of dark flesh, gnawed bone. Barnaby pondered these remains.

"Persephone is more interesting than Mill Town."

"True," agreed Cedric. "But remember when the Goat Girl dressed the cows in Squire Semple's shirts and breeches, led them in parade from the pasture to the manor?"

Barnaby's laugh echoed loud as horse-hooves. "The sight was a wonder. Squire let me take her beating, and worth every blow."

At which epilogue Cedric went silent.

Four armed men now came running up the street, the leader bearing a lantern that cast the glow of authority. While down the street came another band, waving plebian torches.

The two squads all but collided.

"Prisoners have escaped the gaol," came the shout from one set.

"To Infernum with your prisoners," shouted the second. "Someone's nicked the Lady's horse. Find it or she'll sell our corpses to the Tarchs."

News shared, the two bands ran off, leaving the stage to silence again. Then Cedric sighed.

"Barnaby, I came here seeking you."

"Oh? Well, it was clever to find me in this far place. I meant to be on the road to that tower, scooping up gold and jewels."

Again, Cedric went silent.

Something scuttled across the cobbles before them; eight legged like a spider, but near large as hunter's hound. For a moment it waved sacs of glittery eyes in greeting, then hurried off on its own arcane quest.

Barnaby reached for his axe, but Cedric stopped him.

"I believe it harmless," he declared.

"That's good to hear."

Spiders and their webs, thought Cedric.

"Barnaby...I have things to say about your family."

"Oh? Is everyone well? Alf has his bad back and Mother Miller's teeth always taste so sour to her."

"Barnaby, your stepmother and Alf… they wished you harm. As did the Squire, who has long been her leman. They did not send you to find treasure. They sent you away so they might gain the mill which is rightfully yours. And, and I did not stop them."

Barnaby looked at Cedric, then away. He began a stream of chatter quick and light as starlings discussing sparrows.

"Oh, and I want you to meet my new friends. They're all wondrous wise. One is even a cat, if you can believe. Talks and has eyes white as, as something very bright and white -"

"Barnaby."

"- and there is Dark Michael who is a ghost and knows all about blades and fighting and we were in a haunted house and a rat told us poems and can you believe Michael confounded a necromancer just with the salt? My axe isn't magic but it's amazing, I call it Dragontooth and it's like we're friends. And Bodkin is an old thief who's become a kid again and he's also a very good friend. So is Night-Creep who is a witch's cat and a good friend. We're all friends. All of us. Good friends." The rush of words only stopped for Barnaby to breathe; panting hard as if waving Dragontooth at dread foes again.

"I'm sorry."

"Oh, that's all right. Anyways, I've met many interesting folk on the road. Missus Green and Val and St. Herman though he's just a stone. And I became a soldier by accident and lived in a wood. Val might be here in Persephone but I haven't found her yet."

Cedric sighed. *The boy doesn't want to talk about his home. Perhaps that's wisdom, for now. Perhaps.*

He stood, leaning on his staff, offering Barnaby a hand.

"Well, if I can find you half across Demetia, then odds are good you can find your missing friend."

Barnaby nodded, standing with Cedric's help. "First, we should find Bodkin. He went down the sewers but when he comes up again he'll head back to the inn."

The two continued their weary march down the street.

"Would that I could help," said Cedric. "But I must leave the city. It'd go hard on you to be found helping me."

"What? Why?"

"As it happens, I am a wanted man in Persephone. Condemned to death. This very night I flew from gaol along with my fellow gallows birds."

Barnaby stared in surprise. Condemned to death? Escaped gaol? Friar Cedric of Mill Town? The quiet scholar who spent his days arguing arcane learning with the shadows of his tiny cottage?

"Friar, you've been having adventures."

"That I have," Cedric agreed. Giving eye to the tall fellow in fiend-torn armor beside him. Where now, the dream-bound miller's boy who stared into embers?

Cedric thumped the cobbles with his staff. "Seems we both have been on adventures."

At which admission they laughed together.

"Disreputable sorts," observed someone from behind.

"Rogues," affirmed a second voice.

"Ne'er-do-wells," added the first.

Barnaby and Cedric turned. There stood a mud-smeared Bodkin, teeth white in wide grin. Beside him, darker than the night, excepting only the eyes of angel-white, sat Shadow-Creep.

The cat stretched; adjusting whiskers, checking tail, then leapt to Barnaby's shoulder. Settling himself there as king returned to throne.

Chapter 38
The Road of Clever Souls

Crow Swynthe

After you croak you find yourself walking a country lane. Easy and familiar, like all your life you've been on this road. The evening shadows make it just a bit worrisome. You know you want to get on before night comes. And to stay on the path, keep moving forwards.

Oh, and you know there's a gate ahead. Got to pay the toll to pass it. No problem for me. I've begun the journey with pockets jingling rich as the purse of a king's whore.

Other folk on the road eye me, my heavy pockets. I keep head down, not speaking. All that matters is getting past the gate before night catches me.

A fellow clears throat behind and I look back, while another from the side pretends to trip, knocking into me. Old game, but they're good. I shove the closer fellow away, he mutters apologies, slips off. I kick at the fellow behind, he grins, hurries on.

I check the coins in my pockets. Less than before. Shit and shave, who'd have thought I'd be taken so easy?

I continue down the road, keeping wary, worrying whether I can still pay to pass the gate. A fellow in rags sits on the roadside, hand out. I shake my head, avoid his eye. Never minded helping a down-and-out in the sunlit world, so long as I had enough left for beer and bedmate. But not now, not on this road. I've got to keep enough to get past the gate.

Something jingles to the ground. A coin dropped by a woman just ahead. I bend quick, scoop it up.

"That's mine, that is," she shouts.

"Isn't," I grin. "Dropped it myself."

I shove it to a pocket. She steps forwards swinging. I step back, bump into an old man with eyes sly as two rats considering a basket of kittens.

"Here, watch where you go," he curses. Pushes me towards the woman, who kicks my knee. I tumble to the bricks. There comes jangle and clangle as my coins spill out, rolling about.

I scream, grabbing for them the way Magpie did for the rings that got me dead. Other folk scoop them up first, laughing, fighting.

I crawl about like a dog, searching. But my coins have vanished quick as butter before a dog. I sit and howl like a dog. While folk pass as though I were a dog; giving the looks you'd give a dying dog

Finally, I stand, feel in my pockets. One coin left. I walk down the road holding it tight. A fellow ahead is chatting with a pretty girl. I set myself, pretend to trip into him, do a quick withdrawal of funds.

He curses, she laughs, I mutter my sorries, hurry on. Check what I won: four coins. I look ahead, wondering how much farther till the gate, how much longer till the night.

The road becomes more crowded, we now walk within reach of one another. I feel a wind on my person, check pockets. A coin is gone. I curse. The light is fading, night's coming, someone hurries by. I check pockets again. Another gone. I moan and groan, grasping the last two coins. Are they enough for the gate? Best get to work.

I put them deep in a pocket, ready my hands. then I slow, let a fellow pass, and slip what I can from his pocket. He shouts but I dodge behind two fools who've come to blows. Safe in the fuss I count what I took: three coins. I laugh and while I do someone brushes past, apologizing. I curse, check pockets. Pockets are empty.

The road grows more crowded, more shadowed. Easier to bump, to reach, to sneak away with a coin or three but soon as you do you feel a wind, a touch and pockets go light again. I reach to the fellow ahead and empty his pockets, move to the side as he shouts at a woman crying beside him. A man behind pushes me aside, I empty his pocket as he empties mine. We both hurry from one another but I bump into the crying woman, we shove each other away but now my coins are gone again.

The road grows more crowded and the light grows darker and for all I grab and push and tangle and lift, when at last I reach road's end my pockets are empty.

They don't waste time. They slam and lock the gate before me. The last light fades, leaving me here, outside in the dark.

Chapter 39
Just What Lucif Said to the House of Saints

"Harp and swag still safe," declared Bodkin, hanging by fingertips to the rafters of their room in the Pomegranate.

"But the silver piece is gone." Barnaby felt about in the matting of the bed. "How, with door locked and window latched?"

"Ah, that door makes no challenge, even if the innkeeper's cousins' sisters' bedmates don't have another key," scoffed Bodkin. He dropped neatly to the floor again. "And the window sits just below the roof. Could open it with my left foot."

"Well, next time I'll take the harp with me."

"Next time? We can't be staying here, 'less you want to be caught with a fellow fresh slipped from the noose."

"The pyre," corrected Cedric.

"How do they know he's here?"

"Ah, they don't yet. But from what you say, they know their escaped heretic was alongside a big fellow with yellow hair in leather carrying a gory axe. Won't take much asking to track you to this very inn."

"Oh," said Barnaby. "Ha, that's clever." He looked to the door, picturing a crowd of thief-catchers, city guards and Questioners bursting through. "We'd best be off then."

He stood, for all he felt weariness weighing like sacks of mill stones. He gave a longing look to the beds.

"Not you," declared Cedric, rising. "I am the one who must depart. And I leave in joy. I went seeking your bones, Barnaby son of Barnabas, and I find you alive among friends. What comes thereafter for me, is of no import."

"Noble," yawned Night Creep from the rafters.

"Quite," agreed Michael from the shadows.

"Gentlemen, gentlemen, no cause to scamper yet," declared Bodkin. He leaned back in his chair, hands behind head. Enjoying his authority in these matters. "We've a day, at least. Two, more like. Persephone is busy repelling Plutarch invaders. Or so it thinks. No one's going to be on a poor fox's trail tonight."

"Yet there is still a trail," sighed Cedric. "Leading to Barnaby. Best I depart."

"They'll be watching the gates," warned Night-Creep.

"And the walls," agreed Dark Michael.

"I had a different path in mind," declared Cedric.

Bodkin grinned. "Slip into Plutarch?"

"Yes, and by the seven orders of saints who and what are you, child?"

"I'm the clever one of the gang," declared Bodkin.

From the rafters: "The clever one taken prisoner by an old fool and a little girl."

From the shadows: "The clever rogue who lost a fortune in magic property."

From the rafters: "The clever fellow who set the city in a panic."

Bodkin scowled. Cedric looked up to Shadow-Creep, then to the corner where the dim shadow of Michael lounged laconic.

"Is there purpose to your strange cabal?"

At which question Bodkin, Shadow-Creep and Dark Michael looked to... Barnaby.

Barnaby sat again, glad to do so. Dug into his pack, found the wrinkled parchment map. Spread it out.

"We plan to get to the tower, gather all the treasure."

Said aloud, this declaration sounded less sensible than just a few days past, wandering whistling down a summer road.

Cedric frowned at sight of the map.

"Barnaby, I thought you understood. The tale of treasure was your stepbrother's evil jest to ensure your death."

"For sure, Alf gave the map same as handing me horse-piss, calling it ale. But it was my Da's map. And Professor Night-Creep and Dark Michael say it's an honest map."

The boy should return home, thought Cedric; and immediately reconsidered. What home? That house of cruel eyes, dark hearts? Barnaby might claim the mill for his inheritance; but the Squire would contest it. While mother and brother planned anew. Ah, they'd not be sending the boy on a second fool's quest. They'd find him a surer path to the grave.

No, best he stay away, find other purpose, another home. And yet, this journey to the tower... that was madness.

"It's a far and deadly place."

"For sure," said Bodkin. Boy eyes wide and bright. "Cursed by the saints, they say. Shadowed by storms and crows and ghosts and bats. Steps going up and up, with wolves, snakes and spiders sneaking about to trip or bite. No one makes it to the door."

"Some have," said Dark Michael. "And then dared enter. But fewer came out again. And when they did, they bore scars and frightened eyes, not treasure."

"Then why go?" That, from Barnaby.

"You ask me? It's your map. Your quest. Tell this *cabal,* miller's son. Why set yourself to the task?"

Barnaby stared at the map. It still held the glow of mystery that fascinated him as child. He fingered a corner where his father had nailed it to the wall. Before Da had taken sick, and mother had stuffed it into the trunk with his shoes.

"I'm not sure of the why of things now. Starting out, it just made something interesting to do. I didn't think it'd be dangerous, nor crossing some curse of the saints."

There came more chuckling from the rafters.

Barnaby peered up at the cat.

"It's quite vexing when you sit up there just watching and laughing so knowing-like."

"Exactly what Lucif told the Upper House of Saints," replied Night-Creep. At which observation Cedric and Bodkin laughed.

"Well, I'm going to the tower too," said Bodkin.

"You? Why?" That, from Cedric.

"Yes," added Michael, knife-sharp. "Why?"

Bodkin leaned back in pose of confidence, for all he sat on his knees to meet adult eyes.

"I need to set myself to something worthy of old Mercutio Moon. Something with adventure and danger."

This was met with silence, excepting a yawn from above. Bodkin ignored that judgement, addressed Cedric.

"If'n you want to cross into Plutarch, don't try the bridges. They'll be watched. Probably closed, what with thinking the Tarchs are invading."

"You suggest I swim the Lethe?"

"'Course not. But there's boats. Back and forth across the river by night, not under hand nor eye of either side."

"Trade in bodies," growled Cedric.

"'Tis legal, if not over nice." Now came Bodkin's turn to yawn, not in judgment but in weariness. He looked towards the cots. "I'll find passage for us tomorrow."

"Us?" That, from Barnaby.

"If they find you but not your clerical friend, they'll try knocking answers from out your head. Might put you in the same lockup he walked from. Best we all move camp to the other side of the river."

"That is wise," declared the cat from above.

"Almost clever," offered Michael.

"Very well, then," yawned Barnaby. He shook his head, drunk with the need for sleep. The yawn passed around the room again; excepting to Dark Michael, who merely sighed. Night-Creep yawned, probably just to mock.

Rising, Barnaby staggered to a cot, removed his boots, his leather armor. Collapsing with a sigh of relief. Bodkin rose, did much the same.

But Cedric remained at the table, staring at the candle. A tall stalk of fragrant beeswax, the flame a golden flower waving in the draft. Cedric watched it grow shorter, while he considered the events of the night, listening to the snoring breaths of the two boys.

At length he reached a finger to the map upon the table. Tracing the edges. A large parchment, intricately detailed. On one side a rough map of the Saintless Mountains, showing outlines of Martia and Hefestia. The other side showed a grand tower, with portions detailing seven lower floors.

Yellowed with age; but untorn, near unwrinkled. This was no document fading gently into dust. This *thing* waited for completion. He turned gaze from map to candle flame, back to map, pondering completion.

"Unwise," said the cat. No longer in the rafters, but upon the table.

Cedric smiled. "And now I will pretend to wonder what you mean."

"If you burn the map you will not turn the boy from the tower. You only diminish his chances once he arrives."

Cedric replied not; merely continued to contemplate 'completion'. Same end by fire, as the Questioners had intended for his heresies.

Silent as the cat's arrival, the shade of a soldier commanded the chair across from Cedric. Hat now removed, revealing a thick mop of gray and black hair. A handsome face; yet scarred and efficient as Barnaby's axe. When he spoke, voice came low but clear.

"Surely there is some purpose of the saints that so aimless a creature as the miller's son is sent on such path?"

At which question Cedric smiled.

"Mark you two, how the candle flame dances?"

Ghost and cat replied not.

"But good sirs, does it dance to its own will, or to the song of the wind?"

Cat and ghost replied not.

"Poetic question, no? But in truth, the flame knows no dance. Merely flickers with the wind. As the wind knows no song; merely puffs to the weather of the night. And that grand personage 'Night Wind'… we might easily give face, and name, and house. But she is the mindless child of moon and sea, cloud and sun and the turning globe. True things all, and holy for being true. But they know us not, for they know themselves not."

The white eyes of the cat reflected no least candle shimmer. While the eyes of the ghost remained dark caves, returning no least candle glimmer.

But that flame shone bright in Cedric's living eyes. He reached a finger. The flame writhed at the near-touch.

"But we watch a flame and see a dance. We catch the wind's muttering and hear voice. As we gaze up at the far untouchable stars and see the hosts of the Upper House of Saints."

Ghost and cat replied not. Cedric rose from his chair.

"Barnaby has set himself on this path. *That* is what counts. Not the will of saints nor the random winds of the earth. So, I shall go with him on the journey. By my own will, if he will have my company."

That declared, Cedric bent, snuffed the candle's dance with a puff. The room became dark as starless night. He made his slow and mortal way to bed. Ghost and cat replied not.

Chapter 40
Warm Bath, Quick Death

Val the Bard lay in soapy water making a sea froth of bubbles about the islets of knees, the coastal breasts. She leaned back against warm marble, letting the aches and indignities of gaol soak away.

And the dirt. When she'd first settled into the bath, it'd turned brown as a communal chamber pot. Now the water shone clear, smelling of pink flowers, spring blossoms. Val sang aloud, enjoying the echoes.

Miss Fortune chased the grail.
Up and down to no avail.
Kissed St. Bridget, made her fidget,
Said, 'I find her warm and so female'.

She stretched out the 'so' to a long '*soooooooo*'.

"Now that makes a proper entrance," declared Alexandra. Appearing at the door, fingering the ties of her robe.

"Been expecting you," sighed Val. "But there's no lock on the door. Go away. I'm recuperating. I'm having a holy moment. I'm communing with the saints."

"You steal my horse, then my bath including all my salts." Alexandra tossed her robe aside. "Did you go to bard school or the Thief's Guild?"

She slipped legs over the edge of the great marble tub, slid in to sit opposite Val. Grinning over the archipelago of knees, across the soapy waves.

"Oh, I see new scars. Stand and let me appreciate."

"Yeah, no."

"Wimp. I'll show you mine. Look at these slices on my hands from learning the rapier. And this scar by my ear comes from a war lance. We were charging at one another without helms. Kinda stupid, I guess. Oh, and this scar where-"

Val closed eyes, began a loud and rude snore.

"Ah, c'mon, 'Tine. I worked hard to get these. Been waiting forever to show them off."

Val considered. Sighed, opening eyes.

"Sorry, Lex. Don't want to be mean. Those are lovely scars. You look a proper warrior of St. Martia."

"Really? Truly?"

"Absolutely. Dress you in some leather and brass scraps and you can slip over the border, be shouting on the practice fields like the best." *Which is an idiot way to spend one's life.*

"I bet you just added in your head that practicing war all the time is for dimwits."

"No, 'course not. It's just not for me."

"Horse theft is your true vocation?"

Val hesitated. But she could tell Alexandra.

"I saw the cup again, Lexi. This time I was wide awake, in some dull class about theurgy. I looked out the window and there it was. Floating down the road like a soap bubble. I jumped up, ran outside. The headmistress's horse was waiting all nice and saddled. What else could I do?"

"Makes sense to me. Granted, it scheduled you to be branded 'T' for thief. And that's before breaking gaol, assaulting guards, consorting with witches. Change of schedule. Now you're slated for summary execution."

"Wait, what? You aren't going to pardon me?"

"Me? I'm not the duke. Just the daughter everyone says is touched in the head. I have authority to throw tea parties and ride through the streets while waving a sword. I've no power over decisions of the Juditandis, much less the Council of Questioners."

"I killed some of those monsters last night."

"Well done. Maybe they'll give you a softer rope to hang from."

"Shit. Then ask your father to pardon me."

"The man who sentenced his wife to exile for misuse of the rites of St. Dion? He follows the law like a dog follows dinner."

"Not even for the child he used to call *Martia's Little Princess*?"

"Not even. Unless he decides the fate of the prodigal is up to St. Martia. In which case he'll send you back. In chains."

"I'd rather hang."

"Figured so."

"Well, if I'm still a condemned criminal, why am I not behind bars?"

"Ha. I may be a taken for a lightweight mooncalf, but I'm still an officer of the ducal guard. I apprehended you while nobly defending the city. Now I'm keeping you under my... custody."

"Get your pretty foot off now."

"Sorry, sorry. Just illustrating the metaphor."

"How about if you just let me sneak out your window?"

"If you want. I'll send the guards on some errand. And leave some gold and a knife lying around. But the city will howl I'm incompetent, dad will go red-faced with hysterics and the Juditandis will make a point of running you down."

"Shit. Well, either you've gotten cruel in late girlhood, or you have some plan to help me."

"Ha. 'Course I do. Not going to let them hang the only creature in the Middle House crazier than me."

"I'm not crazy. I just chase a floating glowing singing cup that leads me into crazy situations."

"Exactly. Anyway, politically my city is at a tense moment. No one likes Father and everyone thinks I'm touched. Meanwhile in Pomona the army is busy eating its leaders. Can you believe they hung the Cold Major for treason? And after last night, everyone worries a horde from the dark side of Proserpine is about to invade our bright happy half."

"Wasn't much of an invasion."

"Yeah, and that's puzzling everyone. Maybe sending monsters up through the sewers was to test our defenses."

"Let me guess. You want me to stand on the bridge and defy the Tarchs to cross?"

"That'd make a glorious picture, wouldn't it? And you'd do it, Kurgus. It's in your blood."

"My splattered blood being the essential element of the glorious portrait, yes."

"Yeah. No, my plan is less glorious and less bloody. Not that you'll like it. If I suggest something it must be crazy."

"You once tied a Hefestian energy crystal on an arrow and shot it at a statue of St. Apollonius."

"Most obnoxious saint in the Upper House. Grins like knows he can get you legs up and eyes open. And wasn't the boom amazing?"

"My father thought so. Not the bishop of St. Apollonius."

"Your dad was special."

"Yeah. Yeah, he was."

"Sorry. Anyway, *this* plan is sane and sound. Gets you out of Demetia with no thief-catchers on your trail. No Martia ambassador demanding your return. No angry fathers shouting. And I look cold and cruel, which people think means sane and competent."

"And the mad plan is…?"

"We cast an oration of '*Seem Undead*' on you. Announce you've been summarily executed. You lie quiet in the courtyard for all to see. At sundown we cart you away. They take you across river pretending to sell you to the body-traders. You jump up and run away."

"Seriously? That's your plan?"

"Yep. And we'll get the witch you escaped with to recite the spell. That way no one here will know but me and my personal guard."

"Won't people expect to see an execution?"

"Summary means fast. I'll tell everyone your crimes distracted from the city defense in time of emergency. We dragged you to the courtyard, I gave a sword thrust and done."

"So I just lie dead quiet, then get carted across the river to freedom and safety."

"That's about right."

"Well, that is simple. Totally insane, but simple."

"Val, it's the stuff of song. You want to just sing about heroic deeds, or you want to do them?"

"I want to just sing about them."

"Well, maybe your cup wants you to do more."

"You know I could drown you here in your bath."

"Maybe. Or not. Last few years I've been practicing fighting. While you've been practicing harp plucking."

"I wouldn't actually be sold off to twisted monks with a fondness for dead girls, right?"

"'Course not. Once across river, we break the spell, and you're free of the law and familial duties. You can stay in Plutarch or wander back to St. Demetia. Go sing your songs to the trees of St. Silenus, if you want."

I follow the cup, though Val. *If it goes into the wilds of nowhere, I'll go there. But no; the mad thing wouldn't go anywhere so sensible. It led me here.*

"Fine. But I want another corpse for company."

"Whose? Not mine. I need to look alive for this to work."

"The witch. She's fast on her feet. And her feet want out of here as much as do mine."

* * *

Jewel stared about her room in the ducal tower. The chamber had a cot, a table, a lamp. A plate of honest food, clean water for drinking and washing. Far more pleasant than the gaol cell. But the window was barred, the door locked. She was still a prisoner.

She took her necklace, laid it upon the floor. "Periwinkle, awake," she whispered. The thing twitched, growing to become the bigger-than-a-cat spider again.

"Hullo, Perry," she whispered.

It waggled its blue eye-sacs, waved a few legs in greeting.

She sat watching as it scuttered about the wall, under the bed, out again. Then to the bars of the window and through them.

She closed her eyes. A vision came, faint but dizzying. As if she stood on the tower looking down at the city from a thousand connected pictures. She was seeing through the facetted eyes of Periwinkle.

She opened her own eyes, the vision vanished, leaving her trembling.

There came steps and sounds at the door.

"Return," she whispered. At once the spider slipped through the bars. "Periwinkle, sleep.".

The door opened. Jewel stood, attempting not to stagger. She retrieved her necklace from where it now lay on the window ledge. That done, she turned to see the Duke's daughter Alexandra. Behind her came the bard horse-thief. They entered, closing the door firmly behind them.

"Explain this again?" asked Jewel, staring at the floor, the book, the horse-thief. Not at the Lady Alexandra. Noble folk took offense when meeting peasant eyes.

"You'll cast '*Seem Undead*' on us both."

"On you and Lady Alexandra?"

"No, on you and me, for saint's sake. Alexandra isn't a fugitive condemned to death."

"Right. On you and me. Then what?"

"We look dead. She tells everyone she's run us through. Summary execution in time of emergency, etcetera. There's a decent chance no one pays attention while they worry about invasion. Meanwhile we lie still till evening. Then get carted across the river to be sold as corpses. Once in Plutarch, we run away laughing."

Jewel considered this.

"This city is insane."

"Yes."

"I don't know the oration."

Alexandra produced a small but thick leather-bound book.

"I had a prayer book of St. Hecatatia brought from the Cathedral's shelf of forbidden texts. The oration's on this age."

"That's a difficult one."

"So? You broke out of a cell meant to hold mother superiors."

I had help, Jewel thought but did not say. She wondered what happened to the heretic. What was his name? The Questioner called him… 'Cedric'. Where was Cedric now? She could ask. Though that might draw attention to him.

Anyway, probably he lay in a street with his throat ripped by shadow-fiends. If not, then he'd been returned to a cell and his appointment with a pious pyre. Pity. He'd been useful.

He'd been kind, said a voice in her head. Not her usual sort of thought. She looked at her spider-necklace suspiciously. Had that been Perry? 'Course not.

"If you want to help us escape, why can't you just let us sneak out?"

"Because they will come after you," said Alexandra. "Escaping insults the Juditandis. They'll make a point of setting bounties, send out hunters. Even if you get out of Persephone, you'll have to play fox and hounds all the way to Hefestia or Aurelia."

"Might work," said Jewel. Surprised at how easily she argued with a duke's daughter.

She raised her eyes, daring to look Alexandra face to face, as she was oft told not to do as kitchen girl in Stonecroft.

She beheld the noblewoman staring impatiently, but not in contempt. Bigger in build than Val or Jewel. Soldier's tunic, horseman's pants and boots. Hair cut short as a man's, scars on fingers in place of rings.

Bet she likes girls more than boys, thought Jewel. She turned to consider Val. Probably the two were lovers as well as friends. *They need me to cast the oration. But we aren't friends. Good.*

Again, she wished Cedric had made it through the night. Not that he'd been a *friend*. Just, nice. But anyway she had Periwinkle.

"Jewel, right? That's your name?" asked Val.

Jewel nodded.

"If Alexandra just lets us slip out the window, she gets into major trouble, and they'll make an extra effort to run us down. Maybe pass our names to the Friends of Friar February."

"But it's a crazy plan."

"Sister Fortuna has already given all the smiles we can ask of her. Whatever we do next has to be something mad enough to make Fortuna laugh aloud. This plan is simple and quick, and definitely mad."

"You promise we aren't really going to be sold to necromancers?"

"Of course," said Alexandra. "That's just the excuse to get you across the river. Walk away when you get to that side. Or run. Val will have some money sewn in her shirt."

"And a knife," reminded Val.

"Right. A knife. You two will be on your own. But free of pursuit or bounty. At least until Val steals another horse."

Jewel bit lip in thought.

"Plutarch has no laws against orations to Sister Hecatatia."

"They do not. Over there, they are all about the Lower House of Saints."

"Right, then," declared Jewel. Placing her necklace about her throat. "Let me see that prayer book."

Chapter 41
What Dreams May Come

Capitano led two men and a cart into the eastern courtyard of the Ducal Tower. There the bodies lay, exact as reported. Two females lying quiet, hands bound before them, livid faces turned to the afternoon sky. Flies circled and drank from pools of blood fast turning black.

A bored guard leaned against the wall, staring at the same sky, brushing away the flies. At the approach of the officer he straightened coat and spine. Capitano studied the single guard, the two corpses, at length nodding satisfied.

"These will do. Load them into the cart."

The guard cleared his throat. "Begging your pardon, Captain, but Lady Alexandra ordered they not be disturbed till sun comes down."

Capitano smiled "Quite right of her ladyship. All should see the reward for defying law and saint. But tonight Demetia has need of *legally* deceased corpses. So I am authorized to gather such windfall fruit, wheresoever the wind lets it drop."

The guard worked upon this metaphor.

"Authorized?"

"By the Duke. Whose orders precede his daughter's. Correct?"

"Yessir."

"Good man.

They wrapped the bodies in sheets, placed them in the cart, wheeling them out and away.

Beyond the tower gate they made slow progress towards the river. Passersby eyed the cart, turning quick away. At length Capitano directed them into a quiet alley.

"We've time," declared Capitano to the two subordinates. "Put the civilian clothes on."

"Are we going to cross the bridge?"

"Hmm, no. The bridges stay closed. We'll go by the corpse-trader's boats tonight. They don't cease even for war."

"Ah. Reconnaissance, sir?"

"Exact so. His Grace wants to know what the Black Robes mean by sending fiends through our pretty sewers. Maybe they just got lost. Maybe they were practicing invasion. So, we dress as civilians, take a cartload of corpses across river right into St. Plutarch's Cathedral of Resurrection itself."

"Cartload? This is just two."

"Hmm. Good point. Needs at least another body to seem believable cargo, doesn't it? Climb in, soldier. Wrap yourself in a sheet."

"Me? I'm not dead."

"Oh, you don't have to be. We aren't really corpse-trading, We just need a believable cargo to get inside the Cathedral. Then we sniff around, see if they are planning invasion. So climb in, lie down. You'll get to nap beside two pretty things while we do the work and take the risks."

"I guess. I mean, yessir."

The soldier climbed into the cart, twisting a sheet about himself. While Capitano and the other soldier changed to civilian clothes.

Once shrouded, the soldier in the cart lay back. Then shifted, twitching like a caterpillar dissatisfied with its cocoon. Capitano observed this twitching, equally dissatisfied.

"Can't you keep any more still than that?"

"It itches, sir. And its damned uncanny being next to dead ladies. And they smell."

Capitano sighed, produced a pipe, struggled to light it. Watching as the shroud-bound soldier continued to wiggle, occasionally grumbling within his sheet.

"It's important you not speak or move, or we'll look like fools, failing the mission."

"Yessir."

"So don't speak anymore."

"Yessir. I won't."

"You are speaking now."

"Sorry. Itches. And I'd take oath the dead lady next me moved."

Capitano sighed, gave up attempting to light his pipe. He settled for biting thoughtfully on the stem. Leaned against the alley wall, contemplated the fading day.

"Just between us and these deceased lovelies, we've a second mission."

"Another secret mission?" That, from the shrouded soldier. Capitano scowled exasperated.

"Seems there's an old statue in a back chapel of the cathedral. Wears a helmet that's a forgotten relic left behind when Plutarch took that half of Persephone. Gives power over the dead, they say. The Duke's decided we need it back now."

"I'll keep that to myself, sir."

"I don't doubt it."

Capitano put away pipe. Drew knife.

"You took the oath to St. Demetia, didn't you, soldier?"

"Yessir."

"You recall it?"

"Yessir. Pledge life and honor to the flag and sword of the lands of blessed Saint-."

"Good man." Capitano thrust knife into the shroud. There came a gasp, a shudder, then a rush of red into the dirty cloth.

Capitano stood awhile, watching red bleed through white. Definitely a more believable picture of a corpse-cart. He put away knife, returned to the struggle of lighting his pipe.

At sun's setting he and the one assistant led the cart from the alley, bearing three corpses down to the river.

Chapter 42
Sometimes There Are No Words

Bodkin sat to table in the common room of the Pomegranate, chewing on hot sausage, cold thought.

Last night I met my own granddaughter. Don't even know her ma's name. Probably old Mercutio never asked. And years ago, pretty Maggy Swynthe drowned herself cursing him. Cursing me.

He looked about, young eyes appreciating how morning light turned dirty window glass to dusty glory. While the air of the room wafted with flower smells of summer Persephone, mixing with cooking scents from the kitchen, smoke from the hearth. Ghost perfumes of beer and wine rose from the floorboards to haunt the sensitive nose with memory of revels past.

And everywhere sounded a pleasant buzz and bustle of a busy inn on a quiet day. Horses and carts in the street, kitchen clatter of cups and plates, bits of bird song, barks of dogs.

What would this morning seem to old Mercutio? With his rheumy eyes eight decades old, ancient nose twisted large and useless by time. Age-deafened ears catching only weak echo of the sounds of the day.

At which thought, the old man in his head laughed.

At eighty and more, you might as well have your head in a bucket. Not hearing much, not smelling much, not seeing much, not tasting much. It's why we stole the Elixir of Youth. To feel this alive again.

"Yeah? I'm thinking maybe there was another reason you didn't want to be Old Mercutio anymore."

I wanted this. To be young again.

"Maggie Swynthe drowned herself cursing the father of her child. Or her children? Don't know the litter count. Bet you don't know either. After all, according to

Crow, offspring of Old Mercutio came plentiful as kittens in spring."

The old man voice said nothing.

"Maybe old Mercutio reached a day in his long years where it all looked a damned stupid business. Decided to drown himself same as Maggie. Just by a different cup."

Arrogant child, thinking you can understand. A man's life is not a boy's dream. Maggie did as she wished. In girlhood and womanhood. Exact as did I.

"And you both ended yourselves."

Forget about it! That's all washed clean. Over!

"Is it? Is forgotten the same as washed? 'Cause Persephone seems full of your ghosts. Same as my head."

They don't matter! Move on. Regain our skills, not our regrets. Keep head down and eyes sharp.

"To do what?"

To do things right this time! Make ourselves rich and famous and happy! Achieve victories folk will talk about for years. Continue our legend!

"Last night I heard my legend. Says I was a cock, a grin and a light-fingered piece of wandering dogshit."

Stop being childish.

"Sure. Give me a few years and I'll get it done."

Fool. You're arguing with yourself aloud. Drawing attention when you should be sitting quiet. Shut up and listen to the room. Are thief-catchers and the Questioners on your trail?

Bodkin sighed. The old voice wasn't wrong. He needed to be careful, get back to the business of staying alive and on top of things.

He looked about. Finding a few folk eyeing him with mixes of pity or distaste. Seeing a boy in dirty clothes talking to himself. Probably deciding he was cracked.

Perhaps they had the right of it. Maybe the old man in his head was him being bedlam. Fine, he'd make it work to his favor.

He continued eating, no longer speaking, keeping an ear cocked to the chatter and clatter of the room. Not surprisingly, chief topic was the night's bells and watch whistles.

"Invasion and escaped prisoners from the gaol," said a fellow at the bar. "The Duke don't run things right anymore, and his girl don't know how."

"Not her Ladyship's fault what those rotters across the river decide in the night," argued another. "And I heard she caught two of the three prisoners. A witch and a horse-stealing bard. Hung 'em both this morning, quick and done."

Bodkin frowned. Recalling when he'd poked his head up into St. Sidon's courtyard. There'd been two females pretending to be guards. One had even sung with Whisper. Had that been Val?

He recalled him, no, *her*, by the campfire trading songs and jests with the robber band. You didn't need an old man's insight to see she thought Marcus and the gang were yokel fools who mangled the song in their mouth like dogs gobbling ducklings.

Had Val come to Persephone, been arrested, escaped gaol, gone running through the streets same as Barnaby and Bodkin? With less luck than they, if she'd ended kicking from the end of a rope.

"Breakfast!" Barnaby shouted, sitting to table across from Bodkin. Eyeing the plates. "Some of this mine?"

"Some. Just not all. What you been at?"

Barnaby pulled a plate of sausage and baked apples before him, bacon and potatoes to the side.

"Michel gives instructions in the morning, Night-Creep in evening. Except when we're all busy."

"Should think you had practice enough yesterday."

"Just what I said. Could scarce rise from bed. Michael didn't care to hear my plaints. Think we'll have time to look for Val today?"

Bodkin considered sharing his suspicion that the bard dangled like a watch-fob in a courtyard of the garrison.

Don't, advised Old Mercutio. *Boy's mind is full of glorious idiocies. He'd decide to rescue her from the gibbet or retrieve her from the Lower House of Saints. And it might have been some other criminal. Why blacken his morning?*

"Barnaby, if a girl doesn't let you find her, she doesn't want to be found."

To Bodkin's surprise, Barnaby only grinned, not the least disheartened.

"Ah, I know that particular truth, Master Old-Soul. If Val had interest in my miller's person, she'd have stayed for a fare-the-well kiss."

"Then why chase after her?"

Barnaby bit the head off a sausage in sign of deepest thought.

"Not chasing her. She's hunting her magic cup, I'm working sideways towards my tower. It's just that after us crossing paths twice, I've begun looking for her on the road ahead."

He reached for bread and change of subject.

"Ha. Wonder if this was made with flour from Mill Town? Might have ground the wheat myself. What a strange thing that'd be, to meet it again so far away. And why are you staring so glum?"

Bodkin sighed. Old Mercutio was right; no profit to darkening Barnaby's morning with talk of the bard's fate.

"I'm staring because you look like a one of those northern wild men that howl about Holy Bishop Wotan."

"Me?"

"Yeah. And I have the look and smell of a rat drowned in Lucif's saintly sister's chamber pot. First order of business is fresh clothes for us both."

Barnaby fingered his half-healed face, his yellow beard. "I do need a shaving knife. New tunic. And wet stone for Dragontooth. Awl and thread to stich my leathers. A new cloak would be nice. My boots are still good."

"Well, my boots are more full of shit than a fat monk's bowels. Finish up the bacon and let's be off."

"What about crossing the river with-"

"-with our good friend the tailor," interjected Bodkin. Giving a look sharp with warning.

"What tailor?"

"The one who taught you your letters upside down."

Barnaby looked about at the folk of the common room. Noting the eyes and ears fixed upon them. "Oh. Right. Yes. My friend the tailor. He says he'll stay in the room out of sight. We should get him something besides his-"

"-his tailor clothes."

"Yes," agreed Barnaby. "Because they make him look too much like a, a tailor."

Within Bodkin's head, an old man sighed. Same as the outer younger Bodkin did so sigh.

"Good. Mr. *Tailor* can watch our gear. There's no crossing the river till evening. We've time for errands."

Barnaby took last bites, stood.

"What's first and where?"

Bodkin hesitated, then decided. "Let's make a quick visit to an old friend."

Whisper sat on the pathway twixt the gaol and the garrison, blinking in the morning sun, singing bits of song, eyeing the passersby.

She watched a tall man and short companion head down the street towards her. *Time to scamper?* No, they'd not get rough with a poor girl in bright day's shine.

Anyway, you could tell Mr. Barnaby was a good sort, for all the rough look to him. She noted the red lines down one side of his face, wounds mostly healed. *Saint's healing*, that must have been. Hadn't had those marks yesterday.

"Good morning, Miss Whisper."

"Good morrow, Mister Barnaby; and blessings of the Sainted Sister Persephone make your day bright and your night warm."

She turned a wary eye to Bodkin.

"You here for your glitter back? Don't have it now. Anyways I opened the grate exact as agreed. Not my blemish you decide to keep down in the yucky muck."

"You're right there. But I'm just dropping by to inquire upon something else."

At which news she looked down at the hat lying before her. It contained a wooden button, a worn copper and a chicken bone.

Bodkin growled, added a penny to the mix, then proffered his question.

"Did Magpie make it home safe?"

Whisper grinned. "That all? Ha. Mag's fine. She's always fine. You could drop the world into Lucif's soup bowl and Magpie'd come up with the splash, stealing his spoon. Fast and clever, that one is."

"Good to hear."

"But Crow's dead. Things ate him half up right on the cobbles, if'n you can believe."

"I can."

"Also they gacked the two escaped ladies this morning. Quick as snuffing candles. Folk say the Duke did it fast to show he's still got a grip but I think it mean. The witch was a peppery sort but the bard-"

"Right, thanks, Whisper," hurried Bodkin. "We're good. Tell Magpie..." Bodkin paused, searching old soul and young self for message.

"Tell 'er what?"

Yes, boy. What to tell a stranger that accident makes your granddaughter? Will you send your love? Give her wise advice upon keeping nose clean, eyes clean, soul clean? Bah. There are no words. Not from me. Not from you.

Bodkin gave up.

"Ah, never mind. Thanks, Whisper. But you, you take care of yourself."

* * *

Evening covered the flower-scented city with light soft and warm as melting butter poured upon the rooftops, reminding Barnaby that he was hungry again.

He turned from the window, went to the mirror. Studying his reflection, pleased and puzzled. Blond beard trimmed; not shaven clean as his habit in Mill Town. Fresh trousers, clean cotton shirt beneath patched leather vest. He felt different. Maybe because he'd washed for the first time in days?

He reached a finger, tracing the claw marks down the cheekbone to the chin. They resembled wounds from weeks past, for all he'd gained them but the night before.

He turned to Friar Cedric. Now wearing hat, shirt and coat bland as a shop clerk's second best.

"Still see a miller in your mirror?" Cedric asked.

Barnaby laughed. "No sir. That there is a bold adventurer. Scarred and fierce, ready for battle. Or dinner. Can we get dinner first?"

"No," said Bodkin. "You are a bold adventurer, and danger is your meat and drink. Now let's depart before Questioners and thief-catchers dine upon us."

Bodkin led them through winding streets towards the river docks. Less talkative than the day before. Cedric kept head down, face shadowed by hat.

Far ahead walked the shadow of Dark Michael. Barnaby looked behind, spying the dark form of Shadow-Creep. Why did the two keep such distance? But they were a ghost and a cat. Mysterious creatures. No telling the 'why's of either.

I'd like to be mysterious, decided Barnaby. I'd say riddling things. Disappear for days, then reappear at the door. No, at the *window*. During a storm. On a horse with flaming eyes. With strange wounds I won't explain. Wearing a hat from foreign parts. No, from the *moon*.

He pondered what hats they wore so far above. Meanwhile, Bodkin led them downwards, their path ever darker, dirtier. Passing folk on doorsteps who offered no evening greetings. The wind grew colder, damper; the smell of river water and mud diminishing Persephone's flower scent.

"Let me do the talking and we don't get our throats cut," declared Bodkin. "Barnaby, you loom again. Keep silent, threatening blood and war with your menacing looks."

"Very well."

"Remind me why a child is in command?" Cedric wondered aloud. Barnaby gave him a menacing look. Bodkin grinned. Cedric shook his head.

They turned, and turned again, and came of a sudden before the river. Wide, flowing black as an old man's thoughts of death; glimmering white wherever ripples caught the light. A cold wind haunted the water, moaning faint lament. Worn brick steps led down the bank to boat docks where waited a scattering of dismal vessels.

At the bottom step sat a city guard; manning ancient chair beneath ancient post from which hung a lamp, probably ancient. Certainly its light seemed faded by time, weary with shining yet another night. The guard eyed their approach, hand bell ready to ring alarm.

"Looking for the delivery skiff," declared Bodkin.

The guard, being old and scarred, gave an old and scarred look. Suspicion mixed with bitter wisdom and weary disinterest.

"Where's your cargo?"

"Just us, all nice and breathing." He gave a grin to show how very good it was to breathe. The grin took the guard by surprise. He peered closer.

"Hey, now, don't I know you?"

"No."

The man snorted. "Guessing not. Just... you look like a mate of mine when I had your years."

Bodkin hesitated. *Lucif's teeth to my privates, it's Bert. Saints' spit he's old.* He opened mouth to laugh about the day they'd nicked a cart of wine, got all the southern quarter drunk. Emptied a hundred pockets, easy...

Keep quiet, idiot, commanded old Mercutio. *You've nothing to share with him now. He's done! Look at him. Worn as a tossed boot. That's the pox we escaped. Old age!*

"Your mate," asked Bodkin. "He live happy?"

The old man scowled; maybe at Bodkin, else at memory.

"Infernum, he laughed oft enough, if that's your 'happy'. It was the fools trusting him that ended crying in the dock, screaming at the whipping post, choking in the noose. Sure as saints' shit shines, when time came for the bill to be paid, Merc would be safe away and laughing."

"Yeah," sighed Bodkin. "That comes easy in my head to picture. Thank you, then."

The guard growled at any offered 'thank you'. Holding out palm wrinkled and gnarled as an ape's.

Bodkin offered three silvers. The open palm waited dissatisfied. Bodkin nodded, placed two more. Coins pocketed, the guard pointed down the walkway.

"Skiff with red lamp."

Bodkin returned the growl, then led away along rows of boats sharing a common color theme of black, dark black and grayish black. At the end waited a long flat riverboat. On a pole attached to the bow hung a lamp of crimson glass. The candle flickered within like to a trapped insect or troubled soul.

Beyond that faint light stood an eerily tall figure entirely hid within cloak and cowl. He did not turn at their approach. Instead stood watching night come up the river. Beside him waited a large but more human-sized personage; wearing leather as dramatically scarred as Barnaby's. Upon his back was strapped a two-handed sword to rival Dragontooth. He *did* take notice of the newcomers, looming menacing and anxious for violence.

Barnaby studied the crossed arms, the angry frown. Deciding happily that *here* was an expert loomer to follow. He crossed his own arms, frowned his own frown.

The big man's scowl deepened at this imitation. He cocked head, spat angrily into the river, keeping eyes on Barnaby, unblinking. Barnaby appreciated how this gesture expressed both rough manners and inner rage. He cocked head, spat angrily into the river, keeping eyes upon the loomer, unblinking.

Now the fellow growled, scraping one foot back, forth, back; a bull ready to charge. Barnaby growled, scraping a foot forth, back, forth.

"Stop that, you idiot," whispered Bodkin. Then stepped forwards to the silent figure in dark cloak. What conversation followed came in whispers quiet and mysterious as the flow of the river before them.

Meanwhile the loomer began fingering his sword hilt. Barnaby studied this act, then began a careful caress to the hilt of Dragontooth. Cedric sighed, turned to watch a hand cart coming along the walkway. One man pulling; a second walking before it with a lamp, lest the cart tumble into the river. What the cart carried lay shrouded beneath sheeting; but Cedric guessed what it must be.

"Interesting," said a voice close beside him. Cedric all but jumped into the Lethe. There stood the shadow-figure of Dark Michael.

"What interests?"

"The two bringing the cart. They are soldiers, not body traders."

"How can you tell?"

"By how they walk. Keeping backs straight, eyes to shadows. Boots, belts and weaponry are army issue."

"They wear civilian clothes."

"Yes. That is what makes it interesting."

The cart stopped beneath the red lamp. The two began lifting long burdens wrapped in dirty white, bearing them to the boat.

Bodkin came up beside Cedric. "Passage arranged," he whispered. Then eyed the cart. "Crap. Guess that was to be expected."

"Why do we not hire less… *macabre* transport?"

"Because the Duke thinks Plutarch attacked last night. Bridges are closed, river crossing forbidden. It's the charnel skiff or we swim. Hop on board."

Three sheet-wound corpses now lay on the deck of the boat. Cedric stepped around them, disliking the smell. The sheets showed the outlines of feet, of breasts and heads. Not the person within, just the rough idea of the former personage.

The two corpse-dealers took seats on a bench beside their cargo. Eyeing the other travelers.

The loomer gave over menacing Barnaby. He untied the mooring ropes, while the cloaked man pushed off from the riverbank, using a pole long as a beam of light from the moon, black as the dark between the stars.

Cedric eyed the dim figure of Michael, remaining on the dock, observing their departure. Where was the cat? Perhaps the two unnatural creatures could not cross the river. If so, perhaps that was for the best.

The rocking boat persuaded Barnaby to sit. He took a place across from the two corpse-dealers. Trying not to stare at their sad cargo. A bare foot stuck out from a sheet. Pale and thin. *A woman's foot*, Barnaby decided.

Cedric watched the cloaked man patiently poling them downstream, keeping close to the bank. "Why aren't we crossing the river?"

Bodkin had gone silent, staring at the shrouded corpses. A look of old-man worry upon his young-boy face. Barnaby gave a shrug to say *river traffic is mystery to a miller*. It was one of the corpse dealers who answered Cedric.

"Ah, we don't go straight across." The man's voice came loud and happy, for all the setting of shadow and gloom. To Barnaby, the voice sounded familiar.

"See the towers on the bridge? Guards are eyeing us from there now. They'd send shot and arrows our way if we headed straight towards the Plutarch bank. No, we'll float lawfully downriver till we're out of their view. There'll be a ferry rope we'll catch hold of. Pull ourselves across, work our way back upriver."

Barnaby eyed the man. Young, long-nosed. With confident voice and grin. Where had they met?

"Did you kill these people?" he asked, pointing at the shroud-wound bodies.

Cedric took a breath inwards. Bodkin kicked Barnaby's boot. But the man laughed, taking no offense.

"You'll be hearing how folks are murdered on the road, traded as clay to the Tarchs. But if you bring a corpse to the Black Robes, first order of business is they ensure it was a *legal* death. Civilians in their beds, soldiers, hmm, in their duty."

"Or state execution," added his companion, grinning, giving one of the bodies a kick.

"*Shit*," whispered Bodkin. *Quiet,* whispered Mercutio.

The corpse-dealer shrugged.

"Execution comes under the definition 'legal', While any happy matricide bringing in his just-knifed mother will find himself working graveyard shift on the Plutarch docks himself."

Barnaby nodded, feeling a bit relieved.

"Then, who gets traded? I mean, who were they, before they are, well, dead?"

"When poor sorts in sunny Demetia feel pinched for coin, they sign title to their mortal remains whensoever the House of Saints shall decide they're done with it. Wherefore not? Gets some hungry family through hard times."

"Saves on burial expenses," added his companion.

Barnaby worked to picture that. Why not, indeed?

The corpse-trader continued, grinning at the grand jest of Life and Death.

"Then there's the brooding types that live dreading Friar Februarys' bony finger-tap on the shoulder. They breathe easier knowing they'll keep busy for St. Plutarch, stead of lying still for the worms of Demetia."

Barnaby tugged on his beard.

"And yet, just seems wrong somehow."

"Plutarch and Demetia dwell alike in the House of Saints," said Cedric. "Both bearing their different testaments." He studied the corpses lying still and meaningless as lumber put aside. "But I admit, the messages of the Lower House have always confounded my understanding."

Barnaby worked to picture living in his body knowing it was destined to other uses. But wasn't that true now? And did it matter? When he was dead, he'd have no use for it, any more than title.

"How much do the, the Black Robes pay a person for their body?"

"I see you are a businessman," said the dealer. "Excellent question. As in life, so in death. The strong fetch more than the weak. The young more than old. Fair more than the plain. Ah, particularly the females, bless 'em."

"Why so?"

Cedric sighed; Bodkin hissed. The corpse-dealer leaned forwards, giving Barnaby a grin to say they were both *men of the world*.

"Well, now, see, there are houses on the dark side of the river where the clientele seek bedmates that never tire, and never perspire, and never inquire."

He reached to one of the sheets.

"Care for a peek, free of charge?"

"No," said Bodkin, standing. "Stop."

Barnaby turned to Bodkin. The boy looked panicked. Understandable. Barnaby himself felt sickened.

"No, thank you," he said, tone cold as any clay.

The dealer laughed; the sound flying amused across the water, into the night.

"Suit yourselves, dainty masters. But if you aren't in the trade, why take this exciting night excursion?"

Cedric answered, before Barnaby or Bodkin.

"I have appointment with Bishop Democritus in the Cathedral of Resurrection. Alas, the bridges are closed. We must take this roundabout path."

"You don't say. Know the cathedral well?"

"I spent a month in their scriptorium studying variants of the Gospel of St. Orpheus. Fascinating texts."

At which boast, Bodkin sighed.

"Ha. One would almost suppose you cleric, did your clothes not declare you shop clerk. Do you remember a side-chapel for a saintly personage called Yama?"

"Hmm. No, not proper chapel. Brother Yama is a mystery this far north. But I remember his statue in a corner of the Sanctum of Departure, collecting dust with other eidolons of the Lower House."

"Wears armor, shield, spear, helmet?"

"You know, I argued with the Bishop on that very subject. Pointing out that a Demetian helmet was inappropriate for a saint of the Southern Isles. His opinion was that the original home of-"

"Capitano," said Barnaby.

"What?" That, from the corpse-trader. Smile vanished quick as light from candle snuffed.

"That's your name. Capitano."

"We've met?"

"You tried to make me a soldier."

"Tried? How did I fail such grand task?"

"Well, I ran away."

"Ah. Ah, I remember. The miller boy. Sat with us, bright and shiny as new penny. More clever than I took you. That was excellent retreat you made."

Barnaby considered whether to thank him. While Capitano exchanged looks with his friend. They nodded, then stood, drew swords.

Chapter 43
As I am, as You Are

Val the Bard:

Our execution passed dull as buying eggs. No somber ceremony of chanting priest, no solemn drum tattoo nor headsman capering to crowds screaming for blood and justice. Just a march down tower steps, hands bound loosely before us, preceded by Alexandra in armor, sword drawn. Followed by a guard with a pike who sweated dreadfully. A few folk of the castle spied us, saying nothing.

Why did the guard sweat? Did he think this ended with honest blood? More likely he knew it for fraud, and feared being caught in Alexandra's scheme. I longed to turn, kick his feet out from under him, grab the pike and fight my way out. I did not, of course.

We walked to an empty courtyard where pigeons chatted, fountains splashed, a great pomegranate tree presided over dawn's performance. A place for morning tea, not executions.

Granted, in St. Martia we drag the condemned onto the practice fields to serve as targets for arrows and spear-thrusts. But from Demetians one expects drama, ceremony and ritual.

So we stood in morning sunshine beside a palanquin where waited two dirty bed sheets. Innocent sight that yet made me shiver. Again I considered overcoming the guard and making my farewell.

"Don't," whispered Alexandra.

Well, she knew me. I grinned to say '*might*'. We both turned to Jewel. The witch trembled. *Timor Mortis*? Else the fear she'd fail in the prayer. I judged her for the kind that feared failure near much as death. A compliment, by St. Martia's measure.

"Get to it," Alexandra commanded, waving sword. In the back of my head whispered the worry that if Jewel failed the oration, Alexandra would run us through. What choice would she have? If she tried, I'd take the sword away and run her through. What choice would I have?

Jewel took breath, facing her own choices with a nod of head. Cupping a necklace in her bound hands. Where she'd gotten that? Must have hidden it in gaol. Now she whispered to it, eyes closed.

At first I felt nothing, and I doubted. Then I shivered. I watched the sunlight fade to chill shadow, for all the cloudless sky. A whispering wind set the tree branches rustling. Within my chest my heart raced, then slowed, a clock weary of its winding. With a last faint beat, it stopped.

Alexandra lifted sword, thrust to my chest. By reflex I moved to fend; faltering to see the livid skin of my hands. Pale and purpled. The sword did not reach me, yet blood already darkened my jerkin. Not fresh; this seemed the trickle of a wound hours old.

I turned eyes to Jewel, who still stood cupping her relic. She'd become unpleasant to see. Standing as a dead thing, long hair hanging for half a veil. Revealed face pale, lips near white, eyes turned to shadowed bruises.

Alexandra poked her sword tip into Jewel's meager chest. Jewel flinched, gazing down at her own blood-drenched dress.

"Fall down, idiots," Alexandra whispered. Her voice came distant and muffled, as though I lay already shrouded.

Jewel looked at me, then quick away. No doubt disturbed by the sight of seeming death. I felt...

detached, no longer worried, unconcerned with escape or struggle. I let myself fall to the ground; watching Jewel settle herself to the earth with less surrender.

And there I lay, staring up at the morning sky become the gray of autumn. The branches of the pomegranate tree wavered, whispering sad lament. The stones beneath me were cold and hard, yet comforting as no bed ever felt. I settled against the surface of the earth naturally as I must have once rested upon my mother's breast. Was this how real death passed? Not so terrible as one hears, as one fears.

I watched Alexandra kneel beside me, staring close into my face. She looked horrified, as if she'd actually run me through. So help me she had tears, the sensitive nit. I felt an urge to make a face but did not. No doubt I was already making face enough.

At length she bent down, gave my cold morbid lips one soft kiss.

"Later, then, girl. Luck to you."

Goodbye said, she rose, waving sword, walking away, humming of Miss Fortune's comic adventures.

The day passed peaceful as any in my life. I lay in a perfect quiet of body and mind. Feeling no restless urge to shift about. Nor pee nor yawn nor scratch. At times folk would come, gaze down. Some shaking heads in pity for the dead; others grinning for the joy of being yet alive. Some muttered prayers, others kept silent, conducting the usual inner litany of the living beholding the dead: *as I am, so you once were. As you are, so I shall be.*

Meanwhile I stared unblinking at the summer sky, watching birds flitter, clouds shape themselves to the wind. Reviewing my life as though it were a song now sung.

I recalled my father's sunburned face, smiling. Happy to play with me, not games of blade and death but story and adventure. He was not the usual St. Martia warrior, for all he bore a scarred sword, scarred smile. A *kind* smile. Why had I not told him of the cup? It was a thing to be shared, not kept secret. But as a child I'd supposed the cup would be forbidden me, simply because I wanted it. Who knew, perhaps my father wanted the cup as well?

Not mother, to be sure. She had neither patience nor pity for impractical pursuits. Exactly as I; or so I would have said; excepting only the cup. Excepting only the cup.

I recalled Alexandra, close to sister as ever I found. A tall gawky child when we met, running through the house waving swords, shouting war-cries. Lex was obviously intended by the House of Saints to be a warrior of St. Martia. One would think we'd been switched at birth, excepting I fit no better in her castle-lady life than on the practice fields of Martia.

I recalled faces from bard school; casual friends, easy lovers who'd been songs worth singing once or twice; but never entering into the repertoire of my heart. Good metaphor, that.

I thought on the miller boy who'd watched over me when I lay sick. Definitely a song left unfinished. In the clear light of death I saw we'd had much in common. Absurd wanderers pursuing something more inside us than outside. Decent metaphor, that.

And so thoughts passed; clouds passed, hours passed. At noon the guard was replaced. The new guard gave me a kick to show his authority. I did not flinch; the strange languor kept me indifferent. I might have lain in a tomb sealed by stone, safe from all the world's kicks.

Soon after came a cart, a smiling fellow with long nose, officer's wear. At his order, men wrapped us in the waiting shrouds, tossed us to the cart. Not with cruel laughs, much less as lovers into bed. No, they lifted and dropped us same as one might any lumber to be moved. I felt only a vague regret to no longer watch the passing clouds, to stare instead at the rough cloth of a winding sheet.

We trundled through the city, in no hurry. I heard the dim clop, clop of horses, the cry of folk and bird. Pleasant sound, distant as song beyond five doors. At some point another body was added to the cart. Through the weave of my shroud I dimly saw a man, a knife, heard words, then a gasp. The bed of the cart became wet beneath me.

That's not according to plan, I thought. Should I rise up and inquire? But the voices were ones I did not know. For sure someone held a bloody knife. And what did it matter? These were acts on the stage after I'd departed the play.

Still, I pushed myself to awaken, working to fight the peaceful paralysis of indifference. While the cart trundled on, the darkening night paced by the occasional lantern glow.

There came a colder, wetter wind; dank and rank. Surely the river. Then hands lifted, grabbed, carried, dropping me. Two more thumps, one for Jewel, one for our unexpected fellow traveler.

Easy to tell by the rocking motion I now lay in a river boat. That at least was the plan. I wondered how Jewel fared. Did she feel this same indifference to life's pains and thunder? I wondered how long the oration would last.

There came conversation. Not of secret plans to steal relics from St. Plutarch; more casual talk. From voices I knew.

Shit, I thought, and actually shivered. I knew that low, amazed-at-life voice. That was Barnaby. And the older voice? Surely the cleric who'd escaped with us from gaol. Cedric.

I lay contemplating this unlikely meeting, my mind calm, my heart quiet. Was it secret, incomprehensible design of the saints? Or mere idiot accident? Exactly what one could ask about anything in life.

How peaceful it is, to believe one is done with deciphering all the riddles of existing. It grows so quiet, feeling one is done with life.

And it all matters naught, till life says it is done with *you.*

Chapter 44
On the Shore of a Shadowed Land

Capitano stood, drawing sword. Bodkin immediately stepped away, pushing back his oversized coat, revealing his own sword. Barnaby stood as well, unsure. Should he draw his axe? Cedric continued sitting, watching.

"Oy, gentlemen," said Bodkin. "No need to upset ourselves."

"I'm not upset," declared Capitano, and thrust blade towards Barnaby.

But Cedric's broomstick staff swooped down. There came a clang! The blade clattered to the deck. Capitano cursed, stepping back, near tripping on the cargo of corpses. His companion moved towards Bodkin, who backed away, sword drawn.

Now Cedric stood, staff raised. Barnaby pulled his axe. Capitano recovered footing, drew knife, moving to stand beside his friend.

Then came a thundering boot stamp from the front of the skiff. All turned to behold the looming guard, two-handed sword drawn.

Quite intimidating; but behind him stood a figure of far greater menace. The cloaked man poling the skiff had at last turned to face his passengers. Holding the dark pole high. That pole stretched upwards into the night, endless as a beam of light, dark as Lethe's waters. No face showed within the cowl of the cloak; but the eyes gleamed red, two rubies aflame.

When this personage spoke, the voice came low as the floor of Infernum, dark as the caves of Nix. Shaking the boat with one mere word.

"Sit."

Bodkin sat. Capitano sat. His friend sat. Cedric sat. Last, Barnaby sat.

There followed silence. The cloaked figure turned away, continued poling. The looming guard kept sword unsheathed, eyeing the passengers.

For a long while there came only the sound of the river, the night wind, the cry of night birds. At last Capitano gave his easy laugh.

"After all, we leave St. Demetia behind. What quarrels we had are left behind as well, no?"

Barnaby's heart still beat double-time. The man sitting and talking so friendly had meant to kill him.

"How are you so ready to kill and laugh?"

Capitanos confident face went empty as the eyes and mouth of any sheet-wrapped corpse.

"What?"

Barnaby did not repeat the question.

Cedric spoke instead. "Certainly, we have no quarrel with you."

"Exactly," said Capitano, recovering smile. "My apologies. I spied a breaker of oaths to St. Demetia. My fervency to uphold her law overcame my easy practical nature."

Cedric brushed that aside same as he'd done the sword.

"If you wronged the boy in the name of the saint, that remains twixt your conscience and the saint. It need not come between you and us."

"Fair enough. Pax then, while in blessed Plutarch's quiet demesne."

"So be it," said Cedric, stamping the boat deck with his staff.

Bodkin reached to pocket, took coin, tossed it to the air. Catching and slapping it to wrist.

"Call," he demanded.

"For what?" asked Capitano, amused.

"For who leaves the dock first. Winner gets five minutes head start, so there's no arguing over who owns the street."

"Clever child," agreed Capitano. "Heads."

Barnaby, Cedric and Bodkin sat on crates watching Capitano lead a cart from the docks, his morbid cargo piled indifferently within.

Around and about stood warehouses little different from those upon the Demetian shore. Lamps glowed at regular intervals, casting islands of light where workers appeared, only to vanish into the night again. None asked the travelers questions. Barnaby wondered were these dead folk set to tasks for the living? Or living folk set to tasks by the dead?

He watched the river boat splash slowly away, its eerie ferryman speaking no word of farewell. The loomer with the two-handed sword stood steadfast. Barnaby waved goodbye to his mentor in looming. The man hesitated, then waved back. The sight cheered Barnaby; some.

Plutarch's air seemed the same as Demetian. Barnaby puffed a few test notes, found he could still whistle. The moon seemed the same; decorating itself with whisps of tattered cloud. The river Lethe smelled the same.

Perhaps it was just thoughts of the somber *Saint of Holy Ending* that turned lamplight to shades of gray, tainting the summer air with the chill of churchyard stones. When he spoke, it was to the shadowy night, more than to his companions.

"Since I left Mill Town, I've met so many people. Strangers on the road, in fields, in taverns and streets. Wonderful folk, amazing faces. Old and young, even a just-born babe. And yet... it seems now as if a death served for each milestone."

Bodkin and Cedric exchanged looks. Then Bodkin clapped hand to Barnaby's shoulder.

"You're just feeling ol' Plutarch's solemn gaze, Master Miller. This side of the river he's in the wind, under the floor, in the light. Same as Demetia in her green home. But sainted Plutarch sings a colder song to the congregation. Crossing the river from Persephone in high summer is like walking into a brown autumn day."

Barnaby shook his head. It felt more than a change of air. He stared across Lethe, recalling the flower-smells of Persephone, the green farm fields of the lands beyond, all the little houses and woods. Walking the country roads of St. Demetia had been a journey through a green ocean of life; warm, bright and alive. He'd idled along laughing in joy to see each living thing, feeling life itself hot and green within him.

Now, he felt something colder inside.

"Who is Plutarch, exactly?"

"Excellent question," replied Cedric. "He is a Greater Saint of the Lower House. To him is given the *Testament of Ending*. Friar February is his gardener; tending Plutarch's flowered Fields. The mansions of Elysium make Plutarch's quiet city."

"But he is at war with Demetia? As Martia is at war with Hefestia."

"Never think it. It is not the saints that war, but the folk who hear only one saint's voice, denying another. Any farm field, any grave plot, will tell you that life and death make one weave. These lands may seem divided, but the saints themselves are but common servants in the One House of Saints."

Common structures to the reality of existence, he added to himself; but did not share aloud. Absurd to lecture Lucretian truths just now. He turned to Bodkin.

"You palmed the coin you tossed, did you not, young sir?"

"'Course."

"You wished those men to leave first?"

"Aye.

"Why?"

"Ah, best have his sort waiting ahead, not tiptoeing up behind."

"You think he plans ambush?"

"Most like. That one's the sort that can't rest happy till he's pissed on the corpse of whoever's seen him for a snake."

A shadow in the shadows, suddenly opened two angel-white eyes.

"Certainly the rogue has the right of it," said Night-Creep. Leaping to the crate where Barnaby sat. "No doubt Capitano lurks in an alley now, crossbow ready."

Barnaby contemplated scratching his magic-tutor behind the ears. Would it be undignified for such a learned creature?

"If I might suggest," said the cat, "this offers chance of instruction for my master."

"A spell of protection against shite-souls?" This, from Bodkin.

"That would be a most useful oration," agreed Night-Creep. "But no. Pupil Barnaby, if you would open the bag of magical bric-a-brac gifted you by unlamented Pentateuch, you will find a crystal egg."

Barnaby searched his pack, finding that very object. Small and heavy, glittering like ice. He held it, thinking how Da would have placed it on the chimney mantle as one more thing proving to cynical eyes that the world remained a place of wonders.

"As we are now in Plutarch's kindly shadow, it is polite to send him the oration, rather than sainted Demetia. Cup the crystal in your hands, recite these words:"

"Solemn Keeper of the Dead,
Show us our road ahead.
Through all dark and shadow,
Reveal to us the face we know."

Barnaby stared into the crystal, reciting the words.

"What do you see?" demanded Bodkin.

"The lamp reflected above us. My face turned egg-shaped. Uhm, my hands under the egg."

Bodkin laughed.

"Pity," sighed Cedric. "Then best we wait here till daylight. Though I was hoping to rest at an inn."

"Sorry," sighed Barnaby.

"Disappointing, but not unexpected," declared Night-Shadow. "You have affinity with Demetia. Your thoughts turned easily to her green light. Here is a darker realm, miller's son."

"Just as well. I don't want to use magic to see Capitano. Magic should make folk happy. Like that harp, or the Hefestian bird that made Da laugh. Or just healing folk. If I could look in a magic glass egg, I'd want to see something to make me smile."

"Whatever would that be?" asked the cat, licking a paw in casual thought.

Barnaby returned no answer excepting a smile. Gave the crystal a last glance before putting it away. Then he stopped; drawing it close. Stayed gazing a long moment. At last put it into his pack. That done, he stood. Drew his axe.

"Shit," said Bodkin. Standing as well, stepping away.

"Barnaby?" asked Cedric. "What is it? What did you see?"

Barnaby turned, walking quickly into the dark streets of darker Persephone. Axe resting ready on his shoulder.

"Where are you going?" called Cedric.

He answered without looking back.

"Capitano isn't waiting to surprise us. He's hurrying his cart towards a great stone church. The sheets have come loose from the bodies. I saw their faces."

Cedric and Bodkin hurried to catch up, walking to either side of Barnaby.

"Did you know?" he asked, looking to Bodkin. "I've been feeling there was something you didn't want to tell me."

"Know what?" asked Cedric.

"Yes," said Bodkin.

"Yes, what?"

"Yes, I knew the bard-girl was dead. Figured she was lying in front of us on the boat."

"Well, you should have told me."

"Why, so you could fight Capitano? Barnaby, she's dead."

"Bard girl?" puzzled Cedric. "You mean, the horse-thief I escaped with?"

"Yeah. Executed with some witch this morning."

"Oh. Of course. And one was the friend you sought? What a sad, strange coincidence."

"Quite strange," agreed Night-Creep. Somehow he'd maneuvered ahead of the trio. Now he sat on a high doorstep. "No doubt Capitano hurries to the Chapel of Renewal in the Church of Resurrection. Before his goods spoil."

Barnaby stopped, confronting the cat.

"I don't want him selling my friend's remains like a, a sack of carrots. Nor even that Jewel's."

He continued on.

"Barnaby, wait," shouted Bodkin. "We need a plan."

Barnaby did not slow; keeping eyes fixed on the lantern-lit street before him. But a dark figure now walked at his side.

"You cannot rescue the dead, boy."

"Aye, Master Michael. He's a soldier. I'm a miller."

Of all things, Michael laughed, sound echoing against stone walls, cobbled earth.

"If you suppose I argue against battle, you mistake me, miller. Go deal with the man. But do so wisely. Recall your training, and your allies, and the limit of what there is to win."

At which words Barnaby stopped, looking behind. There in the night-street stood Bodkin, sword drawn. And Friar Cedric, staff ready. Between them sat the darker-than-night cat, eyes bright.

"You lot should stay here," said Barnaby. "This is just some tangle I've got myself into. And Michael is right. It's not going to bring anyone back."

At which words came Bodkin's turn to laugh. While Cedric shook head, stamped staff.

"I owe it to those brave women to see their remains are given respect, not merchant valuation."

"And I find I've taken a dislike to this Capitano fellow," declared Bodkin. "Ha, even old Mercutio is saying it's better to front his sort, than have them sneak from behind."

"Excellent attitudes all," said Night-Creep. Striding forwards; leaping to Barnaby's shoulder, settling himself there. "Let us visit the quiet house of Sainted Plutarch. Perhaps he'll be in for us."

Chapter 45
A Secret Refraction of Light

Jewel stared upwards as the cart rattled along. The trip went pleasant enough. Now they rumbled down a boulevard more formal than the dock streets, past solemn statues staring into the distance, indifferent as Jewel to the shadow theatre of the living. Summer stars made a spill of diamonds across black velvet sky. Bats flitting, cloud whisps sailing the night winds that rustled the dark banners of this darker half of Persephone.

When the Infernum's fiery fuck does this oration end? she wondered. An impatient thought, entirely from habit. In truth she felt content just to watch the world roll by. Clearly, the 'seeming death' extended even unto thoughts and feelings. No matter.

It'll end at dawn. I can just sleep.

But she felt as indifferent to sleep as to rising. Gazing open-eyed at the night sky was all she could do, or wanted to do.

She listened to the two soldiers argue. One favored abandoning the cart, going to a tavern, spending coin to gather news, get their spying done while downing ale. The other declined, and he sounded in charge. Probably the one who murdered the third soldier, spilling blood through the cart, turning Jewel's back warm and sticky.

That would upset me without the spell, she observed. Was this peaceful indifference what her father felt hanging from a rope, watching his child struggle to cut him down?

Oh, that should make me furious. Pappa had no right to peace. But this is like being outside myself, just looking in the window. All the anger is in there, not out here.

She felt the soft weight of the spider-necklace upon her chest. Did Perry worry for her? She should explain to it that she was not dead. But what did a magical spider know of life and death? Well, what did a kitchen-girl know?

This feels nice, she informed Perry. *I should cast 'seeming death' on myself every night.*

She pictured lying in her cot in the scullery. Hands folded upon chest, legs straight. Eyes staring fixed into the oblivion of ceiling shadows. No more tossing and turning, gnashing teeth at memories sent from Infernum to make her rage, weep or despair. Just this pleasant cool clay peace.

Memories... she had good ones now. She recalled every step of the glorious escape from gaol. Cedric encouraging her, not calling her a stupid farm-slut. And Val; that mad bard horse-thief friend of nobility, had treated her as an equal.

Best night of my life, she told Perry. *And then I was given you.*

Again, she felt the spider twitch. To say *'glad I found you'*, she decided.

Hey, you think Cedric saw us set fire to a shadow-thing? That oration is called 'Hecatatia's Violets'. Didn't even know for sure I could do that.

Her thoughts turned to the heretic cleric.

I'm sure I heard his voice on the boat. Good to know he escaped. Maybe we'll meet again. Perry, do you think he's too old for me? Thirty or thereabouts. No gray hairs, no paunch. Just that elder attitude clerics put on with robes. But nice. I'd bed him.

That last admission would have embarrassed and angered her if she were inside the house of herself. But outside looking in the window she could be honest. Why the Infernum not?

She stared upwards as the cart rolled through a grand archway of stone, dark as a nether basement of Nix. Folk passing by showed no least interested in the cart's grim contents. Most wore robes of cloth heavy and dark, as though to muffle the life within. *Monks of St. Plutarch,* Jewel informed Perry. *Kids at home scare each other at the hearth fire, telling of their wicked practices.*

The spider pendant twitched. In alarm? No; Jewel decided Perry told her: *don't worry.* Not that Jewel did worry.

Now came distant chanting, falling and rising in pleasant echoes off stone arcs and arches. The light of altar candles did not reach up to the church ceiling, but cast a pleasant glow upon pews, statues and frescoes.

"Don't bring that trash in here," commanded someone. "Go through the side door to the Chapel of Renewal."

"Yessir. Ah, but I was told take it to the Chapel of Departure."

"Truly? Do you know the difference?"

"Ah, one's for leaving, one's about returning?"

"Brilliant. And a corpse is in need of renewal, yes? Already done with departing, no?"

"Ha. 'Course you're correct, holy sir. I'll be on my way."

"See that you are."

The cart rolled on; giving Jewel a glimpse of a great statue of Persephone; looking young as Jewel, and sad as Jewel, defiant as Jewel; but far prettier than Jewel. Behind her loomed a yet taller statue; dark robed, crowned in black iron, stern face shadowed in the folds of stone cowl. One great hand reached out, resting upon the shoulder of Persephone. In ownership, quite clearly.

What a piss-pot saint is Plutarch. Fighting all a war just to force a poor novice of Demetia to join his idiot order. Probably pulling her into his holy bed as well, the saintly cock-shite.

The cart rolled down hallways, coming to a smaller chamber lit by efficient oil lamps, not holy candles.

"See anyone?" asked Soldier One.

"No one breathing," replied Soldier Two.

"Right. I'm bloody tired of this stinking cart. Push it to the wall beside those others, and let's be off. The Chapel of Departure is down the hall. That's where the helmet will be."

"You seen any signs these folk are about to go to war?

"Not here, nor in the street."

"Lot of nonsense, then. Thought so."

Jewel listened to them depart. *Good,* she decided. *They weren't nice.*

Perry tapped agreement. *Not nice.*

I'd be scared if I didn't feel so calm, Jewel admitted. *What happens now?*

The spider gave a light, slight tap. Jewel felt sure it meant *we'll see together.*

* * *

Barnaby, Cedric and Bodkin stood at the archway to the Church of Resurrection. A grand construction decorated in shades of darkness. Black marble steps, funereal banners, basalt statues. Stained glass windows of purple and violet crystals, depicting skeletons and scythes, skulls and roses. The total should have achieved the vision of some grand mansion of Elysium.

But to Barnaby it looked *burned*. Something once bright, long settled into the cold ashes of its own funeral pyre.

Night-Creep leapt from Barnaby's shoulders, darted into the cathedral.

361

"Now where's he off?" asked Bodkin.

"To explore, most like," said Barnaby. "He's fond of twitching whiskers into strange places."

"Better if we stayed together," said Bodkin. "The Black Robes aren't folk to treat light. They're all about silence and sudden death."

"We need not storm the cathedral," said Cedric. "I have a friend within who may aide us."

"Fellow Lucretian?" asked Bodkin.

"Clever lad. My advice: be not too clever and too loud with the same breath. The Society of Lucretius is interdicted in Demetia and St. Martia. It is tolerated in Plutarch. No more than tolerated."

"Why?" asked Barnaby. "Don't the saints agree on such things?"

"My boy, there are no..." Cedric sighed, ended the sentence unsaid. Putting hard truths away for later. Began again.

"Saints may agree, but kingdoms do not. Lucretian thought is popular in Hefestia. So the Deaconry of St. Plutarch find it wise to grudge us our existence, to keep their alliance against Martia and Demetia."

"Strange friendship," considered Barnaby. "St. Martia is all about war. Demetia is a place of peace."

"A place of peace that wished to burn me alive."

"And Hefestia is all about mechanical marvels."

"Marvels that often twirl blades, spit poison, burn men to ash."

"And Plutarch?"

"Is much like all lands. Which is to say, much like all men. Mistaking order for peace, dogma for wisdom, death for victory."

That said, he walked on into the cathedral, followed by Barnaby and Bodkin.

"Can I help you, sirs?" inquired a monk.

"We seek audience with Bishop Democritus."

"*Archbishop* Democritus sees none but the saint."

"He may yet see my profane person. Inform him that one who knows the secret of the rainbow, desires audience."

The monk gave a measuring stare.

"So, you are a seeker of light?"

"Say rather, the truth of light."

The monk nodded. "Very well. The archbishop is that silent figure kneeling to the side of the high altar. But he is not well. Let your audience be short."

Cedric nodded, began the long trek to the high altar, past endless black wooden pews. Barnaby followed, staring about. All was somber silence, candlelight, solemn figures in black performing tasks holy and obscure.

"What secret does a rainbow have?" Bodkin asked Cedric.

"None, in truth. They are not secretive things, rainbows. Infernum, they shout their truth in the sky loud as thunder. But men's minds must see riddles in the sky, as in the earth."

"I don't always understand you," admitted Barnaby. "What did you just say?"

At which declaration Cedric sighed, Bodkin laughed. The sound making heads turn, faces disapproving of frivolous noise, unsolemn spirit.

They continued, approaching the great statue of St. Plutus, forever resting a cold stone hand upon Persephone.

Within its shadow knelt a small figure in simple cloak. At their approach, the figure turned, revealing a face gray with life's fading. Still, he smiled. A living man's smile, no mere symbol carved for a statue's reminder of endings.

"Cedric Weiland," whispered the man. "How pleased I was to hear of your escape from the Questioner's pyre."

"You knew?"

"Of course. We spy upon the doings of the brighter Persephone, as they do the darker. Granted, I must boast that our spying goes far more efficiently. You came with some of their bumbling scouts."

"Then they are apprehended."

"Not at all. They sneak and snoop about the cathedral even as we speak."

"You permit that?"

"Absolutely. Contrary to fearful rumor, Plutarch makes no plan to cross the Lethe. So let their soldiers-in-disguise poke about, and find we have no massed armies ready to march."

"That is good to hear. War is an idiocy of men, not the will of saints."

Democritus gave dusty chuckle. "And what is the will of the saints, oh follower of Lucretius?"

"The random wind and the clever mind of men, oh arch priest of Plutarch."

"Arch, indeed. The saint has promoted me. Quite soon the scythe of his servant February shall promote me further. A seat awaits me upon the Council of the Departed."

"That is sad to hear, my friend."

"To those whose fingers claw at the cliff edge twixt birth and death, it is sad. Not to those who do not fear the fall."

"Excellent metaphor, exactly so long as one stays from the edges of cliffs."

Again the dusty chuckle. "What do you seek, Cedric Weiland? Refuge? You are safe from Demetian Questioners in Plutarch's shadow. But if you seek purpose, we have use for your learning."

"I have found purpose, Excellency."

"I rejoice to hear it. Yours was a mind ever seeking truth. Yet finding no purpose in knowing the truth."

"The seeking is purpose enough, is it not?"

"So I once thought. But now I stand in the doorway that leaves this world. The truths I gathered so proudly, I see now are handfuls of paper scraps. Lines of dramatic math, summing to sand grain facts slipping through my fingers. Bah. Let the wind take it all."

Democritus bowed his head, waving fingers, releasing conceptual trash into the world's wind. Cedric reached a hand to the older man's shoulder, held it. Barnaby looked from one to another, puzzled. The men looked sad. Why? What was their sorrow?

"So," said the archbishop, straightening, recovering himself. "Your new-found purpose. What does it lead you to seek?"

"The spies from Demetia brought two bodies with them, as excuse to enter Plutarch and the Cathedral of Resurrection. We wish to recover these remains."

Democritus tilted his head, unsure his ears heard correctly.

"Why?"

Barnaby answered, before Cedric.

"We wish to bury them proper. They are my friends. Were, I guess. Well, Val is. Was, I mean. That girl Jewel wasn't at all a friend exactly and even stole my luncheon but she was still the first soul I met on the road and by Lucif's kettle I'm not having it."

"Not… having luncheon?"

"No sir, them walking about dead."

Democritus stared a long time at Barnaby, intent as a man seeking secrets in a rainbow. At last turned to Cedric.

"On one condition."

"That being?"

"That you, Cedric Weiland, ordained priest of St. Demetia, high officer in the oh-so-secret Society of Lucretius, pledge here and now that when you pass from this mayfly life, your body shall be rendered to the Chapel of Renewal."

There came silence at that demand. It was Cedric's turn to shake head, clearing it of words surely misunderstood.

"You actually wish me to join Sainted Plutarch's order as one of your undead scholars?"

"I do."

"Why?"

"Potential. I wish to see more upon the Deaconry who know that ghosts are but the figments of our fevered imaginations."

"Ah. I comprehend."

"I don't," said Bodkin. "How can you not believe in ghosts? What about Barnaby's Michael? And aren't your councils filled with the vaporous things? I thought they ran the kingdom."

For reply, Cedric stamped his staff upon the stone floor. Mere broomstick, yet the sound rang through the cathedral, a hammer blow to a mountain.

"Before the saints, I agree to your terms."

"Excellent," said Democritus. "Then I give you leave to wander the cathedral as you wish, claiming what you seek." He reached, replaced cowl about his stone-bald head, returning kneeling to shadows. Giving final words.

"But you, young man with the fearful axe, if you wish burial for your friends, then take what you find to the north court. I shall send word, and none shall hinder you. Whatever you have heard of the acts of our order, we regard burial as a sacred rite."

He turned unseen face upwards, towards the stone face of Plutarch.

"Under the eye of the patron of Holy Ending himself, of course."

* * *

Val lay staring fixedly at a burning candle. Observing it grow shorter. Where did the candle go? Obviously flame turned wax to light. This candle was black; but the light seemed no darker than usual. One would think red wax would make red light. And a black candle should cast a flame black as shadow. Could there be a black flame? You could put the candle into colored glass, of course. But if the glass were black, there'd be no light...

I should be bored to death. Ha. To death. And it isn't that this detachment makes things interesting. I just don't care that I'm bored. How useful it would be back at bard school, studying poetic variants of iambic pentameter.

She pictured a classroom of corpses, flies buzzing about, staring glassily at a droning headmistress. The idea should have made her laugh, but of course did not.

The two soldier-spies had left to go spying, steal a holy relic, whispering sinister things to one other. Val decided she preferred them gone.

Really, they were awful.

A black-robed monk came by, poking about the cart, grumbling of fresh work. He tweaked Val's breast through the shroud, giving her a wink she did not return. Then he yawned, lifted the dead and dripping soldier to a smaller cart, rolling him away.

Just me and Jewel now. She wondered how the witch fared. Did she feel this peaceful indifference to life's cares and indignities? Obviously. She'd hardly be lying still otherwise.

That girl is built of hot anger and cold pride. Hard childhood, no doubt. These words made her laugh within the comfortable silence of her head. Clearly they described herself as much as Jewel.

But I have the cup. Or want the cup. I've seen the cup. I'm looking for the cup. But what is the cup? I bet I won't ever know. Even if I hold the cup.

Voices neared. Familiar ones. Ha, it was the miller boy again. *Bridget's private bits, he must want me.* She pictured kissing him, undressing him, twining naked with him. Broad shoulders, cute freckles and an empty head. It'd be limited to copulating, no clever conversing. Which would be fine. So long as he didn't chatter in wonder... she pictured him chattering in wonder of her body. *Well, that could be fun.*

She watched Barnaby lean over the cart, peering down at her body now. But was this actually the miller's son? Certainly not the gormless face she recalled at St. Herman's font; nor the worried boy chatting with her fevered self in the robber's wood.

This Barnaby seemed older; face etched with beard and worry. Half-healed wounds lined one side of the face, marring the freckles somewhat.

"Yes, it's her," said Barnaby.

Is he going to cry? wondered Val. That would be embarrassing. But he did not. What was in his face?

Anger, decided Val. *At whom, for what?*

But Barnaby reached, covered her with the sheet.

Infernum, don't do that, idiot. I want to watch. But she lacked any will to say so aloud. She lay still as the cart began to roll. *Hey, ho. Off we go again.*

"Mister Democritus said there was someplace to bury them proper."

Shit, don't bury us, thought Val.

Whoever replied did so in familiar voice. Ha; that was her fellow escapee Cedric.

"The north court serves as churchyard for those of the order who decline resurrection of the body. It is straight on this way."

"Where is Bodkin?"

Bodkin? The brigand boy is here too. Why not.

"I would guess the boy has taken Democritus's permission to find what we wished, as license to gather all the wealth of the cathedral into his pockets."

"Well, that's not good."

"Indeed it is not. The riches of St. Plutarch are fabled, as is the ferocity of his guardians."

"Then I'll take the cart to the churchyard. Can you go find Bodkin? He's likely bringing himself into trouble."

"He's likely climbing Plutarch's great statue to pry the jewels from the crown."

"Ha, sounds like him."

"I will find the rogue and meet you in the courtyard."

"Very well."

The cart rattled on. To Val, the dark beyond the shroud lightened, the air cooled, a wind passed about, ruffling the shroud.

We're outside. She heard sounds, faint but recognizable. Bird song, making the twittering just before dawn. Solemn bells tolling matin prayers. A shovel scraping earth and stone...

The cart stopped.

"Hallo," said Barnaby.

"Hello to you, youngster," replied... someone. An old voice; strong and deep. For all her indifference, the voice sent a shiver through Val.

"I see you are digging graves."

"Observant fellow."

"A real archbishop said I might bury my friends here."

"Truly? That is a great honor given you. Or at least to your friends."

"Should have thanked him then. I'll do so very next time I see him."

"Well, this very hole is shallow but wide. I declare the earth ready. Place them in."

Hands reached, grasping the bloody sheet that wound about Val. Lifted her up, placing her down upon cold clods of earth.

She listened as something was placed beside her. The witch, no doubt. *Large grave*, thought Val. *That's lucky. Well, no, it's a horror. Not that I care.*

A hand reached, pulled the shroud back from her face. She stared up at a sky streaked with light, framing Barnaby staring down. Looking grim and sad. He bent down, placing something upon her chest. A thing of soft golden glow, strings of silver humming.

A harp, she thought. *For me? It's beautiful.*

Barnaby sat with a sigh upon the grave's edge.

Someone spoke from beyond Val's narrowed view.

"What sort were your friends, young Barnaby?"

"You know me, sir?"

"Why, you live in Mill Town, do you not? I met your father once."

"Ah, that makes me happy just to hear. Da was a wonder."

"He was indeed. A man capable of finding the highest joy in daily things. That's the secret of living, miller's boy. To laugh, to love, to wonder. All else is trash."

"Just what Da would say. And your name, sir?"

"Hmm, hereabouts I'm called Mister Quiet."

No, seriously? thought Val.

"Proper name for churchyard work," declared Barnaby."

"Bah, I'm not untalkative. It's just the silly monks and nuns must forever chatter."

"Well, Master Quiet, in life these were Val the Bard and Jewel the Witch. Miss Jewel was the very first I met leaving home. She was a sour sort. Stole my lunch and gave a pebble for a kiss. Can't have been pleased I wound up with her cat."

"You don't say."

"I do so say, if you can believe. Still… I liked her fine. Even from high in a tree you could tell she was a farm girl being brave as a queen, crossing arms and stamping foot at witches and the world. One should admire that, I say."

"I'd say the very same."

"And this other, she was Val the Bard. Met her at a fountain riding a horse all decked with silver bells. She being on the horse, I mean, not me. And not her decked in bells, that was the horse, can't remember the beast's name. But the fountain was Herm. We all got on fine. Val says he winked at one of us. Herm winked, I mean, not the horse. But perhaps Herm winked at both of us, why not?"

"Why not, indeed?"

"Anyways, Val was riding the roads on her jingling horse looking for a golden cup that sang. Glorious thing to be at, don't you think? While I had my tower to find. Still we were on the same road. So I found the horse but it was dead. Then I found Val and some robbers and they were dead. Not Val I mean, just the robbers. She's wonderful fierce. Was fierce."

"Remember her so, then."

"That I shall, Master Quiet. Anyways I fixed her up with a wand touched by Missus Green. Special sort of lady. Can't quite figure that one out."

"No more can I."

"And Val popped up healed and ran off to Persephone and got herself killed and carted here. Same as Jewel. Sad thing to happen. And so here I am now. Attending another burial."

"And you are puzzling why the road you wander, has gravestones to mark the miles."

"That is the very thing I do, sir."

"Master Miller, the more one is aware of life, the more one feels the shadow of death. You've been on Demetia's roads delighting in bright life, green life, warm life. Yet doing so you passed as many graveyards as villages. And all the rich warm life you rejoiced in had its roots deep in dark wet bones and rot."

Barnaby laughed, light and sad as faint breeze through churchyard flowers.

"Ah, Master Quiet, that sounds wondrous wise. But it but comes to saying '*what lives was once dirt, and is going to the dirt again.*'"

"Well, now there is wisdom," declared a voice. Not the gravedigger's, but another's.

Him again? thought Val, and almost sighed. *Tedious fool. What was his name? Right. Capitano.*

Chapter 46
Make it Small Bites

Barnaby stood. His face showing no miller's son pondering what the world intended next. Setting his feet, he drew Dragontooth from its sheath. This act made no friendly greeting. In the early light the axe looked dark as the jet eyes of Plutarch's eidolon, jagged as the points of Plutarch's iron crown.

But Capitano laughed lightly, turning to his fellow soldier.

"Ah, now who is so quick to kill and smile?"

Barnaby shook his head, declining the challenge of bantering conversation.

"Go away."

"No time for friendly chat? But who were you just chattering to? The lovely ladies in their graves?"

Barnaby looked towards Mister Quiet. But the man had vanished discreetly as his name. Probably that was wise, though Barnaby wished he'd stayed. Now he had to talk to Capitano. Who would dance clever words around him, grinning as if they were friends at the table. While readying his knife.

"I don't like you. And don't like talking to you."

Capitano started to make reply, hesitated, then waved it all away.

"Fair enough, soldier. In any case I've not come to chat with a dimwit of a rural oath-breaker. No, we've higher purpose among the dead today."

Capitano reached into a pack, drew forth a helmet. Darker than bronze. Iron, perhaps. Though shaped no differently than any brass pot-helmet upon the head of some Demetian foot-soldier.

Capitano stood in the dawn light, grinning at the brightening sky, the courtyard of gravestones.

"Legend says this helmet gives the wearer command of the dead. Perhaps, perhaps. Shall we put it to the test?"

Not awaiting answer, he placed it upon his head.

Barnaby watched, wary of tricks. This was overmuch like talking poetry with the rat Belinda. Distracting, until she'd leapt for his throat. He considered striking at Capitano first. But the second soldier stood ready, sword drawn. It would come to Barnaby fighting both.

"Feels right," Capitano said. "Yes. I can tell. It is right." Voice rising like wind before storm. "Ladies, if you would arise. And I say you must. I command it."

Capitano's purpose became clear to Barnaby then.

"Stop it," he said. Sickened; feeling a dizzying heat. Trembling, though he held the axe steady enough. He repeated the words louder. "Stop it now."

Capitano shook his head; smiling, drawing his own sword. By morning's light the man looked fresh; happy and young. *He's just a boy playing Lucif*, thought Barnaby. *Is that why he smiles? Because he thinks it's all a game?*

There came sounds behind Barnaby. Cloth ripping, earth falling. Whispers.

"Well, now," said Capitano. Sounding pleased; and awed. "Well now. Look who comes to join the dance."

Barnaby recalled what his tutor in weapons advised when facing two foes. *Move to the side. Put one opponent in front of the other.*

But that would mean seeing what occurred in the fresh-dug grave behind him. But he had his Da's advice as well.

Finish the task before you, then turn to the one behind. That would have to do.

"First order of business," said Capitano. "Ladies, feast upon this bumpkin miller. Make it small bites."

Barnaby leaped at Capitano then, axe swinging. Clearly catching the man by surprise. But training brought the man's sword up to block.

Little use in that against Dragontooth. The axe swept the blade from Capitano's grasp. He cursed, stumbling back.

The second soldier thrust at Barnaby. No time to parry. He stepped to the side, keeping feet set as Michael instructed. The strike went to his ribs, sliding along the leather armor, cutting into him. But Barnaby now held the axe high, meeting the man's eyes.

I don't even know his name, he thought. And then struck. The axe shearing away the hand holding sword. The man screamed. Barnaby screamed.

Now Capitano stepped forwards again, wielding knife. No time to swing the axe nor step aside. Barnaby thrust the axe pommel into Capitano's face. The man's knife glanced off Barnaby's shoulder, driving into his forearm. While the axe struck Capitano in the face, hard as hammer blow, sending him reeling.

Barnaby stepped back, panting, knife still fixed in his arm. Capitano cursed, gasping and choking, his nose now a flowing red pit. The man missing his hand moaned, pressing arm to chest, seeking to hold the red life within. And yet, the sound of most significance, the sound echoing with greatest meaning through the churchyard, was *music*.

And at last Barnaby turned, looking behind him.

There in dawn's pretty glow stood two women, bedraggled in old blood, fresh mud. Hollow of eyes, hair tangled, the tatters of shrouds hanging upon them like royal robes of Elysium.

One held a harp close; strumming the strings with quick fingers, plucking notes simple as light summer rain drops, melodious as crystal chimes.

The other figure held hands to her chest, cupping something on a chain; whispering to it some private conversation.

The two blinked beside their common grave, observing the morning light, the three wounded men observing them.

"Kill him," gasped Capitano from a mouth drooling blood. Pointing to Barnaby. "Devour him. Do it. I order you."

The two women looked to one another. And then one laughed, and the other giggled.

"Well, now," said the arisen Val. "He does look delicious." She took a step towards Barnaby, strumming harp, licking lips. "There's just something about those freckles."

"Everyone in Demetia has freckles," argued the arisen Jewel. "You might as well lust after noses." She looked towards Capitano. "Well, not that fellow's, obviously."

"I command," whispered Capitano. A look of desperation took his damaged face, turning it into a mask of tragedy. He tried a stamp of foot.

Jewel nodded. Whispering to what she cupped in her hands. A glow of purple fire appeared, as though she held burning violets.

"Val?" croaked Barnaby. "Miss Jewel?"

"Lucif's thorny cockerel, that boy's polite," said Jewel. "Calls me 'miss'."

Val now stood before Barnaby. Within reach of his axe. *Should I swing?* he wondered.

"Polite, yes. But up close I'm not seeing much boy here," declared Val. She met Barnaby's eyes, gave grin.

She's happy, he thought. *Like when she talked about her singing cup.* He lowered the axe.

"Are you both alive then? I'm quite confused."

"Well, I can understand that," admitted Val.

"It's all mad," said Jewel. "Ask my spider."

"It is all perfectly simple," said a new voice, high and sharp. Professor Night-Creep, perching atop a headstone angel, feline form fitting comfortably into the folds of stone wings.

"An absurd theatre of coincidences," declared Dark Michael. Approaching slowly through the gravestones, hands deep in coat pockets. He kicked at the severed hand upon the ground, sent it flying.

"Then I'll do it myself," hissed Capitano. Reaching down, reclaiming his sword.

"What shall he do?" asked Cedric, entering the churchyard.

"He's going to finish Barnaby," decided Bodkin, skipping cheerfully beside the cleric. "But my money is on millers today."

"Help," groaned the second soldier, pressing his bleeding wrist beneath his good arm. "That man with the axe is, is a Demetian spy. Kill him."

"That's creative," said Cedric. He raised staff to smite the man, then relented. "Hold your arm out while I bind the blood."

Val set the harp on a gravestone. Reaching to Barnaby. "Hold still," she ordered, and plucked the knife from his arm.

"Infernum's mother's thorny teapot," hissed Barnaby. "What?"

Barnaby started to explain. Val waved it aside.

"Behind you."

Barnaby turned to find Capitano staggering forwards, sword high, face a bloody mask.

Barnaby readied himself, feeling weary. He had but one trustworthy arm for the swing. But Capitano looked in far worse condition. Gasping, stumbling, spitting out blood. He brought the sword down in a clumsy slash.

Barnaby blocked with Dragontooth, then kicked the man in the stomach. Capitano gasped, collapsing to the ground. Dropping the sword again. And there he sat, coughing on blood and defeat.

Barnaby raised the axe. Should he end the man? If he did, no mirror nor saint could say it was wrong.

He looked about. There stood Val; a figure of blood and shadow, smiling happy as child freed of chores on a spring morning. Beside her stood Jewel; equally bloody, but unsmiling. She watched all that occurred. While whispering to whatever she held in her cupped hands, telling it what she thought it all meant.

Barnaby turned to meet the eyes of Friar Cedric, wrapping a rough tourniquet for the second soldier. Cedric nodded, keeping silence, giving no advice to the raised axe.

While Bodkin now perched happily upon a gravestone, his boy's feet kicking at ancient epitaph. Clearly indifferent to whether Barnaby struck, or stayed hand.

Dark Michael tipped hat back, letting morning wind ruffle his grayed hair, letting the dark caverns eyes meet Barnaby's. Giving a smile light and slight, both ironic and sardonic. No guidance in that.

Barnaby turned to Professor Shadow Night-Creep. The white angel-wing eyes closed, opened again in a slow blink of greeting. Then the cat yawned, mouth pink as a baby's.

Last, Barnaby looked down at Capitano himself, struggling to rise while holding hands up to fend away the looming axe. Barnaby lowered it.

"Get up. Go away. Leave us all alone. I've had enough of burials. And twice enough of you."

Capitano reached for his sword again. But now a creature scuttled out from gravestone shadows; a spider large as dinner plate, diamond eyes waggling in warning.

Capitano gasped, hissed, abandoning sword, staggering to his feet. He gave all within the churchyard the tearful glare of a furious child. Then backed towards the gate, followed by his unnamed companion.

They gathered under the angelic statue where perched Night-Creep. Barnaby rested gladly upon a cold stone etched with dates from long years past; feeling old as the years inscribed.

"*Seeming Death* was awful," said Val, stretching, shaking her gory locks. "And yet, I've never felt so rested."

"Very awful," agreed Jewel. Looking about at the morning sky, the old stones, the gathered folk. "I'll never wish to be dead again."

"A wise wish," said Cedric, leaning upon his staff. "Live, then, at least until you decide otherwise."

"Master Miller fought well," declared Dark Michael.

"Needs to keep his knees more loose," argued Val. Holding the harp in her lap, fingers petting the strings.

"For knife fighting, perhaps," said Michael. "An axe requires stronger stance."

"Should we worry about those idiots?" asked Bodkin, staring towards the gate.

Jewel perched upon a stone beside Val, attempting to finger-comb dirt and blood from her hair. Now she closed eyes, lowered head.

"Perry is following them. I'm watching through his eyes." She paused, then narrated. "They stopped in an alley to patch their hurts. Arguing what to do next. One wants to rest. The other wants to take the helmet across the river, give it to the duke."

Jewel paused. "Well, now they've come to blows." She raised her head, opened eyes. "Idiots. They're half dead and want to kill each other. I'm not watching anymore. Perry, return."

Leaning forwards on his staff, Cedric reached, put comforting hand to her shoulder. Jewel did not shrug it away. She looked at the hand, then up at him.

"How old are you, exactly?"

At which question Val laughed. Bodkin laughed. Cedric looked surprised. Night-Creep settled for clearing throat.

"And now that the saints have twined the threads of your separate fates into this fascinating tangle, there is a matter of importance to discuss."

"What matter?" asked Val. "Bet it isn't as important as a bath. Not to me, anyway."

"Clean clothes," said Jewel.

"Breakfast," added Bodkin.

"Yes, to breakfast," declared Barnaby. He grasped his wounded arm. "Also bandages. Or a chance to cast healing, though that might put me to sleep."

"Sleep, clothes, food and bandages are irrelevant," declared Shadow-Creep, tail a'twitch in annoyance. "The tower must take precedence."

Barnaby rose. "Sleep, clothes, healing and food come first, Master Cat. The tower will follow after."

Chapter 47
In the Maiden Tavern

Matilda, Tavern Girl:
Oh you could tell they were bold adventurers by the blood and dirt and weary wary way they entered the door of *The Maiden*. Probably been fighting dragons and wolves and wicked kings, bless 'em for it.

"You'll be wanting one room for each?" I asked. Counting five. Also a cat and a ghost but ghosts in Persephone seldom take rooms. Gloomy things, and anyways what coin should a ghost pull from pocket? A cat might pay in mice. Well, but who wants mice? Excepting another cat. I suppose a cat might run an inn for cats, get paid in mice. But felines so seldom get along; a tavern all for cats seems most astonishing doubtful.

"Two rooms will do, girl," said the boy. Cheeky, the beardless thing calling me 'girl'. One of those olive-skinned creatures from the Spice Islands that rule the streets of bright Persephone and smile like summer sun. Handsome as princes but don't kiss 'em or you'll lose what you promised mother you'd keep. He was too young to kiss anyhow but it's a thing you might want to remember.

"One room for the ladies. One for us gentlemen."

"With baths," added the tall thing with boyish hair. She looked half-dead. Granted in darker Persephone you distinguish all sorts of shades and flavors of *deadness*. You have those drafty government counselors all wispy and wise, and then you have your solid-boned revenants cold and calm as statues taking a walk. Then there are the rotting sorts, sometimes just bone and old rags and red eyes. Though that sort keep to themselves and never take rooms, thank the saints.

I wanted to ask questions like *'who are you, what you been at, why so bloody?'* but did not as it weren't polite and they looked weary as the Prophet Sisyphus watching his holy stone roll down Lucif's seventh buttock. So I gave them excellent rooms top floor and brought the tin tubs and began the weary business of heating and porting and pouring hot water while listening as you can imagine. Amazing how folk ignore a body as you come and go setting up baths and beds.

Seems the ladies had been near dead but came back with the sun and had limited funds and both speculated upon bedding the big fellow with the axe as opposed to the older fellow with a staff who was handsome enough but shy. They had that right, You can always tell the shy sort. Makes you want to lean forwards just to see them blush down your blouse.

When the girl with short hair climbed in the bath she showed enough scars to honor all a veteran regiment. A Martia personage, clear enow. I could report her as suspicious to the watch but there's not much trouble on the border twixt Martia and Plutarch nowadays and anyways I'm a proper devotee for Sainted Silene so why should I care for squabbles twixt foreigner saints? I poured the hot water and attended the gents, who declined to bathe before me the shy things. But putting ear to the door I picked up talk of a tower and treasure and destiny and a map. Glorious; Just what a girl wants when she's weary of making beds and boiling potatoes. Damn potatoes to St. Tartarus's tar pot for tax-gatherers, I say.

So I harkened till I spied that feline watching me from top of the stairs. Eyes white as a blind man staring at the moon; just staring and staring. I eyed it right back but you don't win that sort of fight with that sort of creature. And then I got that cold-water shiver that says a ghost is frowning at you from their secret corners. Not that *they* apologize for spying. So I left off listening at doors.

No matter, I'd heard what soul and ears needed. It was decided. For sure when the adventurers marched off from this quaint idiot tavern, I'd be leaving with the bold troop.

To the tower and treasure!

Chapter 48
Under My Own Orders Now

Capitano:

Ah, don't complain of smiling and killing. If a man can do both, why he's proper soldier. If he must sniffle at blood, best he find other employ.

As for the fellow who'd lost his hand, I did him kind favor. He was good as dead anyway, bandage pouring life out fast as wine bottle uncorked. Didn't expect him to do me the same; knife to the ribs, straight up into the lungs.

We sat in the dirt of the alley watching one another bleed out. I tried to recall his name. Decided he'd never had one. Some folk go through life anonymous as a stray dog dying in a ditch. Or alley.

Not me. I am Jolan Caleb, sub captain of the ducal guard. Was. Dead now.

Getting dead was a long slow business. I watched my blood quit pouring. My ripped lungs ceased panting. The panicked heart ended its idiot *thump, thump*. All the world went gray as the face of the dead man opposite me. Gray, but not black. Not what I expected.

Time passed. Some wanderer came into the alley, pissed against the wall. Eyeing us, but not saying anything. He finished up, hurried away, calling for the watch.

Stand up, I told myself. And so help me St. Venus's middle kingdom, I stood. *Take the knife out your chest*, I demanded. And I watched my hand do just that.

Took a while to comprehend. But I wore the helmet. *Command of the Dead*, it gave the wearer. Being dead, I could order myself about.

"You get up too," I told the fellow that finished me. And he twitched, and stumbled, and stood.

Now what? I was in command of myself. Maybe more than I'd ever been. But what the Infernum did I want to order myself to do?

I considered going after the miller. I'd cut his nose off, feed it to crows, make him eat the crows, then cut off more of him, feed the parts to rats. Round and about in a pleasant circle of pain. Exact as life.

Or I could finish my mission for the duke. Go across the river, report no pending invasion; hand over the holy relic helmet. But then he'd order me to go bury myself. Bright side of Persephone didn't have any use for revenants.

I looked to my fellow alley-corpse. He didn't look useful, having just a hand. But he was company of a sort.

"Let's march," I told him. We abandoned the alley, leaving life and blood behind.

Being the dark half of Persephone, folk looked askance at us but didn't go to screaming. We even passed a few fellows just as finished with life as us. In cleaner clothes, granted.

"What's your name?" I asked my companion. He gave me a look, but no answer. Possibly he couldn't speak. Else he'd forgot it, same as I did. As I said, some people just go down the road without a name.

"That's alright," I told him, clapping him on the back. "We'll find you a good name."

Chapter 49
A Sudden Arrow to the Eye

The common room of The Maiden mirrored that of the Pomegranate tavern across the Lethe. Large, with time-blackened rafters, filled with a pleasant air of hearth smoke and sausage, ale and casual conversation. Rough benches set before heavy tables, walls bedecked with honorably tattered flags and banners. The head of a boar above the doorway. Surely brother to the boar above the door of the Pomegranate.

And yet differences remained. Barnaby sniffed, missing the summer-flower perfume of the brighter Persephone. Here the wind carried taints of stone and ash, dust and old wood. Less morning birdsong choired beyond the open window; and that mostly the caw of crow, the croak of raven. The folk passing by wore solemn faces hinting somber thoughts.

"Do you listen, miller's son?"

Barnaby turned gaze from the window.

"Yessir, sorry, sir."

Dark Michael leaned against the wall, comfortably wrapped in shadow. "I said you'll need a horse."

"Well, I don't know how to ride a horse."

"You won't be riding. This shall be for carrying."

"Carrying treasure?"

"No, carrying food, blankets and tools. The journey will take weeks, even without trouble. And there will be trouble."

"Wouldn't a donkey be better?" asked Bodkin. "Horses take more tending and carry less."

Michael remained silent. Barnaby recalled the sad beast bearing the sadder corpse of Michael. Perhaps the ghost disliked the idea of journeying with another donkey.

"Why not a mule?" asked the tavern girl, setting plates of bread and bacon upon the table.

"Who are you and why are you jumping into our talk and where are our eggs?" asked Bodkin.

"Oh, I'm Matilda and the eggs are still in the pot and I don't like donkeys much. Just smart enough to do something stupid. Like dogs, I say."

"Exactly," said a voice in the rafters.

She looked up, smiling to see an agreeable cat looking down.

"Well, hello up there, talking cat person."

Night-Creep returned the slow cat-blink of formal greeting.

Barnaby considered the sharp tips of the woman's ears poking from thick braids. The slotted pupils of her eyes, and the mad manner of conversing.

"You're a Silene."

"Am not."

"You aren't?" He looked down to her feet, which were two polished goat hooves. With little flowers painted upon them, pretty as porcelain pots.

"Not a bit and why are you looking at my feet?"

"I'm not."

"Right then. Meanwhile you're a band of adventurers demanding eggs, so I'm off." That settled, she turned about.

"Perhaps a mule then," agreed Michael, continuing the discussion. "Wayward creatures though they are."

"Cartage is your least concern," declared Bodkin. Seizing bread and the plate of butter. "You need a team."

"A team of mules?" asked Barnaby.

"A team of folk to get there, find the treasure and then get out alive," replied Bodkin. "North of Hefestia are mountains. Little law and plenty bandits. And nastier things than bandits. You'll need folk with skills to fight, to watch your back, to cast spells and throw stones."

Barnaby laughed. "Bodkin, we aren't going to war. Just find a tower, go inside, follow a map, look around, find gold. Then..." There he stopped, unsure. Then what?

Bodkin did not ask. He seized bread, waved it to the air.

"Ignore getting to the tower. Inside will be locks to pick, traps to avoid. Other treasure hunters to fend away. Guards and monsters for sure. Probably magical summoned creatures that have been set to slay all that enter."

"Truly?"

Cedric sipped coffee so hot it burned lips; entirely as a scholar preferred. He set the cup down, licking blisters.

"There is no certainty what we will find. I foresee a ruined tower empty of all but owls and cold wind. No fiends guarding treasure, and the only profit shall be the wisdom gained in the journey itself."

"That's far different from what Master Bodkin predicts."

"And he may have the right of it. Fireside tale though it sounds. The question is: is it worth the journey to find out?"

Barnaby looked about the warm and comfortable tavern, searching for a reason to exchange it for someplace cold and uncomfortable.

"The Maiden looks like The Pomegranate, other side of the river."

"Aye," said Bodkin. "It's a bit like mirrors. The dark side of Persephone tends to copy the bright side. Some say it's the deceased from that bank coming here, repeating what they remember when they breathed."

"You lot sharing your breakfast?" asked Val, descending stairs, approaching the table. Jewel followed behind. They seized a bench, eyeing the plates. "'Course you are."

"'Course we are not," said Bodkin.

"Certainly, we are," said Cedric.

"Morning," said Barnaby, pushing plates forwards.

"You two look quite alive," said Cedric.

Jewel touched hand to hair fresh cleaned and bound. "I still need a comb. A brush. Something cleaner than burial clothes."

"Do you intend to stay in darker Persephone?" That, from Cedric.

Jewel took a roll of bread, broke it, weighing the halves.

"Probably. Best I avoid Demetia for a time. Agat and Hemp would sniff me out quick. Else the Questioners."

Cedric nodded. "Well, if you remain in Plutarch, you might seek employ at the cathedral. The archbishop will value someone with your affinity for the orations of Sister Hecatatia."

But Jewel only shuddered. "Lucif stuff me in his holy chamber pot, I'm not stepping foot near that stone bedlam again. Came near to being buried still blinking."

"Sorry," said Barnaby. "Thought you were dead."

Jewel stared, unsure what to say. In the cemetery thinking her dead, he'd actually praised her. Declared she'd been brave as a queen to face the world and witches. It made no sense for him to be so *nice*.

Suddenly she recalled that she owed him a kiss. Did he want it now?

Jewel felt Perry's heartbeat tap. Why? To reassure her? Maybe just to ask *did everyone have to make sense? Maybe he was just nice.*

"Bah," said Val. "Ignore the witch's whining about being buried alive. You rescued us. Or meant to. And wasn't it glorious when that idiot found his undead minions didn't give a shit for magic helmets?"

"Eggs," declared tavern girl Matilda, setting down a steaming bowl of boiled eggs. "Bacon. Salt. Bow and arrow."

"What?"

"If you're going to storm a magic tower you need someone as can shoot arrows fast and sure."

"This is meant to be a private, secret conference." That, from Bodkin.

Matilda nodded. "Won't tell a soul nor my mother."

Now Michael spoke. "She has a point. Barnaby has his axe, the boy has a sword. The cleric can cast spells, but at no great distance. There will come times you must strike from a distance."

Matilda studied Michael; then bent low, whispering to Barnaby.

"There's a ghostly man in the corner."

"We know," whispered Barnaby right back.

"Why do you now have a bow on your back and a quiver of arrows?" asked Bodkin.

"Who does, now?" asked Matilda, eyes wide, looking behind her.

"In Mill Town I have a friend from St. Silenus," said Barnaby. Taking an egg, cracking the hot shell. "She's good with a bow. Her name is…" he took breath, breathed out, "*Mmahaahahaaah*. But we just call her the Goat Girl."

Matilda put hands to hips.

"'The Goat Girl'? You call her 'The Goat Girl'? That's not a proper name to call a poor thing languishing far from hearth and heart and home."

"Was that Silenian?" asked Val, impressed.

"*Mmaha haha aah*? Of course," said Matilda. "A beautiful wondrous ancient name of great meaning."

"What meaning?"

"Hmm, it means 'The Goat Girl.'"

"We need more coffee." That, from Cedric.

"Then the adventurers shall have more coffee." Matilda turned, left them.

"Silenians are all mad," declared Bodkin. He pulled the plate of bacon from Jewel and Val. "Pass the salt and stop sampling our feast till you put coin upon the table."

"Bodkin, I've been meaning to thank you for giving me that knife in the woods," said Val.

"No need," said the boy, grand as five kings smiling. 'Twas the least I could do."

"Well," said Val, taking up the bread knife. "It was certainly the least you could do without me tracking you down and gutting you like I did Marcus and his band."

The table went suddenly quiet. Excepting a chuckle from the rafters, a chuckle from the corner shadows.

Meanwhile Val used the knife to peacefully spread butter upon bread, exactly as its maker intended. "Still, least though it was, you did save me from a bad end. So, thank you."

Bodkin said nothing, settled for pushing the platter of bacon before her again.

Jewel looked up at Night-Creep, her hand upon her spider necklace. Cat and witch met eyes, unblinking. Till Jewel turned away.

"It's mad how we all have come together like this," she whispered. "Is it the will of the saints?"

"It is our own will," corrected Cedric. "Barnaby determined to seek a tower in the north. I decided to follow after him, Bodkin chose to come as well. While you and the bard pursued your own paths, till they intersected with ours. As paths oft do."

Jewel frowned at Barnaby, recalling the guileless boy fetching her a bucket of creek water.

"Tower? What do you expect to find there? Treasure?"

Barnaby shook his head.

"Bodkin says treasure. Michael says death. Cedric says owls."

Val jumped in.

"We *are* speaking of The Saintless Tower, correct?"

"Yes," answered Cedric. "An ancient site where those called 'saints' are said to have met."

"*Called* 'saints'? What else are they?"

Cedric hesitated, glancing about the tavern for the robes of Questioners.

"Hmm, leave that for another time. But as for *treasure*, there may well be relics. Offerings from ancient times. Even items from the Lands Beyond."

Val turned to stare out the open window. When she spoke, it came touched with tone of bardic dreams.

"Thebes and Rome, Gaul and Xin, Djenné, Abyssinia, Etruria, Athens, Babylon, Teotihuacan, Carthage… I've always wondered if they weren't just names on a mad and imaginary map."

"They are real lands," affirmed Cedric. "Or were. They may be dust now. But long ago their ships came oft to *Terra Sanctorum*, as they named our world on *their* mad map. It was from one of those lands that Brendon sailed to our shores, fervent with holy vision.

"He spoke to the folk of the villages and was ignored. Debated the learned in their towers and was mocked. Preached to princes in castles and was beaten.

"At last he climbed a mountain, battling up a thousand steps, coming before the archons of earth and air, fire and water, life and death. To them he delivered his grand revelation of the House of Saints. The message that all creatures are equal bearers of a holy testament. And the powers of earth and sky, water and fire listened, and humbled themselves and were sanctified by Brendon and became those we call the saints."

From the table came silence. From the rafters: a chuckle.

"Something like that," said the cat.

"Why call it Saintless if it's stuffed with the holy things?" That, from Bodkin.

Again, Cedric glanced about.

"Because unlike most lands, the tower is not under the rule of any one saint. Truly, one might better call it *'The Tower of All Saints.'*"

"Well, I knew about Barnaby's tower already," declared Val. "And I'm inviting myself on the trip."

"Truly?" asked Barnaby. "What about your cup?"

Val laughed. "The cup led me to the fount where I met you. Then you went into the woods and found me. Then we found one another in the same miracle play, enacting 'dead bard and heroic avenger'." She took a bite of sausage. "No, master miller, I'm going to play it safe and follow you to your saints-cursed tower. If I don't, eagles will just swoop down, drop me on my ass back before you."

"Quite likely," said the cat in the rafters.

"Huh," said Jewel. Rolling a boiled egg about her plate, seemingly uninterested in cracking it. "Well, good luck to you all, then."

"Good luck to *us* all. You're coming too."

"Me? You want, you expect, *me* to go?"

"You're tangled in the tale as any, girl. We need a witch. You clearly need something to be a witch for."

Jewel looked down at her lap, letting unbound hair veil her face, her thoughts.

"We need a name for our association," declared Bodkin. "Something that expresses our grand friendship while keeping primary focus on profit."

Barnaby laughed delighted. "The Marauders?"

"The Miller's Marauders," suggested Val.

"Ugh, no," protested Bodkin. "Sound like one of those bands of wandering folk dancers."

Barnaby tried another. "The Fellowship of the Tower?"

"Excepting only some of us are fellows." That, from Val.

"The Companions?" suggested Cedric.

"Ah," replied Val. "In general reference to females, that word has indelicate meaning in terms of profit."

Bodkin thumped the table with boy's fist, man's certainty. "The Society of St. Benefact."

"I'm not familiar with that saint." This, from Cedric.

"'Course not, I just made him up. He's the patron saint of self-benefaction. Under his holy guidance we become... *the Benefactors*. Bravely and boldly adventuring, entirely for our own purses."

This was met with laughter, even from Cedric.

"Here now, boy, toss this apple in the air." That, from Matilda. Placing a fresh pot of coffee upon the table, and an apple.

"Why?" asked Bodkin. Eyeing the bow on the back of the Silene. "You aren't mad enough to shoot an arrow inside a tavern, are you?"

The woman tapped a flower-painted hoof.

"Fine," said Bodkin. "But if you miss, it's a free round of sausage and bacon for the table."

The woman tapped again. Bodkin grinned, tossing the apple high into the rafters.

Near too fast to see, Matilda had the bow from her back, an arrow cocked and loosed.

The apple rose to zenith, where Night-Creep batted it with a paw. Then it descended to fall in Bodkin's open palm. Entirely untouched by arrow.

"Ha," laughed Bodkin. "Missed the apple. Fetch the bacon."

But Barnaby, Val and Cedric stared elsewhere; at the head of the boar above the door. An arrow still quivering in its right eye.

"Who'd be wanting to shoot fruit?" asked the Silene. "Silly thing to be doing." Taking the apple from Bodkin, biting into it with teeth wide and white. Chewing thoughtful, her strange eyes gazing upon the gathering. "And I'm quite very happy to join your Society of holy St. Benefact."

Part II

The Journey to the Tower

Chapter 1
Monsters are Much, Much Easier

The Dark Market of Persephone made no gloom-filled plaza of shadow and silence. Like its twin across the river, it bustled with merchants hawking wares from barrows, blankets and booths. Folk wandered chatting, sampling food and drink; else setting to the work of bargaining, their words spiced with waves of hand, stamps of feet. Children scurried laughing through the crowd like forest creatures twixt the rooted adults. Singers and acrobats performed to claps and shouts, between ceremonial passings of the coin-hungry hat. Same as the Bright Market across the Lethe.

And yet to Barnaby the total held a different feel. On St. Demetia's side of Persephone, the light weighed dense; gold cloth upon the outstretched hand.

Here in St. Plutarch's half of the city, it was the shadows that bore weight; piling thick beneath the garden trees, filling the branches of cypress and yew, their leaves so dark a green as to be near black.

Barnaby noted fewer fountains, more memorials. Less trees; far more statues. All about the market square stood stone and bronze figures on high pedestals, gazing down upon the living. Their fixed faces carrying a clear and common message: *Travelers, life is brief wandering. Keep to serious paths.*

Were these stern figures men and women of Plutarch past? Perhaps their ghosts sat in councils now guiding the land with wisdom gathered across centuries.

Barnaby pictured the robed ghosts coming by night, standing beneath their own images, weighing what they'd gained passing Death's door. Perhaps they laughed to see how wise they'd become since their mayfly days of life.

Then again, perhaps they stared puzzled, seeking connection with the person they'd been, seeing only a stranger's face reflected in stone.

What had Belinda the Rat said? *Death is an ending. What comes after does not continue what passed before.* Talking of Pentateuch's lost love for her. Or hers for him? Surely it came to the same.

He stared up at the statue of a woman in marble robes, her head bedecked with a mother superior's wimple. Stone face; but the sculpting caught wrinkles, dimples, a hundred scars of flesh suffering the outrages of time and heart. The carven eyes narrowed, as if peering into mist. Mouth just slightly, lightly set in smile.

He pictured the statue calling to him from her high, wise pedestal, asking '*Barnaby son of Barnabas, why do you take your friends into deadly danger?*'

He shook his head. "I don't know."

"Don't know what?" asked Cedric. Looking from Barnaby to the statue.

"He talks to himself," replied Bodkin.

"Also to butterflies, axes, candles, hearth fires, cats and ghosts," added Val.

"Who knew millers were such complex fellows?" wondered Jewel.

"It's all them wheels turning round and about," declared Matilda. "Gets in their poor heads, it does."

"Next on the list," read Bodkin, raising voice to override non-essential conversation. "Tents. We'll need two. One for the ladies, one for us masculine sorts."

"And a third to shelter supplies," suggested Cedric.

"Oiled cloth, so rain doesn't leak upon our faces," advised Val.

Cedric sighed. "They always leak."

Barnaby turned from the statue, considering his friends. Should he tell them to end these preparations? Did he have the right to do so? What would they do instead? What would he do?

"I'm off to the horse dealers," declared Val. "I'll shop for a mule."

"No stealing them," warned Bodkin. "You aren't any good at it."

Cedric and Jewel laughed. Val sniffed to say *we shall see*.

"I shall accompany the lady bard," said Matilda. "I've friends at the stables."

"Goats?" asked Bodkin. "Cousins?"

Matilda bent her tall frame downwards, face to face with Bodkin.

"Ho, that was meant to be humorous. I do so love a good jest. Elsewise I'd be kicking your tiny butt to the nether caves of Nix."

"Apologies," said Bodkin.

"Accepted."

Bodkin turned quick to Val. Handing her an underfed purse. "You'll need coin."

"I have what we divvied up this morning," said the bard. Reaching into her jerkin, finding a pocket rich with fishing weights.

"Infernum's fucking fires, you little thief stop *doing* that."

"Have to practice if I'm going to outmatch old Mercutio."

"Who?" asked Jewel.

"Oh, the little snot's all a battle of bedlams in the head," said Val, turning walking towards the market gate. "Same as the rest of us. The Society of St.

Benefact is composed of folk who hear voices and chase fairy lights."

"Not me," said Jewel, following behind. Cupping hand over the spider-pendant upon her breast. She felt sure it gave a reassuring tap to say, *no, not us.*

Barnaby watched his friends go. It felt good to say it within his head: *There go my friends. Val, Matilda, and Jewel. I know all sorts of things about them. Val likes peppery food and music and is angry at her mother. Matilda dances and has brothers who make swords. Jewel has a fear of storms and can't sleep at night. I know them. They know me.*

He considered all they knew of him. What was there to know? Couldn't think of a thing. He looked up again at the statue, still waiting, still waiting, for reply. *Barnaby son of Barnabas, why lead your friends into danger?*

"Still don't know," he told it. "Maybe I shouldn't."

"Trouble approaches," declared Cedric.

"Best to scamper?" That, from Bodkin.

"No, lad. Bide still."

Barnaby looked about. Spying two figures in black robes, carrying staffs of authority; flanked by two of the bone-white Death Hounds. The market crowd parted before these grim officials. Cedric waited, leaning peacefully upon his staff till they halted before him.

"Cedric Wieland."

No question there, but declaration marked with stamp of staff on stone.

"Yes?"

"You are summoned to appear before the Deaconry."

"On what charge?"

The man shook head, smiling benign as the statuary that observed their mortal converse.

"Who spoke of 'charge'? The council merely wishes to speak with you. And so they shall speak with you."

Cedric nodded. "Very well." He turned to Bodkin and Barnaby. "I will find you back at the inn. If I do not return, it will be wisest that you not to inquire."

"We'll come with you," said Barnaby.

"No," said Cedric. "This shall be a discussion between scholars, not battle with monsters." He gave Barnaby a sad grin. "Monsters are much easier."

* * *

"So Bodkin is really an old man?" asked Jewel.

"Hmm, not quite," said Val. "He *was* an old man. Some famous thief, according to him. Now he's a kid giving himself airs. But claims the ancient still lurks in the back of his head, shouting advice."

"What sort of advice?"

"Ah, how to steal the Duke's coronet, rob the bank of Pomona, sass taller folk without being kicked to Nix. That sort of thing. He does have a way with grin and wink, I grant."

"Ah, he's an old soul, then," said Matilda. "Some folk are born so."

"And some are born a pain in the butt. I'm thinking we should buy a cart. Two mules."

"Costly," observed Jewel. "Why not send Bodkin to steal it?"

Val halted, turning frown upon Jewel. Who raised hands in defense. "What? If we've got a clever thief for ally, might as well make use of him."

Val shook head. "Let's not get stuffed into any more cells this week."

Matilda had continued on; now she stood before an array of folded cloths. "I'm needing a blanket, as I leave my comfy tavern bed behind."

Jewel: "And I need a blanket that doesn't serve as a kingdom for fleas."

"Not those cotton things. Wool's warmer," advised Val.

"Six, then, for us and the boys."

"Five will do." Matilda shook her head, pointed ears twitching. "That miller's about to scamper from the venture."

Val stared, disbelieving.

"What? It's Barnaby's map, his tower. Infernum, it's his damned venture. We mad strangers just tag along because the saints decided we're useful to their mill-lacking miller."

"Oi now," declared Matilda, stamping hoof. "I'm no mad tag-along. I do sane and useful tavern work, fine as St. Vitus does a holy jig. Never spill a dram excepting upon the sorts that get fresh because a girl hasn't toes."

"Then why are you off to the wild with lunatics?"

"Well, as it happens, I'm rather bored silly with tavern wenching. Probably same as Mister Barnaby with his milling, and holy cleric heretic Cedric with his clerking. But now for sure your miller's pondering a skip. It's what he's talking to the air about."

Val pulled a blue blanket from a shelf. Thick, decorated with a weave of poppies and pomegranates. Symbols of Persephone; pretty, but funereal as the chiseled frame to a headstone epitaph.

"Maybe you have it right. He has gone all brooding. Boys daydream of slashing foes with swords, until they start picturing themselves wiggling on the sharp end of the blade. Maybe fighting Capitano put the fear of Friar February into our bold miller."

She put away the funereal blanket; fingered another, green as St. Demetian summer.

"Neither of you has ever been lonely, have you?" That, from Jewel. Standing apart, arms folded in sign of defiance.

Matilda turned her mad, slotted eyes upon Jewel. As Val turned her brown and round pupils.

"What's 'lonely' got to do with aught?"

Jewel shook her head, turning away, refusing to say more. But within her head, she gave furious words to Periwinkle.

How do they not see? The miller has friends now. Damned sure he never did before. To him we feel like, like family. He isn't fearing for himself. It's for us. He doesn't want his new family to come to harm. Idiots.

She felt the familiar faint spider-tap of reassurance.

Thanks, Perry. And you're right. We don't want the idiots to die either.

* * *

Cedric stood in a high-ceilinged chamber bedecked with frescoes of the saints performing holy acts, to a background of flaming clouds, marching armies, comets and volcanos in choreographed dance.

Before him waited a table set upon an ebony dais. Tall candles glowed, proud to declare this setting an altar of the saints. Proper stage for a council of figures decked in dark robes, somber faces. Seven ashen thrones; four occupied.

A cautious majority, decided Cedric. This is something of import to them, if not to me.

"Sit, young Cedric," said the central figure. A man showing some forty years of life upon his gray face...and behind his eyes glimmered a hundred years of thought; red embers making no surrender to gray ash.

"Father Egregious," said Cedric. He nodded, sat.

"You and your friends journey north."

"We make no secret of it."

"Treasure hunting?"

"For the younger ones, treasure is the goal. At least, the adventure of seeking treasure. For me, I see the opportunity to learn. Great historical significance lies within *that* tower."

"Hmm. We have been discussing forbidding your journey."

"Alas, the Saintless Tower does not lie within the demesne of Sainted Plutarch, nor the Deaconry of the saint."

"No, and alas, but you and your companions currently do dwell within our purview. More alas."

Cedric smiled, held out his hands to show them empty of recourse.

"But you will not forbid our venture."

"How do you know?"

"Because it is clear to you that the saints intend this journey. Your wise counsel is always to steer with the wind, not defy the storm."

"Neither winds nor storms greatly concerns us," said the cowled personage to the right of Egregious. Face a mere shadow of dark eyes, pale lips. "Think rather, we labor to align the wild winds of the world with the wise will of the saints."

There is no difference, said Cedric to himself. *The one is the other.*

Egregious raised hand to remind all that he held discussion's reigns.

"But as we cannot torment you now with dangling permission and refusal, Wieland, we must settle for stating our terms. We shall give you letters of permit to travel freely through the demesne of Plutarch, patron of Blessed Ending."

"And permit through Hefestia," added Cedric.

The figures exchanged glances.

"We can give you letters of passage across the border of our ally Hefestia. Once there, your steps are between yourself and the Saint of Holy Artifice."

"Excellent. And your condition?"

"You make official visit upon an associate of yours."

"I have many associates within Daedalus."

"No. We mean, here in Plutarch."

For many heartbeats Cedric only stared; while cold seeped from the stone floor, settling like winter rain into his stomach.

"Where?"

"A hermit's cave, not far from the river road. Conveniently on your way north. Truly, the saints have brought you to us so that you might perform this task."

"Whom?"

"The hermitess Beatrice."

"No. No and no."

"Wherefore not?"

For some while Cedric sat silent.

Then, "We promised never to meet again so long as we lived. A promise we have kept."

"Why then, there is no breaking of your oath, young priest. The hermitess has freed herself from mortal coil."

"*Freed* herself?"

"We believe she perished in an act self-directed. Defying the testament of the Saint of Holy Ending. With the dark result that oft occurs to such."

Nachzehrer, thought Cedric. *No.*

"Believe? You do not know?"

"We know only that she preached sermons denouncing this life, this world. Renouncing the flesh as those inclined to a hermit's life oft do. Indeed, many pilgrims journeyed to her cave to hear her words. Seeking enlightenment, and no doubt some token as relic to a saint yet undeclared."

"That, I had heard."

"One of her disciples came to us, fleeing Beatrice's self-declared order of penance. Describing how the novice inflicts ever more terrible trials upon herself, to renounce the flesh, become pure spirit."

At which the figure to the right of Egregious pushed back its cowl. Behold a face like to a skull bound in rags of parchment, eyes dark holes from which a blue light flickered, faint as fox fire in fog.

An eerie thing to see; yet when this personage spoke, it was in voice soft as silk, feminine as a mother's touch.

"Purity of spirit is a most excellent goal. Pity that those who seek it so oft wrap themselves in needless pains, despairing without cause."

These words stirred yet another of the council.

"Life is brief; breath is pain; living is a fool's journey. Beatrice understood that, as much as mortal mind shall do."

It is you that do not understand, thought Cedric. *What do you know of life? Nothing except what you recall in the dust of your graves, the rotted thoughts within your skulls. Bah. You should be swept up with brooms, put to the dust bin.*

Cedric did not speak these words. Merely wiped eyes, staring up at the bright frescoes upon the ceiling.

Egregious cleared throat, continued.

"Since that last novice fled, no further word has come from the hermitess."

Cedric returned gaze to the council.

"Then she might yet live."

"If you wish to think it so. But pilgrims to her cavern shrine no longer are permitted to see her, unless they join her ranks. And those that join, do not return. As well of late, travelers upon the river road have begun disappearing."

"That may be coincidence," said the blue-eyed councilor. "The river road north is perilous."

"Then send soldiers and exorcists to scour her lair." Cedric took breath.

"There are many in Plutarch who regard the hermitess as a speaker for the saints," said the councilor of blue eyes. "As perhaps she is. We are bound to investigate before resorting to exorcism."

"Therefore, we send you as Questioner, young Cedric," declared Egregious.

"Why me?" asked Cedric. "What reason can you have but cruel amusement?"

The council waited in a silence that signaled annoyance. At last the cowled specter spoke.

"Cedric Wieland, we acknowledge you as scholar, a priest, a mind of noble intent. Do us the favor of admitting we are not monsters set upon a feast table, delighting in the pains of the living."

But you are, thought Cedric. *You send me to find love turned to horror. You know it so.*

Egregious continued.

"You gather a company of adventurers. Your journey takes you past a place of danger to the welfare of Plutarch. And you, Cedric, are one of the few who knew Beatrice Lucia by face and heart. It is the belief of the Deaconry that this must be the will of the saints. It is they that set you upon this task, oh priest."

Cedric bowed his head. The council waited; patient as only those can be who do not count time in breath and beat of heart. At last he sighed, raised his head.

"Very well. I and my associates shall take the river road north. Making a visit to Beatrice's shrine. If she has brought harm upon herself, I shall see to ending her pain."

Cedric stood, not waiting for the council to give him leave. "After all, this is Plutarch's realm. Proper endings are his purpose within the House of Saints, are they not?"

To himself adding, *to see that all things reach a proper and holy finish. Even my love for Beatrice.*

Chapter 2
In Which Bodkin Vows to Turn Over a New Leaf

Ptolemy, oldest and greatest of the bells atop the Church of Resurrection, tolled slow and solemn as a bronze heart beating. At the sixth strike Val came half awake. Out the corner of one eye she spied someone upon the floor beside her cot. A shimmering, golden glow of a girl, head thrown back in silent song. At the twelfth toll of the bell, Val came fully awake. She sat up. No girl now upon the floor. Only the harp, resting quiet as any inanimate object.

Val threw aside her blanket. Reached for pants, for shirt; last for the harp.

She sat awhile, tracing a finger along the gilded frame. It shimmered in the light of the room's single candle. The pillar of the harp held the form of a young woman, face tilting upwards, smiling. Small breasts bare, body tapering at the waist into scales and a fishtail that merged into the soundboard.

A mermaid of the southern isles, thought Val. She caressed the strings, savoring how the soft crystal chime seemed a voice, singing soft as surf on a quiet shore.

More than once, when she'd looked at the harp sideways, she'd spied the faint form of the girl. Arms about knees, head thrown back, singing to the sky. And when Val played, she knew the harp itself added to the tune.

Well, any bard could sing of special objects that housed some spirit. Harps and swords, shields and mirrors so wondrously crafted they held life within.

"I know you're in there," she whispered to the harp. "Don't be shy."

In reply the strings thrummed, just faintly.

"Would you like a name? I can't just call you 'harp'."

Again the faint *thrum, hum*.

"Good," said Val. She perused her bardic knowledge. Seeking a name to do with the sea, and with song.

"Thelxipea," she decided. "She's a sea maiden, and her name means '*Charming song*'. That please you?"

In reply the strings twanged entirely upon their own. A quick light tumble of happy notes.

"I'll take that for 'yes'. Thelxipea, then."

Val stood, harp in hand, tiptoeing to the door. Pushing aside the bar, stepping into the hall. A lantern upon a table cast weak light, strong shadow. She listened. Beyond the other doors she heard sounds, quiet conversations. Midnight, and all the *Benefactors* were supposed to be resting. Tomorrow they'd be leaving Persephone, taking the river road north. Beginning the grand adventure.

Val tiptoed down the stairs, through a dark corridor into the common room. A low fire burned in the hearth. Before it sat a figure cross-legged, gazing into the flames. He did not turn at her entrance.

Val took a chair some distance away. Studying Barnaby. Fresh shaven, hair combed, leather armor put aside for simple shirt. No longer the wild man swinging an axe in a graveyard.

There's the dreamer again, thought Val. *The boy from old tales who stares into the embers while the practical world laughs at his foolish soul.*

Val took Thelxipea, strummed. The notes sifted softly together, forming song clear and simple as water trickling from some mountain rill where no clumsy human foot stepped.

For a long while she played so, no tune she could name. Thinking upon her home in Martia, the days in bard school, and the cup, and even the silly miller boy as he'd sat beside the fountain staring into an infinite distance of dreams. Same as he did now. Same as *she* did now.

At length Val ceased playing, unsure how long she had sifted thoughts now lost. There in the shadows now sat Jewel. In simple night-dress, dark hair unbound, left hand cupping the spider pendant.

Jewel did not speak. In the firelight her eyes shone large and mysterious; thin face sharp as knife. Looking every inch the witch.

Cedric entered then, giving nod to Val.

"You play beautifully," he said. "Drew me from my bed."

Val smiled in approval of his musical judgement; then turned, watched Matilda crossing the room, lighting candles.

"Can't sleep, you lot?" the Silenian asked.

Val shook her head; as did Jewel.

"We'd all be wise to rest before tomorrow's journey," Cedric declared.

"But this is our last night of easy beds and free wine," said Bodkin, slipping into the lighted room.

"What free wine?" demanded Matilda.

"Why should you be caring? You've given over being tavern slavey. You now share our astonishing life of adventure. And our common funds. Anyhow, what are locks twixt friends?"

"You will be settling your wine tab tomorrow, young tippler," growled Matilda. Putting hands to hips.

Bodkin put hands to his boy's hips, preparing riposte. But stopped, as Barnaby stirred.

All the room watched as he rose from the hearthside. Stretched, as if ending long labor. Then stood with back to the fire, gazing about the room.

They kept silent, till at last he spoke.

"I am glad we are all here."

"Oh?" That, from Val.

"Yes," affirmed Barnaby. "I have something hard to say. So best said to all, and done."

Val exchanged look with Jewel, who nodded to Matilda, who turned eyes upon Bodkin, who gave grin of mischief to Cedric. That last personage sighed, spoke.

"You have decided not to go to the tower."

Barnaby's mouth opened.

"How were you knowing that?"

Mild laughter filled the room.

"The sad look on your face of late. That, and you've been arguing death and purpose with shadows, statues and chairs."

"Ah. Well. That makes it easier. You are good folk, all of you. I'd dearly love to travel together. See the world, what's down each road. But there's no cause to travel towards likely death. When I left Mill Town, it didn't matter where I wandered. A mad tower made as good a goal as any. But now..."

"Now you don't see any point in risking the lives of friends on your fool's quest."

"That's the very thing, Friar Cedric."

"Well, but we decided to go, Barnaby." That, from Val.

"Only because I am going," insisted Barnaby. "The Friar feels obligated to look after me. *You* think you've been pushed into the venture by a magic cup. Bodkin is being an easy friend. Not sure why Miss Jewel wishes to come."

Jewel sniffed in disdain, looking away. Declining to discuss her motives. While Val Kurgus, bard of St. Martia, set down her harp. Leaned forward as lioness ready to spring.

"Listen well, Master Miller. We are all bound on this venture. If you try and back out, we will tie you down and throw you in the mule cart. By St. Euterpe, that's a promise, and I'll keep it."

Barnaby blinked. Bodkin only smiled, perching upon a table, kicked short legs forth and back.

"The girl's right, Barnaby. "It isn't only up to you, We Benefactors are all in the game together."

"Game," sighed Barnaby. "That's just what it is." He searched pockets, drew forth a roll of parchment.

"This is a game my brother Alf began. Meaning no good by it. Gave me the map, playing me his jest. Had he not, you lot would be pursuing sensible paths."

At which Matilda laughed, stamping a cloven foot.

"Mister Miller Barnaby, does the present company strike you as the sorts to be pursuing sensible paths?"

This comment brought laughter. But Barnaby only looked puzzled.

"To me, you seem very quite sensible." His puzzlement turned to sad grin. "Granted, mother says I don't know sense from St. Lucif's fiery shit."

This rare and coherent profanity impressed the room; they kept silent as Barnaby placed the roll of parchment into the fire. At once it sprang to flame, curling, blackening, gone.

"Well," said Bodkin, almost idly. "Who'd have thought you'd do that?"

Barnaby turned from the fire, keeping face to the floor, speaking to its dusty planks.

"Well, it's done. And should have been done before it came to purchasing mules and tents and such. You lot sell or keep it all. Divide the remaining coin from Pentateuch among yourselves. I won't take a penny."

Looks were exchanged; but Barnaby sighted no great anger or disappointment. Only Cedric staring sadly at the fire, as though imitating a daydreaming miller.

"Calls for wine to mourn the Benefactors," declared Matilda. She brought forth a heavy basket conveniently filled with bottles, jugs and mugs.

"Whatever will I do now that the adventure is off?" Val asked the air. "Become a strolling troubadour, I suppose. Or I might give horse theft another try."

"I'm fated to be mere and drear tavern wench," declared Matilda. "Getting my pretty bottom pinched."

"For me, I'm going to turn over a new leaf," declared Bodkin. "I shall work to affirm the laws of the saints, the authority of the Juditandis."

The room met this statement with dead silence. Barnaby frowned, looking from one to another till Matilda poured a mug of red wine, handing it to him. He felt obligated to take it, drink it. Then fall into coughing.

The others poured their own cups. Jewel taking sips delicate as cat licks.

"Never had proper wine before," she admitted. "Just sherry from the kitchen cupboard."

"What will you do now, Jewel of Stonecroft?" That, from Bodkin.

Jewel stared into the distance, seeing her future. "I think... I shall go home and burn down the neighbors' farms." She extended tongue tip, savoring a drink darker than wine "Then I'll hunt down that Agat and

Hemp. Turn them into something even nastier than their mirrors see now. Next, hmm, I shall call blight and murrain upon the estate that took my family's croft. Oh, then I think I will track down my thrice-cursed mother and–"

"And you, Friar Cedric?" asked Val, bright and loud, cutting off Jewel's dark itinerary.

Cedric only smiled, shook head.

Barnaby frowned. Finding the conversation somehow odd. Well, but no doubt his friends labored to put a good face upon things.

Friends, he thought. *We'll still be friends. Won't we?*

Matilda filled his cup again, smiling. Friendship demanded he empty it. Val began to play the harp; a clever melody of notes winding and twining with the wine. Barnaby laughed, feeling sad, feeling happy, feeling he loved these people more than life itself.

He started to say so; fell into a fit of hiccups. Gave the speech up. The music played, the bottles emptied.

Far away, Ptolemy tolled three solemn beats.

"I'm off to bed," Barnaby declared. Wobbling to his feet, as love and wine bubbled up from his overfilled heart. "Thank you, my friends. I, I am sorry."

"We too, Master Miller," said Val the Bard. For all the bright melody her fingers harped, her eyes glowered upon him, her jaw biting the words. "We too."

No one else spoke. Barnaby departed, making his way up stairs that seemed to shift beneath his feet. Within his room waited darkness, the candle long snuffed. He found his cot, lay down wondering what he would do tomorrow, and all the days after.

It was said there were water mills on the Demetian side of the Lethe. He might seek employ there.

He lay picturing the dark river turning mill wheels, as the wind did the vanes at home. Da said a proper mill was the mating of wind and stone. Said it with a grin, though Mother Miller frowned.

Barnaby wondered if Val would ever want to mate with him. He couldn't picture her being a miller's wife. Nor that Jewel, either. But he decided he could picture mating with either. That was easy to picture.

His thoughts sank into a vision of a mill turned by a flowing river of wine, while naked bards and witches leaped and capered in the wheels. His breath became snores, the occasional hiccup.

At length the door eased open, faces peering in.

"If 'tis to be done, best done quick," whispered Val. She tiptoed in, followed by a scowling Jewel, a grinning Matilda. They stood above the sleeping miller, contemplating.

Bodkin followed after, holding a lamp. He bent low over the cot.

"Barnaby?" he whispered. There came no reply.

"Aye, he's out," declared the boy. "For the night."

"What of the cat and the ghost?" whispered Jewel.

The four looked anxiously about in the shadows.

"Absent," declared Bodkin. "And anyway, they only teach."

Val nodded, turned to Jewel. The witch bit her lip in indecision, then whispered to the night.

"Perry."

Within the dark of the room shimmered the faint star-shine of the spider's clustered eyes. The creature scuttled along the floor, upon the wall, then dropped upon the bed. Val and Bodkin lifted Barnaby's feet; the spider wound them about with thread thin as knife edge. Then they lifted his head and arms; again the spider scuttled circling, winding and binding Barnaby tight.

Matilda shook her curled locks. "Pleasant fellow though he is, shall be angered in the morning, I'm foreseeing and foretelling."

"I gave him fair warning," said Val. Sounding angered herself. "Let's get him to the cart. You two get his feet. Bodkin and I will get his head. Ready, and lift."

Barnaby son of Barnabas, sometime Marquise of the Fief of Millstones, Lord of the Thousand Winds, wielder of Dragontooth, awoke to bird song. A pleasant awakening, though the sound came strangely accompanied by clop of hooves, rattle of wheels.

His bed rocked and rattled as well, as if he'd fallen asleep in a wagon rumbling down the road. It made his stomach queasy. He struggled to open eyes that seemed filmed by a week of sleep.

Opened eyes revealed that the ceiling of the inn had been replaced by open sky; a fresco of clouds painted in the orange fires of dawn.

Puzzled, he struggled to sit up. Finding his legs bound by thread thin as silk, strong as chain. He reached to pull it away, only to find arms bound to sides.

Barnaby looked about. He lay in a cart atop bags and packs. It did not rumble through any busy city street of Persephone. This was some country road lined with dark trees, where crows and ravens cawed a somber *good morning*.

"Saint Lucif's thorned tea kettle," he whispered.

"Awake, are we now?" asked Val. She walked beside the rolling cart, peering in. Dressed for travel in leather jerkin; harp slung across her back.

Barnaby fell back, staring up at the girl. Saying nothing. Then the dark form of Night-Creep leaped past her, landing beside Barnaby graceful as snowflake upon flower petal.

Barnaby met the white, bright gaze.

"Can you free me?" Barnaby whispered.

The cat placed his head against Barnaby's chest. A gesture of affection the cat had never made before.

"You know well that I cannot, master."

"I might ask Dark Michael, as my third request."

"True. If you no longer value his company."

Val gave a command to someone beyond view. The cart halted. She leaned over the edge, joined by Bodkin, Jewel, and Matilda. They stared down upon Barnaby, bound.

He stared up at them. His head ached; his mouth felt horrid and he needed to pee. And more than anything, he felt shamed. And angry.

"We're about five miles north of Persephone, in case you wondered. On the river road, which does not see much traffic."

Barnaby said nothing.

Val sighed, produced a knife.

"No need to demand we free you, Master Miller. We just wanted to get you on the road with no more nonsense of keeping us safe." She passed the knife across the threads, they fell away. Barnaby struggled to sit upright. Val offered him a hand, which he ignored. Finding himself atop the tents and food supplies, rope and blankets, all the wondrous items they'd purchased for the glorious adventure.

He spied his pack, his armor, his axe. Took these things, dropping them over the side of the cart onto the road. Then he clambered clumsily out the cart, stood brushing spider threads away.

"Barnaby, we are sorry," said Bodkin. "But it was the best way to make you understand. We truly wish to go on this journey."

"I did warn him," declared Val to all.

"So you keep reminding," said Cedric. Alone of the company, he stood apart, not facing Barnaby but staring away. Leaning upon his staff as though weary.

Still Barnaby did not speak. He hurried towards the trees that lined the road; vanished in the brush, leaving the others to stand in awkward silence. After some minutes he returned, wearing a face that none had seen upon his cheerful person before.

He pushed past Bodkin and Jewel, retrieving his boots, his leather armor, his axe and sheath. Donned these things; last his pack. Then he turned, walking down the road and away.

"Where you going?" asked Bodkin.

"Ah, he's done with us," sighed Matilda. "Pity, that. Seemed a pleasant sort."

"Shit," said Val. Then shouted. "Come back, dammit up Lucif's third buttock! Do we really have to apologize?"

Barnaby made no reply. Giving no last glance back. Only quickened his pace. Clearly in a hurry to be down the road, beyond their view and gone.

Chapter 3
Smoke, Ash, and Nothing

Alf of Mill Town:

Loved my stepbrother Barnaby with all my heart. Though Mill Town chided me for the endless japes upon him. Horse piss for ale and dead rats in his blankets. Pouring flour down as he passed through the door, putting burrs in his pants, sending him running to the manse with letters instructing the Squire to kiss Lucif's flaming lips.

Folk named me a spirit sent by Infernum itself to torment an innocent. Not that they didn't laugh loud to see Barnaby fall flat, or stand snowed in flour, or watch him spend the day fishing for mermaids in the brook.

What they didn't see was that I did it for my brother's good. Ah, folk are blind that way. They see your acts; not the why of the act.

It was Ma and the Squire's sly plan; raise Barnaby to be a fool. They wanted the mill, of course. She kept promising it'd be mine; though you could tell by his eyes that the Squire had other plans.

So: I set myself to teach my brother wisdom. I tricked my brother again and again, to teach him not to be tricked.

For years I instructed Barnaby to never walk unwary, never trust another's intent. Check under the blanket for rats, in every hat for dogshit. Look in every doorway for a cord to trip a foot. Peer into both boots for a spike before putting foot within.

I did my honest best to make Barnaby understand that folk lied, deceived, cheated. That a stepmother full of affirmations of the saints could be a sly devil. A friar full of knowledge could be spouting blither that even the Goat Girl would know for blather. And that a brother who clapped him on the back, sending him to gather moonlight in a sack by night, was someone he should thump on the head.

He never did once. Thump me, or anyone. For all he was strong as any I've met. Ah, my poor brother would be the butt of some lesson, and his cheerful face would turn surprised. And I'd wait, holding breath, thinking that at last, at last we'd see the cup overflow with anger, with understanding of the world's soul. Then at last would come the righteous thumping! He'd toss Ma out of the house, knock the Squire on his ass. Break my arms, no doubt, and then chase the Friar round the mill.

But no; Barnaby would only shake his head, and then grin, and then go about his chores, humming, watching the clouds. Settling at day's end before the hearth. Whatever cruel trick I played, he smiled; and forgot. Never learned a thing.

At least, never learning any lesson *I* gave. A thousand cruel japes only taught my brother to dream, to turn hearth flames into a window showing a world more real to him than Mill Town.

The last thing I ever gave Barnaby: a scrap of a map his fool Da left. I clapped my brother on the back, told him '*here's your treasure map, be on the road and away.*'

What else to do? If I'd told him Ma was pondering poison in tonight's soup, he'd have nodded, and grinned, and reached for the soup spoon. So I set him wandering from Mill Town and murder.

Ma and the Squire thought sending him off made excellent plan; better than poisoned soup.

So we all waved goodbye, calling him a brave fellow, wishing him well, telling him to travel safe, return soon with our treasure.

What would you have had me do? He had a better chance of seeing the next dawn on the road, than another night in his bed. As for the dangers of that lunatic tower, what of them? It was a thousand leagues away. He'd no more chance of reaching it than if I'd given him a map to the moon.

Soon as Barnaby disappeared down the road, the Squire and mother went off to chuckle and fornicate. The Friar locked himself in his cottage, the shamefaced lackey. I returned to the mill alone, sat before the hearth fire. And there I stared and stared, seeking what Barnaby found here that turned his face to a portrait of dreamy contemplation.

I watched flames devour logs, leaving embers; the embers settling to cinders. Just wood's usually fiery decay into ash and smoke.

And when the last ember died, I found myself alone in the dark of an empty house. Not bit nor wit wiser than before.

And staring into the ashes, it came to me that perhaps Barnaby had gotten the last laugh. All those years I'd worked to make my brother wise. But I never thought to ask him to teach me to be a fool.

Chapter 4
Stars, Scars, Trips, Ships

The Society of St. Benefact made camp within sight of the road, where a line of trees provided shelter from wind off the river. The two mules grazed at peace, disinterested in discussing the day's sad turn.

"It seemed clever at the time," said Bodkin, poking the campfire with a stick. "Amusing, in fact. And Barnaby's an easy-going sort. Saint's truth, I expected him to laugh."

"He had no business calling *our* venture off," insisted Val to the flames. "It was for all to decide."

"Ah, he didn't like looking foolish," said Matilda. "Darkens a boy's mirror to think the ladies have been laughing at what he was up to with a head full of wine."

Cedric sat far from the fire, his back against a tree, staring up at evening stars. None knew he listened, till he spoke.

"Barnaby is quite used to looking foolish, Whether in his mirror or the eyes of others. That is not what hurt him."

"What then?" That, from Val.

The answer came in tone of sad reflection.

"The realization that we tricked him."

Val took Thelxipea up from the ground. *He gave me this,* she thought. *Carried it about hoping to give it to me. Put it in what he thought was my grave.*

She strummed a few notes. They came forth discordant, angry, tangled. The sound made her furious. *Whose side are you on?* she demanded of the harp.

She set the traitorous thing down again, observing aloud. "We treated him fair. In St. Martia, if you flee battle the punishment is death. Not being tied up drunk."

"Not the same," said Jewel. "He thought he was leading us towards danger."

"If we decide to go, what right has he to cry 'halt'?"

If you care about folk, you have the right, thought Jewel. But kept silent. What good saying it? Clearly the bard felt guilty. Like Bodkin, Val had expected the miller to just grin, praising his friends' clever trick.

Jewel recalled stealing Barnaby's lunch. It hadn't troubled her. That was witch-work. But tricking him out of the promised kiss had felt mean. She'd left him staring at the pebble, puzzled as puppy expecting a pat, getting a kick.

"He went north," observed Bodkin. "Maybe we'll catch up when he's in a better mood."

"Well, he'd best walk careful," declared Matilda. "The river road isn't used much nowadays, nor patrolled. Too many nasty things in the water and the ruins."

"Dangerous?"

"Hmm, not for a cautious company. But not the best way north for anyone traveling alone."

"Barnaby has his axe, his magic cat, his ghost and his luck," said Bodkin. "He'll do fine."

"You think he's still going to the tower?"

Everyone looked to Cedric. Who only shook his clerical head.

"I don't know what he will do. I doubt he knows himself."

"Question is, what do *we* do?" asked Matilda. She alone seemed to retain cheerful spirit. "Go on, or give it up?"

"We go on," said Bodkin.

"You still have the map?"

"The copy. He'll find the original in his pack."

"That won't make him any happier," said Jewel. "He'll realize you picked his pocket, gave him a roll of trash to burn. Which tells him we planned it all before his noble announcement."

"Tough for Master Miller," declared Val. "I'm with Bodkin. On to the tower. How about you three?"

"Oh, I'm still in the game," said Matilda. "Who'd be turning back at the first dark cloud?"

Jewel kicked at the earth, scuffing dirt into the fire. She bent head low, hair covering her face. When she spoke, it was low words from behind that veil.

"This venture is something I've been given, as much as I was given Perry. I want to go on." *Also, don't have anywhere else to go.*

Now all eyes turned to Cedric. Who sighed, stood, stretched.

"I began this journey in penance for my cowardice towards Barnaby. And for my cowardice towards the truths I have been given. I would have accompanied him to the tower. But if he does not want my company, I respect his decision."

Shit, sighed Jewel. *It's all falling apart before it began.*

"But," Cedric continued. "I have been given a mission by the Deaconry of Persephone. I must visit a shrine some three days north. So, allow me to continue with you, at least to that point."

"What shrine? What mission?" demanded Val.

"I have been asked to ascertain whether a certain hermitess has become a night-haunt. A *Nachzehrer*, to be exact."

"What is that?" asked Jewel.

"A kind of vampire," said Val. "Happens to suicides. Particularly in Plutarch."

To that bit of lore, Cedric said nothing.

"Well now, that was a thing you might have mentioned earlier," declared Bodkin.

"It was an act I agreed to in return for permission for us all to travel freely through Plutarch and Hefestia."

"And when you've settled this hermitess?"

Cedric turned, staring north. His voice unsure.

"When the Deaconry's question is settled, then we shall see. Who knows where the mad wind called the will of the saints, shall send me next? For now, let us leave it at that."

Val rose now, harp in hand.

"It's pleasant weather. Don't see need to set up tents. I'll keep watch till midnight. Who's up after me?"

"I'll take the second watch if I can ride in the cart tomorrow," offered Bodkin.

"Ride, till noon."

"Deal."

Val took a blanket, folded it out by a tree beyond the firelight. Deciding if trouble came, it'd be from the river. She sat facing that way, knife to her side, harp in her lap.

She strummed a few notes. They sounded lifeless.

"Euterpe blow Taliesin, what the Infernum is wrong with you, Thelxipea?" she demanded.

The strings hummed, faint and angry as bees trapped under a pot.

"What, you think it's my fault he walked away?"

Thrum, went the strings.

"Shit, you've got a crush on the miller."

Humm, sighed the strings.

"Bah. He was an idiot."

At which the harp burst into sound. No faint *thrum, hum.* Now the strings jangled, clangled like lead bells battling tin chimes. Val jumped to her feet, holding the harp from her as if it attacked.

It fell silent.

"What was all that?" demanded Bodkin from his blanket by the fire.

"Trouble?" asked Cedric.

"Some of us are desirous of sleep," observed Matilda.

Val debated what to say.

"Sorry. Thelxipea had a fit."

"Who?"

"My kick-to-Infernum harp! Never mind her. If it happens again, I'll cut the strings."

She gave the harp a look to say *I mean it.* It said nothing. Val dropped it to the grass, where it lay silent and indifferent. Val sat again, leaning against the tree, staring up at the stars. Finding them comforting to consider.

The stars were the inhabitants of the Upper House of Saints, according to standard revelation and common sense. So bright, so cold, so far away and happy. Surely they were holy beings moving to some grand purpose, dancing to music too divine for mortal ears.

Granted, the mad Hefestians and madder Lucretians claimed those tiny points of light were *worlds*. They even talked of building ships to sail among them. A lunatic idea. Any sensible person saw all sorts of reasons the idea was impossible. But perhaps it'd make a good subject for a song.

Val sat seeking rhymes for stars and ships. *Far and sheep? Bizarre and trip, scar and whip.*

Far into the night, with the moon overhead, the campfire sunk to red embers, Val stirred from a half-drowse. Coming aware of a slight sound, a faint motion.

There in the dark sat a dimly glowing girl. Naked, transparent as any ghost. Arms wrapped about knees, face up to the stars where sensible ships could never sail. The girl sang, eyes bright with tears, rocking back, forth in sorrow.

"I'm sorry, Thelxipea," whispered Val. It was all she could think to say. "I miss him too."

The glow of a girl gave her a glance, then disappeared. Val sighed, retrieved the harp, returned to the tree, sitting again. She strummed the strings, just faintly. Making no song, no melody; just petting the strings as one might a cat, telling it with this note and that strum, that it would be better. It would all soon be better, soon, soon.

Chapter 5
The Sly Danger of Radishes

 Barnaby, Marquise of Millstones, Lord of a Thousand Winds, walked a country lane little different from any in Demetia. Just a brick road intersecting byways of dirt and grass. At times he passed bits of woodland where small animals scurried in the brush, while birds argued ownership of trees and skies. Other times the road followed long stretches of fenced fields, orderly crops. Above him arched the robin's egg sky, centered with the familiar yellow sun.

 And yet summer in Plutarch wore a darker green than Demetia. This sun warmed a more shadowed land. To the west the countryside lay dotted with small pools and lakes. Fens and marshes bordered with long dark grasses, where solitary trees stood, twisted and brooding. To Barnaby it looked wet and drear. But he didn't feel in the mood for cheerful views anyway.

 Barnaby spied fewer houses, fewer travelers. On occasion he passed ruins of brick or stone, empty of roof, window or door. Just the bones of houses, looking owl-haunted and forlorn. The river wind blew through untended fields where wheat and weed flourished together, whispering memories of proper farming.

 The river Lethe stayed in view to his right. The dark water shimmered, hurrying south to Persephone, then on to the distant and theoretical sea. The folk he passed nodded heads, keeping on. Just as well. Barnaby did not feel like shouting so much as a 'hallo'.

 He found that swift walking kept thoughts bearable. Just once, he looked back the way he'd come. Far down the road, he spied a shadow in form of a cat. And as he hurried onwards, far ahead walked the shadow of a man in coat and hat, for all the summer day. These sightings cheered him; some.

Barnaby wondered why his instructors kept their distance. Perhaps they sensed he did not want lessons in magic or fighting. Unless they were disappointed in him for ending the *Grand Adventure*? Maybe they'd call him tomnoddy or puddinghead, demand he rejoin the Benefactors.

No telling, as they kept away. Merely letting him know they still journeyed with him, wherever his idiot journey led. He knew he'd have to decide where exactly he went. Not just now.

Barnaby stopped on a bridge crossing a brook anxious to join the river. Frescoes of skulls and poppies decorated the stone arches. He leaned over the edge, watched the water flow, envying its confidence. *It* knew where to go. Across the land, into the Lethe, down to the sea. Then where? The Friar claimed that sea waves rose up into the air as clouds, to rain down upon the land again. Though Alf had laughed, naming it a lunatic insult to the saints that guided storm and rain.

Barnaby wondered what Friar Cedric did now. Maybe they'd all returned to Persephone. No point in going on without the map.

But they'd been on the road north bearing a bound Barnaby. Why? They'd seen him burn the map. Perhaps they'd decided on some fresh adventure? But if they had some new goal, they could have just invited him. Why tie him up, thrown him in the mule cart? Puzzling, but no longer his concern.

Determined to think of other things, Barnaby opened his pack, seeking lunch. There he found a bound sack of cheese, a bag of dried fruit, and a rolled parchment map returned from flames miraculously as rain from the sea.

Barnaby held it confounded. It had hurt to burn something of Da's. But he'd been willing, to keep friends from a mad journey to a cursed tower for no reason except Barnaby's stepbrother thought it amusing.

How was it back in his pack? Not hard to guess. *Clever Bodkin picked his pocket, gave him a roll of paper to burn.* Everyone must have seen exactly what the comic miller was going to do before he'd known himself.

And when he'd walked away, they hadn't gone chasing after him for the map. For sure they had a copy or three. So they still determined to go to the tower; and didn't need Barnaby for the venture.

He closed his eyes, felt the river wind blow his hair. He listened to the water flow, the distant cry of crows and river birds. Then sighed, opened eyes again to the world. It looked the same. He felt rather different.

He wanted to tear the map up, toss the pieces to the wind. But withheld. Best wait till he decided whether to go on to the tower himself, else return to Mill Town. Maybe… neither. Maybe he'd just wander all the roads of all the world, for all his life.

He returned the parchment to his pack. Opened the bags of dried fruits, hard cheese. Then frowned in suspicion. Suppose they'd poisoned it?

Why for the love of the Lord of the House of Saints would your friends do such a fool thing? asked a voice within his head.

Why would my mother and brother? he replied. *Why would my friends pick my pocket, get me drunk, tie me up?* Scowling, he emptied the fruit and cheese over the bridge. The act felt satisfying. That done, he continued on northwards.

Evening shadows lengthened, and Barnaby's stomach lectured in long growls upon the folly of dramatic gestures. He considered where he'd spend the night. Beneath some tree, same as he'd done in the Witches' Wood? Better than in one of the dark ruins beside the river. They'd be haunted for sure.

At least this time I can start a fire, knowing lesser Cast Flame. And he might set a snare for a rabbit; though that was a thing of luck. With the river so close he could catch a fish, excepting he lacked hook or line or bait. Probably there was an oration: *Lesser Catch Fish*. But being lesser, maybe it only caught minnows. Anyway, what sort of fish swam the Lethe? Probably dark things with plenteous teeth. Maybe ghost fish. What sort of bait would one use for ghost fish? Glow worms, maybe.

He mused upon these questions, passing alongside an ivy-laden fence. Beyond stood a small brick-and-thatch farmhouse, looking wonderfully cozy in evening light. Smoke rising from a chimney, a candle already shining in the window. While before the house, an old man worked the ground with a spade. Barnaby waved, walking past, then stopped in surprise to hear his name called.

"Young Barnaby, is it?"

Barnaby turned, studying the man. A tall, bent-backed fellow wearing a straw hat, tattered work clothes. And a cleric's collar...

"Mister Quiet? I am surprised to meet you so far from the cathedral."

The man leaned upon his spade.

"Ah, this cottage's where I most only winter. But I had to make the St.-Erebus-kiss-it journey to catch up on chores I promised the missus."

"Digging another grave?"

Mr. Quiet laughed.

"I'm mucking the wife's roses, youngster. It's not always graves to be dug."

"Ah." Barnaby felt glad to hear it.

"Where are you off to, if you don't mind my busybody inquiry?"

Barnaby hesitated. It felt good to talk to someone beside the angry Barnaby in his head. But there was no explaining things; not yet. He had yet to think it all out. So he shrugged, nodded to the road ahead.

Mister Quiet, straightened, put shovel upon his shoulder, turned towards the house.

"Well, evening's upon us, boy. I don't recommend the river road by dark. You'd be welcome to stay the night here. Give you some supper as well."

The man entered the house, not waiting for reply. Barnaby hesitated, then found the gate, followed after.

Quiet's cottage was a homely place; one main room, a bed chamber to the back. A grand hearth, a rough table, rougher chairs. But Barnaby noted softer touches; curtains of green embroidered with ivy, a porcelain flowerpot set with paper flowers in need of dusting. He examined a set of nick-nacks upon the mantel that would have delighted Da. A seashell twisting to a point sharp as needle; a brass coin with a hole in the center, a peacock feather white as snow, a bronze plaque writ with letters incomprehensible as bird tracks.

Quiet added logs to the hearth while Barnaby laid aside his pack, his leather armor and axe.

"Fearsome blade, that," said Quiet. "Show me."

Reluctantly, Barnaby handed him Dragontooth. The gravedigger pulled it from the sheath. Holding it steady with one hand. He ran a finger along the jagged edge, giving a tap to the tarnished blade. There came a faint chime, as if he'd struck a wine glass. For a second the blade shone red as iron in a forge.

"Hmm," said Quiet, and no more. He returned the axe to Barnaby. Began bustling about the cottage, pulling items from cupboards, setting plates and cups upon the table.

While Barnaby examined Dragontooth, frowning in suspicion. It felt hot, though hardly so heated as to glow.

"The missus is across the river in Demetia," Quiet shared. "Visiting her harridan termagant of a mother. Won't be back till summer's end. So its cold pork, watered cyder and unbuttered bread for our supper."

Barnaby found this entirely to his hunger's satisfaction. The two sat, dining in silence; chewing upon their own thoughts.

Barnaby wondered what Cedric and the others did. By now the Benefactors would be preparing for the night. Setting up the tents, hobbling the mules. Circling a bright campfire, sharing mulled wine and sausage. For sure, Val would be playing her harp, Cedric reciting arcane legends, Jewel sitting shy, Bodkin telling bawdy jokes. Matilda would be laughing at the fun of it all. Probably they agreed how better the journey went without a fool miller.

That isn't fair, his conscience chided.

"Don't want to be," he told his plate.

Mister Quiet snorted, not asking for explanation. At length he rose, declaring himself done. Put cups and cutlery into a tin wash basin.

Barnaby shook himself from dark thoughts, studying his host. Not so old as to be feeble; but still, old. Eyes set deep in the sockets like to Dark Michael's; caverns holding their own inner realms.

"You work at the Cathedral," Barnaby asked. "Are you a cleric?"

Quiet reached to his neck, as though verifying he indeed wore a holy collar.

"Aye, though clerking's an office I neglect worse than the wife's roses. Let the folk in the fancy robes do all the damned chanting and orating, I say."

Finished with the wash-up, Quiet brought out a blanket, laid it by the fire.

"Hearth's yours. Sleep warm." With that, he disappeared into the back room, shutting the door.

Barnaby settled by the fire, enjoying how peaceful the house felt. Far better than curling up beneath some tree, awaiting wolves or witches. He looked about for Night-Creep and Dark Michael, expecting to see them lounging and lurking in the shadows. No sign of either. Well then, no instruction this evening.

He turned eyes from the hearth, determined not to fall into fools' dreams. He should do something sensible. Perhaps practice orations? He took the crystal egg from his pack. It'd only ever worked for him that once. But if mastered, he could use it to check upon Val and the others.

Of course, that'd be an idiot thing. Secretly watching folk you'd said goodbye to meant you didn't really want to forget them.

You don't really want to forget them, said the flames reflected in the egg. Barnaby sniffed, ignoring their opinion.

He studied the crystal, pondering what mad things it could show him if he knew the trick. The sea, perhaps. He knew from stories that'd be endless fields of green-blue water curling high as houses, with mermaids singing and tritons waving spears, whales swallowing ships.

Or he might spy upon the forests of Silenia, where goat-footed folk danced. Mad and happy people born drunken on the communion wine of St. Silenus. Then there were the stone planes of Nix, where beautiful women lurked in holes, scattering treasure upon the ground to lure travelers close to their cannibal arms. Or the grand towers of the Aurelians; tall folk pale as paper, silent as trees, wise as owls. Or why not demand of the egg that it show him the Upper House of the Saints? They'd be gathered at a grand table, princes at a feast deciding the world's wind and weather...

"Here now, who might you be?" demanded someone. Barnaby raised his head, puzzled why he did not see the kitchen of his home in Mill Town. Then sighed. Just staring into the reflections of hearth flames, he'd fallen into dreams again. He shook himself awake, looking to a woman standing in the doorway of the cottage.

Young; plain of face, dressed in the habits of a novice of St. Plutarch. She did not wait for answer, but closed the door. Setting wimple and cloak upon the table, shaking hair free, looking about.

Barnaby rose to his feet, recalling her question.

"I am just Barnaby. I'm a miller though I don't have a mill right this now. Hello."

She looked him up, down, weighing his self-explanation; finally smiled. A wry smile, appreciating a miller lacking mill.

"Well, hello to you, Just Barnaby. Guest of the old fellow, are you?"

"That I am."

"Ah. Well, I hope he's been a half-decent host. For sure, he hasn't talked your ear off."

"No, he's been wondrous polite. Quiet as his name." Barnaby considered. "Though in Persephone he shared his views on graves and life and such."

"And what did you think?"

Barnaby felt an urge to give this woman honest answer.

"Ah, he meant it kindly. But his words summed to *'from dirt, to dirt.'*"

The woman's laugh shook the house.

"Oh, I hope you told him so. My advice, Mister Barnaby. Wisdom from a grave digger is only ever half-wise."

Barnaby considered. "What's the missing half then?"

"Ah, now, didn't say I knew, and never said I'd say." She went to the cupboard, took out the jug of cyder, the bread and cheese. A bowl of raisins. Set it on the table.

"Hungry?" she asked. "I've come straight from Demetia. Famished as the rat catcher in the town of cats."

Barnaby knew he *could* eat more; but it went impolite to devour all Quiet's cupboard. He shook his head.

"Just had supper. You dig in."

So she did exactly that; while he returned to the hearth. Seeking not to stare at the fire, nor the woman. But she showed no inclination not to contemplate *him*, chewing thoughtful as sheep studying sunset. This open scrutiny embarrassed, till he spoke.

"Are you Quiet's daughter?"

She returned a sour look.

"His wife, as it happens. Make sure you ask him the very same, though."

"Sorry, Mistress Quiet."

"Ah, call me Sephie. I'm not near formal as the old bones in his bed." She gave a glance to the closed door.

"Miss Sephie, then. In Demetia the clerics and novices marry. When they want. But I'd heard the St. Plutarch orders kept to single beds."

At which she laughed loud as a grand flock of ducks sharing a small pond.

"Alone in bed isn't what I've heard nor seen of my gloomy-robed brethren," she declared. "But true enow, they seldom marry. Claim they're mated to the saints. And feel free to picture *that* as you wish."

Barnaby struggled *not* to picture it. Failing completely.

"And you?" Sephie asked. "Got a girl? Boy? Saint to keep in holy bed-embrace?"

Barnaby considered. "There was a girl I'd been chasing. But I'm giving it up."

"Ah? Why so?"

"She..." He searched for words. "It's like I'm a slow plow horse and she's a deer running past. Except Val's crazy dangerous with a knife and one can't picture a deer with a knife. Well, no, one can but that's not my point. But she's something with long legs that moves very fast while I stand staring. There's no catching up."

Sephie shook her head. In pity, perhaps; else to clear it of over-many images. Barnaby considered as well, seeing further explanation needed.

"I mean 'fast' in terms of thinking and talking, not actual running. Not that Val couldn't outrun me and not that deer talk any more than they wave knives. But I'm sure they think fast, else how could they run so fast?"

"Somehow that all comes to sense," decided Sephie. "And my wise and sisterly advice is-"

She stopped. First staring, then glaring at the shovel leaning in a corner. Done with glares, she stood.

"Damn the man up all seven holy holes of Lucif," she swore. "Was he only mucking my roses *today*?"

Barnaby swallowed, nodded.

"If there be such a thing as a green thumb, that man has both hands black as the tar pits of Tartarus. Blast him to St. Abaddon's aphotic abattoir, I told and told him to attend my roses first damn day of spring."

Barnaby feared she was going to march into the cottage bedroom, shouting at her husband. It'd be loud and uncomfortable as when his stepmother berated Da. If so, Barnaby'd best depart.

But Sephie only shook her head, took plates and cups to the wash basin. Grumbling to herself about gardens and menfolk.

Finished with wash and grumble, she opened another cupboard, brought forth a lantern. Glass sided, fresh candle within. Then an empty bottle, corked.

She lit the candle, placing it and the bottle upon the table. Crossed arms and addressed Barnaby.

"I'm supposed to be in Demetia. Only snuck over the river on an errand to help out a sister novice. Whole business is against the rules, which bothers me nary and naught."

"Oh?"

"Now I'm thinking, hmm, there's no rule against asking a miller without mill to do this small, tiny task. As merest favor?"

Barnaby hesitated. Once he would have said 'aye' soon as asked. But he recalled too well, agreeing to kill Pentateuch's rat, only to find it spoke poetry. He liked Miss Sephie and Mister Quiet. But best not agree before knowing to what he agreed.

"What would you have me do?"

"Hmm. I keep a garden just across the road. I need a certain flower from it."

Barnaby tried to recall. "Those were radishes."

"No, past the radishes. You follow the path through the field till you come to a second gate. Go through to path's end. You'll be at a field where I grow poppies. I'd be ever so grateful if you'd pick me one."

"Well, sounds simple enough."

"One can hope so. As well, I need this bottle filled with water from the fount thereabouts."

"Is it a special sort of water?"

"Well, clearly, love. Or else I'd use the well out back." She watched him weigh the business. "You'd not just be helping me; but a poor novice fallen into difficult bind."

Barnaby pondered how a flower and a bottle of water would help anyone. Decided it best not to ask. So he stood, gathering his pack, his armor, his axe. Last he went to the table, took up the bottle and lamp.

"Decided quick as that?" asked Sephie.

It's that or fall into dreams, thought Barnaby. But it sounded unheroic to say. Also, he felt the woman spoke true. She'd made a journey to help another. Would be small-souled to decline simple favor, after accepting hearth and supper.

So he nodded, even managing a comic, courtly bow to say '*at your service*'.

Sephie made a dancing step before him, laughing. "Plain to see you're no slow plow horse, Master Barnaby. Behold a hero of the old school. Well then, let's to it."

She went to the door, opened it wide, entered the night. Barnaby following after.

They walked in silence across the lane, where a low stone wall defined a plot of vegetables. Stopping at a rickety stile.

"Now here's some advice for the task," said Sephie. "First and last: stay on the path. It may wind, but it will never grow uncertain. Beware things to left and right that may seek to draw your feet astray."

"In the radish field?"

"*Past* the radishes, dear heart. There's no danger in the radish field. It's just a radish field."

"My Da always said radishes made him break out in sneezes."

"Are you larking with me, boyo?"

"No ma'am."

"Wise. Now, past these innocent radishes is a locked gate. Open it with this key."

Barnaby took from her hand a long black key, heavy and cold.

"Past the gate, talk to whom you must, but stay on the path. At the end will be a field of poppies. I want a particular one."

"How shall I tell one flower in a field of flowers?"

"Excellent question. In the light of this lamp, it will look black as St. Lucif's love for his sister. The other flowers will remain red."

"A black poppy?"

"Yes. Pluck it, put it somewhere safe. There will be many a fountain on the path. The one you want will have the water flowing out a lion's mouth. Fill the bottle with that water, and no other. Cork it tight, put it safe and then hie thee hither back."

"Sounds easily done."

"But you've become wise enough to know it won't be?"

"I'm thinking if it were easy, you'd not be asking."

"Why do it then, Master Miller?"

"Ah, since this morning I don't know what to do with myself. Might as well do something useful. As Da would say, '*if you can't help yourself, then help someone else*'. As well..."

"As well, what?"

Barnaby did not answer. Not till he'd climbed over the stile, stood with feet firm set among the innocent radishes. Then he faced Miss Sephie, holding the lamp high.

"As well, I said I was a slow plow horse. Never said I was stupid. I know right well who you are, ma'am. And Master Quiet as well."

In the shadows of night, by the lamp's simple light, Sephie now seemed taller. Her hair become a waterfall of dark tresses shining with the stars, her plain lips now red as the poppies of her special garden.

"Know us, do you? And don't feel frighted?"

"Should I?"

She arched eyebrows in affront, stamped a foot.

"Well of course you should."

"What was the half missing?

"What half, what?"

"When I said how Quiet's words on life came to '*from dirt, to dirt*'. You said he only had half the wisdom. What's the other half?"

She ran a hand through her hair, as if searching within the tresses for answer.

"Ah, that. Hmm. I think it was something along the lines of '*from dirt, to dirt, but not dirt.*'

Barnaby weighed that. It was rather simple. But simple would do. Da would like it fine.

"Thank you, then." With that, he turned, walking off through the radish field.

Chapter 6
Same as for the Saints

Persephone, Blessed Sister of the Middle House:

Of course, I spied on the boy. I had this mad idea the radishes would rise up and attack just to prove me wrong. But the vegetables left him alone, he arrived safe at the gate.

The second wall looked no higher than his waist. I worried he'd try clambering over it. *That* wouldn't have ended well. But plow horse though he claimed to be, he kept the furrow straight. Went to the gate, set key to lock, opened and entered.

Beyond *that* gate it's anyone's guess what one will meet. Dreams, ghosts, three-headed dogs. Violent giant radishes, maybe. Probably not that last.

Barnaby son of Barnabas followed the path through a peaceful orchard of pomegranates and apples. Stones lined the way, perfectly clear by the lamp. He passed a pretty fountain where a marble hippocampus spat water. I worried. You get fellows who think they are clever, deciding any water will do. But after carefully deducing that a half-horse, half-fish summed to no lion, he went on.

Soon the trees grew thicker, no longer a tended orchard. Just a bramble-filled wood. The prophet Tantalus cook me dinner, but of course *they* set themselves to lead him astray.

First sortie: a pretty girl sitting on a tree stump. Posing for a strumpet in the moonlight. Skirt high, bodice low. She called to Barnaby as he passed.

She was lonely. Did he want to come to her bower just a bit off the path, and make her less lonely?

Well, no he did not. At least, so he affirmed. I watched his eyes trace the moonlit bosom. He did want to, just wasn't going to. The noble boy gave a most polite goodnight, walking on.

She hissed at his back, revealing teeth sharp and thin as a weasel's. Ripping at the stump with nails that'd fright a bear.

Next was the Bloody Wood. I wished I'd spent more time in warning: *draw no weapon, front no foe.* But overmany words just make a mortal defiant to the business. Same as for the saints.

To left and right came shouts, came screams. Of a sudden the dark wood rang with the clash of swords. Men rushing through the brush, falling upon one another. Ragged banners rose and fell, the air awash with bugle calls and battle cries.

Our sweet miller hesitated; looking about with eyes big as the millstones of the mill he lacked.

I could only hold my breath, watching Barnaby reach for his axe… then stop himself. Instead, he raised the lamp high, continuing down the path. Excellent creature.

But now to left and right along the path gathered soldiers and knights, blood-drenched, mortally wounded yet immortally determined. Entrails spilling from their opened guts, arrows still fixed in their angry hearts. They waved fists and blades, shouting for him to fight them, else turn and run.

Through this gauntlet of blood and bluster, Barnaby walked. Trembling; or so hinted the wavering lamplight. Which showed him sensible. And yet he kept on, tremble or no.

When he passed beyond their view, all shouting ceased, each sword fell. The furious warriors crumbled to the earth, mere bits of bone and squirming shadow.

Master Plow Horse continued on, passing a fountain of silvery bowls trickling water that shimmered like liquid diamonds. Quite pretty. He held the bottle, debating whether to fill it here. Surely there could be no water more magical? But in the end he shook his head, walking on.

Beyond the wood lay an open field of lilies and daisies, bright by moon's light. Soft music played from out the shadows. A long table stood decked with candles; set with goblets and dishes glowing glorious and golden, filled with every delicacy of cake and meat, fowl and fruit. About this grand table, dressed in satins and velvets, ermines and sables, sat princely folk with faces declaring them lords and knights, ladies and holy matrons. All gathered together to feast in peace, in honor, in common joy.

Then did noble Sir Barnaby halt, staring at the wondrous food and drink, the fine gathering. The revelers spied him, waving, calling him to join their gay company.

Now a great solemn servant stood forth, to stand just beside the path. With an elegant bow, an eloquent wave, he motioned for Barnaby to take the very chair of honor at the table's head.

Eyes wide with wonder, the miller lifted a foot from the path… a glitter of hunger shone in the servant's eyes, and I trembled. But the boy did not set the tempted foot down. No, our slow plow horse recovered his balance and his sense. Stepping back, shaking head. He would not be joining in the feast.

The servant waved hands to persuade, to cajole; the revelers called for him to return. Still he continued on the path, giving no least glance back. And so did not see the bright company turn to a gathering of hags and ghouls, and the feast to offal and excrement, and the solemn servant into a great toad snapping tongue at its escaped prey.

I watched Barnaby reach the path's end. Only then did I dare take breath. That had made harder trial than I meant to set the boy.

But he came safe to my garden of poppies. Searching about, waving the lamp. Trodding on over-many of my blooms, *dammittoinfernum*. Made me growl, but I suppose it was to be forgiven. At length he spied one poor black poppy, dead yet not dead, curling in upon itself, the suffering thing. Plucked it, put it to pocket.

Only on the return did he spy the font of the lion, pouring out the ever-joyous Water of Life. Not that he knew its name or nature. I suppose he might have guessed. As Master Plow Horse himself said: slow, but not stupid. He filled the bottle exact as instructed.

I watched him cup the water in a hand, take a sip. Well, I hadn't told him not to. His eyes lit up, of course. Excellent. He looked the better for it.

That done, he returned down the path. Encountering no least resistance. No phantoms, no temptations. Even the radishes left him in peace.

* * *

"I've brought the flower, ma'am. And the water." He holds these things out, looking pleased to have the task done right. Making no question of what the Infernum it was all for. You see why Mother took to him?

"Hmm, I'll take my lamp back. You keep the flower and the bottle. And the key. Never know when you need a good iron key. I'm going straight back to Demetia before Mother Superior catches me out of bed."

"What am I to do with these things?"

"Have you not been paying attention, Master Miller? You are to present them to the novice of whom I spoke. She's in dire need of these things."

"What will she do with them?"

"She will choose between them, of course. It's one or the other for the poor thing."

"Where do I even find her?"

"Ah, farther up the road north. Exactly where you were heading, I do meekly point out."

"Well, how shall I even know her?"

"Oh, you just will. But if it helps, her name's Beatrice."

Chapter 7
A Metaphor of Memory

Nightfall of the second day upon the road. Cedric debated with the gathered *Society of St. Benefact*.

"But there is no need for any of you to go to the shrine. If danger awaits it is mine to face. If not, as I expect, it shall be a dull argument upon the wisdom of the prophet Epicurus versus the asceticism of Stylites."

"Lucif's fiery farts, that's become a tiresome song," growled Bodkin. "Hear up, Friar. You let your real friends join your fight, or you are no real friend to them."

"Damn right," said Val. "You're sounding like, like, *you-know-who*." She frowned at her harp, which had a tendency to make sad 'twangs' upon the naming of certain millers.

Cedric opened mouth to argue… then stopped himself. Smiling sadly.

"It was Jewel who explained Barnaby best." *Twang*. "She said he did not fear for himself, but for those for whom he'd come to care."

"I never said Barnaby was scared," said Val. *Twang*. "Just being too Infernum motherly with other people's decisions. So don't you make the same mistake."

"Or I'll awake bound in cobwebs?"

"Could happen," declared Jewel. Giving rare smile.

Cedric hesitated, then nodded.

"You are right. I am wrong. We shall share the task and its hypothetical dangers together, then."

"What exactly *is* the danger?" asked Matilda. "Just out of idle idolatrous curiosity."

"The Deaconry of St. Plutarch fear the hermitess Beatrice pursued a life of self-denial to the point of ending that life."

"Killed herself?" asked Val. "Why does it matter? All mad Plutarch is ruled by ghosts and revenants."

"The Testament of St. Plutarch declares Death the final sacrament. Suicide misuses the rite of life and death. And truly, a spirit obsessed with its own destruction is a thing to be feared. Whether in this world or what dream may follow. Here, such creatures oft become night-haunts."

"You said a *Nachzehrer*," reminded Val.

"So spoke the Deaconry," sighed Cedric. "But such as they assume the worse whenever some devout soul begins to declare truths that threaten dogma and commerce. I suspect we will find poor Beatrice alive, starved and scarred by the violence of her own devotion. No doubt abandoned by the acolytes who could not follow her path of self-denial."

"You knew her." That, from Bodkin.

"Did I say so?"

"Your face says so."

"Well, I make no secret of it. We were students together in Daedalus. The Deaconry sends me now instead of Questioners and exorcists, exactly because I knew her. I can best judge in what state of mind or soul she now stands."

"Then your mission is just to scout," said Val. "You don't have to put down any night-haunts. The Deaconry will send forces to deal with what you find."

Cedric *growled*.

It took a moment for the others to understand it as a sound of anger and pain. The man had never expressed himself so before. When he spoke, the words came sharp, edged with determination.

"If the hermitess is well, I shall wish her well. If she is in need, I will aid her. And if she is dead, I will see to her proper rest. It is nothing for any committee to decide."

"What is that?" frowned Matilda.

Cedric halted, looked about.

"What?"

"Something in the tree branches."

From above came the sound of mocking laughter.

"Shoot it," commanded Bodkin.

Matilda drew her bow quick as rogue picking pocket.

"Stop," commanded Cedric. "We are not at war with every shadow of Plutarch."

"What about the ones surrounding us?" whispered Val. She stood, long knife drawn. "Backs to the fire, all."

The mules brayed in alarm. Matilda started towards them; Val pulled her back. Bodkin drew his sword; Cedric raised his staff, whispering words that set it aglow.

"I see a light," whispered Matilda. "Coming from the river."

"Lot of lights," agreed Bodkin.

They watched a firefly flicker become a candle flame. Then another, and another. Gradually the night wood filled with soft glows moving slowly past their camp. Candles, held by solemn figures walking between the trees. Men and women, old and young; clad in simple white gowns that glowed faint as star shine.

A woman entered the camp, holding taper high, singing soft words without meaning to any but her. Eyes alight, face transfixed with some inner vision.

"Hello," said Val. "Out for a walk?"

The woman smiled to the companions, but did not halt nor turn. She continued on, singing, soon disappearing again into the trees.

Now all through the woods marched similar figures. Filling the night with song that rose and fell, calm as ocean waves journeying to far shores. Moving steadily west through the trees, paying no heed to the Benefactors.

Matilda shouldered her bow, a dreaming look overtaking her usual expression of alert amusement. She took a step to follow the marchers.

"Stop," commanded Cedric. He grabbed Matilda by the arm. She muttered but did not struggle.

"Holy Erebus swallow me whole," whispered Bodkin. "Wake up, idiot." Matilda turned, blinking as though indeed coming awake.

They stood silent, watching the glowing candles disappear with the marchers.

"It's just some ceremony from beside the river," whispered Val. "And I'd guess they're heading to the shrine."

Now one last figure walked through the trees. A young woman, face transfixed with visions of inner wonder. Long hair streaming out behind her, golden rays worthy of a cathedral icon. Simply clad in white gown, barefoot; she glowed faintly in light that seemed to come from deep within her. She walked past the fire, past the companions... then turned. Studying them awhile. Wide eyes fixed as a statue's gaze, yet warmed by kindly smile. She spread her arms wide, speaking a name.

"Cedric."

He was slow to answer. When he did, it was merely to whisper a name.

"Beatrice."

"My Cedric. For too long I have felt your pain and confusion across the Middle House."

His reply came more firmly.

"We vowed not to meet again."

She shook her head. "We never parted, Cedric. Always was my spirit with you, as yours with me."

"A metaphor of memory. But that is not to be together."

She laughed. A pretty laugh; a schoolgirl's laugh.

"Ever the materialist, holding priest's staff."

"A converted broomstick, actually."

To that she made no reply. She began stepping backwards into the trees, eyes still towards Cedric. The faint glow of her form dimming to dark.

"I charge you to come to me, Cedric Weiland. This very night. In the shrine we shall…"

Her voice faded, last words unfinished or unheard. The faint star-shine glow of her form vanished. Beatrice was gone.

Chapter 8
To Mill, or not to Mill

Barnaby lay on the ground, back against a tree. The summer night felt warm now; but he knew that by midnight he'd be shivering in the wind off the river.

Should have taken time to gather proper supplies from the cart, But I felt too angry to think right.

He sat up, adjusted the spit holding a rabbit haunch above the little campfire. Sharing his conclusion with the fire.

"Being angry makes a fellow stupid."

"Truth, that," agreed Night-Creep from the tree branch above him.

"Quite true," agreed Dark Michael. Sitting on the far side of the fire. Barnaby studied how the man's eyes returned no reflection, though he held out large hands to catch the flame's heat.

"Do you get cold, Master Dark Michael?"

Michael considered. "Not as you think it, boy. But yes. In my own way, I know cold."

"Well, we shall get you a better coat at the next town."

At which words, the ghost smiled sad; the cat laughed loud. Barnaby reached, pulled the wooden spit from the fire. Using his knife to cut two portions. Laying one down beside him.

Night-Creep leapt from the branch, hurrying to the still smoking offering. Nibbling here, sniffing there, testing.

"On the whole, I prefer my rabbit closer to raw," he observed. "In the future, just so you remember."

"Bah," said Dark Michael. "You need dinner as much as I need a new coat."

The cat made no answer; mouth now full.

"And I need a blanket or three to go North," observed Barnaby. "And a better cloak."

"Then you still journey to the tower?"

"For sure. I won't be called a quitter, no matter what, what *they* thought of me."

"You do have other choices," observed Dark Michael. "It is best to weigh them, even if only to strengthen your resolve for the choice you make."

"Go back to Val and the others, tell them I've gotten over being angry, want to be their fool friend again?"

"Returning to your friends is a choice before you, yes. Whether they take you for fool is their choice."

Barnaby shook his head, feeling of a sudden hot as the fire before him.

"No, sir. I find I'm still angry. I'd rather go back to Mill Town."

"That too, is a path."

At which Barnaby barked a most un-barnabish laugh. "Return to my loving stepmother and Alf and the Squire? I'll knock on the door of my own Da's house, and they'll open it surprised to see I yet breathe. Then they'll start in with their cursing and cuffing, demanding to know where in Lucif's seventh kettle is the treasure they sent me to fetch."

Cat and ghost said naught to that.

Barnaby took a calming breath. When he spoke again, it came in his usual musing tone.

"But I suppose I could take up milling in some other town. There are those watermills near Persephone. Amazing thing, your watermill."

"Why return to milling?" asked Night-Creep. Delicate tongue licking lips. "Why not be marquise?"

"Is there livelihood in being the Marquise of Millstones, Lord of a Thousand Winds?" That, from Michael.

"No, but there is in being the Marquise of Pentafax Abbey," replied the cat. Now sitting up, curling tail in pride about his feet. "This midnight past I journeyed across the leagues, swift as owl shadow, silent as cat's step, to the very door of Pentafax Abbey."

Barnaby frowned to recall. "The ruined manse of poor Mister Pentateuch? Why?"

"To converse with Sexton, the caretaker."

"Upon what?" demanded Michael.

The cat sniffed at tone of *demand*.

"Obtuse things of no concern to brute spirits. Sexton and I spoke long upon the will of the angels and the whiles of devils, the ways of witches and the world's tangled tales. The laws of necromancy particularly concerned us, with all their ten-fold twists of posthumous property and propriety. Truthfully, I consider Sexton almost a peer."

"Why?" asked Barnaby, as Michael growled "To what purpose?"

"We discussed unto happy agreement, that as you, Barnaby son of Barnabas, defeated the previous master, the late Pentateuch Draconicus, in fair combat, that you, the heretofore cited Barnaby son of said Barnabas, are now by chthonic law the rightful master of the Demetian estate known as Pentafax Abbey."

Barnaby answered this complex statement with simple head shake.

"Didn't mean to slay anyone."

"Entirely to your credit, but not to any lessening of your claim. As your representative, once title was affirmed, I took the liberty of directing Sexton to make the grounds suitable for your future habitation."

Barnaby tried to picture the dark, haunted ruin as 'suitable'. Impossible. Then he tried picturing himself sitting at the head of that ancient table in the grand feast hall. Also impossible. And yet, and yet...

He pictured Val and Cedric, Bodkin, Matilda and Jewel standing in awe before a rebuilt Pentafax Abbey. Fountains flowing, gardens full of blooms. They'd wonder what noble fellow owned so grand an estate? And when ushered inside, they'd gasp astounded to see... the M*arquise*.

Should he rise from his chair, welcoming them with grand words? Or order the vagabonds from the premises? Why not pretend not to recall their names? Oh, that last held wonderful taste of satisfaction.

"I see lights by the river," observed Michael.

Barnaby freed his mind from the glories of noble indifference to former friends. Peering between the shadows of the trees, spying faint glimmers, distant figures.

"Folk with lights. Are they singing?"

"Some ritual of the locals," yawned the cat. "A river baptism, no doubt."

"At night?" wondered Barnaby. "Baptism's a thing for the dawn. So all know in Demetia."

"This is the demesne of St. Plutarch," reminded Michael. "His disciples follow a more shadowed revelation."

Barnaby returned to staring into the fire. Working to picture his friends confounded by the glory of *Marquise Barnaby*. Exactly how did one look glorious? No doubt by wearing heavy robes and diamonds, waving hands in gestures of command.

The image made him blush. Feeling more foolish than when he awoke tied up and thrown in a mule cart. He gave it up, stood, stretched.

"I've restless soul and feet tonight. I'm going to have a look upon the doings by the river."

He expected his advisors to argue. But,

"Curiosity kept more cats alive, than ever slew them," declared Night-Creep. And leapt to Barnaby's shoulder, settling himself.

Dark Michael continued to sit by the fire, hands held to flames, gathering what light and warmth he could.

"Remember your lessons in moving through trees," he said, and no more.

Barnaby made his way towards the river, now wishing he'd finished the rabbit. Still, a shiver of excitement took him. The distant candles mirrored the stars of the night sky, as the eerie singing rose and fell with river wind. Finding what wonder lay ahead felt infinitely better than brooding into embers.

"Will you be advised by me now, master?" whispered the cat.

"That's a warning that something dangerous lies ahead."

"Hmm, yes."

"Well, let's have it."

"Do not directly approach the celebrants. See that flat rock? Upon it lie white robes. Take one, don it. Bring forth your candle, light it. Then walk to the back of these creatures, allowing yourself to be taken for one of the congregation. Speak to none, smile to all."

"You want me to pretend to be one of them?"

"Not if you are content to watch mouth agape from distant shadows. But if you wish to understand what they do, then you must stand among them. To do that, you must seem one of them. For the folk of belief oft give false smiles and hard eyes on those not of their company."

Barnaby hesitated. He'd only wanted to watch a bit of foreign doings. Still, Professor Shadow Night-Creep was wise to the world's ways. And so he nodded, continued on.

Close to the river, the water made its own song; a flowing melody that spoke of long journeys, inevitable windings, and the final sea.

"Have you ever been to the sea, Master Night-Creep?"

"Many a time, and in many a weather, by sun and storm, winter wind and spring shine. Oft beneath the green waves. to dance with the merfolk in their treasure caves. Else advising grave sea kings in their coral palaces, seated upon thrones decked with pearls and the bones of drowned men."

Barnaby considered asking about baby mermaids; decided not. Instead, he approached a great flat rock upon which lay piles of white robes.

He took one, pulling it over himself, tangling his pack, his axe and the cat on his shoulder. The cat struggled, scratching its way out the tangle.

"Put those things down first," instructed the cat from the ground. Voice dry.

Barnaby did so, then donned the robe. It glimmered in the summer starshine, making him feel ghost-like, less Barnaby-like. He wished for a mirror. Lacking one, he took up axe, cat and pack again.

"These burdens make you stand out somewhat," sighed the cat. "But it would not do to leave them. And I spy a few among the congregants who also go armed.

Officers, perhaps. So light the candle, and let us see what these happy folk do on the shores of somber Lethe."

The folk sang, as Barnaby already knew. They stood upon the slope of the riverbank, humming, swaying, focusing upon a person standing waist deep in the shallows. He found a quiet edge of the crowd where he could watch and listen.

"You'd best sing," whispered the cat.

Sing what? Barnaby wondered. He heard no sense in the words of the congregants. Probably it didn't matter, so long as he sang. He could think of no hymn but Val's bawdy adventures of Miss Fortune. She'd sung half a hundred verses that night in The Maiden, setting Matilda to snort ale from nose.

"Hmm, hmm, sought a cup,
Hmm, hmm, bare feet up."

The cat sighed. No one else took notice.

Barnaby watched a white-robed figure hurrying through the crowd, near running downhill in haste to reach the water. Splashing through the shallows where stood the focus of the crowd: a woman glowing bright as the moon. Her wet robe flowing in the current, her gold hair streaming like sunrays about her face. She held out arms to the newcomer, laughing happily.

"Here's one in a hurry to be clean," she announced. The crowd laughed as well, mixing amusement with song.

The woman put one hand to the man's back, one to his chest, bending him backwards, lowering him gently into the dark water. The crowd sang louder.

Barnaby watched, whispering Val's lyrics to their holy melody.

Miss Fortune did all she could
Crossing mountain, sea and wood.
Met a druid of morals fluid,
Said, 'Miss, dismiss this maidenhood'.

He'd seen such ceremony enacted before among the penitents who came to the Jahrmarkt, Da thought little of it, though he'd agreed it made pretty theatre.

Barnaby waited for the woman to raise the fellow's head from out the dark Lethe. And waited yet longer, while the crowd sang, the river flowed. He found his own breath catching in sympathy. Barnaby stared, unsure whether he saw the man's hands now flounder, struggling to rise from the Lethe.

Instead, the woman bent down, putting her own head beneath the water. For a long while the two seemingly consulted in the privacy of the dark river.

Barnaby ceased all song, feeling his breath grow narrow in his chest. As though he too were held overlong underwater. While the crowd sang yet louder.

At last, at last, the woman rose up, hair not a bit confounded by the wet. She seemed to shine the more. While the man in her arms worked to stand, wavering in the river current. Finally he raised pale face to the starry sky, singing. Then splashed his way to rejoin those upon the shore.

Another celebrant walked down the slope, joined the shining woman in the shallows. The ceremony repeated; again with the unbearably long immersion, the hint of struggle.

Barnaby realized he'd left off singing. Found he didn't want to anymore.

"Something not right here," he whispered to the cat.

"My master is wise," returned the cat.

At length the congregants began streaming up the riverbank into the trees. Seemingly, the night's ceremony had concluded.

Barnaby decided it'd look suspicious to remain behind, or to leave in a different direction. So, he followed, humming, holding candle high, confident he could slip away in the trees.

He hesitated when he spied a campfire, no mere candle's flame. Five figures standing silhouetted, orange light aglow upon a short sword, a long knife. From nearby, mules brayed in alarm.

"Kick Lucif's mother's tea kettle to Infernum, have they been as near as that?"

The cat said nothing. Barnaby watched as the last of the candle-bearing celebrants marched on, leaving the five members of the Society of St. Benefact to their campfire. But they did not rest for the night; instead they stood, waving arms, clearly debating.

At length, the silhouette bearing a clerical staff walked into the trees. Followed by three others, shouting words Barnaby could not catch.

He edged nearer, using what tricks of silence and shadow Michael had drummed into him. Close to the fire, he spied Matilda standing with back to a tree, bow in hand. Eyes watching the shadows, looking wary and angered.

"Come out now, you" she called. "I see you lurking." She put arrow to string, though pointing towards the dirt.

"I'm holding a candle," said Barnaby, stepping forth. "And wearing a white robe. Doesn't come hard to spy me."

"So you are. Oi, is it the young miller? Joined these mad folk, have you?" Matilda tone turned amused.

"No, I was just, I mean, well, it was the cat's idea."

"Well of course. A proper puss must always be up to mischief."

Night-Creep sniffed.

"Where have the others gone?" asked Barnaby.

"Hmm, seems their leader is some old bedmate of Mister Friar Priest Cedric. His holiness went after her. The others went after *him*. I'm staying to watch the cart and gear and mules."

"Oh. Well, I don't think these are good people," declared Barnaby. "To me it looked like they drowned folk in the river, brought them from out the water different."

"Well, that's not a bit good," decided Matilda.

"No, it isn't," agreed Barnaby.

They stood a moment considering how very *not good* it was. Then Barnaby took breath.

"So, I think I'd better go rescue the innocent things."

Chapter 9
Round and Round and Down

"Your friends been missing you, rather," said Matilda, as they hurried through the trees.

"Have they?"

"Entirely. And they oh-so regret the silly business of tangling ale and spider webs about your fondly regarded personage."

"Don't care."

"Granted, you were being a proud ass, as I'm sure you've already admitted to your miller's mirror."

"Was not. And haven't one. And won't."

They ceased whispers, reaching the road. Some distance away waited a once-grand stone arch, looking sad and broken as old bone in the light of a single torch. Guarding that gateway stood two of the White Robes. Drawn swords reflecting the sputtering fire.

"Guess I can spare two arrows," whispered Matilda. Barnaby blinked, turning to study the friendly tavern girl. Tall, curly hair, brown slotted eyes. Strong looking, cheerful seeming... and ready to drop two strangers dead same as partridges in the brush.

"We aren't here to kill folk at their posts."

At which words she focused slotted eyes to study *him*. Adding a sad smile.

"You're a kindly sort, Master Miller. But you've already mentioned they were doing evil at the river. And mark how they stand?"

Barnaby frowned, returned gaze to the guards. They stood with swords ready, staring inwards toward the shrine. That did seem odd.

Matilda put it to words. "They aren't there to keep folk from getting in. They keep any from getting *out*."

Barnaby shivered, perhaps with the chill of the river wind. Then,

"For sure, these folk are up to twisted things. But we can't be putting arrows into them without cause."

"*Cause*, meaning wait till they've sliced a lovely miller liver first?"

"If I may advise," interrupted the cat upon Barnaby's pack. "I suggest my master feign to be one of the congregants of authority. You, Silenian, can be a new disciple to be brought before the hermitess."

"Don't think much of playacting into a dragon's den."

"Your opinion is not unwise," agreed the cat. "But an honest charge into a dragon den shall end in the dragon's gullet. You've not enough arrows to take down a congregation of mad cultists."

Matilda bit lip. "Maybe sneak sly round the back?"

"Hmm, there is indeed a back entrance. But it will be sealed. This shrine is an old fortress of St. Plutarch You cannot enter except by the front door."

She stamped a hoof.

"How do you know so much, Mister Kitty?"

The cat sniffed.

"When your great-grandmothers' baby hooves danced to Sainted Silenus's mad piping, *Mister Kitty* watched war and slaughter upon this very spot. A day the dirt turned red, and the river ran red, and even the gore-affrighted sky shone red."

"Fine," growled the Silenian. "Let's walk up smiling then."

Barnaby nodded, wanting to draw his axe. But that would put the guards on alert. So he strode across the road, telling himself he walked up to the millhouse at home. Granted, that'd been full of folk wishing him dead.

"*Call out to them first,*" whispered the cat.

"Ho, there," Barnaby shouted.

The two guards turned, swords raised. Eyeing him.

"*She's to see the lady,*" suggested the cat.

"She's to see the lady," declared Barnaby. Jabbing a thumb at Matilda. The Silenian waved cheerfully.

The guards nodded, lowering swords.

But as they walked through the arch, one called out.

"What of the pass phrase?"

"Pass phrase?" asked Barnaby, turning what he hoped were indifferent eyes to the guards.

"*No idea,*" sighed the cat. "*Good luck.*"

"Yessir." The guard stood in formal pose and recited. "*Pilgrim, what do you bring the Hermitess Beatrice?*"

"Oh," said Barnaby. "Her. Those. Yes." He took a breath. "I bring a poppy from the garden, and water from the fountain."

The guard frowned. "Not exact. Should go '*I bear the Poppy of Death, the Water of Life.*'"

But the other guard disagreed. "No, it's '*I bring poppy from Death's Garden, water from Life's Font*'."

The two debated. Barnaby and Matilda backing away, continuing down the lamplit path, coming soon to a great doorway built into a stony hillside. The doors were open, and from within came bright light, the sound of singing.

"How by Saintly Silenus's sacred sack did you know the pass phrase?" whispered Matilda.

Barnaby wondered where to begin to explain. Night-Creep spared him the effort.

"My pupil has a sense for the right path," he declared proudly.

Matilda gave Barnaby a look of respect he was not sure he deserved.

"I just wander into these things," he admitted.

Within the shrine waited a large hall. Windowless, but lit by plentiful candles. The chamber was set with rows of benches upon which a scattering of folk sat, heads bowed, whispering prayers to the saints above or the floor below. Most wore usual clothes; seldom the white robes.

A statue stood to the front; a woman with arms outstretched, head tilted to the sky, or at least the ceiling. But the features of the face were cruelly hammered away. The outstretched hands likewise vandalized, fingerless to grasp whatever they reached out to touch. Barnaby felt a twitch of pity for the statue. It stood as a stone in pain.

The air tasted cloth-thick with fire smoke, candle-smoke, altar incense, human sweat and the dust of years. Barnaby sniffed a farther smell of food cooking. The whole made a homely mix. But beneath, behind, these understandable smells wafted something less pleasant; a taint of decay.

Barnaby looked about for Cedric, for Val and the others.

"Should we ask where the visitors went?"

"We know where they went," replied the cat. "Down to the hermitess. Go left along the wall, then into that doorway."

Barnaby did so, coming to a candlelit hallway. Following past doorways where he spied folk sitting to table, else working at shelves and benches. He heard only whispered words, and the ever-present rising, falling song. No one withing the shrine simply chatted or chattered. But perhaps that was how devout folk vowed to pass their hours.

They came to the hallway's end, where waited steps downwards. A White Robe leaned beside a lamp, holding sword.

"She's to see the hermitess," said Barnaby.

The guard looked to Matilda. Mouthed something, then motioned for them to pass. They began descending the stone steps.

"What did he say?" asked Matilda, looking back.

Night-Creep answered.

"He said, '*poor her*'."

"Oh."

The stairs spiraled down into dark; the air growing thicker; more clearly tinged with rot. And now came strange noises. Cries, moans, words of imprecation neither chanted nor sung.

"Smells foul," whispered Barnaby.

"That is blood, among other things," observed Matilda, sniffing. "And plentiful shit."

The stairs opened to a large chamber. Warm, and darkly illuminated by the flames of a central fire. The walls writhed with the shadows of some twenty men and women in near-clockwork motion. Some flailing whips at their own bared backs. Others striking their flesh with bundles of thorned sticks. A few stood bowing up, bowing down, bowing up.

"Penitents," remarked Night-Creep. White eyes bright, unblinking.

"Seen such at the Jahrmarkt," whispered Barnaby. "But just regular folk fasting for a season, marching about in hair shirts. Naught so bloody as this. Are they mad?"

"Yes," answered Matilda.

"It's a point of view," whispered Night-Creep. "Granted, it's a point of view I share. Walk through the room to that far door. It leads further down. And speak to none."

Don't want to go further down, thought Barnaby. *I want to get out.* He exchanged a look with Matilda. She now breathed fast and shallow, eyes wide. Clearly feeling the same horror and repulsion. Yet, she waited for him to declare the path.

"Let's go on," Barnaby whispered.

And so they went. Walking with care through the busy, bloody folk. None spoke to them, nor paid them mind.

Halfway through the room Barnaby passed a woman holding a knife. Her naked torso shone with trickling blood, as she nicked and cut, nicked and cut.

He met her eyes, and could not keep silent.

"Why are you doing that?"

The woman paused, smiling at Barnaby friendly as if they exchanged words on the weather.

"This flesh disgusts me, sir. This heavy warm stinking mud buries me, sir." She writhed arms and legs, seeking to shake herself free of flesh. "With every cut I loosen another cord binding my true self. Soon, soon I shall be a pure beam of light to serve the Hermitess, sir."

She took the knife, digging the point across a breast. Mouth agape, eyes turning upwards, she panted as though in the throes of love.

Matilda grabbed Barnaby's arm, pulling him forwards.

"Going to be sick," whispered Barnaby.

"Not here you aren't," growled Matilda. And gave him a kick. Which being from a Silenian hoof, hurt.

"Ow," he hissed, ready to return the blow. He met her goat eyes, daring him to retaliate.

She's wise, he decided. *Knows a good kick can help more than words.* He considered giving the woman with the knife a kick. But it'd do her no good. Nor him either. So he limped onwards, towards the doorway where steps wound round and round, down and yet farther down.

A cloud of decay welcomed them to the next chamber of the hermitess's shrine. Foul air carrying a low and constant wind-mutter moan.

They peered into a room quieter, darker than the one above. Here the candle flames burned blue-tipped, as if fire itself choked and gasped for air. The dim glow shone on rows of low cots, upon which lay folk resting. Or corpses lying?

Difficult to tell, for each body looked ravaged beyond possibility of the heart still beating or lungs still breathing. The naked limbs were mere bones wrapped in parchment skin, where flies hovered, settling maggots into the seeping wounds.

A sickly-sweet smell of rot rose from these bodies as flower scent from a dark garden of Infernum.

"Hold your breath, then move through fast," recommended Night-Creep.

Barnaby and Matilda nodded. Hurrying, stumbling, mouth's tight shut. Barnaby struggled not to look left nor right; but of course he did. And saw these were not corpses. The open eyes turned this way and that, staring into worlds beyond the foul dark of the chamber. Their lips moved in secret conversations. From some came low moans, a faint wind-echo of the happy song upon the riverbank.

Barnaby sought to turn his own inner vision to green fields and warm sun, the chatter of birds in the woods about Mill Town, the smell of fresh-cut hay. But the thick air seeped into nose and mouth, turning heart's blood black, breath to a mere wind of rot.

Halfway across the chamber his steps faltered. Trembling, gasping, no longer able to hold breath. As did Matilda. Her eyes turning upwards, lips mouthing silent words, as if sharing the dark visions of the corpse-dreamers.

For a second they stood so, trembling. Then Night-Creep bent forwards and bit Barnaby hard upon an ear.

"Move, idiots!" the cat commanded.

Barnaby jumped, one hand at his bleeding ear. But the other hand reached, grabbing Matilda's hand. Tugging her forwards, reaching the doorway where waited steps that wound round and ever further down.

"Hear voices," muttered Matilda, pulling her hand from Barnaby's.

"I hear Cedric," he declared.

Heartened some, they dared descend yet farther. Round and round, at last coming to a great doorway. Wooden door thrown open. Barnaby peered within.

Chapter 10
What Lies Beneath, Behind, Ahead

Friar Cedric:

Foolishly, I did not await the dawn. No, I insisted I must follow Beatrice. Wherefore not? That shining vision was no *Nachzehrer,* no night-haunt. She yet lived. All was well.

And so I rushed heedlessly towards the shrine; followed by a grumbling Val, a silent Jewel, a cursing Bodkin. They gave over arguing me into sense; though doubtless they weighed knocking me down, binding me till sense returned of its own. Well, but the *Society of St Benefact* had sworn off such methods of debate.

The Silenian remained with the mules and our gear. At the time, I thought that wise. I did not foresee battle; only theologic debate.

Word must have been given, for no guard challenged our entry to the shrine. No, they ushered us on, smiling, welcoming us in the name of the hermitess.

Whenever I doubted the path, I spied the glow of her white dress, the shine of her gold hair, leading me on. Reminding of summer days in Daedalus, when we sat on the grass of the aerodrome, comparing the power of steam to the power of the saints.

And so I hurried after, seeing her face before me, eyes stern, chastising me for my long delay. I pursued her through the room of devotions, and down through the chamber of penitence, and then through the nightmare chamber of sleepers. By then I understood I had erred. Not all was well, at all.

And so at length we stood in the lowest room of the shrine. 'Lowest', in every sense of the word. A long stone chamber lit by plentiful candles, but lacking chair, table or least ornament. Baren as a tomb. Only a rough stone altar lurked in the back, far from the candles, where shadows ruled.

I stood before Beatrice, staff in hand. Not to lean upon it in weariness; but as symbol of authority. For though I had rushed in as a lovelorn fool, still my duty remained clear: I stood now before the hermitess Beatrice as Questioner.

Granted, behind us now gathered white-robed disciples, weapons drawn. I had not just walked into a child's model of Infernum. I'd led my friends into a trap.

And yet, looking upon Beatrice, still it came difficult to distrust, to fear.

Though the room glowed with bright candles, she shone the brighter. The thin white robe shaped a form young, and womanly as any marble angel. Her golden hair radiated outwards, making a halo worthy of a stained-glass saint.

She held hands out to me, ignoring the others of my company, and the white-robed followers who stood at the door, swords ready to prevent exit.

"Cedric Wieland, you must choose. Is it to be the flesh that rules, or the spirit?"

I worked to meet her eyes. Wide and open, gazing intent and stern. Yet not truly meeting mine. Did she even see me? I considered her words; mere echo of those we'd exchanged when parting years passed.

But I stood now as Questioner, not lover. I gave a stamp of my staff, broomstick though it was.

"The choice is not flesh or spirit, Beatrice Lucia. It is Life, or Death. Which have you chosen, Sister of the Order of St. Plutarch?"

Beatrice gave her gentle laugh, passing hands over breasts and groin to remind me of the shapely form shining bright within this tomb.

"Man, you see I glow with life. Behold me now, Cedric. You have never known life so pure."

"Life is never pure, Beatrice Lucia."

"But the saints call us to make it so, Cedric Wieland."

"The saints..." At that I halted. What servant in all the House of Saints did Beatrice now serve in her proud madness? My eyes looked past her to the shadowed altar at the far room. In the dark where no candle shone.

I raised my staff, commanding *light*.

"Do not," she ordered, raising hands high to hold back the light. Still, it came, filling all that tomb-chamber.

And so revealing what lay upon the stone altar. Nothing dramatic. Just a pitiful scarecrow form shaped of sticks, parchment and cobweb hair. Alive; if twitches indicated life.

"What lies behind you, Beatrice Lucia? Or rather, who?"

Beatrice turned her heaven-blinded eyes upwards, opening mouth wide, and gave a scream to tremble the candle flames.

Trembling myself, I leaped backwards, colliding with the friends I had entirely forgotten. Brave souls who'd descended with me through horrors to this chamber of death.

Beatrice completed her scream, which surely must have carried through all the shrine. She faced me again; and again I felt her eyes did not see me. Not as we call *seeing*.

There came no more sweet looks, no stern chiding in her expression. Only mad fury.

"Kill," growled my lost love. "Kill. Kill."

* * *

Val the Bard:

I never took Cedric Wieland for fool. The man walked calmly, talked wisely; displaying an understanding of the world's ways near practical as mine. Even if he did flirt with a martyr's pyre for absurd theologic reasons, still I felt he was *reasonable*. A counter to daydreaming Barnaby, secretive Jewel, mad Bodkin, madder Matilda. Yes, and to any crazed bard chasing golden cups.

But a proper bard should have understood the man better. Within Cedric's head debated a host of dead scholars; more warring voices than in silent Jewel or old-soul Bodkin. Sense he might talk; but in the end, he was more the dreamer than Barnaby, more the pilgrim pursuing incomprehensible vision than me chasing the cup of dreams.

In the Spice Isles they say of some mystery: '*seek the woman.*' Clearly there in the woods that night stood the female who explained Friar Cedric's mad debate against the existence of the saints, his march towards martyrdom and cursed towers.

Could he not see that his Beatrice was a pretty illusion? Forget that her damned bare feet left no print. And that her long hair had no slightest worry for wind or wet. Did men actually think a real girl *glowed*?

We followed along, urging him to think upon it as he might consider propositions of logic, paragraphs of thesis. To no point; he sought the girl.

Within the hermitess's lair waited bland folk smiling peacefully, muttering to saints and shadows. But below *them* waited a chamber of torture ruled by the tortured.

We hurried past the bleeding fools, down to a foul den of dead-alive dreamers. And yet farther down, farther down.

And so we came at last to a crypt where Cedric's dream girl awaited. She stood golden, glowing, and false as a penny whore's moan of ecstasy. While between us and the path back now gathered eight White Robes. Swords out, faces proud to be in sight of their hermitess's smile.

I exchanged glances with Bodkin. Wise soul, he nodded, hand seeking the short sword forever dragging beneath his coat. I worked to catch Jewel's eye; but she stared fixedly at Cedric, scowling. Well, she'd decided she fancied the man. Though he had ten years on her, and was a scholar, she a kitchen-witch. Now she kept one hand upon her spider-pendant. I hoped she prepared battle orations, not debated whether to enchant her own hair gold.

Meanwhile Cedric and Beatrice debated spirit and flesh. I waited, hoping it might yet conclude in words. Though the path to this tomb omened the way out would be a path of blood. We stood at the bottom of a shrine of mad folk. To leave would mean fighting past them all.

I scowled to see yet another White Robe enter. With a tall personage whose footsteps went *clop, clip*, upon the stones. Matilda?

And oh, by the Great Gold Hammer of St. Martia Patroness of Just Causes herself and no least other, but the fellow in white robe with her was *that son-of-a-miller Barnaby*.

I laughed loud, same moment as Beatrice screamed. Cedric raised staff high, casting light that far outshone the candles, the glowing hermitess.

Her scream shook Benefactors and White Robes alike. But the woman followed it with clear words of command: *Kill.*

At which I turned, thrust long knife into the throat of the fellow behind me, same moment he raised sword to strike my pretty head.

The battle went quick. The first true fight with all the Society of St. Benefact taking part. Jewel cast no orations to prettify herself. No, she tossed purple fire upon the fellow behind her, then very sensibly backed from his flailing blade. While her pet spider Periwinkle leaping upon another White Robe.

Bodkin turned, struggling to draw his sword, And Lucif bang me in the basement, he had to go tangle the pommel in his coat! Then just stood gaping at the sword of a White Robe coming for his head. It did not strike, for Cedric pulled the little rogue back by the scruff. Our cleric had rushed to defend his friends, not debate with lost love. I never called him fool.

The White Robes did not understand that Barnaby was of our company. I watched him strike one in the head with the heavy pommel of his axe. Same as he'd done to the blowhard Capitano. But the minion beside the falling man cursed this treachery. He rushed to strike... and our miller swept that dreadful axe down, cutting the man's head away neat as scythe to barley stalk.

Ah, poor Barnaby. He stared in horror at the fountaining trunk; eyes wide, mouth open as though it were his own head sent rolling. While he stood so, blinking, another White Robe rushed to cut him down. An arrow to the chest ended the brave charge. From Matilda, sensible girl. She backed into a corner and readied another. And still Barnaby stood blinking at the man he'd slain. The first, no doubt.

The fellow who'd menaced Bodkin now kneeled upon the ground, moaning with hands to face. I believe Cedric cast a spell of blinding upon the man. Bodkin kicked him, and then for luck kicked the one now struggling in spider web.

One White Robe remained. He turned and ran for the door. I slashed with my knife, but it was Matilda's arrow that took him down.

And that was that. Battle done. At least with the servants before us. But I heard shouts from the floors above. Orders, calls to arms. No doubt all the hive of lunatics would come in answer to Beatrice's scream.

I watched the cat upon Barnaby's back whisper into his ear. Barnaby shook himself awake, turned to the door. Pushing it closed; slipping the iron bar into position. Wise, I suppose. It would keep them out for a bit. Granted, it would keep us in.

Now we all looked to Cedric, who turned towards Beatrice. She stood with head now down, golden tresses hiding her face. Hands wringing, twisting, as though in heartfelt sorrow. Slowly she knelt, a flower folding in upon itself at sun's setting. The golden glow faded to shadow, to dust; she vanished entirely.

Cedric walked past, staff raised high, casting light. Stopping before the stone altar at the far end of the tomb-chamber. There upon it lay a woman, of sorts. Rag-clad, with skin just as tattered. Hair a thread-tangle of cobweb locks. Face skeletal, sunken eyes staring, hands clawing, twitching, working at the festering wounds that decorated the sad remains of her person.

"Beatrice," said Cedric.

She struggled to see with eyes filmed by illness, by pain, by confusion. But did see. At last meeting eyes.

"This flesh is a mere vessel, Cedric," she whispered. "Not the spirit. I am the spirit."

"Spirit should be kinder to its vessel, and more honest to its friends."

The withered lips twitched; I understood it to be a smile. Well, they were continuing their debate, it seems. Easy to see them as theologic students slyly flirting in some classroom, citing this testament, that poet.

"True kindness, Cedric, is to lead our spirits from the degradation of soul we call flesh."

"What you call 'degradation', is the dignity of living."

"Dignity?" she spat, rejecting the word.

"Beatrice," began Cedric. But,

"Are you Beatrice, then?" asked an interloper.

I turned, Cedric turned, the tattered, tortured creature turned. All turned to study Barnaby of Mill Town. He'd sheathed his bloody axe; now he held two absurd objects. A poppy bloom, and a bottle of water.

"These are for you, Ma'am. From Sephie. And Mister Quiet, I suspect."

"Mister Quiet," repeated Cedric.

"Sephie," whispered Beatrice.

"Yes'm." He looked ready to go into long explanation, thought better of it, thank the saints. Instead he offered the two objects. Not to Beatrice, but to Cedric.

Who laid aside his staff, hesitated, then accepted the Flower of Death, the Water of Life. Weighing them as though they were choices offered him, not another. He made no choice; instead, held bloom and bottle out to his once love, current opponent in theologic debate.

For a long while Beatrice's sunken eyes stared, considering. We watched, while the room echoed with attempts to open the barred door. Fists pounding, voices shouting for the hermitess. Still, we stood watching Beatrice, waiting.

At last one claw-like hand reached, declaring choice. She held the poppy bloom close to her sunken eyes, studying its petals, its meaning to her. At length, she placed it into her mouth.

That done, she closed eyes, sighing. Ceasing any last, least labored breath.

Bodkin:

My view is same as Mercutio's. You live for the saints, you die by the saints. That's to say, make the mistake of getting indebted to those holy riffraff and soon or late they will eat you up. Maybe order you to give all your coin to the poor and go freeze in an alley. Else send you off to preach love to the cannibal girls of Nix. Maybe just stand in a bonfire to prove your devotion.

If I understand the hermitess's particular lunacy, she tortured herself till body and spirit separated, sick of one another. The glowing golden girl being spirit, the festering thing on the altar being body. Interesting trick. But when I feel a need to put mind and body in separate rooms, I'll stick to wine or hemp.

But it was good to see Barnaby again.

Damn me to high summer in the Lower House, it was good to see him walk into the crypt. And mad Matilda with her bow. Our odds of keeping our own flesh and spirits united improved. My view of the whole venture improved. I admit it: I'd been contemplating a scamper from the Benefactors. It didn't feel a lucky caper without our gormless miller in the front.

Pity that when it came to the fight, I tangled the damn magic sword in my coat. Old Mercutio just laughed, though a sword edge was about to open the head we shared.

But that Cedric yanked me out of the way. Making up considerable for the fact he'd gotten me into the basement of a bedlam where a sword wanted my head.

They weren't proper fighters, those White Robes. The battle went quick. Once done, we stepped over the dead and twitching, watched Cedric and his lost lunatic love exchange last arguments to their churchly debate.

And then Barnaby produced a flower, a bottle of water. Flower of death, water of life: easy to picture the choice. But why did she choose death?

Life hurts, boy. Beatrice thought she could escape the pain of existing, by separating herself from her body. But she found that the agonies of the spirit are hundredfold those of the flesh. Life hurts. There is no escape but death. Thus, the flower.

That's Old Mercutio talking. Ignore him, he shat all over his own idiot life. Makes him feels better saying that all life is shit.

Foolish boy. But you will learn. And one day you will crave a poppy from Persephone's garden, same as any, same as all.

The crazy cultists pounded fists on the door. Echoing like heartbeats in the stone chamber. Or maybe that was my heart. Friar February's white grin, I was still seeing that sword coming for my face.

"What now?" I asked. "When they think to fetch a few axes, they'll have that door down and find their beloved hermitess dead."

"So we open it first," declared our Martia bard. "Fall upon them, fight our way out. Let's do it."

"Not advisable," remarked a voice from the shadows. Michael, Barnaby's ghostly advisor in weaponry; now leaning against the altar, disinterested in its offering of dead hermitess. "There will be a priest's hole somewhere about. Best seek that."

That cat of Barnaby's leaped from his shoulder. Sauntered about the altar, speaking casual as Tuesday tea.

"No, a priest's hole is for hiding. Recall, this is a former fortress. Seek the hidden escape passage."

I felt an urge to joke about *priest's holes;* but the only priest present, Cedric, had saved my brains from stirring by a sword. So I let the idiot jest pass.

We wandered about. Cedric waving his glowing staff here and there. I kicked at walls, hoping to hear a hollow thump. A sensible thing in wooden houses; not so much for stone crypts.

The pounding on the door sounded deeper and louder. Shaking it. Well, they'd brought something to batter it down. The guard tied with webbing shouted incoherent curses, as did the blinded one.

I kicked a shadowed section of stone. The old man in my head laughed.

These walls are carved from rock, he declared. *There is nothing hidden there.*

Then where? I demanded.

Did you not see the scratches in the floor to the left of the altar?

Shit, of course. I rushed to the altar, pushed the stone block. It moved, slightly. Built on low wheels. The others saw, rushed to add their shoves. Altar moved, we found a narrow stairway. Going yet farther down.

The Society of St. Benefact stared into the depths. The pounding on the door booming loud as if we stood inside a drum, or the heart of a saint.

Cedric went first, holding his glowing staff to light the way. Giving no last, loving glance to the offering upon the altar.

Chapter 11
Assume It So

Narrow steps descended to narrow tunnel. The Benefactors stood at the bottom, staring up as they might from the bottom of the grave.

"Tug on that chain," instructed Cedric. "It will move the altar back into position, hiding our escape."

"And cut off our air," pointed out Bodkin.

"No, this air is wet, not stale. Doubtless it leads to an opening by the river.

Barnaby and Matilda pulled the chain. The altar declined to move. Bodkin and Val joined in. The altar scraped, rolled... then the chain snapped, tumbling them all back upon one another, cursing. Leaving a strip of light above, their exit not fully hidden.

"St. Sheol shove me in the Styx," growled Val. "No help for it. Let's go."

Cedric lighting the way, they followed the tunnel. Splashing at times through puddles of dank water, brushing through tree roots that poked from the walls. At length,

"Light ahead," declared Cedric.

They kicked their way through old branches, tangles of brush, at last emerged into open air. Stood blinking within a copse of oaks. The light of dawn just yellowing the top leaves. Close by, they spied the river Lethe, its black water looking chill and unconcerned with the pains of life.

Everyone took long breaths of clean air untouched by the miasma of the shrine.

"All clear," said Val, at length. "Let's move."

"Where's the camp?" demanded Bodkin.

"That way," pointed Matilda. They hurried through the trees, wary of ambush. But there waited their cart, the hobbled mules, the still smoldering campfire.

"I don't credit those folk with much sense," observed Val. "There's no telling what they'll do when they find their hermitess all flesh, no spirit. Let's get on the road fast."

They hitched the mules to the cart, loading what gear lay about. Val smothered the fire.

"Bodkin, take the reins. Matilda, you ride in the back keeping bow ready. Don't shoot just because you see a target. Cedric and Jewel, we walk. If you have any orations to speed us or slow them, call them up."

She turned last to Barnaby, leaning against a tree, indifferent to this martial preparation. Her eyes met his.

"Master Miller, can we assume you are with us for the present?"

Barnaby gave the slightest of nods to say *'assume it so'*.

"Then you keep to the front. If they come out of the trees, your axe will be better use than my knife."

For reply, Barnaby drew Dragontooth. Still sticky red.

They hurried the cart to the road. No one in sight; yet.

"Which way?" asked Bodkin. "Back to the city, or north to the tower?"

"North," declared Matilda.

"North," added Cedric.

"Agreed." That, from Jewel.

"My view as well," declared Val. "What about you, miller?"

"Let's get St. Lucif's thorned cockerel away first," said Barnaby. Looking up and down the road. "Talk later."

The Society of St. Benefact stared surprised. It was not a Barnabish thing to say. Then Bodkin snapped the reins, setting the cart rumbling down the road. The rest trotted alongside, eyes and ears wary for attack.

An hour down the road, Matilda called out. "I see a fellow on horse, backaways. Seems to be alone."

Val stared behind. "He's keeping his distance. Might be trailing us for the madmen. Might have nothing to do with us."

They rumbled on through the morning, not resting. At times they passed stone ruins; other whiles farms where folk worked, giving scant greeting, eyeing them warily.

At noon they halted where a creek offered a chance to water the mules. Barnaby knelt on the bank, splashing Dragontooth in the water, scrubbing it best he could with sand and grass.

Val watched him, saying nothing. At last turning away to see Bodkin, Cedric and Matilda watching her watching Barnaby. She blushed, scowled, pointed north.

"Those hills ahead are the border to St. Martia, We don't want to get too close, or we'll run into a border patrol. We need to turn east soon, and cross the Lethe into Demetia. Then run north fast, get into Hefestia."

"Why not go on into Martia?" asked Matilda. "I thought you were from there."

"I am from there. And so I don't want to go there. You don't want to go there either."

"We are all weary," sighed Cedric. "Including the mules. Let us find a place out of sight of the road, where we can rest, eat and watch."

In the end they choose a ruined farm with a standing wall, surrounded by trees that must have once made a fruitful orchard. Barnaby did not assist in the preparations for camp. Instead he walked to a great flat rock, surely the ancient hearth stone of the house. There he sat, looking eastwards towards St. Demetia.

Across broken stonework, past fields long turned fallow and weed-filled, he studied the dark ribbon of the Lethe, flowing south like a road of shadow.

From the corner of one eye he noted that Night-Creep now perched upon the stone beside him. The cat sat tall and elegant as a flower vase for the table of a king. Tail wrapping about feet, white eyes staring towards the same distant river.

From the corner of the other eye Barnaby spied the shadow of Dark Michael, arms folded across chest, hat slanted over eyes. Quietly meditating upon the very same distant river.

And so the three stayed silent, watching the water flow. When at last Barnaby spoke, it was in voice slow and casual as words upon some distant dream enacted in the embers of the hearth.

"I wonder what his name was."

He did not say whom he meant; and neither cat nor ghost asked whom he meant.

"Names," said Night-Creep, licking a paw in consideration. "Sounds that give the illusion of knowing persons, places, worlds. But the man you slew was a stranger. No more, no less. A stranger who intended to kill you because a glowing woman screamed 'kill'."

"That makes him sound mad and evil," mused Barnaby. "But maybe he just wandered into it all. Not wanting to be where he was."

"Such is war," said Michael. "And do not reply that you were not at war, boy. You descended into a pit of lunatics to rescue your friends. What steps brought the man to blindly serve madness, are his to answer for, not yours. You did right to stop him from killing your friends. And yourself."

Barnaby nodded. "Knew that. And I'd do the same again. If I had to. No, good masters, I'm not repenting the strike. Still, I just wonder what his folk called him when they sat to supper."

They contemplated the distant river in silence, weighing the absence of a name in silence. At length Val approached. She stood a bit off, looking at him, hands on hips. Night-Creep yawned, slipping away into evening shadows. Dark Michael's lounging form disappeared from sight.

"Can I sit?"

For reply, Barnaby shifted, making space upon the hearth stone. There she sat. Hands on knees; her turn to ponder the distant Lethe.

"First one?"

Barnaby did not ask what or whom she meant. He went back to staring out over the fields, watching the setting sun repaint the water, the banks, the clouds. Speaking at last in words calm and unhurried as the river's journey to the sea.

"One year in the Jahrmarkt, Alf set me to fight in a rope circle. I found myself facing a crazy fellow near big as me. Folk shouted while Alf took wagers on who'd win. The fellow and I hit each other with our fists bound with cloths, so as not to break fingers."

"Did you win?"

"No. I was stronger, had the longer arm. But I didn't want to hurt him. Or anyone, much."

"Ha. Serves your brother right to lose his coin."

At which words, Barnaby laughed low.

"Ah, no. Alf wagered against me. Knew me, he did."

"Seriously? What a miserable shit."

"A clever one, though." He looked about. "This seems nice country, though darker and wetter than Demetia. Why are so many of the farms empty?"

He doesn't want to talk about it, she decided. So she answered his question.

"It's the river. Folk fear it. The Tarchs avoid the river road as well. They use another one farther west."

"Why?"

"When Demetia and Plutarch warred, there were battles all along here. The Black Robes summoned creatures from places lower than the basement of the seventh Tartarus. They say those horrors still lurk in the waters. Come crawling out if you spill blood or spit wrong."

He shook his head. "Maybe we should camp elsewhere?"

"Maybe. But if we have the river at our backs, we only have our front to watch."

"Sounds a soldierly opinion."

Val shifted. "So. I wanted to thank you for coming to our rescue."

Barnaby shrugged. "Didn't really. You'd have won without me. Those white cloaks weren't like you." For a moment he looked at the ground, as though picturing a severed head bouncing. Then he gave a soft laugh. "They were more like me."

Val crossed arms, kicked at the same ground, striking a weed poking its own innocent head out from the stones.

"Barnaby, I'm sorry we tricked you, tied you up," she said, delivering the words fast. "It was mostly my idea. Cedric voted against. And Jewel, actually."

Barnaby considered. It felt less important now than when he'd walked down the road, head aching with ale, face burning with shame.

"I think... I'm over being angry about it. Anyways, you were right. I shouldn't have tried to make the decision, when it was up to us all." He turned, looking directly at her for the first time.

"So, if I'm still in the Society of Saint Bonefract, I'll go along to the tower."

"*Benefact*," corrected Val. "The holy patron of self-benefaction. Proper guide for adventurous treasure hunters."

She started to say more; but from the bag upon her back, music began to play. Loud and wild, a rushing stream of notes. Val jumped, then reached to the sack, extracting her harp. She gave it an angry shake.

"Stop that, Thelxipea," she commanded.

The harp twanged happy, ignoring her.

"Thelx-who?"

"That's her name," explained Val, near shouting over the outpouring melody.

"Well why is it doing that?" he asked, also near shouting.

"She's happy you've rejoined us," shouted Val.

Chapter 12
Beneath the Threads that Weaves the World

Democritus, Archbishop of St. Plutarch:

Light traversing a properly shaped crystal shall divide into separate beams. Red, orange, yellow, green, blue, purple, violet. Pose a second crystal of correct shape, and these beams shall reunite into a single beam of white.

And if your light be the sun itself, and your crystal be ten million drops of rain? Why, behold the rainbow. The symbol of hope sent by the saints to remind the Middle House how those above watch over us through every storm.

We creatures of clay move through textures of light woven together as silk threads of a tapestry. As our clay is itself but a further winding of endlessly divisible threads.

Consider a grand cathedral orchestra playing a masterpiece of music. A clever ear can isolate the flute from the oboe, the trumpet from the harp, the drum from the cymbal.

All things observed, touched, known, can be so divided, identified, analyzed. And yet, what does it mean? What is the worth of dissecting a symphony, a tapestry, a beam of light?

The Lucretians see the light, touch the clay, hear the music. And they alone dare test, divide, identify. And so they alone know that beneath every thread that weaves our world, is a separate, secret realm of rules. The smallest grain of sand shall obey the same laws as a mountain or the whirling moon itself.

Even unto the saints. They too are divisible, of parts identifiable. Though they may appear to us as golden beams of light or marble statues, a stranger on the road or a voice in a dream. The saints are the construction of rules twining together like light, like grains of a rock, like melodies of music.

When the Deaconry decided to send Cedric as Questioner to his former love Beatrice, I did not object. The mission was valid; to inquire upon a dangerous cult corrupting doctrine, leading folk to destruction. If it ended with Cedric's death? Well, he had agreed to join the service of St. Plutarch. Such ending would be his gain, and ours.

And yet as I watched the proceedings, I felt able to divide their wisdom into smaller, meaner parts. They of the Deaconry are wise spirits; but never forget: *they are dead*. Truly, they recall love, and all the fires of desire and ache of loss. But only recall. Never more than recall. And that recollection of love is to them at once burning agony, and sweet perfume.

Well, if you were starving, and could only smell fresh bread, but never taste the least crumb... might you not sit in command of a bakery ordering this sweet cake, that fresh loaf be baked and brought before you, so that you might inhale the warm memory?

At heart, the Deaconry sent Cedric to Beatrice to torment a living man with agonies horrible as Beatrice and her devotees inflicted upon themselves. So that at the table of the high council, they might, just briefly, close dead eyes to the living world, and recall the sweet, wonderful, unbearable pain of life.

Chapter 13
They Smell the Blood

Matilda stood on watch, her back to the remains of the farmhouse chimney. The campfire had settled to orange embers. No moon shone to charm with glow, nor distract with shadows. Silent as the stones she leaned against, the Silenian tipped head, listening. Hearing wind in tree branches, the distant flow of water. Choirs of crickets and frogs making their nightsong, owls, moths and bats debating ownership of the night air. And a distant crackle of crushed leaves.

Matilda waited motionless till it came again. Then notched arrow to bow. Tiptoeing best one can with hooves, crouching low, finding Val wrapped in blanket.

"Pssst," she whispered. "Wake up."

"The cup?" asked Val.

"What?"

Val shook herself awake, pushing off the blanket.

"Never mind. What is it?"

"Folk gathering in the trees. I think. Coming from the road south."

Val drew her knife. "I'll wake the others. You keep watch from someplace where they can't come behind you."

Matilda nodded, edging away. Val shoved her feet into boots, crept to the blanket where Cedric lay huddled. She knelt, shook him by the shoulder. Finger pressing to her lips in sign for quiet. He blinked himself awake, nodded.

Val did the same with Jewel, who lay conveniently close to Cedric. The bard wondered if and when those two would begin sharing a blanket. Who'd make the first move? Seemed more likely to be Cedric. He was older, more confident. Well, but Jewel was more direct. Or was that pose? Infernum, who knew. They were both unfathomable as the nether pits of Nix.

Before she had time to wake Barnaby, something flew over her head. An arrow, slaying a pine tree. If she'd not been moving in fast crouch, it would have slain a bard.

"Wake!" she shouted to all, and rolled from firelight into shadows. Finding herself on her back, staring up at a stranger holding an axe. Nothing so fearsome as Barnaby's butcher blade. This was just something for chopping wood, the heads of chickens. Still, it looked perfectly lethal raised above her. She waited for the downward strike, preparing to roll. But the man decided to drop the axe, then drop himself, Revealing Bodkin behind him, holding a short sword darkened with blood.

Val rolled to her feet. The camp now filled with shouts. A man in white robe strode into the firelight, swords in both hands.

"Suffer and die, defilers of the spirit!" he shouted, and leaped into the campfire. At once his robe burst into flames. He screamed, but continued standing, waving swords, burning like an avenging paper angel.

"Die!" he repeated.

Val turned from him to a woman rushing through the trees, waving a kitchen knife. Val waited, and as the woman neared she sidestepped, reached, slicing the attacker's throat neat as scissor snipping thread. The attacker continued onwards, colliding into a tree; falling to the ground. There she knelt slashing at the trunk, determined to take the tree with her to Elysium.

More mad cultists emerged from night shadows; while the fellow in the flames screamed in an ecstasy of pain and devotion. One and then another fell with arrows calmly placed by Matilda.

Val watched Barnaby leap into the firelight, swinging his axe, striking the chest of a man holding a pitchfork. The man screamed, fell, began crawling towards shadows. Barnaby raised the axe to finish the man; then turned away, letting him retreat.

Bodkin waved his magic blade at two attackers, backing away till one fell writhing in Jewel's purple flames. The other collapsed with a blow to the head from Cedric's broom-stick staff.

Now the man screaming in the campfire knelt, his white robe ashes, his skin a black-red painting of some denizen of Infernum. Swords dropped, arms out, he continued calling for death. Perhaps for the company, perhaps for himself. Slowly, he toppled onto his side, began crawling from the fire, making moans distant as wind from the river.

Val put her back to tree, looking about. No more enemy in sight. She walked to the fire, knelt by the burning man and cut his throat. His moans ceased.

"Everyone alive?"

"I saw more out there, gathering in the trees," declared Bodkin. "I think these first were just the crazy ones who couldn't wait for a sensible attack."

"Sounds likely. Haven't seen the one with a bow yet. Let's get the cart hitched and get out of here."

But from the trees they could hear Matilda cursing.

"No, no, no!"

"What? What is it?"

"My mules are dead. Throats cut! Damn these lunatics to the shit pits of Sainted Sheol!"

"Right," growled Val. "Everyone gather what you need first. Take whatever we can all use. Food and blankets for sure. Take one tent. Leave the water."

"What is that?" asked Barnaby.

"What is *what* now?"

"Somethings coming out from the river. Shining all green."

"More than one," said Matilda. "Well, of course it would go so. They smell all the blood."

"They?"

"Twisty things that haunt the Lethe. Arms like snakes, teeth like spikes. Spilling blood on Lethe's bank is like ringing a bell calling 'em to dinner."

From the trees about them now came shouts and calls. The fanatics of the shrine were preparing a more organized attack.

"Let's move before they surround us," said Val. "We head west, away from the river. Across the road. Now."

Backs burdened with what supplies they could carry, they hurried through the trees. Behind them, within the ruins of the farmhouse, beside the smoldering campfire, came shouts; then screams.

"I think they've fallen to fighting each other," declared Matilda, stopping to stare backwards. "Squiggly things against crazy folk."

"Well, that's a bit of luck for a change," said Bodkin.

"Quiet," ordered Val. "Let's scamper before they notice we aren't at the party. With our usual luck, they'll become fast friends and chase us down."

They marched the rest of the night west through the marshlands of St. Plutarch, fleeing the river and the road. Making their slow way across tussocks of marsh grass, splashing through pools and puddles of stagnant water. To left and right, the glow of will-o-whisps teased them to lose their way. Fireflies danced about, pretty as stars; but so did endless flies that bit and stung. A congress of croaking frogs began a deafening debate upon their trespass.

They stepped beneath trees bearded with dripping moss that tangled in hair, painting slime across face and shoulder. Tree roots poked high as if to escape the wet earth, tripping the unwary. Mud sucked at each step, attempting to seize boots. Pools and rivulets kept forcing them steadily uphill, northwards.

Dawn found the company muddy and weary, resting upon a rocky hillock overlooking a land of somber ponds reflecting pink sky. The newly-revealed St. Plutarch looked green; but not the same summery hues of Demetia. This was the verdant of scum across stagnant ponds, and the pallid green of marsh grasses, the dark green of ash and cypress. Dull-feathered birds circled the quiet sky, wide wings near motionless... till they dropped, seizing the unwary fish or frog.

Behind the company, the hills northward rose yet higher. Becoming rock scapes where scrub trees grasped tight wherever wind and rain allowed.

The company sat considering the land, the night, the strange battle and their muddy selves.

"You look a mucky mess," declared Bodkin to Val.

She started a casual obscenity; then recalled him stabbing the fellow about to chop her with a farm axe. Settled for a weary grin.

"Well, you look no better."

"So where are we?"

"Toss a rock over these hills and it will land in Martia. East and north lies Hefestia, where we want to go. I suppose in a pinch we could cross the Lethe into Demetia first. Easier now we've no cart. But there'd still be Demetian patrols to avoid. I'm hoping we aren't still sought by thief-catchers and Questioners."

"Is there a bridge across the Lethe?" That, from Jewel.

"This far north? Not till the Debated Circle. Just ferries, and some shallow places that can be forded."

"I thought the Tarchs had a town on the border with Martia. Where they let folk cross."

"Orpheum. It's days west of here. Has a road going south to Pleasance. That's the road used by most going north and south, instead of the river road. Has proper inns along it."

Cedric emptied a boot of mud and water. "An inn sounds rather appealing at the moment."

"Yeah, but it'd be a week of marching across muddy ground like what we just tasted. And in the wrong direction. We want to go east, not west. Anyways, we can't be spending coin at inns if we're going to purchase new supplies."

Barnaby poked a finger across the dirt, sketching the world as he knew it. Not a complex map, at all.

"Isn't there a place where the corners of Hefestia, Demetia, Plutarch and Martia all touch?"

Val pointed northeast.

"That's the Debated Circle. Used to be a city, though nobody remembers when nor whose. Just burned ruins. Still has some skirmishing going on. Festians against Martia, Demetians 'gainst Tarchs. My father died there. For a worthless field of rocks and bones."

Bodkin laughed. "So, we can't afford to go west, don't dare step north. Monsters and cultists to the east, mud and flies to the south. Looks like we're trapped on this hillside."

"Not trapped," replied Val. "Just sensibly dodging trouble. We'll camp tonight in these hills, somewhere out of sight. Tomorrow we'll work our way east back to the road. The cultists will be eaten and the squiggly things will have gone back to the river, stomachs full. We'll hike the road north to the Debated Circle. Once a week there's a truce. Travelers can cross twixt Plutarch and Hefestia, or Martia and Demetia."

"Is that safe?"

"Pretty much. We'll have to wait in the caravan camp. And pay a toll for the escort."

"What's our plan when we get to Hefestia?"

"Hmm. Restore supplies. Maybe in Daedalus. North of that are the mountains. And in the mountains, sits our double-damned tower. Waiting impatient for us, no doubt."

They emptied their boots of mud, then gathered up their things again. Lamenting the ease of travel with cart and mule. Val leading, they worked their way ever higher into the hills, at last finding an isolated gully that cut deep into the hillside, A pleasant place of vines and scrub, where rock walls shielded from easy view. Barnaby drew his axe to cut wood for a fire; but Val stopped him.

"We're on the border between two lands at war. We can't risk a fire being seen by wandering patrols."

"Thought we had papers of permission?" said Matilda, looking to Cedric.

"We do," sighed the cleric. "But the bard is wise. A patrol finding us in the border hills might fill us full of arrows before properly requesting our documents."

"Or they might shout we're spies and smugglers," declared Bodkin. "Confiscate our supplies. Never, ever wise to catch the eyes of soldiery at war."

"War," considered Barnaby. "That's been puzzling me. Plutarch and Demetia are supposed to be at war, but folk cross back and forth in Persephone easy as going from kitchen to barn. And Plutarch and Martia are at war in these very hills, yet we haven't seen a solitary flag nor soldier."

For answer, Val bent down, pulling back branches just where Barnaby had prepared to chop.

"See that?"

Barnaby puzzled, studying a heap of gray-white rubble pleasantly wrapped in flowers, decorated with vines. Of a sudden, though they did not move, they took different form, different meaning. Becoming a man; or the scattered remains of one. Ribs crushed, skull turned up to the sky. The hilt of a sword still clasped in twig-like grasp.

"In my father's father's time, these hills were full of flags and soldiers, prayer and spell, horn calls and screams. All the dance of war."

She bent down, picked up the sword hilt. A harmless thing, bladeless and pathetic.

"Haven't been real battles twixt Plutarch and Martia, Hefestia and Demetia in ages." She poked at the bones with a foot. "Even in the Debated Circle they call truce one a week, to let people pass through. Nowadays, the lands would rather sit quiet, trade peaceful."

"Then why have borders and patrols, all that dispute and worry?" asked Barnaby.

"Shear habit of distrust. To the folk of Demetia, the Black Robes of Plutarch are bloody necromancers wanting to feed children to St. Erebus. To the folk of Martia, the Hefestians are lunatics who mate with clockwork. To the folk of Hefestia, you simple Demetians are superstitious savages."

She bent, carefully returning the sword hilt to the bony grasp. "No doubt our Cedric now wishes to remind all, it is the folk of the lands who argue, not the saints."

"Would it were so," said Cedric. "But as it passes in the Middle House, so it goes in the Upper House. They war up there as well."

"No fire then," sighed Barnaby. "This high, the night wind shall blow cold." He sat, shaking head rueful. "Hermits, saints, wars, kingdoms. Flies and glowing things from rivers. They conspire to keep a body up at night."

"If it grows cold, we'll just have to lie all snuggly close and warm together," declared Matilda. Giving grin sharp as the tips of her ears. Bodkin laughed; Jewel looked aside. Cedric smiled. Val frowned.

While Barnaby said nothing. Just found his blanket, placed his pack for a pillow to his head. Then closed eyes best he could. Listening as the others settled themselves, sharing food, idle talk. It all wound together as a pleasant background sound; far better than the wind in the trees when he'd slept alone.

I'm back with my friends, he thought. He opened eyes to take a last look. Bodkin sat with Matilda, tossing a coin while she called 'heads' or 'tails'; always incorrectly. Cedric sat with back to a rock beside Jewel. They paged through her book of orations, arguing this spell from point of view clerical, that oration from point of view occult.

And Val the bard stood some feet away, holding her own blanket, looking at him. When their eyes met, she immediately looked away. He closed his own eyes, feeling he spied. He waited, considering whether to open his eyes again, find if she'd returned to looking at him again. He decided to wait and catch her off guard. He'd count to fifty. At twenty-five he drifted off to sleep, unaware she'd returned to staring at him.

Chapter 14
Ba'al Bogramoth Holds a Tea Party

Ba'al Bogramoth:

Frogs are dull. I like mice. Mice are warm and quick and furry. Fur is fascinating. Whiskers too. So fascinating! Plenty of frogs in the liquid. No mice. Have to grab them fast from the gaseous. Have to play with them in the gaseous. Not in the liquid. Can't squeeze mice. Can't show too many dimensions or little squeaky minds go 'pop'.

Frogs... you can show frogs things. They're solid. But so dull! Cold and wet and stupid. Like litter spawn that never went past larval stage. Mice are better. Mice are *nice*.

Blood summoned us from the liquid the two-legs call 'Lethe'. We squiggled along their little dimensions of forward, sideways and upwards, into the gaseous. I saw fire, felt warm things dying. Blood calling us, we hurried. Past trees. Bah. Dull things, trees.

My nest mates grabbed what they found, dragging them squirming and screaming back into the liquid. Greedy things, nest mates. I looked for mice. Caught a bat with a tentacle.

"Hello," I told it. It squeaked. Bats look like mice but are not fun like mice. I ate it, looked around. A two-leg lay half in the fire. I picked him up.

"Hi," I said. "I'm Ba'al Bogramoth." He didn't answer. He was burned and his throat cut. I propped him up with tentacle eight. Making his head waggle to show he talked.

"Hi, Ba'al Bogramoth! I'm Mister Burned Man. Let's be friends!"

"That is good idea, Mr. Burned Man. Let's find more friends."

I found a four legs all cold. I dragged it near the fire, set it next to Mister Burned Man. Jiggling the long head with tentacle twelve.

"Hello, Ba'al Bogramoth! I am Meat-with-fur. Do you like my fur?"

"I do like your fur, Meat-with-fur. Do you like it, Mr. Burned Man?"

Mr. Burned man said he liked the fur because it was like mice fur. We were getting along fine. I reached for more bats, and more friends. A two-legs hid behind a tree, still squiggling and gas breathing. I brought him close to join us.

I jiggled Mr. Burned Man, making him wave in welcome.

"Hi! I am Mr. Burned Man. What is your name?"

"Help me," said the newcomer. I jiggled the four-legs to show how happy he was.

"Hello, Mr. Help-me. I am Mr. Meat-with-fur. Will you be our friend?"

"Please," said Mr. Help-Me.

I brought another of the two legs to our circle. She lacked a head. But I wiggled her with tentacle seven, showing she too was excited.

"I don't have a head but I am very happy to be friends," I had her say.

"Hi, No-head! I am Mr. Burned Man. Do you like mice?"

"Oh, yes I do, Mr. Burned Man. I like mice fine."

"Help me."

"Let's all eat our bats," I had Meat-with-fur say. "Dig in!"

"No, no, Meat-with-fur," I said, rapping him with tentacle eleven, which hurts. "Remember our manners."

"Oh, yes, Ba'al Bogramoth. You are right. Let us say thank-you's first."

"Bow heads, all." No-head did not, but I made her sort of bend. Mr. Help-me did not bow his head not till I rapped him with tentacle ten, which does not hurt. Not much.

So we all bowed our heads and chanted.

"Saint Cthulhu, bless this feast,
Cxaxukluth, bless each beast.
And crawling Nargalothetep take the least."

Then we dug into our bats.

"I like bats because they are like mice," No-Head said. "But I like mice better."

"Mr. Help-me likes mice too," I told the others. "We all like mice. Don't we, Meat-with-fur?"

"Yes, Ba'al Bogramoth. But I don't think Mr. Help-me really likes mice."

This was getting interesting. I wiggled tentacle seven, so that Miss No-head said, "Are you sure, Meat-with-fur?"

Meat-with-fur nodded sadly.

We all turned to Mr. Help-me. He wiggled, though I did not wiggle him. That was Mr. Help-me wiggling himself. He made noises.

"No, I don't like mice," he said.

We all went quiet.

"That makes me sad to hear, Mr. Help-me," said No-head.

"Me, too," agreed Meat-with-fur.

"I don't think Mr. Help-me is our friend," said Burned Man.

"I don't care!" shouted Help-me. He wiggled out my grasp and ran for the trees. I don't know why. Trees are dull. I grabbed him and brought him back and sat him down again. Then I ate him up.

For a while we all sat silent, excepting Mr. Help-me, who wiggled in gullet six, the way they do when you swallow them whole.

"This has been a very nice time," I told my friends.

Mr. Burned-man agreed. Mr. Meat-with-fur agreed. Miss No-head agreed. It had been a very nice party.

I went back to the liquid of the Lethe and my nest mates. I could feel Mr. Help-me squiggling within, the way they do. I wondered if I ate a few mice, whether they would all get along in gullet six? He might come to like mice.

I mean, mice are just *nice*.

Chapter 15
In Which a Line is Crossed

For once, the Society of St. Benefact rested all the night in peace. Bodkin keeping watch till moonrise; passing the duty on to Matilda. At sunrise they took their time awakening, breakfasting, preparing for the day. A rock pool farther into the gully was declared the public bath. A coin toss designating it the men's' for the first hour.

"I'm trusting Bodkin's coin tosses as much as a handshake from the Spice Isles snake-saint," declared Matilda. "Next time it's my coin and my call."

She sat with Jewel and Val on a rock ledge, staring out over the somber countryside.

"The little thief will just steal the penny from the air before your eyes," predicted Val.

Jewel sat motionless, hair hanging down over her face. Matilda cocked head, concerned.

"Here now, are you feeling unwell, Miss Witch?"

Jewel did not answer. Val did.

"I asked her to send her spider round about, scout for us. She's seeing what it sees."

"Oi, now that's a useful sort of thing. I'd send it to spy on that dog."

"What dog?"

"Down a ways, towards the rock shaped like a duck. A bit like a duck."

Val stared. Far, far down the slope, among the stagnant pools and twisted trees, loped the form of a dog. Bone white, long-legged. The creature trotted steadily through marsh grass, leaping the smaller pools, sniffing, gazing, hurrying on.

"A death hound," said Val. "It's picked up our trail. There'll be a patrol following behind."

Matilda held her bow, weighing the challenge.

"Too far for an arrow."

"Seriously? You harm that dog and you'll have half Plutarch after us."

"Pleased to hear they love their pets. But if we can't send it away, best we get away."

They stood. Jewel remained seated till Val reached down, shook her.

"Wake up, farmgirl."

Jewel's head rose, looking about, shaking away Val's hand, her own veiling hair.

"What is it?"

"A death hound. Why didn't your spider see it?"

"Uhm," Jewel blinked her eyes to simplify it from reality divided into a thousand facets. "Perry, I, we were looking, scouting I mean, uhm, elsewhere."

"Where?" demanded Val. "What did you see?" At which question Jewel blushed, looked away.

Matilda's nose was a pretty girlish thing, not a bit goat-like. But now it began to puff goatish sounds, '*mah*'s and '*hah*'s piping Capricornian mirth.

"Oh, no, no you weren't," said Val. "Seriously?"

Jewel hid her face in her hands.

Val growled, turned and hurried into the sheltering rock gulley. Till she heard the splash of water, the conversation of Cedric and Barnaby just past a bend of rock. There she halted, risking shouts.

"Sorry to interrupt your bath, boys, but a Tarch patrol is sniffing about. We need to hurry back to the road where travelers belong. If they catch us here, they're likely to act rude."

"Fine," shouted Barnaby. "Give a moment."

Bodkin added further opinion.

"And keep that damned spider from its spying or I'll put a rock atop it!"

The Benefactors hurried best they could eastwards. But the land defied their progress. The hillside grew ever steeper, cut with arroyos and gullies they could not cross, forcing them yet higher into the hills.

At noon they came in sight of the river road and the Lethe. But it was distant, far below the ledge where they perched. So they rested, contemplating their distant goal, till came the faint echoing howl of dogs.

At Val's nod, Matilda rose. Crouching, she hurried back along the path they'd come. Her hooved feet moving more sure than boots on the rough path, her slotted eyes spying all that moved. The others stood, readying to fight or flee.

When the Silenian returned, she whispered, curt for one so fond of words.

"Five soldiers. Two of 'em walk strange. Three dogs. I'm thinking we might surprise 'em."

"You can't surprise those dogs," said Val. "And the two walking strange are dead folk. Fill them with all your arrows and they'll just smile." She considered that. "Well, no, not smile. Actually, they wouldn't do anything but keep walking forwards to squeeze your throat."

Bodkin leaned down the dark stone crevice before them, examining the sides, where ferns and mosses kept a small green world, secret and peaceful. At the distant bottom water trickled, wending its way to the marshes, to the river, on to the sea.

"We might be able to get down here."

"You could, maybe," declared Val. "Not the rest of us."

"I've rope," declared Matilda.

"But nothing to tie it to," pointed out Bodkin.

"We could hold it while some of us got down."

"Leaving the rest to fend for themselves? Anyways we don't know where this crevice leads. Might be trapping ourselves down there."

"Then we go around again," sighed Cedric, staring up the hill slope. "That's manageable.:

"We've come too far north already," said Val. "Any farther and we'll be in St. Martia."

There came the howl of dogs on the wind.

"Shit," cursed Val. "Yeah, I see where this is going. Fine. Infernum. We climb."

They clambered up a rocky slope, came to a ledge that led into a canyon so narrow as to be almost a tunnel. It made an easy path through the hillside.

"Looks like it goes all the way through the hills," said Barnaby.

"That's what I'm afraid of," said Val. She looked behind. "Maybe we could front them here."

"Battle is not a wise option, if we have a path forwards." That, from Cedric.

"Agreed," said Bodkin.

"Also agreed," said Jewel.

Val looked to Barnaby. He shrugged. "I don't want to fight. But Miss Val is our guide in these things. If she says it comes to fighting, I'll trust her on it."

She stared at him. Shaking her head in sign she was absolutely bewildered by life and millers. No words followed; she led them onwards through the passage.

It opened at last upon a little cup-shaped valley, peaceful and green, sheltering fern and flower. Tumbled rocks stood about posing pretty as statues. Birds sang, bees buzzed. It might have been some secret garden of the saints.

"Does it go on through the hills?" asked Barnaby.

"Probably," said Val. "But we aren't."

"We could manage a climb up that side," declared Cedric, eyeing the rock walls. "But I want a rest first."

"Me too," declared Matilda.

"Fine," growled Val. "But a damned quick one. And by the Patron Saint of Just Shits, no one steps a foot farther north. Or someone in St. Martia will cut it off."

"Ha, too late for that."

Barnaby looked about, not sure who spoke.

Quick as blink, Matilda had her bow out, arrow nocked. Seeing that, Barnaby drew Dragontooth. Cedric raised his staff. And Val... did nothing. Except swear.

"*Shit-shit-shit.*" She turned to the Benefactors. "Put down your weapons, idiots. And no one move."

"Wisdom, there," declared the voice.

Now a man stepped from behind a standing stone. He held a short spear, twirling it easy as juggler in the market. Done twirling, he tapped it thrice on the rock. The taps surely making signal. Out from behind boulders and up from high grass appeared others. A dozen men and women. Dressed alike in leather kilts braced with strips of bronze; wearing leather armor little different from Barnaby's. They bore plentiful swords, spears, knives, and bows. Ready for war as a flock of crows for an autumn wheat field.

But it was not weaponry that made them seem so fierce. These folk circled about the Benefactors with the confidence of wolves facing house dogs.

The man with the spear stepped forwards, giving each separate companion a measuring look, a bright smile. Stopping last before Val the bard. She waited, silent, meeting eyes till the man ceased smiling.

For just a second, it seemed the two would come to sudden blows. Then the man recovered his grin.

"Lady Valentine Kurgus, blood descendent of the Patroness of Worthy Battle." He followed these words with a short bow. "Welcome home."

Chapter 16
Never Take Her for a Maid

Dark Michael, known in life as 'The Cold Major' (for all that he was once a general of the quiet land of Saint Demetia), sat upon a simple and civilian stone. Wrapped in heavy solder's coat, defying the warm summer sun.

Beside him perched Professor Shadow Night-Creep, supernatural summoning from the moon. The familiar of devils, advisor to angels, companion of haunts and Fae, consultant to witches, warlocks and all folk enamored of arcane secrets.

Together they stared out over the land of St. Martia. Not from any great height. For the hills marking the northern border of Plutarch did not descend again. They continued as a bare and rocky tableland, far less green than Demetia or Hephestia.

The two watched the Society of St. Benefact marched away, guards upon all sides.

"So much trouble to get them this far," said the cat. "I feared they'd wander Plutarch till they joined the local ghosts."

"What shall pass with the brave band in the land of the Saint of Worthy Battle?" wondered Michael.

"No telling. Martia is a strange place, a strange person. More primitive than Demetia. More rule-bound than Plutarch, more idealist than Hefestia."

"All their lives the folk of Martia train to fight," mused Michael. "And yet to no purpose but decorate one another with scars. Never any grand march of conquest to justify the bother."

"Fortunate for its neighbors."

"True. Though to live forever beside the dangerously mad, must incline the neighboring kingdoms to madness themselves."

"That can be said of any kingdom in the Land of Saints, and every last nation beyond the sea."

"What? That their neighbors are mad?"

"No, that they are mad themselves. And so gaze upon their neighbors as a man holding a bloody knife might stare into a mirror."

Cat and ghost pondered this striking image in silence, gazing upon the high and stony land.

The Society of St. Benefact marched along a dusty path that never quite became proper road. Before and behind, to left and right, walked soldiers of Martia.

These soldiers made indifferent guards. Seemingly content to have the Benefactors keep to the same pace. The soldiery sang as they walked, nonsense words not meant to keep a common step, but a common humor.

One, two, three, four,
Why Infernum go to war?
Stone, mud, storm, flood,
Drown us all in fire and blood.

Five, six, seven, eight,
Who did Martia copulate?
Sword, spear, bow and shield,
Heels high to say you yield.

Jewel whispered to Cedric. "Are we prisoners?"

"No," said the man carrying the short spear of authority. Hypo, as he'd named himself.

"Yes," growled Val.

"We didn't confiscate your weapons," pointed out Hypo.

"Because you hope we'll fight you," sighed Cedric.

"You actually think we *hope* you will lift your staff and burn us with Demetia's flames? While that Silenian fires arrows fast as pigs fart and our glorious Kurgus goes into a battle rage that rips half the patrol to scraps so small a cat wouldn't need to chew first?"

"Yes," declared Cedric. "Exactly. You were hoping exactly that. You are still hoping exactly that."

Hypo looked hopeful. "Well? You going to?"

"No."

"Shit. What a bunch of lambs you bring home, Kurgus."

"They aren't lambs. Just not stupid." *And this isn't home.*

Hypo shrugged, twirled the spear, stopping when it pointed north.

"Guests of Lady Kurgus, we escort you all to her mother in Demos. She'll want to meet her daughter's friends."

"She'll want to order their throats cut in front of me."

"Does that sound like her?"

Val considered. "No, my mistake. She'll cut their throats herself."

"Yes, that's more like."

Jewel peered between her hanging hair, looking from Val to Hypo. Seeking some sign this was exaggeration. But she could not read these folk.

Soldiers of Demetia were different, she thought. When they marched down a road they went in rows and files. Wearing bright clothes, shiny helmets and stony looks. They didn't smile and chat with regular folk. Though they were casual about grabbing kitchen girls' asses. They sure never sang funny songs.

Nine, Ten, Eleven, twelve,
Never born to plow or delve.
Take the blade Martia made,
But never take her for a maid.

Captain Hypo led the song as they marched, conducting with short spear.

Twelve, eleven, ten and nine,
Friar February's come to dine.
Eight, seven, six and five.
Never ask to leave alive.

"I'm of St. Martia," said Val. "I have right to trial."

Hypo waved the matter away.

"Ah, your trial's over and done. While you were in some land called Absentia, wherever that is. Naturally your mother petitioned for your death. Said you'd abandoned your post of Dutiful Daughter. While your uncle argued that you were called by the saints to special purpose. Something about chasing a holy cup? Sounded mad. But we rather like that sort of madness, at least in Martia's bloodline."

"What was decided?"

"Why, that you were insane. And therefore innocent. Logical. Who'd be innocent in this world, excepting the insane?"

"Mother must have been furious."

"She took it calm as a rib takes knife. Granted, later that day she sliced your uncle to strips of sandal leather. Wears him about the house, one hears."

"Shit."

Hypo nodded, threw back his head and sang further.
Two, four, six, eight,
Kiss, fuck, eviscerate.
Three, five, seven, nine,
Lucif pregnate Valentine.

That sung, he turned to Cedric. "It's said Lady Valentine made up half the verses. Bet that surprises you."

"It really does not," said Cedric.

Barnaby stared about as he walked, curious to see a land he'd so long imagined. St. Martia appeared to be a plane of reddish rock and reddish dirt. Not the red of blood. Rather, it seemed Martia was in a state of rust.

Wind and rain sculpted rock scarps to strange shapes, oft resembling man or beast. These stood like giant statues in a garden of the saints. Stunted trees grew where and as they wished; but never close enough to form proper woods. Clearly, the trees preferred to keep a certain distance from one another. Exact as did the soldiers.

The path now followed the rocky edge of a cliff. Beyond and downwards, Barnaby could see the Lethe. A shiver took him as he realized that the land across must be Hefestia. He searched for great flying eggs shooting out beams of light. Seeing nothing but clouds. *Storm approaching*, clearly. He wondered if they'd spend the night camping in the rain.

"You a Demetian?" asked one of the soldiers, keeping pace beside him. A woman Barnaby's age. Not pretty by Demetian standards, which preferred a female to have a roundish solidity. This creature looked constructed of wire, leather and muscle. Hair cropped short, cheekbones sculpted high. Reminiscent of Val. But on her back she carried no harp. Instead, there hung a war hammer, incongruous on such small frame. The hammer glimmered golden as the summer sun.

"I am Demetian," affirmed Barnaby. "From a place we call Mill Town because it has a mill which isn't mine. The mill, I mean not the town. Though I am a miller. Like my da."

He pondered adding that he was also the marquise of a haunted abbey, deciding to skip the whole business. Instead he waved towards the East and South, where mill and town and abbey must lie, impossible as that seemed. "Have you heard of it?"

"Demetia?"

"No, Mill Town."

She laughed. "Is it likely?"

He considered. "Ah, no. 'Course not. Too small, too far away." *Too peaceful,* he thought but did not say.

"I'm Barnaby," he declared. "You?"

She gave a glance to the other soldiers, who ignored them. "Huh, call me Maris. Welcome to St. Martia, Barnaby."

"Thank you, Maris."

They walked on. Barnaby watched Cedric and Val talking with the Martia leader Hypo. Val looked grim. And angry. Her hand kept drifting between the harp at her back, the knife at her side. He watched that hand, till Maris poked him with a finger.

"You Demetians are supposed to be our allies against the Tarchs and Festians. But you don't take the fight seriously."

Barnaby considered. It sounded true. In Mill Town no one worried about borders and foreign lands,

Plutarchian invasions or Hefestia outrages. But who expected them to? What good if they did?

"Well, we take other things seriously."

"Ah? Like what?"

"Serious things." He considered what was serious in the daily life of Mill Town. "Milling. Plowing. Sowing. Harvesting. Ah, we tend plentiful sheep and goats and pigs. And we have summer dances and the spring Holy Service. Then all the folk of Mill Town go to the Jahrmarkt where we see puppet shows and eat cakes baked with berries and sell clothes wove from wool. Sometimes colored pretty though the stockings will itch no matter the color." What else did his people do? "We raise excellent chickens."

Maris shook her head, rejecting these fine things.

"That's all for servants and thralls. Not for a body with pride. How'd you get the scars? Fighting chickens?"

Barnaby touched his face.

"Some astonishing creatures from Nix. Ah, they stepped like dancing shadows with beautiful eyes but their claws... ouch." He raised hands to imitate high curled claws, stepping to show how graceful the creatures moved.

Maris laughed. "Now you're talking. Did you chop them with that bloody great axe?"

Barnaby nodded. "Till they downed me. Ten cats on the one brave mouse." He drew Dragontooth. It looked darker and uglier that it should have by daylight. Catching all the reds of the countryside, returning nothing of the sun.

Maris reached a finger, all but touching the dark metal. Then gave a very Val-like grin.

'Careful now, Master Miller. I might say 'aye'."

"To what?"

"In Martia, when a body offers their blade of choice, it's invitation to bed or battle."

"Oh?"

Barnaby continued holding out the axe. Not that he wanted to battle Maris. She'd mince him for a pie. But bed her? Skinny, but it came easy to picture holding her, kissing her. She'd twine around him like an amorous weasel...

Maris might have been picturing that same amorous winding; for her face reddened. Of a sudden she looked a shy girl, not fearsome warrior. Barnaby took a deep breath, embarrassed. He sheathed Dragontooth.

She took her own breath, began a casual lecture.

"When you challenge me, I choose the type of fight. It goes Claw, Point, Crow or Eagle. 'Claw' is any blade you want. 'Point' is spear, 'Crow' is bow. 'Eagle', you get up someplace high and shove at one another. Which lacks style, in my opinion."

She mused a bit, studying Barnaby as a horse trader might, were he a horse, not a miller.

"Were you challenging me, I'd choose 'Claw'. My pretty hammer against your hideous axe. That's a mating for the ages."

Barnaby laughed, picturing his axe and her golden hammer naked of sheaths, tussling, clanging, panting.

"Suppose you challenge me?" he asked. "What should I choose?"

"Well, you'd be a tomnoddy to raise blade against any St. Martia fighter. Unless millers are trained for more than grinding grain." She pondered his long arms, broad shoulders. "Hmm, you'd have the best chance with 'Eagle'."

"That's where you push one another?"

"Yeah. Not much to it. Get up on a watchtower, shove away till one falls. Excepting sometimes both fall."

Barnaby watched Matilda and Bodkin marching side by side, whispering. They were keeping worried focus on Val and Hypo. Barnaby managed to catch Cedric's eye. The cleric gave wave meant to reassure. Barnaby waved back, not really reassured.

He walked awhile in silence, till Maris spoke, voice thoughtful.

"Those were serious things, too."

"What were?

"Ah, all the ordinary things you described. Tending house. Raising chickens and cows, growing crops and flowers. Enjoying the seasons. Enjoying family. I've daughters, if you can believe." She looked at him in defiance, as if sure he would scoff.

He considered the fierce heat of *experience* she emitted. Found he could easily believe she had children.

Maris scowled at a rock in the path. Kicked it, sending it rolling towards the cliff edge. There it stopped, exactly on the edge.

"When you have children, there's a question that haunts a body in the night. Do you want them to live right, or to live happy?"

Barnaby puzzled. Made no sense to him.

"Isn't it the same?"

She shook head with enough certainty to swing her short bangs about.

"'Right' and 'happy' meet neither oft nor long in the Middle House, Mister Miller. Soon or late, the choice comes. Fight and maybe die, else lose for sure what makes life worth the living."

"That's a hard view."

"Wake up, Demetian. Right now you may be marching towards years of servitude. They might put you on a farm, make you tend their chickens and mill their wheat. Teach you to keep your humble head down when someone important passes."

"Sounds like home."

"Seriously? You've no more backbone than that?"

Barnaby pondered his quantity of backbone. He'd worked dutifully under the cuffing and cursing of his stepmother, Alf and the Squire. Never complaining. Never raising voice nor fist. But now...

Maybe it was the change of lands. Here was not the peaceful fields and woods of Demetia, nor even the somber marshes of Plutarch. He walked in the sunlight of St. Martia, A stone-filled land, stark and red. The air he breathed inspired thoughts long avoided by staring into hearth-flames. Of a sudden, recollections of his old life angered him. *Shamed,* even. Why had he been so meek, retreating into dreams? Infernum, they'd taken Da's mill. Still, as Da would say, -

No. Don't. Da didn't always have the right of it.

This thought shocked him, and saddened him, and yet... he felt a burden lifting. It did Da no disrespect, for Barnaby to walk by his own words...

Or the words of others. Michael, Night-Creep, Bodkin, Val, Cedric... Barnaby had a wise set of teachers, each with their own wisdom. Da would get on fine with them, as one of them. But only as one.

When at last Barnaby answered Maris, it was in tone cautious yet decided.

"I don't like being ordered about. But our Val is wise in matters of fighting. She said to keep peaceful. So here we are walking and talking peaceful. For now."

"That peace is about done. Look at *our* prodigal Kurgus."

Barnaby studied Val, still walking beside Hypo. She smiled now, no longer twitching hand between harp and knife.

"She looks calmer."

"She's been deciding whether to fight or surrender. She just decided."

"What did she decide?" But, of course he knew.

"You got millstones for brains? It's choosing to live that puts worry in the face. Her smile says she decided to fight and die, rather than go home to sweet mother. You'd best do something fast."

He turned puzzled eyes upon Maris.

"If she starts fighting, I'll do the same. So will we all."

Maris yawned. "And you'll lose."

"Well, you're one of the folk we'll fight."

She stamped foot to indicate the dirt beneath them, the rocks around them.

"This is Martia's land. Don't you know her testament to the Middle House?"

"Ah, she's patroness of Worthy Battle."

"Damn right. She shouts what sleeping souls forget. Life is birth, copulation and death. Same for any dog. And all your pleasant Demetian days have the same value as any dog's. Unless you prove to your mirror that you are the master of your life, not life's servant."

"I don't have a mirror."

"You have the Upper House of Saints, boyo. That's your mirror, staring down."

"You sound like Friar Cedric. Which means I don't understand you much."

"Bah! It's no riddle. Decide what in your life is worth losing your life. And then *fight to keep it.*"

She uttered that last with teeth clenched, as though thrusting blade into guts. Barnaby's guts, maybe.

He blinked. Was Maris challenging him? Should he attack first? Give her a kick, draw Dragontooth, chop off her pretty head?

Maris grinned, reading his thoughts. Waiting, watching.

Instead, Barnaby quickened his pace, moving away from her, passing other soldiers who eyed his approach in hope of trouble. He slowed again behind Val and Cedric.

Hypo gave a warning growl. Barnaby ignored it; instead putting hand to Val's shoulder.

"Hey," he whispered. If she drew knife and slashed the hand from arm... well, it would have hurt but not surprised. But she did not. She glanced back, fey smile vanishing. She looked suddenly weary and sad.

Hypo raised his own hand, halting all, soldiers and company alike. That done, he turned to Barnaby.

"Keep to the back and stop troubling your betters," he ordered. No longer the smiling fellow welcoming travelers to Martia. "Go."

And still Barnaby ignored him. Speaking to the bard, meeting her eyes.

"Remember when you said it was wrong for one of us to decide what concerns all?"

Val blinked. Bit lip, and then, just barely, nodded.

"Shit", she whispered. "I hate this."

"Well, *I* was enjoying it," said Hypo. "Until now." Quick as Bodkin withdrawing pocket change, he held a knife. Point just before Barnaby's nose. He opened mouth to deliver some jest before thrust or slice.

Barnaby spoke first.

"Eagle."

"What?" That, from Hypo.

"What?" That, from Val.

"Eagle," said Barnaby. Crossing his arms, peering cross-eyed at the knife. "You're challenging me. I choose 'Eagle'."

Hypo looked outraged.

"Where'd you learn that, you Demetian bumpkin?"

Barnaby wanted to look toward Maris, but feared it'd bring her trouble. So he shrugged, casual as tinker taking tea.

"No point to wandering about unless you're ready to learn new things."

Chapter 17
Not the Moves She Meant

The Society of St. Benefact, holy patron of self-benefaction, gathered in a large wooden barn. Resting in a circle upon a floor of dirt and old straw. A lantern sat in place of proper campfire. Evening sun streamed through the doorway, sending yellow rays through chinks in wall and roof, revealing dust motes floating bright and significant as the stars of the Upper House.

Upon a barrel perched Night-Creep, angel-wing eyes following a mouse as it scuttled through shadows. Dark Michael sat before the lamp, holding hands to it just as he would to a campfire.

Val took a breath of mold and old manure, opening discussion and debate.

"Questions?"

"Sure," said Bodkin. "First, where in Infernum's five thousand and forty-three fornicatoriums are we?"

"Looks like a barn," said Barnaby. "Smells like a barn." He sniffed. "Horse barn."

"Yes, we are indeed in a barn," affirmed Val. "And the barn is in what we, I mean *they*, call a holding. Half farm, half fort. Not many servants. It's just an outpost to keep watch on the border with Hefestia. This particular holding is called Edgestead, if you care."

"I don't," said Jewel. "What I care about is what in the tangle of Sister Gorgodaemon's seventy snakes am I doing here?"

"Blame Barnaby," said Val. "For reasons clear only unto the milling wheels within his head, he challenged Hypo to see who could shove whom off a watchtower. As it happens, Edgestead has a wonderfully high watchtower. You get a breathtaking view of Hefestia, not to mention anyone being shoved off it."

"Saw the tower. Right on the cliff. If he falls, he dies."

"Yes. That's the idea. Tomorrow."

"Well, why in the name of all the saints of the Lower House did he do it?"

The Benefactors stared at Barnaby, who shook his head, and all the millwheels within.

"It just, well, happened. I was talking with Miss Maris and she told me about challenges. Its goes Paw, Cow, ah, Bear then Eagle. Then when I saw Val was going to attack the soldiers- "

"How did you see that?" interrupted Val.

"You wore your scary smile."

"Oh."

"Anyway, I went to stop you and Hypo jumped in and 'Eagle' just jumped out."

"Maris?" asked Cedric.

Barnaby nodded. "One of the soldiers. Walked with me for miles. Told me things about St. Martia. She was awful fierce but nice. I liked her."

"All I saw was you talking to yourself," said Bodkin.

"Which the dear boy does, rather oft," added Matilda.

"She was the lady soldier with the gold hammer," said Barnaby, puzzled. "You didn't see that?"

"Maris, with a gold hammer," said Val. Exchanging looks with Cedric. "Well, of course. Shit, millers tangle these things fast."

"Leave it tangled," said Bodkin. "Vital question is are we free to walk?"

"You can go where you want in the holding. If you try and go out the gate, they'll stop you. Politely, maybe."

"So, we're prisoners? But they haven't separated us. Haven't tied us up nor locked us in. No guard at the door. Haven't even taken our weapons."

Val sighed. "It will sound mad to outsiders. But we-I-mean-they, of St. Martia let servants, thralls, even prisoners carry whatever weapons they want."

"Then how come the servants and thralls don't just rise up and slaughter the sleeping Martia gentry?"

Val laughed. "Oh, they try. Every few years. As far as Martia is concerned, that's carnival time. Understand, the constant chance of attack and revolt reminds us that we are warriors, not weaklings playing at nobility."

"St. Silenus kiss me in the sheets twixt the cheeks," said Matilda. "And I thought Plutarch was scrambled as any land could get." She looked at the open doorway, whispered. "So, we sneak over the wall tonight?"

"No. They'll be watching. Don't think because they like the taste of risk, that they're careless."

"Well, what exactly do they want with us?" asked Cedric. "Besides lure us to battle?"

"They want to take *me* back to my mother in Demos. I doubt they've decided what to do with you lot. Excepting Matilda, you're all Demetians. Allies. They might escort you to the border. Else, set you to work for a few years just to make a point about trespassing."

"I'm not going to cooperate," declared Bodkin. "It's the free life for me, or nothing."

"Nor me," said Jewel. Hand to her spider-pendant. "I've had my fill of tending scullery while some fat farm wife beats me with the laundry stick."

"Then we should have fought on the way here," said Bodkin. "There are far more in this holding. Our odds are worse now."

Val shook her head.

"If Barnaby hadn't stopped me, we'd be cold corpses now."

"But what *good* did it do, except put off the fight?" demanded Matilda. "I'm not going to allow my bold and pretty self to be set to peeling carrots." Val started to reply but Matilda continued. "And don't be going all noble and tell us to let them march you away. We aren't going to allow it. So, it all still comes to a fight."

"If we fight here, now, we die. If Barnaby wins tomorrow, which he has a, a decent chance of doing, then he and the rest of us have a chance to make a break for the border, or talk our way out of this idiot land."

"So you're fine with him going up against some crazy soldier atop a tower?" That, from Jewel.

"I'm fine with it," said Barnaby, before Val could reply. "And I can beat this fellow. We should believe Val when she says it's our best chance."

This was met with silence. Barnaby looked to Shadow Night-Creep upon the barrel. Hoping to hear of some oration that would rescue them.

The cat crouched, tensed, wiggled hind legs, then leapt into the dark. Disappearing from view and council entirely. Out from the dark came the death-cry of a mouse.

Barnaby turned to Michael, who met his gaze, returned a rare smile; and said... nothing. Barnaby sighed, giving up hope his unnatural counselors would offer some mad and clever solution.

Cedric broke the silence.

"I agree, Barnaby's brave act has given us time to consider options, awaiting better odds. And that it brought us to the border is also to our gain. We might yet escape into Hefestia."

"That's down a cliff you need rope to descend. Then across a river needing prayers to swim," said Val. "While archers shoot arrows from the cliff edge. Not easy. And once across the Lethe, we deal with being taken prisoner by suspicious Hefestian patrols."

"What if I beat Hypo tomorrow?" asked Barnaby.

"Nothing," said Val. "What did you expect? That they'd declare us free guests of the land?"

"Would be nice."

"Nice people don't have customs about shoving each other from towers."

"Don't want to, anyway," said Barnaby. "So, what if I tell Hypo I changed my mind?"

"He'll hamstring you, drag you screaming to the cliff, piss on you then shove you over."

"Oh."

When Cedric spoke next, he kept voice low.

"I am not knowledgeable about this land, But I know much of Hefestia. With Miss Jewel's help, there *might* be an oration to aid us."

Val shook head. "If you attempt spells to harm Hypo or strengthen Barnaby, they'll know. And be very insulted."

"But will they know or care about a change of weather?"

"Huh. Not that I can see."

Cedric nodded. He stood, stretched, then held hand down to Jewel. She stared surprised. Then reached, allowing him to help her rise.

"Let us find a quiet corner and consider your book of orations to Sister Hecatatia."

The Benefactors watched them take a candle to a far corner.

Next Bodkin rose. "Well, if we aren't prisoners, then I'm going to stroll about. Make friendly with folk, eye the weak points of the walls. Anyone want to accompany me?"

"I'll come," declared Matilda. "But you'd best keep from picking pockets."

"Fine. Want your comb back?"

"What? St. Charon paddle your behind, that was my ma's. Return it forthwith."

The two stepped into the evening light, arguing the concepts of property, the contents of pockets. Val rose next. She looked down at Barnaby, shaking her head for sad conclusions. Followed the shake with a thoughtful kick.

"Ow," he complained.

"You come with me. I'm going to show you the moves Hypo expects will throw a *normal* miller down to the Lower House."

They departed, leaving Dark Michael to sit before the lamp alone. Muffled in coat and shadow, hands out, seeking what warmth it had to give.

Val and Barnaby found a storage room in back of the barn. Pushing aside rubbish, clearing a space. Taking stand in this arena, Val put hands to hips. Barnaby could only half see her by what light entered a narrow window.

"This is all the space you'll have on the tower. And there are no railings. You afraid of heights?"

"I get up atop the mill to fix the vanes. And the millhouse to fix the slates, and even the Squire's manse to clean the chimneys in the spring."

"While someone tries to push you off?"

"Ah, no. Though Alf put grease on the tiles once. Well, twice. And cut half through the top rung of the ladder, though Mother angered for the waste of a good ladder. Also once he caught my foot in a snare. It was clever how he hid the rope in a bird nest. Also, once-"

"Right, that's all perfectly awful but put it aside and step in."

Barnaby walked into the conceptual arena. Staring down at the woman before him, as she stared up at *him*.

"First off, you've got more weight, more strength and longer arms than Hypo."

"Sounds near to unfair of me."

"Yes, but smart bets are still on Hypo. He has training. Has your soldier-ghost given any lessons about fighting with hands and feet?"

"Some. Don't breathe fast, don't tense up. Strike with a straight wrist. Quick low kicks are best. Use the other fellow's move to get him off balance. Don't wear lavender."

"All good except why the saint's shits should you not wear lavender?"

"Just joking. Made that up."

"*You* made a joke? I don't remember you ever making a joke."

He shrugged to say *what of it?* She frowned to say, *it puzzled*.

She began moving left along the square, still facing him. He stepped to the right, still facing her.

"Now, two fighters oft circle so. They don't generally stand still because going from move to move is a bit faster than going from a still position to moving."

Barnaby stopped his sideways stepping.

She grinned.

"Putting it to the test?"

"No, I'm waiting for you to come closer."

"To kick, punch or grab?"

"None of those."

"What, then?"

"Come closer and see."

She sidestepped closer, wary.

"You know, since we crossed the border you've been acting very-"

Barnaby reached, putting hands to Val's shoulders, drawing her yet closer.

"-very strange lately," she continued. Staring up to his face in the half-light.

He bent down, kissed her shadowed lips. Her hands grabbed his shoulders. He waited for her to shove him away, else flip him upon his head.

Instead, she pulled herself against him, standing on tiptoe to place the kiss more on even footing. Adjusted so, the kiss continued for some time. She felt him shaking; same as he felt her shake.

Finally, she pulled back, panting as a good fighter shouldn't. Then crossed arms.

"That is, is not what I wanted to, to show you."

"But it's what I wanted to show you."

"Show me, show me what?"

"That I think you are pretty. That I think you are amazing. That I want to undress you. Ah, I'd put you on a chimney mantel as a wonder for folk to admire. Excepting I'd rather be holding you."

She stared; mouth open to speak, finding it empty of reply.

This silence did not dismay Barnaby. He stepped close again, ran a finger across her cheek. Making her shiver. She grasped the hand; not pushing it away, but holding it tight.

"Yes, definitely you very are, are acting today strange," she declared. Then stepped closer still, thumping his armored chest with a ladylike fist. "Fine. Fine. Armor will tire you fast. Best take it off."

He nodded. Began undoing the leather from his chest and arms. Nervous fingers fumbling at the fastenings. Armor gone, he thought it best to remove breeches as well. Letting it all drop to the floor.

"Your turn," he told her.

She stared at him, looking up and down. Not speaking, neither to argue nor agree.

He turned deliberately away, looking about. The storage room had plentiful straw, and convenient piles of old horse blankets. He selected the cleaner blankets, laying them atop straw for a rough bed. Taking his time. Only when done, did he turn back to Val.

She now stood naked in the center of the conceptual fighting square. Hands refusing to cover herself. Rather, she held clenched fists to either side. *Ready to fight*, said her stance.

He returned to stand before her. Looking down while she stared up. Both trembling. At last he reached behind her back, behind her knees, lifting her easy as an armful of pretty air. Cradling her thus awhile. She studied him, then gave study up. Snuggled close as cat in lap, growling into his chest.

"You'd best understand this is *not* how a death-fight atop a watchtower shall go."

He bent head, giving quick kiss. She returned it. That done, he carried her to the makeshift bed, laid her down. Stood looking awhile upon her shadowed body. Bending low, he breathed her breath, she breathed his. At last, he whispered to her upturned face.

"Maris told me that to fight, you have to decide what makes it worth the fight."

That explained, that decided, he laid himself down beside her.

The harp beside Val's pack began to play. At first a low shy melody, touching, testing notes and quick themes; gradually repeating, merging themes, rising towards a crescendo that at last shouted through the barn.

"What's that?" asked Barnaby, breath ragged.

"It's, ah, it's Thelxipea," replied Val. "Ignore her. Don't stop, don't stop."

"Won't."

"Good, good."

Cedric and Jewel sat by themselves, leafing pages of her forbidden book of orations in the light of a candle. Searching for references to cloud and fog, mist and wind. When the harp began to play from the dark of the barn, they stopped. Jewel looked at Cedric, who stared puzzled into the shadows.

"What in the world?" he wondered.

"Val's harp," explained Jewel. "Thelx-whatever. She's happy."

"Why in the name of St. Taliesin would a harp be happy?"

Dimwit, thought Jewel. She put hand to spider pendant, bending head to consult with it.

Cedric observed, puzzled, till the two reached conclusion. Then Jewel reached, snuffing the candle.

"What are you doing?" asked the dimwit in the dark.

"Taking off my dress. And don't you dare ask why, cleric, or I set Perry to bind you tight as your vows of chastity."

"I would never take any such fool vow."

"Excellent."

Cedric sat silent till she moved, settling herself into his lap as queen to throne.

At which settling, Cedric put away the book, put away wondering; and put arms about the girl. Feeling, testing, finding a different Jewel. No more hard eyes and sour silence; just this being of softness, of warmth.

Across the barn, the harp strummed, thrummed, hummed in a quickly rising fugue approaching completion.

"You seriously want me?" Cedric asked. "I'm ten years older and dull as a tome on Stygian optics."

Jewel's answer came firm, nothing soft nor weak.

"If I want you, will you have me?"

"Absolutely."

"Then shut up and have me."

Bodkin and Matilda wandered Edgestead. Studying the ramparts, eyeing possible weak points. Noting a useful coil of rope beside a well. Stopping at a smithery where Matilda chatted with an apprentice upon sword crafting. No one asked their business. None shouted for them to cease spying, return to the barn.

But both noted the wary looks, the ready stances, how every hand checked the pommel of knife or sword. Each proper citizen of Martia was ready to smile and chat; and equally ready to draw blade and fight.

Pirate tavern, whispered Old Mercutio.

"Exactly," agreed Bodkin.

"Exactly what?" inquired Matilda.

"Ah, this holding. It's like one of the nastier taverns by the docks of St. Parvati. Everyone going about their business pleasant as can be. But eyes watching, ears twitching, ready for knives to fly."

"I'd wager all St. Martia follows the same," agreed Matilda. "Explains our mad bard-girl nicely."

They passed a barracks, a granary, a goat pen. Following wind-wafting dinner scents till they came to a great fire pit where a pig roasted. There at table beneath evening stars sat Hypo with fellow soldiers. Bodkin and Matilda hesitated, till he waved for them to come join the feast.

They did. A servant promptly brought mugs of ale, plates of pork. This servant being a middle-aged woman in plain dress who carried no weapon but the carving knife. The woman kept silent, eyes upon her work.

Matilda pictured her suddenly shouting *'freedom!'* And cutting the nearest Martia throat. Perhaps as signal for other servants to do the same.

Studying the faces at the table, she understood that such an act would not take a single soul by surprise.

Bodkin sipped ale, observing Hypo. He laughed and chatted, not the picture of a man expecting death tomorrow. Was that confidence? Or just indifference to death? Probably the first. Barnaby looked a fighter, but down deep he was just a village boy carrying armor, axe and smile. He'd been tricked into that challenge by some chit of St. Martia.

Always a girl behind these things, chuckled Old Mercutio.

"Is there a soldier named Maris about?" asked Bodkin.

Hypo nodded. "She's beneath your feet."

Bodkin did not look down. Matilda did. Hypo laughed, then explained.

"Maris is just a pet name for Sainted lady Martia. And her land, her air, her rocks, her folk."

"Ah. Carries a golden hammer?"

"In icons and statues. Absurd. A gold hammer would be heavier than iron and softer than lead. But saints shall do as a saint will do. Now, regale the table of your journeying with our Kurgus."

Bodkin described the wild night running through the streets of Persephone. The table laughed at the theft of the Lady Alexandria's horse.

"Kurgus actually thinks she's a bard?" wondered Hypo. "That's mad, even for one of her blood."

"Does the cup come from the Upper House?" asked someone. "Perhaps the saints have some mission for Valentine Kurgus."

Bodkin noted there were no truly old at the table. Did Martia warriors die upon graying? Else kept to corners, ashamed to have survived all their battles. But a man who seemed eldest present, now spoke.

"Long ago I heard of *that* cup. 'Tis said to be from a place as far above the Upper House, as the Upper House lies above us."

"Nonsense," scoffed Hypo. "All nations know there are three Houses. Upper, Middle, and Lower. Nothing higher, nor lower."

The two men eyed one another. The table waited eagerly for challenge. None came. The older man merely smiled to dismiss the argument. Disappointed silence followed, till Matilda launched a blood-filled description of the mad hermitess Beatrice and her insane followers, the battle by the Lethe, the attack of the tentacled fiends, the dreadful murder of her mules.

"Sounds exactly like those Tarchs," said a soldier down-table. "Evil fools who don't understand life. Only death."

"They take an overlong view," declared Bodkin, setting down his mug. "While you folk live entirely for the moment. Clear to see who must be the wiser."

He stood. Matilda following suit. Bidding all good night, leaving the folk at the table frowning, unsure the boy's observation slighted the wisdom of St. Martia.

The two returned to the barn. Stopping at the door, surprised to hear Val's harp playing far within the dark. Peering in, they no longer spied the candle of the studious cleric and witch. Michael had vanished into the night; Shadow-Creep disappeared to hunt mice, else visit the seven queens of the moon.

"Ah," decided Matilda. "By the excited melody of that there harp, I'm guessing miller and bard are not practicing arts to be defined as martial."

"Yeah. And by the sounds from our cleric and witch's darkened study corner, they have given over researching prayers to the saints. Excepting perhaps Bridget, patroness of proper copulation."

The two relit the lantern, settled in its light as they would a campfire, wrapping themselves in their separate blankets. Properly placed to keep watch upon the open door. Still, ears and thoughts kept turning toward the dark of the barn, the muffled noises of appreciation, exhalation and exertion.

Val's harp began a new, more measured melody. Accompanied by further rustlings and whispers of prayer best relegated to Saint Bridget.

"That is all so entirely not to any purpose for the benefit of the Benefactors," complained Bodkin.

"Truly," said Matilda, "yet it makes a heart bright as sunrise behind church window to see, well, *hear* them finally getting to what matters to a body's soul."

"You aren't about to go frisking for *my* body, are you, Miss Silenian?"

She laughed. "Might. When said body's got hairs where needed."

"Your loss, girl. Stored in my head is all the fleshly wisdom of the ages."

"To be sure," yawned Matilda. Wrapping herself tighter, closing eyes tighter. "Keep practicing that wisdom a few more years. Then, come find me."

Chapter 18
She Gets in Your Head

Matilda:

Never been to St. Silvanus, where folk have eyes like mine, hooves like mine, hearts like to mine. Was born in Pomona, king's seat of St. Demetia. Pleasant old lady of a city, full of brick streets for a kid to stamp and run upon, with plentiful flower gardens setting eyes and nose twitching for the wonder. Quite like to Persephone, excepting without that stain of dark past, shadow of dark present.

It were my parents as kept memory and custom of the forests of Silvanus. Taught me to shoot a bow, kick a boy, gather herbs. Then it was *off you go now, girl.*

Sounds a mite rough, but they were thinking in Silvanian. In that grand eastern wood, when a child grows tall enough to pick their own spring apple blossoms, why you send 'em off through the trees to find their own grass to stamp. In a year or three the happy thing wanders back with kids and tales. Then comes a grand party beneath the woods, all the relatives singing and dancing, with maybe Sainted Silvanus himself fetching the communion wine.

My folks saw all the world as forest, with trees or without. Gave me the seven blessings and off I went, west and north, looking for fun and trouble. Finding both, oft enough.

Fun or not, one can't just wander through towns as one would trees. I needed purpose, occupation. Upon quite sober and mature reflection, I decided to become... *an assassin.*

Tavern tales are stuffed with the creatures. Call themselves the *Friends of Friar February*, a nicely sinister name when you recollect February is St. Plutarch's reaping monk. Fascinating work, the *friends* do. Meet in crypts and masked balls, learn to crawl on ceilings and undo locks with just a curly hair from their crotch. Why, your proper assassin gets paid in diamonds to scale a castle wall, dance past guards, slip poison into a king's cup and then vanish 'poof' up the chimney.

Oh, and I chose a glorious nom-de-guerre for my future career. An assassin has to call her pretty self something that exemplifies her cunning, her deadly sense of style. Just the right name came to me daydreaming, walking from Pomona, going nowhere in particular.

Noctilucatilda.

Tasted wonderful to the tongue. *Noctilucatilda!* Ware thee, kings and bankers and bishops and pirate lords. *Noctilucatilda* is in the shadows. Who's that under the bed? *Noctilucatilda.* Who's that in the closet? Could it be the shadow lady Noctilucatilda? Ha! Closet's empty. I'm behind you holding my dagger.

I just needed to join my fellow assassins, and I'd be set. But how to find such happy folk? Asking the whereabouts of a secret tribe of killers seemed tomnoddy as wandering the night woods calling for wolves and witches. Best I could do was keep eyes peeled, ears pricked for *mysterious strangers*. For sure they'd lurk in tavern corners, faces shadowed, smiling with professional pride whenever someone important turned green, fell dead.

Which led me to be wearing an apron in a tavern on the shadowed side of Persephone. Pouring beer, ale, wine. Seeking dark mystery in grumbling tradesmen, blue-nosed clerics, staggering tipplers. Bah! Dull as counting flies on a plow horse's ass.

Noctilucatilda started putting pepper into the mugs of customers overfond of pinching a girl's person. Silly old sots never noticed. If it'd been poison and they'd been kings, why, they'd have turned green and tumbled from their thrones. And serve them right.

I decided to move on from Persephone; maybe south to the Spice Isles where folk are said to be more honestly unlawful. Oh, but then the tavern door opened and in came the muddy and bloody, mysterious and delirious magic and tragic folk of the Society of Glorious and Uproarious St. Benefact.

Not assassins, but proud treasure hunters. Excellent; that suited my sensible sensibilities fine. Noctilucatilda wasn't a bit downhearted. These new folk had a map and a mission, plus a magic cat and a glowering ghost. Not to mention all kinds of tangles of flirtation and argumentation with one another, and with the law and even with the saints if you can believe. They weren't your usual folk at all. Excellent, neither am I. I jumped right in.

So came the morning in St. Martia when I woke to Mister Hypo shouting loud 'shine and rise' at the door of the barn.

I disliked the fellow. Always cheery but keeping eye to the distance twixt your throat and his knife. Seems all the folk of Martia think so. Even our bard.

He had a servant lady put down some baskets of food for breakfast. Bread and sausage, mostly. No coffee, curse it. But also some water and cloths for a washup, which would be twice useful for four of us six Benefactors.

I wondered if Miss Bard would emerge all sulky, shaming and blaming Mister Barnaby for seducing a poor unmade maid? Or maybe go all dewy-eyed, holding his hand, calling him her sweet honey millerman. Both seemed unlikely. But unlikely happens all through the Middle House, or where'd be the fun?

It was Mister Friar Father Reverent Cleric Cedric and his bonny bedmate Miss Farm-witch Jewel who first emerged from the amorous dark of the barn.

Dressed, and looking business-like as bankers on a bench. Not a paintbrush touch of embarrassed blush upon either, which pleased and yet disappointed this girl a tad. I so wanted to get both aside and ask questions pertinent and impertinent. But the two were deep into academic discussion of orations, the studious things.

First they did was walk to the barn door, gaze out.

"Fog," declared Cedric; voice satisfied as a fellow stating 'gold' after examination of his pocket pennies.

"St. Lucif take me upside down but that's a damned heavy fog," agreed Jewel. And then did the sweet dear thing let her hand wander into his. Gave me a glow to see.

I hadn't paid a farthing of attention to the weather; but now I noted how beyond the barn door, the air'd gone thick and gray. Seems a storm cloud had decided to rest upon St. Martia awhile. Bit ominous, that.

Cedric:

In seminary, Beatrice and I seemed two beings formed of one clay. Devout, studious, greedy for the secrets of the saints. We worried and quarreled over flesh and faith, same as our fellow students, same as our teachers. Beatrice would seek my touch by night; and then on the morrow weep for her weak flesh, my tempting words. Drove me mad; and eventually drove us apart. In hindsight, we only appeared of similar soul. Beatrice Lucia sought purity. I sought truth. And when is truth ever pure?

Came the day I stood in a gaol cell, seeing Jewel of Stonecroft scowling behind her own bars. In her I saw nothing in common with my academic self. Just a farm girl, a mutterer of dark prayers to the shadows of the Lower House.

But by the hour of our escape I knew her for a soul of fire, determined to defy authority. Whether of oafish farmers, dark witches, holy Questioners or the Upper House of Saints itself.

Did she look into my cell and see a spark of her own defiant flame? If so, it shall make my mirror proud.

The flying mechanisms of Hefestia are miracles. Not of the saints, but of the human mind. As the saints themselves are miracles sprung from human thought.

Would you argue it? Excellent. Do so now. Wax upon the glories of the House of Saints; its shining denizens and all their mysteries. Expound their separate testaments with reference to proofs ontological, epistemological and historical.

Then ask the enlightened air: did your words just prove the saints, or merely construct the saints? An honest mind must admit the second.

The Hephaestion *directables*, as they are called, are wondrous flying ships; but large and brittle, moving slow as oxen-cart trudging uphill. Vulnerable to a well-aimed trebuchet or ballista. Therefore, the folk of St. Martia place throwing machines along the cliff-edge of their eastern border. Keeping the *directables* deep within Hefestia... excepting when chance weather allows them to swim the border. Then they glide like great hollow whales through storm or mist, detected only by a faint and ominous hum.

After our lovemaking, Jewel and I composed ourselves, reciting formal orations to Sister Hecatatia to bring fog upon Edgestead. We hoped this might delay Barnaby's brave but foolish challenge. It might even bring the distraction of Hephaestion incursion. Allowing us a chance of escape.

Of course, it did not go so easily as that.

In the morning, there came no talk from Hypo of delaying breakfast nor death-challenge. We finished the first, prepared for the second.

Barnaby and Val emerged from out their love nest of a storage room; straw in their hair, sleep in their eyes. He looked grim; as did she. Well, the world's wisdom said they were about to part. Hard wisdom, when they'd only just united.

Granted, the threat of parting hung over us all. But I made no pledge of love to Jewel of Stonecroft, kitchen girl, novice of St. Hecatatia, member of the absurd Society of St. Benefact. Nor did she make least expression of love to me. In truth, we scarce knew one another. We only wished for time to know one another, to forge a common bond that concourse only symbolized.

Perhaps the one night was all we'd share. And that only because she'd the courage to offer; I, the need to accept.

And so on a mist-wrapped dawn the Society of St. Benefact awoke, granting solemn 'good morning' each to each. Making no jests on how any passed the night. We knew ourselves on a knife edge twixt death and life. The white fog, the deadly cliff made mere theatre backdrop; the overwrought metaphor of some antique miracle play.

Val:

After seeing the fog Cedric and Jewel had brought about, I instructed all to bring their packs as we left the barn. With luck, we were leaving this place.

We stood apart from the folk of Martia gathering 'neath the watchtower. Bodkin approached, whispered close.

"Why not fight now, before Barnaby gets himself killed?"

"Because we'd lose," I replied. "But he has a, a decent chance of winning. Then we all go on towards Demos. That gives us days and miles to watch for a chance where fighting has a chance."

He wanted to argue. The little thief has the soul of an ancient reprobate; but he's loyal to our miller. I reminded myself to ask him why, someday. Not that day.

I tapped Barnaby on the shoulder, led him to the foot of the watchtower. Others already stood near, grumbling how the fog meant there'd be no clear sight of his body falling to the ground.

We watched Hypo climb first. The man whistled as he went, waving in cheer down to us all before vanishing into the mist.

"Won't he kick my face as I reach the top?"

"No. Fighting can't begin until the bell is sounded. You'll have time to climb, take your position. Remember, don't get overclose to the edge. There's no safety in corners up there."

He grinned. "Is anywhere safe in St. Martia?"

The answer was *no*. But I didn't want to spend last words discussing the land of my idiot birth. Infernum unto Infernum, I'd be fine never hearing of it again.

"You can do this," I told him.

"I can," he agreed. His confidence surprised me, same as it'd done last night. Clearly, he was feeling the aura of the saint. That crazy bitch Martia gets in your head, turns heart beat to war drum. Makes you want to fight and fornicate, wrestle bears, dance with swords. Fun things that get you killed.

"Sure you can," I said, clapping him on the back like we were old drinking buddies.

We exchanged a look that turned of a sudden to shared laughter. Why? Part shyness, to see each other by light, remembering last night's naked touch, raw smell, salty taste. And we laughed for the sorrow that we might not ever so touch and taste of one another again. Ever. And last, for sure, we laughed for the damned dance we saw we'd been set by the saints since our first meeting.

When Barnaby spoke, his voice came wry and sad, nostalgic as some ancient miller in a rocking chair recalling harvests long passed.

"Come a ways from St. Herm's font, we have."

At his words, the memory of our meeting struck me, clear as any vision of the Cup. I saw Herm's wry stone grin again, smelled Demetia's green fields. Heard Destrier's bells tinkling light and happy, water from the font trickling while a butterfly circled Barnaby, fascinated with the wonders within his head.

The total hit me in the gut, and I put fist to mouth, biting hard. No more words, no more words. He saw, and turned away. Up he went, up and up, out of sight into the mist. Giving no last look behind.

Chapter 19
The View from the Back of a Dragon

Mist turned the rungs slippery. Barnaby climbed slowly, not wanting to fall before ever seeing the top. Soon reaching a point where end and beginning were equally lost in bright mist. And there he paused. Appreciating how he perched in as unlikely a place as any miller had ever found themselves. On a ladder in a glowing cloud twixt earth and sky... quite interesting, if shadowed by mad and bloody purpose.

"I don't want to push anyone to their death," he told the fog. "Makes me almost a murderer."

"No, it does not," argued a voice. "Makes you a fighter."

"That you, Mr. Hypo?"

"No one but me and Friar February up here, and he's quiet as his master."

Barnaby sighed; continued climbing. Came to the ladder's end, where Hypo leaned over, observing his progress. Smiling, of course.

"I worried you'd got lost climbing in the fog."

"How shall I be getting lost?"

"Ah, that was jest."

"Oh." Barnaby hesitated. "Would you mind backing away a bit?"

"Not at all." Hypo stepped away, Barnaby completed the climb. Clambered upon a square of wooden boards lacking railing. This square perched in a sea of white mist glowing with the dawn. Hypo now sat at the far end.

"Rest a bit," he suggested.

It seemed rude to refuse. Barnaby sat. They contemplated one another.

"You aren't any kind of soldier," decided Hypo.

"No sir, I am not. I'm a miller, actually."

"Oh? Water or wind?"

The question delighted Barnaby. "Wind, as it happens. We don't have river enough in East Demetia. But I've heard of water mills on the Lethe. Like to see those, I would."

Hypo laughed. "I'd wish that you do someday. But the wish would put a halt to the things I'm looking forward to seeing myself."

Barnaby nodded. "Understood. What things were you wanting to see?"

Hypo fingered his chin.

"A dragon," he decided.

Barnaby laughed. "Me too! The fiery red ones of the mountains? Or the green worms of the southern sea?"

Hypo prepared to answer, when from beyond the mist tolled a leaden bell, sounding slow and solemn as funeral march. The signal to *begin*. The man sighed, rose to his feet.

"And now to our work, Mister Miller."

Barnaby jumped up. Feeling sick to his stomach. Hypo stood with feet spread even, hands to side, palms open. Still smiling pleasantly. He took a casual step to the side, as though to get a better view of Barnaby.

Moving comes quicker when you are already moving. So Val instructed last night. And they'd proven it true, though the motions had not been those of fighting. Barnaby stepped to the side, matching Hypo's pace.

Think on her, he told himself. *Live to get back to her. Live for her mad smile. The way her brows rise when you say something foolish. The way she bites lip playing the harp. That sound she gave like a petted cat when you ran your hand down her stomach...*

Of a sudden Hypo pivoted, kicking a heel towards Barnaby's knee. Barnaby stepped, not backwards nor to the side, but closer in. Punching fist up into Hypo's face.

The man staggered back surprised, near going over the edge. Barnaby waited till Hypo regained his balance.

Should have rushed him then, he told himself.

But he would have fallen, he replied.

Yes. Think on her. Think on her. Think on her.

I don't want to kill this man.

"She only told me the half," complained Barnaby. "Same as Mr. Quiet."

Hypo reached hand to lip; the hand came away bloody. "Who, what?"

"Maris."

"Maris?"

Barnaby began to explain, but Hypo stepped forwards, making a feint of a fist strike. Barnaby circled, kicking low. Hypo blocked with his own kick, nearly knocking the leg out from under Barnaby. His turn to stagger back, balancing upon the edge.

Hypo leaped forwards as Barnaby had not.

Live, he thought, and fell to the floor, rolling forwards. Hypo tripped, flipping over Barnaby and rolled beyond the edge of the platform -

-catching onto it with flailing hands. Barnaby stood, panting, watching. His first thought: *help him up*. His second thought: *stamp on his hands*.

Hypo pulled himself upwards, getting his arms to rest on the platform. And there he hung, looking up at Barnaby.

"Well, that was humiliating."

"Sorry," said Barnaby.

"This is where you kick me and end the fight, if you wondered. While I settle for grabbing your foot, taking you with me to Infernum's finest fornicatoriums."

"I don't want to make you fall," said Barnaby. "Nor fall myself."

"You're going to let me rest, then get up and go another round?"

"Does sound foolish, doesn't it?"

"It sounds strange," said the man. They rested silent, contemplating the strangeness. "What were you saying about Maris?"

"That she didn't say anything about deciding to kill. She talked about deciding to live."

"Doesn't need to be said. Can't blame you for not noticing but I *was* trying to kill you."

"Yes, but I was trying to live. What is that?"

"Living?"

"No, the thing in the fog coming up behind you. Must be bigger than a house." Barnaby's eyes grew round. "Oh, you don't think it could be a dragon?"

"Well, for the love of Lucif's mother's dog. Should have expected them."

"Who? Dragons?"

Before Hypo could answer, light blazed through the mist. The tower shook. Barnaby struggled to stay upright, but the tower did not. It tottered, then tilted. Hypo scrabbled to hold on, then slid away, disappearing into the mist. Barnaby tumbling after him.

With a crash, the watchtower toppled.

I didn't kill him, thought Barnaby, tumbling through the fog. *Should I have? Of course. But then the dragon would still have killed me. Still, I'm glad I didn't.*

He lay on his back, considering it all. Then wondered what exactly he lay on, and when had he come to lay upon it? Not the ground. Something more comfortable. Not feather-bed comfortable; but equal to a good cot. He stared at the white sky, the white air, then sat up to study the gray cloth construction upon which he sat.

About him lay pieces of the tower, fragments still smoldering. Not far away, Hypo pushed aside boards, struggling to stand.

"Where are we?" asked Barnaby.

"On top of it."

"Of the dragon?" Barnaby gaped, astonished and delighted.

"No, you cow-manure-for-brains farm bumpkin Demetian dimwit, we're on top of the Hefestian *directable* that just burned down the watchtower. Stand up."

Barnaby stood, annoyed he couldn't have more time to appreciate the wonder of riding such a fabled mechanicalism. Hypo limped to a heavy piece of wood. Hefted it for a club.

"Find something to fight with," he ordered.

Barnaby picked up a board still burning on one end. Prepared his stance for Hypo's attack, which didn't come. Instead, the man turned, walking carefully into the mist.

"Step on the raised areas," he instructed. "Those are struts. Avoid putting weight on the cloth. Might fall through."

Barnaby hesitated, looking behind. Far in the mist, just visible, sat the dark form of a cat. Beside it stood the dark silhouette of a man. Well, his teachers were observing their student. Barnaby waved to them, wondering what they thought.

"You coming?" called Hypo.

"Yes."

Barnaby followed carefully, staring about. They moved along the spine of a long construction of stiff cloth, curving downwards left and right. Through his feet he felt it vibrate. Almost a living thing, swimming through the air.

"They keep to a chamber on the bottom," explained Hypo. "With a tunnel that leads up here so they can do repairs. They'll show up soon to clear the rubble before anything catches fire. They won't be expecting us, I hope."

Barnaby understood. '*They*' must be Hefestians.

"Edgestead has two arbalests which can take these things down. We have to get off before the ship turns tail to Hefestia."

At which words, the ship shook; fires blazed in the lower distance where the holding of Edgestead must lay. Hypo stared into the fog, growling.

"Correction, it won't turn tail because it just destroyed both arbalests. Shit. Now they're going to take their time setting fire to Edgestead and everyone in it. This is becoming a difficult day."

Barnaby considered words of sympathy; dismissed them.

"Here it is," said Hypo, stopping at a round metal plate set into the construction. "Hinges are on this side, so when they pop up they'll be facing that way. We crouch low behind in the fog, wait for them to stand. Then we hit them."

At which instruction, Barnaby began to laugh. Laughing till he shook. He felt weary past standing, dizzy with the mad turns of a mad land ruled by mad winds.

"Are you going to fight, miller?" asked Hypo. "I need to know now."

"Aren't we supposed to be fighting each other?"

"Forget that game. We're atop a Hefestian war machine that attacked us both. Now they're going to slaughter all they can in Edgestead. Including your friends."

"Oh." Barnaby sighed, put away the weighing of life and death. "Right. Understood. Kill or be killed."

"Damn right and welcome to blessed Martia's warm and lively bed," said Hypo. Then whispered. "Quiet. Here they come."

The hinges of the metal plate creaked, the round portal rose. A leather-helmeted head rose from the hole, like a mole popping up from its burrow.

This personage clambered up and out. Followed by a second. Hypo did not hesitate; he stepped forwards, clubbing the second hard in the back of the head.

The man fell, but not silently. The other Hefestian turned at thump, at gasp. For a moment Barnaby recoiled to meet a face lacking humanity. Bulbous frog-like eyes stared at him, while a gloved hand reached to a belt, seeking a tool. A weapon, surely.

Barnaby leaped forwards, swinging the still smoldering board, sparks flying in the air.

The Hefestian jumped backwards, cursing. Only to trip upon debris. He shouted, went rolling down the sloping side of the *directable,* vanishing into the fog.

"Good work," said Hypo.

"His eyes."

"Hefestian goggles. No idea why they wear them. Fashion, one supposes."

Hypo bent down to the remaining Hefestian, removed a knife from the belt. Then with a kick, sent the man rolling into the mist.

Barnaby closed his eyes to steady himself. Opened them when there came the same bright flash, the crackle and boom of fire that took the tower.

This time came screams from the distant ground. Orange glows of fire appeared, where the Hefestian bolt must have set a building of Edgestead ablaze.

"There's usually a crew of six," shouted Hypo. "Two down. Four to go. Ready?"

Barnaby wanted to ask '*ready for what*'? But the answer was obvious. Descend the tunnel, take the ship before it slaughtered all the holding. Fight more strangers he'd rather talk to. Asking them about their strange eyewear, what it was like to fly the night sky...

"Ready," said Barnaby. Paused, then added. "For the patroness of Worthy Battle."

Hypo grinned.

"Just a few more scars and you'll make a soldier worthy of Martia's smile. Her bed too, maybe."

That said, he climbed down into the portal. Barnaby followed, privately thinking he didn't want any more scars.

Chapter 20
To Find, or Just to Seek?

"We need to get closer," said Val, peering up at the fog-shadow of the *directable*.

"Closer? We need to get the Lucif's flaming lips away," said Jewel.

"Why closer?" asked Bodkin.

Cedric explained. "We wish to steal that airship."

Bodkin's eyes grew wide, voice excited.

"Steal a war machine twenty feet in the air that shoots fire? Great idea. Let's get closer."

The crowd had fled the vicinity of the fallen watchtower. Not in panicked rout, but as organized groups with different tasks. Some carried away the wounded; others formed bucket lines to put out the fires cast by the Hefestian machine. Some with bows took defensive positions behind buildings and rubble, firing defiant but ineffective arrows up to the fog.

"What about Mister Barnaby?" asked Matilda.

"He's dead, child," said Cedric. Voice hoarse. "The upper half of the tower fell over the cliff."

"Don't believe it," scoffed Bodkin. "Our miller has the luck of all the saints, including a wink from Lucif and a pat on the ass from February."

"Saints' luck leaves you when you need it most," said Val. "But... bring his axe and pack. Just in case."

They hurried towards the fire, the remains of the watchtower. The barn where they'd spent the night now blazed, adding smoke to fog. The *directable* hummed half-seen, some twenty feet above.

"So what's our plan, Bodkin?" asked Val. "How do we steal that thing?"

Bodkin took breath.

"Jewel ties her spider pedant to an arrow. Matilda shoots it into the air-machine. The spider fixes web to the ship, then jumps back down to us. Then we do it over hmm, fifty times. Till we have enough thread to pull the air ship low. Then we climb aboard free and easy as St. Priapus with the novices."

This plan would have been met with silence, excepting the shouts, sounds of burning buildings, varied bells ringing, the intermittent screams.

"That is the most puddinghead idea, ever." This, from Jewel.

"Don't have any fifty arrows." That, from Matilda.

"We can't pull that thing down on spider web." This, from Val.

"It's light," insisted Bodkin. "Look at it, people. It floats in the air."

"Right," sighed Val. "Change of plan. We're going over the part of the stockade that's fallen. We run, following the cliff edge, looking for a place to climb down. Maybe, maybe we'll meet up with Mr. Miller." *In the fields of Elysium, most like.*

Screams came from beyond the smoke. They watched as three women with kitchen knives pursued a man waving sword. He threatened with it while they circled, cutting and slicing pieces of him as though he were pork on a plate. When he collapsed all a red mess, they howled like wolves, ran off through the smoke.

"What?" asked Matilda.

"Ah, appears the servants see this as ripe opportunity to shout 'freedom'," said Val. "Good for them."

"Fine," said Bodkin. "I've another plan."

"What?"

"We climb the rope ladder the air ship is lowering."

Val, Cedric, Jewel and Matilda looked upwards. Half hidden in the smoke, there now descended just this very thing.

"Why would they do that?" asked Val.

"Could they be descending to fight on foot?" wondered Cedric.

"Maybe they see we aren't from Martia?" asked Matilda.

Shouts from the holding said that the proper folk of Martia had noted the descending ladder.

"Right," ordered Val. "Everyone ready to climb."

Bodkin leaped, grabbing a rung soon as it came in reach, clambering easy as squirrel up oak. Jewel followed, less quick, more cautious. The ladder twisted with each step. Next came Cedric, slowly, bearing his pack and Barnaby's.

Matilda hesitated.

"'Tis a damnable difficult thing when a girl's got sensible Silenian feet."

"But it's pretty how you paint them. Climb quick, else your hooves get used for decorative door handles."

"That's quite awful," said Matilda. Hurrying to climb.

Val remained alone on the ground, watching as different groups rushed through smoke and mist. Some were servants in rebellion; others were soldiers stamping out fire and rebellion alike. But several crept steadily closer, sheltering from the *directable's* flame weaponry. Val waved to let them know this was a routine maneuver, not an escape. Then she turned, began hurrying up the ladder herself.

Below and behind, her former countrymen shouted, demanding she return. She watched an arrow appear by her head, quick as any thought within her head, only to disappear again into the fog. With clearer air it'd have hit the target, that being her head full of thoughts.

I'm not going to make it, she thought. Pity. I wanted more time with Mr. Miller. Will we meet again in the Fields? Bah. Too sensible an end. They say the Lower House is near as mad as the Middle House, which is near as mad as the Upper House. But will I see the cup? Hear it sing again?

The ladder jerked, nearly throwing her off. Then it pulled upwards, making her stomach sink. The ground fell away. Well, the *directable* was moving. She watched a few more arrows fly. Wasted shots; she now made a very difficult target.

Granted, it was difficult to climb. Infernum, it was difficult to just hold on.

Of a sudden, the *directable* emerged from smoke and fog, leaving Val dangling in clear air. Dangling as a pendant from the Upper House of Saints itself. Beneath, the distant ground offered an illuminated map of the border twixt Martia and Hefestia. The Lethe shone like a roadway paved in onyx; the smoke of Edgestead wafting for a distant hearth fire.

"What exactly did I want from the cup?" she asked the fog, the smoke, the fire, the wind. A passing crow. "And did the cup want anything from me? Did it want me to find it, or just to seek it?"

The crow circled round, considering the airship, the dangling bard and her question. Val felt obligated to explain further.

"All I know is I felt that the cup knew me. And that it, it loved me, and wanted me to be happy. Isn't that reason enough to seek it?"

Whatever the crow knew of wanting, of seeking and finding, it did not share. It gave a yawp, flew on and away. No doubt deep into its own amazing quest. Val looked back to the smoke of burning Edgestead, the rocky red land of Martia.

When Mother hears I escaped, she's going to howl till her eyes bleed. The thought made Val smile. She prepared to climb again, gazing upwards... and there within the door of the airship she spied a pale freckled face staring down. The shock near made her drop.

Val started laughing, shaking, knowing she approached a dangerous state of overmuch battle and blood, fear and hope. If she swooned, she'd awaken in the Fields.

So she closed eyes, taking ten slow, deep breaths, exactly as taught on the practice fields of Martia. Then opened eyes, her calm recovered. That done, she continued her climb.

Beneath the *directable* hung all a house, woven of rope and wicker. Val climbed in, helped by Cedric and Bodkin.

Within, the humming of mechanicalisms set her teeth vibrating. Hands now free, she drew knife, seeking the source of the smell of fresh blood. Not far away, a man in Hefestian army clothes lay with throat cut.

Barnaby, wandering miller of fabled Mill Town, sat on the floor amidst blood-spattered machinery. Jewel and Matilda leaned over him, discussing a Hefestian dart projecting from his back.

"I've cut the leather around the dart," offered Matilda. "Not sure what to do next."

"I am," said Val, pushing her aside. Kneeling beside Barnaby, she touched fingertips to the wound. He hissed in pain, but she smiled.

"Not too deep. The leather slowed it, or you'd be dead. Wasn't poisoned or you'd also be dead."

"Well, I'm not dead either way," Barnaby growled, panting. "Have Jewel or Cedric cast some oration to fix it magical and quick. It hurts."

"Cedric is busy steering this thing," said Jewel. "I'm no good with healing."

Val frowned. "Our cleric knows how to fly Hefestian *directables*?"

"He studied in Daedalus itself," said Jewel. Possibly proud.

"Studied theurgy. What part of the curriculum is mad machinery?"

"I don't want to interrupt all selfish like," said Barnaby, "but I'm still hurting here aplenty."

"Oi, Mister Miller," said Matilda. "Brother Reverend Clerical Heretical Cedric kindly brought your pack." She rummaged through it, seeking the wand made in the robbers' wood. "Can you heal yourself?"

"Not a good idea," said Val. "Healing orations have a heavy cost. Casting when you are the one hurt, can knock you dead. I'll handle it."

To the surprise of all, she bent down, gave Barnaby a quick kiss.

"Was that supposed to be magic?" he grumbled. "Didn't work."

"Lucif's mother's dog bite me but you whine," she observed. Then took harp from her pack. Fingered the strings.

"I *am* the bard of the group. 'Bout time I did some cantrips with Thelxipea. Matilda, be ready to pull the dart out."

"Ready," said the Silenian.

"I'm not," growled Barnaby.

"Hush. Close your eyes. On count of five, Matilda."

"You're going to do it on three," growled Barnaby.
"We aren't."
"Are."

"One," said Val. Nodding to Matilda. Who nodded, then pulled hard upon the dart shaft. Barnaby screamed. Blood poured easy as wine out uncorked bottle. Jewel looked away, feeling sick. Met the glassy eyes of the dead Hefestian, sliced throat still trickling. She turned again, staring out a window into the bright sky. Listening as Val strummed her harp, singing with the humming of the *directable*.

To the saint of song appealing,
Lady of lyre and harp, we beseech,
Your melody sending, our pain ending.
Music is the sweetest healing,

Her voice harmonized with a second, softer song. Jewel turned, puzzled. For just a moment she spied the golden shadow of a young woman kneeling beside Barnaby, hand to his shoulder, singing.

The oration ended. Barnaby sighed, falling slowly forwards, curling in upon himself. Val muttered something, letting the harp drop. She lay down, curling close beside Barnaby.

Matilda hurried to check breath and pulse of both.

"Hmm, he's stopped bleeding. Wound looks better. Not quite closed. She seems well. I think the two dear sweethearts are simply tuckered."

"Hard day after long night."

Jewel put hand to mouth, surprised she'd just said that aloud. On her breast the spider pendant gave a soft tap in reminder that *their* night had passed long; and pleasant. Jewel whirled back to the window to hide her smile. Matilda grinned; not hiding hers a bit.

"No doubt the poor things took no sleep, though 'tis entirely indecorous to speculate upon their private doings until we can pry the salient and salacious details from out them. Let 'em rest for now, whilst you inform me about *your* night, Miss Witch."

Hours later, Barnaby opened eyes. Still on the floor of the corridor. A darker place now; the glass portals of the airship granting mere twilight's glow. But he lay far more comfortably, in far less pain. Wrapped in a blanket, head pillowed in Val's lap. She sat cross legged, leaning over him, tapping his face with a finger.

"Twenty-seven," she declared. "Twenty-eight. Twenty-nine."

"What are you doing?"

"Counting your freckles. Been wanting to since we met. Thirty. Wait, did I do this one by your ear?"

"Dunno. You should mark them with a quill as you go. Would turn me spotted blue. Unusual thing to see."

There came grumbling in the corridor beyond. He turned. There, Matilda and Bodkin struggled to drag the dead Hefestian, who'd gone stiff as wooden church effigy.

"What are you two doing?" asked Barnaby.

"Putting this fellow out the door," replied Bodkin. "He's unpleasant to pass, and soon he'll be getting ripe. Same for the other."

"No," said Barnaby.

"What? Why?"

Barnaby considered. The nameless Hefestian had thunder-clapped him out a tower. Meaning to kill him without so much as asking his name. Maybe in Hefestia they didn't even have the name 'Barnaby'.

Still, it was wrong to treat a body as trash. Wrong, as too much of life went. Even in this fabulous flying magical mechanicalism of a *directable*.

"Because we can't treat him so, just dropping him down to the dirt."

"Sure we can. For sure he'd do the same to us or his favorite brother."

"Maybe. Still wrong. Leave him till we can bury him proper. And the other."

"Seriously?"

Val cut in. "Mr. Miller has the right of it. We've all had the saints' luck. Let's keep on Master Quietus's good side, so he stays on ours."

"Fine," growled Bodkin. "There's a storeroom to the side, next to the engine room. Let's put him and the other in there, if no miller complains of the disrespect of not giving him blanket and pillow."

"Thank you, Bodkin," said Barnaby.

"Thank you, Bodkin," said Val.

"Ha," said Matilda.

"Hmph," said Bodkin.

Val returned to her census of freckles. "Thirty-one. How do you feel?"

"Awful. Which is still better than before. How about you?"

"Ah, I just needed a rest. My spirit is not tuned to healing."

He reached up, traced a finger along her freckle-less cheek.

"Not true. You've been healing something in me since we met."

Val found no reply to that. Others did.

"So romantic," whispered Matilda.

"But now she'll argue it," whispered Bodkin. "Watch. She'll insist she's a rough sort unworthy of his kind miller's heart. Girls never just take the damned compliment."

"Both of you find some other part of this ship to pester," said Val, still counting freckles. "Thirty-two."

Bodkin and Matilda dragged the body down the corridor, leaving them in peace to meet one another's eyes.

"Your homeland is an interesting place," he said at last. "I liked the people. Fierce but friendly. And I never saw such rocky land. Is all St. Martia like that?"

Val considered. "Thirty-five. No. Yes. Most of it is like Edgestead, maybe less nice. Hypo turned out to be a decent sort. Crazy, but decent. Thirty-six."

Of a sudden, Barnaby recalled Hypo lying wounded. He tried to sit up. Val pushed him right back down.

"Is he still alive? I should heal him."

"No need. Matilda and Jewel kept him from bleeding out till Cedric could take time for an oration. The man's hurt, but alive."

"Ah. That's good."

Val grinned.

"Granted, he's not pleased about where he finds himself. Thirty-Seven."

"Where? On an airship?"

"On *our* airship. Fifty miles into St. Hefestia, as *our* prisoner. Done. You've exactly thirty-nine freckles."

Chapter 21
Someone Entirely from Somewhere Else

Hypo:

Thank the saints for the fog. Would have humbled my proud soul to have all St. Martia see me hanging from the tower like Demetian washing.

After the tower fell, as the saints placed us atop the *directable*, as the mad miller and I crept upon the crew, I asked myself: what error had I made in the challenge? Hadn't forgotten training. Hadn't violated a single rule of attack.

And of a sudden, in glorious revelation, I saw *training* was the mistake.

The Demetian had fought to live. We of Martia are taught to kill. Fuck me in all Infernum's fifty thousand furnaces, the first word we teach a babe is 'attack'. Not 'mama", not 'papa'. '*Attack!*' our offspring shout before putting toothless mouth to mother's teat.

My head hummed with a new philosophy of combat. Not working to beat down the foe, but letting them defeat themselves while you saved your breath. A fascinating heresy to our holy training fields, where we dislike even carrying shields.

Further pondering would wait. The Demetian and I crept from the ladder tunnel to find ourselves in a narrow corridor at the bottom of the *directable*. Around us the ship hummed. We'd been swallowed by a purring whale.

A Hefestian stood with back conveniently to me. I considered testing my new strategy, let him attack till he wore himself out. But experimenting is more of a Hefestian art. Besides, the noise would alert the crew. I put off the trial, cut the man's throat.

We stepped over his twitching body, continued on to the control room door. There'd be three left. I peered through a glass portal, spying two Hefestians. Worrisome; where was the third? I knew behind us were storerooms, crew cabins and the engine room. Didn't like enemy ahead and behind. Still, easier to deal with smaller bites.

"Ready?" I asked the mad miller.

He was staring back at the dying Hefestian. Saying something to someone. To the corpse? No idea what, no idea who, no idea why. The man was mysterious as purring whales.

"Demetian. You going to fight? Or just talk to yourself?"

He turned; face showing anger enough that I readied knife. For the first time I could believe this pleasant foreigner might have met Maris. The saint of Worthy Battle her very own, very bloody self.

"I'm ready," he said. "Never wasn't ready. Let's go."

"Right. Two Festians ahead. Dart guns on their belts. If we hit them before they draw and aim, then we live."

The mad miller nodded. I eased open the door and in we went.

Hefestians call it 'the bridge', as if it were a sea ship. A narrow chamber paneled in panes of glass. Bright by day, crowded with brass instruments, chimes, pipes and bells, various tools of Hefestian madness.

One man stood before a ship's wheel; the other sat in a chair pulling levers, turning knobs. The first paid no attention to our entrance. The second turned, looking properly astonished. He shouted. By then I was rushing forwards while he scrabbled for his dart gun. I leaped and stabbed. He drew and fired.

There's no *style* in Hefestian dart guns. Just gas cartridges, a crossbow trigger. But I admit they are efficient in close quarters. There came that meek 'click-puff' the guns make. Then the dart ripped into my gut. Nothing meek in *that*.

Not that it kept my knife from piercing the man's throat, slicing across.

That done, I wanted to charge the other Festian but delayed, feeling of a sudden I'd feasted on thorns, hot coals and angry vipers. My dear sweet belly was now a world of hurt. I fell atop the Festian. He was trying to scream with throat sliced. Never, ever is that a pretty sound. We both bled, twitched and moaned together. No, not like lovers. Just two fools dying.

I watched the other Hefestian abandon the wheel; hands seeking his own dart gun. The mad miller stepped forwards, sweeping down the tower-fragment club. Knocking the gun away. A good start.

The Festian I'd killed still held his dart gun. I ordered my trembling hands to take it. They were slow to obey. Meanwhile the standing Hefestian raised his fists.

"Get out, you!" he shouted. "You aren't allowed here!"

"Why not?" asked the mad miller. He had the wooden club raised to strike again, but in the tradition of mad millers, remained open to conversation.

"Regulations!" shouted the Festian. "Rule #47, section six. *'Strictly no non-authorized personnel in the control room during course of official maneuvers.'*"

The mad miller pondered Rule #47. The club waited, smoldering impatiently. At length the miller offered his thoughts.

"Well, but see, you are trying to kill people down there. From way up here. Some of them are my friends.

Not that it is not also wrong to kill folk who aren't my friends, I'll add."

The Festian shook head, crossing arms. "Rule #35, section seven: '*strictly no discussions of saints, politics or war in the control room.*'"

"Who's talking saints, politics or war? I'm talking you setting people's houses on fire."

The Festian hesitated, unsure. "Well, that's the same as politics, isn't it?"

The miller frowned, equally unsure. At last he prepared rebuttal; but did not deliver it. There came a *click-puff*, and he gasped. He turned around, revealing a dart now projecting into the leather armor of his back.

Shit. At the control-room door stood the missing sixth Festian. Grinning, understandably. Till *click-puff*, I shot him in the grin. A lucky shot, I'd aimed for the chest. No matter. Hands scrabbling at his face, he fell forwards.

The remaining Festian shouted some rule concerning *altercations in the control room*. I shot at him. Hitting an arm, doing little damage. Still, it kept him from recovering his own dart gun. The miller had time to turn, striking the man with the club. Thankfully, that concluded the debate.

And there stood the mad miller, master of an Hefestian *directable* control room. Dart in his back, bodies scattered about, mysterious dials twitching, the whole edifice humming. He looked lost as lamb in the slaughterhouse. I struggled to speak, mouth now drooling with blood.

"Miller. We passed a door. As we came. There's a rope ladder. Rolls to the ground. Pull the lever. Open the door. Let the ladder down."

He tried to reach the dart in his back, but it was in that place between the shoulder blades you can never quite scratch. Gave it up, nodded, staggered away. I closed my eyes, expecting when next I opened them it'd be to see the *Fields*. There'd be a crowd awaiting. Not all of them friends. But such is life and war. Not that the one, isn't the other.

When next I opened eyes I beheld… the same Infernum-kissed control room. Still stinking of spattered blood and emptied bowels. At least now I lay on the floor, not atop a Festian with cut throat. Not as soft, but far preferable.

I felt better. Not recovered. But the pain had backed off, the creeping cold retreated.

The Demetian priest knelt beside me, staff in hand. He looked wearied. Obvious he'd been doing *saint's healing*. Officially, we don't approve of orations in Martia, excepting for weapon-craft. Though soon or late everyone seeks out some surreptitious healing or blessing.

I considered thanking him. Then I considered what in the name of the balls of Sainted Mithras' bull was he doing on the Hefestian airship *I'd* taken. I then considered the little rogue from the Spice Isles who now sat at the control board, moving levers and buttons with the confidence of a graduate of Daedalus Air Academy. While the Selenian stood at the wheel, humming to herself, tapping her flower-painted hooves.

Yes, I pondered these observations; coming to easy conclusions.

"Kurgus's wandering lunatics have stolen the ship I captured."

The little rogue replied without turning. "We aren't her lunatics. She's our lunatic. We are the Society of St.

Benefact. Val's the society's mad bard. And this is the society's airship."

I thought about asking who the Infernum was 'Benefact'. But the Upper House alone has exactly as many saints as stars. One might as well inquire the holy identity of a random sand grain from the dunes of St. Psamathe.

"Clever escape," I admitted. "Well done."

The priest smiled. "We enjoyed our stay in Martia. But proper guests never overstay their welcome."

I looked about for the Hefestian dart gun. Gone, of course. As was my knife.

"Where is Kurgus now?"

"Tending Barnaby."

"Tending," chuckled the Silenian. "Ha."

"Glad to hear he breathes," I said. It was true. That miller was a strange creature, yet likeable. I never met anyone so entirely from somewhere else.

"So," I asked the cleric. "What do you intend to do with *your* ship? And *your* prisoner?"

"We plan to continue into Hefestia. As for you, we will set you on the ground tonight. Wishing you good day, good luck, farewell. As we did earlier with the surviving Hefestian, Sub-Lieutenant Thuro. Though the man kept complaining how we violated rule number *this*, section number *that*. Dogmatic as a Demetian bishop."

"You let him live?"

"We are adventurous treasure hunters, not wandering murderers."

"Thuro will run to the nearest town, alert the authorities that a pack of Demetian lunatics have stolen a military airship."

"As a wise band of adventurers, we keep on hand a skilled rogue." The boy at the controls waved. "Under his advice, we bound, blindfolded and secluded Mr. Thuro. He knows nothing of our appearance, names nor purpose. The Hefestian authorities will assume you of Martia captured the ship. Hardly expecting us to continue into Hefestia."

I considered warning him that a *directable* did not fly unseen nor unquestioned, even in Hefestia. Decided that was the problem of their St. Benefact.

"How far past the border are we now?"

"Some fifty miles."

"Can I have a knife for the journey home?"

"Of course. When we are waving farewell."

"Wise of you." Which sounded threatening. And really, with recovered strength and a decent sword I would have cut all their throats. Even the miller's. Even Kurgus's.

Not out of resentment. Who wouldn't admire these bold folk? Wonderful how they'd seized their chance of escape. That, and my warship. But their courageous nonsense meant I now faced a three-day march through Hefestian territory, then a swim across a haunted river, then a climb up a deadly cliff. And when I reached the top...

My heart sank, stomach feeling an echo of the razored dart. Lucif's flaming lips kiss me quick... when I returned to Martia I'd have to march to Demos. And there report to Kurgus's mad bitch mother that her mad bitch daughter had floated away like a dandelion puff on the wind. I pictured that discussion. And debated telling the folk of St. Benefact *not* to give me a knife.

I'd be too tempted to cut my own throat first.

Chapter 22
Breakfast Strategy, with Coffeeish

Barnaby lay in a narrow bunk, peering out the window beside him. The land below the *directable* looked green as his homeland. But Demetia had the orderly flatness of a well-tucked blanket embroidered with farms and woods. This countryside rose and fell in swells of gentle hills crisscrossed by strange lines. A soft green quilt of a land, decorated with strange patterns and devices.

"What are the lines along the roads?"

"Rails," Val informed him. Lying close, one arm settled across his chest. "Most are iron. They chain carts together, then pull them along with horses. Using sails when there's a proper wind. A few carts even move on their own, pulling other carts. Like this airship. Except the front carts blow out smoke like a dragon."

"Huh. Like to see that. What about the trees waving their arms?"

"Semaphore towers. People pull ropes to raise and lower the arms. Different combinations make letters, sending a message from hill to hill."

"Astonishing land, Hefestia." He tapped on the glass. "Even their windows."

"They call them portals."

"Why?"

"Hmm, because they are round? Don't really know."

"In Mill Town most windows just have wooden shutters. Sometimes we cover them with oiled fish skin. But the Squire's manse has glazed windows. Diamond-shaped glass fitted together with lead. Amazing how they let in the light, keep out the wind."

Val slipped atop him.

"Is everything new to you?"

Barnaby turned, considered Val's nose, her eyes, all the pleasant press of *her* atop *him*.

"I spent overlong hours daydreaming. Still catching up on things. Windows. Foreign lands. Kisses and such."

"Oh, was that catching up? Not the first time?"

"Well, I've kissed the Goat Girl plenty. Though she'll give you a kick to say '*quit now*'. And there's a weaving prentice I'd meet each year at the Jahrmarkt. We'd partner for the dances, go for walks through the tents. Behind the tents, a'times."

Val propped elbows on his chest, resting chin in palm. From this position, she gazed down with critical eye.

"Oh, yes, clearly you are quite the experienced lover."

For reply he reached, traced a finger along a cheekbone, down her neck to the back. There he scratched between her shoulder blades. She shivered, emitting bardic purrs.

"You are new to me," he replied. "But I think... I could lie like this with you for years and years, and it would still astonish. Like a, a sunrise. Some things are just always new."

There came admiring whispers from beyond the door.

"I hear you out there," growled Val. "Prurient sneaks."

"I deny it," shouted Bodkin. "But we need everyone up and about. Captain Cedric's calling a meeting. Dress first, please."

The Society of St. Benefact gathered in the control cabin. Cedric stood by the wheel, gazing out portals, tapping a brass spyglass thoughtful as king wielding scepter.

"You look a proper and proprietary captain," declared Matilda.

"Just the pilot," replied Cedric. "Bodkin commandeered the captain's hat. And coat. And goggles. Possibly the boots."

Jewel went to the wall, released a catch. Down unfolded a short table. This short table expanded to become a long table. While from beneath unfolded small stools. Barnaby laughed, poking fascinated at different joints and hinges.

Now Bodkin entered with a tray. Wearing an overlong blue coat, frog-like lenses and a Hefestian officer's cap. He set out wooden cups upon the miraculous table. Empty of liquid; each cup held spoonfuls of brown crystals.

"What is this shiny dirt?" growled Matilda.

"Coffee," declared Bodkin.

"Doubtful," she doubted.

"Observe," he commanded. Crossing arms, nodding to Jewel, who took up a pitcher of clear water. She filled Matilda's cup, then stepped quick away to avoid explosion.

The cup hissed, steamed, foamed; the air filling with a smell reminiscent of coffee.

"Oi, that's quite astonishing," declared Matilda. Touching finger to the liquid. "How is it being hot if the pitcher wasn't?"

"Hefestian wonder," declared Bodkin, tipping back hat. "How's it taste?"

Matilda sipped. "Hmm. Like a cup full of the ghost of coffee." He looked disappointed. She added kindly, "But still hot. Wondrously fine, actually."

Jewel filled the other cups, set them foaming. The company sampled the almost-coffee while Bodkin and Jewel placed more Hefestian delicacies upon the magic table.

Barnaby pondered the letters upon his cup, working not to turn it upside down.

"'*Phaethon*'. Are all the cups belonging to this personage?"

"That's the name of this directable," explained Val.

"They name them?" asked Barnaby. "Excellent thing." He sipped, pondering what he'd name a directable warship. Something grand, as a flying ship deserved. '*Dragon Egg*' sounded strong. '*Thunder*'? Rather too simple. '*Thunder Dragon*', maybe.

Or was it time to move on from dragons? The name '*Sky Lion*' held strong appeal. Stronger on the tongue than the coffee, anyway.

Meanwhile the company tasted, tested, debated the Hefestian breakfast offerings. Sampling ingots of grain and honey in tin boxes, and breads wrapped in waxed paper. Strips of unidentifiable meat cut neat and dry as leather for belts. Colored cubes that reminded nose and tongue of various fruits.

"It's like a strawberry has been dried, ground fine, given oil and reshaped to a square," declared Matilda. "Hmm."

"How do these purple squares taste almost like grapes?" puzzled Barnaby. "I'd call them '*grapeish*'.

"Is this why the meeting was called?" asked Matilda. "Not to complain of a free breakfast."

"But is it breakfast?" asked Val. "More like '*breakfastish*'.

Cedric had remained standing, staring out the portals. Now he turned to address the Society.

"We are pursued."

"Hypo's folk?" wondered Barnaby. "How can they follow so fast?"

"No, not them. We are followed by another Hefestian *directable*. Perhaps by several."

"Oh. Will they attack?"

"I do not know. For the moment, they flash signal lamps, demanding we identify ourselves."

"You can read Hefestian signal code?" That, from Val.

"Not their battle codes. But yes, the simple communication signals."

Val nodded. "Thought so. You were spying on Demetia for Hefestia."

There came an uncomfortable silence. Jewel glowered at Val, putting hand to spider-pendant. But Cedric merely smiled, taking no offense.

"So the Questioners suspected. As did the Deaconry of Plutarch. To my mind, I worked with my fellow Lucretians across the imaginary lines we call *borders*. But I grant the Society of Lucretius resides chiefly in Hefestia."

"Can you use your contacts here?" That, from Bodkin.

"We are Demetian trespassers in possession of a Hefestian warship. The blood of its crew still staining walls and floors. No philosophical alliance will keep us from arrest and trial."

Matilda stamped a hoof.

"Would be nice if we could find some magical land where a body can rest in peace for five minutes before the constabulary shout for a meek girl's hooves."

Cedric nodded. "I'd hoped we might ride this ship north, perhaps even unto the tower. But it is clear we must abandon it soon, continuing on foot."

"This is a war ship," pointed out Val. "We could wait for them to get close, then attack with the same fire they used on Edgestead."

"No," said Cedric.

"No," said Bodkin.

"No," said Barnaby.

"No," said Jewel.

"No," said Matilda.

"Fine. Fine. Just an idea."

"My proposal," declared Cedric, "is we continue north and east with all the speed we can push from the engines. When night falls, we descend, leaving the ship to wander where wind and saint wish. The Hefestians shall pursue it, while we continue peaceably on foot."

The Benefactors frowned, muttered and sighed at the thought of a return to marching. But no one offered a better path.

"That's the plan, then," declared Val. "People, search the ship for what seems worth carrying away. We can replace what we lost with the cart. Food, blankets, rope, tools, weapons."

"What about the captain's trunk?" asked Bodkin. "Can't be leaving till I get that lock open."

"Then stay till you do," shrugged Val. "Or carry it on your back."

"What about borrowing their fire-throwing gunnery?" That, from Matilda. "Come in useful, it would."

"Definitely. You just need an elephant to port it about."

Bodkin looked dissatisfied with the total plunder.

"Then what about the dart pistols?"

"If you want," said Val. "But those gas cartridges are glass. They break easily. And when one shatters, they generally all do. You hear of Hefestians taking a tumble, going 'boom' like thunder. Leaving just Festian scraps floating down."

"Ah," sighed Bodkin. "Wondered why the things weren't more popular than sharp metal sticks. Well, perhaps I'll take just a few, and walk careful."

"Just not too close to the rest of us."

"The ghost of coffee," mused a voice.

All turned, beholding a newcomer who had not entered by the door.

Dark Michael now leaned against a portal.

"Well good morning, Mr. Spooky Person," said Matilda, customarily friendly. "Would you like some *coffeeish*?"

"No," said Michael, customarily curt. Then, uncustomarily relenting. "But thank you, Miss Silenian."

He turned to Cedric. "You do not have till nightfall. They shall attack within the hour."

"How do you know?"

Michael did not answer. Another did. In high voice, lecturing and amused.

"Mr. Spooky Person is a proper Demetian officer. They learn Hefestian battle codes in the unlikely case they ever war against some army other than their own."

All gazes turned to the control board, where Night-Shadow lay, sprawling atop the knobs and buttons.

"Here, off that," shouted Bodkin. "I've said before about you lying there. You'll be sending us crashing."

At which concern, Night-Creep yawned.

"But their ship keeps far away," declared Cedric. Gazing out the window. "How will they attack?"

Dark Michael smiled. "You think as a man on the ground. But in the air you must consider not just what is before and behind, but what is below and above."

"I don't understand."

"A second directable is high above this ship now," explained Night-Creep. "At their leisure, they can blast you to Infernum's bloodiest midden."

"Then best we blast them first." That, from Matilda.

Val growled.

"Can't. The mechanism is beneath the directable. They do not fire upwards. Their ship can strike us; we cannot strike them."

"Then why haven't they struck?"

"No doubt they want the Phaethon back. And intend to take it. Also take us."

"How?" That, from Bodkin.

Val considered, trading glances with Michael. "*Fliedermenchen*," she declared. He nodded.

"Which are what?"

"Flying soldiers in gear with wings like bats. They make short trips to and from *directables*. You see them flitting about the border with Martia. Scouting, St. Lucif take them home to bed with him."

"They fly?" asked Jewel. "Some kind of oration of levitation?"

Val shrugged. Night-Creep licked paw, happy to explicate.

"Hmm, not exactly an oration. As many of the wonders of Hefestia, the principle is closer to clockwork bolstered by the *aura* of the patron saint of artifice. The *fliedermenchen* do not function well beyond the borders of his demesne."

"Just as orations to Demetia are weakened here and in Martia," sighed Cedric. "It near ended me to heal Hypo. And came to only half-healing."

"Our fog oration worked," said Jewel.

"We made appeal to Sister Hecatatia," reminded Cedric. "She makes no kingdom her own, and so resides in the night of any land."

"Pity it's daylight," said Val. "At least I should be still able to make a cantrip to Euterpe."

"You going to sing them a song?" That, from Bodkin.

Val smiled. "Might."

"What will these flying men do?" asked Matilda.

"I have read their signals," said Michael. "They have exact orders. Recover the Phaethon. Take you prisoner. Interrogate you, then execute you."

"What?" That, from Bodkin. "How about first discussing the whole innocent misunderstanding?"

"No slightest chance. The Hefestians are outraged that their warship was captured, the crew slaughtered. Someone must pay. It will be you."

"Can we outrun them?"

Cedric considered.

"We can move quite fast for a short time. But the ship hovering above would destroy us before we were beyond range of its fire."

"Very well," said Val. "Can't bargain. Can't run. So, we fight." She worked to avoid grinning; failing this noble work.

"Seriously?" asked Bodkin. "This is their kind of battle. Flying men, fire bolts, dart guns and engines."

"Then we make it our kind. First task is, repel the *fliedermenchen*. Second task, take down the directable above before it burns us alive."

"But we can't." That, a whisper from Jewel.

"Sure we can. We'll start simple. I want you to send your spider to the top of the ship. That's where the *fliedermenchen* will land. Warn us soon as you see them."

Jewel looked to Cedric, who gave encouraging nod Same as he'd done between the bars of the cells of Persephone. She nodded back.

"Cedric, can you strengthen Barnaby's armor against darts?"

"I can do that much. But it will only last a short while."

"That's all the time we have anyway. Master Miller, I want you to guard the access tunnel doorway. Keep them from getting to the control room or to the engine room."

Barnaby said nothing; had said nothing. Merely gazed out the portals to the clouds, the innocent sky.

Val frowned.

"Now you are going to say you don't want to kill anyone."

Barnaby nodded, still not turning.

She took a breath clearly meant to become a string of curses; then released it in a sigh of calmer words.

"Barnaby, these Festians are at war with your Demetia. They would have burned us to ashes in Martia. They are coming to end us now. They are trained and willing killers, not strangers to befriend."

Still gazing out the window, Barnaby rose. Drew his wand from the woods of Demetia, pondering the green leaf sprouting from the tip. When he spoke, it was to that leaf.

"I don't want to kill anyone. But I'll fight when it comes to fighting." That said, he turned to Val. "But I can't swing an axe in close quarters. I need to be outside, atop the ship."

"They'd see you and just shoot you beyond the swing of your axe."

"Professor Night-Creep taught me a spell of hiding. I'm going to cast it, then wait atop by the portal. Same as Hypo and I did."

The Society of St. Benefact turned from Barnaby to Val, studying the faces and eyes of both. Not a one spoke. Until,

"There is little time," reminded Dark Michael.

Val nodded.

"Fine. Right. That's, that's a better plan, Barnaby. Good luck."

His cat-tutor jumped down, strode to Barnaby. Leaping to his shoulder, making himself comfortable for the delivering of lectures.

"Now. Remember that the spell only lasts while you remain still. Once you strike, they will see you."

"So, I will remain still, then strike hard."

Val turned to the rest.

"Bodkin, gather everyone's packs and put them close by the ladder door for a quick escape. Search the ship for whatever else we can use."

"I do have a magic sword, you know."

She began a sarcastic reply; then recalled the boy saving her the night of the cultists' attack.

"So you do. If they, if they get past Barnaby, you'll be the one keeping them from the control room and the engine room."

He made a face. "Old Mercutio doesn't think much of that. Says I should jump ship, leave you lot to pay for the piper's lunch."

"You going to listen to him?"

Bodkin laughed. "Nah. I've grown to enjoy listening to him whine how I'll get us both killed."

Val blinked. "You are a very strange boy." That declared, she turned to Cedric.

"Can you be ready to move the ship fast and away?"

"Yes; but not so swift as to avoid their fire."

"Then I'll give them something else to fire at." Val took her harp from the sling on her back, brushing fingers across the strings. "Euterpe is no battle saint. But she will hear me even in the sky of Hefestia. And the theatric dear has a fondness for a dramatic show of seeming."

"A cantrip of illusion?" asked Cedric. "It will have to be quite good."

"Then I'll make it good." She turned to Matilda. "You come with me to the engine room. I'm going to show you how to make some special arrows."

"Oh, I do like the sound of that," declared Matilda. "Though I'm both pondering and wondering if I *should* like the sound of that."

"Anything else?" Val asked the Benefactors.

None spoke. She clapped hands.

"Battle stations, all, then."

Chapter 23
The Battle of the Phaethon

Jewel of Stonecroft:

I have to say it in small pieces. To take it all in.

Cedric and I are not alike. He's a scholar. An ordained priest. I'm a kitchen girl. A farm creature. He, almost thirty. I, almost twenty. He is kind. I am not. Never wanted to be.

In the barn in St. Martia when we touched, difference didn't matter. When he was inside me, difference didn't matter. When I lay atop him, difference didn't matter. When he lay atop me. The differences? Didn't. Matter

I needed. He needed. Not just pleasure. I wanted to be loved. Touched. Cared for. So also, him. We had that in common. Needs of the flesh. Needs of the heart.

We both feared to meet eyes afterwards. Would he push me away? Dismiss me as something done with? And would I scowl for my weakness? Perhaps I'd turn ice. Or cry. Or mutter *'well, that's over'*.

We didn't. We didn't do those things. None of it. No, we set about the tasks of the society. Composing an oration to Hecatatia. *Holding hands.* Worked. Like in Gaol. The saint heard me. Us.

Ah, I've been so very weary of wanting. Of hating. Of being empty. Since forever I've chewed on old hates, cold angers. Sitting to feast from my poisoned plate.

Feeding your soul on rage? Same as feeding a dog on bread. Oh, it thinks it is full; but it is starved, ready to fall dead. That has been my feast in Infernum since childhood.

And Cedric? For years he's lived as a hermit locked with his books, his fears and regrets. Gnawing on the memories of lost love, brooding on the will of the saints, debating with shadows the meanings of texts dry as the sands of Psamathe.

So: we had that in common. Our feast time in Infernum. And our hope to get out.

Together, why not.

The day of the air battle I sent Perry through a window. He scuttled up the side of the directable, perching atop, keeping low. While I sat in the control room, eyes closed, seeing through Perry's thousand facets. I recited what I saw.

"No flying men yet. Don't see Barnaby. Either his hiding oration worked, or he's tumbled off the ship. But there is another directable above us. Like Michael said."

'How high above?" That, from Val.

I tried to guess. "Sixty feet. Maybe more."

"Matilda, think you can hit that with our special arrow? Straight up from the top of this directable?"

"You're insulting to the pride of my bow, not to forget the honor of my Silenian blood and my papa's training. Also you wound my-"

"Right," interrupted Val. "Get up the ladder before the *fliedermenchen* show. Shoot that ship. Jewel, keep watching. Cedric, be ready to-"

"Uhm," I interrupted.

"What?"

"There's a third directable to the south. And a fourth to the west. They're far away but moving closer fast."

"Shit," said Val. "They aren't taking chances. Matilda, go take out the ship above us. Cedric, when you hear thunder, then move us fast. Northeast is best."

"They will pursue. No doubt cutting us off."

"I'm going to make a distraction that will confuse things. It'll probably put me out of the fight. Everyone, get to it."

"Uhm," I said.

"What? What now? What?"

"Four men with wings like bats. Just settled atop our directable."

I waited for Val to panic; to curse. She did neither. When she spoke, it was calm as weak tea with milk.

"Barnaby will handle them."

The miller and the bard made a strange pair. I'd thought him a daft child. As I'd taken her for a bossy bitch with a head full of mad dreams.

I don't like mad folk. They leave you to go dancing with the moon. I don't like childish folk. They ruin things. Love, farms, lives. Ruin your life if you let them.

But whenever I saw Barnaby and Val Kurgus together, heard them argue together... they seemed right for one another. Right as flame and candle. For all that a mad bard and a dreamy miller are such different animals. Maybe differences don't always matter?

Barnaby's kindly like Cedric. Val's practical, like, well, like me. And if those two can belong together... why can't Cedric and I?

I watched through Perry's eyes what happened atop our directable. Watching four men wearing armor that seemed padded cloth. Leather helmets with those strange eyeglasses Hefestians fancy. Three worked to free themselves from their great wings, fold them into packs upon their backs.

The fourth kept guard on the portal to the ladder. Wings still spread, dart gun ready. Though none looked concerned. Seemingly they had the field to themselves.

Until of a sudden there stood Barnaby, swinging his horrible axe. Out from his spell of hiding. Cutting down the one holding gun ready. Striking neat as scythe to wheat stalk. Staining the gray directable cloth red.

The others shouted; caught tangled in their wing harnesses like men challenged to fight just as they are pulling off their trousers. Ha. Well done, Mister Miller.

But proper soldiers, they didn't panic. One fellow backed away, knife drawn to cut the straps of his wings. The second moved to the side, risking the fatal slope of the directable. The third ignored his dragging wings, rushed to tackle Barnaby.

The miller had no time to swing again. He met the man's charge with the axe pommel, striking the fellow's head. The man staggered but continued forwards into Barnaby, sending both tumbling atop one another. Wings fluttering in the wind, tangling them both.

That was not good. Perry-me had been watching at a safe distance. We decided to scuttle to the rescue quick as all our legs could take us.

The Hefestian who'd first backed away, now stood freed of his harness straps. Dart gun in one hand, knife in the other, he approached the tangled Barnaby. The fellow to the side struggled with the wind catching in his half-folded wings, threatening to slide him beyond the curve of the directable.

Which was when the portal opened and Matilda poked her head up and out, a gopher checking for hounds. Soon as she spied the fellow with knife and gun she ducked head. Good thing. A dart went 'ping' upon the portal door.

Barnaby succeeded in pushing aside the Hefestian atop him, rose to his feet. A dart struck him in the chest armor, bounced away. Cedric's protective spell, no doubt.

Barnaby rushed forwards, swinging his axe. The man stepped aside wonderfully quick. Moving to put knife to Barnaby's throat, but halting to consider an arrow fixed of a sudden in his left eye. Through the glass lens. Making a bloody broken mess.

Matilda had popped up from the portal again, put arrow to bow and fired fast as Bodkin could pocket another fellow's penny.

The man attempted to ignore the arrow, continuing waving knife at Barnaby. But his heart was no longer in it. The knife dropped; he dropped.

The fellow who'd moved to the side freed himself from his wings; let them tumble from the ship. He drew his dart gun, taking stance to target Barnaby's head. But the shot went into the sky, the man staggered. He waved arms, screaming. Afraid of spiders, clearly.

Perry-me circled him, wrapping thread about his legs. He attempted to shoot us while hopping away. Legs tangled, he toppled, tumbling from the ship.

Matilda now rose from the portal. Grinning, she studied the directable hovering above us. Then from her belt pulled an arrow with an absurd burden upon its front. Long blue stones that shimmered in the noon sun. The shaft of the arrow was bound with cylinders mysterious as tokens to a saint no mortal ever revered.

Perry-me looked up with our shared eyes. Spying a new squadron of flying men flittering about the directable above us. No chance to take them by surprise.

The Silenian set her hooves firmly into the canvas of the directable. Notched the strange arrow to string, stuck tongue out to the side of her mouth in concentration... and then her hooves went through the cloth skin of the directable. Her turn to shout, wave arms while her legs disappeared. She dropped the bow, the special arrow went tumbling.

Barnaby rushed forwards, grabbed the bow. Perry-me scampering along the side. Catching the arrow.

Later I learned it was bound with one of the crystals the Hefestians use to move their mechanicalisms. Weighted with the gas cartridges they used for their dart guns.

Heavy, Perry let us know. *Tired now.* Well, it was the sunlight, as much as the work. Perry is a night creature.

We can get this done, I told Perry. We have to. Then rest. Then Cedric.

We checked the sky. The second team of flying men were circling, spiraling closer.

Perry-me scampered to the top of the ship again, arrow in our mouth. Kind of a mouth. In our front fangs anyway.

There Matilda waited, lying on her back, staring at the sky. Legs still stuck below the outer cloth skin of the directable. She glared angrily at the sky, the enemy ship. But brightened to see us bring the arrow. Took it quick, with nary a 'thank you'.

Barnaby stood a bit away, lest the cloth tear further beneath his weight. Wise of him. He pushed the bow towards her. She took it, set the arrow to string, gazing upwards. It looked to be a difficult shot; but the Silenian grinned for the fun. And then, she fired.

Perry-me and Barnaby and Matilda and the flying men and all the saints twixt the Upper and Lower Houses watched that arrow fly. I had no least idea what it was meant to do. One arrow would hardly bring down a warship. Or so I thought.

Though my body sat in the control room beside Val, my spirit watched through Perry. So I missed witnessing the bard take her harp, sing her oration to St. Euterpe. Sister Lilith eat my liver, it's twisted that so warlike a creature as Val Kurgus serves some mousy lesser patroness of music. Why ignore her own bloody ancestral saint? Pride, for sure. Lady Valentine doesn't want anything to do with her family.

Well. I can understand *that*.

So. I didn't see her strum her strange harp, pronouncing the oration, then fall overcome to the control room floor. But Perry-me did have the fun of seeing St. Euterpe's response. Not so mousy as I'd expected.

Perry-me watched Matilda's arrow rise, up and up, same as a holy prayer to the Upper House. But I turned some of our eyes away, when about us appeared half a dozen Infernum-fucking airships. Illusion copies of our Phaethon. Well done, Sainted Euterpe.

I was so smacked to see them appear I missed when Matilda's arrow struck. Only looked when a new sun burst above us. Followed by a thunderclap that shook Phaethon. Shook the Middle House.

"Be getting inside!" shouted Matilda. She scrambled to regain footing upon the airship. 'Course each time she stepped a hoof, the cloth ripped beneath. Same as struggling out from thin ice on a winter pond. Finally Barnaby grabbed her hands and dragged her. They reached the portal, clambered down and away.

Perry-me remained, staring in amaze through our thousand-windowed eyes. The burning ship above rained down burning debris. It would have fallen upon Phaethon, set it ablaze as well. But with a sudden jerk to tumble anyone lacking eight legs, we rushed away. Clever Cedric whipping the engines like horses of a war chariot.

We left the illusory directables behind, swarming the air like giant hornets. At times they fired bolts of fire to the sky, or to the ground or upon one another. Wherever they struck, they left no mark, began no fires.

While the real airship struck by Matilda's arrow sank same as a setting sun. Flaming, smoking, crashing upon the earth. Black smoke rose, incense to please the bloodier sort of saints. The flying men circled about, flies pondering a dog fresh dead.

And now the true Hefestian ships joined the party. Attacking the illusory ships. Firing the same bolts that burned Edgestead. Some of the illusory ships fired back. Their flames doing no more damage than shadows. Still, the air became thick with smoke, bright with fire, loud with thunderclaps.

I watched the Hefestians wage the illusion of a grand battle. Perhaps it made no difference to them whether they fought real foes or shadows. Maybe they just needed to see enemies burn. Destroy them, crush them, grind them to ash and dust...

Leave them to it, I thought. No, that was Periwinkle thinking. Chiding me. Reminding me.

"You're right," I whispered. "Let's get back."

Perry and I left the Hefestians to their battle. We had better things to see, to do.

Chapter 24
The Stuff of Ancient Humor

"Why in Lucif's mother's dog's darkest love should we leave the Phaethon?" asked Bodkin. "We won it fair as a toss from a paladin's dice. Here we've got bunks. A private room to shit in. Stores of food and drink. Not to forget the flame guns. We'll need 'em when we're next in trouble."

"Which will be within the hour," prophesized Matilda.

"We have little fuel left," said Cedric. "We traded it for the speed of our escape. And the reserves went to Matilda's wonderful arrow."

"Was a bit astoundingly wonderful, was it not?" asked the Silenian, grinning. "Ah, that was like sending the sun a kiss, seeing it laugh fire in return. And I did it lying on my back. Not the usual fun a girl has in that position, though similar."

"Right," said Val. "Without more energy crystals, Phaethon is a deathtrap wandering with the wind. Their signal towers will be sending out the word. All Hefestia will be looking for it. We need to get off and away while it is still dark. Tonight."

"Couldn't we get more crystals?" asked Matilda.

"Doubtful," said Cedric. "They guard them like a dragon guards its eggs." Bodkin started to speak; Val cut him off.

"Spare the saints' ears from hearing how you can steal dragon eggs with eyes closed and hands tied. Disregarding certain death, stealing crystals is more Lucif-kissed *work* than just walking calmly where we want to bloody *get*."

"Yeah, but walking's a bore," said Bodkin. Giving a yawn to demonstrate the agony of ennui.

"I could use a bit of boredom," declared Cedric. "Once again, we barely avoided the swing of Friar February's harvest scythe. And only now approach the tower."

"Approach?" asked Barnaby, eyes widening. "Are we finally near?"

"Hmm, relatively. Were it daylight, you'd see a line of blue mountains to the north. The tower is within those very peaks, beyond the Hefestian border. A week or three away. But autumn approaches; it shall get cold."

Barnaby shivered at thought of the cold, at thought of the tower. The tower that waited in the cold. Waited for them. Maybe it shivered too? Barnaby pictured a tower shivering in cold wind, thinking how each day Barnaby and his friends neared it. Did the tower await them eagerly? Or in fear?

"Shall we put it to vote?" asked Cedric. "Stay on the ship, or leave?"

"Stay," declared Bodkin. "Let's see where the wind takes us."

"Stay," agreed Matilda. "Just another night."

"Leave," voted Cedric. "The Hefestians are not fools. They will not fall for the same tricks twice. They will find this ship. We'd best be away when they do."

"Leave," said Jewel.

"You're just agreeing with Cedric," growled Bodkin.

Jewel leaned forwards towards the rogue. He leaned back and away. She hissed.

"We had saint's luck today. Would anger Sister Hefestia to be asking for the same luck tomorrow. She'd name us fools. And the good Sister leaves fools to drink wisdom from a deep cup of tears."

"Fine," said Bodkin. "Fine. Fine."

Val turned to Barnaby.

"What about you, Miller?"

Barnaby looked about the control room. Counting the different places blood still stained. There by the control board, and in the corridor, and atop the ship...

"Staying on Phaethon means fighting to keep it. Today we did what we had to. But we don't have to stay now. And we shouldn't. I vote we leave."

"And I vote the same," said Val. "That settles it. Grab your gear, whatever you think you can carry. Admiral Cedric, find a quiet field and put us near enough to the ground to use the ladder."

Barnaby listened to the night sounds of Hefestia. Crickets aplenty. Night birds; but he only recognized the owl calls, the nightjar songs, the bats' near-inaudible squeak. What was the bird going '*thweep, thweep*?

He sat on dew-wet grass with the rest of the Society of St. Benefact, in a circle with Jewel for a center. Above them hovered the great gray whale of Phaethon. Drifting just slightly in the night breeze.

"What do you see?" demanded Bodkin.

Jewel kept head bent, hair veiling face. Her answer came slow, voice the whisper of a dreamer.

"Perry-me is tired. Today was hard. Too much sun."

"Just push the button," said Bodkin. "Then you can scamper off to bed."

"Which button? Are dozens."

"Lucif's flaming lips kiss my innocent mother, the red one of course."

"What is red? Our eyes see depths of green. Bright green. Leaf green. Cricket green. Flame greens..."

"Well, that's daft."

"No matter," said Cedric. "We can let the ship drift away."

"Bad plan," argued Bodkin. "There's little wind. The constabulary will find it floating in the next cow pasture. Be on our trail by breakfast, pop us in the gaol wagon by lunch."

"Could we not beseech some nice saint for a wind to blow it far and friendly away?" That, from Matilda.

"No beseeching from me," said Val. "I'm empty as Peri-Jewel. Or Jewel-Periwinkle. Whoever she is. I just want to sleep. For a year. Right here, now."

"I don't know any orations for wind," said Barnaby. "Pretty tired as well."

"Ah, *Luciftakemesideways*," muttered Bodkin. He stood, set his pack on the ground. Ran for the rope ladder.

"Oi," said Matilda. "Where you off?"

Bodkin made no answer. He clambered up, disappearing within the ship. Then,

"The boy's here," whispered Jewel. "Good. He can push things. We will sleep now."

"No, no," chided Matilda. "Don't go to sleep yet, Miss Spider-and-Witch. The lad's showing you which button to push. But he has to get properly down off the ship first or he'll float away to Nix and our sad loss."

Jewel did not answer, save with soft snore. She bent forwards, curling upon the grass.

They waited. Of a sudden, the ship began to hum. Then to move. Slow at first, but picking up speed. The ladder dragged along the grass.

"Is he leaving?" wondered Barnaby.

"He's stealing the ship we stole," giggled Val. She found herself leaning against Barnaby. He put an arm about her shoulder to prop her up.

Bodkin appeared at the directable door. Climbing down the ladder. But the ship now rose fast as he descended. At the ladder's end he dangled twenty feet above the ground.

"He's going to break his neck if he drops," predicted Val. Then shouted. "Bodkin, don't!"

"Patience," said Cedric. "The little rogue knows his business."

The ship passed over a stand of oaks marking the field's end. Bodkin dropped, disappearing into the branches. The Society gathered up their packs, hurrying best they could towards the trees. Cedric and Matilda aided Jewel, who stumbled sleepily.

They halted before a world of tree-shadow and bracken. Cedric raised his staff, muttered. A weak shine came forth. They stumbled farther.

Not far within, not far above, they heard cursing.

"Bodkin, boyo, that you?" inquired Matilda.

"No, it's Lucif's mother's owl," snarled a voice down from the dark branches.

"Owl?" asked Barnaby. "I thought she had a dog."

"I'm dropping the witch's spider pendant. Catch it."

A silver-glittering object fell from the branches. Jewel shook herself awake, ran to scoop it up.

"Can you get down?" asked Cedric.

"My trousers are speared on a branch. Ancient stuff of humor. I'm having to cut them away, so be ready to mock my boyish legs and butt."

The Benefactors waited. Till from the branches dropped a pair of tattered breeches. Bodkin followed more slowly, his climbing moves uncharacteristically slow.

When at last he reached ground, Cedric's faint light shone on fresh blood across Bodkin's face. The naked legs trembled, scratched and bleeding. The rogue crossed arms, glaring at all.

"Well, get your laughing done."

The Benefactors traded glances.

Matilda picked up the torn trousers.

"I'll sew these up fine for you," she promised.

"Here's your coat till then," said Val. She stepped beside him, draping the overlarge coat across his skinny shoulders.

Barnaby drew his wand, tapped it on a tree.

"This wood makes a good place for a quiet word with the Green Saint. Sit while I ask her to fix up those scrapes."

Now Jewel stepped forwards, pendant on chest again.

"Thank you, Bodkin." She said, then bent down, put a pebble of a kiss upon one bruised cheek. "That was brave of you. Now we can all rest for the night."

Cedric stamped his staff upon the forest dirt. Turning the dim glow to a bright flash.

"Three cheers for St. Benefact's finest rogue!" he shouted.

Bodkin stared at the Benefactors, surprised. Of a sudden he looked entirely and only his age, which was firmly in the realm of boyhood.

"Thanks, I suppose," he said. Wiping at his face. "Ha. Woods always make my eyes tear up."

Chapter 25
Of Pots and Punishments

Saint Lucif, Patron of Just Penance:

Yes, I have a tea kettle. There is nothing special about my tea kettle. Bronze, with floral design of ivy and flame. Made by Hefestus himself. A going-away present from the Upper House. Signed by all the old gang. Michael, Uriel, Ariel… I make *tea* with it. Just tea.

No, I do not have seven asses. Just one. Really, who would want more? With seven complete sets of buttocks, how would one sit? As for my primary generative organ… I refuse to discuss it. Thorns, spikes, snakes, flames? No business of any but myself. Well, and whoever I'm with, going about the business. House politics aside, St. Bridget *adores* me. Ask her.

My lips? are just lips. Quite nice, actually. Yes, they flame some. I'm not embarrassed by that. What fool wouldn't want flaming lips?

Yes, I, Lucif, do have a mother. No, she does not have an unhealthy relationship with her dog though she cares for the thing far more than she values *me* not that I care. Don't care at all. It has two heads, not three. One ass, one tail. A fondness for peeing in important places such as the Conference Room of Judgement. On my rugs. Not that I complain.

Yes, I have a sister. No, I do not have an unnatural relationship with her. We correspond affectionately. She sends me small gifts. Flowers carved from souls, and montages of living hearts torn from sinners' breasts. I send her boxed spirits I know she will enjoy. The saltier sorts, mostly.

The endless '*Lucif take this*', '*Lucif kiss that*', '*Lucif stuff him/her up all seven asses*'… These curses never amuse me. Never. They *puzzle*. Even if one were provided with six extra anuses, how does one go about the simultaneous stuffings? And more importantly, *why* do such stuffing? Forcing struggling, screaming, writhing sinners up my alleged seven personal orifices would punish *me* more than *them*.

Yes, I have a chamber pot. I'm a traditionalist. The modern fad of water pipes and dainty porcelain mechanicalisms annoy me. Chamber pots were fine in the old days before we began playing *saint this* and *sister that*. Simple; not to forget *environmentally friendly*.

Yes, I use my chamber pot to punish the wicked. Just not the tea pot. The tea pot is strictly for tea. If you wish to know, my chamber pot is five miles across, deep as Abaddon's eyes and filled daily with excrement so foul as to make harpies regurgitate the bones of mortals devoured when St. Chronos was a youngster.

I fill the chamber pot myself, most mornings. Usually while reading. I take my time. It's a moment of quiet, which Infernum knows, Infernum lacks. Often I have my most inspiring thoughts right there atop the pot. While it fills with the digested remains of the nastier souls I've devoured. They still wiggle and whine, of course. They scream endless curses. *Lucif bite so-and-so's privates. St. Lucif take me for his sister. Lucif's mother's dog bite their behind. Lucif stuff his thorned cockerel up me.*

As if I would!

Chapter 26
The Magic of Forward Motion

A patchwork of different materials formed Hefestia's roads. Brick, at times. Else flagstones, else pebbles mortared tight as grains on a wheat stalk. Otherwhiles the road became smoothed mud mysteriously solidified to stone.

That last surface puzzled Barnaby. He kicked at the gray substance, thinking it made a strangely dull path to walk. Like traveling a road paved with autumn cloud.

Same as the country lanes, the houses scattered left and right kept to no common design. One would be an egg-like construction with a domed roof of metal and glass. The next would be a wooden box with tilting towers, each topped with metal ornaments that spun and glittered. Beyond that waited a cottage of wattle and thatch looking to have been stolen from some croft of Demetia... excepting the bronze man by the gate that waved with clockwork friendliness. When the wind blew, this mechanical man bowed deep as courtier to king.

Delighted, Barnaby waved and bowed right back, till his friends pulled him on down the road.

The road itself was not left to Benefactors. They stepped aside to let quicker folk pass. These might be walking by sane and proper feet. Or astride horse, else in carts. And every so often would come some astonishing new method of travel.

Barnaby gawked at a man seated on a spider-web of wheels. He sat high as lord on horse, pumping legs up, down, up. Clearly this propelled the miraculous thing.

The others made way for the marvel to pass; but Barnaby stood in the road staring so delighted that the man turned his wheeled steed about, circling Barnaby, tinkling a tin bell. Barnaby laughed, the man laughed. Then waved goodbye, farewell, continuing on down the road.

"How does he not fall over?" demanded Barnaby addressing the sky he credited with such wonders.

"How do you not fall over?" demanded Bodkin. "What with you staring like a kitten on a church spire."

They walked on. Barnaby pondered exactly why he *didn't* fall when walking. It'd never occurred to him before. But on sober consideration, walking was a precarious business. One leaned forwards till about to topple; then shot a foot out, shifting to balance atop that foot while tipping forwards yet more, all while preparing to catch oneself with the other foot...

Barnaby stumbled, his feet tangling with the consideration of their work.

"Do be more careful," demanded the magical tutor upon his shoulder. "I might have been injured."

Barnaby prepared to share his observations of walking, but down the road now came a carriage. At first Barnaby thought it a cart rolling free and afire, for no horses pulled it, and smoke trailed behind.

But no, a man sat in the front, leading invisible steeds. He wore goggles and helmet same as a proper directable pilot. Barnaby waved, but the mechanism did not slow, the man did not wave back.

"How?" he asked the world.

"The wheels turn by burning coal under a kettle of water," said Cedric.

"Ah," said Barnaby. "That explains it nicely." He returned to the study of how he walked. Step, step. Dull business. But suppose... suppose *he were to put wheels on his feet?*

"Maybe we could obtain a steam car," mused Bodkin. "Get us north fast as blink."

"First," said Cedric, "There shall be no thieving, absconding, nor least illegal alteration of ownership within Hefestia. We have been chased like foxes in a house of hounds across three lands. Let us for this one day walk in peace."

"Bah," said Bodkin. "We stole a warship. You going to fret over a mechanical cart?"

"Second," continued Cedric. "The steam cars are insanely dangerous. Pressure oft builds in the kettle till it bursts, sending man and machine to the Fields."

"Then why do Festians ride them?"

Cedric gave e a pondering 'hmm' before reply.

"Daily custom shall make any danger seem a natural part of life. The Hefestians have a love of mad speed and machinery magic. To fly, to glide, to be served by clever wheels and humming engines... For all that every day in Hefestia one will hear a clap of thunder, as some overwrought mechanicalism scatters parts of man and machine."

"Entirely and completely a mad sort of land," declared Matilda.

"The Festians enjoy the taste of danger," offered Val. "Same as the folk of Martia. Comes from the spirit of the blasted saints."

Cedric nodded. "As the folk of St. Plutarch enjoy life all the more for dwelling in the shadows of death. Only Sainted Demetia calls her folk to enjoy life for its light, not its risk of ending."

Barnaby pondered that. Life in Mill Town seemed a dull thing when one walked with adventurers on a road of mad machines. He looked about Hefestia's countryside. Something caught his eye: a dark tunnel-opening on a hillside. Stones lined the entrance, while a faint line of smoke trailed forth.

"Are there Undermen in Hefestia?"

The cat perching lordly upon his shoulder deigned to give answer.

"The term is inexact. In the Middle House, several quite distinct races commonly dwell below the earth. All lazily mislabeled '*Undermen*'. For example, recall the Arachnae of Nix. Women who sit in the mouth of caves, luring their dinner of uncooked adventurer with scattered treasure."

"Do they have men folk?"

"Hmm, of a sort. But the males are timid things, keeping below ground even at night. They mate but once. Then the females devour them."

"Oi, that's more awful than very awful" declared Matilda.

"Not at all," said the cat. "The men sit in their bachelor quarters daydreaming of their wedding nights. Composing beautiful verses upon devotion, consummation and completion. To love once to perfection, and then join forever with the beloved... is that not an apotheosis to be envied?"

"No," said Barnaby.

"No," said Bodkin.

"No," said Cedric.

"Oh, I don't know," said Val. "Sounds rather romantic."

"Poetic," agreed Matilda.

"Sweet, really," said Jewel.

She, Matilda and Val traded laughs. Barnaby laughed too, just slightly unsure he should. Val offered him a toothy smile. The cat continued exposition.

'Then there are the Gobelin of various sub-groups. Generally shorter than mankind; of pale complexion, often of greenish hue. Disliking sunlight. They revere Saint Hob of the Lower House, whose testament is the sacredness of service."

"Mad folk, my dad says." That from Matilda. "Live in the hills northeast of Silenia. Raid our orchards at night for the sour greener sorts of fruit. Singing daft songs, if you can believe."

Barnaby pictured a race that Silenians such as Matilda or the Goat Girl would consider mad. Perhaps Silenians considered Demetians mad. But why? For milling, for farming, for living in villages instead of a sensible forest thicket? Perhaps for wearing boots. Barnaby considered his boots, and whether they argued for his madness.

The cat corrected the fur upon his proud tail, pleased as always to conduct class.

"The Gobelin tribes east of Silvanus are primitive creatures. Those this far west are more civilized. Or at least more circumspect. They have holdings in the mountains north of Hefestia. Perhaps we shall encounter some."

At which words Matilda fingered her bow, thinking happy things.

"In Darker Persephone," offered Bodkin, "they call 'Undermen' the critters that live below graves and crypts. Come out at night to sit on headstones, munching the bones of our grandparents, gibbering comments on the epitaphs."

"Bah, those are mere Ghouls," sniffed Night-Creep. "Scavengers originating from Nod, far, far to the south. They pop up in most any churchyard. Harmless, mostly; but inclined to give themselves airs. Moping in graveyards was never source nor sign of wisdom."

Barnaby pictured himself sitting on a gravestone chatting with Ghouls. At night, of course. A foggy night, while whisps of ghosts flittered, bats chittered. What would he say to such creatures? Or they to him? Perhaps they could talk of stones. The separate qualities of millstone as opposed to gravestone.

Then he shook himself, returned to practical thoughts.

"By 'Undermen', I mean the folk that are short and strong and bearded and make magical things. They live under hills and mountains and you hear their hammers beating like a dragon's heart."

He mimicked hammering an anvil.

"You refer to the Dwarrow," said Night-Creep. "Your description is accurate, if limited. They do prefer to live in caverns. Some within the mountains to which we journey."

Barnaby pointed into the distance, towards the dark tunnel opening upon the hillside. "I asked 'cause that looks to be one of their doorways."

"Ah, no," said Val. "That's a tunnel dug through the hill. For the iron rail paths I told you of."

"Dug through the hill?" wondered Barnaby. "Why not just go round?"

"The rails do not function well except with a level gradient," said Cedric. "And with overmuch curvature of the rails, friction will slow the train of carts and wear upon the wheels."

"I see," said Barnaby, nodding wisely.

"I see a directable," said Matilda. She pointed South.

"The Phaethon?" wondered Bodkin. "Be annoying for it to follow us about like an overfond dog."

Cedric produced a war trophy; the brass spyglass from Phaethon. He studied the distance for awhile. Then nodded, satisfied.

"This directable is decorated blue and red. Signs it belongs to the constabulary patrolling the roadways. Nothing to do with us."

"But if they've retrieved the Phaethon, they'll be looking for the suspicious strangers that departed it," declared Bodkin. "And as 'suspicious goes, we're all that. Best we get under cover before it's above us."

"Our next destination is not far," declared Cedric. "The town of Salmoneus. Once there, we can rest. Then plan our journey north in peace."

"Seems unlikely, that last part," said Matilda.

Cedric prepared to answer; but there came a loud rumble, and out from the hillside rolled a bronze dragon upon wheels.

Barnaby halted, astonished, delighted. Wishing Hypo, his fellow admirer of dragons were present to share the glorious vision. The beast followed the parallel lines, chugging smoke from its metallic muzzle.

The ground shook; just slightly. Behind the dragon came a long line of carts, wheels set to the rails. Barnaby rushed to the side of the road to get a better view.

A cloud of smoke and steam shot from the mouth, lit by sparks worthy of Infernum's ovens. And then from the beast came a glorious battle-worthy whistle-blast.

Barnaby wondered if it meant to attack. Should he draw Dragontooth, front the beast? But really it would be more fun to talk to the dragon, explain the axe's name and his deep admiration for all dragon-kind. As it neared, he saw the different metallic plates and pieces, rivets and bindings...

"Isn't a real dragon," he said. Not overly disappointed. Really, a bronze mechanical dragon was a fine thing to see in the morning.

"No," said Cedric. "The Hefestians delight in decorating their mad mechanicalisms in dramatic ways. Shaping the engine like a dragon head, or a lion or an angel. For them it must look dramatic, not merely serve for utilitarian purpose."

"Hefestians are children, and their land a nursery room of toys." That dismissive judgement from Val.

Barnaby's cat-tutor responded.

"They have a testament from their saint that they express in artistries. Same as all peoples." He gave a lick to a paw. "Excepting cats, of course."

* * *

Afternoon came, bringing weary feet, growling stomachs. On the road ahead waited yet one more Festian mystery to puzzle Barnaby.

"Is that the city wall?"

"In a way," answered Cedric. "Hefestians do not protect themselves with stone defenses as do the Demetian cities. Nor wooden ramparts such as St. Martia prefer; nor yet the moats that circle even the smaller Plutarchian villages. The Hefestians merely pile their refuse upon the outskirts of their towns, till it encircles them."

"Does that protect from attack?"

"Indirectly. So many Hefestian goods are volatile, flammable, or simple toxic that their habitations would choke and burn if they did not regularly dispose of anything that began humming loudly, spinning blades or emitting glowing gasses. Thus, their towns are ringed with ages of lethal debris. A wise invading army shall not step foot upon it."

The Benefactors proceeded down the road. The lowering sun stretching their shadows. Soon they entered a canyon bordered with scrap metal and broken glass. Weeds and even trees grew from the rubble, making it seem the ancient ruins of some time-lost city. The air grew thick with fumes of oil, of soot, of mold and rust; stenches of decay both organic and inorganic. Here and there, paths led from the road, rising into these hills of mechanical trash.

"Who goes up those paths, if it is so dangerous?" That, from Val.

"Trash pickers, of course," said Cedric. "People making their living scavenging parts and materials. As they do in many a city midden or river flat."

Val halted. She traded a look with Bodkin. A secret conversation ensued. Then the two nodded.

"This way, Benefactors," declared the bard. Turning from the nicely paved road onto a rough pathway upwards into the hillside of rubbish.

"What?" demanded Cedric. "Why?"

Bodkin answered, following after Val.

"We're going to find a nice comfortable place to camp for the night." He waved about. "Somewhere in all this lovely uninhabited wilderness."

"Hoof and head of this weary child were hoping for a tavern," declared Matilda. Stamping said hoof, shaking cited head.

Bodkin shook his own head.

"The inns are where constabulary types will be making inquiries concerning bands of mysterious strangers," replied Bodkin. "We camp here tonight. Tomorrow we enter the town separately, do our business as innocent individuals."

Matilda, Cedric and Jewel traded disappointed glances.

"I suppose we'll have to trust our foxes, that they know best how to avoid the hounds," sighed Cedric.

They followed Val up the rough path as it switched back and forth. The footing was precarious, with bits of metal and glass poking like teeth and claws from the dirt and rubble.

Barnaby stopped to study a heap of tangled metal. Within the scrap pile lay a giant face, rusted and tarnished yet smiling beyond the injuries of time. It lay sideways, one cheek buried in dirt. Two eyes large as dinner plates stared into the distance.

Had this been the head of a colossus fit with great iron trunk and legs? Perhaps it had walked in great clockwork steps, making the ground tremble. A clockwork giant.

He reached to touch the face, then stopped. Drawing his hand back. The fallen thing stared across the hills of trash with noble wisdom. At rest, sinking into the world's decay. And yet still worthy of respect. Not something to just poke in curiosity.

Barnaby settled for making a bow. Then backed away, waving farewell, hurrying after his friends.

He found them gathered in a large hollow where debris merged with dirt. A tree grew at the center, holding branches high over the crater.

"These rubble hills occasionally burst in fire and thunder," declared Cedric. "Leaving craters such as this. It shall make excellent place to camp."

"Unless it goes 'boom' again," said Bodkin.

"Unlikely," declared Cedric.

"*How* unlikely?" asked Bodkin.

"Hmm. Decently unlikely."

"Well, that's better than fairly unlikely," said Val. "If not as excellent as 'extremely unlikely'."

"Better than our chances if we just marched into town," declared Bodkin. "Those semaphore towers are probably clicking and clacking warnings to all good Hefestians: beware wandering bands of airship thieves."

The night was warm and the hollow sheltered from the wind. But a campfire was a thing of comfort that declared they rested in a place of safety. Therefore, Val and Bodkin consulted, allowing a small fire to center their camp.

They sat grateful for fire and rest, sharing rations. A mix of foods that declared them proper travelers. Demetian apples, and wrapped Hefestian breads from Phaethon. Wine from Plutarch; even some sausages saved from Martia.

Every so often, a steam-dragon would whistle in the distance, shaking the ground slightly as it pulled its string of carts towards far and exotic places.

Barnaby sat on his blanket, feeling as satisfied with existence as any miller ever felt. Watching sparks fly up like angels to the Upper House. He contemplated all he'd seen today. The steam dragon and the spider-wheeling man and the bizarre paving of petrified mud and the bronze bowing man...

Val sat upon her own blanket, comfortably near to his. She strummed Thelxipea. Humming softly, then shifting to song.

I left my home, left my saint and people.
A child set climbing the cathedral steeple.
Searching haystacks for the holy needle.
Encountering souls both good and evil.
Questioning every angel, every devil.
Toppling the pillars of each temple.
Seeking a truth I knew was symbol.
Thirsting for a thing quite simple.
To find the cup and then drink...
And that's enough, I think."

The Benefactors pondered the song and the singer, the melody and the words.

"Are you thinking your magic holy glowing singing cup is awaiting you in the tower?" asked Matilda. "That would have a quite fine neatness to it."

Val smiled, shook head, declining to say. Put down the harp, yawned. Barnaby studied how firelight and night shadow painted her face. The plain features turning of a sudden noble and tragic as the clockwork giant's. He shivered at the transformation. Turned to the others, wondering if they also saw a Val transfigured.

There sat Bodkin, staring into the fire same as any daydreaming miller. While Jewel gazed downwards to her spider pendant. Cedric stared as well; not at the spider but at Jewel. Matilda stretched out, grinning at the stars of the Upper House of Saints. Beside her sat Dark Michael, hands out to catch the memory of warmth.

Bodkin, Jewel, Cedric, Matilda, even Michael… the same trick of light and shadow placed dramatic masks upon all their faces. Or did it?

No, Barnaby decided. The firelight *removed* the masks. Revealing the souls of his friends as noble actors in life's absurd magic theatre.

Wonderstruck, near trembling, Barnaby lay back, gazing at the quiet stars. Till Val leaned from her blanket to put her ennobled face close to his. Grinning down, she granted him a single chaste kiss.

"Night, you," she whispered. Then she wrapped herself in her own blanket, curled into her own thoughts and slept.

Barnaby wondered about his own face. She'd kissed it. Maybe he'd looked noble himself, transfigured like an ancient statue. Or not. He didn't much mind either way. Satisfied with the kiss, he wrapped himself in his own blanket, his own thoughts, and slept.

Chapter 27
Things at Rest

Barnaby wandered from dreams to the awareness of weight upon his chest. Hoping to see Val, he opened eyes, meeting the angel-wing gaze of his tutor in magic.

"Lesson time," declared Professor Night-Creep.

Barnaby sighed, nodded. He sat up, sending the cat leaping. He looked about the sheltering crater. The other Benefactors still slept, campfire long settled to dim embers. The sky in the east turning pale at the threat of dawn. He stood, stretched, taking up axe and wand.

The cat walked into the night. Barnaby followed, stopping to pee. He noted how the wind blew chill. *Autumn coming*, he thought. Harvest time. At home, who'd be grinding the grain, fixing the vanes and cogs, sacking the flour? Couldn't picture Alf or Mother Miller doing such labor. Mill Town had best call off autumn, go straight to winter.

He looked about, spied Night-Creep springing effortlessly beyond the hollow, following a path clear to cat eyes. Man-eyed, Barnaby stumbled after him.

"Do you ever have to pee?" he asked the cat.

"Hmm, yes. In an intellectual sense."

"Oh." Barnaby pondered exactly what that meant. Considered asking, decided not. "Where are we going?" he asked instead.

"First to gather our tools. Retrieve that metal rod you just stumbled over. It has excellent properties that will serve nicely for a wand."

"I have a wand."

"Yes, but it is attuned to Demetia. Here plays the music of a different conductor."

Barnaby searched the dark ground, fingers finding a cold metal rod. Lighter than iron or bronze.

"What is it made of?"

The cat tutor stood on hind legs, sniffed at the bar.

"Several metals, alloyed. Your friar might be able to tell you of its forging. I limit my interest to detecting potential for magic."

He descended to four feet again.

"Now go to the right past that tangle of spikes. Seek in the shadows. You will find a small pool. Dip the wand in, stir it about. Try not to breathe overmuch."

Barnaby stepped forwards, cautious of sharp objects to left and right. Past piles of debris, he spied a small pool glimmering in dawn's growing light. He approached; ears catching a faint *drip, drip* of seepage from geologic strata of mechanical beasts long buried and forgot.

Wafting vapors of oil and metallic ichors thickened the air. Holding his breath, he bent over the pool. It looked black, glistening with rainbow streaks. He reached the wand downward, stirring the florescent lines. The liquid moved sluggishly, thick as cloth.

When he could hold breath no longer, he retreated, gasping, coughing, head turning light with strange fumes.

"That shall do," said the cat. "Now raise the rod high."

Barnaby did so.

"Recite after me: *"Things at rest remain at rest. What moves shall continue to move, constant in goal and speed. Let this be your first law, sainted Hefestus."*

Barnaby repeated these unlikely words, offering the rod to the dawn. It glimmered with peacock streaks, same as the pool.

"Excellent. Now follow."

Barnaby followed; not far, but downwards into a crater deeper than where they'd camped. The brightening sky revealed the path sufficiently that Barnaby no longer stumbled. At the bottom of this crater, Night-Creep halted.

"Behold our classroom. Now, search for some mechanism not entirely fallen to pieces. We shall attempt a lesser *Oration of Repair*."

Barnaby nodded; began wandering about, kicking here, poking there. Rejecting jumbles of cogs, rusting boxes of wire and glass. He considered something embedded in the hillside. It resembled a coffee grinder fit with a crossbow. Surely some clever Hefestia weapon. Barnaby pulled it loose. The object fell to pieces, then the slope of debris crumbled, sending dirt and trash down upon him. Barnaby jumped back.

"Do strive not to bury us alive," admonished the cat.

Barnaby nodded, dropping the fragments of the dread weapon. He stared into the newly created hole. There in the debris waited a head. Not of a man, but a dog.

He reached, brushing dirt and trash away, revealing something like a bronze statue. No memorial to the noble canine. This beast looked large and rough-furred, with a blunt, bear-like muzzle. A mechanical mongrel, good for guarding a farmyard. The joints of leg, head and jaws looked cleverly articulated. Barnaby waited, hoping it would stir itself.

But the beast's eyes and jaws stayed closed. Clearly it slept away the ages. Night-Creep approached, sniffing warily.

"Hmm. You do continue with your penchant for finding rarities. Granted, we are in a hillside composed of broken rarities."

"It's a clockwork dog," declared Barnaby. "Like Da's clockwork owl. Is it fixable?"

Night-Creep batted a paw at the thing. There came a faint chime.

"Doubtful. It's astonishingly ancient. The insides must be jumbles of rust. Still, for demonstration failure is as educational as success. Raise your wand."

Barnaby raised his wand.

The cat circled him once, twitching whiskers. Then,

"Recite after me: "*Decay stays or advances, never lessening, never yielding. Save only when you, oh Saint of Artifice, hear our pleading.*"

Barnaby repeated the words, his tutor twitching his tail in time to the words.

"Now tap the wand to the head, hmm, the heart, the tail of the beast. Then each leg."

Barnaby so did. With each tap came a pleasant chime, as though the bell of a clock were struck.

That done, they waited. Barnaby watched the eyes, hoping to see them flicker. Perhaps the legs would move like a dog running in dream? But nothing happened. Barnaby listened to a distant steam-dragon clattering. Birds announcing the dawn. The rumble of his hungry stomach.

"Pity," declared Night-Creep at last. "But keep the wand. We shall try again on an easier subject."

Barnaby nodded, disappointed but not surprised. He could not imagine this bronze effigy moving. One might as well appeal to a statue of a saint to descend from their pedestal, come take tea. He gave a farewell tap of the wand to the mechanism's bronze nose, then followed his tutor up the side of the crater.

They were half-way to the camp when from behind came a rumble. Then a roar.

"Run," suggested Night-Creep.

Barnaby leaped to do so. Promptly stumbled, falling to the ground. Behind came a thunderclap, followed by a rain of debris. Barnaby curled in a ball, covering head with arms till the trash-fall ceased. Then he uncurled.

"Did I do that?" he asked.

Night-Creep sat ordering the fur of his tail, not a bit discomposed.

"Likely," he said. "We did petition that energy be transferred. Seemingly it was."

"A dangerous sort of magic," said Barnaby. Rising, brushing himself off. He studied the oily metal wand. In dawn's light it shimmered with rainbow-metallic streaks.

"St. Hefestia is a land of wonders," said his teacher. Walking onwards. "Today's lesson has been: *there comes a risk with wonders.*"

"You're quite alive," declared Matilda happily. "There were doubters, for folk must do their doubting."

"We feared you'd been caught in one of the periodic conflagrations of mechanical refuse." That, from Cedric.

"Almost," said Barnaby. "Breakfast?"

"We've had ours," said Val. "But I saved you scraps." She handed him a bowl; adding a kiss in contribution. It started as a scrap of a peck to the cheek, but he turned, meeting her lips with his. Lips merged, tongue tips tapped. It went on a pleasant while.

From her pack, Val's harp began to sing.

Matilda laughed in delight.

Night-Creep yawned.

Jewel giggled.

Bodkin cleared his throat. The two separated, red-faced but unabashed.

Bodkin sighed. "Benefactors, if I may have your attention?"

Barnaby nodded. Val nodded. Thelxipea quieted.

"Right," said Bodkin. "First off, let's get our story set. Remember, all. We're travelers from Persephone. Crossed the border during the weekly truce at the Disputed Circle. *Not* on a stolen warship. Never heard of Phaethon nor nary any airy battle. And never ever never stepped a foot in St. Martia."

"Martia?" asked Val. "Where's that? One of your Spicy Islands?"

"*That's* the spirit of dishonesty the day calls for. And Cedric, you're a professor from Pomona visiting old school friends."

Cedric rolled eyes, released sighs. "I have papers declaring me a legitimate emissary from the Deaconry of Plutarch."

"Oh, well done. I believed you."

"But, but it is true."

"Too forceful. Now I'm doubting."

"Can I still be a proper and pretty Silenian?" asked Matilda. "Going to need boots and hat quick otherwise."

"Be Silenian," advised Bodkin. "But a peaceable one. You deal only in the softer sort of fruits and the quieter vegetables."

"And I'm a not a miller," declared Barnaby. "I am..." He took a deep breath of dishonesty. "I'm a hat smith."

"A which?" asked Jewel.

"No, a maker of hats." She looked doubtful. He clarified for her. "Special hats."

Bodkin nodded. "You do that. While we whisper to folk how you took a blow to the head. That way, they'll believe you and us together."

It seemed a fair compromise. Barnaby nodded.

"Now," continued Bodkin. "Here is today's plan. We go into, into… what's the town again?"

"Salmoneus."

"Right. That place. We go in pairs an hour apart, so no bells ring at sight of a criminal band of airship thieves. Myself and Matilda go first. We'll do some supply shopping and some scouting. First sign of the hunt and we scamper back here. Next comes Jewel and Barnaby. Do what shopping you need. If there's no trouble, head to the, the… what is it called?"

"The iron rail port. At the north end of town."

"That place. We meet there before sunset. Going to buy seats on a steam dragon wagon. We'll ride north in style."

"Being blown to tatters is style?" That, from Val.

"That seldom happens," Cedric hurried to say.

Val looked doubtful. Then,

"Well, it'd best be Cedric who goes with Jewel."

"Why so?"

"Jewel and Barnaby are the least traveled. While Cedric and I know the basics of Hefestian customs. With one of us, there's a better chance of walking through town without drawing suspicion."

"Ah," said Matilda. "But that leaves you and Mister Barnaby here just sitting about, sitting about for hours."

Val shook her head in sorrow.

"We'll find something to do."

Matilda and Bodkin departed, arguing the dynamics of steam dragon wagons as opposed to sane mule carts. Leaving Cedric and Jewel sitting across from Barnaby and Val. The smoldering campfire sent wafts of smoke to give their eyes something to pretend to watch, made crackles of embers to pretend to listen to. Still, it all summed to awkward silence.

"Those two," said Val at last. "Matilda and Bodkin. They keep things lively and easy. Without them, we're four folk with astonishing little to share or say."

Cedric looked to the sky, spying nothing to share. Barnaby searched the embers for topics of conversation. Finding nothing he wished to share. Jewel sighed, produced her book of orations; stared intently at the pages. Not sharing what she read.

"I could make more coffeeish, if any would like," offered Cedric.

"I do like watching it bubble and fizzle," said Barnaby. "But it gives my stomach a sour burn."

"Mine too," admitted Cedric.

"You don't suppose it bubbles and fizzles inside us?"

"It could well do so," agreed Cedric.

"What was that?" asked Val, standing up.

"What?" asked Barnaby.

"Oh, I'm sure I heard something. Just over the rise. C'mon, we'd best check it out." Val grabbed Barnaby's arm, pulled him to his feet. Turned to address Cedric.

"You two stay here, guard our gear. If we aren't back in an hour, then, hmm, well, remember us fondly."

Jewel did not look up from her reading; but gave a vague wave of her hand to say *'farewell, bye, good fortune'*.

"I heard a steam dragon go by," said Barnaby, following Val. "But they stay on their iron paths." He weighed that statement. "Don't they?"

"That is just the very question," replied Val. "Do they stay on their path? Or do they wander from their iron rails, go sneaking after innocents to devour?"

Beyond the crater, out of sight of the others, she halted, leaning against a wall of dirt and jumbled debris.

"We'd best make plans before it comes to battling dragons."

"Well, it wasn't a mechanical dragon that made the noise," said Barnaby, staring ahead.

"What noise? Wasn't any noise. I made that up, come here."

"It was a mechanical dog."

"What?"

Barnaby pointed. There, farther down the path, stood the bronze figure of a dog. It took a tentative step forwards, as if recalling how to walk. Then shivered, shaking the dust of ages from the curls of its metal fur.

"*What. Is. That?*" demanded Val. Each word enunciated in sharp annoyance.

"Oh, it is the mechanicalism that Professor Night-Creep and I repaired. Not that we knew. That we repaired it, I mean. I cast '*Oration of Repair*' upon it. Which made things thunderclap if you recall. But I guess the spell worked. Night-Creep will be pleased. I think. If he likes dogs. He being a cat, I'm unsure."

The dog worked to open jaws wide, revealing steely teeth. Then made a sound that might have been a bugle barking happily, if a bugle were so inclined to express itself.

Val sighed, drew knife.

"Is it dangerous?"

"Dunno. Looks strong. Being metal and all. But it doesn't sound angry." Barnaby stepped towards the creature, holding his hand out and down as he would to any dog at a farm gate demanding to know his business and his scent.

The dog moved forwards. The first steps stiffly; but soon moving with a more natural gate. It came up to Barnaby, turning gaze from the hand to Barnaby, back to the hand. Clearly considering.

The eyes were dark crystals shining wet as polished jet. Shimmering with the same rainbow skeins that covered Barnaby's new wand. These eyes focused upon the offered hand.

"You're going to get your hand bit off," predicted Val. "And I had plans for it today."

Barnaby hesitated. But it felt wrong to withdraw the offered greeting. He shrugged; and the dog made a shiver of shoulders that echoed the shrug. Then the beast poked cold iron nose into Barnaby's palm. For a moment they stood so; then the dog backed away, taken suddenly shy. It sat on its haunches, staring upwards at him. Opening jaws to give a satisfied grin.

"Good boy," said Barnaby happily.

"That's settled, then," said Val. Held out arms. "Now come here."

Barnaby did so.

"Good boy," said Val.

"It's watching us, Send it away."

"Go play, dog, Shoo."

"Woof."

"Still there."

"Maybe Professor Night-Creep knows how to command it?"

"What? Is your damned magic cat watching too?"

"I am, as it so happens. Entirely disinterested. Continue. For once, I am being educated."

"Shit. Euterpe beat my butt for a drum. That's it. Taliesin take my tits for a tambourine. Done. Move away, miller. We'll try again *alone*."

"Woof."

Val and Barnaby returned to camp, trailed by cat and dog. Val announcing their approach with a long loud string of oaths to the saints of song.

There before the ashes of the fire sat Cedric and Jewel, just as before. Jewel leafing her book, Cedric staring at the sky.

Unlike before, Cedric now showed face flushed pink; while Jewel leafed pages studiously, for all she held her book upside down.

"We found a dog," announced Barnaby. "Unless it found us."

"So I see," said Cedric, rising, straightening his disordered robe. He studied the mechanical beast. "Hefestia is fond of such devices. Some are quite clever mechanisms."

"This one is a bother," growled Val.

The beast took no offense. It wagged a bronze tail, making the *squeak, creak* of a rusty hinge.

Cedric gathered up his things. "The hour has passed. Our turn now to venture into Salmoneus. We shall meet you at the iron rail port."

"Take the dog," said Val. "Dog, go with the nice priest."

But the creature settled itself beside Barnaby firmly as garden statue. He gave it a tentative pat. The beast opened jaws wide for grin. Showing plentiful teeth, centered by a thick cloth tongue, black as its eyes. The tongue shifted sideways to hang casual over steely fangs.

The creature looked entirely satisfied with existence. Barnaby laughed in equal delight; leaned close, listening.

"Hey, he ticks and hums," he announced.

"Wonderful," growled Val.

Barnaby picked up a stick, tossing it across the crater. The dog jumped up, ran after it, trotted proudly back, trophy in mouth. Barnaby took the stick, threw it yet farther.

"Woof!"

"Good dog!"

"Bridget butter my butt and bite it," sighed Val.

"Bye, all," said Jewel. "Have fun." She took Cedric's hand, hurrying him away. Skipping, some.

Val glowered, beginning a mystic bardic sign towards Jewel's back. Then repented, turned it into a weak wave of farewell.

Two hours later, Val and Barnaby stood upon a busy street of Salmoneus, staring, studying. The buildings rose tall as those of Persephone. But each held to that defiant nonconformity he'd seen in Hefestian houses upon the road. Some constructions were all of glass. Others, brick boxes plain as Demetian dirt. Many were quarried stone ornamented with faces that frowned, goggled or grinned in fixed astonishment, same as Barnaby.

Sensible walkways bordered the sides of the smoothly paved street, so that those afoot would not be trampled by the variety of transportation rushing to and fro. Carts and horses, wheeled mechanicalisms peddled and pulled, pushed or propelled by inner fires. Many puffed oily clouds of smoke that hovered in the air like spirits of mad invention.

Yet more walkways stretched *above* the street, connecting buildings same as bridges across a busy river. At times winged men flittered from one rooftop to another, gliding smooth as swallows. Higher still floated the occasional directable, humming its sky-whale song to the clouds.

The total made a mechanical hubbub difficult to ignore. Barnaby stared, smelled, listened, till Val reached, pushing his jaw up to close it.

He grabbed the hand, held it; still staring about. Then turned happy eyes upon her, leaning close.

"Amazing place."

"Yeah, yeah."

He shook his head, clasped the hand, meeting her eyes.

"But you still stand the more amazing."

She blinked, her turn to gape astonished.

"Just occasionally, Mr. Miller, you say the right thing. That was one of them, and just in time, boyo."

They walked on. Val contemplated holding Barnaby's hand the way Jewel had held Cedric's. So very sweet; and yet absurd. Might as well start skipping.

I'm not a dewy-eyed thing in love. I'm... fond of the boy. His sweet nature. And the freckles, the shoulders, all good. But there will be no skipping. No holding hands, arms swinging. None of that. Bah to that.

"Rusty," said Barnaby.

"What is?"

"The dog."

Val turned, looking at the creature trailing happily behind. The faux fur looked tarnished, certainly. But lacked the flaking of rust.

"I mean a name for it. Because, you see, he's made of metal."

"Oh. Well, it has a tag hanging from the collar."

Barnaby stopped, knelt down, peering. The dog grinned, holding still as statue.

"Huh. You're right. Didn't see that."

"What's it say?"

"Festus." He patted the dog. "Greetings, Festus."

Creak, squeak, went the dog's tail.

Val walked on, Barnaby and Festus following.

"Might just mean it's an Hefestian artifice," said Val. "Not that any other folk are so loon as to make such toys."

She halted of a sudden before an open doorway. Music sounded within.

"I know that tune. I know the instruments. Why does it sound so strange?"

Barnaby shrugged. Pondered the front of the building. Colorful walls, with glazed windows revealing the silhouettes of folk inside sitting to table, lifting cups.

"I think it's a kind of tavern."

"Right," said Val. "Let's get a decent meal. Scout a bit. Ask if anyone wants a dog."

Not waiting, she stepped warily in. Barnaby and Festus following.

A Hefestian tavern was like to a real tavern, as Hefestian *coffeeish* was like to real coffee. That is, it reminded of the real thing.

Here were tables and benches, a bar serving beverages, the air thick with the smells of hot food. A pleasant buzz of happy folk talking, and the flow of music.

But the benches and tables were spider-thin constructions of metal and impossibly white stone. The scents were strange and chemical, reminiscent of the food cubes upon Phaethon. While the music came tinkling and jangling from out a great box of brass and glass.

Val went straight to it, staring horrified at what she saw within. Wheels turned, pumps rose and fell, gears spun. Jointed hands moved in clockwork precision. All to pluck strings, tinkle chimes, beat drums, puff pipes. Behold all an orchestra reduced to the essential moving parts.

"This, this is madness," whispered Val.

"*Civic Ordinance 37#, section seven,*" declared a voice behind them. "No dogs allowed in places of public food consumption."

Val ignored the admonition. Barnaby turned. There stood a man of middle years in Hefestian soldier's uniform. A bandage across his forehead.

"Here now, do I know you?" asked the man, peering at Barnaby.

"Possibly. My name is Barnaby. I'm a hat smith."

"Thought you fellows called yourselves hatters?"

"Not us makers of *special* hats."

"Why, what's so special about 'em?"

"Well, they are... fire hats. Excepting the water hats."

"You mean fireproof, waterproof?"

"No, no. I mean they are on fire. Except the water ones. Those drip water like, like a fountain."

"Now that'd be something to see," admitted the man. He reached down, petted Festus. "Hmm. Clockwork dog? Used to be popular. My granddad had one. Guess it can stay. Ordinance #37 is just for the organic sort."

Val continued staring in outrage and fascination into the mechanical orchestra box, ignoring them entirely.

"Barnaby, is it? Well, I'm Sub-Lieutenant Thuro. On leave under Regulation #72, Section 23: *Recuperation from injury in course of duty.*"

"It is very nice to meet you, Sub-Lieutenant," declared Barnaby. "We were just going to have lunch. Will you join us?"

* * *

"I thought for sure you were going to get us arrested," declared Val. Walking from the tavern, checking backwards for constables blowing whistles.

"For having lunch?"

"For talking with that Hefestian air soldier. He almost recognized you from the Phaethon."

"Mister Thuro. I hit him in the head when Hypo and I took the control room. That's why he's on leave, wears that bandage. Funny coincidence we meet here."

"Oh, don't bother calling it coincidence. There's chapter and verse in the testament of Sister Fortuna to clarify such absurdities. *'Blessed be the mysteries of meetings, for soon or late all threads will cross to the will of the weaver.'* It's the saints messing with us, miller."

"Oh. Well, he wanted to buy one of my fire hats."

"Barnaby, you don't actually make hats. Fire or water or whatever."

"Well, but I could. It came to me while we were eating that strange lunch. I could store lantern oil in the brim of the hat, then have wicks poking out the top like altar candles on a saint's day."

"That's the Festian spirit," sighed Val.

"Woof!"

"Not you, you clockwork pest. But the saint of Holy Artifice gets in your head. Sets your spirit afire to build things. Mad things. Things that will probably set your head on fire."

She grabbed his hand, tugged him down the street.

"Let's get you out of this land before you put wheels on your feet."

"I thought of that very thing. I think it's quite doable."
"Woof!"

Chapter 28
Where Parallel Lines Meet

Dark Michael:

Hear then, a strange truth: *ghosts fear death more than do the living*. Death is a gate; and the innocent mortals fear the brief crossing of that boundary. Ah, but once passed beyond, spirit eyes now open to eternity, a soul gazes down a long and perilous road; and trembles at the journey yet to begin.

In life I was not a kindly man. Nor yet unkind, excepting to myself. Excepting to myself. I worked hard, living harsh. I believed in duty. To Demetia, to my king and fellow soldiers. To the House of Saints, I suppose. Though in life I thought little of that grand construction.

The witch spawn cat and I labored to gather companions for the boy. Folk that would keep him alive on his noble quest. It proved absurdly easy. Hard not to imagine that as we worked in shadow, we in our turn were guided from yet deeper shadows.

A strange group, the gathered *Benefactors*. Lonely sorts, of the kind that talk to themselves as much as to another. The Silenian excepted. She seemed so sound of mind that one wondered was she the maddest of them all?

She sat on a bench in the steam wagon depot of Salmoneus. Grinning to watch the boy-rogue pace up and down, looking from the clock to the grand entrance of the station. Arguing with his ancient inner ghost, waiting for the rest of his band to show; else the gendarmes of Hefestia.

I found myself sitting beside her. Recalling for a second the memory of hard benches. Splinters in the ass, aches in the feet, the back of one's head uncomfortably pressing against brick. Ears drumming with the echoes of the depot hall, the hiss of the steam engine, the clatter and chatter of travelers.

The recollection faded, leaving me to sigh. At which sound the Silenian's sharp ears twitched; her slotted eyes turned upon me. As always, she acted as though it were a grand pleasure to behold my glowering shadow.

"Well, hello, Mister Deceased Soldierly Person."

Hard not to smile at such welcome.

"Miss Silenian."

"And how do you fare this fine day wherein we gird our souls to travel by magic mechanical teakettle upon flame?"

I contemplated the question and the questioner. The creature was no fool. No, she chattered pretty nonsense to put others at ease. A clever strategy when one differs from the norm by shape of foot, ear and eye. Doubly so when one is a pretty female serving ale in taverns.

"I have ridden in Hefestian steam wagons," I shared. "They require no special girding of soul."

"Oh, have you now? Is it like riding in a box carriage? Did that very thing once outside Pomona. Till the driver got frisky, the way they will do with a poor girl on the road. I had to kick him into sense and sensibility, let the horses wander." She gave a demonstrative kick of flower-painted hoof.

I recalled an adjunct with a Silenian wife. He made her wear wool stockings to bed, lest her hooves tear his legs as they mated. Later I wondered if Silenian couples followed the same custom; or was the plaint mere human softness?

"This is a primitive affair," I told her. "Merely a chain of enclosed carriages pulled by the steam engine. In

Daedalus you see more advanced ones with doors connecting the wagons like separate rooms of a stretched house. Some for passengers; some for dining. Quite elegant."

She studied me awhile with her goat-slotted eyes.

"Really, you're quite the well-traveled ghost. Seeing so many different lands and folks, not to mention all that coming and going twixt life and death."

To that I said nothing. Though I might have said much. Too much, in truth. She filled the silence easily.

"I've been round and about Demetia. And in and out of that old boneyard Plutarch. And once as far east as Artemisia. Never up to St. Silenus proper, though I've plenteous cousinry there. Have you family still on live in the world's wild woods, Mister Soldier Michael?"

I'd had a wife. Pity her, saints; espoused to the Cold Major. Forget the discomfort of hooves in bed. What joy in mating with a man known for his soul of ice?

"No," I said. "No family. The army was my life." *As it was my death*, I could have added. But such words are a bore. Save them to mutter into a tankard.

"That sounds a mite lonely. Happier now to have a band of mad folk to sit with?"

Happiness. Not a thing I'd coveted in life. Still less in death. A trivial thing, happiness. A soap bubble of laughter floating through existence's garden of thorns. Bah; more brooding words.

"I have purpose. For souls such as mine, purpose is as close to happiness as we shall reach. In life or what comes after."

She nodded. "That's just about exactly what and how and who I took you for. A soldierly sort of fellow and spirit. Not happy lest you've the orders in your pocket, reigns in hand and enemy ships on the horizon."

I almost asked why I'd hold reigns in a naval battle. But she grinned to say she knew she spoke nonsense again. Disconcerting. Could she be trying to *amuse* me?

But then into the station walked Friar Cedric and the farm-witch Jewel. Hands clasped, feet in step. I shook my head at that unlikely coupling. Clearly based on two lonely souls sharing their need to be needed. How long could such binding last? As long as the binding of the Benefactors, no doubt. These were all folk who needed purpose; needed family.

But whether they died in the tower, or walked from it with pockets full of gold... what then? And when I fulfilled my third task for the boy... again, what then?

Matilda nodded at the approaching Cedric and Jewel.

"Does me good to see them cuddling and coupling all lovebird-like. Not even to mention the hot fiery ferocious flirtation of our bard and miller mixing. Makes me want to find a body to share a body in the nights, if you contemplate my meaning."

I contemplated her meaning. It seemed clear.

Now she stood, peering at me with eyes mad as the prophet Endymion chasing the moon he took for the Lord of the House of Saints. Then leaned close to whisper.

"If you feel a'nights that cold eternal wind giving chills, a girl like myself won't be minding your request to share a warm blanket."

She followed these words with a wink, then turned away.

The hours passed; the chain of steam wagons puffed in preparation to depart. Passengers climbed into the joined carriages, maneuvering packs and bundles. But the Society of St. Benefact waited, worrying. Miller and bard were yet to arrive.

The rogue and the cleric argued whether to return to town to rescue them, else retreat to the hill of mechanical waste. There came no discussion of leaving any behind. Excellent. They had learned loyalty.

I sat, observing, considering. I did not seek the boy. I forever knew his location, his condition. He shone as a bonfire on the empty plane of my soul. Binding me to the Middle House, as we call the strange realm of life.

So I turned to the entrance, knowing he would appear. He and the bard hurried into the station. Followed by a mechanical beast. The Benefactors exchanged expletives, excuses and explication, then gathered up their things, boarded the wagons to take them north.

The mechanical dog halted at the steps of the wagon; cocking its head to consider me. Eyes black as jet, touched with colorful glow. The strange construct gave a wag of its tail, then bound up the steps after its master.

The steam engine blew its call to charge. The wheels shifted, beginning to slowly, slowly turn. Then faster, growing confident. At last hurrying out of the depot and away.

Watching it disappear left me feeling vaguely lonely, even abandoned. For all that I would be upon it when I wished.

Though the seat beside me had been empty, of a sudden someone made a dry observation. The witch-spawn, of course.

"Just the final touch. A loyal, faithful, comical mechanical mut."

"That was not the usual automaton," I observed.

"Certainly not. Has a name on the collar."

"And that is?"

"Festus. Consider that."

I considered that. "You don't think it could be...?"

The cat gave an ordering lick to its chest fur.

"I do think it. He's known for his humor. Recall when he caught his wife and Martia in a net?"

"This business began strange and grows ever stranger. What are the saints up to?"

"The saints only know."

We watched the train disappear, puffing and chugging down the twin lines of rails towards the horizon. Hurrying to reach the impossible, inevitable point where even the most unlikely lines must meet.

Chapter 29
Where They Put the Important Stuff

The Benefactors seized a carriage with papered walls, leather-padded benches and a paneled ceiling centered by skylight. The air within wafted thick with ancient smoke, kerosene, old leather and unwashed travelers. Still, the glazed windows opened to lessen the fug. Arranging their packs to serve as pillows, they settled themselves comfortably, listening to passengers up and down the wagon train do the same.

Nervous Jewel sat facing lackadaisical Bodkin, grave Cedric across from amused Val, happy Matilda grinning at a vibrating Barnaby.

He gazed out a window, eyes wide. Leaping up when the dragon engine blew its battle whistle. Tumbling to his seat again when the carriage lurched, rumbling and rattling out the station and into the open world.

"The ride shall be rough," warned Cedric. "You must learn to brace yourself at stops and starts."

Barnaby nodded, thinking it small price to speed through life pulled by a mechanical dragon. He judged they moved at the pace of a trotting horse. Far faster than his amiable striding; if slower than the windborne velocity of the directable.

After a few minutes the changing view, the constant rolling, rocking vibration left him feeling at once sleepy and slightly ill.

The carriages entered the debris hills marking the outskirts of Salmoneus, then exited into open land, passing farms and fields, cows and crops. The strange semaphore towers waved greetings from the hilltops. A directable hummed amiably as it passed. A flock of crows raced the directable; wind-borne clouds outpacing the crows and mechanism together.

At times the wagons halted at lesser stations than Salmoneus's grand depot. Folk descended, dropping packs so to have two arms to embrace some welcomer at journey's end. It gave Barnaby a shiver to sit watching those greetings. As though he were peering into a window, seeing lives.

More than once the wagons halted suddenly in the middle of farm-field oblivion. Throwing drink from cup, butt from seat. These stops came augured by a screech of wheels, a whistle-blast of dragon-steam. Then folk would curse, peer out windows, spying a cow on the tracks mooing defiantly at the fuss.

For all the fitful stops, starts and rumbling clatter, Barnaby decided steam-dragon to be the perfect way to travel. Sitting in a carriage with friends, snacking on strange delicacies, enjoying a panorama of the world unrolling.

Granted, afoot a fellow could greet those he met. Stopping for a chat with some farmer, tinker, cowherd or wanderer like himself. Sitting in the steam wagon, Barnaby had to settle for waving to all he saw.

More oft than not, folk waved back. Then they went on to the rest of their lives, as he went on to his. Probably to never cross paths again. But still, but still, they'd acknowledged one another's existence in the Middle House of Saints. Princes on the road of life saying, *I greet thee, brother, sister.*

Evening came. The benefactors shared rations. Settling into naps and quiet conversations. But Barnaby could not long turn eyes from the window.

Every so often he'd put head out to peer northwards. Checking if the line of blue mountains grew higher, grew closer. Sometimes he thought it did; other times not. But sparks and cinders from the dragon engine would fly into face and eye; he could not stare so for long.

"They are called the Septentrional by Martia mapmakers," said Professor Night-Creep, perching upon the shelf for packs. "The desert folk of Psamathe refer to them as the Moon Black Mountains. Interestingly, the Aurelians name them the Moon White. While the folk of Nix give no name at all."

"What name for what?"

"The mountain range where waits your tower. Only the Hefestians refer to them by their proper name: *the Saintless*. To other lands, the label sounds overly ominous."

"Cedric said they call them the Saintless because no saint makes them their special demesne. Why is that?"

"Probably no one wants 'em," answered Bodkin. "What is there but rock, snow and a cursed tower full of nasty gold and jewels?"

"There are Gobelin holdings," observed the cat. "Not to mention Dwarrow mines. And plenteous bandits that plague the passes, hoping to ambush unwary mining expeditions from Hefestia, or better, a fat caravan from St. Psamathe."

"What is Psamathe like?" That, from Barnaby.

"Hmm. Hot summer in the day, cold winter in the night. An ocean of sand, where dust storms turn the sky to orange flame, burying the unwary without trace. Great hills of rock rise like islands above the dunes. Oft these rocks are carved with face and form of forgotten saints, ancient kings. Indifferent to time and empire, their stony gazes stare out at a world empty of all but wind, sand and silence. More significantly, the folk of St. Psamathe are quite respectful towards cats. As is proper to the land where St. Bast keeps her high cathedral."

"Will our wagon-dragon go all the way to the tower?" That, from Matilda.

"No," replied Cedric. "The rails end at a mining town on Hefestia's northern border. There we can purchase more supplies, possibly a mule or horse. Then, alas, we continue afoot."

Festus made a sudden leap into Barnaby's lap. A thing of metal, his was no easy weight to take.

"Ow!"

The beast struggled across him to push its head out the window. Jaws wide to bite the wind. The bronze tail wagging *creak, squeak* into Val's face. She cursed, moving back, shoving Bodkin, who added curses.

Just then the wagon wheels screeched, the carriage shuddered, throwing the dog to the floor again, claws digging into Barnaby's leg again.

"Ow!" again.

The train halted. Barnaby sighed at the tear in the legs of his breaches. Then looked out the window. No town to be seen. All about lay quiet countryside.

"Why have we stopped?"

"Perhaps it's robbers," said Bodkin. "They pile rocks upon the tracks, and when the wagons stop, they leap out like highwaymen demanding money or life."

"Did your Old Mercutio get up to such shenanigans?" asked Matilda.

"'Course not. Weren't his style. He'd have been making friends up and down the carriages, selling gold pieces for a silver."

"That's not sound trade," objected Barnaby.

Bodkin laughed. "You'd think. And yet, he never failed to smile when reckoning the ledger."

Val yawned. "I'm off to give my legs a stretch." She extended these very legs, one foot accidentally kicking Festus. He gave a flute-like yelp she ignored. Instead, she stood, exited the carriage singing.

There was a miller had a dog.
All of rusty wheel and cog.
He kicked the pest,
And said 'Tis best
We drown you in the bog.'

Barnaby rose, patted Festus in apology, followed after her. Festus following after *him*.

Outside, the late summer sun shown on a field of corn, an orchard of apples. The apples were fast red; the cornsilk darkening from yellow to brown. Crows held raucous congress in the air, debating changes in wind and sunlight. *Harvest time soon*, Barnaby thought. It gave his stomach a twist to realize it'd all have to go on without him. He fought an urge to run back to Mill Town, get wheels and stones, bags and barrels ready.

He watched other passengers descend the carriages, stretching, grumbling, giving wagon wheels a kick to start it up again. The news spread down the line that a tree branch blocked the way. The steam dragon tenders worked to drag it off.

Meanwhile two children with baskets went to carriage windows, selling boiled eggs, boiled corn, fresh bread, ripe apples.

Bodkin leaned out, chatting amiably.

"Clever wind, to blow that great branch from those trees all the way to the rail path."

The children exchanged looks. Then the eldest replied, solemn as sexton at a bishop's funeral.

"That's the work of Sainted Boreas. She's a most clever servant to the glorious and holy House."

"Ah," replied Bodkin. "And was it Boreas that tipped you to be ready with baskets of eggs and corn before we'd even stopped?"

This time the younger child answered, voice sweet as sun on honey.

"Yessir. Holy Sister Northwind whispers us wisdom down the chimney. By nights. Kindly of her, it is."

Bodkin nodded entirely in approval of wind's kindness and child fabrications; buying a full silver's worth of apples and bread. Barnaby watched hoping the silver would not somehow turn to a fishing weight once settled into the children's pockets.

Val sat on the sunlit grass, the clever north wind blowing her hair. Strumming her harp, singing to the sky.

There was a miller, had a mut,
Clock for brain, spring for gut.
Told it sadly, "I feel quite badly,
It's time to boot your sorry butt.

Festus sat beside her. Lifting head, he began howling between the choruses.

There was a miller, had a hound,
Arrooooooo.
A dimmer beast was never found.
Arrooo, roooo, rooo, roh.
All agreed that what we need,
Aaaar aaaar, aaaarr aaaar.
Is see the beast Infernum bound.
Aroooooo!

Bard and dog exchanged looks. It grinned, she frowned. Both opened mouths for a further chorus. But then the steam-dragon whistle blew, drowning words and barks, calling for all to board again.

Returned to his seat, Barnaby resumed watching the passing world. Now, evening swept over fields and woods, towns and hills. First the hosts of the Upper house took the stage, then the moon leapt over the world's edge to seize the proscenium. While on the floor of the undramatic Middle House, the lights of farmhouses shone from far hills, lonely and distant as hearths beyond the stars.

The other benefactors slept, drowsing, leaning upon one another. But Barnaby found himself rising, stepping quietly out the door of the carriage. The wagons now went so slow it took no effort to walk beside them, peeking into windows. Some were dark within; others illuminated by candle or lamp.

He peered into a carriage, surprised to see the Squire himself. There sat the man in a pile of gold glittering by candle shine. Testing, weighing, stacking each coin, recording grand numbers in a ledger book big as a bishop's gravestone.

"You owe me one penny," said the Squire, not looking up. "Two now, as interest has accrued."

"It was painted tin," objected Barnaby. "Meant to get me hanged."

"Bah," said the Squire. He grabbed a handful of coins, tossing them at Barnaby. They did not jingle, but splattered upon him like mud. "Tin? These are all gilded shit. What of that?"

Barnaby stared at the coins. They *did* glisten unpleasantly, rather like wet shit. He hurried to brush the coins off his arms and chest best he could. While the Squire sighed, cold face turned of a sudden full of tender pity.

"Poor young miller. Never heard the secret? Hear it now. There is only one rule for wolf or sheep, for saint or man or worm. *Take all you can and keep it.* How much you take is the only honest measure of what life is worth. All else is the whimpering of cowards feigning kindness to flatter their mirrors and flee the dreadful battle of life."

Barnaby nodded, unsure what to reply. He considered asking about Mother and Alf and the mill, decided not. So, he waved goodbye, walking on, scraping golden excrement from his leather armor.

The darker-than-night shape of Night-Creep perched upon the next carriage top. As Barnaby approached, he leapt to the miller's shoulder. There came a growl; he turned. Behind strode the mechanical dog Festus. Grown near large as a horse. Rainbow-glimmering eyes flickering, jaws wide in grin.

"Good boy," said Barnaby. Hoping it was true.

Festus gave a friendly tail wag. Barnaby walked on, reassured.

He passed another window, then looked back astonished. Within the carriage sat Mr. Quiet and the Goat Girl herself. With a chess board between them. Barnaby gaped. Who'd have guessed the girl knew the game?

The Goat Girl lifted a knight, sent it prancing into Quiet's pieces. The old gravedigger frowned, then pushed a pawn forwards, sly and soft as earth settling into a grave.

Barnaby waved to cheer her on; she ignored him, her attention on the game. So he continued till he came to Jewel leaning out a window, exactly as she'd leaned on a fence the day they'd met. They traded smiles, both thinking on pebbles. Barnaby peered past her into the carriage. A man hung from the ceiling, body swaying back, forth, back, with the rocking of the wagon.

Friar Cedric stood on a seat, knife in hand, sawing at the rope. At last the body fell to the floor, making a final 'thump'.

"That done, then?" asked Jewel, not turning.

Cedric nodded. "Just about."

Jewel moved to the carriage door, throwing it open. Cedric huffed and puffed to push the corpse out. Barnaby helped; pulling on the feet, wondering who the man had been. When at last the body tumbled to the ground, Jewel slammed shut the door. Returning to the window, she gave Barnaby a wave. Then she snuffed the lamp, leaving herself and Cedric alone in peace.

Barnaby smiled, continued on. Looking back, he saw the hanged man come to his feet, stagger into the night. Trailing the noose like a disconsolate scarf.

The chain of wagons began to increase speed. Now Barnaby had to trot to reach the next window. There a man leaned, taking in the fine night.

"Da," said Barnaby, pleased as the bear finding the bees away from their honey-comb home.

"Well now, here's my boy," said Da, every bit as pleased.

"Here I am," Barnaby agreed. "On my way to that tower, I am."

"Are you now?" asked Da. "That's an adventure. Who's minding the mill?"

"Oh, Alf and Mother, I suppose. No doubt 'twill be a month of sweat and swearing to set things right when we get home again."

"Ah, well," said Da. "Take your time on that. *'Best let the bested worker rest, and better to let the over-rested work.'*"

They laughed together at that tongue-twister wisdom. A favorite of Da's. While the dragon engine gave a whistle blast; chugging and huffing ever faster. Now Barnaby sprinted to keep up.

"Da?"

"Aye, son?"

"Da, why did you never get mad? At mother, at Alf, at the Squire. At the other folk of Mill Town. At the saints, even. Never telling you what needed hearing."

Quick as sun's shine behind coming storm, the happy glow upon Da's face darkened; turning it tragic as the iron giant's in the debris hills. The face of an honest man taking in all the world's sorrow in a glance. And still the train clattered fast, rumbled faster. Barnaby could no longer keep up. Da had to shout to give Barnaby an answer.

"Here's a secret for you, boy."

"Aye?"

"At the bottom of the tower-"

"Yes?"

"-begins the stairs to the top of the tower."

Now the carriages sped fast as horse at gallop. Barnaby stopped, turned, seeking his own carriage. Which was it? A door thrust open, and there stood Val. She reached, he reached, but then Festus leapt past. Pushing Barnaby aside, knocking Val back.

Before Barnaby could recover, the wagon sped on, leaving him behind. He stood on the still shivering rails watching the final wagon disappear in the night.

He began trudging after it, following the rails.

"Now that we are alone," whispered the cat on his shoulder, "if you would be guided by me?"

"Yes?"

"Then do not over-trust the dog. The beast has its own agenda; and is far more than it seems."

Barnaby pondered these words, unsure. What secrets did a mechanical dog have?

Before he could ask, the cat spoke again.

"And here comes my carriage." With that, Professor Night Creep leapt; not to the ground but up into the sky. Disappearing towards the just-risen moon. Leaving Barnaby alone in the night.

Far ahead in the night, the dragon engine blew a whistle blast, a lonely sound that made Barnaby shiver. Feeling he'd been left behind in a spot more empty and distant than the moon.

"Wait for me!" he shouted, and began to run.

"Wake up, miller," demanded Val. Thumping a bardic fist upon his head.

Barnaby blinked to see the dark cabin, the resting Benefactors. Above and across, the angel-wing eyes of Night-Creep studied him. From the floor, the rainbow shimmer eyes of Festus studied him. As Val's brown eyes studied him, close enough they shared breath.

Barnaby took a deep breath of her breath, infinitely glad to be back with friends. Not left behind in the night.

"Sorry to wake you. But you were kicking and shouting."

"Oh. Sorry. Strange dream."

She nodded. "Mine too. Must be the motion of the carriage."

"I guess." He struggled to remember the dream. Night-Creep's warning, and Da's last words.

"Do you think we aren't supposed to just get to the bottom of the tower, but the top?"

"Hmm," she *hmmed*, snuggling head into his shoulder. "Might be. I mean, the important stuff is always up high out of reach, right?"

He could think of no answer to that. But his tutor in magic could.

"So the Upper House of Saints believes," said the cat.

"Woof," agreed the dog.

Chapter 30
Songs Wrestling like Snakes in the Head

Two days later, the Benefactors returned to the dull and dusty work of traveling by setting one foot before another, then another and then another. Behind, the sounds and smells of the mining town faded, the last house vanishing with a turn of the road. Before them now ran a wheel-rutted way of flattened dirt, flattened rock. Upon each side rose stone hills, rising to mountain cliffs.

"And so farewell to St. Hefestia," declared Val. "Welcome to the Saintless Land."

"*The Land of All Saints*," corrected Cedric. "If here no saint rules, neither is any absent."

"You don't believe in the saints, Master Cleric."

"True; but I faithfully affirm the conceptualization you call a 'saint'. The wind blows, the grass grows, the sun shines. And so a child's mind ascribes these acts to Saint Boreas, Holy Mother Demetia, and Blessed Helios. But the adult mind deduces deeper causes. All the more powerful, even the more holy, for that those causes are not mere persons but grand laws. They act; but know themselves not."

"I see now why the Questioners wished to roast you," replied Val. "I'm thinking of casting a cantrip of flame right now."

Cedric laughed, undeterred.

"Oh, spare me. Every bard is a heretic. You change the saints to fit your tales; alter their divine testaments to please your rhymes. You are the very folk who give face and name to wind and sun, my fellow member of the Society of imaginary St. Benefact."

To which Val replied with something sharp and clever; but Barnaby lost the thread of discussion. His attention upon the mountains ahead. No longer a mere teasing line of blue. Now they were great stone monsters, near impossible for a miller's mind to accept. How could anything be so big? Some stood closer, some farther. Some rose high, others crouched lower. A few peaks held touches of white upon their tops. *Snow,* Barnaby thought. Ice and eagles, crags and cliffs and caves with Dwarrow kingdoms of jewels ashine in lamplight, and Gobelin halls where the wild-eyed creatures twirled and whirled in circles like mad children round and round the solstice bale fire.

And ever and again, his eye sought a tower atop a thousand black steps. Not in sight yet. But he felt it, just behind the next rise, just beyond the next turn of the path.

"Will we reach the tower today?" he asked.

"Hmm, no," said Cedric. "This road winds north another day, then divides. The main route heading towards Psamathe, the city of Sphinx. The second choice leads to mining settlements with quite a mixed population. Gobelin, Dwarrow, and less likely sorts. The third path will take us into the mountains where the tower patiently awaits us. That trail is not traveled much, save by wandering sorts and the occasional pilgrim."

"Or bandits," added Val.

"They are hereabouts," agreed Cedric. "Or so I was warned. But one can assume they watch the caravan road to Psamathe. They'll have no interest in those on a lonely mountain trail to owl-haunted ruins."

"Well, but for now it's the same path," observed Matilda.

"True," said Val. "Cedric, what orations have you of use against multiple attackers?"

"A blinding light worked well in the crypt. Less effective in open daylight. I do know Demetia's Protection from the Unlawful. But how such prayers work in the Saintless Mountains is theologically complex to predict."

"Then we'd best test. Prepare that oration. What about you, Miss Jewel?"

Jewel did not answer at once. She pushed hair from face, turned gaze up to the sky, studying the day.

"My orations are less effective in sun's light. Up close I'd throw violet fire. Otherwise, I'd keep low, sending Perry off to do mischief."

"Excellent. Barnaby, if robbers attack us on the road, what's your move?"

Barnaby tapped chin in thought, then drew his axe. "I'd show them Dragontooth to scare 'em."

"Good start. Then what?"

"Ah, then I'd loom to make them shiver like Bodkin instructed. And if that didn't work..." He paused, pondering.

"Yes?" asked Val. Asked Bodkin. Asked Matilda.

"I'd make conversation?"

"No." That, from Bodkin.

"No." That, from Matilda.

"He's teasing," said Val. Giving a look that said, *better be teasing*. Barnaby did not reply. He rested the axe upon his shoulder and gave Val a menacing looming glower. And a wink.

Bodkin shook his head at discussion of battle.

"Were I so small-souled as to take to hill banditry, I'd ask myself why get into nasty fights? Just wait till the marks are in a narrow spot like the one ahead. Then roll rocks down. At the least it'd distract from an attack from behind."

"That's the very sort of thing we need to watch for," agreed Val. "Like up there." She pointed. "See where that fallen tree is holding back rocks from tumbling down?"

Barnaby studied the slope ahead, the rocks, the helpful log. It did look ready to come tumbling.

"Another thing," said Val. "Practice keeping an eye open for sudden arrows."

"Voice of experience there," observed Bodkin.

She nodded. "So everyone practice spying for where a conceptual archer might be hiding to ambush us unwary innocents."

"How about that brush up ahead to the left?" asked Matilda. "Has the advantage of height, and some nice rock cover."

"Excellent example. What would you do if a fellow or five hid there now, ready to send death with the twang of a string?"

Matilda drew her bow, considered. "Well, I wouldn't go any closer for sure. The clever rogues will be peeking twixt the brush, waiting for us to pass by so they can shoot us in the backs. That puts them on the lower, forward side. So... I'd send an arrow thereabouts first, just to poke around for me."

"Not to waste resources, but give it a try."

Matilda nodded, notched, fired. The arrow disappeared into the brush; producing a rustle of branches and a scream.

As though surprised by the scream, the log upon the hillside rolled away, releasing large rocks and small boulders that tumbled and rumbled into the road before them, setting up a cloud of dust.

While from behind the Benefactors now came shouts, the sounds of men coming at a run.

"Practice time," said Val.

Timaeus, bandit chief of the Saintless:
We'd been tipped to a fat caravan coming south from Sphinx. 'Cept they didn't show. Boys got bored, fretting about winter coming, drink getting short. Half took off for easier pickings nearer to civ.

The ten that remained were pushing to raid a Gobelin hold. I kept talking 'em out of it. Not smart, messing with creatures who know the mountains better than us, and have cousins in every hole. I played my *Pipes of Persuasion* to calm 'em, but things were heading towards mutiny. Then we got word of travelers coming north.

Scout vowed only three looked dangerous. A Silenian bowman, a big fighter with an axe and a cleric. You got to assume clerics can pass out some harm, though most times they're a joke. The others were just a kid, two women. And a dog. Scout said it wore armor, which was mad.

No horses, no cart, just packs. Who were these fools? I decided they were treasure hunters, heading into the haunted parts of the Saintless.

I told the boys we'd best let 'em pass peacefully. Let them gather their treasure. We'd keep watch, and when they came back pockets jingling, we'd jump 'em.

But they pointed out the idiots weren't likely to return. If they headed into all that tales say is up there, then the fools were already good as potted for Quiet's garden. Best harvest them now.

I saw where this was going. They'd worked themselves up to do some fighting. I'd best lead the charge, else lose the reins. So I agreed. Even slipped in the idea in that the strangers carried Hefestian power crystals. I didn't believe it for a second. But you have to tease dogs with a juicy bit of meat if you want 'em to fight.

Anyways, never can tell what fools on the road were carrying. Not till you are looking in the corpse's pockets.

So we set up just before the Throat. Which is where the road splits twixt Psamathe and Nix. With that third trail to nowhere sane.

We piled up the usual rocks, set a fellow to let 'em roll when the travelers came to the right spot. Which pretty much never works. The one holding the rope always get excited, lets 'em roll too soon. It still helps. Your targets are staring at the avalanche that just missed them, while you're coming up behind.

Or so it should've gone. *These* targets stopped too soon. Something tipped them off. They sent arrows into the brush, planting one of my bowmen in the Fields. Then the rocks rolled down. Too Infernum soon, raising dust that helped them more than us.

A bad start. But we rushed on, and St. Taliesin twist my mother's tits but they were already in a circle of protection. Weapons ready.

Yeah, I know. We should have backed off then. That kind of magic hinders us souls committed to making a hard living in a hard land. But we had the numbers. Nine of us, in good armor. I figured we could sweep over them.

I figured wrong. My best spearman rushed the fellow with the ugliest saint-cursed butcher blade ever. Went through my man's shield, leaving the spear, the arm and half a shoulder in the dust.

My knife man saw the problem, bless 'im. Went for the fellow casting the circle. But the cleric fended with his staff while one of the women gathered pink fire in her hands, tossing it to the knifer's face.

Sacred Erebus eat my liver, they had a cleric and a fuckin' *witch*. The knife man did his best to scream with half a face burned to jelly. Ugly thing to see.

"Retreat," I shouted. Which is when the dog leapt out of the circle. Hit me like a cart of bricks, knocking me flat. But I did a roll, came to feet again neat as dance. Slashed for the thing's throat and it went *clang* like I'd tried to gut a church bell. Shit; it was a Hefestian windup. Worth a fortune. I stood there staring the way you'd consider a bag of diamonds lying on the road.

The circle of protection had faded, the targets moved to new positions. Bruiser with the bloody axe jumped in front of me. The cleric flanked my left, staff ready. Even the little kid had a sword pointed at my throat. While the damned windup dog grinned steel fangs.

The axe guy was enjoying himself, just waving that evil thing in front of my face as though deciding where to start cutting.

My gang were running down the road. I wanted to join 'em. But the Silenian put an arrow into the back of the slowest. Our healer, who was pretty useless anyway, no loss. So I wised up. Dropped sword, raising hands, feeling damn stupid.

But I didn't beg, didn't whine. Already been stupid. No point in adding weakness to the cup.

"We kill him?" asked the Silenian. Giving me a kick with a hoof. Hurt plenty.

"'Course you do," I said. Taking off my helmet like I was at home with family. Dropping it to the dirt, giving myself time to think. "That's the dance. You gut me good. Then my boys trail you, wait for you to sleep and cut your throats."

The child with the sword laughed.

"Their older brothers, maybe. Not that litter of pups."

And still the bruiser with the axe didn't blink. Just loomed before me. That axe going back, forth, back. You could tell that killing didn't mean a thing to him. For all I've seen an' done, the sight gave me chill. Like I was standing before Friar February himself.

The blond female came up.

"Spare a wolf, slay a flock," she declared. She held a harp under an arm. Beautiful thing, gold gilt and carving, silver strings. Harp's not my favorite instrument but just looking at it made me hard.

"Fellow troubadour, are you?" I asked. Getting an idea.

She shrugged. "I'm a bard. You're a hill bandit."

"We don't all hang around taverns wearing velvet and bells."

"True, that," she admitted.

I reached, slow so they wouldn't gut me. Took out my Pipes of Persuasion. Greater relic of Sainted Herman himself.

"*Rosg Catha*," I said. Loud and proud, like I was laying down winning cards on the table.

She threw head back and laughed. I waited for the laugh to end. Took a while. Found myself counting the blade scars on her face. Her hands. A Martia girl? Shit. Who were these creatures?

The rest waited for her to finish. Obviously she was in charge. Made sense, if she'd wandered from bloody St. Martia.

"Bard challenge?" she asked. "Seriously?"

"Before the eye of Sainted Taliesin, within the court of Blessed Euterpe, let the prophet Orpheus hear my challenge."

"He can hear me yawn," she snapped. "I don't have to accept." But I saw in her eye, she wanted to.

"True, you can gut me here. But I've got twelve good friends on the road behind, another five ahead. Accept the challenge, and win or lose you have my word as a bard. We'll leave you in peace."

"No, you've got seven former mates still cleaning shit from their pants," said the boy. Smart mouth on him. "And right now they're arguing who's in charge once you're squiggling in Infernum's hotter midden."

"Maybe. Or maybe my mates have more to them than your sort."

"Didn't show such when they left you behind."

Which was true. Didn't argue it. Just stood with my arms crossed like an honest taxpayer on his doorstep. Trying not to watch that dripping axe shift back, forth.

No, I watched the bard. Her eyes showed that fey look you see when folk who like risk stand on a cliff, or the doorstep of a bear cave. Else at the game table with stakes high, breaths held.

I knew exactly what to say.

"I understand, miss. Saints gave you a magic harp that scares you. It hurts folk like us, knowing talent ain't up to the instrument."

"Fine," she said.

"Why does this not surprise me?" asked the cleric; looking up to the sky. Addressing the Upper House, I guess.

"Because she's nuts?" That from the smart-mouthed boy.

Now the axe bruiser backed from me, turning his stony look to the bard. She gifted him a smile warm as a fresh loaf of bread. Or her ass in bed. Whichever warmth you want.

Smile done, she started barking orders.

"Bodkin, keep a lookout for this fool's friends sneaking back. Matilda, keep an arrow ready. Cedric, prepare your blinding light."

That done, she traced fingers across that harp.

"Terms. You lose, you empty all pockets, leaving your armor and sword. And pipes. You hi-thee-hither back to whatever hole you came from, promising as a bard to keep your friends from following us."

I nodded, liking where this was going. Liking it *fine*.

"Good enough. And if I win, I keep my things. And I want fifty gold and your harp."

"Yeah, no."

"I've got to have enough coin to persuade the fellows that it's all good business. Or they'll just overrule my oath. And bardic challenge says one of us walks with the other's instrument."

She hesitated. I saw the others preparing to argue her out of it. She saw it too.

"Fine," she growled. Taking a stance to please any sword master. "Ready?"

I nodded, closed eyes. Had to get myself in the right frame of mind. Which comes with the right rhythm of breathing, thoughts fixed on what's important to your heart, not your gut.

I put my pan pipes of St. Herman to my lips, kissing them soft. Old Herm's a thief with a wink and no conscience. But a true saint, no dim brigand. He keeps to his testament: to be easy in taking and in giving. To live for the moment, catch the fun of life. Not a bard's best friend; but when you sit at a fire laughing with folk who'll cut your throat for your boots if you drink too deep, your eye follows the campfire sparks to the Upper House of Saints, and you hear Herman laughing with you.

It's about life. And life is about the music. And the strongest song? Well, that's about strength. Doing what's needful. Told myself that, and began.

Didn't even notice the bard girl start. I gradually realized she'd already been playing. A simple tune, like the first raindrops on a summer day. Like first bird song at dawn. A tune about easy things, daily things, kind things. From a Martia girl, if you can believe.

Her tune got in my head, my breath, threatening to take it over, turn it to *her* tune.

I thought on when I'd led thirty mad fellows to take a caravan in the night. Sent the fifty guards to Infernum, tied up the fat merchants. What a party we held. The wind in the mountains breathing soft and warm as a lover in a green field of clover...

No! That thought was from her song, not mine. I don't give a shit about lovers in summer clover. Her damned harp kept singing of kindly days, warm sun, sweet kisses. Lucif feed such tripe to his mother's dog.

I blew louder, pipes now almost shouting the tune, thinking on when I'd faced three rivals with knives; and left 'em gutted. All the roisterers shouting for me to be captain of the gang. I'd gone about the room clasping hands to each brave fellow, promising I'd make him rich and happy. We were brothers forever against the world, seeking joy, finding family..

No, that was her tune again. Brotherhood? Joy? Family? What the Infernum were those things to me?

But my breath rebelled; couldn't get her tune out my head. At last I left off, gasping like I'd run a race.

Fine. Knives make a song too. I reached for mine.

Then stopped, studying the arrow ready for me, the axe ready for me, the staff ready for me. The weird girl with hair veiling her face probably readying something nasty too.

Yeah. It was over. I'd lost. I'd ended playing her tune, not mine. That's how high bardic duels go. So I dropped the knife, handed over the pipes. Took off the armor. They let me keep my pants and shirt. Didn't send me down the road naked, anyway.

I took my time on the walk back. Was sunset when I reached the mine where the gang holed up. I stood outside it awhile, listening to the grumbles and swearing within. The boys weren't happy. Wasn't going to be easy, walking in on them in that kind of mood...

Years back I'd had an associate who was one of those troglodytes from Lod. Live their lives in lightless caves. He used to do night-work for us. We shared a bottle once, and I asked if he'd ever go back to the lightless life.

He said he *had* gone back. Stood in the front cave of his home and stared into the dark, and realized he was too scared to go in. Gotten too dependent on lamps and candles.

I'd laughed then. Now I knew how he felt. I had to go into a cave of angry killers and persuade them I was still in charge, though I returned as a bootless beggar. *Without my pipes of persuasion.*

Yeah, that was not going to be easy. Twixt you and me, it scared. I tried to calm my breath... and found I was still humming that bard-girl's tune about friendship and love. Lucif's hottest poker, that wasn't the tune needed now.

I took a deep breath of rage, indifference and greed, and entered the cave to face the music.

Chapter 31
The World as Holy Mill

Two days of cautious hiking brought the Benefactors to a winding valley empty of all voices but their own. No birds crossed the sky, nor sang from the gnarled trees. No animals eyed their passing from brush or burrow. This silence weighed heavy, declaring them trespassers in the hall of a grand but empty house, closed and barred to outsiders.

At times the path wandered beneath giant faces carved into the cliffsides. Many of these monuments showed features implying stern and noble thought. Other times... the stone visage twisted in some expression of divine madness, staring down upon the travelers with no emotion mortal tongue could name. Eyes wide, great mouths gaping to shout revelations certain to shatter stones and souls.

Barnaby shivered in the gaze of these effigies, keeping eyes down. While Friar Cedric glared up at them in challenge.

At times the path wound past old shrines. Crumbling steps led to toppled pillars, faceless statues wound about with vine. These places did not make picturesque ruins. They seemed warnings set to remind passersby that *here* no saint tended, no king reigned, no law ruled. Only wind and ice, sun and storm, stone and empty sky held mastery.

Barnaby cast an awed glance up to a carven profile. Great as the mill house; female seeming, rich lips pursed in thought. Yet for all her fixed gaze, the smooth stone eyes gave an impression of blindness.

Emboldened, Barnaby stared openly, feeling defiant. The great face was stone, and only stone. This ancient saint could not see him, would not hear him. Whether he shouted to her in praise, prayer or insult.

Barnaby pondered Cedric's view that the saints were only natural things to which clever bards and dreaming millers added face, name and testament.

If wind and storm, birth and death, sun and moon were not wise beings to honor and beseech... what then? The world would still run, there would still be *order*. Just no longer mysterious wisdom directing that order. All the grand House of Saints would become a thing of weights, pulleys, cogs and wheels. Exact as his mill.

Barnaby walked on, turning this idea about in his head. Supposing he were to name the vanes of his father's mill? Paint faces upon the greater and lesser wheels and gears? Give holy titles to the grinding stones? And declare the threshed grain an offering, the returned flour a blessing... He'd have to wear holy robes while working. And a great grand sacred hat.

The picture made him laugh aloud. The laugh echoed through the valley, up to the blind stone face and down again.

The same mood turning Barnaby's thoughts solemn, had fallen over all the Benefactors. When he laughed now, it made them jump as if he'd sounded a dragon-engine whistle.

"You gone off your head?" asked Bodkin, annoyed.

"Sorry. Thinking about hats."

Evening came early, the sun sinking behind mountains same as into storm cloud. A chill breeze wended through the quiet valley, muttering of trespass and its consequences. The benefactors took shelter in a hollow hidden from wind and the mad gaze of mountain faces alike. Yet still they felt the brooding stillness of the valley; warning they camped in a place not meant for mortals to wander.

When the fire was built and supper passed round, the Society of St. Benefact sat quiet. Their thoughts turned inwards, staring into the embers like six Barnabys before the kitchen hearth.

In the morning, the Society awoke to feathers of white drifting down from a sky gone the gray blue of a frost giant's frown. Flakes hissed as they fell into the campfire embers.

"What happened to autumn before winter?" grumbled Barnaby, cocooning himself into his blanket, cold caterpillar into warm silk.

Val stood weary with keeping the night watch. She looked down upon the would-be butterfly Barnaby, and with no lover's gaze.

"We're in the mountains, not the kindly fields of your flat Demetia." She gave miller and blanket a poke of boot toe. "Up, boy."

Across the fire, Bodkin growled.

"I'll be sleeping in today." That said, he curled the tighter into his blanket.

"Exactly," shouted Matilda from her cocoon. "Cold out there. Let's at least wait for the St. Lucif-take-it sun to rise."

"Seriously?" demanded Val. "Out of those blankets, all of you. St. Euterpe blow her oboe up my ass, in Martia no one sleeps with a blanket until November."

"Just another reason to leave the mad place," grumbled Barnaby.

Val tendered him another boot poke. At which he gave up, uncurling from blanket. Rose grumbling, wandered shivering into the brush. Returning with tinder to build up the fire. That done, he sat down to hot Hefestian coffeeish, warmed bread and sausage. Watching the snowflakes settle; not yet enough to whiten the earth.

"Might be smart to camp here till the sky clears," said Bodkin, sitting before the fire wrapped in his blanket. "You hear how travelers get caught by snow in mountains. Eat each other up." He bit into a sausage to illustrate this sad fate.

"All the more reason to keep moving," said Val.

"If we are on the right path, the tower might be in another day's walk." That, from Cedric.

"If?" echoed Matilda. "What means this 'if'?"

Cedric gave an uncharacteristic growl. "Yes, '*if*'. I am a stranger here, as is anyone sane. Nor am I experienced in traveling mountain terrain. The proper trail might have been the one leading south, where the stone had a face carved like a Xin Pixiu."

"Which face of what?"

Cedric began describing winged lions while Val began kicking dirt upon the campfire. They all sighed to see this insult to warmth; but none argued.

She gathered up her pack and blanket.

"If we're on the wrong path, best find out sooner than later. Let's go, you whining lot."

Barnaby began packing, pondered wearing his blanket as a second cloak. Something felt missing. He looked about.

"Where's Festus?"

Val shrugged. "Haven't seen the beast since sunset. Knew there was a reason I felt so cheerful."

"Should we wait for him?"

"No."

"Maybe he just went off to pee." That, from Matilda.

"Pee what? Lamp oil?" That, from Bodkin.

Barnaby frowned, recalling Night-Creep's dream-warning: *do not over-trust the dog.* Granted, Night-Creep was a cat.

"He's clever," sighed Barnaby, picking up his pack, setting it to his shoulders. "He'll find us when he wants."

The mountain trail grew narrow; high cliff on one side, steep precipice upon the other. After arguing, they proceeded single file. First went Val, wary for ambush. Last came Matilda, equally wary. Barnaby came behind Val, eyes seeking Dark Michael and Professor Night-Creep. But cat and ghost were as absent as the mechanical dog. He wondered if it all made an ominous sign.

The snow fell thicker, hindering sight. While the trail became an ever-thinning path between chasm and mountain. Barnaby pictured the way at last so narrow they'd edge sideways, backs to the mountain, toes over the abyss. Their faces staring into the void same as the mountain-carved effigies...

But no, they'd turn back before that. No quest for treasure required they march into empty air.

The wind had left them in peace all the morning. Now it pounced. Stabbing through coat and breeches, shivering skin, chilling bone. Tossing ice grains into eyes, slowing their march, teasing feet towards a wrong step. The Benefactors began to spread out along the trail, till Barnaby could scarce see Val ahead.

She shouted words Barnaby could not catch. Were they warning? Perhaps he'd best draw Dragontooth. But if threatened, for sure she'd have halted. Unless she'd drawn knife, rushed towards the foe like a good Martia soldier. Like a mad bard.

He drew his axe, hurrying forwards, one shoulder keeping touch with the mountainside. Now he could not see Val at all. Perhaps the trail ended at a cliff edge. Perhaps she'd tumbled over, and he rushed to do the same. They'd fall spinning and whirling together, reaching hands out to one another as they plummeted. A romantic sort of ending, if disappointing.

The wind wove falling snow into cloths of white that confused the eye. He edged forwards till the trail opened upon a wide flat shelf going deep into the mountain.

Here the falling snow and hovering clouds glowed bright by the light of the unseen sun. Barnaby walked with slitted eyes, feeling he stumbled through a hall decked with altar veils of white fire. He called out for Val.

Someone answered; no telling who, nor where. He turned in circles, axe raised. Perhaps it'd only been the wind. He continued wandering, cautious of precipices and monsters.

He only stumbled when the way forwards rose, not fell. Rose in shelves of fresh-fallen snow, where wind-swept patches showed black stone beneath. He recovered his footing, stood considering the slope before him.

Bending down, he scraped snow away. Revealing stone, smooth and black. Clearly a carven step, as was the next stone above and beyond it, and the one beyond that.

Barnaby's eyes followed what was suddenly not a mountain slope, but a stairway winding upwards. He began counting steps, giving up at fifty. No doubt they numbered a thousand. And still his eye traced upwards, till at last, far and high, all but hidden behind glowing snow fall, rose a construction of white stone. Reaching from mountain into clouds, perhaps unto the Upper House of Saints itself. A tower, indifferent to his presence as the sky to a worm.

When at last he looked down again, he beheld the black form of Night-Creep upon his left. While on the right stood the tall shadow of Dark Michael, hat low over eyes, soldier's coat wrapped tight.

Dark Michael spoke not; merely stared up the endless steps. But the cat leapt nimbly to Barnaby's shoulder, making itself comfortable. Turning eyes whiter than snow upon the miller, speaking with a whisper that yet pierced the mad wind.

"Behold your high tower, Master Barnaby."

Part III

Happenings at the Tower

Notes on an Unknown

Plato, 500 BCE
Concerning Atlantis

... for beyond the mouth which you Greeks call the pillars of Heracles, there lay an island larger than Libya and Asia together...

The god of gods, who rules according to law, and is able to see into such things, that they might be chastened and improve, collected all the gods into their most holy habitation, which, being placed in the center of the world, beholds all created things. And when he had called them together, he spoke as follows...

The Voyage of St. Brendan
(Navigatio Sancti Brendani Abbatis, 600 CE
Excerpt

They took sail with provisions for forty days, sailing west for that space of time; during which their guide went before them. At the end of forty days, towards evening, a dense cloud overshadowed them, so dark that they could scarce see one another. 'This darkness,' said their guide, 'surrounds the Land of Saints you have sought full seven years.'

And after an hour had elapsed a great light shone around them, and the boat stood by the shore. When they disembarked, they saw a land, extensive and thickly set with trees, laden with fruits, as in the autumn season... And for forty days they explored in various directions, But never could they find the limits thereof. At last they came to a large river flowing towards the middle of the land, which they could not by any means cross over...

Letter to Ricci, *aprox date: 1610 (?)*
Vatican Archives

Miscellaneous Incunabula: #Bi:161

To Matteo Ricci, mathematician, cartographer, brother in the Society of Jesus, I send the kiss of friendship, my fraternal love, and the peace of God, trusting this letter finds you, and finds you well.

Brother, the Lord has brought my unworthy person to astounding things, and the news must reach you in Macao, and our Father in Rome, and our brothers scattered across the waves and mountains of the earth. For but four years ago, sailing west from Lisbon towards Vera Cruz, the Lord of Storms thought it wise to drive our vessel South. After much tribulation our prayers led us to a coast marked upon no chart. An island like unto no other; for a galleon might circle round about it in three days' time; and yet within its bounds lies a vast land of many kingdoms that weeks of journey could not cross.

From various signs I believe this unnatural isle to be the fabled Atlantis spoken of by Plato; else the Hi-Brazil whispered of among the Irish monks, if the two lands be not the same.

But I give it no pagan name; we have christened it 'Terra Sanctorum', for it is a land rich in thought of divinity, awaiting only holy revelation.

The continent is divided into many and various kingdoms, some pleasantly wooded, others settled into peaceful farms, else busy towns, even cities. The folk seem a mix of all the lands of the world, as if we stood at the foundation of the Tower of Babel. I deduce that once there was communication between 'The Land of Saints' and the empires of the Caesars and Greeks, the Phoenicians, even the forgotten Etruscans. For in matters of worship the folk here speak of Jupiter and Demeter, Apollo and Venus. Yet they refer to these ancient deities in terms of orders of saint and angel, church and society. As have done other lands seeking to graft old errors onto the new revelation.

I am convinced those of faith came here long before me. They speak of a Saint Brendan, who reformed their old beliefs, creating the facade of a proper church.

We must have more workers in the fields herein, lest the harvest be heresy, not faith.

In short, this land, my brother, requires teachers, apostles, and Church Law. In hope of these good things I shall sail with the spring, bringing my maps and notes to Rome.

But I request your wise support, Brother Matteo, lest upon arriving the society think me mad, my maps mere lunacy. I beseech you, write to the college and affirm that we who wander in strange and distant lands are worthy of trust.

Your fellow laborer in the fields of faith
Benedictus

Summation of client's request:
Research and Application
Apr 12th, 2023

The phenomenon: the NSA has recently detected sporadic radio messages from the mid-Atlantic. Messages in a home-made tongue of Greco-Roman, German, Arabic, Chinese and other languages never meant to by nature to mix.

The source claims to be from a nation named 'The Republic of St. Hefestia'. Their *University of Daedalus* has recently discovered our own transmissions, and wishes to establish regular communication.

Their messages reference a continent never known, with nations, histories and cultures equally mysterious. Seemingly agrarian, pre-electric, highly religious. They inquire of our forgotten empires and dusty kings as if they'd heard of the outer world from ancient travelers, yellowed texts.

The request: the NSA asks us to compose a *rational explanation* that takes these messages seriously; with no consideration of hoax or delusion. They give no explanation of the point of the strange assignment; nor do we ask.

In sum, our client requests a straight-faced serious-voiced *hypothesis* explaining how an invisible continent exists where satellites and sanity insist is only empty ocean.

Raw material for rationalization abounds. From classical myth to modern schlock, legends place a magical land exactly in the Mid Atlantic where the signals originate. Atlantis, High Brazil, the Earthly Paradise, Lemuria and Avalon. Let's throw in the Bermuda Triangle as well. A grand warehouse of lore awaits the solemn researcher ready to sift fact from folderol.

And diligent sifting done… no fact remains. It is all and only folderol. In the 1500's a sane mind might believe in a lost land between Europe and the Americas. Not in the third millennium.

Well, but the request remains. As do bills to be paid. Ergo:

Our rational explanation:

I am proud to say the team quickly agreed that wormholes and Einstein-Rosen bridges were *passé*. A sad faction lobbied for magic of the sort that protects Oz, Xanth and Diagon Alley from mundane eyes. An even sadder minority favored placing the continent underwater, perhaps in a hollow Earth.

Fortunately, the Mid Atlantic Ridge came to our rescue.

We submit our 134-page *rational hypothesis* with impressive graphs correlating seismic activity along the Mid Atlantic Ridge with satellite detection of *surface plasmon* phenomenon integrating nicely with the time-periods of Hefestian radio transmissions. We suggest that oscillating geo-magnetic waves periodically achieve quantum resonance with *another continent of Earth's distant past or future*, herein referred to as 'Space-Time X'.

When the above-cited geo-magnetic forces achieve harmonic resonance, access between our reality and Space-Time X becomes possible. In fact, the mix of languages and cultures implied by the messages, plus the nagging endurance of Atlantean legends across multiple eras, implies that regular animal and human interaction has in fact occurred across millennia.

Afterword:

The *Hefestians* propose standardizing access between our separate realities. Briefly, they invite us to visit, and hope to visit us.

Tentative hypothesis: if access is established, these charming folk will sail into our harbors in quaint wooden galleons. We, of course, will enter theirs in nuclear warships.

Chapter 1
It's Been Waiting for You

Axe at ready, cat on shoulder, ghost at side, Barnaby the miller's son set foot upon the first step to the saint-cursed Saintless Tower... then paused. Recalling all he'd heard of these very stairs. A thousand black steps guarded by snakes, spiders and wolves. He looked about; spying cold stone beneath fresh snow. No wolves, no spiders, no snakes.

He felt he could handle a wolf or two. But what good was Dragontooth against snakes and spiders? Unless they came big as wolves. Which would be easier to strike. Yet more fearsome for being so terribly unnatural. Ah, but suppose the wolves came small as spiders? All too easy to picture swarms of tiny wolves tearing at one's ankles...

"Barnaby!" shouted Val.

He turned to see her appear through curtains of falling snow.

"Where you been?" he asked.

"Chasing your dog."

"Festus? Where is he?"

"Dunno. Ran this way. See the tracks?"

Barnaby studied the steps. Spying no regular trail; but every fifth or sixth step showed a brushing of snow.

"Must have been going fast," declared Val. Then went silent, following the snowy steps higher and higher.

"Euterpe sing me to sleep offkey. That's, that's your tower, isn't it?"

Barnaby nodded.

Voices behind announced Cedric and Jewel, Matilda and Bodkin. They gathered before the steps, gazing upwards through the falling snow.

"So we have arrived," said Cedric. Tone solemn, face solemn. "And it is no owl-haunted ruin."

"I smell treasure," declared Bodkin, nose twitching same as rabbit in unguarded garden.

"Strange to see it up there, isn't it?" asked Val. "After coming all this way."

"It's been waiting for us," mused Barnaby.

"Let's get on," said Jewel. "Be warmer inside."

"Oh, sure to be," laughed Matilda.

And still they lingered. Till Val gave Barnaby a shove. "Your privilege, Mister Miller. Go first."

He considered. Then turned to face the Society of St. Benefact. "Right. But listen, all."

The company waited, shifting and shivering. While Barnaby struggled with all he wanted to say. Finding the total beyond a miller's tongue. He settled for the important part.

"Let's just remember that gold isn't worth a one of us dying."

"How much gold, exactly?" asked Matilda. "Per hypothetical deceased Benefactor, I mean."

"Personally," said Bodkin, "I never consider dying for anything less than a basket of diamonds."

"How big are these theoretic diamonds?" asked Val. "I'm not dying for tiny diamonds slipping through the basket bottom."

"Suppose it's just one diamond, basket-sized?" That, from Bodkin. "I'll trade one Benefactor for that. Not me, of course."

"How big a basket?" countered Matilda. "We talking egg basket, or bushel basket?"

Barnaby smiled to hear his friends' jests. He looked to Dark Michael; standing off from the group. Gazing up at the tower. Hands deep in pockets, in search of the warmth he'd left in the grave.

Barnaby's smile died.

He recalled the battered corpse buried in a potato field. What did Michael think of jests upon death? Did he think the Benefactors foolish? More likely, he saw them as brave children dancing before the mouth of the dragon's cave.

"Right, then," said Barnaby. He turned about, began the march up the steps. Determined to keep his friends safe. No wolves leapt, no spiders scuttled, no snakes wiggled. The Benefactors followed.

"Assuming there even is treasure," mused Cedric aloud. "I remain doubtful."

"I believe you mentioned relics," replied Bodkin.

"Ah, yes. Holy trash of the saints is perfectly likely."

Barnaby began counting steps. Five, ten, fifteen. At step thirty Val began to sing.

Past bog and fog, rain and flame,
 Through the Middle House to gain
Victor's crown and hero's fame,
Our Barnaby to the tower came.

"When were we in a bog?" he asked.

"Plutarch, running from the cultists."

"Oh, right." He continued counting. Thirty five, forty steps. At fifty Matilda paused, ears twitching.

"Hear that?" she asked. "Know that sound, we do."

Barnaby listened. Within the snow-heavy clouds something hummed and purred. He looked up, spying a whale-shaped shadow hovering above the distant tower-top.

"A Hefestian directable?" asked Val. "What business has it here?"

"To catch directable thieves?" That, from Matilda.

"Unlikely," said Cedric. "It didn't follow us, and clearly arrived earlier." He produced his battle-trophy spyglass, focused upon the sky.

"Ah. The markings say it is from the University of Daedalus. Nothing to do with us."

"Why's it here then?"

"Research, no doubt. The location has historical significance and unusual qualities." Cedric put away the spyglass.

"They may not be looking for our merry band," said Bodkin. "Doesn't mean they'll be glad to see us."

They continued their climb. Barnaby found his knees growing sore, his pack growing heavy.

"*Directable*'s a clever way to reach the top."

"We going there?" asked Bodkin. "I thought the map says treasure is in the basement."

"I *think* it does," admitted Barnaby. "I just have this idea we are supposed to get to the top eventually."

He resumed counting. Seventy, eighty, ninety. At one hundred and fifty they reached a wide square shelf cornered with statues of sinister beasts. Black stone snow-bedecked, with jaws wide to bite.

"Nice doggies," yawned Bodkin.

"Wolves," corrected Matilda. "Not doggies. Probably not nice either."

"Oh?" said Barnaby. He walked to one, brushing snow from the head. Pondered the stone fangs, wide wild eyes. "Here is why tales say the stairs are guarded by wolves."

Now spoke Night-Creep from his perch upon Barnaby's shoulder; voice dry as St. Psamathe counting the grains of his desert.

"I feel it is within the parameters of my duties as your summoned tutor in magic to suggest an alternate origin for macabre rumors of guardian wolves in this present location."

Barnaby struggled to decipher this lecture. Val and Bodkin, quicker students, stepped back, drawing blades. While the stone form began to shiver.

"Specifically," continued the cat, "I would suggest these are not mere stairway ornaments but in fact charmed effigies ready to attack trespassers."

Now the statue shook itself, sending snow flying Barnaby stepped back, setting his feet, steadying his axe. The wolf head turned, focusing ember eyes upon him. It gave low growl, then leapt. Barnaby swung.

The creature was not stone, nor any mechanical beast. The blade cut it same as any being of flesh. But as it fell, there came growls from behind. Panting, Barnaby turned to see Cedric flanked by two more wolves. A third rushed upon Bodkin.

Barnaby hurried to help. But the little rogue did not waste time drawing sword. He threw himself backwards, rolling to a ball. The wolf leapt past, snapping jaws at the air. Landing in anger, it began a howl cut short by Val's long knife.

Barnaby turned from that to see a wolf writhing in Jewel's purple flames. No need for his axe. But the last wolf had seized Cedric by the leg, shaking him across the stones, sending his staff rolling.

Barnaby menaced it with his axe, fearing he'd strike Cedric. Then an arrow took the beast in the chest, driven so deep only the feather showed.

The wolf released Cedric. Attempted to bite the arrow; then sank down, lying still as stone upon the blood-dotted snow.

The Society formed a circle about Cedric, Panting, weapons ready for the next attack. No charmed statues remained, no further enemies showed. Barnaby and Jewel turned to kneel beside Cedric, checking his torn and bloody leg.

"That needs healing," declared Barnaby.

"Then bandage it," grasped Cedric. "I can't call such healing upon myself without killing myself. And it would put you out of any fighting to come."

"We could camp here for the night," suggested Barnaby. "Set up tents."

"Not smart," declared Val. "We don't know how long till these sendings return for another round. Nor what else prowls these stairs. We either go on or back."

"Then back," said Jewel. "Try again tomorrow."

"We'd face the same risk with less supplies," argued Bodkin. "We aren't going to get up these stairs without a scratch."

Jewel pushed her veiling hair aside, staring upon Bodkin with unfriendly eyes.

"Easily said, little thief. Wait till it's your flesh torn to the bone."

"Calm down, witch-girl," said Bodkin. "I'm quite fond of our cleric. Even if I'm not sharing his holy blanket."

Jewel hissed, curling fingers to scratch. Bodkin reached hand to sword. Val growled, stepped between the two.

"Stop that nonsense, both of you." She sheathed knife, took out her harp. "I'll cast a cantrip of healing. Then we bandage whatever still bleeds. That will be enough to get Cedric on his feet again."

"Good plan," said Cedric, unaccustomedly concise. "Do it. Hurts."

When Cedric stood again, he looked pale and bloody. Leaning upon his staff. Still, he smiled, giving a nod of thanks to all.

"Right," said Val. She looked weary herself. "Master Barnaby, you take the lead. Bodkin, you keep watch behind. With sword *drawn* this time. Ready, all? On and up."

Barnaby continued counting steps. Cedric's staff went *thump, thump.* The wind blew colder, singing of lonely valleys, icy peaks, desolate chasms. Val began to sing to counter its wintery song.

Our heretic cleric of views eccentric,
Cedric the Doubter, of courage authentic,
Of face majestic, with mind ascetic,
Reached the tower by pure dialectic.

"What does that mean?" asked Barnaby of Matilda. She shook head. "I only follow her saltier verses."

Cedric said naught; but reached a hand to rest upon Jewel's shoulder. Perhaps for support, more like for comfort, one to the other. Val continued singing over the wind, not asking its opinion.

The nightshade's a lovely flower,
Fitting bloom to Hecate's bower
Our novice Jewel a maid of power,
Reaching at last the Saintless Tower.

At step five-hundred and ninety-seven, assuming he'd kept proper count, Barnaby halted. Before them waited another flat shelf, cornered with suspicious statuary. He eyed a snow-bedecked knot of black stone coils.

"Snakes," he sighed. "Had to be."

Matilda studied the scene. "Couldn't we run fast past? Or tiptoe, those that have toes with tips?"

"No," said Val. "Getting ourselves chased up icy steps by swarms of snakes is folly. We settle them first."

Dark Michael was suddenly beside Barnaby, hand to chin, pondering.

"Not work for arrows or knives," he declared. "An axe swing could take them coiled. But once on the move, the strike is doubtful."

Night-Creep leapt from Barnaby's shoulder. Stood on hind feet, paws folded across chest, peering ahead. Barnaby resisted urge to reach down, scratch the magic-tutor's tummy.

"The witch's flames would serve best here," the cat decided.

"I could do one," growled Jewel. "Not four. Takes too much out of me. Particularly in sunlight."

"I might manage a bolt of flame," sighed Cedric. "But like Jewel, only the once."

There came a long silence. Then Val stamped foot.

"Here's the battle plan. Barnaby, you go to the far left corner. Soon as the things twitch, you strike. Jewel, prepare to cast your purple fire on the far right corner. Don't get closer than you have to. Cedric, you burn the nearer left snake pile. Bodkin and I will take on the last corner."

Bodkin swallowed. "Old Mercutio has a suggestion. I don't like it, but he makes a good point."

"What's that?" demanded Val.

In answer, Bodkin held out the magic sword.

"This will serve better than your knife against such creatures. And you know better how to use it. So I'll take your knife, guard your back."

Val considered, then nodded.

"Tell the old reprobate it's past time he made himself useful."

Bodkin grinned.

"He says, stuff Gabriel's bugle up your butt and fart revelry to the Lower House."

"That act would definitely please the tavern crowd," agreed Val. "Right. All ready?"

It went well for Barnaby. He hurried across the square, took position before the snow-covered coils. There came a shiver of snow, a glow. He waited till he saw a jaw open, white fangs dripping venom. Then he swung Dragontooth with all his strength. Segments of snake went flying, writhing and twisting in the snow.

It passed well for Jewel. She gathered her violet flame in hands, then stood before the stone coils. When they twitched she threw the fire, backing away from what became a knot of snakes writhing, wiggling, withering to purple ash.

It went well for Cedric. He did not need to near the coils in his assigned corner. Merely waited till the guardians awoke. Then he raised staff high, whispering. There came a burst of green fire enveloping the knot of snakes. Turning them to emerald tentacles hissing and twisting in summery flame.

For Val and Bodkin, things passed less well. She stood before the stone coils, shining sword raised. Soon as they shivered, she struck. But the blade lacked the weight of Barnaby's axe. It cut through half the coils, - then slowed, then stopped. She cursed, struggling to draw it free. One serpent, then another slithered from the knot, hissing, eyes glimmering red.

Just as she freed the blade, a scaled head struck, fangs biting into her side. Val screamed. Bodkin sliced with the long knife, severing the snake behind its head. But still the fangs held fast to her flesh.

"Help here!" shouted Bodkin. Leaping back as another snake menaced. Val retreated as well, staggering, waving the sword blindly. Two serpents coiled and wiggled in pursuit.

But down upon the first came Cedric's staff, crushing the spine with a *snap!* Down upon the second came Dragontooth, slicing through the sending, then deep into the black stones. While Val flailed the sword at the snake head still chewing into her side.

Bodkin grabbed the creature by the neck, pulling it away, tearing her flesh. Val screamed, falling back. The snake segment writhed in Bodkin's hand, seeking to bite. He tossed it far and away upon the mountainside.

Val lay trembling on the snowy stones, eyes rolled up to whites. Panting, flecks of froth spotting her lips.

"Sweet Sainted Silenus, the damned things were poisonous," whispered Matilda.

Barnaby dropped his axe, knelt beside Val, asking advice of none. He produced his wand. Bowed his head, muttering, whispering. Now a green light flickered from the willow stick. He tapped it solemnly upon her forehead, her mouth, then above the heart. Lastly to the wound in her side. Whispering all the while, to the saints or to her or perhaps himself. For a dreadful second nothing passed; and the certainty came to each Benefactor that nothing would pass but death.

Then came a burst of blinding green, bright as Cedric's flame. When the Benefactors could see again, they stared down at Barnaby collapsed beside Val.

"They need to rest," said Bodkin. "We all do."

"Can't be resting here," said Matilda. "We'll freeze. And how long till those snaky guardians come alive again?"

"Sunset," said Cedric.

"Wolves, too?"

"Yes."

"Right. That gives us an hour, tops."

They stared down at Barnaby and Val; wrapped in blankets. Both breathed; and that was good. But neither would awaken.

Jewel spoke. "Can we carry them?"

Cedric leaned upon his broomstick staff. Testing his bandaged leg. When he spoke, the words came low and weary.

"Even if I were fully healed, I could not long carry Barnaby."

"You just keep on your priestly feet yourself," said Matilda, kindly. "We'll sort this problem out."

Jewel spoke, not kindly but curt.

"Can't stay and can't carry. So we wake them."

"How?" demanded Bodkin. "Put fire to their feet?"

Jewel pushed veiling hair aside, giving a very witch-like look.

"If that were the only way, aye. But I've an oration that'll wake 'em. Well, it should get them walking anyways."

"What spell and why am I feeling I won't like it?"

"*Hecatatia's Fever*. Draws sleepers to their feet, sets them wandering."

"Off the mountainside?"

Jewel put hands to slender hips, staring down at the unconscious bard and miller.

"We'll have to lead them down. Slow. Maybe on a rope. Like blind beggars down the road."

Bodkin looked about for Night-Spore and Dark Michael. Surely they'd have some advice, practical or arcane. But of course the mystic creatures and their wisdom had vanished. No, it was up to the mortal Benefactors still standing.

"Fine," said Bodkin. "But we go upwards. Going slow, there's no chance of reaching the bottom before sunset. We'll be caught twixt wolves and snakes."

Jewel looked to Cedric; but he said naught. Clearly struggling to remain standing. She bit lip in thought.

"Upwards means another fight. Probably worse than the last. Downwards we know what we face."

At which Bodkin bowed polite, as though introducing himself to an innocent on Bright Persephone's high street.

"You and the Cleric get these two on their feet. Matilda and me, we'll go ahead and handle the next exciting challenge."

"Sure, an' we will," declared the Silenian. Stamping a confident hoof. The sound rang loud in the icy air. She grabbed her pack, repeating the declaration. "Surely, we will. Oh yes, for sure."

Bodkin did not hear this repetition, already hurrying up the steps. Matilda stamped after him, muttering more *'sure's*.

After endless steps, repeated mutterings, they slowed, knees aching, chests panting. The snowfall ceased, clouds thinning to reveal blue sky fast fading to twilight's gray. Spiked by the looming tower before them, the tower that gazed indifferently down upon the lives seeking its entrance.

Boots and hooves cautious, they approached a third landing. Wide and square as the previous places of attack. But here waited no guardian statues. Only a flat blue-white blanket of snow.

"Oh, looks wonderfully innocent, don't it?" asked Matilda.

"Which means it isn't."

Bodkin paced the edge of the square, not stepping upon it. He bent down. "Hmm."

"What?"

"Snow's blown away here. Shows a spider carved into the stone."

"Ah." She considered the number of stones in the square. "That should come to a nice warm swarm of nasty things."

"Yep."

"I suppose we could stamp on 'em. If they aren't venomous. 'Course they *will* be venomous."

"Oh, no stamping needed. Just one arrow. And a clever girl with a steady aim. Ah, but where to find one this time of day?"

Matilda pondered the need of such a person, and smiled.

"You have a plan, Master Rogue?"

"Naturally. But first, the lamp oil." He searched his pack, producing two flasks. These he emptied across the steps below the square.

"That was meant for the dark of the tower," reminded Matilda.

"Worry about tomorrow's dark, tomorrow. Now hand us an arrow."

Matilda produced one quick as Silenian wink. Bodkin took it, reached into inner pockets. Bringing forth a small and innocent box.

"What's that?"

"Just a souvenir from the captain's trunk on Phaethon."

"Thought no one could open that."

"No one not talented and handsome, no."

Bodkin's talented and handsome hands swiftly bound something blue and glowing to the arrow.

Matilda shook her head, aghast and delighted.

"Seriously? You've been skipping alongside us with one of them inflammatory to Infernum Festian crystals in your pocket?"

"And now you are very, very appreciative I so did. Take the arrow. Go down, hmm, twenty steps. I'm going to trigger the guardian charm, then come running to bravely hide behind you. Soon as they swarm over the lamp oil you shoot, and all is merry and bright."

Matilda laughed, setting the arrow to bow string.

"You are a strange old child, Mister Bodkin. But it's been an honor to know you."

"Just what my mirror said this morning. Ready?"

"Just so," she answered, taking position, drawing back the string.

Bodkin nodded, said something aside to his inner old man, then stepped upon the waiting snow.

* * *

Jewel sat on her pack, book of prayers upon her lap, pendant clutched. Chanting softly. Cedric stood leaning on his staff, observing. Clearly too weary to aid with more than his presence.

Wind blew, snowflakes drifted. Jewel muttered, at times dangling her pendant over the two sleepers. At some point the wind silenced, the light darkened. Jewel began rocking back, forth, back. No longer a witch chanting dark spells. In evening's light she looked a lost child on a cold hill.

And then Barnaby stirred. Jewel kept eyes shut, still rocking, still whispering. Cedric bent down, putting hand to the miller's chest.

Now Barnaby's eyes opened unblinking to the sky. He struggled to rise, as did Val beside him. Their faces flushed, foreheads damp with sweat despite the icy air. Eyes fever-bright, mouths muttering words unheard.

Jewel opened her own eyes. Gazed upon the risen sleepers. Then stood, scarce more steady than they.

"You guide the miller," she told Cedric. "I'll help the bard."

Cedric nodded. Putting a hand to Barnaby's shoulder. His eyes darted about, tracking things of waking dream. Cedric pulled his arm, coaxing him sternly forwards.

"Step up," he said.

Barnaby blinked, clearly wondering where he was, who he was and why. Still, he nodded, began climbing steps. Behind, Jewel led Val, whispering similar instruction.

When a thunder-blast of flame shook the darkening air, Cedric and Jewel jumped, nearly falling. Their sleep-walking charges took no note.

"What?" That, from Cedric.

"Bodkin being Bodkin, I'm guessing," said Jewel. Staring upwards. And there appeared the very boy, beside the tall Silenian.

"Path's clear till sunset," shouted the rogue.

"Which is about ten minutes, give or take ten minutes," declared Matilda. "Move your hooves."

The conscious Society of St. Benefact hurried up the Saintless stairs, leading their sleep-walking charges. Approaching the third square, they found the stones blasted clear of snow. Puddles of lamp oil still flaming. Tiny ashen bodies scuttled in the wind like dead leaves in winter wind. A few still wiggled. Bodkin made a point of stamping them as he passed.

"Sorry, Perry," said Jewel. Stopping in the middle of the burned area. "No, I don't think they were nice. They were going to sting us. Well, I am always careful of regular spiders. No, of course you aren't regular. You're quite special."

Matilda went back. Jewel looked fevered and weary herself, little better than Val beside her. Matilda coaxed the two on. Bodkin doing the same with Cedric and Barnaby.

Far behind the mountains, the setting sun declared itself done with the Middle House of Saints. And so day's last light died.

And still they climbed, step after step; staggering and stumbling. The night wind granting no least mercy from icy embrace, chilling caress. Ever farther up they climbed. Cedric and Jewel staggering half asleep, same as Val and Barnaby.

Bodkin looked back, spying Cedric come to a halt, leaning on his staff. While Barnaby wandered perilously near a precipice. Bodkin leaped down steps to grab the miller, guiding him back to Cedric.

He coaxed both on and up; Matilda doing the same with her drowsing charges. They took turns encouraging somnolent Benefactors onwards with well-meaning lies.

"Soon we'll rest and have coffeeish and a fire and blankets," promised Matilda. Voice lacking her usual jaunty cheer. No doubt encouraging herself, as well.

"Exactly so," affirmed Bodkin. "Rest. Blankets. Fire. Just a few more steps." It sounded a falsehood unworthy of his talent. He decided to try a game of numbers.

"Just five more steps. One, two, - "And then he stumbled, finding no third stair step. Surprise shook him, and the realization he'd been near sleepwalking himself.

Awake, he found himself on a grand flat square. Across it waited the tower, grown mountainous. Glowing a ghostly white by starshine. A grand archway waited, open. Open like a shadow-filled mouth.

"Spy any last trap?" wondered Matilda aloud.

"Don't see any," replied Bodkin. "Which granted isn't worth half the tin shat by the Prophet Tophet."

In full agreement of that summation, Matilda laughed, notched an arrow.

"You're a very strange tavern girl," observed Bodkin.

"Ah, waiting tavern is dull as dull as dull. I wanted to be *Noctilucatilda the Assassin*. Just couldn't ever find the folk of St. February to apply my wares."

"Find them? They met in the wine cellar of the Maiden. Right beneath your flowery hooves."

"What? No, truly?"

"Didn't you note how the barkeep kept tugging his left ear lobe while tapping right foot? 'Tis the very secret assassin's sign."

"Really? I thought him just a twitchy sort."

Now Jewel whispered. "Cold. Tired. Angry."

"Then we'll get you warm and peaceable inside, Miss Witch-girl."

"Not so fast," cautioned Bodkin. He bent down, pulling away a boot. This he tossed into the shadows of the waiting archway.

It clattered undramatic as a boot dropped to bedroom floor. Nothing happened... until two rainbow eyes appeared. Bodkin sighed, drew sword. Matilda chuckled, drawing back bowstring...

There came the *clink* and *clank* of metal paws. And then out from the dark walked the figure of a dog, Bodkin's boot in its mouth. The bronze tail wagging a happy *creak, squeak*.

"Barnaby's Festus, isn't that?" declared Matilda.

In answer the mechanical dog dropped the boot. Then it bowed head, stretching front legs forwards in obeisance. Welcoming them all to the Saintless Tower.

Chapter 2
The Infinite Library

Friar Cedric:

A dream wolf shook me by the leg. I awoke thrashing, gasping, staring up into a grand vaulting of arches, pillars and marble stairways. Through high windows I spied dawn's pink light. Clearly I lay within the tower itself. My torn leg throbbing as though ghostly teeth still chewed upon it. Perhaps they did.

I pushed away blankets, struggling to sit. About me lay the scattered followers of imaginary St. Benefact. Blankets wrapped tight, packs for pillows. Did we resemble defeated soldiers? No; we'd won the battle, ascended the mountain, reached the tower.

Granted, that was yesterday's victory.

Observing the sleepers, I contemplated their separate faces. They looked tired, dirty, and weary. As did I, no doubt.

I am the oldest of the band. In truth I think myself the only adult. The rest... innocents dancing in the storm, leaping to catch the fire of the saints in upraised hands. Even our bard. She bears plentiful scars and worldly views. But at heart she's as much a daydreaming waif as the boy I put a dunce hat upon at lessons. Just so his cruel family would see him as dunce, and leave him be.

And Jewel? I watched her breathe in, breathe out. In the hall's half-light her face looked pinched, worn as any farm wife after a week of weary work. Jewel is grown woman, no child. And yet could I see her spirit as I'd beheld Beatrice's... surely Jewel would appear a glowing, glowering girl-child. Arms crossed, angry foot stamping at the adult world.

Or did I do her wrong? And all the Benefactors, seeing them as wandering innocents? Condescending of me, certainly. These people were not fools; for all they'd come to a cursed tower for unlikely treasure, certain adventure.

Perhaps the wrong lay in not including myself in the category *'wandering innocent'*. Surely every soul is a lost child; and all our years are the long miles we wander. Whether alone or with friends.

Ah, but the road is so much easier with friends.

To study faces seeking visions of the soul within... a fool's game. But still I gazed down on Jewel of Stonecroft. If she saw *my* spirit, what would she see? Probably a dreary man grown gray in library dust. Tottering on his cane, snapping yellowed teeth at the saints.

The thought made me growl. Enough brooding! I stood. Feeling sore and weary, cold but *not* old. Bah.

I set to the repairing of my leg. Beneath the bandages waited dried blood and fresh pain, pink scars and leaking wounds. Unpleasant. I closed my eyes, trembling to recall the wolf shaking me back and forth.

I pronounced what healing oration I dared, feeling the green warmth lay like a kind hand upon the wound. And yet draining me afresh of what strength I'd recovered in sleep. My blanket siren-called me to return. I resisted.

Instead, I stood, began exploring the hall. Tapping my staff against white stone walls. Stark masonry that glowed wherever sunbeams splashed. But not the floor: rough black rock that ignored sun's golden touch.

The hall itself confused the eye. Spaced regularly with great pillars through which a maze of spiral stairways wound to higher levels.

I followed a cool wind to the tower entrance. Dim memories of last night returned. Matilda and Bodkin coaxing us up and ever on through the dark. Shepherds leading befuddled sheep to safety. How by St. Typhon had those two rogues thunder-blasted the third trap?

Beyond the archway, I stood outside the tower. In open air, gazing at a peaceful panorama of mountain and cloud, shadow and light, ice and stone. The sun rising in triumph, painting clouds with orange fire softened with salmon pinks, dove grays.

A humming sound on the wind drew my attention upwards. There floated the Hefestian directable, the markings of the University of Daedalus upon its side. A line moored it to the tower top. What did they do here? Research, of course. But historical, theological, political, practical or academic?

The directable could not have been here long. Unless supplied by yet another directable. Costly business, that.

Strange coincidence they should be here upon our arrival. I watched, spying no movement but the craft shifting position as the wind blew.

I entered the tower again, stood in the grand hall, pondering the different stairways. Some merely led to balconies. But central to the hall wound a great spiraling set of steps, offering the choice of descending to the depths, or rising to the top.

The rising steps were pretty marble; those downwards, black and uninviting. How much more pleasant was the path upwards; for all that the map sent us to seek the lower levels.

I climbed upwards, the stairs curving so that one never saw far ahead nor behind. My leg complained, while an unpleasant taint upon the air worried me. I climbed farther, soon spying the corpse I expected.

Poor fellow, he lay sprawled face down. A rich red-black trail declared he'd come from higher floors, struggling, ending here, so near the tower exit.

The robes were familiar. I'd worn them myself as a student of the University of Daedalus. Perhaps I knew this man, had shared a class or glass of beer. Cautiously I turned the body over.

No longer stiff; faintly wafting of decay. This man died some two days past. The livid face: not one I knew. A dart-end protruding from his stomach declared his manner of death. I searched pockets. Finding parchment and quill. A shattered ink bottle. Behold: a dead scholar. The blue ink bleeding into the blackened blood.

A pocket of the robe held two stones that glittered bright by the dim light. Diamonds, I decided. They weighed ominous for their probable worth. Another item interested me more: a book. I leafed through it puzzled. A dictionary of an antique language from the lands beyond the sea. *Anglish*? The folk far north of Psamathe speak a dialect of Anglish; but it is no scholars' tongue. Why carry it to this tower?

Mere academic interest, most like. A true scholar carries a book to learn from, not to crack nuts. I sighed, raising my staff over the man.

"May the one true Saint be your guide through the Infinite Library," I intoned. Not truly a sacramental oration. In fact, a Lucretian farewell. Who knew, perhaps he was my fellow heretic.

And if you wonder, the Infinite Library is this world. Your world, my world; our shared existence. No grand marble edifice in the glorious but doubtful Fields of Elysium. This world itself is the One Library containing all books. And all your life you wander the aisles, perusing ancient texts and strange pictures, filling pockets with bits of wisdom and science, truth and fable. There is no greater purpose, for all that the truths you gather shall return to the shelves upon your passing. So be it.

So I sighed, signed goodbye to the dead man, turning with weary steps downwards. I did not note how he rose and followed after me.

I came in sight of the Benefactor's makeshift camp. Val and Matilda stood yawning, searching packs for breakfast items.

Soon as I came in sight, the Silenian shouted. She drew bow, notching an arrow. Val lifted her knife.

"Peace," I said, surprised at their alarm.

But Matilda sent an arrow near enough my head I felt the feather kiss my cheek. I shouted, ducked.

Val hurried forwards, knife ready. While the other Benefactors struggled to awaken, pushing aside blankets and dreams.

I prepared to retreat, thinking my companions gone mad. Turning about at a sound behind me. There stood the dead Hefestian scholar, hands curled into bloody claws. Mouth open to bite. But instead of falling upon me, he sank to the floor, Matilda's arrow through his dull white eye.

Chapter 3
Where Spirits Build Houses of Moon and Wisp

Val the Bard:

When battle comes, I take the lead. Wherefore not? I am a bard. I sing of battles and so of course I know all about them unless I lie.

Therefore, it came humbling to awaken, find I'd been led up the mountain like a child. While the two Benefactors I considered least responsible had taken sober charge.

Lucif's flaming lips to my private bits, but that snake bite hurt. And Bodkin ripping it from my side hurt worse. Granted, he saved my life. He, and Barnaby. And Jewel. And Cedric and Matilda. Ah, I owed them all.

First thing upon waking in the tower hall, I heard Matilda hiss warning. I jumped up, drew knife, watched her put arrow to eye of some wandering revenant. If you wonder, we dragged the body out of the tower.

Second thing I did was move our camp somewhere more defensible. We chose a balcony looking down over the hall and the entrance. Narrow and easily defended, with plentiful window light.

Third thing: I went back to sleep. So did the others. Kick Lucif in all seven asses, but we were worn and weary. With wounds still healing. We needed rest.

Only as evening came did I stir. Daring to stretch, check my side. Welcome, new scar. Alexandra would be impressed, the battle-besotted lunatic.

The other Benefactors rose as well. We sat wrapped in blankets sipping hot coffeeish, supping on rations from various nations. Alas, no wood for a campfire. We discussed our climb to the tower, and the map, and the dead Hefestian.

"Shouldn't we tell his friends atop the tower?" That, from Barnaby. I shook my head.

"No point. They're dead."

"All of them?" That, from a horrified Cedric. "The whole expedition? Crew and scholars alike?"

I nodded.

"Consider. The man lay dead some two days. The blood trail says he came from the upper floors. His friends haven't sought him. We haven't seen anyone, heard anyone. Though they must have spied us come up the mountain, battle the guardians."

"What would have killed them?" That, from Barnaby.

Bodkin gave quick answer, the same I'd give.

"One another, most like." He held the two diamonds in his hand, rattling them together same as dice in an alley game. "The dead fellow was hurt, but going from his friends, not to them. With a Hefestian gas dart in his belly. Probably the studious folk stumbled across glittery things, came to open murder."

"That rings true," sighed Cedric. "Greed is a more powerful trap than any magical sending."

"Easy enough to find out," declared Matilda. "Tomorrow let's go up the stairs. Lot more light upwards than that dark passage down."

"But the map says downwards," pointed out Barnaby.

"Don't need the map if we don't go there," argued the Silenian. "And if there's treasure up in the air and light, why seek it in the nasty dark?"

These words impressed the Benefactors, myself included.

"Might be treasure upwards," said Bodkin. Giving the diamonds another dice-rattle. "But old Mercutio is saying the easiest paths have the nastiest traps. The Festians thought they could just float to the top of the Saintless Tower. That kind of clever never ends well. Folk don't naturally get up and walk, two days dead."

My bard instincts chimed in, agreeing with the old rogue in the young rogue's head. Not that *I* have a bard in *my* head whispering advice. That'd drive a soul mad sooner than all the lead bells of Infernum clanging, jangling, jingling.

No, I just had a *feeling* that in some things, shortcuts were cheating. And in places *significant* as the Saintless Tower, cheating would be punished.

"Let's table discussion for the morning sunshine," I ordered everyone. I mean, I advised.

"Where is Festus?" asked Barnaby.

"Run off again," said Bodkin. "With my boot, blast the beast."

The others laughed at his bare foot. I did not.

"How was Festus waiting for us past the traps of the mountain steps?"

Barnaby shrugged. "Maybe the guardian magic doesn't care about bronze windup dogs?"

Possible. But the repeated disappearances of that dog bothered me; almost as much as its presence. Another worry that could wait till morning.

Night fell, filling the tower hall with cold drafts, black shadows. We wrapped ourselves in coats and blankets, settling around an imaginary campfire. Matilda and Bodkin argued how many diamonds it took to make a person properly rich. I wondered what a Silenian did with wealth? Buy a forest? Well, what would a bard do? I decided I'd buy a nice casing for Thelxipea. And a peacock embroidered cloak. A horse. Black leather boots shiny as obsidian...

Barnaby volunteered for the first watch. I *advised* him to keep an eye on the central stairway. Any trouble would come from there. That said, I fell asleep mid-yawn, to dream of buying boots.

When he shook me awake, the hall was darker, the night deeper. For an annoyed-but-not-uninterested moment I supposed he wanted to slip under my blanket. But no.

"On the stairs," he whispered. Pointing through the railing of the balcony to the hall below. I sat up, peering past the bars.

Down the spiral steps now flowed a soft red light, a carpet of ember glow to mark a solemn and eerie pathway.

And then a bell rang, one long toll that shook the soul. Surely a great metal bell, struck once. The slow solemn wave of sound passed through the tower, shivering stone and bone and soul. And it did not ring from above, but below.

My fellow Benefactors awoke, wondering, reaching for weapons. The magical cat leapt onto the railing, white eyes shining, observing what now passed below. I lifted hand in sign for all to keep silent.

Down the spiral stairs came a figure, aglow with the same ruddy shine. A man, dressed in scholarly robes. Eyes wide and unconcerned for a throat slashed open to the bone. Behind him in stately march came a second dead Hefestian. Then more.

Beside me, Jewel and Cedric now stood. Farther off, Matilda drew her bow.

"Keep still," I whispered. For the red glowing path did not lead towards us; rather through the archway leading out the tower. And so we watched as one and then another marched down, and out, and away.

Cedric started. "That man with the knife in his chest," he whispered. "I know him. A great teacher from Daedalus."

"Wish we students could ask the teacher some questions," I sighed.

"What was his name?" asked Jewel.

Cedric gave a puzzled look.

"Sigmund."

She nodded, bent head, hand to her spider pendant. I wanted to tell her to cease whatever dark oration she pronounced. But the little witch was no fool. I waited.

"Sigmund," she called. "By Blessed Sister Hecatatia, patroness of the night, shadow in the tomb, the dark of the moon. I command you, Sigmund. Halt and speak."

At his naming, the bloody figure staggered, stopped. Turning the gaze of empty eyes towards us. The other figures passed him by, paying no mind.

At length he stood alone. No further uncanny folk remained on the stairs. Only then did Sigmund speak.

"Release me." A seeming whisper; and yet echoing through all the hall, same as the bell.

"Sigmund, what do you here?" demanded Cedric.

"Marching to the summoning."

"Who summons?"

"A fellow corpse who wears the Helm of Command."

At naming of that dark relic, those of the Society of St. Benefact with quick memories frowned, recalling the graveyard of the Cathedral in Persephone, the bloody soldier Capitano.

"To what purpose does he summon you?"

"To aid his passage up the mountain stairs. Then to take this tower. And last to destroy you. He has gathered many dead upon his journey here."

Well, Taliesin take me with a trombone. That Capitano idiot has followed us all the way here?

I listened for Cedric to swear; but he settled for a sigh.

"Sigmund, my poor friend. Why did you come to this cursed tower?"

"To speak to the lands beyond the sea."

That was not any answer we expected.

"How?"

"A clever mechanicalism casting unseen light, that from this place can be received by scholars beyond."

"That, that is strange purpose."

"Indeed. The folk beyond the sea have strange minds. Wise in a thousand ways to bend and break a world."

Again rang that solemn bronze bell from far, far below. The dead man's eyes were filmed white as the cataracts of an ancient; but now they widened as though beholding the wonders of Infernum.

"Release me, Wieland! The bell summons."

"Ask how he died," I whispered.

Cedric nodded.

"What slew you, scholar?"

The dead man trembled, putting hand to knife-pierced heart.

"Ambition. Fear. Greed. Some among us rebelled, declaring we invited mad and dangerous nations to our shores. Others coveted the knowledge the outsiders offered. And some among us merely lusted for the treasures found in this accursed tower."

"Oh ho," whispered Bodkin.

"Free me, Wieland!" repeated the dead man.

I had more questions. But,

"Do so," said Cedric to Jewel.

The witch nodded, whispered to her pendant.

Freed, the dead scholar staggered away on his blood-shine path. Not speaking further, giving us no least glance. He followed the others and was gone.

We returned to our blankets, if not to sleep. I lay pondering the dark end of the Hefestian scholars.

Could I picture the Benefactors quarreling over treasure? Certainly. But never drawing knives upon one another. Not for chests of gold nor bags of glowing magical relics. And yet… any bard can sing a dozen songs of glorious friendships that failed when temptation whispered.

"We have to move," I told the others. "We don't want to be trapped here by an army of undead fools."

"Where would we prefer to be trapped?" asked Bodkin.

I considered. "They'll be weakened by the guardians. The tower entrance is narrow. We could front them there."

"We don't want to front them," pointed out Cedric. "We want to avoid them."

I started to return words that insulted his courage and manhood; then reconsidered. He had a point.

"The Saintless Tower is not for taking by armies," continued Cedric. "Let the cursed construction defend itself. But I agree we'd best keep moving."

I was still tired, still hurting. No doubt the others felt the same. But I prepared to rise, order the rest to rise, gather things and march.

"If I might offer the class some magical instruction," interposed the cat upon the railing. "The Helm of Command is a great and powerful relic. But its usage has cost, same as the least kitchen oration. Capitano will not have the strength to mount the stairs this night. He must rest, even as you."

"I don't think I can rest waiting for an army of revenants to corner me here." That, from me.

"Me neither." That, from Barnaby.

"Where do we go, anyway?" asked Jewel. "Up the tower, down the tower, or out the tower?"

"Out isn't an option unless we fight past him and the guardians. It's up or down."

"Down means we are cornered in the basement in the dark," said Matilda.

"I think at the bottom there is a stairway up again," replied Barnaby.

"Is that on the map?"

"No. But I had a dream. Of my da. He told me. Hinted it, anyways."

This was met with polite doubt.

"Put it to vote." That, from me.

"Up," Matilda declared with a stamp of hoof.

"Down," countered Barnaby. Stamping his boot.

Cedric sighed. "We have done well by keeping to our goal. Let us continue to follow the map. Therefore, down."

Jewel: "Up." Which surprised all. She could disagree with Cedric? Seeing our surprise, Jewel raised her head, defiant.

"I don't want to go down those awful stairs. For sure to an awful end."

We looked to Bodkin.

"I've already expressed my wise opinion. Up looks easier. So, we'd best sly our way downwards."

Benefactor gazes settled upon me. I could tie the vote, which would lead to who-knew-what sort of fight. Or I could say what bard-guts told me was the right choice.

"Down."

That settled, we decided to wait for dawn. Resting best we could. I lay in my blanket doubting I could sleep.

And yet deeper into night, I awoke again. This time to the tower hall echoing with laughing folk greeting one another. Not voices I knew, nor liked. I sat up, spied Barnaby with axe drawn, peering downwards.

The newcomers came through the entrance archway. These were not staggering undead. Far stranger folk, and more sinister. Reminding of the shadow fiends we'd fought in Persephone. Same dark forms, with eyes of flaming flowers. But these stood far larger, leathery wings overarching.

Two such beings chatted like bakers meeting upon a street corner, inquiring politely of one another. Their voices echoed sweet and musical as oboes in love, whispering to one another a'bed.

"Where have you been, Melchizedek, and what prize do you bear in that great sack?"

And indeed both carried bags upon their backs; sacks that twitched and thrashed, clearly containing items that did not wish to be in a sack.

"Ah, this night I flew high into the night, so high one cannot hear the ever-groaning earth. Higher than the clouds where lost spirits build themselves houses of wisp and moon beam, only to have cold Boreas tear them to tatters again. High I flew, till the song of the stars of the upper house set my dark soul a'tremble. Far I flew, and East into Demetia, seeking a widow snug in bed with her leman. She poisoned her mate, and he profited by the act, and now both are in the sack. And you, Hieronymus? Where have you been and what do you bear?"

The other laughed.

"To sword-blessed Martia I've been, to fetch a fierce thing of knives and curses. No sluggard in bed, she! The proud thing stood on a tower top staring at the moon, wishing she could lead an army against Cynthia's seven kingdoms. I came from behind and bagged her, but not before she bloodied me like an angered she-bear."

And the shadow-man Hieronymus gestured to wounds upon his side, that bled flames rose-pink as the fire of his flower petal eyes.

The two laughed, while their burden bags twitched and struggled. From within came curses and cries.

"Let me out!" demanded a woman's voice.

"I did not do the deed!" shouted a man. "It was her evil hand!"

"This I swear on Martia's golden hammer, spawn of Infernum. I will gut you and wrap the entrails seven times about my house."

The two shadow men gave fond thumps to their separate burdens, till the cries ceased. Then they continued through the hall. It did not surprise me that they went to the dark stairway, disappearing downwards.

I sank to the floor. Considered my knife, wishing I had something to kill. But I did not. So I put it aside, reached for Thelxipea. And there I sat, back to the wall, strumming. Petting the strings as one might caress a cat, not to calm it, but to comfort oneself.

Barnaby stood at the railing, looking down into the dark hall. When he spoke, his words came measured as a man reading his own stone epitaph.

"The voices. In the bag. That was Mother Miller. And the Squire."

I strummed the harp, drawing notes slight as night wind through a spider's web.

"Yes. I heard my mother, as well."

Barnaby sighed, came and sat beside me. Laying axe aside, putting an arm about my shoulder. We sat together so, not speaking. Just drowsing. Not sleeping, till finally our trembling ceased.

Chapter 4
Would I Ever Eat a Fly?

Jewel of Stonecroft:

It's about family, Perry. There are the folk you matter to, and the folk you don't. And when others matter to you, why then they are family.

Yes, of course *you* are family. No, not just to me! The others are all very fond of you. You were so brave on the directable. I think Val's harp was jealous. And what can Barnaby's cat or ghost do? Just talk and grumble. But you were quite wonderful.

Thelxipea sings? What of that? No, I don't think you need to learn to sing. Are you teasing me?

When we woke and breakfasted and said to one another, '*now it begins',* I didn't want to take the stairs downward. There was no light. The stones were cold. Gave shivers to touch the walls. And last night all those awful creatures went that very same way. Why follow them?

But everyone except me and Matilda voted to go downwards. Even Cedric. Don't tell, Perry. But sometimes our Cedric gets a black mood inside him. He wants to give up life's worries, go be a spooky scholar in a tomb library. Why? Well, being alive hurts. Any kitchen girl knows that. Probably knows it better than a bookish cleric. Don't tell him I said that.

Even lying with me, poor Cedric's head is too full of thoughts. Not anger or hate or anything sensible. Just, well, *thoughts*. No, it doesn't make sense to me either.

Anyway, it was brave of you to go first down the stairs, looking for traps. Were you scared?

Scared for me? That's so sweet! But no need. I've learned quite a lot since I left Stonecroft with a cat-scratched face. And I have friends now. Yes, you included, silly spider.

So: the map told us the stairs went down to a big round room with three doors. Yes, exactly what you told us you saw. But it made us feel better about following the map, knowing it wasn't making things up.

No, we still needed Cedric to make that light with his staff. Bodkin and Matilda used up half our lamp oil. You know very well we can't see in the dark like you. Well, I *like* having just two eyes. No, your eye clusters are all quite pretty. Like tiny blue jewels. Yes, I'm a jewel. You're teasing again.

Oh, we knew which door to open because the map had skulls over the first two doors. What is a skull? A kind of bone inside our heads. No, people heads. Spiders don't have them, I guess. But skulls on the map meant danger. So that's why we didn't open the first two doors. For sure something nasty waited behind them.

And so, you our brave friend went right through the third door and down the stairs like a very brave spider. And we followed you to that room with all the boxes that idiot Bodkin wanted to open but the map warned were traps.

No, I like Bodkin. He makes me laugh. But he's trouble, no point denying it. He's one of those people that the mischief just bubbles up inside every so often. And then watch out, 'cause they're going to do something mad. That's why he opened that box.

Yes, it was a nasty fight. No, they weren't people. Not exactly. A vampire is a kind of blood sucking human. Well, yes, I suppose that makes them like a spider. They are very strong and fast, and the older ones can't be killed except by strong orations or a major relic.

No, I don't think you could have talked to them. Perry, they weren't nice. You saw how the first one grabbed Bodkin by the throat. Matilda's arrows and Val's knife just sort of went through it. Cedric's staff hurt it, or it would have throttled the boy. Then sucked him dry as a fly. Do you eat flies? Really? No, I will not try one. Are you teasing again?

Yes, I was slow to help. It's hard for me to talk to you and summon *Hecatatia's Violets*. Then I decided her *Bind the Dead* oration would serve better, and wouldn't burn a friend. By the time I was ready the second vampire was out of their box and had Val by the throat. But that bard's very tough. Gouged its eyes with her thumbs. Then I bound it. Yes, yes, two eyes are not as good as a thousand. You've made your point.

Then Barnaby cut their heads off. That axe is scary. No, Barnaby isn't scary. That's crazy. Barnaby's so nice he's simple-minded. What? Why is *that* scary?

I suppose I see what you mean. Things do happen around him, while he just smiles like a lamb that doesn't know what's for dinner. Yes, I've eaten lamb. No, that is *not* worse than flies!

Pretty obvious that the saints are leading Barnaby around like a lamb. And maybe this tower is the kitchen. You think they will eat him up? Could be. Well, they'll have to eat us up too, then. No help for that. It's about family, Perry.

Chapter 5
Like Lips and Loves

Bodkin:

Yeah, the vampires were nasty. And yes, they probably wouldn't have stirred if I hadn't opened one of the boxes.

Boxes? They were coffins. They were obviously coffins. Not treasure chests. Coffins.

Whatever. Fancy boxes for rich men's bones. Always worth seeing what the noble deceased hoped to take with them to the Fields.

Idiot. Almost got us sent to the Fields.

Calm yourself, oldster. I took a calculated risk. We were fresh and ready, and it made a good test of the map to verify that indeed, indeed, the boxes were deadly.

Bah. Don't pretend you were being clever. You couldn't bear leaving loot behind.

Ooh, you make me sound like some old fellow who spent a lifetime squirreling coins under rocks for the worms to covet.

I never buried a penny, whelp. I spent every coin I ever won on something worth having. Beds and mates and bottles. A horse and a house in Pomona, fountained and gardened to please a prince.

Truly? Didn't think you so sensible.

We were never a miser, boy. A full fifth of all I stole, I tithed yearly to beggars in the name of St. Herman.

Ah, buying the patron's favor? But I'm not thinking the sly fellow's smile is so easily won.

*No! Not for his smile. For our own. To remind myself, **our** self, that loot is not the point. Only the deed counts. The defiance of guard and bar, noose and whip, law and propriety. Style and* *glory are the point. Not weight of pocket change! And so I call you greedy idiot for seeking treasure in a box marked by death. You cannot deceive me. I am you.*

Fine. True. I was hoping for glitter. But I wouldn't have done so if it wasn't a reasonable risk. And didn't I help take down the second vampire? Got him fine, in the back with the short sword. Maybe I should give it a name, like Barnaby's Dragontooth.

We once named a long knife taken from the altar of St. Hermaphroditus.

What did you call it?

St. Venus's Penis.

Well, that's just sad.

No, it's mocking. Professionals never name their tools, boy. Nor chat with their horses nor boast in taverns nor trust a smiling stranger. And professionals never ever get greedy during a job.

Fine. It ended well enough. And you saw how well I did on the next floor down. Professional to the core.

No, I closed my eyes. You'd embarrassed me past bearing with the vampires. It was like watching my mirror be an idiot.

Liar. Sure you watched. It was that big round chamber lit by a glowing stone in the ceiling. Thirteen different doors.

Oh, I know the map, same as you. Doors are marked with skulls promising death. Excepting the first, fifth and ninth doors, which are marked with sun signs.

Which promised treasure. Except they'd been sly. Put a bit of stain on the floor before the first and ninth.

Blood, or fire?

Hmm, Black like old blood.

Any on the doors?

No.

Well, lack of splatter makes a good hint that the stains are fake. But not a sure bet.

Yeah, and we argued whether to take the bet. After the vampire battle, Val and Barnaby didn't want to open anything interesting. It required unto Matilda and I to remind all that we'd come for treasure. If the map said 'glitter', the faithful followers of St. Benefact were honor-bound to fill our pockets with his blessings. Cedric agreed, bless 'im, so of course Jewel agreed. That settled that.

You know your friends didn't come for treasure. They came because they were lonely and needed purpose.

Oh, for sure. And myself among them. Seriously, old man. If I didn't have a flock of lost sheep to guide through dangerous alleys, you'd have swallowed me up by now.

I am you, boy.

Nah. You're just who I used to be.

What you are, I once was. What I am, you shall be.

Surely. Unless I catch the ambition to do better. No offense, of course.

I never take offense. Just other things. What waited behind the three safe doors?

Hmm. Matilda opened the first. Nothing jumped out. Was just a closet. Ah, but holding a present for our Silenian. A longbow, relic of St. Artemisia her blessed self.

Ah, truly? Quite valuable.

Yeah, but no good to me. I took it upon my brave self to open the fifth door. Well now, and what did I find?

What?

Oh, you don't want to know.

Probably I don't. If it was anything worth a boast, you'd have bragged of it already.

Well, it was my missing boot. That weird mechanical dog of Barnaby's ran off with it in the night.

And left it in a closet of a deadly chamber of a cursed tower? A strange jest. Beware that beast. It has its own mind, and its own purpose.

I do believe I agree, old man.

What lay behind the ninth door?

Oh. Six bars of silver, big as bricks and ten times as heavy.

Ha. That's a trap. Something just valuable enough the greedy can't bear to leave behind. But guaranteed to weigh them down when they need to run.

I suppose.

No. You didn't put them in your pack, did you? Tell me you aren't so completely an idiot.

Treasure and packs, they're like lips and loves, cocks and coquettes.

Get rid of them.

No. If I leave this tower with an empty pack, you'd mock me for all I left behind. I may have come for the fun and company, but I'm not leaving without heavy pockets.

Then you probably aren't leaving.

That's 'we', you mean. And twixt us, it's easier to carry silver bricks in your pack than a sad old man in your head.

Silver weighs plenty. Life's wisdom weighs nothing.

Ah, now, there you're mistaken. The longer I carry you, the more you weigh on me.

You prefer to carry metal bricks than overmuch knowledge of life?

Depends on the knowledge. Were you satisfied with the life you lived? Saints' shit, no. You drank a magic cup to forget it. Same as any tippler in a tavern.

There is no escaping one's self.

Hmm. Well, I'll grant that it can't be easy. But maybe that's why I've come to the tower. To leave *you* behind. Just a thought.

Chapter 6
All the World's a Wood

Matilda:

Circling down and down that cursed tower, a band of undead rotters on our trail, I felt less and less like *'Tilda the Tavern Girl*. And ever more the sly assassin *Noctilucatilda*. Feared and revered member of the fulsome Friends of Friar February. Excellent!

Helped to have a new better-than-butter bow upon my back. For sure touched by bonafide blessed Saint Artemisia. Ooh, gave me an amorous tingle just to hold.

I never had overmuch to do with Artemisia. Patroness of the Hunt, you know. The shy thing has a stick up her butt, always chastising a girl for overmuch charity with her chastity. Still, every Silenian knows Artemisia is a lady's best friend in the woods.

And this tower *is* the woods. Full of pretty things in the open, and hungry things in the shadows. Mister Holy Father Cedric says the world's a library. Let's call the world a wood and have done. That's Silenian philosophy, that is.

After the chamber of thirteen doors, we wound down and round. Passing plenteous doors and hallways the map warned us to leave alone, At last we came to a large hall, bright with fresh-lit candles. A pretty fountain made a welcoming splash and plash into a basin.

"Nice of them to light the room, see to drinks," said Bodkin. Dear boy was being ironic, if you wondered.

"Is the fountain poisoned?" asked Jewel. "I'm parched. We've not much water left."

"What says the map?"

Mister Barnaby answered with his knowledge of the very same mad map, not bothering to produce said sacred text.

"There are three exits. The ones left and right of us have death heads, so we don't take those. The archway on the far end has a sun sign. We go there."

"What about the fountain?"

Barnaby scratched a chin in miller's sign of grinding rough thoughts to floury conclusions.

"It shows this fountain with a sun sign and a death's head together. What does that come to?"

That magic kitty of his did not wait to debate. He leapt to the font rim, put head low, began to lap. All very well for him. But what served a mystic feline for drink might not do for a sensible Silenian; nor those near-as-good-as-Silenian.

I approached the fountain. Sniffed. Reached a fingertip, tested with a tap to tongue.

"By the authority of my pretty nose I declare this safe drink. Has a wine touch, I shall add."

Jewel produced her horn cup, dipped, sipped with a slurp. Then *laughed aloud*. Saintly Silvanus nip my mother's nethers, who'd ever heard the sour and dour little witch laugh?

"Ha," she declared. "It's good. I feel less tired. Stronger. And my knee where I fell yesterday isn't hurting anymore."

"A healing font," declared Cedric. "Let us rest here."

Our growling scowling bard argued against rest. "Capitano may have already passed the outer guardians. In which case we've a horde of undead behind us."

"Perhaps he'll assume we went upwards," considered Cedric.

"Else he'll split his troops," suggested Bodkin. "Then we'll only be facing a mere half an undead horde."

"Up or down, he has no map," our Barnaby pointed out. "He'll have to try different doors, different paths."

"Oh, and that will cost him," agreed Bodkin.

"Fine," said the Bard. "Fine. We rest. But not overlong."

So we sat and snacked, drinking the font's wonderful offering. Made this girl feel wonderful; like I'd had a bath and a good night's sleep. A happy mood took us all. The growly bard and the frowny witch started singing racy ditties with rhymes like 'miller and fill her', 'cleric and derrick'.

I giggled, feeling dizzy. *Tipsy*, I realized, alarmed. Not always a safe thing, as any tavern girl knows. Particularly for girls in taverns. I stood, wobbling a bit, dratting the floor that had turned ship deck in storm. Walking towards the darker side of the chamber.

I'd thought the far half of the room the same black stone as elsewhere. A closer view showed that there wasn't much of a floor. Just a narrow black bridge over a deep empty dark. I meditated upon that awhiles; then saw the trap and shouted.

"Shit, shop dunking I mean stop drinking! Not another sop I mean sip. Stop."

"Why?"

"Why, 'cause we've got to cross this bridge. You wanting to walk it drunken as Friar Bacchus on the feast day of St. Silenus?"

"How drunk is that?" asked Jewel, giving rare and ragged giggle. A sound to bring joy to my stern Silenian heart, upon another time. Not just then.

Bodkin and Barnaby came, stood beside me, studying the dark situation. The rogue shook his boyish head.

"Now here's a clever snare. We have to go single file on a path for sober feet. Thirty steps, no missteps or its drop into February's bed."

"Well, but hey now, I can do that," declared Jewel. "Watch!" The little witch-lady skipped towards the chasm edge. Barnaby grabbing her just before she stepped into air.

She giggled in his arms.

"Don't I owe you a kiss?" she asked.

"No, I don't think so."

Val the Bard jumped up.

"Let's make some coffeeish, get it down her, get it down, uhm, I'm going to sit awhile," said Val. So saying, she did so sit again. Dropping her cup.

Of the Benefactors, Jewel and Val seemed the most muddled and befuddled. Cedric and Bodkin the least. Barnaby looked awake but kept shaking his head to clear it, same as a horse bebothered by flies.

Cedric turned towards the door.

"I hear steps," he announced. Well, of course. Never rains but rocks fall from the sky. I drew my bow, moved towards a wall. Val struggled to stand, draw her knife. She seemed unsure how to do both at the same time. But,

"Rope," said our rogue. Searched his pack, finding the very thing. Looked for something in the chamber to tie it to. Spying nothing firmer than a miller.

"Barnaby, stand here. Wrap this about your waist, hold tight and brace your feet."

He nodded as if he understood. I kept an arrow and an eye on the stairs. Meanwhile Bodkin stepped upon the bridge confident as Lord Mayor down the High Street. Trailing the rope. Thirty dancing steps later he stood on the far side, back to a dark doorway. There he looped the rope about a torch sconce. Waved to Cedric.

The holy fellow grasped the rope in one hand, taking hesitant steps. I didn't see him finish, as the eye I charged with watching the stairs now spied someone coming to join our party.

Was a soldierly-looking fellow, pale with a tad of green to the face. Clothes declared him Demetian when alive; for all he'd obviously emigrated to the Fields of Elysium.

I aimed for the right eye. But that font water still babbled and burbled making bubbles within the heart's soul of my brain's spirit. My arrow took the fellow in the forehead. Soon as hit, the man's head burst into flame.

Well now. That was a pleasurable surprise. I credited St. Artemisia's probable opinion upon the undead. She's all about nature, and you can't argue but that dead folk afoot are quite unnatural. Not that *that*'s an opinion to opine in Dark Persephone. Least if you want tips from the paler tavern custom.

The creature howled, clawing at its head. Tumbled down the steps, causing the two behind to stumble.

"Be hurrying," I warned my fellow Benefactorials. Not that I couldn't fill that doorway with nasty burning dead folk; but only exact so long as my quiver didn't empty. It felt over-light now.

I put down two more, setting them afire. Which brightened the room considerably. More dead folk struggled to pass, grumbling and grousing for the business.

I checked on the rest. Cedric was safe across. Jewel now inched along the bridge, holding to the rope. Bodkin encouraging her. Mister Barnaby working to keep the rope taut.

I turned back to the doorway blocked by burning dead. Newcomers worked to push them aside. I added two more arrows to the business, two more corpses to the fire. I had to keep them on the steps. Once they entered the room, the world's forest would go dark for *this* Silenian.

"Excellent work," observed someone observant. A man leaned against the wall beside me, slouching easy as morning toper beside tavern door.

Well, of course it was that Dark Michael. Just as nonalive as these undead fellows. But far different. Michael was a person without a body. They were bodies without the person. So I granted him a grin, fixed another arrow into a dead man's head.

"Don't suppose you can fetch more arrows?" I inquired.

He shook his handsome hatted head.

"Ah, no harm. Didn't expect so."

I checked the others. Jewel had now crossed the bridge. Val now stood in the middle, arms out, wavering this way and that. I watched Barnaby drop the rope, rush to her, grab by the waist just before she toppled over the edge. Then he slung our bard over his shoulder as a proper miller might do with a sack of endangered and feminine flour. In thanks she cursed, beating his back with dainty girl fists. A sight to make my sober soul howl with laughter.

"Beware," hissed Dark Mister Michael.

I turned from that show to see the dead folk pushing aside the burning bodies. They staggered into the chamber.

"Retreat, girl," ordered the ghostly major general sergeant lieutenant Mr. Michael.

Ah, it was that font-wine buzzing within my shy Silenian self that gave reply.

"Kiss me first."

The man stiffened, if not with the stiffening a girl prefers. Pushed his hat back in astonish.

"What?"

I stamped a dainty hoof. "Kiss me quick else I stay."

He looked at the dead folk staggering forwards; returned to frowning at me. Then by St. Hyman's maiden aunt, he dared bend close. For a second my pretty eyes met his round brown orbs. Like staring into two caverns where candles dare not tread. Then came... the kiss!

His lips felt a bit dry, a bit cold. But perfectly manly and fine. Not much time to test and taste, Lucif take the hurry.

Kiss done, I gave a shy wink then high-tailed it to the bridge.

Chapter 7
We Can't All Be Cats

Professor Shadow Night-Creep:

Not to boast, but I am a supreme connoisseur of dark places. Lightless domains call to me, saying *'come, noble cat, wander within our mystery'*. Perhaps a chasm on the moon where beings from the stars sleep till world's end. Else the city sewers of Persephone, Pomona, Pleasance, with their liquid trill of pungent waters. Or the caverns of Nix, dark and stark, where cannibal maidens sing sweetly as sirens upon the sea; and with the same hungry purpose. And true afficionados of darkness shall always appreciate the catacombs beneath the Temple of St. Bast. There one tastes time itself in the dry dead dust, the cold stone must, the old bone musk. Then of course there are the warehouses of Sister Parvati in the warm Spice Isles, with their delightful mix of cinnamon and pepper, clove and coffee, rodent and rot...

In brief: darkness enhances appreciation. Spicing the senses of whisker, nose, tongue and ear that overmuch light diminishes. What is a rustle of leaves by day's illumination? Bah, a trivial insect, meriting yawn. But in the depths of a necromancer's dungeon or farmer's barn, the slightest *scritch, scratch* makes all a symphony to a cat's ears, setting tail and soul a'twitch.

Therefore did the lower depths of the Saintless Tower call to me. Alas, the humans followed their map, avoiding a dozen opportunities to wander places of darkest fascination. True, they would have perished. Screaming spitted on stakes or struck down by razor pendulums, seized by tentacled summonings, else driven mad by music too eldritch for mortal minds. In particular, the eighth option of the Chamber of

Thirteen doors led to a plane of existence entirely beyond the stars. Quite fascinating, if lethal.

But no, the party took the safe path. Sensible and boring. Even the vampire-in-a-box was ho-hum. Granted, I suppose the safe paths are intended to bore.

So I blame mere ennui that when the Benefactors came to the Chamber of the Font, I did not spy the clever trap. I knew the font water granted healing, with a side-effect of inebriation. What of that? The bridge made no challenge. A one-eyed kitten could tumble back and forth all night.

I did not consider the potential risk in context of large clumsy bipedal creatures with heads swimming. Ah, no matter; they managed.

I would like to mention that once we all stood safe upon the far side of the pit, observing Capitano's undead minions enter the chamber, I made a casual observation: the bridge was wooden.

The rogue was quick to grasp my clever point. He took the remaining lamp oil, pouring it across the bridge. Then my pupil Barnaby son of Barnabas pronounced a perfectly decent *Oration of Flame*, upon which the bridge burst into fire.

That done, the humans thought it wise to flee the chamber, continuing down ever more stairs. Exactly as I would have advised. Really, they were doing fine. One can't be forever waving the instruction rod or the students will never learn.

So I lingered to observe some of the less-aware undead wander onto the bridge, setting themselves alight. They flailed, tumbling into the chasm. Far, far below, these corpses were snatched from the air by tentacled things. Devoured still struggling, still burning. Mildly interesting.

At length a new personage entered the chamber of the font. Wearing excellent armor, a general's red cloak, waving proud saber. Behold the undead Capitano, wearing the Helm of Command and a proud swagger he'd yet to earn.

He searched about, hoping to see the scattered limbs of dismembered Benefactors. Alas, finding only smoldering minions, a burning bridge. He counted his still-functioning revenants, cursing the sum. Well, but he was finding that the Saintless Tower was no place to storm by mere numbers. Each wrong choice would devour half his servants.

No doubt he believed he came on a mission of dark vengeance. But it was the Powers themselves that gave Capitano the Helm of Command, and set him upon the Benefactor's trail. But was their intent to stop the heroes, or to drive them on?

I awarded the question a yawn. Either way he was an idiot. Just a puppet, as these undead were puppets. Yawn completed, I rushed away to see what the next level offered. The map had shown a mere circle centered with a death's head. Interestingly ominous, if scarcely informative.

The humans were taking their time, recovering sobriety on the winding stairs. I passed through their stumbling feet to find the witch's spider had assumed the party lead *again*. Annoying creature. But it was young. I nobly declined to take offense. Instead I raced past, arriving first to the next chamber.

Well, but this was more interesting. The chamber was pleasingly lightless. Filled with a quality of dark that hinted of menace, with a touch of otherworldly monstrosity spiced with spiritual madness.

If that challenges the whiskers of your imagination... *hmm*; picture a curtain of blackest sable, sewn from shrouds stolen from the corpses of dead titans buried beneath the dark plane of the third Tartarus. Good. Now stare into that black cloth, seeking stars or sparks, searching with frighted eyes for the least sign of light… finding only deeper, softer, ever more velvet night.

Excellent! Now, if you dare: pull aside the curtain, face what lurks beyond.

Just so did I prowl the dark, sniffing, catching scents of burning revenant from above. Dust; and a touch of old blood long seeped into stone. And just a faint tang of sulfur. Ah; always something interesting, when sulfur is in the air.

My sharp ears caught the voices of the humans behind me. And a low, sad, dismal song from the dark before me. I approached, wary and wise. Behold a large circle glowing dim as just-heated iron. In the circle sat… a child. Humming softly to the dark.

To judge human age and gender, a girl some ten years old. Plain dress. Sweet eyes, unless you caught the glimmer. Pretty smile, unless you spied the sharp incisors. Not that I don't have glimmering eyes and sharp incisors myself. Truthfully, the teeth of humans remind of sheep. And their eyes? Dull pebbles. But I suppose we can't all be cats.

I sat and studied, seeking what lurked beneath the mask of humanity. It ignored me; though it knew I observed. And hated me for so doing.

Always amuses, to sit staring, staring, just beyond the length of a guard dog's chain. How shall any cat resist?

Dull-toothed and dull-eyed the humans might be, but not dull-witted. When at last they entered the chamber, it was with light from the cleric's staff.

Nor did they immediately approach the Cursed Child. First, they circled about, examining the chamber. Two passageways offered easy exit. Naturally the map designated them *deadly*. A closed door at the far end from the stairs offered the only exit marked *safe*.

I watched the thief approach the door, examine the lock, give experimental tug to the handle. To no one's surprise, it did not open. He tapped a finger to the dark iron keyhole, then turned to consider a large iron key lying beside the Cursed Child.

The creature ignored the humans. She rocked back, forth, humming her desultory tune, lonely as night wind 0through gravestones. She grasped something, singing to it: a wooden ball. Before her on the cold floor lay a scattering of small square bones. From the ankles of sheep, if you wondered.

The child tossed the ball high, then reached to scoop up a bone with the same hand, then catch the descending ball. Behold a lonely innocent playing a child's game in a basement of the Saintless Tower. How very sad. How very dark.

My pupil approached her. No doubt intending to make friends, exchange hugs and happy chatter. I interposed myself, which near caused his limited feet to stumble into the thrice inscribed circle. When he recovered his balance, I granted instruction.

"The circle around her is a powerful charm of protection. Do not to touch it with foot or hand."

"Does it protect her?" asked Barnaby.

I sighed. I'm fond of my pupil, but his thoughts turn like the stones of his mill. Properly and to profit, but not over-swift.

"No, it protects *you*."

"Oh."

"Hey, girl," called out Bodkin. "Lend us that key, will you?"

The child did not look up to answer.

"No." That said, she placed hand upon the key to confirm she'd be keeping it.

The thief nodded unsurprised. Gathered his fellow followers of the patron saint of self-benefaction. Huddling close, they plotted.

Meanwhile, I circled the girl, working to guess what creature hid within the innocent form. Watching her play her game of ball and bones. *'Knucklebones'* in western lands. In the south it is *'astragalus'*, or *'jax'*. Amusing, no doubt, if one has hands and is trapped in a charmed circle in a dark basement of a cursed tower.

From the stairway came wafts of smoke, unpleasantly tinged with burning revenant. But no sounds of pursuit. Yet.

Bored, I joined the plotting Benefactors, curious what wild plan they weighed.

"On the eighth, you shoot," the thief told Matilda.

That sounded unwise. Time to instruct.

"If you cross that circle with hand, blade or even arrow, it shall cease to imprison her. And once unbound, she shall seek to slay all within the chamber."

Cedric nodded. "So I informed them."

But they continued with the steps of their plan. My pupil put away axe, drew forth his relic wand of St. Demetia. Began the calming breaths his excellent tutor taught him to practice before the more difficult orations.

Meanwhile the cleric Cedric moved across the room, taking position before the locked door. The Silenian girl taking position on the opposite side. The bard stationed herself by the stairs, knife drawn. Was she now sober? I watched her wobble some. Ergo, not quite.

While the thief Bodkin approached the charmed circle, stopping just outside it. There he sat, confident as cat. Whistling happily, just a schoolboy skipping class. The

Cursed Child watched him, darting glances about the room, one hand on the key. Pretty eyes narrowing, wondering what sinister challenge unfolded.

Bodkin took from his pack a dozen Hefestian fruit cubes, and scattered them before him, Next he produced a Demetian half-sovereign, which he placed upon the back of his hand.

The girl eyed these actions, frowning.

The rogue gave her a winning smile, then flipped the coin into the air. He reached, scooping up *one* fruit cube. Then caught the coin with the same paw. Hand, that is.

The girl sniffed in disdain. She took her wooden ball, rested it atop her hand, then sent it upwards. Scooped up *two* of the knuckle bones, in time to catch the descending ball.

Bodkin nodded approving. He replaced the coin upon the back of his hand, let fly upwards. While it rose, he scooped *three* fruit cubes. The same hand then catching the descending coin quick as cat paw. Near quick, anyways.

The girl growled in equal appreciation and annoyance. Brushing pretty curls aside, she resettled herself, placed the ball atop her hand again. Then sent it flying upwards, scooping up *four* knuckle bones.

This duel interested me enough I only half-observed the Silenian Matilda notch arrow to bow. I did spy my pupil Barnaby raise wand to pronounce oration. I sighed, assuming they prepared to attack the Cursed Child. That would not end well.

But I withheld my call to *halt*. There was discernable discipline to what they did. I watched as the Cursed Child now scooped up *six* knuckle bones. Giving a low, very low chuckle of triumph. Her form shivered some, letting the human mask slip. For a moment the sulfur-hint in the air grew thick.

Bodkin took a breath, coughed, tossed the coin up, reaching to scoop *seven* fruit cubes. The descending coin landed on edge, bounced from his hand. But the rogue managed to reach out, catching it again before it hit the stones.

Now the Cursed Child shook her curls, sat up on her knees, stretched her tiny arms to ready herself. With a defiant smile to Bodkin she set the ball upon her hand. Then let it fly upwards -

At which Matilda shot her arrow. Not at the girl, but the key lying forgotten beside her. The arrow struck true, sending the key flying beyond the circle.

The girl scooped up *eight* bones, giving a high laugh of delight cut short by the passing of the arrow. She reached for key, arrow and ball, catching none. Knuckle bones rolled and rattled away, the ball descended uncaught, bouncing, bouncing. The key clattered on the stones far beyond her reach.

The Cursed Child howled, a sound to shake the foundations of the tower. Bodkin rolled away quicker than the wooden ball.

Meanwhile Cedric, positioned behind her, seized the key where it clattered. He then rushed to unlock the door.

But with the trespass of the arrow, the glow of the charmed circle faded, flickered, vanished. The girl rose to feet, raising hands high. She shivered, casting aside guise of humanity for something shadowed and shapeless, tall as the ceiling, with multi-jointed arms that stretched out –

-and stopped. For a new and wider circle now bound the angered fiend. This circle glowed green and gold, a masterfully cast barrier clearly the product of *excellent instruction*.

The shadow-being thrashed and howled within its new cage.

"Excellent work," I informed my pupil. For proper praise in moderate measure is as instructive as harsh critique. I leapt, returned to my customary place upon his shoulder. "But it will not long hold such a creature."

"Good," said the Bard, still standing by the steps. "I hear Capitano approaching."

"Ah," I said. Comprehending.

We rushed to the now-unlocked door and out the chamber. I observed the first revenants enter, just as the Tartarus-fiend broke free of the circle.

Then Cedric slammed shut the door. Put key to keyhole, locking it. Beyond the door we heard the howls of the shadow-creature, the growls of the revenants, the shouts of their unhappy commander Capitano.

And then did I, creature of power and purpose that I am, deign to purr; that glorious feline sound that declares, '*I find myself pleased*'.

For I had come to consider the miller's mad friends as my students. And stern teacher that I am, I found myself pleased. It's all very well to appreciate darkness. But learning is a thing of light. And these mad followers of an imaginary saint had just shone brilliantly. Clearly, they had a bright beacon of a teacher.

Myself, that is to say.

Chapter 8
In a Mist of Glass and Mirror

Dark Michael:

Absurd, that a man such as I should be put into position of *supernatural adviser*. I've attended a thousand funerals, never once lingering graveside to brood on life's dark end. I've slept in haunted ruins, less concerned for ghosts than for rats. Dreams I have had, as any man. And on awakening I left them behind, refusing to sift for revelation. I've gazed unmoved upon apocalyptic wonders in the sunset sky. Never feeling least shiver for life's Glorious Mystery.

Alive, I never had use for the unknown, the unseen. The world I knew and saw made challenge enough. *And that was wisdom.* Life's daily truths are the only real concerns of the living. Never the trash of mysteries beyond the veil. For all that I now stand on the far side of that curtain; one more of its mysteries. Now I peer through the curtain into Life, spying upon the magic theatre beyond. And so for me, daily life is become the realm of Mystery. Nearly too bright and holy for my sight to bear.

I trailed the adventurers as they descended yet deeper down winding stairs, through dank halls dimly lit by unlikely sources. Passing side corridors whose cold winds chuckled of death to those who came without map.

At length we came to an archway opening onto a grand chamber; so large and bright within that it gave the illusion of open air. On a misty day, perhaps; as the distance soon faded to gray blur.

"Last floor before the bottom," declared Bodkin.

"I see folk moving," whispered Matilda.

"That's us," countered the rogue. "Our reflections. There's mirrors set about. And walls of glass."

The company stepped into the chamber, finding themselves in a corridor of glass. The miller boy tapped upon a panel, face showing his usual delight at anything new and absurd.

"It's like the amazement tent at the Jahrmarkt, where you wander through twisty hallways bumping your nose where you think the path goes but doesn't."

"Oi, is my hair so tangly as that?" asked the Silenian, pondering a reflection. As it happened, it was. *Tangled*, I mean. Yet fetching. Her hair curled like wood shavings. No doubt softer to touch than wood shavings.

I almost did. Reached out to touch, that is. But I withdrew the hand. Absurd act. From either side of the veil. Absurd.

The Benefactors stepped into the chamber, finding themselves entering a corridor of glass. Tapping produced the faintest of chimes. Beyond could be seen yet more glass walls, interspersed with mirrors. The total effect could only mystify those wandering within.

The adventurers came to an intersection, pondered choice.

"Time for the map?" asked the warrior Valentine. She seemed to have recovered sobriety. Looking flushed and angered for having lost sobriety. What a soldier she'd have made. Give me a platoon of Martia bards and I could conquer Terra Sanctorum. If I wanted. I don't, as it happens.

"Ah, no need for the map," said the boy thief. "It makes things easy here. Always take the left. Right means death."

"Suspiciously easy," observed the witch-spawn cat. Ominous words; not that we needed omen. The band went on, taking the left way.

Strange, to see multiple sets of Benefactors wandering the labyrinth. Amusing to ask myself, *did I follow the true band?* Perhaps I trailed mere reflections. How should a ghost know what is real?

I considered testing. I walked unseen behind the Silenian; studying her tangled curls. Perhaps if I reached, my hand would touch glass, or pass beyond as through mist. But would that be a measure of her unreality, or of mine?

Idiot thought. And yet inevitable. Death must turn the most practical spirit to philosophy. Same as it turns the body to worm and dust.

Bored with philosophy, I reached. Touching a single curl of the girl. Soft, and real. Ergo, she was real. I suppose it confirmed I was real, not that I doubted *that.*

Matilda turned at the touch. She looked surprised; then gave me her mad Silenian smile. I did not speak. What was there to say? Nothing. She went on, hooved feet stamping in something close to dance.

"Trouble," declared our bard-warrior. She pointed. There in the much-reflected distance staggered several armed men. At their lead came a red-caped figure in the armor of a Demetian general. I wondered where Capitano had obtained high officer's uniform. Did the former owner now stumbled behind the man, demoted to foot soldier? The thought angered me. Capitano had not merited military honor in life. Certainly not since.

Glorious uniform aside, he made a pitiful sight. The armor dented, the cloak ripped. A jagged wound in one leg left him limping. Behind him followed a ragged remnant looking no better. Staggering into one another, else into the glass walls. Waving swords to menace reflections. No army marching to war; this was a routed remnant lost in the maze, seeking retreat from the field.

Benefactors and undead minions wandered the glass labyrinth, at times coming nearer, readying arms, then finding themselves forced to follow another path. Till at last the twists of hall and destiny brought the two bands side by side, separated by a single transparent wall.

The Benefactors halted to consider their pursuers, unimpressed.

"Not much left to that lot," remarked the rogue.

"Surprised any still walk," said the bard. "This madhouse tower has been dangerous enough, even following the map."

Capitano approached the glass wall, studying each of the Benefactors. Up close, he did not resemble a defeated general. No, he looked a battered toy. The plaything of a cruel child, who'd subjected this wooden soldier to ten thousand flames and blows, kicks and insults.

Capitano snarled something unheard. No doubt proud words of defiance. The Benefactors merely shook their heads. He drew his sword, beat the pommel against the glass wall. The glass chimed mockingly, giving no hint of cracking. Seeing this, the creature dropped the sword; then sank to the floor beside it.

His remaining band of revenants stood contemplating these actions, dead faces declaring their hearts unmoved. On the faces of the Benefactors, I marked the emotions of contempt, of horror, of pity.

"Leave the idiot," said the bard. She ushered all down the hallway. But the miller looked back, hesitated, then returned. Of course he did.

He drew forth the wand he'd crafted in the woods of St. Demetia. His friends watching; the witch-spawn upon his shoulder whispering. No doubt advising that he save his strength and pity. The miller shook his head; lips silently pronouncing oration.

There came a flash from the wand; warm light, green as summer sun through forest leaves. It crossed the glass, shining upon the kneeling man beyond.

Flames wound about Capitano, vines of emerald fire. He did not struggle, nor scream any last curse. Instead he closed eyes, whispering words for himself alone. And then the light faded, and he fell to dust. The black helmet upon his head rolled away across the floor.

The remnants of his dead followers sank to the ground, no longer under command, no longer part of the mad theatre of the labyrinth.

Barnaby leaned against the glass a long moment, wavering, recovering his strength. His friends waited, patient. At last he nodded, putting away the wand, rejoining their company.

At length they came to a new intersection. The rogue turned left - and then things changed.

"*Oh*," said the bard. Voice low, yet so heartfelt that all turned in fear she'd found an arrow in her chest.

She had not. She held eyes wide, face turned up, radiant as mirror before the sun.

"What?" asked the miller, and the rogue, and the cleric and the witch and the Silenian. I, the ghost, did not ask. Though I wondered as well.

The bard lifted a hand towards the passage to the right. Clearly reaching for some object of her inner vision.

"You're back," she whispered. "You're back, you're back, you're back."

"Who's back now?" asked Matilda, looking about.

The bard stepped forwards, gazing upon something unseen to other eyes. Including mine. Annoying, to be a ghost, and yet have no insight to mystic visions.

"We don't want to go that way," said Bodkin, putting his boy's hand to her shoulder. She shrugged the hand away.

"I do," she said. "I must." The tears upon her face shone bright, more real than anything in the mist of glass and mirror. She continued down the hall.

"Val?" called Barnaby. He rushed to stand before her. She moved to step around. He put out an arm to block the way.

It would have alarmed all and surprised none, if she had drawn knife. She did not. She put hand to his face, stood on tiptoe, gave a kiss.

"Love you," she whispered. "Love you all. But the cup is calling. Hear it? See it? That's my path."

That said, she stepped around him, continued on. He stood watching, no longer seeking to hold her back.

If there had been least glimmer in the air before her, least hint of music, then all would have believed. There was not. Just the light of her joy. And how to tell that from madness? No way I know, one side of life or the other.

The thief Bodkin formed quick plan. "I trip her. Barnaby, you keep her from drawing knife. Kiss her or whatever. Meanwhile, Jewel's spider wraps her legs tight. Cedric, you be ready to give her head a whap."

"I don't think we can do that," said Barnaby. Watching Val wander on through the glass maze. Her lips moving, singing now, too low to reach us.

"Don't have time to do aught else," argued Matilda. "If Mister Map says that way lies disaster, we're bound to take the papery thing at its word."

"Well, but maybe her magic cup knows something not on the map," countered Barnaby.

"What cup?" demanded Matilda, stamping hoof. "Don't see anything but air and a silly look on a girl's pretty face."

"It's stop her or let her go," said Jewel. "What choice is that?"

There came a silence. Each thinking of a third choice. Barnaby said it aloud.

"Can't leave her. And don't have the right to stop her. But we can go with her."

"But, the map," whispered Jewel.

"It got us this far," said Cedric. "But perhaps for the last step we have a different guide."

"One we don't know, see, or hear," pointed out Bodkin.

"Perfect guide for the lot of us," sighed the miller. Then grinned. "All said, we've none of us been knowing what nor where nor why as we went, now have we?"

A pointed question that pricked all souls present. Mine included. Sharp point made, the miller turned, striding through the maze of misty glass and diminishing mirrors.

The others hesitated, exchanging doubting looks. Then sighed, turning to follow. I also followed. Not doubting, but wondering.

The Society of St. Benefact, sadly imaginary patron of Self Benefaction, hurried to rejoin their wandering bard.

Catching up to her standing before a grand wooden door. Face turned upwards, hands clasped at her chest.

She stared into the air, singing softly. Barnaby stopped, stood beside her, studying her face.

"This door isn't even on the map," said Bodkin, puzzled.

"Looks quite impressive," observed Matilda. "I'd keep treasure behind it."

Val took a deep breath, turned to the others.

"Here we go," she said. Then reached to Barnaby, grasping his hand. Then reached to Bodkin, taking his hand. Barnaby nodded. He reached, took Jewel's hand. She in turn took Cedric's; who reached for Matilda's hand.

And Matilda the mad Silenian turned, holding out hand to me, the sane ghost. And I the ghost studied that offered hand, and the others a moment; then reached, clasped.

As if in acknowledgment of that final gesture, the door before us trembled. Slowly, in no hurry, it swung inwards, revealing a dark stairway. Leading, of course, yet further down.

At which sight all dropped hands and drew weapons. Axe drawn, sword drawn, knife drawn, the company stared down this new path.

"Last level," whispered Cedric.

We Benefactors nodded to one another, took breaths, and walked forwards. Hearing the door closing softly, firmly, irrevocably behind us.

Chapter 9
All the Underworld's a Stage

Beyond the last step of the final stairway to the lowest level of the Saintless Tower, waited a wide corridor. Chill drafts ran up and down, muttering of mysteries. Sconced candles flickered, setting shadows dancing to the mad music of flame and wind. The passage stank of the dust of ancient stones, the mold of forgotten cells where lay forsaken bones. At times a sulfur-taint wafted past, reminding of the Cursed Child's desolate chamber.

This atmosphere weighed heavy upon heart and spirit, as though all the levels of the tower above pressed down upon the company. Fixing each where they stood, stone figures gazing down the corridor, seeking an end hidden in the curving distance. No one seemed able to move, nor willing to take the next step.

Till Shadow Night-Creep leapt from Barnaby's shoulder.

"Look for me, by and by," he informed all; and darted ahead. With this farewell, the strange paralysis of the company ceased.

"Annoying pet, that," observed Matilda. "Impersonally, I find Miss Witch's spider more utilitarian, not to mention egalitarian."

"Thank you," whispered Jewel.

Val stood with eyes closed. Her face no longer alight; no longer gazing upon a vision for her alone.

Barnaby put a hand to her shoulder.

"Cup vanished again?"

She nodded. Took breath, wiped eyes, blinking puzzled at cold stone world and worried friends. When she spoke, it came in surprised whisper.

"Are we still in the tower?"

"Yes."

"Seems ages ago." She put a hand to Barnaby's face, studying it. "You haven't changed a bit."

"No, no. I'm older and wiser," Barnaby affirmed. "By full five minutes."

"Did he just make a joke?" wondered Jewel. "I never heard him make a joke."

"It's the second I've heard out him," affirmed Val. Her eyes still upon Barnaby's face. "The first was that night in the barn in Edgestead."

"Oi, I am very much desiring to hear that particular jest," declared Matilda.

"Valentine Kurgus, do you need rest?" That, from Cedric.

Val shook her head, then her whole self. Dream visions cast away, her face returned to present worries. She studied the hall before them.

"Let's go on."

And so they went; warily, weapons ready, hearing only the echoes of their own footsteps, the rasp of their own breaths. At times to left or right a side passage offered choices they pondered, then declined.

Some fifty such wary steps brought into sight a desk high as a judge's bench. Behind it sat a figure beside a lamp, paging through a book. The company halted to consider.

"Do I take him down?" asked Matilda, fingering an arrow.

"No," said Cedric and Barnaby.

"Not yet," said Bodkin.

They looked to Val. She studied the distant personage.

"Seems peaceable. Let's seem peaceable too."

They approached the desk, wary for sudden attack. The reader ignored them till they stood within the light of the desk lantern. At which point he put down the book, gazing upon the newcomers with large and watery eyes.

"*Gobelin*," whispered Matilda to the Benefactors.

Barnaby stared delighted; studying the man's rough complexion, indeed tinged green. Scant locks of hair sprouted across the round head like unprosperous weeds. Sharp teeth gleamed, frog-like eyes meeting his in equal curiosity.

Barnaby weighed all he wanted to ask this personage. What was it *like* being a Gobelin? Did they sleep in beds or in nests? Tell tales by the fire? Did they have Spring Festivals and did they like cake? But of course *everyone* liked cake. Though perhaps Gobelins did not fancy cinnamon sugar cakes which were surely the favorite of all sensible folk. But did the Gobelin consider themselves sensible? For that matter, did they consider Barnaby sensible? Still, cake required flour and flour needed grain and grain required milling and how on earth did they get the work done under the earth?

When the Gobelin spoke, the voice rasped rough as toad with croup.

"May I help you?"

Barnaby prepared to ask about cakes but Bodkin stepped forth first, making a quick bow.

"We're just wandering through. No need to trouble yourself."

"Ah, treasure hunters, are you?"

The question took Bodkin aback not nit nor wit. He returned boyish smile and roguish wink.

"Well, I've never been known to pass by the loose penny or wandering diamond."

"Hmm," said the Gobelin. "Well, continue on down the hall. Grand vault is second to the left."

That said, he returned to his book.

The companions exchanged looks, uncertain what to reply. Meanwhile Cedric posed a question as dear to his heart as cake to Barnaby's.

"May I inquire what tome you read, Master Gobelin?"

The creature peered over the top of the book.

"*Baptismus Deorum*'. By Brendan himself. Or so they say. Personally, I find several passages to be obvious insertions by later and lesser authors."

"Oh, yes, chapter seven in particular," agreed Cedric. "But what has clearly been removed is the more serious textual problem."

The Gobelin nodded. "There's said to be an original copy in the Temple of Twelve Riddles. Not that anyone would be daft enough to go *there*."

"A true treasure, surely."

The Gobelin looked about to see who eavesdropped. Spying none but the wandering treasure-hunters, he dared a conspiratorial whisper.

"*Mister L* insists we all study this antique folderol. He's become obsessed with turning it into..." Here the Gobelin shuddered. "- into a theatre play."

"The Baptism? Into a *play*?"

"Indeed. See you avoid his eye. Else he'll draft you into the performance."

"We shall."

The Gobelin returned to his reading; the adventurers returned to walking warily down the hall.

"Who's Mister L?" asked Barnaby.

"I'm afraid to guess," answered Val.

At length they came to a passage where a second Gobelin waited. He slouched against the wall, attempting to twirl a short spear. At the sound of their steps he jumped, straightened like a proper guard; dropping the spear.

Spearless, he settled for giving the company a stern and looming look. While Barnaby bent down, recovered the spear, handing it back. Val sighed, the Gobelin nodded thanks. He returned to slouching and spear-twirling.

A certain glittering light from farther down the side passage drew the Benefactor's eyes. They wandered forwards, stopping before a gate of thick iron bars. Beyond this barrier waited a long, well-lit chamber. Shelves lined the walls, heaped with jewels twinkling like evening stars. Upon the floor waited opened chests of metallic shimmers that hummed with the promise of incalculable worth. Scattered across tables lay rings and wands, necklaces and brooches, crowns and amulets. Some shone soft and warm as glowworms on a summer night; others flickered bright as torches tossed to the air signaling battle victory.

The Benefactors crowded against the gate, peering upon a feast of wealth and magic. Nearly seeking to press themselves through the bars.

"That's moon-silver," whispered Bodkin. "Beams of moonlight hammered into magic ingots. See how they shine?"

"Oi, and do you spy that pretty quiver of golden arrows?" asked Matilda. "Saintly Apollonius made just such for pretty Artemisia. Each arrow returns with the dawn. One can guess what he wanted in return, the holy old fornicator."

Cedric studied a book upon a pedestal. Leather bound, golden letters across the spine. It glowed with mysterious wisdom as the summer sun shone with life.

"That's no alphabet I've can read," he whispered. "And yet, there are carvings of just such characters in the oldest temples of Psamathe."

Jewel whispered excitedly to her spider pendant. "No, it's a true potion cauldron of Hecatatia, I'm sure. See the snakes?"

Barnaby studied a thick wooden box, the lid thrown back. It sat stuffed with golden coins as a bushel basket from a harvest of bankers.

What in the world would one do with so many coins? he wondered. Half a hat-full would buy all of Mill Town. He pondered what he would do if he owned all Mill Town. Certainly he couldn't live in every house at once. And where would the previous owners live? They'd be sleeping in the woods with pockets full of gold. Seemed a poor trade.

Val growled. "Stop. Wake up. Let's not get dazzled by the glittery stuff."

Bodkin pushed upon the grating. It did not move in the slightest. He tapped upon the lock, which was large, bronze and inscribed with symbols that hinted magical laughter to thieves.

He turned to the guard still practicing his spear-twirl.

"Hey," he said. "How do we get in?"

In answer the guard pointed the spear to a sign beside the gate; a sign they'd ignored, eyes caught by the wonders of the glimmering vault.

Attention, Treasure Hunters.
For the key, see Mr. L.

"Where can we find this mysterious Mister?" asked Matilda.

In reply, the Gobelin merely gave her a long, pitying stare. Then he closed his round eyes and shuddered.

The Society of St. Benefact held formal consultation.

"This is mad," whispered Val. "They aren't going to just let us walk into their vault and fill our pockets."

"They might," argued Barnaby. "As a reward for getting past all the dangers." Said aloud, these words sounded unlikely even to his optimistic ears.

"Yes, yes, of course it's a trick," said Bodkin. "But a smile and a nod gives us chance to play some trick of our own."

"Why play?" asked Matilda. "We could take out the two Gobelins, then break down the gate."

"There are a good many more about," said Val.

"How are you knowing that?"

"Because here they come."

Now they all noted the *tramp, tramp* of boots upon stone. Val pulled and pushed the fellowship deeper into the side passage. Barnaby started to draw Dragontooth; she shook her head. They waited, weapons sheathed.

With a rumble of conversation, a rumble of feet, a strange assembly tramped down the hall before them. Not a disciplined regiment of soldiers in formation. More like a congregation preparing to assemble in some hall, grumbling over the inconvenience of the assembly.

Gobelin, primarily. Armored and bearing spears, swords, axes. Some few bore crossbows.

But others among the throng were larger, leather-winged, with eyes of flower-petal fire. Same sort of Shadow-folk as the Benefactors had observed entering the tower.

This crowd flowed by, ignoring the humans watching from the alleyway. Last came stragglers led by a man and a bronze dog.

The man stood tall as Barnaby, seeming no older. But far leaner, wearing silk shirt and vest embroidered with peacock feather designs. He danced along in excited steps, elegant boots stamping upon the stone floor, while waving a hand before him to conduct the symphony of his own words.

"How does this sound?" he asked. Cleared throat, deepened voice.

"*You speak, Brendan, of existence as one grand House wherein every least being is holy messenger, each to each. But in truth we all float alone in the void, falling through the dark. And there is no message from one life to another, saving the common scream of that forever falling.*"

A Shadow-Specter rubbed chin. "Is it floating, or falling? Can't be both, I'd say."

"I like it," said a Gobelin juggling sheaves of ink-stained paper. "Works for me."

"Write it in, then," ordered the tall man. The Gobelin began scratching a quill across parchment. The bronze dog trailing behind yawned, possibly in subtle critique. Its metal claws going 'click, click' upon the stone floor.

Then these beings passed from the sight of the Benefactors. Who sighed with relief… until the *click, click* returned.

The bronze dog reappeared, sniffing at the ground. Then the head turned upwards, rainbow eyes spying the huddled Benefactors. The tail began to wag with a loud *creak, creak*.

"Sshhh," said Barnaby, putting finger to lip.

"Woof," barked the dog, wagging the louder. *Creak, creak*. "Woof!"

"Son of a bitch," muttered Val.

And now the tall man poked his head around the corner, studying the Benefactors in pop-eyed delight.

"Ah ha! Wondered when you lot would show."

The Benefactors exchanged looks. No one drew weapons; though all kept hands ready to so do.

"You know us?" asked Val.

"Well, of course," said the man. "Been saving the best parts in the play for you adventurers. You, Lady Kurgus, shall make a perfect Saint Martia. Scarce requires practice, I should think."

"What?" whispered Jewel.

The tall man nodded to her. "And you, Miss Stonecroft, are the very depiction of dour Sister Hecatatia."

"Who shall I be?" asked Barnaby, fascinated.

At which question, the tall man rose up on a polished boot toe, twirling once entirely about, in order to express his glee.

"Ah, Master Miller Barnaby. There's but one soul in all the alleged House of Saints, Upper, Middle or Lower, who I want to play the role of Saintly Brendan. That's your very person."

Barnaby grinned, flushed with delight.

"Why should we act in your play?" demanded Val.

The man tapped his nose in thought, as though asking himself *indeed, now why should they?*. Then he reached to vest pocket; producing the answer in form of long bronze key.

"Because you want entry to the tower vault, do you not, oh followers of the saint of self-benefaction? The door shall be opened. Merely act in my little theatre. What harm in that?"

The Benefactors studied the key, watching hungrily as it returned to pocket.

"And what role do you play?" asked Bodkin.

"Myself, of course." That declared, the tall man turned away, striding down the hall.

"Come along," he called back, without waiting to see they obeyed. "I'll find you a quiet room to rest and practice your lines. First rehearsal's tomorrow morning."

The company exchanged looks that signaled quiet agreement: *follow along for now.*

"You must be Mister L," said Bodkin, short legs working to catch up.

"So I'm oft called, Young Master Moon. If not to my face."

"What does the 'L' stand for?" That, from Barnaby.

At which the man halted, turned. When he spoke, it was to the bronze dog, as it *click, clicked* to a stop.

"We forgot to introduce ourselves. Quite rude."

The beast gave a yawn to express its opinion of propriety. The tall man sighed to the company, waving hand to the bronze dog.

"To begin, this assemblage of bolts, gears and lunacy is Saint Hefestus, patron of Holy Artifice."

"Woof," said Saint Hefestus.

"Knew it," growled Val.

"No, truly?" asked Barnaby. Frowning at his dog. "So you were just pretending to be a mechanical creature fetching sticks, running off with boots, barking to wake us?"

The patron saint of Holy Artifice lowered head and tail in shame.

"Woof."

"And you?" asked Matilda. "Who are you being?"

At which inquiry, the man bowed deep; deep as the pits of Erebus, deep as the nether caves of Nix.

"Lucif, patron saint of Just Penance, at your service."

The company stared, saying nothing. The man met their silence with his own silence. This quiet continued some while. At last he nodded to say *that's done, then.* He continued down the hall with his long-legged stride. St. Hefestus following, *click, click*.

And still the company stood, motionless, staring. After ten long strides, Lucif looked back, surprised to see they yet lingered.

"Come along, now," he called. Giving a warm and winning smile. "I'm just about to put the teakettle on the fire."

Chapter 10
Preliminary Reading of the Script

Our Cast
Barnaby: St. Brendan the Navigator
Valentine Kurgus: St Martia
Cedric Weiland: St Plutarch
Jewel of Stonecroft: Sister Hecatatia
Matilda: St Demetia
Bodkin: St Herman
Festus: St. Hefestus (playing himself)
Lucif: St. Lucif (playing himself)

Scene 1, Act 1: *a pillared hall. Long table at which gather the Powers. A feast is before them. Yet the Powers sit dejected, staring into cups.*

Martia: Bored.
Hefestus: Drink up.
Martia: Drink bores me.
Hecatatia: Start a new war.
Martia: War bores me more.
Apollonius: *(stands, raising goblet)*
    This eternal bliss
    Is nothing I would miss.
    My revels through eternity
    But sum to empty ennui.
    (drinks, throws aside his cup)
    Better a bad couplet out of me,
    Than this eternal cup in front of me.
Enter Herman, messenger of the powers.

Herman: Arch Lords and Ladies, High Powers and Principalities, Virtues, Thrones and Dominations. A mortal man knocks upon the door.

Plutarch: Oh, feed him to the dog.

Hecatatia: Dull. No, turn him to a monster that devours what he loves.

Martia: Drop him from the mountain?

Hefestia: Give him words of truth that bring only sorrow?

Plutarch: Set him to roll a stone uphill forever.

Martia: No, let him starve before a feast, thirst in pools of wine.

Demetia: All these things have been done.

Apollonius: And are only shadows of our own sad condition. Fixed in bliss, perfected and purposeless. Set to eternal feasting, sitting, satiated, draining infinite cups...

Herman: I shall send him away, oh Powers.

Hecatatia: Wait. Bring him before us. We shall listen to his mortal plaint, and weigh the cries of his heart. And then he shall with trembling knee and soaring spirit hear our judgment, the very wisdom of the Powers.

Martia: And we grant his prayer?

Hecatatia: No, we feed him to the dog.

(Company laughs)

(Enter Brendan, stage left)

Brendon: Oh avatars of life and death, wind and wave, war and peace, wood and mountain, fire and light. Peace be with you.

Plutarch: Oh, and also with you , little man.

Brendan: Through storm and wrack have I sailed to reach your shore. For weeks I walked the roads of your kingdoms, through field and wood, plane and mount.

Preaching to the workers in the fields, the hunters in the woods, the lords in their castles."

Martia: I'm sure they were fascinated.

Brendan: No, they listened not. '*We have the Powers, and they suffice,*' all said. So I come to you, whose spirits are in the air and water, the storm and shadow of this land. And I bring message.

Apollonius: Do you indeed? Let us hear this message.

Brendan: That you must die, and be reborn sanctified.

(Silence)

Demetia: You make strange request.

Brendan: It is no request. It is the merest truth of being. All things perish, even the gods. To surrender willingly is the only path of rebirth. Humble yourselves with a touch of water, a mortal's blessing, and you shall be reborn. Then this your golden prison will open, and you will find yourselves unbound. Free dwellers in the Grand House of Saints."

All: House? Of Saints? What is that?

Brendan waves hand in explication as the stage darkens.

   Lucif put aside the wrinkled mass of parchment. Looking about the room to measure his audience's opinion.

   The Benefactors reclined in carved chairs bedecked with silk cushions. Plates of wondrous foods placed within reach, goblets of chilled wines reflecting the bright candlelight. The total might serve as the setting for the play just read.

   But none spoke. Not a theatric line occurred to any. At last Lucif cleared his throat,

   "So. Ah, how does it sound so far?"

Each of the company pondered how it sounded, and how they'd best say it sounded. At last,

"How can Festus be declaiming speeches?" asked Barnaby. "All he ever says is 'woof'."

Lucif brushed that away. "He's quite a talkative fellow when the mood takes him."

"So," said Val, setting down her cup untouched. She crossed legs, leaning forwards to express a proper business attitude. "We recite these lines, perform your theatre piece. Then you give us the key to your treasure vault?"

Lucif's chuckle bubbled pleasant as spring water out a mountain rill.

"It's not *my* treasure. Really, what in the name of my own dear mother's chamber pot would I want with a lumber room of heavy metal and shiny rocks? For that matter, this isn't even my tower. Just visiting, same as you. On my own personal adventure."

"To put on a play? Is that why we were led here?"

Lucif rolled his eyes, large, round and boyishly sincere.

"None of that *divine conspiracy* nonsense. You came of your own choosing. Seeking treasure, purpose, friendship and adventure. Excellent goals, all. But it just so happens you now need a key. It just so happens I now need actors. It's all, all, just fortunate coincidence."

"What has Saint Hefestus to do with this fortunate coincidence?" That, from Cedric.

For a moment Lucif paused. Then shrugged. "Ask him."

"He'll say 'woof'."

Lucif laughed. "Probably."

He stood, stretched. "Make yourselves free of the floor. Just remember it's the darkest level of a cursed tower full of deathtraps. Water closet is down the hall to the left. Theatre is up the hall to the right. First rehearsal is tomorrow. If that goes well, and by my six mythical asses it *will* go well, then in a month we'll start on tour."

That declared, he headed towards the door.

Val called out.

"Tour? What tour? To where? For how long?"

Lucif's long strides had already brought him to the exit. He paused mid-step to answer.

"What would be the point of putting a play on *here?*"

"None, that I see," replied Cedric.

Lucif nodded. "Exactly. We'll be touring Infernum. Perform in all the important spots. Pandemonium, Tartarus, Dis. Also some stops in the rural circles. Though theologic enactment will be over the heads of that sort of crowd. Even the ones who aren't stuffed upside down in a fire pit."

That said, he vanished out the door. Leaving a very quiet room.

At last Val spoke.

"All in favor of not going to Infernum with a mad saint, say 'aye'.

"Aye."

"Aye."

"Aye."

"But, treasure," said Bodkin.

Cedric picked up the sheaf of script, perused.

"Act Two is Lucif alone on stage. Giving a long, very long soliloquy on the glories of existential defiance. It continues," he leafed pages, "till act four. Hmm. Ah. Then I deliver an impassioned speech upon the logical nature of reality."

"Just another reason to skip out," said Val.

"As well, he did not inform us of the entire cast."

"Who else is in the play?"
Cedric read aloud.

Squire Semple: St. Apollonius
Madam Kurgus: St. Euterpe
Sister Agat: Maid in waiting
Mother Hemp: Persephone

"Hemp and Agat?" whispered Jewel. "Here?" She jumped up from her pillows, looking about the room.

"They might be," said Val. "I'm pretty sure my mother is somewhere about. And Barnaby heard two of his folk from Mill Town. Being brought in bags by those shadow-fiends."

"Why in Lucif's name would Lucif bring them here?"

"To torment us, I'd guess."

"He seemed nice." That, from Barnaby.

"He is nice, dear." That, from Matilda. "He's a saint. He just happens to be the saint of tormenting souls."

"Only the bad ones."

"Well, but that's anybody, pretty much. If you're a stickler for the rules, as saints shall be."

Cedric rubbed chin in thought.

"Barnaby's stepmother and the Squire were evil creatures. I will wager that Agat and Hemp were no better. And of what I hear, while Valentine's mother is to be admired for martial virtues, she is a, a *fearsome* person to stand near."

"A homicidal lunatic bitch, to be exact," explained Val.

"Then let us assume that Lucif, patron saint of Just Penance, felt it within his authority to bring those four here. Whether to torment us, or to torment them."

Val stood, hand on knife hilt, pondering the door, and all that might wait just beyond it.

"He did say we could go where we wished. Barring the occasional deathtrap."

"Same as in Martia," said Bodkin. "We aren't prisoners. Just *strongly* advised not to rabbit for the exit."

"The rabbit is overcooked," observed a voice. "Again."

All turned to spy the black form of Night-Creep upon a table, nibbling at dainties.

"Mister Magic Kitty is back," observed Matilda. "One wonders if the mad saint has a part for a feline?"

Night-Creep sat up, licking whiskers.

"Indeed it happens that I have graced various theatre performances across the years. In all three recognized themes: Mystery Play, Morality Play, and Miracle play. For my last piece, I played Everyman's Cat."

Here the little feline stood on hind legs, one paw to chest, the other stirring the air as he declaimed.

"I pray you all give audience,
And hear this matter with reverence,
By figure a morality play.
The Tale of Everyman called it is,
That of our lives and purpose show
How we wander, and never know.
This theme is wondrous precious,
The telling of it loquacious.
A tale to while away the day.
And shall be sweet to bear away.

The company pondered cat and speech.

"You know, I used to wash clothes, scrub pots, weed gardens," mused Jewel. "When did my life get so strange?"

The cat sniffed.

"You face two challenges before returning to scrubbing pots, plucking weeds. First: gain access to the treasure vault. Second, escape from the tower."

"Suppose we skipped the treasure?" argued Jewel. "Just run back up the stairs, out the doorway screaming?"

"Looks silly to come all this way, then turn tail," declared Matilda.

"Agreed," said Bodkin. "Bad style."

Cedric hesitated, then nodded.

"We have done well marching forwards. Retreat must end with us cornered by forces unimpressed with our strength of purpose."

Jewel scowled at him. Cedric returned wry smile.

"In any case, Jewel of Stonecroft, you are wasted scrubbing pots."

At which words she covered face with her hanging hair.

Bodkin: "Might help deciding what to do, if we knew why we were here. It's not all coincidence. What in Lucif's name does Lucif want?"

"Lucif wants mischief, no doubt," said Cedric. "For me, the mystery is what Hefestus desires."

The cat pondered a paw; gave it a thoughtful lick.

"I suspect the answer to why you have been brought to the bottom of a cursed tower, awaits you at the top of the cursed tower. It's mere symmetry."

"What about all that blither of the climb up being more fatefully fatal than the route downwards." That, from Matilda.

"I think..." Barnaby spoke slowly, "I think there is a second stairway. The only safe way to the top. Starting from somewhere here at the bottom."

"Is that even on the map?" asked Bodkin. "For this floor I only remember a main hallway, and a red circle with a sun in the center. Where we decided the treasure was."

Barnaby began emptying his pack, scattering souvenirs about. The glass scrying egg. A coffee mug with 'Phaethon' on the side. His metal wand. A blood-red rock from the road to Edgestead. A bright blue feather found near Herm's Font, which he intended for a hat if he ever had a hat.

"What's this?" asked Bodkin. Scooping up a heavy iron object.

Barnaby considered. Where had he gotten a key?

"Ah, that. It opens the gate past the radish field of Miss Sephie. You needn't fear the radishes, by the by. But she told me 'never can tell when you need a good key'."

"Yeah, I'm going to pocket this innocent bit of iron for now," declared Bodkin.

"You do that," agreed Barnaby. He found the map, unfolding it before all.

Bodkin leaned over it, tracing with a finger. "This is the main hall. The treasure room we saw would be here. No sun sign."

"Oh, that room," yawned Night-Creep. "Ignore it. Enchanted, showing what appeals to covetous thoughts. The real contents were pots of Gobelin dung, old bricks, worn out shoes. Chicken bones. Adventurer bones."

"You might have mentioned so before." That, from Matilda.

"Normally, I would not have mentioned it at all," said the cat. "The rules of my summoning limit me to instruction. But as the topic is 'magical enchantment', I feel allowed to share bits of wisdom upon this subject. That room was not the treasure vault."

"Where is it, then?" That from Bodkin.

The cat licked paw, enjoying being the center of attention.

"Really, you should have guessed. That circle is clearly the amphitheater."

"The theatre where we are to put on a mad play writ by a yet madder saint." said Val.

"Exactly." The cat gave a last dismissing sniff to overcooked rabbit, then jumped to the floor.

"Best you gather your things. Curtains about to rise. You are all due on stage."

Chapter 11
The Faces in the Fire are the Real Ones

Scene: a high-domed chamber ringed with benches. The stage itself: a grand circle, wooden-floored. A long table set with empty cups, barren plates.

Barnaby considered the table, picturing the play read aloud by Lucif. A glowing gathering of saints would be staring in mockery at his entrance. He cleared his throat, tried an awkward bow to the imagined assemblage.

"Uhm. Hi. I'm Brendon, not Barnaby. I sailed on a real ship! Just to bring you holy persons a message. Except I also walked too because you know the sea's a long way. Anyhow, here I am. With a, a message."

Bodkin laughed, shook head. Leaped to perch upon the table. Crossing arms, he awarded Brendon-not-Barnaby a look of noble disdain.

Bodkin: "Message? From whom?"

Barnaby: "Ah, I don't know that."

Bodkin: "Then why should we harken?"

Barnaby: "Ah. Because... it's very mysterious?"

Bodkin: "Mysteries weary our saintly ears."

Barnaby: "But it's about important mysteries."

Bodkin: "Such as?"

Barnaby: "Uhm. Stars. Graves. Millers. Which are important even though I'm not one. And cake. And babies, they're important, I'm sure. Oh, and cats and ghosts and chickens and roses and crops and directables and fountains and folk singing on street corners and selling flowers and the fields with wheat waving like sea waves. Oh, and woods at night with the moon and owls and wolves acting all story-like. And the roads you go walking down, just meeting anybody, everybody."

Bodkin: "We are the powers. We rule these things already. What message could tell us more?"

Barnaby: "Well, because...the message puts them all in one great grand house. And in that, that home everyone knows they are family. And so we all mean something to each other and sit by the hearth and eat cake and tells stories."

Cedric smiled. "This messenger is wiser than he seems."

Bodkin: "Tedious." He clapped hands. "Guards, throw this dogsbody to the dogs. Seneschal, send the next pilgrim before us."

Matilda laughed. "Seems a more likely ending."

Val ignored this impromptu dialogue; pacing the stage, studying the floor. Finally peering under the table.

"Ah. There it is."

"What?" That, from Matilda.

"The star trap." She knelt down, prying at the boards of the floor.

"That's not explaining much." Matilda bent down to help Val raise a hinged square.

"A star-trap is the trap door that actors use to come onstage from below.

"Ah. I see. Theatrical places, your theatres."

"Not to forget comical and dramatic. Get some candles. Mister Bodkin, you may have the honor of checking for surprises."

"What about the spider?"

"Perry's tired," said Jewel. "Must be daytime outside."

Bodkin held a candle into the dark below the stage. Before he could pronounce judgment, Professor Night-Creep leapt past, down into the shadows.

"Show off," groused the boy. Then jumped after the cat.

Val peered down. "There *is* a ladder, people." She backed downwards upon this practical thing, followed by the rest.

They stood in a chamber round as the stage above. Two doors, on opposite sides of the room. One a grand oaken portal, the other a small, humble door. Matilda went to that second door, holding a candle to letters upon it.

"*Properties Room*. Now what properties could that be, and whose?"

Val went to the door, gave it a suspicious kick. "It's just where they store things for plays."

She pulled the handle, found it locked. Started to dismiss it; then reconsidered.

"Mister Bodkin, can you apply Mister Miller's mysteriously convenient key here?"

Bodkin stepped forth, applying the iron key.

"Fits," he declared, twisting. At the *click* he leapt back for caution and drama.

The door of the properties room swung open, releasing a musty smell, a swarm of moths. Cedric lifted his staff, whispering. The light shone faintly within, unable to find anything worth illuminating.

The room was long, lined with sagging shelves of cobwebbed knickknacks. Baskets and boxes lay open, stuffed with the tatters and toys of a thousand theatre scenes. From racks hung moth-eaten cloths garishly dyed to appear royal robes and martial cloaks. Wooden swords dangled from strings, gold paint flaking. Bits of quartz and mica glittered from tin crowns and wooden tiaras. Piles of colored glass waited to be taken by credulous eyes for fabulous jewels.

A sickly rat limped across the dust, ember eyes glaring at the intrusion.

"Trash," sighed Val. "The other door looks more promising. Bodkin, let's try the key there." The company turned from the dusty closet.

But now Night-Creep leapt to his customary place upon Barnaby's shoulder.

"If I may advise?"

Barnaby laughed. "You may advise, oh advisor of mine."

"What comes next shall require *Greater True Sight*."

"Understood." Barnaby brought forth his wand of Demetia, then hesitated.

"What about the warning that I might go mad?"

"Ah, let's risk it. All said, the mad enjoy life as much as the sane. Quite often more."

"Very well, then." Barnaby whispered to the wand. A green light played upon the tip. He raised it to his left eye, tapped. Doing the same for the right eye.

For a moment the world grew dark; then brightened again. But with a different cast of light. No longer just a mix of candle shine and the glow of Cedric's staff. Now shadows seemed sharper, the light brighter, revealing every crack in the stone floor.

"Behold the chamber of theatre props. Is it still a collection of trash?"

"No, sir."

Barnaby gazed into a room that surpassed the treasure vault they'd seen entering the tower depths. The chests of gold coins made mere backdrop to more valuable, glorious, glittering things. A storm of golden sparkles warred with the steady glow from magical swords, cups and crowns. Jewels glimmered and shimmered in piles or alone, from plates and bowls that hummed and thrummed with secret aethereal powers.

Barnaby turned to tell his friends of the revealed treasure. Then gasped, frozen. Standing, staring, trembling; till they sensed his silent gaze.

"Barnaby?" That, from Val.

"You alright, Mister Miller Man?" asked Matilda.

"Probably sees a monster behind me," said Bodkin. "When I turn about, there it'll be."

"I don't see a monster behind you," said Matilda.

"That's because I haven't looked behind me yet. It won't be there till I turn about."

"Entire books have been written, explaining reality just so." That, of course, from Cedric.

Bodkin, Cedric and Matilda argued reality while Barnaby whispered; to himself, or his friends, else the cat upon his shoulder.

"I didn't know."

The cat reached, put paw to one of Barnaby's eyes, forcing it closed. Then the same for the other. When he stood with eyes shut, the cat whispered.

"A word to the wise: do not make habit of gazing upon the truth of others. It will not always be a vision of wonder. And whether the sight be good or ill, sweet or foul, overmuch gazing shall overthrow your mind."

Barnaby nodded. "I understand that now." He opened his eyes. Finding them wet with tears.

Turning away from his friends, he gazed upon the treasure room. It had lost none of its glittering splendor. Yet the sight of piled wealth could not shake his soul with wonder, as had the vision of the company.

He cleared throat, as if delivering lines upon the stage above.

"I think we want to give this room a second look," he announced.

* * *

"Still see just trash," said Bodkin.

"Because the vault is under many and various enchantments," declared Night-Creep. The cat stood just before the door, enjoying the opportunity to share his advanced understanding.

"Hear then, the rules. First: only one at a time can be within the vault."

"Why?"

"Because a spell of mad greed will be triggered when two or more enter. They will grow enraged, determined to keep the treasures for their own."

"Oh."

"Now, if I may *continue*, the bard shall stand at the doorway playing a cantrip of *True Seeing*. While she plays, her target will see items as they are. Do not be within when she ceases to play."

"Else what?" asked Matilda.

"Else the illusions will return a hundred-fold, assaulting your senses with hideous sights, infernal scents and sounds to shatter your reason."

"Fair enough. Don't want to be caught in such cacophonous riotous."

"Thirdly, for any item you take, you must leave something behind. It need not be an object of worth. Any trash of similar size, weight or number should suffice."

'Should?"

"That is the qualifying word I used, yes." Night-Creep's tail twitched, annoyed.

"Sorry, Mister Professor," said Matilda.

"In light of the last requirement," he continued, "I suggest you make six equal collections of what you are willing to exchange for treasure."

"Not too much food," warned Val. "Plenty of tales mocking the fools who starved in the wild, chewing on gold coins."

Bodkin laughed. "Knew these were worth bringing." He emptied his pack, placing six silver bricks separately on the floor. To these he added a coffee mug, eight half-pennies, a pair of socks still smelling of Persephone's sewers, a shaving razor he had yet to need.

Each of the others followed, adding items they'd carried across kingdoms, through battles, but felt willing to exchange for gold and jewels. Making the six piles roughly equal in weight and quantity.

That done, everyone but Val chose one, placing the items in their packs. She took position by the vault door, whispering to her harp in preparation.

"Who's first?"

"I'll go," said Barnaby. "But you don't need to play for me. Professor Night-Creep says the wand-touch to my eyes will serve."

"That why you aren't looking at any of us?" asked Val. Tone mocking; yet touched with hurt. "Truth of us too nasty to behold?"

"Oi, it's my hair, I wager," sighed Matilda. "A tangled mess to horrify a soul."

"The truth of people is ugly," said Jewel. Everyone turned in surprise to her. She crossed arms, refusing to speak more.

"No," declared Cedric. "I know what I see looking at you. I see beauty. I see strength."

She stared away, frowning, refusing to hide her face nor meet his gaze. The company kept silent, awkwardly observing.

Excepting Barnaby, who stared at his feet. They were good feet. True feet, for all that their beauty hid in truly tattered boots. Barnaby turned from the vision of his feet and entered the vault.

Not far in, a chest of small gold bars caught his eye. He picked an ingot up. Heavy and cold, with a buttery shimmer comically innocent for something that led folk to do so much evil. He judged six would match the weight of the silver brick; made the exchange.

Going farther, he stopped before a bowl of sparkling stones. Story-book items beyond a miller's ken. But no doubt the clear stones were diamonds. The green would be emeralds, the blue sapphires, the blood-red stones the rubies of pirate tales. He selected five of each color. Leaving behind ten copper pieces, nine Hefestian fruit cubes gone hard as stone, and the blue feather intended for a hat.

Farther in, he gaped before a pedestal displaying a pair of boots. The leather shone lustrous black as the river Lethe. He pulled off his own tattered pair, donning these. They fit as if specially crafted for a miller's feet.

A chest of gold coins sat humbly in a corner. Barnaby traded ten gold pieces for his rock from St. Martia, four Plutarchian half-pennies, two socks not worth darning and three blocks of cheese gone moldy.

He moved on to a chainmail coat ornate with silver filagree and tiny jewels. But taking it would require he leave his leather armor behind. Unthinkable.

For a moment his eyes itched, and he saw two scenes. One the glowing treasure vault, the other the cluttered room of trash. The *True Seeing* spell was fading.

Heart beating loud, he looked for some last bit of treasure. A bowl of strangely wrought rings caught his eye. He placed his Phaethon coffee cup down in exchange, grabbed the rings, then rushed for the exit.

Beyond the door his friends waited, faces anxious. Those faces looked dirty, weary, and friendly; exactly the faces he was used to seeing.

"What did you get?" asked Bodkin.

Barnaby caught his breath. "New boots."

Bodkin groaned; Matilda laughed. Val shook her head.

"Across a thousand leagues and down a cursed tower for... new boots?"

"They are *good* boots. I ran very fast in them. But also I got some jewels and some gold bars and some rings."

"That's a bit better. Who goes next?"

"Me," declared Bodkin. "Start your tune."

Val nodded, whispering to her harp. "You get six minutes."

"What? I've heard you play for hours."

"This is an oration. Takes it out of me quick. I've also got to play for Matilda, Jewel, and Cedric. And they only get three minutes."

"Smart and good looking though I am, why should I get twice the time?"

"Because you're going to gather loot for yourself and for me. As I can't gather gold and play the harp at the same time."

"Sensible. But suppose, oops, I bring you back Barnaby's old boots?"

"You won't. You're just that smart and good looking. Also, we'll be making two piles of the loot you bring back. I choose which pile is mine."

Bodkin laughed.

"I've been teaching you lot proper, 'tis clear. Fair enough. Old Mercutio once emptied an archbishop's seven purses, tupped his whore and put pepper in the communion wine all while the holy man closed eyes once to sneeze. This makes scarce challenge."

Cedric kept a measured count; at each 'sixty' he stamped his staff upon the floor. Exact upon the sixth stamp Bodkin sauntered from the vault.

"Wasn't silly enough to settle for overmuch gold," he declared. "Nor too many loose jewels. Pretty sure I've got a greater relic necklace; just not sure what saint. And a long knife I'll see you drooling for, Kurgus."

"Who's next?" said Val, not drooling yet. She looked wearied.

"Can you play more?" asked Cedric. "Perhaps you should rest."

Val shook her head. "I'm fine. And I'm doubting we can loiter long before Lucif and Festus come to fetch us. No, we stick to the plan. Grab the loot and run the saintly fuck away. Who's next?"

Cedric handed his staff to Bodkin. Val began to harp, Bodkin began to count… but Cedric did not rush into the vault. Instead he stood gazing straight at Jewel of Stonecroft.

She moved to hide her face, then stopped, crossing arms. Staring back in defiance, enduring this magical scrutiny for all that she trembled, as he trembled.

At Bodkin's count of thirty, Cedric turned away, eyes shining, and entered the treasure vault.

At count of sixty Bodkin stamped the staff. At the second sixty, he stamped again. Still Cedric did not return. At the third stamp, the companions exchanged worried glances. Jewel looked ready to rush in after him; Barnaby and Matilda readied to stop her.

Then the cleric came hurrying out with a bag of scrolls in his arms, careful as mother with babe.

"Apologies," he declared. "I fell into reading."

Bodkin gave a disdainful snort.

"Did you get any gold? Any non-scholarly valuables to buy your breakfast tomorrow?"

"Plenty," replied Cedric. "Enough to buy breakfast and a castle. But it is the knowledge within these scrolls that justify all the journey here."

He pondered his own words, making correction. "That, and the treasure I found on the way."

"He means you," whispered Matilda to Jewel.

"Shut up," said Jewel.

Jewel herself went next. Returning at the third stamp of the staff. She now wore a shimmering cape upon her shoulders, a red circlet about her forehead. In her hands she bore a wand carved in shape of two snakes twining.

Her eyes shone. "These are relics. Greater ones."

"You look like a queen," declared Barnaby.

"So she did already," said Cedric.

"That's him being complimentary," whispered Matilda.

"Shut, shut, shut, up, up, up," growled Jewel.

"My turn now," declared Matilda. "You ready, Miss Bard?"

Val nodded; Matilda tapped hoof to the floor once; then dashed within the treasure room. Barnaby watched, feeling both elated and wearied. He looked about; spying in the shadows the figure of Dark Michael. Not leaning in customary slouch. No, now the ghost stood straight as soldier at the front of battle, waiting for the bugle to sound *charge*.

Why? wondered Barnaby. And then came footsteps stamping the stage above their heads. Several pairs of feet. And voices calling. Barnaby and the others looked to the trap door. Unwisely left open.

"Not in the theatre, then," shouted someone. "Where else shall they be?"

Cedric gestured for all to remain quiet. Val played more softly, eyes wide in alarm. The footsteps on the ceiling began to diminish, the folk above departing...

And then came a sound of pans and bells clattering and clanging. Everyone jumped. Barnaby groaned to see Festus tumbling down the ladder from the stage above.

The bronze creature recovered its feet, shaking itself.

"Ssshh," said Barnaby, pressing finger to lip.

The mechanical dog/holy saint replied with a loud and happy '*woof.*'

Now someone new descended the trap door. A stout woman of middle years; familiar to Barnaby for all he'd only seen her once in moonlit woods.

"Why, here the darlings are, hiding under the table and the floor," declared Agat.

"Timid things," said Hemp, appearing next. "Why so fearful of old friends?"

Behind Hemp appeared a great black boar, eyes and mouth full of red flame. While beside Agat now stood a night-dark goat, open maw a forge of yellow fire.

Two more people descended the ladder, less agilely than the others.

"Here the lad is at last," sighed his stepmother. "Up to nonsense, as always."

Beside her stood the Squire, holding a crossbow.

"Same as his fool father," the man agreed.

Last but not at all least, down the trap door came a woman thin and wiry as a racing hound. A creature of middle years, face sculpted in scars and hard expressions. She grasped a knife in either hand, balancing on toe-points graceful as a dancer.

For a moment the room stayed silent, the two groups pondering one another. Festus tried a tail wag, making a dismal *creak, creak*.

"Bad dog," said Barnaby, drawing his axe.

Chapter 12
On Stage: Thunder, Alarum, Battle

Everything that happened afterwards, occurred in one long sequence. Like a great clap of thunder that shakes the sky, rolling steadily from East to West.

Val dropped her harp, drew long knife. Moving towards the woman so obviously her mother, making exactly the same sideways steps the other made towards her.

With that halting of the harp, there came a scream from the treasure vault. Magic song no longer protecting Matilda, she found herself of a sudden in dark nightmare.

"Michael, help Matilda!" Barnaby shouted. He had no time to see what followed. The flame-mouthed boar rushed upon him. Barnaby stepped aside with a swiftness that surprised boar and boy alike. The boar went rushing past, grunting.

Barnaby expected the creature to wheel about, but it went rushing straight up the wall. Nor did it slow as it came to the ceiling. Merely continued running upside down.

Fascinated by this magical act, he missed the charge of the goat. It butted him hard, sending him flying. He tumbled, holding tight to his axe, rolling upright again with back to the wall. The goat gave a bleat of triumph, lowering its head for a second attack.

Just as the goat charged, the boar dropped from the ceiling. Barnaby dodged sideways, again with a swiftness that surprised his enemies and himself.

The goat swerved just as the boar dropped from the ceiling, landing upon the goat. The two witch-spawn tangled in a storm of grunts and bleats, horns and tusks.

Barnaby took breath, took stance and swung Dragontooth through the tangle.

There came a burst of yellow sparks, a flash of red fire. The two creatures dissipated in swirls of smoke, twirls of flame.

Barnaby coughed, looking about. Bodkin now chased the Squire and Mother Miller around the room with his sword. They cursed him while he laughed, slashing at their butts. A sight more astonishing than any magical boar running across the ceiling.

Dark Michael strode across the room, indifferent to battle, holding a twitching Matilda in his arms. He stepped over Agat wiggling upon the floor. The witch lay bound tight in cobwebs of white. Periwinkle the Spider danced upon her chest, waving his many sapphire eyes. She held her mere two eyes wide in terror.

Beyond the bound Agat, Jewel and Hemp faced one another. Jewel held her snake scepter high, new cape waving in a wind only magic cloth could feel. Streamers of violet fire flowed from out the scepter, circling ever closer about Hemp. Hemp beat at them with a wand. Whenever wand touched streamer there came a purple flash; but evermore streamers reached out. The older witch retreated as Jewel advanced. Till she stood in range of Cedric's staff.

"Do it," said Jewel.

"Do what, you little upstart?" hissed Hemp.

In answer, down came Cedric's staff with a crack! upon Hemp's head. Then down went Hemp.

At which Jewel threw back her head and laughed. Barnaby had never seen her so happy, and so absolutely self-assured, and so obviously a creature of the Witches' Wood. The sight slightly frightened.

In reply to the laugh, a screech sounded across the shadowed chamber. Barnaby dashed forwards fast as thought. At the far end he found Val and her mother circling one another, knives dripping. At every third breath they tangled too fast for eye to follow. Then they stepped back, panting, new blood upon one or both.

Seeing Barnaby approach, Val's mother scowled. Her face so like to her daughter's he felt hurt by the look. Jewel and Cedric followed to take stand beside him.

Now Madam Kurgus retreated, eyes narrowing. Not fearing; but seeking new strategy for multiple foes. She backed from her daughter till she stood before the open door to the treasure vault.

Of a sudden, it shone clear to Barnaby what to do. He dropped his axe, rushing forwards with that heightened speed that had aided him twice now.

In range of the woman, he leapt, leg extended, kicking her in the chest, sending her tumbling backwards into the treasure vault.

To all eyes, the vault had returned to a vision of dust and shadowed trash. The woman lay upon the floor, knife still in hand, gasping for breath, glaring defiance.

Val approached. Holding her bloody knife, she slashed the air, cutting some connection visible only to her and the woman glaring up at her. Then with a grin, Val kicked shut the door.

The company stared, turning gazes from Val to the closed treasure chamber. First came silence. Then sounded faint curses. These soon rose to screams, a scrabbling of fingers... at last came silence again. Everyone backed away, shivering to imagine what occurred within. A scream from behind made them whirl about.

"Barnaby! Stop him, you wretched boy!" shouted the Squire. Barnaby turned to see Bodkin still chivying his stepmother and Squire Semple in circles. The two were lagging, and Bodkin growing bored. On the next circuit he allowed the prey to reach the ladder. The Squire began climbing, panting for breath.

"Wait for me, you coward!" shouted Mother Miller, following behind.

Bodkin laughed, poking her with his sword. She yelped, climbing faster. Both disappeared above, footsteps echoing retreat. *Exeunt Mill Town villains, stage left.*

For a moment the company stood still, the room silent but for their panting breaths. Then out from shadows came the *click, click* of bronze claws on stone floor.

Barnaby turned to see Festus standing, studying the Benefactors with his rainbow-shimmer eyes. The creature gave no tail wag, offered no friendly bark. It opened mouth, showing black leather tongue, sharp steel incisors.

Barnaby glanced to the axe he'd left upon the floor. But Festus made no move to attack. Instead, he began walking in circles, growling to himself.

The tail rattled, drooping in sorrow… then fell clattering to the floor. Next went an ear, with a clank upon the stones. Then a bronze panel opened, revealing sparking wires and clashing gears. Now oily smoke poured out Festus's muzzle. The mechanical beast halted. Throwing back its head it gave a howl to shake the room. A mournful cry loud as any steam dragon. Slowly the echoes faded away, followed by silence and puffs of white smoke.

Howl done, the beast burst into sparks and flame. The company leapt back, as bits of bolt, cog and gear flew clattering and jangling. The Benefactors watched till

Festus the Mechanical Dog collapsed into a smoking jumble of metal parts.

Barnaby sighed to see it. Not so, Val.

"Never did trust that beast."

"He was amazing," lamented Barnaby. "A glorious thing. Better than Da's windup owl. Even if he was also a saint up to mischief. Hey, I think my new boots are magic. I move faster. Might just be better boots."

Val started to laugh, then suddenly gasped.

"Oh Infernum, where's Matilda? Is she alright?" She looked in alarm towards the closed door of the treasure vault.

"Michael rescued her." Barnaby pointed towards the shadows. There Michael sat with back to the wall, hat thrown aside. Matilda lay on the floor, head in his lap. They did no speaking; just rested quiet. Might have been some exchange of whispers.

"Oh, thank sweet St. Euterpe. I might have got her killed or sent to madness."

"Not your fault," said Barnaby. "They had this planned to drive us mad. Whoever 'they' are."

"But now you've used your third request for Michael's help."

Barnaby shrugged. "Proper use, I'd say."

"Michael's still here," said Bodkin. "I thought it was three favors and then off to the Fields?"

"I asked him to help Matilda. Maybe that task requires he remain awhile."

"Lots of ways to be helpful to a pretty young thing," observed Bodkin.

"We *can* hear you, you know," said Matilda. "Really its most perniciously prurient of you to so specifically speculate."

Lord Michael, late of the Grand Army of St. Demetia, put finger to Matilda's lips.

"Let them talk."

"Excellent attitude," said a new voice. Though none had heard him enter, St. Lucif now stood at the far end of the room. Holding Festus's bronze head.

Lucif raised it high, addressing it in dramatic tones. "Alas, poor Festus. A dog of infinite wag."

"Is he dead?" asked Barnaby. "I mean, the saint Hefestus that was being the mechanical dog Festus?"

"No, of course not," said St. Lucif. He dropped the dog's head, booted it across the floor. "Just this toy avatar he made to stop you."

"Stop me from what?"

"Going through the door I'm about to open."

That said, the man went to the grand oaken door. Producing the key he'd shown earlier, he unlocked it. Then with a dramatic wave of arm, swung the door wide.

Beyond waited... a set of winding steps, leading upwards.

Chapter 13
What Exactly Are the Questions?

Enter four Gobelins, *center stage*, descending the ladder. The Benefactors watched, ready for further battle. But the newcomers lacked weapons or air of menace. They took up the wiggling form of Agat, the limp form of Hemp, carrying them away. Barnaby wished they'd stay so he could ask about Gobelin lives and loves. But they were busy at work; he settled for a wave goodbye. The leader returned the gesture, adding a roll of frog-like eyes.

Barnaby wondered if they'd collect Val's mother. He turned to the door; and continued turning.

"The treasure door's gone," he whispered.

"Magic tower, magic door," shrugged Matilda.

"We were finished with it anyway," said Val. "And everything in it."

Meanwhile St. Lucif, patron of Just Penance, leaned beside the grand portal he'd dramatically opened. Posing as a street-corner lounger enjoying a quiet morning. Humming, tossing a bronze gear from the departed saint of Holy Artifice.

Val called a quick meeting as far from Lucif as the chamber allowed.

"Anyone think it safe to go up through that door and up those stairs?"

"Maybe," said Jewel.

"Agreed on the maybe," said Bodkin.

"I do," said Barnaby.

"I also," said Cedric.

"Well, I don't," replied Val. "We are missing what this is all about." She began pacing, waving knife to conduct her thoughts. "They brought my bitch-mother here and Jewel's coven and Barnaby's stepmother. Why?"

Bodkin shrugged.

"For the fun of seeing us jump, obviously."

"But why would two saints play such idiot tricks? Don't tell me Lucif and Hefestia care a shining shit about treasure or miracle plays. This has all been about something else."

"No great surprise if Lucif is up to mischief," mused Cedric. "The mystery is his unlikely partnership with Hefestia. Who *didn't* want us going up the stairs, according to Lucif."

Barnaby gave a sad glance to the pile of bolts and wires. Shadow Night-Creep now sat atop the jumble, ostentatiously washing his fur. Bath completed, he stepped to the side, scraping hind legs back and forth in pantomime of kicking dirt upon the remains.

Disrespect asserted, he deigned to approach the company, assuming his customary throne upon Barnaby's shoulder. There, of course, he began to declaim.

"As I previously stated, if you want answers, you are most likely to find them at the tower top."

"*Do* we want answers?" asked Matilda. "What exactly are the questions?"

In answer, the cat merely blinked in sign of secret knowledge, as cats oft do.

"Darned if I know the proper question," growled Val. "I just feel we won't rest safe till we know why a handsome but gormless miller was sent wandering the world with a mad map, gathering all a tribe of talented associates."

"You *could* try asking," said St. Lucif from across the room. "Not that I'm eavesdropping. But seriously?"

Val faced him, arms crossed.

"Fine. First, suppose we just want out of this asylum. Can we skip your mysterious new stairway and leave the way we came?"

Lucif nodded. "I my own saintly self shall conduct you past every last trap and trick. To the very doorway you entered, then down the mountain steps without fear of snake, spider, wolf." He tossed the gear, caught it with a Bodkin grin. "After that, you are back in the wide world and on your own."

"Sounds good to me," said Jewel. "What about your mad play?"

Lucif brightened. "Oh, that offer stands, as does the reward. Tour Infernum but a year or three, enacting my brilliant rendition of the *Baptismus*. In return I promise you another go with the treasures of the tower."

"No."

"No."

"No."

"No."

"Well, maybe," said Bodkin.

"But what about the stairway to the tower top?" asked Barnaby. "Why didn't Festus the Bronze Mechanical Personage want us to go there?"

"That question, as your tutor in magic stated, can only be answered, *if* at all, by taking the stairs to the tower top."

Val turned back to the company.

"Well? Do we exit stage right, alive with pockets full? Or do we risk everything for no reason but curiosity on one last idiot dance to the lunatic piping of the House of Saints?"

* * *

Barnaby approached Lucif, axe upon one shoulder, magic cat on the other.

"I'll pretend I didn't hear, and ask," said Lucif. "What, what is the fateful decision?"

"We want to go to the top of the tower."

"No, really?"

"Yes. We fought our way to the bottom. Might as well see the top."

Lucif studied Barnaby a moment, then shook his head. "Ah, no, young miller. This is indeed as far down as your map went. But, the bottom?"

He gestured. "Come." That said, he took long-legged steps to the center of the room; searching about the floor. Then reached, pulling up a trap door exactly like the one they'd descended from the stage above.

Barnaby approached in cautious steps; followed by the others. He peered warily through the opening.

Below was a winding stairway that continued downwards. And downwards. And downwards yet more. Illuminated by a red glow from a distance great as Mill Town from the farther stars.

Lucif dropped the Festus gear into this abyss. It tumbled, shining faintly, disappearing into the red glow. They waited, but no distant clang sounded.

"If you are about to ask in the name of Lucif's mother's thorny chamber pot just how far down the tower goes," mused Lucif, "save your breath. Not Lucif nor mother nor pot has least idea." He let the door drop with a *bang* that made all jump.

That done, he turned towards the stairway upwards. Making a low bow, waving them forwards.

"I applaud your decision. Off you go now. Farewell, so long, take care." He gave a wave of hand. "Shoo."

Val looked towards the blank stone wall where before had been the door of the treasure vault.

"What about *her,* wherever she is?"

St. Lucif tendered the blank stones a mild frown.

"Hmm. Currently, Madam Kurgus curls in a ball, eyes shut, listening to a thousand battle screams within her head. Feeling the imaginary stings and slither of adders and serpents, recalling when you were fresh-born babe."

"Really?"

"Yes. Wishing she'd tossed you down a well."

"Ah, that's the woman. Out of mild curiosity and no concern, what happens to her?"

"She, Agat, Hemp, Mother Miller and Squire Whatshisname have all done sufficient evil unto the day, that they come under the purview of myself, Patron Saint of Just Penance. For all that they yet breathe. Ergo, I shall draft them for my production." He sighed. "Alas, for *your* roles, I must settle for Gobelin stand-ins." He shook his head. "Studious creatures, but they entirely lack the dramatic persona I saw in you Benefactors."

That said, the saint turned and climbed the ladder to the theatre above. The company listened to his confident steps fading away. *Exit St. Lucif, stage left.*

"You're bleeding," said Barnaby to Val. "Let me do a heal."

"Later, later," she replied. "Let's get started."

"Exactly," added Bodkin. "No sense hanging around *here.*"

The company gathered at the first step of the stairway. Contemplating what mysteries it dared them seek above.

"Probably leads to the clouds," speculated Matilda. "Where giant creatures shining like lamps declare which folk live, and who shall perish, who gets pox or just a pebble in their shoe."

"Well, but why not a grand party?" asked Barnaby. "All the saints singing and laughing, making the Upper House a glorious spring carnival in the sky."

"Doesn't sound properly holy," argued Bodkin. "No, atop these stairs is a church bigger than the world, with statues staring solemn, choirs of angels chanting, bronze bells chiming, incense rising up like prayers, candles tall as trees all aglow..."

"Only one way to find out," declared Val.

Still, no one took the step to find out.

Matilda turned to Dark Michael beside her. "By the by, I'm still feeling quite femininely faint and shall require your constant concern upon the way."

Michael nodded, staring up the stairs. "I remain at your service. And I am as curious as any, to find what waits at the top."

All nodded, agreeing how very curious they were. And still, and still, no one took the step -

-till Val shoved Barnaby in the back. He stumbled forwards. Up one step, then another, followed by the rest. Once in motion, they all continued climbing. Winding round and round a spiraling wall. Cedric holding his staff high to light the way.

They climbed in peace. No side corridors offered dark choice; no sly monsters leapt from shadows, not a single trap made sinister *click*.

"Bit dull, this," observed Matilda,

"Dull is fine," declared Val. "Up Lucif's seven asses with more blood, sweat and adventure."

"He only had the one ass, though," observed Matilda.

"No doubt the remaining six were metaphysical," mused Cedric. "One hears of these mystic appendages."

"By the by, Mister Barnaby," said Matilda, "What did you see when you were looking at us with mystic vision?"

"Something really fine and good and beautiful and amazing and astonishing."

"Just what I see in my mirror," declared Bodkin. "Hey, miller, slow your magic boots. We can't walk as fast in our cheaper shoes."

"Sorry."

"My knees are beginning to ache," admitted Jewel.

"Oi, there's a window." Matilda stopped before a narrow opening in the outer wall. "Ha. I see the very hall where we camped the first night."

After that, Cedric extinguished his staff, for the stairway grew light from regular windows. The stones no longer black, but white, bright and clean as bridal veil, as mountain snow. Barnaby put a hand to the wall; feeling it hum faintly. The tower might have been a giant bell struck ages past, still vibrating with the chime.

A sense of lightness filled the company, as though they left their hurts and weariness below in the dark. The air grew colder, but not numbing with chill. This was like to the cool touch of rain refreshing the weary traveler. And still on they climbed, round and up, round and up. Making no idle chatter now, sensing they approached a place worthy of silence.

At each window they stopped to gaze outwards into blue sky, white cloud, snowy peaks and green valleys. Each view seeming a mile farther from the earth, a mile deeper into the sky.

And still they climbed, round and up, round and up. Feeling no weariness nor sense of impending danger. Only the certainty that something important waited ahead. And the air grew yet colder, clear as the sky from mountain peaks.

Barnaby in the lead, they circled, circled the ever-winding wall... at last to stop in a wide archway. No further steps left to climb. The company gathered close, peering within.

Beyond waited a circular chamber with a high vaulted roof, bright with sunlight, fresh with mountain air. A long table crossed the chamber, lined with ornate chairs. Behold the feast hall of the saints; the truth copied in child's play far, far, far below.

Upon all sides, windows arched from floor to ceiling, open to the panorama of earth and sky. Here the world itself served as mere decoration for something more important: the gathering of arch lords and ladies, powers and principalities, virtues, dominions and archons.

But no such beings sat in the thrones, conversing in holy wisdom. Here ruled only the empty sunlight, the wind, the shadows of passing clouds. Nothing more.

Yet the chamber was not entirely vacant. A man sat on the floor by a window, face gaunt, eyes so open they seemed removed of eyelid.

He sat in a pile of vandalized books; the pages torn away, leaving empty shells showing titles that declared only what was lost.

Beside him hummed a strange mechanicalism of wires, tubes and flickering lights.

The man ignored the Benefactor's entrance. He held a book with one last page. He pulled it away. working to fold the paper this way and that. Reshaping it to something sharp, winged, reminiscent of a diving hawk.

"Sir?" asked Barnaby.

The man raised finger in sign for attention and silence.

"Observe." He thrust the paper dart forwards into the air. To the surprise of all, it did not tumble to the floor.

Instead, it glided across and away, out a window and into the sky.

Barnaby laughed delighted. At which the man tossed aside the ruined book, turning his over-stressed eyes upon Barnaby, and laughed as well. A long laugh that carried a note of mad desperation.

"The folk beyond the sea have machines that speed and glide just so, just so, through the sky."

"Do they?" asked Barnaby. "I should dearly like to see that."

The man nodded. "Soon, you shall. Soon." That foretold, he rose. Pointed to the humming mechanicalism.

"I've kept watch three nights. Or was it three years?" He turned mad eyes to the table, as if asking the empty chairs. Then whispered aside to Barnaby. "*They* never tire. They sit and sit and sit and sit and sit, staring, staring. All very well for *them*, but mortal flesh must rest. Mustn't it?"

He trembled, as if indeed he'd spent years releasing pages of books to the wind.

"Then you should rest," affirmed Barnaby, voice coaxing.

"Thank you, young sir," said the man. "I feel I can leave the last task in your hands. The outsiders shall contact us within the hour. Flip that blue switch when you hear the bell, and they will follow the signal to our shores."

"The blue switch," repeated Barnaby. "After the bell."

"Just so. It will serve as a beacon from their reality to ours. Their ships shall come as a grand fleet, a glorious procession, a marauding host of wise and princely wolves."

"Wolves?" puzzled Barnaby.

"Just so. The blue switch, remember. Now I'm going to step out for a bit of fresh air."

That said, the man turned. Before anyone thought to stop him, he stepped through the arched window and disappeared. A faint laugh rose up; ending far away, far below.

Barnaby rushed forwards, nearly following the man into the air. He held back, peering down the great height of the tower. At last he shook his head. Turned to stare at the Benefactors, faces equally horrified.

"Why did he do that?"

Bodkin sighed.

"Because he was barking mad?"

Cedric picked up the outer leaves of the vandalized book. "'*Secrets of Psamathe*'. A lost work, thrown to the winds. I concur. The man was mad."

"One of your Hefestian scholars," sniffed Val. "Must have sat here alone, last of his expedition. Waiting for his magic signal from the lands beyond the seas."

Matilda looked about and shivered. "This place seems wonderfully nice, but it's not for people. At least not for them with ambition to keep their brains from bubbling."

"Right," said Val. "This is as high as the tower goes. I declare the adventure officially done excepting our exciting and successful exit."

"Ah, no," declared the cat upon Barnaby's shoulder. The creature leapt to the table, sat with tail curled primly about paws. "Look upwards."

Val and the rest obediently gazed up. In the center of the vaulting, the stonework opened to reveal... *another floor of the tower*. Stairways winding, pillars arching to a yet further level; and beyond that yet another. And more still past that, rising, diminishing in the distance.

"No end below, and no end above," declared Cedric. "This tower is a grand metaphor in stone. If only one knew what grand truth it represented."

"I see why that fellow went mad," declared Jewel. "Makes me dizzy to look up."

"Right," said Val. "Back to nobly running away. That far door must lead to the stairs down to the entrance hall."

"More stairs?" asked Bodkin. "No thank you. There's our carriage." He pointed to the directable.

Val started to argue; then laughed. "You know, I don't see why not. Ship should be empty and full of supplies, if that fellow was alone for days."

Bodkin tested a foot to the walkway, pronounced it good. Skipped along to the door of the directable, disappearing inside.

Barnaby stared sadly at the empty chairs about the table. Wishing for the scene of gathered saints, as in Lucif's play.

Something flew back through the window. The folded paper the mad Hefestian had released to the wind. Now it glided, faltered, circled, dropping at last to rest upon the table. Barnaby picked it up. He unfolded it, turning it this way and that, puzzling at what he saw.

"Well, it's a map. But these words make no more sense right-side up, than up-side down."

"Another map?" groaned Val. "Someone grab it from him quick."

Cedric peered over Barnaby's shoulder, declining to grab. "Hmm. The map holds no great mystery. That is the land of Psamathe. The script, their strange hieroglyphs."

"What does it say?"

"Hmm. Ask me later. Let us not linger till some last jest of chance restrains us."

Just then, a small bell chimed. Everyone stared at the mechanism upon the floor.

"Oh," said Barnaby. "That's the bell. Now I'm supposed to push the blue lever?"

"Yes, if you want to invite a host of mad outsiders to come for lunch."

"Well, but need they be mad? Perhaps they'll be nice."

"Perhaps," mused Cedric. "My deceased friend Sigmund did say the Outsiders offered wondrous knowledge."

From the table, Night-Creep yawned, generously offering his opinion.

"Great knowledge is best earned and learned. Merely given, it makes an inheritance of fire."

Again rang the tiny bell. The company contemplated the mechanicalism till Bodkin returned, whistling.

"Ship's empty, pockets full, let's fly."

"Right," said Val. "Time to leave."

And still Barnaby hesitated, undecided.

"What about the guiding signal? Shall I pull the blue lever, or no?"

Val growled.

"Fine. Put it to vote. All in favor of inviting the lands beyond the seas to come visit our own bedlam world, say 'aye'. I'll go first. I vote 'Infernum, no'."

Jewel: "Agreed. The world is mad enough."

Bodkin laughed. "'Never open wide the gate to strangers bearing gifts', as old Mercutio would advise. I say 'no'."

Matilda turned gaze to Michael, who stood smiling at the sun in the clouds, hands before him as though at last he'd found a fire that properly shared its warmth. But when he spoke, it was with a tilt of head to Matilda.

"My advice is to leave each world to mend its own sorrows, and to find its own wisdom."

Matilda nodded. "And same for *their* world, bless the adventurous outsider darlings. I'm voting 'no'."

Now Friar Cedric groaned, so deeply did he feel the choice. He stamped his staff, which did not help.

"This decision is hard. My colleagues perished in a grand effort. And yet, and yet... they were mad to come here." He took breath, decided. "I also say no. We've no right to put entire kingdoms in peril out of academic curiosity."

And now all turned to Barnaby.

Again rang the innocent chime of the bell; as if the outsiders waited on the doorstep of the world, impatient to enter.

Barnaby held the flying paper in his hand, contemplating its mystic folds.

"I'd dearly like to see the wonders of the lands beyond the seas. I've already seen so many amazing things, met such astonishing folk. But... I don't like that bit about 'wise and princely wolves.' Gives a miller shivers. And we've no right to stand in a tower deciding the world' winds. Let the door of the world stay as it is. Closed."

"Unanimous, then," said Val. "No pushing the blue lever and let's be off."

Evening on the airship. From the control room they watched the tower recede in the distance. Bodkin at the control board, Cedric at the wheel.

Barnaby stared at the diminishing spike of stone in the days' last light. When he spoke, it was to that tower.

"We spent so long to reach it. Now there it goes."

"Good riddance," said Val. Struggling to wrap a bandage about her arm. "It was a mad cursed double-damned death trap."

"One that made us rich," pointed out Bodkin.

"While near murdering us," pointed out Matilda. "Why, I might have gone quite entirely mad, mad, mad."

Barnaby nodded to all points made.

"Yes. But when we climbed up the stairs, I felt sure at the top we'd find the saints sitting at their grand table. Just like in, in *Mister L's* play. And they'd invite us to join the feast, and answer all our questions and tell us secrets to make us wise and happy."

"I'm plenty wise already," Bodkin declared. "And heavy pockets are making me fabulously happy."

"Well, you'd have liked meeting Missus Green and Mister Quiet. And Sister Sephie. Maybe Mister Hefestia would have left off saying 'woof'. Oh, and Maris. She was quite like Val, but not as pretty."

Valentine Kurgus tried to frown; it slipped to smile. Matilda and Bodkin laughed. Cedric kept hands to the wheel, speaking in musing tone.

"We were told we'd find answers at the tower top. And so we did. We came to a chamber of wind and light, air and earth, shadow and stone. Infinite sky above, endless earth below. And indeed, these things hold great truths. Alas, they cannot share their truths with mortal minds. Not in plain words nor mad feast."

"If I say I didn't understand that, are you going to rap my knuckles?"

Cedric laughed. "I'd dare no such offense against the barbarian warrior you've become."

"He's my heroic miller," said Val. Taking seat in Barnaby's lap, holding out an arm. "Tie this bandage and I'll give you a kiss."

"Might mean a pebble," warned Jewel, giving Barnaby a grin.

She's happy now, he thought. Remembering the sour-faced girl on the road from Mill Town. He looked about, counting smiles. If grand purpose had to be declared for a journey, surely that sufficed. To be happy.

He began tying the strip of bandage across Val's much-scarred arm.

"Da used to ask does the wind turn the mill, or the miller turn the wind?"

Val snorted.

"What did he mean by it?"

"Da would never say, though I asked. It sounded wondrous wise. Now I'm sure it meant naught. Just words to make him laugh. And that's wisdom enough."

Cedric cleared throat to gain attention.

"There remains the question of 'where to now?'"

"Will folk suppose we stole this airship?"

"We are stealing this airship," pointed out Matilda. "Not that I'm feeling significantly guilty."

"We might return it to the University," replied Cedric. "I feel obliged to report the demise of their expedition. But there will be questions. No doubt confiscation of our more interesting finds."

"That's out, then," declared Jewel. Adjusting her circlet, her cape. Protective hand over spider pendant.

"We could head back to Persephone or Pomona," said Bodkin. "With our winnings, we could live like the bankers that kings want to live like."

"Oh, I have a ruined manse," remembered Barnaby. "I'm the Marquise of Pentafax Abbey. If anyone wants to go there."

"Isn't that a haunted ruin full of mad ghosts?"

"It is," said Night-Creep. "What of that?"

"Off my control board, you witch's pet of a feline showoff," chided Bodkin.

The cat yawned to say he'd leave of his own will, not for the noise of apish boys. Then leapt to the table. There lay the parchment glider, forgotten. He batted at it with a paw, whiskers twitching.

"Interesting," declared the cat.

"Psamathe script," declared Cedric. "Can you read it?"

The cat answered with a dismissive *sniff*.

"Of course. It's a list of twelve questions."

"What sort of questions?"

"Riddles. Alas, it lacks the answers."

"Ah," said Cedric. "I recall a shrine in the lore of Psamathe. The 'Temple of the Twelve Riddles'. Fable, I've been told."

"Oh, quite real. A great library holding the treasures of ancient empires. Guarded by a dozen immortal sphinxes, each presenting a riddle to those who would pass. Lost in the sands centuries past, though this map gives a decent idea of where to seek."

"Stop. Right. There," said Val. Making each word distinct as slash of knife.

"What?" asked Barnaby, looking at the bandage. Had he tied it wrong?

"Why?" demanded Bodkin. "Seems a shame to disband the Society of St. Benefact after one measly act of self-benefaction. Now we've had some practice, the next job will be cake and wine served free all the night."

"I don't want to disband," whispered Jewel.

"Nor does my adventurous Silenian self wish to go separate ways so soon," affirmed Matilda. She looked towards Michael, leaning against the wall. "Concerning which, I'm feeling mad and faintish again. Prepare to catch me."

The ghost nodded, solemn face saying he readied himself should she faint or go mad.

Slowly, Barnaby followed their point. If the Benefactors had no goal, they'd soon go separate ways. Rich, granted. Friends for sure. But still, separate.

He pictured returning to Mill Town. Squire Semple and Mother Miller would be absent, busy touring Infernum. But what would Barnaby do? Mill grain in the day; by nights he'd be back to staring at the hearth fire, picturing the very faces about him now.

He finished knotting the bandage. Val started to rise, but he reached to hold her where she sat. She did not resist, for all she *could* have resisted.

Instead, she gifted him a fond and mocking smile. He returned a fond and honest smile. She spoke first.

"I suppose we *could* give Psamathe a visit. How about you, wandering Barnaby? What do you say?"

"I say..." he looked about the room, studying the faces of the friends. Not faces dreamed in flame and shadows, but real faces. The truth past even *Greater Spell of Seeing*.

"I say let's go to Psamathe, look for a lost shrine. If we have the riddles, how hard can it be to find the answers?"

Nighttime. The directable hummed through a cloudless sky, making stately progress northwards. Professor Shadow Night-Creep, consultant to warlocks, initiate to ancient mysteries, confidant of saints, devils and millers alike, sat atop the directable, adjusting the fur of his tail. Clearly indifferent to the mountain winds, the stars blazing like a mad host of angels. Beside him stood

Dark Michael, hands in coat pockets, gaze turned to the Upper House of Saints.

"I assume Hefestia wished the Outsiders be shown how to cross to our world," said the ghost.

"Oh, for sure," agreed the cat. "The Saint of Holy Artifice could hardly be expected to resist the temptation of new sciences. Improved forms of fire and light, astonishing devices for flying the skies, swimming the seas, overturning the occasional mountain or city."

"Not something the other saints would favor."

"Yes. One will assume Martia, Plutarch and Demetia opposed the contact. Rather than go to war, the saints must have put it to trial."

"Choosing a daydreaming miller for their coin toss?"

"Well, both sides played fair. Reasonably fair. Letting the mortals decide. With Lucif serving as neutral referee. An amusing role for him, no doubt."

"I don't think the Benefactors grasped what it was all about."

"They did not. And I find that for the best. You might tell them *The Grand Plan*. But it would seem absurd, would it not? Led across kingdoms, battling fiends, ghosts, monsters and machines, all to spend half a minute deciding whether to push a lever when a bell rang."

"Absurd, yes. And yet by deciding *not*, they shut a door to war, invasion, the ruin of two worlds."

"True."

The night wind sang of bright stars, lonely peaks, empty vales. A beautiful song, for all that the night wind knows no song, for it knows itself not. But from below, cat and ghost heard the strum and hum of Thelxipea. Val and Matilda choiring bawdy verses. Of a sudden the glorious sky, the dramatic earth seemed mere theatre backdrop. Far less than the glories of the mortal company below.

The two supernatural creatures retreated into the airship. Into the hearth-fire warmth of life, of light, of family.

The End

Notes on Terra Sanctorum

Concerning Magic

'Magic' in the Land of Saints is primarily the practice of *theurgy*. That is, an appeal to divinity to perform a supernatural action. This appeal is essentially a prayer; usually referred to as an *oration*.

Style of orations vary between lands and their tutelary saints. Three ceremonial elements are commonly required.

First requirement: a relic. This shall be an item touched or at least associated with a saint. Relics are of lesser and greater sort. *Lesser* relics are objects conceptually associated to the domain over which the saint resides. Thus, a bone from a grave can serve for a lesser relic of St. Plutarch. A sheaf of wheat from St. Demetia, a bronze gear from Hefestia, a sword from St. Martia. Relics aide the petitioner in making their oration.

Greater relics have been touched by the saint themselves. These are rare and valuable; guarded for their direct connection to a saint.

Second requirement: the supplicant must have a spiritual or vocational affinity with the saint to whom they appeal. Farmers, shepherds, millers and those who live close to nature can feel St. Demetia's presence, when merchants and soldiers might not. Gravediggers, necromancers, executioners and all who mourn are most likely to be heard by St. Plutarch, Patron of Blessed Endings.

Third requirement: a proper casting requires a formulated oration. These have lesser or greater wording. The lesser are mere recitation of ad-hoc rhymes expressing the concepts of a saint's domain. But greater orations require exact recitation in the original wording affirmed by the saint themselves. *Greater orations* are seldom shared among magic-workers.

Once an oration is performed successfully, it becomes bound to the relic used. Thereafter the petitioner no longer needs to recite the oration when using the relic. However, if the recitation of a new oration thrice fails, the relic will never afterwards function for that oration. For which reason magic-workers are cautious in what new spells they apply to relics.

Note: the casting of an oration places a cost upon body and mind of the petitioner. The cost of greater orations can be fatal.

The Saints

Saints are assigned higher or lower honorifics in accord with their standing. Important female saints are often referred to as 'Mother'; the lesser as 'Sister' or 'Novice'. Male saints of lower status are generally given the honorific 'Brother' or 'Friar', instead of 'Saint'.

Often referred to as the Hosts of the House of Saints, they are equated with the stars. Some saints take kingdoms of the Middle House (the Earth itself) as their special domains. Each saint is said to have a message for all other beings in the House of Saints; this is referred to as their *testament*.

A Sampling of Saints, and their Dominions

Saint Demetia

Patroness of Birth, Growth, Healing.

Sister Hecatatia

Patroness of night, of dark, of boundaries between the natural and supernatural world.

Saint Plutarch

Patron of Holy Ending; rules over burials, the quieter realms of the afterlife (often called the 'Fields'),

Friar February

Assistant to Plutarch; carries the scythe oft associated with death itself.

Saint Martia

Patroness of Worthy Battle. Her domain is any physical struggle for life, for honor, for acts of courage.

Saint Hefestia

Patron of Holy Artifice; presides over creation of machines, engineering, the physical sciences.

Sister Persephone

Patroness of travel between life and death, dream and waking; growth and decay, spirit and flesh.

Saint Lucif

Patron saint of Just Penance; ruling over the darker realms of the afterlife such as Infernum, Tartarus and Erebus. A feared personage, yet often the subject of comic curses.

Brother Silenus

Patron of wine, drunkenness, of mad dancing, of forest revels; testifying to the wisdom of life lived without care for the morrow.

Saint Apollonius

Patron of epic poetry, prophecy and the lyre. Also known to be a skank.

Sister Euterpe

Patroness of Music, of female bards, minstrels and troubadours. Very loyal to musicians who wander singing songs, seeking glory.

Saint Bridget

To the reverent, she is the Patroness of Worthy Desire. To the irreverent, her dominion is inarguably: copulation.

The House of Saints

Essentially all of existence; divided into the Upper, Middle and Lower House. The Middle House is where mortal beings dwell; the Upper House is inhabited by the brighter saints; the Lower House by the darker, as well as the spirits of the dead.

It is argued whether the 'lands beyond the sea' are included in the House, or they represent a separate reality.

Some Kingdoms, Nations, Realms
The Kingdom of Saint Demetia

Monarchy. Capital is Pomona. The largest, oldest city is Persephone, straddling the River Lethe. An agricultural land, populated with small woods and villages. Nominally at war with Plutarch and Hefestia.

The Dimarchy of St. Plutarch

Capital: Pleasance (formerly known as Necropolis).

A misty, swamp-filled land dark with black forests, fens and valleys of fog. Ruled by a shared council of dead and living known as The Deaconry. Nominally at war with Demetia and Martia.

Free State of St. Martia

Capital: Demos. A land of spartan lifestyle, ruled by a nobility of warriors constantly at war with the servant class. Nominally at war with Hefestia and Plutarach.

The Republic of St. Hefestia.

Capital: Daedalus. More mechanically advanced than other kingdoms. Roads are paved, steam-powered transportation is present but not omnipresent. Hefestia values learning and free-thinking; frequently suffering minor explosions. Nominally at war with Demetia and Martia.

About the author:

Raymond St. Elmo wandered into a degree in Spanish Literature, which gave no job, just a love of Magic Realism. Moving on to a degree in programming gave him a job and an interest in virtual reality and artificial intelligence, which lead him back into the world of magic realism. Author of many fantasy books, possibly comic, certainly unusual. He lives in Texas.

Printed in Great Britain
by Amazon